T10649882

SUSAN LENOX:
HER FALL AND RISE

THE LAST PORTRAIT OF
DAVID GRAHAM PHILLIPS

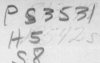
David Graham Phillips

SUSAN LENOX

HER FALL AND RISE

VOLUME I

WITH A PORTRAIT
OF THE AUTHOR

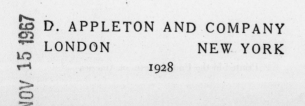

D. APPLETON AND COMPANY
LONDON   NEW YORK
1928

Printed in the United States of America

DAVID GRAHAM PHILLIPS

A TRIBUTE

Even now I cannot realize that he is dead, and often in the city streets—on Fifth Avenue in particular—I find myself glancing ahead for a glimpse of the tall, boyish, familiar figure—experience once again a flash of the old happy expectancy.

I have lived in many lands, and have known men. I never knew a finer man than Graham Phillips.

His were the clearest, bluest, most honest eyes I ever saw—eyes that scorned untruth—eyes that penetrated all sham.

In repose his handsome features were a trifle stern—and the magic of his smile was the more wonderful—such a sunny, youthful, engaging smile.

His mere presence in a room was exhilarating. It seemed to freshen the very air with a keen sweetness almost pungent.

He was tall, spare, leisurely, iron-strong; yet figure, features and bearing were delightfully boyish.

Men liked him, women liked him when he liked them.

He was the most honest man I ever knew, clean in mind, clean-cut in body, a little over-serious perhaps, except when among intimates; a little prone to hoist the burdens of the world on his young shoulders.

His was a knightly mind; a paladin character. But

he could unbend, and the memory of such hours with him—hours that can never be again—hurts more keenly than the memory of calmer and more sober moments.

We agreed in many matters, he and I; in many we differed. To me it was a greater honor to differ in opinion with such a man than to find an entire synod of my own mind.

Because—and of course this is the opinion of one man and worth no more than that—I have always thought that Graham Phillips was head and shoulders above us all in his profession.

He was to have been really great. He *is*—by his last book, "Susan Lenox."

Not that, when he sometimes discussed the writing of it with me, I was in sympathy with it. I was not. We always were truthful to each other.

But when a giant molds a lump of clay into tremendous masses, lesser men become confused by the huge contours, the vast distances, the terrific spaces, the majestic scope of the ensemble. So I. But he went on about his business.

I do not know what the public may think of "Susan Lenox." I scarcely know what I think.

It is a terrible book—terrible and true and beautiful.

Under the depths there are unspeakable things that writhe. His plumb-line touches them and they squirm. He bends his head from the clouds to do it. Is it worth doing? I don't know.

But this I do know—that within the range of all fiction of all lands and of all times no character has so overwhelmed me as the character of *Susan Lenox*.

She is as real as life and as unreal. She *is* Life. Hers was the concentrated nobility of Heaven and Hell. And the divinity of the one and the tragedy of the other. For she had known both—this girl—the most pathetic, the most human, the most honest character ever drawn by an American writer.

In the presence of his last work, so overwhelming, so stupendous, we lesser men are left at a loss. Its magnitude demands the perspective that time only can lend it. Its dignity and austerity and its pitiless truth impose upon us that honest and intelligent silence which even the quickest minds concede is necessary before an honest verdict.

Truth was his goddess; he wrought honestly and only for her.

He is dead, but he is to have his day in court. And whatever the verdict, if it be a true one, were he living he would rest content.

ROBERT W. CHAMBERS.

BEFORE THE CURTAIN

A few years ago, as to the most important and most interesting subject in the world, the relations of the sexes, an author had to choose between silence and telling those distorted truths beside which plain lying seems almost white and quite harmless. And as no author could afford to be silent on the subject that underlies all subjects, our literature, in so far as it attempted to deal with the most vital phases of human nature, was beneath contempt. The authors who knew they were lying sank almost as low as the nasty-nice purveyors of fake idealism and candied pruriency who fancied they were writing the truth. Now it almost seems that the day of lying conscious and unconscious is about run. "And ye shall know the truth, and the truth shall make you free."

There are three ways of dealing with the sex relations of men and women—two wrong and one right.

For lack of more accurate names the two wrong ways may be called respectively the Anglo-Saxon and the Continental. Both are in essence processes of spicing up and coloring up perfectly innocuous facts of nature to make them poisonously attractive to perverted palates. The wishy-washy literature and the wishy-washy morality on which it is based are not one stage more—or less—rotten than the libertine literature and the libertine morality on which it is based. So far as degrading effect is concerned, the "pure, sweet" story or play, false to nature, false to true morality, propagandist of indecent emotions disguised as idealism, need yield nothing to the so-called "strong" story. Both pander to different forms of the same diseased craving for the unnatural. Both produce moral atrophy. The one tends to encourage the shallow and unthinking in ignorance of life and so causes them to suffer the merciless penalties of ignorance. The other tends to miseducate the shallow and unthinking, to give them a ruinously false notion of the delights of vice. The Anglo-Saxon "morality" is like a nude figure salaciously draped; the Continental "strength" is like a nude figure salaciously distorted. The Anglo-Saxon article reeks the stench of disinfectants; the Continental reeks the stench of degenerate perfume. The Continental shouts "Hypocrisy!" at the Anglo-Saxon; the Anglo-Saxon shouts "Filthiness!" at the Continental. Both are right; they are twin sisters of the same horrid mother. And an author of either allegiance has to have many a redeeming grace of style, of character drawing, of philosophy, to gain him tolerance in a clean mind.

There is the third and right way of dealing with the sex relations of men and women. That is the way of simple candor and naturalness. Treat the sex question as you would any other question. Don't treat it reverently; don't treat it rakishly. Treat it naturally. Don't insult your intelligence and lower your moral tone by thinking about either the decency or the indecency of matters that are familiar, undeniable, and unchangeable facts of life. Don't look on woman as mere female, but as human being. Remember that she has a mind and a heart as well as a body.

BEFORE THE CURTAIN

In a sentence, don't join in the prurient clamor of "purity" hypocrites and "strong" libertines that exaggerates and distorts the most commonplace, if the most important feature of life. Let us try to be as sensible about sex as we are trying to be about all the other phenomena of the universe in this more enlightened day.

Nothing so sweetens a sin or so delights a sinner as getting big-eyed about it and him. Those of us who are naughty aren't nearly so naughty as we like to think; nor are those of us who are nice nearly so nice. Our virtues and our failings are—perhaps to an unsuspected degree— the result of the circumstances in which we are placed. The way to improve individuals is to improve these circumstances; and the way to start at improving the circumstances is by looking honestly and fearlessly at things as they are. We must know our world and ourselves before we can know what should be kept and what changed. And the beginning of this wisdom is in seeing sex relations rationally. Until that fundamental matter is brought under the sway of good common sense, improvement in other directions will be slow indeed. Let us stop lying—to others —to ourselves.

D. G. P.

July, 1908.

SUSAN LENOX

I

"THE child's dead," said Nora, the nurse.

It was the upstairs sitting-room in one of the pretentious houses of Sutherland, oldest and most charming of the towns on the Indiana bank of the Ohio. The two big windows were open; their limp and listless draperies showed that there was not the least motion in the stifling humid air of the July afternoon. At the center of the room stood an oblong table; over it were neatly spread several thicknesses of white cotton cloth; naked upon them lay the body of a newborn girl baby. At one side of the table nearer the window stood Nora. Hers were the hard features and corrugated skin popularly regarded as the result of a life of toil, but in fact the result of a life of defiance to the laws of health. As additional penalties for that same self-indulgence she had an enormous bust and hips, thin face and arms, hollow, sinew-striped neck. The young man, blond and smooth faced, at the other side of the table and facing the light, was Doctor Stevens, a recently graduated pupil of the famous Schulze of Saint Christopher who as much as any other one man is responsible for the rejection of hocus-pocus and the injection of common sense into American medicine. For upwards of an hour young Stevens, coat

1

off and shirt sleeves rolled to his shoulders, had been
toiling with the lifeless form on the table. He had
tried everything his training, his reading and his experience suggested—all the more or less familiar devices similar to those indicated for cases of drowning.
Nora had watched him, at first with interest and hope,
then with interest alone, finally with swiftly deepening
disapproval, as her compressed lips and angry eyes
plainly revealed. It seemed to her his effort was degenerating into sacrilege, into defiance of an obvious
decree of the Almighty. However, she had not ventured to speak until the young man, with a muttered
ejaculation suspiciously like an imprecation, straightened his stocky figure and began to mop the sweat from
his face, hands and bared arms.

When she saw that her verdict had not been heard,
she repeated it more emphatically. "The child's dead,"
said she, "as I told you from the set-out." She made
the sign of the cross on her forehead and bosom, while
her fat, dry lips moved in a "Hail, Mary."

The young man did not rouse from his reverie. He
continued to gaze with a baffled expression at the tiny
form, so like a whimsical caricature of humanity. He
showed that he had heard the woman's remark by
saying, to himself rather than to her, "Dead? What's
that? Merely another name for ignorance." But the
current of his thought did not swerve. It held to the
one course: What would his master, the dauntless, the
infinitely resourceful Schulze, do if he were confronted
by this intolerable obstacle of a perfect machine refusing to do its duty and pump vital force through an
eagerly waiting body? "He'd *make* it go, I'd bet my
life," the young man muttered. "I'm ashamed of myself."

As if the reproach were just the spur his courage and his intelligence had needed, his face suddenly glowed with the upshooting fire of an inspiration. He thrust the big white handkerchief into his hip pocket, laid one large strong hand upon the small, beautifully arched chest of the baby. Nora, roused by his expression even more than by his gesture, gave an exclamation of horror. "Don't touch it again," she cried, between entreaty and command. "You've done all you can—and more."

Stevens was not listening. "Such a fine baby, too," he said, hesitating—the old woman mistakenly fancied it was her words that made him pause. "I feel no good at all," he went on, as if reasoning with himself, "no good at all, losing both the mother and the child."

"*She* didn't want to live," replied Nora. Her glances stole somewhat fearfully toward the door of the adjoining room—the bedroom where the mother lay dead. "There wasn't nothing but disgrace ahead for both of them. Everybody'll be glad."

"Such a fine baby," muttered the abstracted young doctor.

"Love-children always is," said Nora. She was looking sadly and tenderly down at the tiny, symmetrical form—symmetrical to her and the doctor's expert eyes. "Such a deep chest," she sighed. "Such pretty hands and feet. A real love-child." There she glanced nervously at the doctor; it was meet and proper and pious to speak well of the dead, but she felt she might be going rather far for a "good woman."

"I'll try it," cried the young man in a resolute tone. "It can't do any harm, and——"

Without finishing his sentence he laid hold of the body by the ankles, swung it clear of the table. As

3

Nora saw it dangling head downwards like a dressed suckling pig on a butcher's hook she vented a scream and darted round the table to stop by main force this revolting desecration of the dead. Stevens called out sternly: "Mind your business, Nora! Push the table against the wall and get out of the way. I want all the room there is."

"Oh, Doctor—for the blessed Jesus' sake——"

"Push back that table!"

Nora shrank before his fierce eyes. She thought his exertions, his disappointment and the heat had combined to topple him over into insanity. She retreated toward the farther of the open windows. With a curse at her stupidity Stevens kicked over the table, used his foot vigorously in thrusting it to the wall. "Now!" exclaimed he, taking his stand in the center of the room and gauging the distance of ceiling, floor and walls.

Nora, her back against the window frame, her fingers sunk in her big loose bosom, stared petrified. Stevens, like an athlete swinging an Indian club, whirled the body round and round his head, at the full length of his powerful arms. More and more rapidly he swung it, until his breath came and went in gasps and the sweat was trickling in streams down his face and neck. Round and round between ceiling and floor whirled the naked body of the baby—round and round for minutes that seemed hours to the horrified nurse— round and round with all the strength and speed the young man could put forth—round and round until the room was a blur before his throbbing eyes, until his expression became fully as demoniac as Nora had been fancying it. Just as she was recovering from her paralysis of horror and was about to fly shrieking

4

from the room she was halted by a sound that made her draw in air until her bosom swelled as if it would burst its gingham prison. She craned eagerly toward Stevens. He was whirling the body more furiously than ever.

"Was that you?" asked Nora hoarsely. "Or was it——" She paused, listened.

The sound came again—the sound of a drowning person fighting for breath.

"It's—it's——" muttered Nora. "What is it, Doctor?"

"Life!" panted Stevens, triumph in his glistening, streaming face. "Life!"

He continued to whirl the little form, but not so rapidly or so vigorously. And now the sound was louder, or, rather, less faint, less uncertain—was a cry—was the cry of a living thing. "She's alive—alive!" shrieked the woman, and in time with his movements she swayed to and fro from side to side, laughing, weeping, wringing her hands, patting her bosom, her cheeks. She stretched out her arms. "My prayers are answered!" she cried. "Don't kill her, you brute! Give her to me. You shan't treat a baby that way."

The unheeding doctor kept on whirling until the cry was continuous, a low but lusty wail of angry protest. Then he stopped, caught the baby up in both arms, burst out laughing. "You little minx!" he said—or, rather, gasped—a tenderness quite maternal in his eyes. "But I got you! Nora, the table."

Nora righted the table, spread and smoothed the cloths, extended her scrawny eager arms for the baby. Stevens with a jerk of the head motioned her aside, laid the baby on the table. He felt for the pulse at its wrist, bent to listen at the heart. Quite useless.

That strong, rising howl of helpless fury was proof enough. Her majesty the baby was mad through and through—therefore alive through and through.

"Grand heart action!" said the young man. He stood aloof, hands on his hips, head at a proud angle. "You never saw a healthier specimen. It'll be many a year, bar accidents, before she's that near death again."

But it was Nora's turn not to hear. She was soothing and swaddling the outraged baby. "There—there!" she crooned. "Nora'll take care of you. The bad man shan't come near my little precious—no, the wicked man shan't touch her again."

The bedroom door opened. At the slight noise superstitious Nora paled, shriveled within her green and white checked gingham. She slowly turned her head as if on this day of miracles she expected yet another—the resurrection of the resurrected baby's mother, "poor Miss Lorella." But Lorella Lenox was forever tranquil in the sleep that engulfed her and the sorrows in which she had been entangled by an impetuous, trusting heart. The apparition in the doorway was commonplace—the mistress of the house, Lorella's elder and married sister Fanny—neither fair nor dark, neither tall nor short, neither thin nor fat, neither pretty nor homely, neither stupid nor bright, neither neat nor dowdy—one of that multitude of excellent, unobtrusive human beings who make the restful stretches in a world of agitations—and who respond to the impetus of circumstance as unresistingly as cloud to wind.

As the wail of the child smote upon Fanny's ears she lifted her head, startled, and cried out sharply, "What's that?"

6

"We've saved the baby, Mrs. Warham," replied the young doctor, beaming on her through his glasses.

"Oh!" said Mrs. Warham. And she abruptly seated herself on the big chintz-covered sofa beside the door.

"And it's a lovely child," pleaded Nora. Her woman's instinct guided her straight to the secret of the conflict raging behind Mrs. Warham's unhappy face.

"The finest girl in the world," cried Stevens, well-meaning but tactless.

"Girl!" exclaimed Fanny, starting up from the sofa. "Is it a *girl?*"

Nora nodded. The young man looked downcast; he was realizing the practical side of his victory for science —the consequences to the girl child, to all the relatives.

"A girl!" moaned Fanny, sinking to the sofa again. "God have mercy on us!"

Louder and angrier rose the wail. Fanny, after a brief struggle with herself, hurried to the table, looked down at the tiny helplessness. Her face softened. She had been a mother four times. Only one had lived— her fair little two-year-old Ruth—and she would never have any more children. The tears glistened in her eyes. "What ails you, Nora Mulvey?" she demanded. "Why aren't you 'tending to this poor little creature?"

Nora sprang into action, but she wrapped the baby herself. The doctor in deep embarrassment withdrew to the farther window. She fussed over the baby lingeringly, but finally resigned it to the nurse. "Take it into the bathroom," she said, "where everything's ready to feed it—though I never dreamed——" As Nora was about to depart, she detained her. "Let me look at it again."

7

The nurse understood that Fanny Warham was searching for evidence of the mysterious but suspected paternity whose secret Lorella, with true Lenox obstinacy, had guarded to the end. The two women scanned the features. A man would at a glance have abandoned hope of discovering anything from a chart so vague and confused as that wrinkled, twisted, swollen face of the newborn. Not so a woman. Said Nora:

"She seems to me to favor the Lenoxes. But I think—I *kind* o' think—I see a *trace* of—of——" There she halted, waiting for encouragement.

"Of Galt?" suggested Fanny, in an undertone.

"Of Galt," assented Nora, her tone equally discreet. "That nose is Galt-like—and the set of the ears—and a kind of something to the neck and shoulders."

"Maybe so," said Fanny doubtfully. She shook her head drearily, sighed. "What's the use? Lorella's gone. And this morning General Galt came down to see my husband with a letter he'd got from Jimmie. Jimmie denies it. Perhaps so. Again, perhaps the General wrote him to write that, and threatened him if he didn't. But what's the use? We'll never know."

And they never did.

When young Stevens was leaving, George Warham waylaid him at the front gate, separated from the spacious old creeper-clad house by long lawns and an avenue of elms. "I hear the child's going to live," said he anxiously.

"I've never seen anything more alive," replied Stevens.

Warham stared gloomily at the ground. He was evidently ashamed of his feelings, yet convinced that they were human and natural. A moment's silence between the men, then Stevens put his hand on the gate latch. "Did—did—my wife——" began Warham. "Did she say what she calculated to do?"

"Not a word, George." After a silence. "You know how fond she is of babies."

"Yes, I know," replied Warham. "Fanny is a true woman if ever there was one." With a certain defiance, "And Lorella—she was a sweet, womanly girl!"

"As sweet and good as she was pretty," replied Stevens heartily.

"The way she kept her mouth shut about that hound, whoever he is!" Warham's Roman face grew savage, revealed in startling apparition a stubborn cruelty of which there was not a trace upon the surface. "If I ever catch the —— —— I'll fill him full of holes."

"He'd be lynched—*whoever* he is," said Stevens.

"That's right!" cried Warham. "This is the North, but it's near enough to Kentucky to know what to do with a wretch of that sort." His face became calmer. "That poor little baby! He'll have a hard row to hoe."

Stevens flushed a guilty red. "It's—it's—a girl," he stammered.

Warham stared. "A *girl!*" he cried. Then his face reddened and in a furious tone he burst out: "Now don't that beat the devil for luck! . . . A girl! Good Lord—a girl!"

"Nobody in this town'll blame her," consoled Stevens.

"You know better than that, Bob! A girl! Why, it's downright wicked . . . I wonder what Fanny allows to do?" He showed what fear was in his mind by wheeling savagely on Stevens with a stormy, "We can't keep her—we simply can't!"

9

"What's to become of her?" protested Stevens gently.

Warham made a wild vague gesture with both arms. "Damn if I know! I've got to look out for my own daughter. I won't have it. Damn it, I won't have it!"

Stevens lifted the gate latch. "Well——

"Good-by, George. I'll look in again this evening." And knowing the moral ideas of the town, all he could muster by way of encouragement was a half-hearted "Don't borrow trouble."

But Warham did not hear. He was moving up the tanbark walk toward the house, muttering to himself. When Fanny, unable longer to conceal Lorella's plight, had told him, pity and affection for his sweet sister-in-law who had made her home with them for five years had triumphed over his principles. He had himself arranged for Fanny to hide Lorella in New York until she could safely return. But just as the sisters were about to set out, Lorella, low in body and in mind, fell ill. Then George—and Fanny, too —had striven with her to give them the name of her betrayer, that he might be compelled to do her justice. Lorella refused. "I told him," she said, "and he—I never want to see him again." They pleaded the disgrace to them, but she replied that he would not marry her even if she would marry him; and she held to her refusal with the firmness for which the Lenoxes were famous. They suspected Jimmie Galt, because he had been about the most attentive of the young men until two or three months before, and because he had abruptly departed for Europe to study architecture. Lorella denied that it was he. "If you kill him," she said to Warham, "you kill an innocent man." Warham was so exasperated by her obstinacy that he was at first for taking her at her offer and letting her go away. But Fanny would not hear of it, and he acquiesced. Now—"This child must be sent away off somewhere, and never be heard of again," he said to himself. "If it'd been a boy, perhaps it might have got along. But a girl——

"There's nothing can be done to make things right for a girl that's got no father and no name."

The subject did not come up between him and his wife until about a week after Lorella's funeral. But he was thinking of nothing else. At his big grocery store—wholesale and retail—he sat morosely in his office, brooding over the disgrace and the danger of deeper disgrace—for he saw what a hold the baby already had upon his wife. He was ashamed to appear in the streets; he knew what was going on behind the sympathetic faces, heard the whisperings as if they had been trumpetings. And he was as much afraid of his own soft heart as of his wife's. But for the sake of his daughter he must be firm and just.

One morning, as he was leaving the house after breakfast, he turned back and said abruptly: "Fan, don't you think you'd better send the baby away and get it over with?"

"No," said his wife unhesitatingly—and he knew his worst suspicion was correct. "I've made up my mind to keep her."

"It isn't fair to Ruth."

"Send it away—where?"

"Anywhere. Get it adopted in Chicago—Cincinnati—Louisville."

"Lorella's baby?"

"When she and Ruth grow up—what then?"

"People ain't so low as some think."

11

" 'The sins of the parents are visited on the children unto——' "

"I don't care," interrupted Fanny. "I love her. I'm going to keep her. Wait here a minute."

When she came back she had the baby in her arms. "Just look," she said softly.

George frowned, tried not to look, but was soon drawn and held by the sweet, fresh, blooming face, so smooth, so winning, so innocent.

"And think how she was sent back to life—from beyond the grave. It must have been for some purpose."

Warham groaned, "Oh, Lord, I don't know *what* to do! But—it ain't fair to our Ruth."

"I don't see it that way. . . . Kiss her, George."

Warham kissed one of the soft cheeks, swelling like a ripening apple. The baby opened wide a pair of wonderful dark eyes, threw up its chubby arms and laughed—such a laugh! . . . There was no more talk of sending her away.

II

NOT quite seventeen years later, on a fine June morning, Ruth Warham issued hastily from the house and started down the long tanbark walk from the front veranda to the street gate. She was now nineteen—nearer twenty—and a very pretty young woman, indeed. She had grown up one of those small slender blondes, exquisite and doll-like, who cannot help seeming fresh and sweet, whatever the truth about them, without or within. This morning she had on a new summer dress of a blue that matched her eyes and harmonized with her coloring. She was looking her best, and she had the satisfying, confidence-giving sense that it was so. Like most of the unattached girls of small towns, she was always dreaming of the handsome stranger who would fall in love —the thrilling, love-story kind of love—at first sight. The weather plays a conspicuous part in the romancings of youth; she felt that this was precisely the kind of day fate would be most likely to select for the meeting. Just before dressing she had been reading about the wonderful *him*—in Robert Chambers' latest story—and she had spent full fifteen minutes of blissful reverie over the accompanying Fisher illustration. Now she was issuing hopefully forth, as hopefully as if adventure were the rule and order of life in Sutherland, instead of a desperate monotony made the harder to bear by the glory of its scenery.

She had got only far enough from the house to be

visible to the second-story windows when a young voice called:

"Ruthie! Aren't you going to wait for me?"

Ruth halted; an expression anything but harmonious with the pretty blue costume stormed across her face. "I won't have her along!" she muttered. "I simply won't!" She turned slowly and, as she turned, effaced every trace of temper with a dexterity which might have given an onlooker a poorer opinion of her character than perhaps the facts as to human nature justify. The countenance she presently revealed to those upper windows was sunny and sweet. No one was visible; but the horizontal slats in one of the only closed pair of shutters and a vague suggestion of movement rather than form behind them gave the impression that a woman, not far enough dressed to risk being seen from the street, was hidden there. Evidently Ruth knew, for it was toward this window that she directed her gaze and the remark: "Can't wait, dear. I'm in a great hurry. Mamma wants the silk right away and I've got to match it."

"But I'll be only a minute," pleaded the voice—a much more interesting, more musical voice than Ruth's rather shrill and thin high soprano.

"No—I'll meet you up at papa's store."

"All right."

Ruth resumed her journey. She smiled to herself. "That means," said she, half aloud, "I'll steer clear of the store this morning."

But as she was leaving the gate into the wide, shady, sleepy street, who should come driving past in a village cart but Lottie Wright! And Lottie reined her pony in to the sidewalk and in the shade of a symmetrical walnut tree proceeded to invite Ruth to a dance—a long story, as Lottie had to tell all about it, the decorations, the favors, the food, who would be there, what she was going to wear, and so on and on. Ruth was intensely interested but kept remembering something that caused her to glance uneasily from time to time up the tanbark walk under the arching boughs toward the house. Even if she had not been interested, she would hardly have ventured to break off; Lottie Wright was the only daughter of the richest man in Sutherland and, therefore, social arbiter to the younger set.

Lottie stopped abruptly, said: "Well, I really must get on. And there's your cousin coming down the walk. I know you've been waiting for her."

Ruth tried to keep in countenance, but a blush of shame and a frown of irritation came in spite of her.

"I'm sorry I can't ask Susie, too," pursued Lottie, in a voice of hypocritical regret. "But there are to be exactly eighteen couples—and I couldn't."

"Of course not," said Ruth heartily. "Susan'll understand."

"I wouldn't for the world do anything to hurt her feelings," continued Lottie with the self-complacent righteousness of a deacon telling the congregation how good "grace" has made him. Her prominent commonplace brown eyes were gazing up the walk, an expression distressingly like envious anger in them. She had a thick, pudgy face, an oily skin, an outcropping of dull red pimples on the chin. Many women can indulge their passion for sweets at meals and sweets between meals without serious injury—to complexion; Lottie Wright, unluckily, couldn't.

"I feel sorry for Susie," she went on, in the ludicrous patronizing tone that needs no describing to anyone

15

acquainted with any fashionable set anywhere from China to Peru. "And I think the way you all treat her is simply beautiful. But, then, everybody feels sorry for her and tries to be kind. She knows—about herself, I mean—doesn't she, Ruthie?"

"I guess so," replied Ruth, almost hanging her head in her mortification. "She's very good and sweet."

"Indeed, she is," said Lottie. "And father says she's far and away the prettiest girl in town."

With this parting shot, which struck precisely where she had aimed, Lottie gathered up the reins and drove on, calling out a friendly "Hello, Susie dearie," to Susan Lenox, who, on her purposely lagging way from the house, had nearly reached the gate.

"What a nasty thing Lottie Wright is!" exclaimed Ruth to her cousin.

"She has a mean tongue," admitted Susan, tall and slim and straight, with glorious dark hair and a skin healthily pallid and as smooth as clear. "But she's got a good heart. She gives a lot away to poor people."

"Because she likes to patronize and be kowtowed to," retorted Ruth. "She's mean, I tell you." Then, with a vicious gleam in the blue eyes that hinted a deeper and less presentable motive for the telling, she added: "Why, she's not going to ask you to her party."

Susan was obviously unmoved. "She has the right to ask whom she pleases. And"—she laughed—"if I were giving a party I'd not want to ask her—though I might do it for fear she'd feel left out."

"Don't you feel—left out?"

Susan shook her head. "I seem not to care much about going to parties lately. The boys don't like

16

to dance with me, and I get tired of sitting the dances out."

This touched Ruth's impulsively generous heart and woman's easy tears filled her eyes; her cousin's remark was so pathetic, the more pathetic because its pathos was absolutely unconscious. Ruth shot a pitying glance at Susan, but the instant she saw the loveliness of the features upon which that expression of unconsciousness lay like innocence upon a bed of roses, the pity vanished from her eyes to be replaced by a disfiguring envy as hateful as an evil emotion can be at nineteen. Susan still lacked nearly a month of seventeen, but she seemed older than Ruth because her mind and her body had developed beyond her years —or, perhaps it would be more accurate to say beyond the average of growth at seventeen. Also, her personality was stronger, far more definite. Ruth tried to believe herself the cleverer and the more beautiful, at times with a certain success. But as she happened to be a shrewd young person—an inheritance from the Warhams—she was haunted by misgivings— and worse. Those whose vanity never suffers from these torments will, of course, condemn her; but whoever has known the pain of having to concede superiority to someone with whom she—or he—is constantly contrasted will not be altogether without sympathy for Ruth in her struggles, often vain struggles, against the mortal sin of jealousy.

The truth is, Susan was beyond question the beauty of Sutherland. Her eyes, very dark at birth, had changed to a soft, dreamy violet-gray. Hair and coloring, lashes and eyebrows remained dark; thus her eyes and the intense red of her lips had that vicinage of contrast which is necessary to distinction.

17

To look at her was to be at once fascinated by those violet-gray eyes—by their color, by their clearness, by their regard of calm, grave inquiry, by their mystery not untouched by a certain sadness. She had a thick abundance of wavy hair, not so long as Ruth's golden braids, but growing beautifully instead of thinly about her low brow, about her delicately modeled ears, and at the back of her exquisite neck. Her slim nose departed enough from the classic line to prevent the suggestion of monotony that is in all purely classic faces. Her nostrils had the sensitiveness that more than any other outward sign indicates the imaginative temperament. Her chin and throat—to look at them was to know where her lover would choose to kiss her first. When she smiled her large even teeth were dazzling. And the smile itself was exceedingly sweet and winning, with the violet-gray eyes casting over it that seriousness verging on sadness which is the natural outlook of a highly intelligent nature. For while stupid vain people are suspicious and easily offended, only the intelligent are truly sensitive—keenly susceptible to all sensations. The dull ear is suspicious; the acute ear is sensitive.

The intense red of her lips, at times so vivid that it seemed artificial, and their sinuous, sensitive curve indicated a temperament that was frankly proclaimed in her figure—sensuous, graceful, slender—the figure of girlhood in its perfection and of perfect womanhood, too—like those tropical flowers that look innocent and young and fresh, yet stir in the beholder passionate longings and visions. Her walk was worthy of face and figure—free and firm and graceful, the small head carried proudly without haughtiness.

This physical beauty had as an aureole to illuminate it and to set it off a manner that was wholly devoid of mannerisms—of those that men and women think out and exhibit to give added charm to themselves—tricks of cuteness, as lisp and baby stare; tricks of dignity, as grave brow and body always carried rigidly erect; tricks of sweetness and kindliness, as the ever ready smile and the warm handclasp. Susan, the interested in the world about her, Susan, the self-unconscious, had none of these tricks. She was at all times her own self. Beauty is anything but rare, likewise intelligence. But this quality of naturalness is the greatest of all qualities. It made Susan Lenox unique.

It was not strange—nor inexcusable—that the girls and their parents had begun to pity Susan as soon as this beauty developed and this personality had begun to exhale its delicious perfume. It was but natural that they should start the whole town to "being kind to the poor thing." And it was equally the matter of course that they should have achieved their object —should have impressed the conventional masculine mind of the town with such a sense of the "poor thing's" social isolation and "impossibility" that the boys ceased to be her eagerly admiring friends, were afraid to be alone with her, to ask her to dance. Women are conventional as a business; but with men conventionality is a groveling superstition. The youths of Sutherland longed for, sighed for the alluring, sweet, bright Susan; but they dared not, with all the women saying "Poor thing! What a pity a nice man can't afford to have anything to do with her!" It was an interesting typical example of the profound snobbishness of the male character. Rarely, after Susan was sixteen, did any of the boys venture to ask her to dance and so give himself the joy of encircling that lovely form of hers; yet from babyhood her fascination for the male sex, regardless of age or temperament, had been uncanny—"naturally, she being a love-child," said the old women. And from fourteen on, it grew steadily.

It would be difficult for one who has not lived in a small town to understand exactly the kind of isolation to which Sutherland consigned the girl without her realizing it, without their fully realizing it themselves. Everyone was friendly with her. A stranger would not have noticed any difference in the treatment of her and of her cousin Ruth. Yet not one of the young men would have thought of marrying her, would have regarded her as his equal or the equal of his sisters. She went to all the general entertainments. She was invited to all the houses when failure to invite her would have seemed pointed—but only then. She did not think much about herself; she was fond of study—fonder of reading—fondest, perhaps, of making dresses and hats, especially for Ruth, whom she thought much prettier than herself. Thus, she was only vaguely, subconsciously conscious of there being something peculiar and mysterious in her lot.

This isolation, rather than her dominant quality of self-effacing consideration for others, was the chief cause of the extraordinary innocence of her mind. No servant, no girl, no audacious boy ever ventured to raise with her any question remotely touching on sex. All those questions seemed to Puritan Sutherland in any circumstances highly indelicate; in relation to Susan they seemed worse than indelicate, dreadful though the thought was that there could be anything worse

20

than indelicacy. At fifteen she remained as unaware of even the existence of the mysteries of sex as she had been at birth. Nothing definite enough to arouse her curiosity had ever been said in her hearing; and such references to those matters as she found in her reading passed her by, as any matter of which he has not the beginnings of knowledge will fail to arrest the attention of any reader. It was generally assumed that she knew all about her origin, that someone had, some time or other, told her. Even her Aunt Fanny thought so, thought she was hiding the knowledge deep in her heart, explained in that way her content with the solitude of books and sewing.

Susan was the worst possible influence in Ruth's life. Our character is ourself, is born with us, clings to us as the flesh to our bones, persists unchanged until we die. But upon the circumstances that surround us depends what part of our character shall show itself. Ruth was born with perhaps something more than the normal tendency to be envious and petty. But these qualities might never have shown themselves conspicuously had there been no Susan for her to envy. The very qualities that made Susan lovable reacted upon the pretty, pert blond cousin to make her the more unlovable. Again and again, when she and Susan were about to start out together, and Susan would appear in beauty and grace of person and dress, Ruth would excuse herself, would fly to her room to lock herself in and weep and rage and hate. And at the high school, when Susan scored in a recitation or in some dramatic entertainment, Ruth would sit with bitten lip and surging bosom, pale with jealousy. Susan's isolation, the way the boys avoided having with her the friendly relations that

spring up naturally among young people—these gave
Ruth a partial revenge. But Susan, seemingly unconscious, rising sweetly and serenely above all pettiness—

Ruth's hatred deepened, though she hid it from
everyone, almost from herself. And she depended more
and more utterly upon Susan to select her clothes for
her, to dress her, to make her look well; for Susan
had taste and Ruth had not.

On that bright June morning as the cousins went
up Main Street together, Susan gave herself over
to the delight of sun and air and of the flowering
gardens before the attractive houses they were passing; Ruth, with the day quite dark for her, all its
joys gone, was fighting against a hatred of her cousin
so vicious that it made her afraid. "I'll have no chance
at all," her angry heart was saying, "so long as Susie's around, keeping everybody reminded of the family shame." And that was a truth she could not
downface, mean and ungenerous though thinking it
might be. The worst of all was that Susan, in a simple white dress and an almost untrimmed white straw
hat with a graceful curve to its brim and set at the right
angle upon that wavy dark hair, was making the
beauty of her short blond cousin dim and somehow
common.

At the corner of Maple Street Ruth's self-control
reached its limit. She halted, took the sample of
silk from her glove. There was not a hint of her feelings in her countenance, for shame and the desire to
seem to be better than she was were fast making her
an adept in hypocrisy. "You go ahead and match
it for mamma," said she. "I've got to run in and see
Bessie Andrews."

"But I promised Uncle George I'd come and help him with the monthly bills," objected Susan.

"You can do both. It'll take you only a minute. If mother had known you were going uptown, she'd never have trusted *me*." And Ruth had tucked the sample in Susan's belt and was hurrying out Maple Street. There was nothing for Susan to do but go on alone.

Two squares, and she was passing the show place of Sutherland, the home of the Wrights. She paused to regale herself with a glance into the grove of magnificent elms with lawns and bright gardens beyond —for the Wright place filled the entire square between Broad and Myrtle Streets and from Main to Monroe. She was starting on when she saw among the trees a young man in striped flannels. At the same instant he saw her.

"Hel-*lo*, Susie!" he cried. "I was thinking about you."

Susan halted. "When did you get back, Sam?" she asked. "I heard you were going to stay on in the East all summer."

After they had shaken hands across the hedge that came almost to their shoulders, Susan began to move on. Sam kept pace with her on his side of the carefully trimmed boxwood barrier. "I'm going back East in about two weeks," said he. "It's awfully dull here after Yale. I just blew in—haven't seen Lottie or father yet. Coming to Lottie's party?"

"No," said Susan.

"Why not?"

Susan laughed merrily. "The best reason in the world. Lottie has only invited just so many couples."

"I'll see about that," cried Sam. "You'll be asked all right, all right."

"No," said Susan. She was one of those whose way of saying no gives its full meaning and intent. "I'll not be asked, thank you—and I'll not go if I am."

By this time they were at the gate. He opened it, came out into the street. He was a tallish, athletic youth, dark, and pleasing enough of feature to be called handsome. He was dressed with a great deal of style of the efflorescent kind called sophomoric. He was a Sophomore at Yale. But that was not so largely responsible for his self-complacent expression as the deference he had got from babyhood through being heir apparent to the Wright fortune. He had a sophisticated way of inspecting Susan's charms of figure no less than charms of face that might have made a disagreeable impression upon an experienced onlooker. There is a time for feeling without knowing why one feels; and that period ought not to have been passed for young Wright for many a year.

"My, but you're looking fine, Susie!" exclaimed he. "I haven't seen anyone that could hold a candle to you—even in the East."

Susan laughed and blushed with pleasure. "Go on," said she with raillery. "I love it."

"Come in and sit under the trees and I'll fill all the time you'll give me."

This reminded her. "I must hurry uptown," she said. "Good-by."

"Hold on!" cried he. "What have you got to do?" He happened to glance down the street. "Isn't that Ruth coming?"

"So it is," said Susan. "I guess Bessie Andrews wasn't at home."

Sam waved at Ruth and called, "Hello! Glad to see you."

Ruth was all sweetness and smiles. She and her mother—quite privately and with nothing openly said on either side—had canvassed Sam as a "possibility." There had been keen disappointment at the news that he was not coming home for the long vacation. "How are you, Sam?" said she, as they shook hands. "My, Susie, *doesn't* he look New York?"

Sam tried to conceal that he was swelling with pride. "Oh, this is nothing," said he deprecatingly.

Ruth's heart was a-flutter. The Fisher picture of the Chambers love-maker, thought she, might almost be a photograph of Sam. She was glad she had obeyed the mysterious impulse to make a toilette of unusual elegance that morning. How get rid of Susan? "*I'll* take the sample, Susie," said she. "Then you won't have to keep father waiting."

Susie gave up the sample. Her face was no longer so bright and interested.

"Oh, drop it," cried Sam. "Come in—both of you. I'll telephone for Joe Andrews and we'll take a drive —or anything you like." He was looking at Susan.

"Can't do it," replied Susan. "I promised Uncle George."

"Oh, bother!" urged Sam. "Telephone him. It'll be all right—won't it, Ruth?"

"You don't know Susie," said Ruth, with a queer, strained laugh. "She'd rather die than break a promise."

"I must go," Susan now said. "Good-by."

"Come on, Ruth," cried Sam. "Let's walk uptown with her."

"And you can help match the silk," said Ruth.

"Not for me," replied young Wright. Then to Susan, "What've *you* got to do? Maybe it's something I could help at."

"No. It's for Uncle George and me."

"Well, I'll go as far as the store. Then—we'll see."

They were now in the business part of Main Street, were at Wilson's dry goods store. "You might find it here," suggested the innocent Susan to her cousin.

Ruth colored, veiled her eyes to hide their flash. "I've got to go to the store first—to get some money," she hastily improvised.

Sam had been walking between the two girls. He now changed to the outside and, so, put himself next Susan alone, put Susan between him and Ruth. The maneuver seemed to be a mere politeness, but Ruth knew better. What fate had intended as her lucky day was being changed into unlucky by this cousin of hers. Ruth walked sullenly along, hot tears in her eyes and a choke in her throat, as she listened to Sam's flatterings of her cousin, and to Susan's laughing, delighted replies. She tried to gather herself together, to think up something funny or at least interesting with which to break into the *tête-à-tête* and draw Sam to herself. She could think nothing but envious, hateful thoughts. At the doors of Warham and Company, wholesale and retail grocers, the three halted.

"I guess I'll go to Vandermark's," said Ruth. "I really don't need money. Come on, Sam."

"No—I'm going back home. I ought to see Lottie and father. My, but it's dull in this town!"

"Well, so long," said Susan. She nodded, sparkling of hair and skin and eyes, and went into the store.

Sam and Ruth watched her as she walked down the broad aisle between the counters. From the store came a mingling of odors of fruit, of spices, of freshly ground coffee. "Susan's an awful pretty girl, isn't she?" declared Sam with rude enthusiasm.

"Indeed she is," replied Ruth as heartily—and with an honest if discouraged effort to feel enthusiastic.

"What a figure! And she has such a good walk. Most women walk horribly."

"Come on to Vandermark's with me and I'll stroll back with you," offered Ruth. Sam was still gazing into the store where, far to the rear, Susan could be seen; the graceful head, the gently swelling bust, the soft lines of the white dress, the pretty ankles revealed by the short skirt—there was, indeed, a profile worth a man's looking at on a fine June day. Ruth's eyes were upon Sam, handsome, dressed in the Eastern fashion, an ideal lover. "Come on, Sam," urged Ruth.

"No, thanks," he replied absently. "I'll go back. Good luck!" And not glancing at her, he lifted his straw hat with its band of Yale blue and set out.

Ruth moved slowly and disconsolately in the opposite direction. She was ashamed of her thoughts; but shame never yet withheld anybody from being human in thought. As she turned to enter Vandermark's she glanced down the street. There was Sam, returned and going into her father's store. She hesitated, could devise no plan of action, hurried into the dry goods store. Sinclair, the head salesman and the beau of Sutherland, was an especial friend of hers. The tall, slender, hungry-looking young man, devoured with ambition for speedy wealth, had no mind to neglect so easy an aid to that ambition as nature gave him in making him a lady-charmer. He had resolved to marry either Lottie Wright or Ruth Warham—Ruth preferred, because, while Lottie would have many times

more money, her skin made her a stiff dose for a
young man brought up to the American tradition that
the face is the woman. But that morning Sinclair
exerted his charms in vain. Ruth was in a hurry, was
distinctly rude, cut short what in other circumstances
would have been a prolonged and delightful flirtation
by tossing the sample on the counter and asking him
to do the matching for her and to send the silk right
away. Which said, she fairly bolted from the store.

She arrived barely in time. Young Wright was
issuing from Warham and Company. He smiled
friendly enough, but Ruth knew where his thoughts
were. "Get what you wanted?" inquired he, and went
on to explain: "I came back to find out if you and
Susie were to be at home this evening. Thought I'd
call."

Ruth paled with angry dismay. She was going to
a party at the Sinclairs'—one to which Susan was
not invited. "Aren't you going to Sinclairs'?" said
she.

"I was. But I thought I'd rather call. Perhaps
I'll go there later."

He was coming to call on Susan! All the way down
Main Stree. to the Wright place Ruth fought against
her mood of angry and depressed silence, tried to make
the best of her chance to impress Sam. But Sam was
absent and humiliatingly near to curt. He halted at
his father's gate. She halted also, searched the
grounds with anxious eyes for sign of Lottie that
would give her the excuse for entering.

"So long," said Sam.

"Do come to Sinclairs' early. You always did dance
so well."

"Oh, dancing bores me," said the blasé Sophomore.

"But I'll be round before the shindy's over. I've got to take Lot home."

He lifted the hat again with what both he and Ruth regarded as a gesture of most elegant carelessness. Ruth strolled reluctantly on, feeling as if her toilet had been splashed or crushed. As she entered the front door her mother, in a wrapper and curl papers, appeared at the head of the stairs. "Why!" cried she. "Where's the silk? It's for your dress tonight, you know."

"It'll be along," was Ruth's answer, her tone dreary, her lip quivering. "I met Sam Wright."

"Oh!" exclaimed her mother. "He's back, is he?"

Ruth did not reply. She came on up the stairs, went into the sitting-room—the room where Doctor Stevens seventeen years before had torn the baby Susan from the very claws of death. She flung herself down, buried her head in her arms upon that same table. She burst into a storm of tears.

"Why, dearie dear," cried her mother, "whatever is the matter?"

"It's wicked and hateful," sobbed the girl, "but—— Oh, mamma, I *hate* Susan! She was along, and Sam hardly noticed me, and he's coming here this evening to call."

"But you'll be at Sinclairs'!" exclaimed Mrs. Warham.

"Not Susan," sobbed Ruth. "He wants to see only her."

The members of the Second Presbyterian Church, of which Fanny Warham was about the most exemplary and assiduous female member, would hardly have recognized the face encircled by that triple row of curl-papered locks, shinily plastered with quince-seed liquor.

She was at woman's second critical age, and the strange emotions working in her mind—of whose disorder no one had an inkling—were upon the surface now. She ventured this freedom of facial expression because her daughter's face was hid. She did not speak. She laid a tender defending hand for an instant upon her daughter's shoulder—like the caress of love and encouragement the lioness gives her cub as she is about to give battle for it. Then she left the room. She did not know what to do, but she knew she must and would do something.

III

THE telephone was downstairs, in the rear end of the hall which divided the lower floor into two equal parts. But hardly had Mrs. Warham given the Sinclairs' number to the exchange girl when Ruth called from the head of the stairs:

"What're you doing there, mamma?"

"I'll tell Mrs. Sinclair you're sick and can't come. Then I'll send Susan in your place."

"Don't!" cried Ruth, in an agitated, angry voice. "Ring off—quick!"

"Now, Ruth, let me——"

"Ring off!" ordered Ruth. "You mustn't do that. You'll have the whole town talking about how I'm throwing myself at Sam's head—and that I'm jealous of Susan."

Mrs. Warham said, "Never mind" into the telephone sender and hung up the receiver. She was frightened, but not convinced. Hers was a slow, old-fashioned mind, and to it the scheme it had worked out seemed a model of skillful duplicity. But Ruth, of the younger and subtler generation, realized instantly how transparent the thing was. Mrs. Warham was abashed but not angered by her daughter's curt contempt.

"It's the only way I can think of," said she. "And I still don't see——"

"Of course you don't," cut in Ruth, ruffled by the perilously narrow escape from being the laughing stock of the town. "People aren't as big fools as they

31

used to be, mamma. They don't believe nowadays everything that's told them. There isn't anybody that doesn't know I'm never sick. No—we'll have to——"

She reflected a moment, pausing halfway down the stairs, while her mother watched her swollen and tear-stained face.

"We might send Susan away for the evening," suggested the mother.

"Yes," assented the daughter. "Papa could take her with him for a drive to North Sutherland—to see the Provosts. Then Sam'd come straight on to the Sinclairs'."

"I'll call up your father."

"No!" cried Ruth, stamping her foot. "Call up Mr. Provost, and tell him papa's coming. Then you can talk with papa when he gets home to dinner."

"But maybe——"

"If that doesn't work out we can do something else this afternoon."

The mother and the daughter avoided each other's eyes. Both felt mean and small, guilty toward Susan; but neither was for that reason disposed to draw back. As Mrs. Warham was trying the new dress on her daughter, she said:

"Anyhow, Sam'd be wasting time on Susan. He'd hang round her for no good. She'd simply get talked about. The poor child can't be lively or smile but what people begin to wonder if she's going the way of —of Lorella."

"That's so," agreed Ruth, and both felt better. "Was Aunt Lorella *very* pretty, mamma?"

"Lovely!" replied Fanny, and her eyes grew tender, for she had adored Lorella. "You never saw such a complexion—like Susan's, only snow-white." Nervously and hastily, "Most as fine as yours, Ruthie."

Ruth gazed complacently into the mirror. "I'm glad I'm fair, and not big," said she.

"Yes, indeed! I like the womanly woman. And so do men."

"Don't you think we ought to send Susan away to visit somewhere?" asked Ruth at the next opportunity for talk the fitting gave. "It's getting more and more—pointed—the way people act. And she's so sweet and good, I'd hate to have her feelings hurt." In a burst of generosity, "She's the most considerate human being I ever knew. She'd give up anything rather than see someone else put out. She's too much that way."

"We can't be too much that way," said Mrs. Warham in mechanical Christian reproof.

"Oh, I know," retorted Ruth, "that's all very well for church and Sundays. But I guess if you want to get along you've got to look out for Number One. . . . Yes, she ought to visit somewhere."

"I've been trying to think," said her mother. "She couldn't go any place but your Uncle Zeke's. But it's so lonesome out there I haven't the heart to send her. Besides, she wouldn't know what to make of it."

"What'd father say?"

"That's another thing." Mrs. Warham had latterly grown jealous—not without reason—of her husband's partiality for Susan.

Ruth sighed. "Oh, dear!" cried she. "I don't know what to do. How's she ever going to get married!"

"If she'd only been a boy!" said Mrs. Warham, on her knees, taking the unevenness out of the front of the skirt. "A girl has to suffer for her mother's sins."

Ruth made no reply. She smiled to herself—the comment of the younger generation upon the older. Sin it might have been; but, worse than that, it was a stupidity—to let a man make a fool of her. Lorella must have been a poor weak-minded creature.

By dinner time Ruth had completely soothed and smoothed her vanity. Sam had been caught by Susan simply because he had seen Susan before he saw her.

All that would be necessary was a good chance at him, and he would never look at Susan again. He had been in the East, where the admired type was her own—refined, ladylike, the woman of the dainty appearance and manners and tastes. A brief undisturbed exposure to her charms and Susan would seem coarse and countrified to him. There was no denying that Susan had style, but it was fully effective only when applied to a sunny fairy-like beauty such as hers.

But at midday, when Susan came in with Warham, Ruth's jealousy opened all her inward-bleeding wounds again. Susan's merry eyes, her laughing mouth, her funny way of saying even commonplace things—how could quiet, unobtrusive, ladylike charms such as Ruth's have a chance if Susan were about? She waited, silent and anxious, while her mother was having the talk with her father in the sitting-room. Warham, mere man, was amused by his wife's scheming.

"Don't put yourself out, Fanny," said he. "If the boy wants Ruth and she wants him, why, well and good. But you'll only make a mess interfering. Let the young people alone."

"I'm surprised, George Warham," cried Fanny, "that you can show so little sense and heart."

"To hear you talk, I'd think marriage was a business, like groceries."

Mrs. Warham thought it was, in a sense. But she would never have dared say so aloud, even to her husband—or, rather, especially to her husband. In matters of men and women he was thoroughly innocent, with the simplicity of the old-time man of the small town and the country; he fancied that, while in grocery matters and the like the world was full of guile, in matters of the heart it was idyllic, Arcadian, with never a thought of duplicity, except among a few obviously wicked and designing people.

"I guess we both want to see Ruth married well," was all she could venture.

"I'd rather the girls stayed with us," declared Warham. "I'd hate to give them up."

"Of course," hastily agreed Fanny. "Still—it's the regular order of nature."

"Oh, Ruth'll marry—only too soon," said Warham. "And marry well. I'm not so sure, though, that marrying any of old Wright's breed would be marrying what ought to be called well. Money isn't everything —not by a long sight—though, of course, it's comfortable."

"I never heard anything against Sam," protested Mrs. Warham.

"You've heard what I've heard—that he's wild and loose. But then you women like that in a man."

"We've got to put up with it, you mean," cried Fanny, indignant.

"Women like it," persisted Warham. "And I guess Sam's only sowing the usual wild oats, getting ready to settle. No, mother, you let Ruth alone. If she wants him, she'll get him—she or Susan."

Mrs. Warham compressed her lips and lowered her eyes. Ruth or Susan—as if it didn't matter which! "Susan isn't *ours*," she could not refrain from saying.

"Indeed, she is!" retorted George warmly. "Why, she couldn't be more our own——"

"Yes, certainly," interrupted Fanny.

She moved toward the door. She saw that without revealing her entire scheme—hers and Ruth's—she could make no headway with George. And if she did reveal it he would sternly veto it. So she gave up that direction. She went upstairs; George took his hat from the front hall rack and pushed open the screen door. As he appeared on the veranda Susan was picking dead leaves from one of the hanging baskets; Ruth, seated in the hammock, hands in lap, her whole attitude intensely still, was watching her with narrowed eyes.

"What's this I hear," cried Warham, laughing, "about you two girls setting your caps for Sam Wright?" And his good-humored brown eyes glanced at Ruth, passed on to Susan's wealth of wavy dark hair and long, rounded form, and lingered there.

Ruth lowered her eyes and compressed her lips, a trick she had borrowed from her mother along with the peculiarities of her mother's disposition that it fitted. Susan flung a laughing glance over her shoulder at her uncle. "Not Ruth," said she. "Only me. I saw him first, so he's mine. He's coming to see me this evening."

"So I hear. Well, the moon's full and your aunt and I'll not interrupt—at least not till ten o'clock. No callers on a child like you after ten."

"Oh, I don't think I'll be able to hold him that long."

"Don't you fret, Brownie. But I mustn't make you vain. Coming along to the store?"

"No. Tomorrow," said Susan. "I can finish in the morning. I'm going to wear my white dress with embroidery, and it's got to be pressed—and that means I must do it myself."

"Poor Sam! And I suppose, when he calls, you'll come down as if you'd put on any old thing and didn't care whether he came or not. And you'll have primped for an hour—and he, too—shaving and combing and trying different ties."

Susan sparkled at the idea of a young man, and *such* a young man, taking trouble for her. Ruth, pale, kept her eyes down and her lips compressed. She was picturing the gallant appearance the young Sophomore from Yale, away off in the gorgeous fashionable East, would make as he came in at that gate yonder and up the walk and seated himself on the veranda—with Susan! Evidently her mother had failed; Susan was not to be taken away.

When Warham departed down the walk Ruth rose; she could not bear being alone with her triumphant rival—triumphant because unconscious. She knew that to get Sam to herself all she would have to do would be to hint to Susan, the generous, what she wanted. But pride forbade that. As her hand was on the knob of the screen door, Susan said: "Why don't you like Sam?"

"Oh, I think he's stuck-up. He's been spoiled in the East."

"Why, I don't see any sign of it."

"You were too flattered by his talking to you," said Ruth, with a sweet-sour little laugh—an asp of a sneer hid in a basket of flowers.

Susan felt the sting; but, seeing only the flowers, did not dream whence it had come. "It *was* nice, wasn't it?" said she, gayly. "Maybe you're right about him, but I can't help liking him. You must admit he's handsome."

"He has a bad look in his eyes," replied Ruth. Such rage against Susan was swelling within her that it seemed to her she would faint if she did not release at least part of it. "You want to look out for him, Susie," said she, calmly and evenly. "You don't want to take what he says seriously."

"Of course not," said Susan, quite honestly, though she, no more than the next human being, could avoid taking seriously whatever was pleasantly flattering.

"He'd never think of marrying you." Ruth trembled before and after delivering this venomous shaft.

"Marrying!" cried Susan, again quite honestly. "Why, I'm only seventeen."

Ruth drew a breath of relief. The shaft had glanced off the armor of innocence without making the faintest dent. She rushed into the house. She did not dare trust herself with her cousin. What might the demon within her tempt her to say next?

"Come up, Ruth!" called her mother. "The dress is ready for the last try-on. I think it's going to hang beautifully."

Ruth dragged herself up the stairs, lagged into the sitting-room, gazed at the dress with a scowl. "What did father say?" she asked.

"It's no use trying to do anything with your father."

Ruth flung herself in a corner of the sofa.

"The only thing I can think of," said her mother, humbly and timidly, "is phone the Sinclairs as I originally set out to do."

"And have the whole town laughing at me. . . . Oh, what do I care, anyhow!"

"Arthur Sinclair's taller and a sight handsomer. Right in the face, Sam's as plain as Dick's hatband. His looks is all clothes and polish—and mighty poor polish, I think. Arthur's got rise in him, too, while Sam—well, I don't know what'd become of him if old Wright lost his money."

But Arthur, a mere promise, seemed poor indeed beside Sam, the actually arrived. To marry Sam would be to step at once into grandeur; to marry Arthur would mean years of struggle. Besides, Arthur was heavy, at least seemed heavy to light Ruth, while Sam was her ideal of gay elegance. "I *detest* Arthur Sinclair," she now announced.

"You can get Sam if you want him," said her mother confidently. "One evening with a mere child like Susie isn't going to amount to much."

Ruth winced. "Do you suppose I don't know that?" cried she. "What makes me so mad is his impudence —coming here to see her when he wouldn't marry her or take her any place. It's insulting to us all."

"Oh, I don't think it's as bad as all that, Ruthie," soothed her mother, too simple-minded to accept immediately this clever subtlety of self-deception.

"You know this town—how people talk. Why, his sister——" and she related their conversation at the gate that morning.

"You ought to have sat on her hard, Ruth," said Mrs. Warham, with dangerously sparkling eyes. "No matter what we may think privately, it gives people a low opinion of us to——"

"Don't I know that!" shrilled Ruth. She began to weep. "I'm ashamed of myself."

"But we must try the dress on." Mrs. Warham spread the skirt, using herself as form. "Isn't it too lovely!"

Ruth dried her eyes as she gazed. The dress was indeed lovely. But her pleasure in it was shadowed by the remembrance that most of the loveliness was due to Susan's suggestions. Still, she tried it on, and felt better. She would linger until Sam came, would exhibit herself to him; and surely he would not tarry long with Susan. This project improved the situation greatly. She began her toilet for the evening at once, though it was only three o'clock. Susan finished her pressing and started to dress at five—because she knew Ruth would be appealing to her to come in and help put the finishing touches to the toilet for the party. And, sure enough, at half-past five, before she had nearly finished, Ruth, with a sneaking humility, begged her to come "for half a minute—if you don't mind—and have got time."

Susan did Ruth's hair over, made her change to another color of stockings and slippers, put the dress on her, did nearly an hour's refitting and redraping. Both were late for supper; and after supper Susan had to make certain final amendments to the wonderful toilet, and then get herself ready. So it was Ruth alone who went down when Sam Wright came. "My, but you do look all to the good, Ruth!" cried Sam. And his eyes no less than his tone showed that he meant it. He hadn't realized what a soft white neck the blond cousin had, or how perfectly her shoulders rounded into her slim arms. As Ruth moved to depart, he said: "Don't be in such a rush. Wait till Susie finishes her primping and comes down."

"She had to help me," said Ruth, with a righteous-

40

ness she could justly plume herself upon. "That's why she's late. No, I must get along." She was wise enough to resist the temptation to improve upon an already splendid impression. "Come as soon as you can."

"I'll be there in a few minutes," Sam assured her convincingly. "Save some dances for me."

Ruth went away happy. At the gate she glanced furtively back. Sam was looking after her. She marched down the street with light step. "I must wear low-necked dresses more in the evenings," she said to herself. "It's foolish for a girl to hide a good neck."

Sam, at the edge of the veranda, regretting his promise to call on Susan, was roused by her voice: "Did you ever see anything as lovely as Ruth?"

Sam's regret vanished the instant he looked at her, and the greedy expression came into his sensual, confident young face. "She's a corker," said he. "But I'm content to be where I am."

Susan's dress was not cut out in the neck, was simply of the collarless kind girls of her age wear. It revealed the smooth, voluptuous yet slender column of her throat. And her arms, bare to just above the elbows, were exquisite. But Susan's fascination did not lie in any or in all of her charms, but in that subtlety of magnetism which accounts for all the sensational phenomena of the relations of men and women. She was a clever girl—clever beyond her years, perhaps —though in this day seventeen is not far from fully developed womanhood. But even had she been silly, men would have been glad to linger on and on under the spell of the sex call which nature had subtly woven into the texture of her voice, into the glance of her eyes, into the delicate emanations of her skin.

They talked of all manner of things—games and college—East and West—the wonders of New York—the weather, finally. Sam was every moment of the time puzzling how to bring up the one subject that interested both above all others, that interested him to the exclusion of all others. He was an ardent student of the game of man and woman, had made considerable progress at it—remarkable progress, in view of his bare twenty years. He had devised as many "openings" as an expert chess player. None seemed to fit this difficult case—how to make love to a girl of his own class whom his conventional, socially ambitious nature forbade him to consider marrying. As he observed her in the moonlight, he said to himself: "I've got to look out or I'll make a damn fool of myself with her." For his heady passion was fast getting the better of those prudent instincts he had inherited from a father who almost breathed by calculation.

While he was still struggling for an "opening," Susan eager to help him but not knowing how, there came from the far interior of the house three distant raps. "Gracious!" exclaimed Susan. "That's Uncle George. It must be ten o'clock." With frank regret, "I'm so sorry. I thought it was early."

"Yes, it did seem as if I'd just come," said Sam. Her shy innocence was contagious. He felt an awkward country lout. "Well, I suppose I must go."

"But you'll come again—sometime?" she asked wistfully. It was her first real beau—the first that had interested her—and what a dream lover of a beau he looked, standing before her in that wonderful light!

"Come? Rather!" exclaimed he in a tone of enthusiasm that could not but flatter her into a sort of intoxication. "I'd have hard work staying away. But Ruth—she'll always be here."

"Oh, she goes out a lot—and I don't."

"Will you telephone me—next time she's to be out?"

' Yes," agreed she with a hesitation that was explained when she added: "But don't think you've got to come. . . . Oh, I must go in!"

"Good night—Susie." Sam held out his hand. She took it with a queer reluctance. She felt nervous, afraid, as if there were something uncanny lurking somewhere in those moonlight shadows. She gently tried to draw her hand away, but he would not let her. She made a faint struggle, then yielded. It was so wonderful, the sense of the touch of his hand. "Susie!" he said hoarsely. And she knew he felt as she did. Before she realized it his arms were round her, and his lips had met hers. "You drive me crazy," he whispered.

Both were trembling; she had become quite cold—her cheeks, her hand, her body even. "You mustn't," she murmured, drawing gently away.

"You set me crazy," he repeated. "Do you—love me—a little?"

"Oh, I must go!" she pleaded. Tears were glistening in her long dark lashes. The sight of them maddened him. "Do you—Susie?" he pleaded.

"I'm—I'm—very young," she stammered.

"Yes—yes—I know," he assented eagerly. "But not too young to love, Susie? No. Because you do—don't you?"

The moonlit world seemed a fairyland. "Yes," she said softly. "I guess so. I must go. I must."

43

And moved beyond her power to control herself, she broke from his detaining hand and fled into the house. She darted up to her room, paused in the middle of the floor, her hands clasped over her wildly beating heart. When she could move she threw open the shutters and went out on the balcony. She leaned against the window frame and gazed up at the stars, instinctively seeking the companionship of the infinite. Curiously enough, she thought little about Sam. She was awed and wonderstruck before the strange mysterious event within her, the opening up, the flowering of her soul. These vast emotions, where did they come from? What were they? Why did she long to burst into laughter, to burst into tears? Why did she do neither, but simply stand motionless, with the stars blazing and reeling in the sky and her heart beating like mad and her blood surging and ebbing? Was this —love? Yes—it must be love. Oh, how wonderful love was—and how sad—and how happy beyond all laughter—and how sweet! She felt an enormous tenderness for everybody and for everything, for all the world—an overwhelming sense of beauty and goodness. Her lips were moving. She was amazed to find she was repeating the one prayer she knew, the one Aunt Fanny had taught her in babyhood. Why should she find herself praying? Love—love—love! She was a woman and she loved! So this was what it meant to be a woman; it meant to love!

She was roused by the sound of Ruth saying good night to someone at the gate, invisible because of the intervening foliage. Why, it must be dreadfully late. The Dipper had moved away round to the south, and the heat of the day was all gone, and the air was full of the cool, scented breath of leaves and flowers and grass. Ruth's lights shone out upon the balcony. Susan turned to slip into her own room. **But** Ruth heard, called out peevishly:

"Who's there?"

"Only me," cried Susan.

She longed to go in and embrace Ruth, and kiss her. She would have liked to ask Ruth to let her sleep with her, but she felt Ruth wouldn't understand.

"What are you doing out there?" demanded Ruth. "It's 'way after one."

"Oh—dear—I must go to bed," cried Susan. Ruth's voice somehow seemed to be knocking and tumbling her new dream-world.

"What time did Sam Wright leave here?" asked Ruth.

She was standing in her window now. Susan saw that her face looked tired and worn, almost homely.

"At ten," she replied. "Uncle George knocked **on** the banister."

"Are you sure it was ten?" said Ruth sharply.

"I guess so. Yes—it was ten. Why?"

"Oh—nothing."

"Was he at Sinclairs'?"

"He came as it was over. He and Lottie brought me home." Ruth was eyeing her cousin evilly. "How did you two get on?"

Susan flushed from head to foot. "Oh—so-so," she answered, in an uncertain voice.

"I don't know why he didn't come to Sinclairs'," snapped Ruth.

Susan flushed again—a delicious warmth from head to foot. She knew why. So he, too, had been dreaming alone. Love! Love!

"What are you smiling at?" cried Ruth crossly.

"Was I smiling? . . . Do you want me to help you undress?"

"No," was the curt answer. "Good night."

"Please let me unhook it, at least," urged Susan, following Ruth into her room.

Ruth submitted.

"Did you have a good time?" asked Susan.

"Of course," snapped Ruth. "What made you think I didn't?"

"Don't be a silly, dear. I didn't think so."

"I had an awful time—awful!"

Ruth began to sob, turned fiercely on Susan. "Leave me alone!" she cried. "I hate to have you touch me." The dress was, of course, entirely unfastened in the back.

"You had a quarrel with Arthur?" asked Susan with sympathy. "But you know he can't keep away from you. Tomorrow——"

"Be careful, Susan, how you let Sam Wright hang around you," cried Ruth, with blazing eyes and trembling lips. "You be careful—that's all I've got to say."

"Why, what do you mean?" asked Susan wonderingly.

"Be careful! He'd never think for a minute of marrying you."

The words meant nothing to Susan; but the tone stabbed into her heart. "Why not?" she said.

Ruth looked at her cousin, hung her head in shame. "Go—go!" she begged. "Please go. I'm a bad girl —bad—*bad!* Go!" And, crying hysterically, she pushed amazed Susan through the connecting door, closed and bolted it.

IV

WHEN Fanny Warham was young her mother
—compelled by her father—roused—"routed
out"—the children at half-past six on week
days and at seven on Sundays for prayers and breakfast, no matter what time they had gone to bed the
night before. The horror of this made such an impression upon her that she never permitted Ruth and
Susan to be awakened; always they slept until they
had "had their sleep out." Regularity was no doubt
an excellent thing for health and for moral discipline; but the best rule could be carried to foolish
extremes. Until the last year Mrs. Warham had made
her two girls live a life of the strictest simplicity and
regularity, with the result that they were the most
amazingly, soundly, healthy girls in Sutherland. And
the regimen still held, except when they had company
in the evening or went out—and Mrs. Warham saw to
it that there was not too much of that sort of thing.
In all her life thus far Susan had never slept less than
ten hours, rarely less than twelve.

It lacked less than a minute of ten o'clock the morning after Sam's call when Susan's eyes opened upon her
simple, pale-gray bedroom, neat and fresh. She looked
sleepily at the little clock on the night stand.

"Mercy me!" she cried. And her bare feet were on
the floor and she was stretching her lithe young body,
weak from the relaxation of her profound sleep.

She heard someone stirring in Ruth's room; instantly
Ruth's remark, "He'd never think for a minute of

marrying you," popped into her head. It still meant
nothing to her. She could not have explained why it
came back or why she fell to puzzling over it as if it
held some mysterious meaning. Perhaps the reason
was that from early childhood there had been accumulating in some dusky chamber of her mind stray
happenings and remarks, all bearing upon the unsuspected secret of her birth and the unsuspected strangeness of her position in the world where everyone else
was definitely placed and ticketed. She was wondering
about Ruth's queer hysterical outburst, evidently the
result of a quarrel with Arthur Sinclair. "I guess
Ruth cares more for him than she lets on," thought
she. This love that had come to her so suddenly
and miraculously made her alert for signs of love elsewhere.

She went to the bolted connecting door; she could
not remember when it had ever been bolted before,
and she felt forlorn and shut out. "Ruth!" she called.
"Is that you?"

A brief silence, then a faint "Yes."

"May I come in?"

"You'd better take your bath and get downstairs."

This reminded her that she was hungry. She gathered her underclothes together, and with the bundle
in her arms darted across the hall into the bathroom.
The cold water acted as champagne promises to act
but doesn't. She felt giddy with health and happiness. And the bright sun was flooding the bathroom,
and the odors from the big bed of hyacinths in the
side lawn scented the warm breeze from the open window. When she dashed back to her room she was
singing, and her singing voice was as charming as her
speaking voice promised. A few minutes and her hair

had gone up in careless grace and she was clad in a fresh dress of tan linen, full in the blouse. This, with her tan stockings and tan slippers and the radiant youth of her face, gave her a look of utter cleanness and freshness that was exceedingly good to see.

"I'm ready," she called.

There was no answer; doubtless Ruth had already descended. She rushed downstairs and into the dining-room. No one was at the little table set in one of the windows in readiness for the late breakfasters. Molly came, bringing cocoa, a cereal, hot biscuit and crab-apple preserves, all attractively arranged on a large tray.

"I didn't bring much, Miss Susie," she apologized. "It's so late, and I don't want you to spoil your dinner. We're going to have the grandest chicken that ever came out of an egg."

Susan surveyed the tray with delighted eyes. "That's plenty," she said, "if you don't talk too much about the chicken. Where's Ruth?"

"She ain't coming down. She's got a headache. It was that salad for supper over to Sinclairs' last night. Salad ain't fit for a dog to eat, nohow—that's *my* opinion. And at night—it's sure to bust your face out or give you the headache or both."

Susan ate with her usual enthusiasm, thinking the while of Sam and wondering how she could contrive to see him. She remembered her promise to her uncle. She had not eaten nearly so much as she wanted. But up she sprang and in fifteen minutes was on her way to the store. She had seen neither Ruth nor her aunt. "*He*'ll be waiting for me to pass," she thought. And she was not disappointed. There he stood, at the foot-path gate into his father's place. He had arrayed himself in a blue and white flannel suit, white hat and shoes; a big expensive-looking cigarette adorned his lips. The Martins, the Delevans, the Castles and the Bowens, neighbors across the way, were watching him admiringly through the meshes of lace window curtains. She expected that he would come forward eagerly. Instead, he continued to lean indolently on the gate, as if unaware of her approach. And when she was close at hand, his bow and smile were, so it seemed to her, almost coldly polite. Into her eyes came a confused, hurt expression.

"Susie—sweetheart," he said, the voice in as astonishing contrast as the words to his air of friendly indifference. "They're watching us from the windows all around here."

"Oh—yes," assented she, as if she understood. But she didn't. In Sutherland the young people were not so mindful of gossip, which it was impossible to escape, anyhow. Still—off there in the East, no doubt, they had more refined ways; without a doubt, whatever Sam did was the correct thing.

"Do you still care—as you did last night?" he asked. The effect of his words upon her was so obvious that he glanced nervously round. It was delightful to be able to evoke a love like this; but he did wish others weren't looking.

"I'm going to Uncle's store," she said. "I'm late."

"I'll walk part of the way with you," he volunteered, and they started on. "That—that kiss," he stammered. "I can feel it yet."

She blushed deeply, happily. Her beauty made him tingle. "So can I," she said.

They walked in silence several squares. "When will I see you again?" he asked. "Tonight?"

"Yes—do come down. But—Ruth'll be there. I believe Artie Sinclair's coming."

"Oh, that counter-jumper?"

She looked at him in surprise. "He's an awfully nice fellow," said she. "About the nicest in town."

"Of course," replied Sam elaborately. "I beg your pardon. They think differently about those things in the East."

"What things?"

"No matter."

Sam, whose secret dream was to marry some fashionable Eastern woman and cut a dash in Fifth Avenue life, had no intention of explaining what was what to one who would not understand, would not approve, and would be made suspicious of him. "I suppose Ruth and Sinclair'll pair off and give us a chance."

"You'll come?"

"Right after din—supper, I mean. In the East we have dinner in the evening."

"Isn't that queer!" exclaimed Susan. But she was thinking of the joys in store for her at the close of the day.

"I must go back now," said Sam. Far up the street he saw his sister's pony cart coming.

"You might as well walk to the store." It seemed to her that they both had ever so much to say to each other, and had said nothing.

"No. I can't go any further. Good-by—that is, till tonight."

He was red and stammering. As they shook hands emotion made them speechless. He stumbled awkwardly as he turned to leave, became still more hotly self-conscious when he saw the grin on the faces of the group of loungers at a packing case near the curb.

Susan did not see the loafers, did not see anything distinctly. Her feet sought the uneven brick sidewalk uncertainly, and the blood was pouring into her cheeks, was steaming in her brain, making a red mist before her eyes. She was glad he had left her. The joy of being with him was so keen that it was pain. Now she could breathe freely and could dream—dream —dream. She made blunder after blunder in working over the accounts with her uncle, and he began to tease her.

"You sure are in love, Brownie," declared he.

Her painful but happy blush delighted him.

"Tell me all about it?"

She shook her head, bending it low to hide her color.

"No? . . . Sometime?"

She nodded. She was glancing shyly and merrily at him now.

"Well, some hold that first love's best. Maybe so. But it seems to me any time's good enough. Still— the first time's mighty fine—eh?" He sighed. "My, but it's good to be young!" And he patted her thick wavy hair.

It did not leak out until supper that Sam was coming. Warham said to Susan, "While Ruth's looking out for Artie, you and I'll have a game or so of chess, Brownie." Susan colored violently. "What?" laughed Warham. "Are *you* going to have a beau too?"

Susan felt two pairs of feminine eyes pounce—hostile eyes, savagely curious. She paled with fright as queer, as unprecedented, as those hostile glances. It seemed to her that she had done or was about to do something criminal. She could not speak.

An awful silence, then her aunt—she no longer

52

seemed her loving aunt—asked in an ominous voice: "Is someone coming to see you, Susan?"

"Sam Wright"—stammered Susan—"I saw him this morning—he was at their gate—and he said—I think he's coming."

A dead silence—Warham silent because he was eating, but the two others not for that reason.

Susan felt horribly guilty, and for no reason. "I'd have spoken of it before," she said, "but there didn't seem to be any chance." She had the instinct of fine shy nature to veil the soul; she found it hard to speak of anything as sacred as this love of hers and whatever related to it.

"I can't allow this, Susie," said her aunt, with lips tightly drawn against the teeth. "You are too young."

"Oh, come now, mother," cried Warham, good-humoredly. "That's foolishness. Let the young folks have a good time. You didn't think you were too young at Susie's age."

"You don't understand, George," said Fanny after she had given him a private frown. Susie's gaze was on the tablecloth. "I can't permit Sam to come here to see Susie."

Ruth's eyes were down also. About her lips was a twitching that meant a struggle to hide a pleased smile.

"I've no objection to Susie's having boys of her own age come to see her," continued Mrs. Warham in the same precise, restrained manner. "But Sam is too old."

"Now, mother——"

Mrs. Warham met his eyes steadily. "I must protect my sister's child, George," she said. At last she had found what she felt was a just reason for keeping Sam away from Susan, so her tone was honest and strong.

Warham lowered his gaze. He understood. "Oh— as you think best, Fan; I didn't mean to interfere," said he awkwardly. He turned on Susan with his affection in his eyes. "Well, Brownie, it looks like chess with your old uncle, doesn't it?"

Susan's bosom was swelling, her lip trembling. "I —I——" she began. She choked back the sobs, faltered out: "I don't think I could, Uncle," and rushed from the room.

There was an uncomfortable pause. Then Warham said, "I must say, Fan, I think—if you had to do it —you might have spared the girl's feelings."

Mrs. Warham felt miserable about it also. "Susie took me by surprise," she apologized. Then, defiantly, "And what else can I do? You know he doesn't come for any good."

Warham stared in amazement. "Now, what does *that* mean?" he demanded.

"You know very well what it means," retorted his wife.

Her tone made him understand. He reddened, and with too blustering anger brought his fist down on the table.

"Susan's our daughter. She's Ruth's sister."

Ruth pushed back her chair and stood up. Her expression made her look much older than she was. "I wish you could induce the rest of the town to think that, papa," said she. "It'd make my position less painful." And she, too, left the room.

"What's she talking about?" asked Warham.

"It's true, George," replied Fanny with trembling

lip. "It's all my fault—insisting on keeping her. I might have known!"

"I think you and Ruth must be crazy. I've seen no sign."

"Have you seen any of the boys calling on Susan since she shot up from a child to a girl? Haven't you noticed she isn't invited any more—except when it can't be avoided?"

Warham's face was fiery with rage. He looked helplessly, furiously about. But he said nothing. To fight public sentiment would be like trying to thrust back with one's fists an oncreeping fog. Finally he cried, "It's too outrageous to talk about."

"If I only knew what to do!" moaned Fanny.

A long silence, while Warham was grasping the fullness of the meaning, the frightful meaning, in these revelations so astounding to him. At last he said:

"Does *she* realize?"

"I guess so . . . I don't know . . . I don't believe she does. She's the most innocent child that ever grew up."

"If I had a chance, I'd sell out and move away."

"Where?" said his wife. "Where would people accept—her?"

Warham became suddenly angry again. "I don't believe it!" he cried, his look and tone contradicting his words. "You've been making a mountain out of a molehill."

And he strode from the room, flung on his hat and went for a walk. As Mrs. Warham came from the dining-room a few minutes later, Ruth appeared in the side veranda doorway. "I think I'll telephone Arthur to come tomorrow evening instead," said she. "He'd not like it, with Sam here too."

"That would be better," assented her mother. "Yes, I'd telephone him if I were you."

Thus it came about that Susan, descending the stairs to the library to get a book, heard Ruth say into the telephone in her sweetest voice, "Yes—tomorrow evening, Arthur. Some others are coming—the Wrights. You'd have to talk to Lottie . . . I don't blame you. . . . Tomorrow evening, then. So sorry. Good-by."

The girl on the stairway stopped short, shrank against the wall. A moment, and she hastily reascended, entered her room, closed the door. Love had awakened the woman; and the woman was not so unsuspecting, so easily deceived as the child had been. She understood what her cousin and her aunt were about; they were trying to take her lover from her! She understood her aunt's looks and tones, her cousin's temper and hysteria. She sat down upon the floor and cried with a breaking heart. The injustice of it! The meanness of it! The wickedness of a world where even her sweet cousin, even her loving aunt were wicked! She sat there on the floor a long time, abandoned to the misery of a first shattered illusion, a misery the more cruel because never before had either cousin or aunt said or done anything to cause her real pain. The sound of voices coming through the open window from below made her start up and go out on the balcony. She leaned over the rail. She could not see the veranda for the masses of creeper, but the voices were now quite plain in the stillness. Ruth's voice—gay and incessant. Presently a man's voice—*his*—and laughing! Then his voice speaking—then the two voices mingled—both talking at once, so eager were they! Her lover—and Ruth was stealing him from her! Oh, the baseness, the treachery! And her aunt

was helping! . . . Sore of heart, utterly forlorn, she
sat in the balcony hammock, aching with love and
jealousy. Every now and then she ran in and looked
at the clock. He was staying on and on, though he
must have learned she was not coming down. She
heard her uncle and aunt come up to bed. Now the
piano in the parlor was going. First it was Ruth
singing one of her pretty love songs in that clear small
voice of hers. Then Sam played and sang—how his
voice thrilled her! Again it was Ruthie singing—
"Sweet Dream Faces"—Susan began to sob afresh.
She could see Ruth at the piano, how beautiful she
looked—and that song—it would be impossible for him
not to be impressed. She felt the jealousy of despair.
. . . Ten o'clock—half-past—eleven o'clock! She
heard them at the edge of the veranda—so, at last he
was going. She was able to hear their words now:

"You'll be up for the tennis in the morning?" he
was saying.

"At ten," replied Ruth.

"Of course Susie's asked, too," he said—and his voice
sounded careless, not at all earnest.

"Certainly," was her cousin's reply. "But I'm not
sure she can come."

It was all the girl at the balcony rail could do to
refrain from crying out a protest. But Sam was saying to Ruth:

"Well—good night. Haven't had so much fun in
a long time. May I come again?"

"If you don't, I'll think you were bored."

"Bored!" He laughed. "That's too ridiculous. See
you in the morning. Good night. . . . Give my love to
Susie, and tell her I was sorry not to see her."

Susan was all in a glow as her cousin answered, "I'll

tell her." Doubtless Sam didn't note it, but Susan heard the constraint, the hypocrisy in that sweet voice.

She watched him stroll down to the gate under the arch of boughs dimly lit by the moon. She stretched her arms passionately toward him. Then she went in to go to bed. But at the sound of Ruth humming gayly in the next room, she realized that she could not sleep with her heart full of evil thoughts. She must have it out with her cousin. She knocked on the still bolted door.

"What is it?" asked Ruth coldly.

"Let me in," answered Susan. "I've got to see you."

"Go to bed, Susie. It's late."

"You must let me in."

The bolt shot back. "All right. And please unhook my dress—there's a dear."

Susan opened the door, stood on the threshold, all her dark passion in her face. "Ruth!" she cried.

Ruth had turned her back, in readiness for the service the need of which had alone caused her to unbolt the door. At that swift, fierce ejaculation she started, wheeled round. At sight of that wild anger she paled. "Why, Susie!" she gasped.

"I've found you out!" raged Susan. "You're trying to steal him from me—you and Aunt Fanny. It isn't fair! I'll not stand it!"

"What *are* you talking about?" cried Ruth. "You must have lost your senses."

"I'll not stand it," Susan repeated, advancing threateningly. "He loves me and I love him."

Ruth laughed. "You foolish girl! Why, he cares nothing about you. The idea of your having your head turned by a little politeness!"

"He loves me—he told me so. And I love him. I

told him so. He's mine! You shan't take him from me!"

"He told you he loved you?"

Ruth's eyes were gleaming and her voice was shrill with hate. "He told you *that?*"

"Yes—he did!"

"I don't believe you."

"We love each other," cried the dark girl. "He came to see *me*. You've got Arthur Sinclair. You shan't take him away!"

The two girls, shaking with fury, were facing each other, were looking into each other's eyes. "If Sam Wright told you he loved you," said Ruth, with the icy deliberateness of a cold-hearted anger, "he was trying to—to make a fool of you. You ought to be ashamed of yourself. *We*'re trying to save you."

"He and I are engaged!" declared Susan. "You shan't take him—and you can't! He *loves* me!"

"Engaged!" jeered Ruth. "Engaged!" she laughed, pretending not to believe, yet believing. She was beside herself with jealous anger. "Yes—we'll save you from yourself. You're like your mother. You'd disgrace us—as she did."

"Don't you dare talk that way, Ruth Warham. It's false—*false!* My mother is dead—and you're a wicked girl."

"It's time you knew the truth," said Ruth softly. Her eyes were half shut now and sparkling devilishly. "You haven't got any name. You haven't got any father. And no man of any position would marry you. As for Sam——" She laughed contemptuously. "Do you suppose Sam Wright would marry a girl without a name?"

Susan had shrunk against the door jamb. She understood only dimly, but things understood dimly are worse than things that are clear. "Me?" she muttered. "Me? Oh, Ruth, you don't mean that."

"It's true," said Ruth, calmly. "And the sooner you realize it the less likely you are to go the way your mother did."

Susan stood as if petrified.

"If Sam Wright comes hanging round you any more, you'll know how to treat him," Ruth went on. "You'll appreciate that he hasn't any respect for you—that he thinks you're someone to be trifled with. And if he talked engagement, it was only a pretense. Do you understand?"

The girl leaning in the doorway gazed into vacancy. After a while she answered dully, "I guess so."

Ruth began to fuss with the things on her bureau. Susan went into her room, sat on the edge of the bed. A few minutes, and Ruth, somewhat cooled down and not a little frightened, entered. She looked uneasily at the motionless figure. Finally she said,

"Susie!"

No answer.

More sharply, "Susie!"

"Yes," said Susan, without moving.

"You understand that I told you for your own good? And you'll not say anything to mother or father? They feel terribly about it, and don't want it ever mentioned. You won't let on that you know?"

"I'll not tell," said Susan.

"You know we're fond of you—and want to do everything for you?"

No answer.

"It wasn't true—what you said about Sam's making love to you?"

60

"That's all over. I don't want to talk about it."

"You're not angry with me, Susie? I admit I was angry, but it was best for you to know—wasn't it?"

"Yes," said Susan.

"You're not angry with me?"

"No."

Ruth, still more uneasy, turned back into her own room because there was nothing else to do. She did not shut the door between. When she was in her night-gown she glanced in at her cousin. The girl was sitting on the edge of the bed in the same position. "It's after midnight," said Ruth. "You'd better get undressed."

Susan moved a little. "I will," she said.

Ruth went to bed and soon fell asleep. After an hour or so she awakened. Light was streaming through the open connecting door. She ran to it, looked in. Susan's clothes were in a heap beside the bed. Susan herself, with the pillows propping her, was staring wide-eyed at the ceiling. It was impossible for Ruth to realize any part of the effect upon her cousin of a thing she herself had known for years and had taken always as a matter of course; she simply felt mildly sorry for unfortunate Susan.

"Susie, dear," she said gently, "do you want me to turn out the light?"

"Yes," said Susan.

Ruth switched off the light and went back to bed, better content. She felt that now Susan would stop her staring and would go to sleep. Sam's call had been very satisfactory. Ruth felt she had shown off to the best advantage, felt that he admired her, would come to see *her* next time. And now that she had so arranged it that Susan would avoid him, everything would turn out as she wished. "I'll use Arthur to make him jealous after a while—and then—I'll have things my own way." As she fell asleep she was selecting the rooms Sam and she would occupy in the big Wright mansion—"when we're not in the East or in Europe."

RUTH had forgotten to close her shutters, so toward seven o'clock the light which had been beating against her eyelids for three hours succeeded in lifting them. She stretched herself and yawned noisily. Susan appeared in the connecting doorway.

"Are you awake?" she said softly.

"What time is it?" asked Ruth, too lazy to turn over and look at her clock.

"Ten to seven."

"Do close my shutters for me. I'll sleep an hour or two." She hazily made out the figure in the doorway. "You're dressed, aren't you?" she inquired sleepily.

"Yes," replied Susan. "I've been waiting for you to wake."

Something in the tone made Ruth forget about sleep and rub her fingers over her eyes to clear them for a view of her cousin. Susan seemed about as usual— perhaps a little serious, but then she had the habit of strange moods of seriousness. "What did you want?" said Ruth.

Susan came into the room, sat at the foot of the bed—there was room, as the bed was long and Ruth short. "I want you to tell me what my mother did."

"Did?" echoed Ruth feebly.

"Did, to disgrace you and—me."

"Oh, I couldn't explain—not in a few words. I'm so sleepy. Don't bother about it, Susan." And she thrust her head deeper into the pillow. "Close the shutters."

"Then I'll have to ask Aunt Fanny—or Uncle George—or everybody—till I find out."

"But you mustn't do that," protested Ruth, flinging herself from left to right impatiently. "What is it you want to know?"

"About my mother—and what she did. And why I have no father—why I'm not like you—and the other girls."

"Oh—it's nothing. I can't explain. Don't bother about it. It's no use. It can't be helped. And it doesn't really matter."

"I've been thinking," said Susan. "I understand a great many things I didn't know I'd noticed—ever since I was a baby. But what I don't understand——" She drew a long breath, a cautious breath, as if there were danger of awakening a pain. "What I don't understand is—why. And—you must tell me all about it. . . . Was my mother bad?"

"Not exactly bad," Ruth answered uncertainly. "But she did one thing that was wicked—at least that a woman never can be forgiven for, if it's found out."

"Did she—did she take something that didn't belong to her?"

"No—nothing like that. No, she was, they say, as nice and sweet as she could be—except—— She wasn't married to your father."

Susan sat in a brown study. "I can't understand," she said at last. "Why—she *must* have been married, or—or—there wouldn't have been me."

Ruth smiled uneasily. "Not at all. Don't you really understand?"

Susan shook her head.

"He—he betrayed her—and left her—and then everybody knew because you came."

Susan's violet-gray eyes rested a grave, inquiring glance upon her cousin's face. "But if he betrayed her—— What does 'betray' mean? Doesn't it mean he promised to marry her and didn't?"

"Something like that," said Ruth. "Yes—something like that."

"Then *he* was the disgrace," said the dark cousin, after reflecting. "No—you're not telling me, Ruth. *What* did my mother do?"

"She had you without being married."

Again Susan sat in silence, trying to puzzle it out. Ruth lifted herself, put the pillows behind her back. "You don't understand—anything—do you? Well, I'll try to explain—though I don't know much about it."

And hesitatingly, choosing words she thought fitted to those innocent ears, hunting about for expressions she thought comprehensible to that innocent mind, Ruth explained the relations of the sexes—an inaccurate, often absurd, explanation, for she herself knew only what she had picked up from other girls—the fantastic hodgepodge of pruriency, physiology and sheer nonsense which under our system of education distorts and either alarms or inflames the imaginations of girls and boys where the clean, simple truth would at least enlighten them. Susan listened with increasing amazement.

"Well, do you understand?" Ruth ended. "How we come into the world—and what marriage means?"

"I don't believe it," declared Susan. "It's—awful!" And she shivered with disgust.

"I tell you it's true," insisted Ruth. "I thought it

65

was awful when I first heard—when Lottie Wright took me out in their orchard, where nobody could listen, and told me what their cook had told her. But I've got kind of used to it."

"But it—it's so, then; my mother did marry my father," said Susan.

"No. She let him betray her. And when a woman lets a man betray her without being married by the preacher or somebody, why, she's ruined forever."

"But doesn't marriage mean where two people promise to love each other and then betray each other?"

"If they're married, it isn't betraying," explained Ruth. "If they're not, it is betraying."

Susan reflected, nodded slowly. "I guess I understand. But don't you see it was my father who was the disgrace? He was the one that promised to marry and didn't."

"How foolish you are!" cried Ruth. "I never knew you to be stupid."

"But isn't it so?" persisted Susan.

"Yes—in a way," her cousin admitted. "Only—the woman must keep herself pure until the ceremony has been performed."

"But if he said so to her, wasn't that saying so to God just as much as if the preacher had been there?"

"No, it wasn't," said Ruth with irritation. "And it's wicked to think such things. All I know is, God says a woman must be married before she—before she has any children. And your mother wasn't."

Susan shook her head. "I guess you don't understand any better than I do—really."

"No, I don't," confessed Ruth. "But I'd like to see any man more than kiss me or put his arm round me without our having been married."

"But," urged Susan, "if he kissed you, wouldn't that be—like marriage?"

"Some say so," admitted Ruth. "But I'm not so strict. A little kissing and that often leads a man to propose."

Susan reflected again. "It all sounds low and sneaking to me," was her final verdict. "I don't want to have anything to do with it. But I'm sure my mother was a good woman. It wasn't her fault if she was lied to, when she loved and believed. And anybody who blames her is low and bad. I'm glad I haven't got any father, if fathers have to be made to promise before everybody or else they'll not keep their word."

"Well, I'll not argue about it," said Ruth. "I'm telling you the way things are. The woman has to take *all* the blame."

Susan lifted her head haughtily. "I'd be glad to be blamed by anybody who was wicked enough to be that unjust. I'd not have anything to do with such people."

"Then you'd live alone."

"No, I shouldn't. There are lots of people who are good and——"

"That's wicked, Susan," interrupted Ruth. "All good people think as I tell you they do."

"Do Aunt Fanny and Uncle George blame my mother?"

"Of course. How could they help it, when she——" Ruth was checked by the gathering lightnings in those violet-gray eyes.

"But," pursued Susan, after a pause, "even if they were wicked enough to blame my mother, they couldn't blame me."

"Of course not," declared Ruth warmly. "Hasn't everybody always been sweet and kind to you?"

"But last night you said——"

Ruth hid her face. "I'm ashamed of what I said last night," she murmured. "I've got, Oh, such a *nasty* disposition, Susie."

"But what you said—wasn't it so?"

Ruth turned away her head.

Susan drew a long sigh, so quietly that Ruth could not have heard.

"You understand," Ruth said gently, "everybody feels sorry for you and——"

Susan frowned stormily. "They'd better feel sorry for themselves."

"Oh, Susie, dear," cried Ruth, impulsively catching her hand, "we all love you, and mother and father and I—we'll stand up for you through everything——"

"Don't you *dare* feel sorry for me!" Susan cried, wrenching her hand away.

Ruth's eyes filled with tears.

"You can't blame us because everybody—— You know, God says, 'The sins of the fathers shall be visited on the children——' "

"I'm done with everybody," cried Susan, rising and lifting her proud head, "I'm done with God."

Ruth gave a low scream and shuddered. Susan looked round defiantly, as if she expected a bolt from the blue to come hurtling through the open window. But the sky remained serene, and the quiet, scented breeze continued to play with the lace curtains, and the birds on the balcony did not suspend their chattering courtship. This lack of immediate effect from her declaration of war upon man and God was encouraging. The last of the crushed, cowed feeling Ruth had inspired the night before disappeared. With a soul haughtily plumed and looking defiance from the violet-gray eyes, Susan left her cousin and betook herself down to breakfast.

In common with most children, she had always dreamed of a mysterious fate for herself, different from the commonplace routine around her. Ruth's revelations, far from daunting her, far from making her feel like cringing before the world in gratitude for its tolerance of her bar sinister, seemed a fascinatingly tragic confirmation of her romantic longings and beliefs. No doubt it was the difference from the common lot that had attracted Sam to her; and this difference would make their love wholly unlike the commonplace Sutherland wooing and wedding. Yes, hers had been a mysterious fate, and would continue to be. Nora, an old woman now, had often related in her presence how Doctor Stevens had brought her to life when she lay apparently, indeed really, dead upon the upstairs sitting-room table—Doctor Stevens and Nora's own prayers. An extraordinary birth, in defiance of the laws of God and man; an extraordinary resurrection, in defiance of the laws of nature—yes, hers would be a life superbly different from the common. And when she and Sam married, how gracious and forgiving she would be to all those bad-hearted people; how she would shame them for their evil thoughts against her mother and herself!

The Susan Lenox who sat alone at the little table in the dining-room window, eating bread and butter and honey in the comb, was apparently the same Susan Lenox who had taken three meals a day in that room all those years—was, indeed, actually the same, for character is not an overnight creation. Yet it was an amazingly different Susan Lenox, too. The first crisis had come; she had been put to the test; and she had not collapsed in weakness but had stood erect in strength.

After breakfast she went down Main Street and at Crooked Creek Avenue took the turning for the cemetery. She sought the Warham plot, on the western slope near the quiet brook. There was a clump of cedars at each corner of the plot; near the largest of them were three little graves—the three dead children of George and Fanny. In the shadow of the clump and nearest the brook was a fourth grave—apart and, to the girl, now thrillingly mysterious:

LORELLA LENOX
BORN MAY 9, 1859
DIED JULY 17, 1879

Twenty years old! Susan's tears scalded her eyes. Only a little older than her cousin Ruth was now—Ruth who often seemed to her, and to everybody, younger than herself. "And she was good—I know she was good!" thought Susan. "*He* was bad, and the people who took his part against her were bad. But *she* was good!"

She started as Sam's voice, gay and light, sounded directly behind her. "What are you doing in a graveyard?" cried he.

"How did you find me?" she asked, paling and flushing and paling again.

"I've been following you ever since you left home." He might have added that he did not try to overtake her until they were where people would be least likely to see.

"Whose graves are those?" he went on, cutting across a plot and stepping on several graves to join her.

She was gazing at her mother's simple headstone. His glance followed hers, he read.

"Oh—beg pardon," he said confusedly. "I didn't see."

She turned her serious gaze from the headstone to his face, which her young imagination transfigured. "You know—about her?" she asked.

"I—I—I've heard," he confessed. "But—Susie, it doesn't amount to anything. It happened a long time ago—and everybody's forgotten—and——" His stammering falsehoods died away before her steady look. "How did you find out?"

"Someone just told me," replied she. "And they said you'd never respect or marry a girl who had no father. No—don't deny—please! I didn't believe it —not after what we had said to each other."

Sam, red and shifting uneasily, could not even keep his downcast eyes upon the same spot of ground.

"You see," she went on, sweet and grave, "they don't understand what love means—do they?"

"I guess not," muttered he, completely unnerved. Why, how seriously the girl had taken him and his words—such a few words and not at all definite! No, he decided, it was the kiss. He had heard of girls so innocent that they thought a kiss meant the same as being married. He got himself together as well as he could and looked at her.

"But, Susie," he said, "you're too young for anything definite—and I'm not halfway through college."

"I understand," said she. "But you need not be afraid I'll change."

She was so sweet, so magnetic, so compelling that in spite of the frowns of prudence he seized her hand. At her touch he flung prudence to the winds. "I love you," he cried; and putting his arm around her, he tried to kiss her. She gently but strongly repulsed him. "Why not, dear?" he pleaded. "You love me—don't you?"

"Yes," she replied, her honest eyes shining upon his. "But we must wait until we're married. I don't care so much for the others, but I'd not want Uncle George to feel I had disgraced him."

"Why, there's no harm in a kiss," pleaded he.

"Kissing you is—different," she replied. "It's—it's —marriage."

He understood her innocence that frankly assumed marriage where a sophisticated girl would, in the guilt of designing thoughts, have shrunk in shame from however vaguely suggesting such a thing. He realized to the full his peril. "I'm a damn fool," he said to himself, "to hang about her. But somehow I can't help it—I can't!" And the truth was, he loved her as much as a boy of his age is capable of loving, and he would have gone on and married her but for the snobbishness smeared on him by the provincialism of the small town and burned in by the toadyism of his fashionable college set. As he looked at her he saw beauty beyond any he had ever seen elsewhere and a sweetness and honesty that made him ashamed before her. "No, I couldn't harm her," he told himself. "I'm not such a dog as that. But there's no harm in loving her and kissing her and making her as happy as it's right to be."

"Don't be mean, Susan," he begged, tears in his eyes. "If you love me, you'll let me kiss you."

And she yielded, and the shock of the kiss set both to trembling. It appealed to his vanity, it heightened his own agitations to see how pale she had grown and how her rounded bosom rose and fell in the wild tumult of her emotions. "Oh, I can't do without seeing you," she cried. "And Aunt Fanny has forbidden me."

"I thought so!" exclaimed he. "I did what I could last night to throw them off the track. If Ruth had only known what I was thinking about all the time. Where were you?"

"Upstairs—on the balcony."

"I felt it," he declared. "And when she sang love songs I could hardly keep from rushing up to you. Susie, we *must* see each other."

"I can come here, almost any day."

"But people'd soon find out—and they'd say all sorts of things. And your uncle and aunt would hear."

There was no disputing anything so obvious.

"Couldn't you come down tonight, after the others are in bed and the house is quiet?" he suggested.

She hesitated before the deception, though she felt that her family had forfeited the right to control her. But love, being the supreme necessity, conquered. "For a few minutes," she conceded.

She had been absorbed; but his eyes, kept alert by his conventional soul, had seen several people at a distance observing without seeming to do so. "We must separate," he now said. "You see, Susie, we mustn't be gossiped about. You know how determined they are to keep us apart."

"Yes—yes," she eagerly agreed. "Will you go first, or shall I?"

"You go—the way you came. I'll jump the brook down where it's narrow and cut across and into our place by the back way. What time tonight?"

"Arthur's coming," reflected Susie aloud. "Ruth'll not let him stay late. She'll be sleepy and will go straight to bed. About half past ten. If I'm not on the front veranda—no, the side veranda—by eleven, you'll know something has prevented."

"But you'll surely come?"

"I'll come." And it both thrilled and alarmed him to see how much in earnest she was. But he looked love into her loving eyes and went away, too intoxicated to care whither this adventure was leading him.

At dinner she felt she was no longer a part of this family. Were they not all pitying and looking down on her in their hearts? She was like a deformed person who has always imagined the consideration he has had was natural and equal, and suddenly discovers that it is pity for his deformity. She now acutely felt her aunt's, her cousin's, dislike; and her uncle's gentleness was not less galling. In her softly rounded youthful face there was revealed definitely for the first time an underlying expression of strength, of what is often confused with its feeble counterfeit, obstinacy—that power to resist circumstances which makes the unusual and the firm character. The young mobility of her features suggested the easy swaying of the baby sapling in the gentlest breeze. Singularly at variance with it was this expression of tenacity. Such an expression in the face of the young infallibly forecasts an agitated and agitating life. It seemed amazingly out of place in Susan because theretofore she had never been put to the test in any but unnoted trifles and so had given the impression that she was as docile as she was fearful of giving annoyance or pain and indifferent to having her own way. Those who have this temperament of strength encased in gentleness are invariably misunderstood. When they assert themselves, though they are in the particular instance wholly right, they are regarded as wholly and outrageously wrong. Life deals hardly with them, punishes them for the mistaken notion of themselves they have through forbearance and gentleness of heart permitted an unobservant world to form.

Susan spent the afternoon on the balcony before her window, reading and sewing—or, rather, dreaming over first a book, then a dress. When she entered the dining-room at supper time the others were already seated. She saw instantly that something had occurred—something ominous for her. Mrs. Warham gave her a penetrating, severe look and lowered her eyes; Ruth was gazing sullenly at her plate. Warham's glance was stern and reproachful. She took her place opposite Ruth, and the meal was eaten in silence. Ruth left the table first. Next Mrs. Warham rose and saying, "Susan, when you've finished, I wish to see you in the sitting-room upstairs," swept in solemn dignity from the room. Susan rose at once to follow. As she was passing her uncle he put out his hand and detained her.

"I hope it was only a foolish girl's piece of nonsense," said he with an attempt at his wonted kindliness. "And I know it won't occur again. But when your aunt says things you won't like to hear, remember that you brought this on yourself and that she loves you as we all do and is thinking only of your good."

"What is it, Uncle George?" cried Susan, amazed. "What have I done?"

Warham looked sternly grieved. "Brownie," he reproached, "you mustn't deceive. Go to your aunt."

She found her aunt seated stiffly in the living-room, her hands folded upon her stomach. So gradual had been the crucial middle-life change in Fanny that no one had noted it. This evening Susan, become morbidly acute, suddenly realized the contrast between the severe, uncertain-tempered aunt of today and the amiable, altogether and always gentle aunt of two years before.

"What is it, aunt?" she said, feeling as if she were before a stranger and an enemy.

"The whole town is talking about your disgraceful doings this morning," Ruth's mother replied in a hard voice.

The color leaped in Susan's cheeks.

"Yesterday I forbade you to see Sam Wright again. And already you disobey."

"I did not say I would not see him again," replied Susan.

"I thought you were an honest, obedient girl," cried Fanny, the high shrill notes in her voice rasping upon the sensitive, the now morbidly sensitive, Susan. "Instead—you slip away from the house and meet a young man—and permit him to take *liberties* with you."

Susan braced herself. "I did not go to the cemetery to meet him," she replied; and that new or, rather, newly revived tenacity was strong in her eyes, in the set of her sweet mouth. "He saw me on the way and followed. I did let him kiss me—once. But I had the right to."

"You have disgraced yourself—and us all."

"We are going to be married."

"I don't want to hear such foolish talk!" cried Mrs. Warham violently. "If you had any sense, you'd know better."

"He and I do not feel as you do about my mother," said the girl with quiet dignity.

Mrs. Warham shivered before this fling. "Who told you?" she demanded.

"It doesn't matter; I know."

"Well, miss, since you know, then I can tell you that your uncle and I realize you're going the way your mother went. And the whole town thinks you've gone already. They're all saying, 'I told you so! I told you so! Like her mother!'" Mrs. Warham was weeping hysterical tears of fury. "The whole town! And it'll reflect on my Ruth. Oh, you miserable girl! Whatever possessed me to take pity on you!"

Susan's hands clutched until the nails sunk into the palms. She shut her teeth together, turned to fly.

"Wait!" commanded Mrs. Warham. "Wait, I tell you!"

Susan halted in the doorway, but did not turn.

"Your uncle and I have talked it over."

"Oh!" cried Susan.

Mrs. Warham's eyes glistened. "Yes, he has wakened up at last. There's one thing he isn't soft about——"

"You've turned him against me!" cried the girl despairingly.

"You mean *you* have turned him against you," retorted her aunt. "Anyhow, you can't wheedle him this time. He's as bent as I am. And you must promise us that you won't see Sam again."

A pause. Then Susan said, "I can't."

"Then we'll send you away to your Uncle Zeke's. It's quiet out there and you'll have a chance to think things over. And I reckon he'll watch you. He's never forgiven your mother. Now, will you promise?"

"No," said Susan calmly. "You have wicked thoughts about my mother, and you are being wicked to me—you and Ruth. Oh, I understand!"

"Don't you dare stand there and lie that way!"

raved Mrs. Warham. "I'll give you tonight to think about it. If you don't promise, you leave this house. Your uncle has been weak where you were concerned, but this caper of yours has brought him to his senses. We'll not have you a loose character—and your cousin's life spoiled by it. First thing we know, no respectable man'll marry her, either."

From between the girl's shut teeth issued a cry. She darted across the hall, locked herself in her room.

VI

SAM did not wait until Arthur Sinclair left, but, all ardor and impatience, stole in at the Warhams' front gate at ten o'clock. He dropped to the grass behind a clump of lilacs, and to calm his nerves and to make the time pass more quickly, smoked a cigarette, keeping its lighted end carefully hidden in the hollow of his hand. He was not twenty feet away, was seeing and hearing, when Arthur kissed Ruth good night. He laughed to himself. "How disappointed she looked last night when she saw I wasn't going to do that!" What a charmer Susie must be when the thought of her made the idea of kissing as pretty a girl as Ruth uninteresting, almost distasteful!

Sinclair departed; the lights in parlor and hall went out; presently light appeared through the chinks in some of the second-story shutters. Then followed three-quarters of an hour of increasing tension. The tension would have been even greater had he seen the young lady going leisurely about her preparations for bed. For Ruth was of the orderly, precise women who are created to foster the virtue of patience in those about them. It took her nearly as long to dress for bed as for a party. She did her hair up in curl papers with the utmost care; she washed and rinsed and greased her face and neck and gave them a thorough massage. She shook out and carefully hung or folded or put to air each separate garment. She examined her silk stockings for holes, found one, darned

79

it with a neatness rivaling that of a *stoppeur*. She removed from her dressing table and put away in drawers everything that was out of place. She closed each drawer tightly, closed and locked the closets, looked under the bed, turned off the lights over the dressing table. She completed her toilet with a slow washing of her teeth, a long spraying of her throat, and a deliberate, thoroughgoing dripping of boracic acid into each eye to keep and improve its clearness and brilliancy. She sat on the bed, reflected on what she had done, to assure herself that nothing had been omitted. After a slow look around she drew off her bedroom slippers, set them carefully side by side near the head of the bed. She folded her nightgown neatly about her legs, thrust them down into the bed. Again she looked slowly, searchingly, about the room to make absolutely sure she had forgotten nothing, had put everything in perfect order. Once in bed, she hated to get out; yet if she should recall any omission, however slight, she would be unable to sleep until she had corrected it. Finally, sure as fallible humanity can be, she turned out the last light, lay down—went instantly to sleep.

It was hardly a quarter of an hour after the vanishing of that last ray when Sam, standing now with heart beating fast and a lump of expectancy, perhaps of trepidation, too, in his throat, saw a figure issue from the front door and move round to the side veranda. He made a detour on the lawn, so as to keep out of view both from house and street, came up to the veranda, called to her softly.

"Can you get over the rail?" asked she in the same low tone.

"Let's go back to the summer house," urged he.

"No. Come up here," she insisted. "Be careful. The windows above are open."

He climbed the rail noiselessly and made an impetuous move for her hand. She drew back. "No, Sam dear," she said. "I know it's foolish. But I've an instinct against it—and we mustn't."

She spoke so gently that he persisted and pleaded. It was some time before he realized how much firmness there was under her gentleness. She was so afraid of making him cross; yet he also saw that she would withstand at any cost. He placed himself beside her on the wicker lounge, sitting close, his cheek almost against hers, that they might hear each other without speaking above a whisper. After one of those silences which are the peculiar delight of lovers, she drew a long breath and said: "I've got to go away, Sam. I shan't see you again for a long time."

"They heard about this morning? They're sending you away?"

"No—I'm going. They feel that I'm a disgrace and a drag. So I can't stay."

"But—you've *got* to stay!" protested Sam. In wild alarm he suspected she was preparing to make him elope with her—and he did not know to what length of folly his infatuation might whirl him. "You've no place to go," he urged.

"I'll find a place," said she.

"You mustn't—you mustn't, Susie! Why, you're only seventeen—and have no experience."

"I'll *get* experience," said she. "Nothing could be so bad as staying here. Can't you see that?"

He could not. Like so many of the children of the rich, he had no trace of overnice sense of self-respect, having been lying and toadying all his life to a father who used the power of his wealth at home no less, rather more, than abroad. But he vaguely realized what delicacy of feeling lay behind her statement of her position; and he did not dare express his real opinion. He returned to the main point. "You've simply got to put up with it for the present, Susie," he insisted. "But, then, of course, you're not serious."

"Yes. I am going."

"You'll think it over, and see I'm right, dear."

"I'm going tonight."

"Tonight!" he cried.

"Sh-h!"

Sam looked apprehensively around. Both breathed softly and listened with straining ears. His exclamation had not been loud, but the silence was profound. "I guess nobody heard," he finally whispered. "You mustn't go, Susie." He caught her hand and held it. "I love you, and I forbid it."

"I *must* go, dear," answered she. "I've decided to take the midnight boat for Cincinnati."

In the half darkness he gazed in stupefaction at her —this girl of only seventeen calmly resolving upon and planning an adventure so daring, so impossible. As he had been born and bred in that western country where the very children have more independence than the carefully tamed grown people of the East, he ought to have been prepared for almost anything. But his father had undermined his courage and independence; also his year in the East had given him somewhat different ideas of women. Susan's announcement seemed incredible. He was gathering himself for pouring out a fresh protest when it flashed through his mind—Why not? She would go to Cincinnati. He could follow in a few days or a week—and then—

Well, at least they would be free and could have many happy days together.

"Why, how could you get to Cincinnati?" he said. "You haven't any money."

"I've a twenty-dollar gold piece Uncle gave me as a keepsake. And I've got seventeen dollars in other money, and several dollars in change," explained she. "I've got two hundred and forty-three dollars and fifty cents in the bank, but I can't get that—not now. They'll send it to me when I find a place and am settled and let them know."

"You can't do it, Susie! You can't and you mustn't."

"If you knew what they said to me! Oh, I *couldn't* stay, Sam. I've got some of my clothes—a little bundle—behind the front door. As soon as I'm settled I'll let you know."

A silence, then he, hesitatingly, "Don't you—do you —hadn't I better go with you?"

She thrilled at this generosity, this new proof of love. But she said: "No, I wouldn't let you do that. They'd blame you. And I want them to know it's all my own doing."

"You're right, Susie," said the young man, relieved and emphatic. "If I went with you, it'd only get both of us into deeper trouble." Again silence, with Sam feeling a kind of awe as he studied the resolute, mysterious profile of the girl, which he could now see clearly. At last he said: "And after you get there, Susie—what will you do?"

"Find a boarding house, and then look for a place."

"What kind of a place?"

"In a store—or making dresses—or any kind of sewing. Or I could do housework."

83

The sex impulse is prolific of generous impulses. He, sitting so close to her and breathing in through his skin the emanations of her young magnetism, was moved to the depths by the picture her words conjured. This beautiful girl, a mere child, born and bred in the lady class, wandering away penniless and alone, to be a prey to the world's buffetings which, severe enough in reality, seem savage beyond endurance to the children of wealth.

As he pictured it his heart impulsively expanded. It was at his lips to offer to marry her. But his real self—and one's real self is vastly different from one's impulses—his real self forbade the words passage. Not even the sex impulse, intoxicating him as it then was, could dethrone snobbish calculation. He was young; so while he did not speak, he felt ashamed of himself for not speaking. He felt that she must be expecting him to speak, that she had the right to expect it. He drew a little away from her, and kept silent.

"The time will soon pass," said she absently.

"The time? Then you intend to come back?"

"I mean the time until you're through college and we can be together."

She spoke as one speaks of a dream as to which one has never a doubt but that it will come true. It was so preposterous, this idea that he would marry her, especially after she had been a servant or God knows what for several years—it was so absurd that he burst into a sweat of nervous terror. And he hastily drew further away.

She felt the change, for she was of those who are born sensitive. But she was far too young and inexperienced to have learned to interpret aright the

84

subtle warnings of the nerves. "You are displeased with me?" she asked timidly.

"No—Oh, no, Susie," he stammered. "I—I was thinking. Do put off going for a day or two. There's no need of hurrying."

But she felt that by disobeying her aunt and coming down to see him she had forfeited the right to shelter under that roof. "I can't go back," said she. "There's a reason." She would not tell him the reason; it would make him feel as if he were to blame. "When I get a place in Cincinnati," she went on, "I'll write to you."

"Not here," he objected. "That wouldn't do at all. No, send me a line to the Gibson House in Cincinnati, giving me your address."

"The Gibson House," she repeated. "I'll not forget that name. Gibson House."

"Send it as soon as you get a place. I may be in Cincinnati soon. But this is all nonsense. You're not going. You'd be afraid."

She laughed softly. "You don't know me. Now that I've got to go, I'm glad."

And he realized that she was not talking to give herself courage, that her words were literally true. This made him admire her, and fear her, too. There must be something wild and unwomanly in her nature. "I guess she inherits it from her mother—and perhaps her father, whoever he was." Probably she was simply doing a little early what she'd have been sure to do sooner or later, no matter what had happened. On the whole, it was just as well that she was going. "I can take her on East in the fall. As soon as she has a little knowledge of the world she'll not expect me to marry her. She can get something to do. I'll help her." And now he felt in conceit with himself again—felt that he was going to be a good, generous friend to her.

"Perhaps you'll be better off—once you get started," said he.

"I don't see how I could be worse off. What is there here for *me?*"

He wondered at the good sense of this from a mere child. It was most unlikely that any man of the class she had been brought up in would marry her; and how could she endure marriage with a man of the class in which she might possibly find a husband? As for reputation—

She, an illegitimate child, never could have a reputation, at least not so long as she had her looks. After supper, to kill time, he had dropped in at Willett's drug store, where the young fellows loafed and gossiped in the evenings; all the time he was there the conversation had been made up of sly digs and hints about graveyard trysts, each thrust causing the kind of laughter that is the wake of the prurient and the obscene. Yes, she was right. There could be "nothing in it" for her in Sutherland. He was filled with pity for her. "Poor child! What a shame!" There must be something wrong with a world that permitted such iniquities.

The clock struck twelve. "You must go," she said. "Sometimes the boat comes as early as half-past." And she stood up.

As he faced her the generous impulse surged again. He caught her in his arms, she not resisting. He kissed her again and again, murmuring disconnected words of endearment and fighting back the offer to marry her. "I mustn't! I mustn't!" he said to himself. "What'd become of us?" If his passions had been as virgin, as inexperienced, as hers, no power could have held him from going with her and marrying her. But experience had taught him the abysmal difference between before and after; and he found strength to be sensible, even in the height of his passionate longing for her.

She clasped her arms about his neck. "Oh, my dear love!" she murmured. "I'd do anything for you. I feel that you love me as I love you."

"Yes—yes." And he pressed his lips to hers. An instant and she drew away, shaking and panting. He tried to clasp her again, but she would not have it. "I can't stand it!" he murmured. "I must go with you—I must!"

"No!" she replied. "It wouldn't do unless we were really married." Wistfully, "And we can't be that yet —can we? There isn't any way?"

His passion cooled instantly.

"There isn't any way," he said regretfully. "I'd not dare tell my father."

"Yes, we must wait till you're of age, and have your education, and are free. Then——" She drew a long breath, looked at him with a brave smile. The large moon was shining upon them. "We'll think of that, and not let ourselves be unhappy—won't we?"

"Yes," he said. "But I must go."

"I forgot for the minute. Good-by, dearest." She put up her lips. He kissed her, but without passion now.

"You might go with me as far as the wharf," she suggested.

"No—someone might see—and that would ruin everything. I'd like to—I'd——"

"It wouldn't do," she interrupted. "I wouldn't let you come."

With sudden agitation she kissed him—he felt that her lips were cold. He pressed her hands—they, too, were cold. "Good-by, my darling," he murmured, vaulted lightly over the rail and disappeared in the deep shadows of the shrubbery. When he was clear of the grounds he paused to light a cigarette. His hand was shaking so that the match almost dropped from his fingers. "I've been making a damn fool of myself," he said half aloud. "A double damn fool! I've got to stop that talk about marrying, somehow —or keep away from her. But I can't keep away. I *must* have her! Why in the devil can't she realize that a man in my position couldn't marry her? If it wasn't for this marrying talk, I'd make her happy. I've simply got to stop this marrying talk. It gets worse and worse."

Her calmness deceived her into thinking herself perfectly sane and sober, perfectly aware of what she was about. She had left her hat and her bundle behind the door. She put on the hat in the darkness of the hall with steady fingers, took up the well-filled shawl strap and went forth, closing the door behind her. In the morning they would find the door unlocked but that would not cause much talk, as Sutherland people were all rather careless about locking up. They would not knock at the door of her room until noon, perhaps. Then they would find on the pincushion the letter she had written to her uncle, saying good-by and explaining that she had decided to remove forever the taint of her mother and herself from their house and their lives—a somewhat theatrical letter, modeled upon Ouida, whom she thought the greatest writer that had ever lived, Victor Hugo and two or three poets perhaps excepted.

Her bundle was not light, but she hardly felt it as she moved swiftly through the deserted, moonlit streets toward the river. The wharf boat for the Cincinnati and Louisville mail steamers was anchored at the foot of Pine Street. On the levee before it were piled the boxes, bags, cases, crates, barrels to be loaded upon the "up boat." She was descending the gentle slope toward this mass of freight when her blood tingled at a deep, hoarse, mournful whistle from far away; she knew it was the up boat, rounding the bend and sighting the town. The sound echoed musically back and forth between the Kentucky and the Indiana bluffs, died lingeringly away. Again the whistle boomed, again the dark forest-clad steeps sent the echoes to and fro across the broad silver river. And now she could see the steamer, at the bend—a dark mass picked out with brilliant dots of light; the big funnels, the two thick pennants of black smoke. And she could hear the faint pleasant stroke of the paddles of the big side wheels upon the water.

At the wharf boat there had not been a sign of life. But with the dying away of the second whistle lights—the lights of lanterns—appeared on the levee close to the water's edge and on the wharf boat itself. And, behind her, the doors of the Sutherland Hotel opened and its office lit up, in preparation for any chance arrivals. She turned abruptly out of the beaten path down the gravel levee, made for the lower and darker end of the wharf boat. There would be Sutherland people going up the river. But they would be more than prompt; everyone came early to boats and trains to begin the sweet draught of the excitement of journeying. So she would wait in the darkness and go aboard when the steamer was about to draw in its planks. At the upper end of the wharf boat there was the broad gangway to the levee for passengers and freight; at the lower and dark and deserted end a narrow beam extended from boat to shore, to hold the boat steady. Susan, balancing herself with her bundle, went up to the beam, sat down upon a low stanchion in the darkness where she could see the river.

Louder and louder grew the regular musical beat of engine and paddle. The searchlight on the forward deck of the *General Lytle,* after peering uncertainly, suspiciously, at the entire levee, and at the river, and at the Kentucky shore, abruptly focused upon the wharf boat. The *General Lytle* now seemed a blaze of lights —from lower deck, from saloon deck, from pilot house deck, and forward and astern. A hundred interesting sounds came from her—tinkling of bells, calls from deck to deck, whistlings, creaking of pulleys, lowing of cattle, grunting of swine, plaint of agitated sheep, the resigned cluckings of many chickens. Along the rail of the middle or saloon deck were seated a few passengers who had not yet gone to bed. On the lower deck was a swarm of black roustabouts, their sooty animal faces, their uncannily contrasting white teeth and eyeballs, their strange and varied rags lit up by the torches blazing where a gangplank lay ready for running out. And high and clear in the lovely June night sailed the moon, spreading a faint benign light upon hills and shores and glistening river, upon the graceful, stately mail steamer, now advancing majestically upon the wharf boat. Susan watched all, saw all, with quick beating heart and quivering interest. It was the first time that her life had been visited by the fascinating sense of event, real event. The tall, proud, impetuous child-woman, standing in the semi-darkness beside her bundle, was about to cast her stake upon the table in a bold game with Destiny. Her eyes shone with the wonderful expression that is seen only when courage gazes into the bright face of danger.

The steamer touched the edge of the wharf-boat with gentle care; the wharf-boat swayed and groaned. Even as the gangplanks were pushing out, the ragged, fantastic roustabouts, with wild, savage, hilarious cries, ran and jumped and scrambled to the wharf-boat like a band of escaping lunatics and darted down its shore planks to pounce upon the piles of freight. The mate, at the steamer edge to superintend the loading, and the wharf master on the levee beside the freight released each a hoarse torrent of profanity to spur on the yelling, laughing roustabouts, more brute than man. Torches flared; cow and sheep, pig and chicken, uttered each its own cry of dissatisfaction or dismay; the mate and wharf master cursed because it was the custom to curse; the roustabouts rushed ashore empty-handed, came filing back, stooping under their burdens. It was a scene of animation, of excitement, savage, grotesque, fascinating.

Susan, trembling a little, so tense were her nerves, waited until the last straggling roustabouts were staggering on the boat, until the deep whistle sounded, warning of approaching departure. Then she took up her bundle and put herself in the line of roustabouts, between a half-naked negro, black as coal and bearing a small barrel of beer, and a half-naked mulatto bearing a bundle of loud-smelling untanned skins. "Get out of the way, lady!" yelled the mate, eagerly seizing upon a new text for his denunciations. "Get out of the way, you black hellions! Let the lady pass! Look out, lady! You damned sons of hell, what're you about! I'll rip out your bowels——"

Susan fled across the deck and darted up the stairs to the saloon. The steamer was all white without except the black metal work. Within—that is, in the long saloon out of which the cabins opened to right and left and in which the meals were served at extension tables—there was the palatial splendor of white and gilt. At the forward end near the main entrance was the office. Susan, peering in from the darkness of the deck, saw that the way was clear. The Sutherland passengers had been accommodated. She entered, put her bundle down, faced the clerk behind the desk.

"Why, howdy, Miss Lenox," said he genially, beginning to twist his narrow, carefully attended blond mustache. "Any of the folks with you?"

She remembered his face but not his name. She remembered him as one of the "river characters" regarded as outcast by the Christian respectability of Sutherland. But she who could not but be polite to everybody smiled pleasantly, though she did not like his expression as he looked at her. "No, I'm alone," said she.

"Oh—your friends are going to meet you at the wharf in the morning," said he, content with his own explanation. "Just sign here, please." And, as she wrote, he went on: "I've got one room left. Ain't that lucky? It's a nice one, too. You'll be very comfortable. Everybody at home well? I ain't been in Sutherland for nigh ten years. Every week or so I think I will, and then somehow I don't. Here's your key—number 34—right-hand side, well down toward the far end, yonder. Two dollars, please. Thank you —exactly right. Hope you sleep well."

"Thank you," said Susan.

She turned away with the key which was thrust through one end of a stick about a foot long, to make it too bulky for absent-minded passengers to pocket. She took up her bundle, walked down the long saloon with its gilt decorations, its crystal chandeliers, its double array of small doors, each numbered. The clerk looked after her, admiration of the fine curve of her shoulders, back, and hips written plain upon his insignificant features. And it was a free admiration he would not have dared show had she not been a daughter of illegitimacy—a girl whose mother's "looseness" raised pleasing if scandalous suggestions and even possibilities in the mind of every man with a carnal eye. And not unnaturally. To think of her was to think of the circumstances surrounding her coming into the world; and to think of those circumstances was to think of immorality.

Susan, all unconscious of that polluted and impudent gaze, was soon standing before the narrow door numbered 34, as she barely made out, for the lamps in the saloon chandeliers were turned low. She unlocked it, entered the small clean stateroom and deposited her bundle on the floor. With just a glance at her quarters she hurried to the opposite door—the one giving upon the promenade. She opened it, stepped out, crossed the deserted deck and stood at the rail. The *General Lytle* was drawing slowly away from the wharf-boat. As that part of the promenade happened to be sheltered from the steamer's lights, she was seeing the panorama of Sutherland—its long stretch of shaded waterfront, its cupolas and steeples, the wide leafy streets leading straight from the river by a gentle slope to the base of the dark towering bluffs behind the town—all sleeping in peace and beauty in the soft light of the moon. That farthest cupola to the left —it was the Number Two engine house, and the third place from it was her uncle's house. Slowly the steamer, now in mid-stream, drew away from the town. One by one the familiar landmarks—the packing house, the soap factory, the Geiss brewery, the tall chimney of the pumping station, the shorn top of Reservoir Hill —slipped ghostlily away to the southwest. The sobs choked up into her throat and the tears rained from her eyes. They all pitied and looked down on her there; still, it had been home—the only home she ever had known or ever would know. And until these last few frightful days, how happy she had been there! For the first time she felt desolate, weak, afraid. But not daunted. It is strange to see in strong human character the strength and the weakness, two flat contradictions, existing side by side and making weak what seems so strong and making strong what seems so weak. However, human character is a tangle of inconsistencies, as disorderly and inchoate as the tangible and visible parts of nature. Susan felt weak, but not the kind of weakness that skulks. And there lay the difference, the abysmal difference, between courage and cowardice. Courage has full as much fear as cowardice, often more; but it has a something else that cowardice has not. It trembles and shivers but goes forward.

Wiping her eyes she went back to her own cabin. She had neglected closing its other door, the one from the saloon. The clerk was standing smirking in the doorway.

"You must be going away for quite some time," said he. And he fixed upon her as greedy and impudent eyes as ever looked from a common face. It was his battle glance. Guileful women, bent on trimming him for anything from a piece of plated jewelry to a saucer of ice cream, had led him to believe that before it walls of virtue tottered and fell like Jericho's before the trumpets of Joshua.

"It makes me a little homesick to see the old town disappear," hastily explained Susan, recovering herself. The instant anyone was watching, her emotions always hid.

"Wouldn't you like to sit out on deck a while?" pursued the clerk, bringing up a winning smile to reinforce the fetching stare.

The idea was attractive, for she did not feel like sleep. It would be fine to sit out in the open, watch the moon and the stars, the mysterious banks gliding swiftly by, and new vistas always widening out ahead. But not with this puny, sandy little "river character," not with anybody that night. "No," replied she. "I think I'll go to bed."

She had hesitated—and that was enough to give him encouragement. "Now, do come," he urged. "You don't know how nice it is. And they say I'm mighty good company."

"No, thanks." Susan nodded a pleasant dismissal.

The clerk lingered. "Can't I help you in some way? Wouldn't you like me to get you something?"

"No—nothing."

"Going to visit in Cincinnati? I know the town from A to Izzard. It's a lot of fun over the Rhine.

I've had mighty good times there—the kind a pretty, lively girl like you would take to."

"When do we get to Cincinnati?"

"About eight—maybe half-past seven. Depends on the landings we have to make, and the freight."

"Then I'll not have much time for sleep," said Susan. "Good night." And no more realizing the coldness of her manner than the reason for his hanging about, she faced him, hand on the door to close it.

"You ain't a bit friendly," wheedled he.

"I'm sorry you think so. Good night—and thank you." And he could not but withdraw his form from the door. She closed it and forgot him. And she did not dream she had passed through one of those perilous adventures incident to a female traveling alone —adventures that even in the telling frighten ladies whose nervousness for their safety seems to increase in direct proportion to the degree of tranquillity their charms create in the male bosom. She decided it would be unwise regularly to undress; the boat might catch fire or blow up or something. She took off skirt, hat and ties, loosened her waist, and lay upon the lower of the two plain, hard little berths. The throb of the engines, the beat of the huge paddles, made the whole boat tremble and shiver. Faintly up from below came the sound of quarrels over crap-shooting, of banjos and singing—from the roustabouts amusing themselves between landings. She thought she would not be able to sleep in these novel and exciting surroundings. She had hardly composed herself before she lost consciousness, to sleep on and on dreamlessly, without motion.

VII

SHE was awakened by a crash so uproarious that she sat bolt upright before she had her eyes open. Her head struck stunningly against the bottom of the upper berth. This further confused her thoughts. She leaped from the bed, caught up her slippers, reached for her opened-up bundle. The crash was still billowing through the boat; she now recognized it as a great gong sounding for breakfast. She sat down on the bed and rubbed her head and laughed merrily. "I *am* a greenhorn!" she said. "Another minute and I'd have had the whole boat laughing at me."

She felt rested and hungry—ravenously hungry. She tucked in her blouse, washed as well as she could in the tiny bowl on the little washstand. Then before the cloudy watermarked mirror she arranged her scarcely mussed hair. A charming vision of fresh young loveliness, strong, erect, healthy, bright of eye and of cheek, she made as, after a furtive look up and down the saloon, she stepped from her door a very few minutes after the crash of that gong. With much scuffling and bustling the passengers, most of them country people, were hurrying into places at the tables which now had their extension leaves and were covered with coarse white tablecloths and with dishes of nicked stoneware, white, indeed, but shabbily so. But Susan's young eyes were not critical. To her it all seemed fine, with the rich flavor of adventure. A more experienced traveler might have been filled with gloomy forebodings by the quality of the odor from the cooking. She found it delightful and sympathized with the unrestrained eagerness of the homely country faces about her, with the children beating their spoons on their empty plates. The colored waiters presently began to stream in, each wearing a soiled white jacket, each bearing aloft a huge tray on which were stacked filled dishes and steaming cups.

Colored people have a keen instinct for class. One of the waiters happened to note her, advanced bowing and smiling with that good-humored, unservile courtesy which is the peculiar possession of the Americanized colored race. He flourished her into a chair with a "Good morning, miss. It's going to be a fine day." And as soon as she was seated he began to form round her plate a large inclosing arc of side dishes—fried fish, fried steak, fried eggs, fried potatoes, wheat cakes, canned peaches, a cup of coffee. He drew toward her a can of syrup, a pitcher of cream, and a bowl of granulated sugar.

"Anything else?" said he, with a show of teeth white and sound.

"No—nothing. Thank you so much."

Her smile stimulated him to further courtesies. "Some likes the yeggs biled. Shall I change 'em?"

"No. I like them this way." She was so hungry that the idea of taking away a certainty on the chance of getting something out of sight and not yet cooked did not attract her.

"Perhaps—a little better piece of steak?"

"No—this looks fine." Her enthusiasm was not mere politeness.

"I clean forgot your hot biscuits." And away he darted.

When he came back with a heaping plate of hot biscuits, Sally Lunn and cornbread, she was eating as heartily as any of her neighbors. It seemed to her that never had she tasted such grand food as this served in the white and gold saloon with strangeness and interest all about her and the delightful sense of motion—motion into the fascinating golden unknown. The men at the table were eating with their knives; each had one protecting forearm and hand cast round his arc of small dishes as if to ward off probable attempt at seizure. And they swallowed as if the boat were afire. The women ate more daintily, as became members of the finer sex on public exhibition. They were wearing fingerless net gloves, and their little fingers stood straight out in that gesture which every truly elegant woman deems necessary if the food is to be daintily and artistically conveyed to her lips. The children mussed and gormed themselves, their dishes, the tablecloth. Susan loved it all. Her eyes sparkled. She ate everything, and regretted that lack of capacity made it impossible for her to yield to the entreaties of her waiter that she "have a little more."

She rose, went into the nearest passageway between saloon and promenade, stealthily took a ten-cent piece from her pocketbook. She called her waiter and gave it to him. She was blushing deeply, frightened lest this the first tip she had ever given or seen given be misunderstood and refused. "I'm so much obliged," she said. "You were very nice."

The waiter bowed like a prince, always with his simple, friendly smile; the tip disappeared under his apron. "Nobody could help being nice to you, lady."

She thanked him again and went to the promenade.

It seemed to her that they had almost arrived. Along shore stretched a continuous line of houses—pretty houses with gardens. There were electric cars. Nearer the river lay several parallel lines of railway track along which train after train was speeding, some of them short trains of ordinary day coaches, others long trains made up in part of coaches grander and more beautiful than any she had ever seen. She knew they must be the parlor and dining and sleeping cars she had read about. And now they were in the midst of a fleet of steamers and barges, and far ahead loomed the first of Cincinnati's big suspension bridges, pictures of which she had many a time gazed at in wonder. There was a mingling of strange loud noises—whistles, engines, on the water, on shore; there was a multitude of what seemed to her feverish activities—she who had not been out of quiet Sutherland since she was a baby too young to note things.

The river, the shores, grew more and more crowded. Susan's eyes darted from one new object to another; and eagerly though she looked she felt she was missing more than she saw.

"Why, Susan Lenox!" exclaimed a voice almost in her ear.

She closed her teeth upon a cry; suddenly she was back from wonderland to herself. She turned to face dumpy, dressy Mrs. Waterbury and her husband with the glossy kinky ringlets and the long wavy mustache. "How do you do?" she stammered.

"We didn't know you were aboard," said Mrs. Waterbury, a silly, duck-legged woman looking proudly uncomfortable in her bead-trimmed black silk.

"Yes—I'm—I'm here," confessed Susan.

"Going to the city to visit?"

"Yes," said Susan. She hesitated, then repeated, "Yes."

"What elegant breakfasts they do serve on these boats! I suppose your friends'll meet you. But Mort and I'll look after you till they come."

"Oh, it isn't necessary," protested Susan. The steamer was passing under the bridge. There were cities on both shores—huge masses of dingy brick, streets filled with motion of every kind—always motion, incessant motion, and change. "We're about there, aren't we?" she asked.

"The wharf's up beyond the second bridge—the Covington Bridge," explained Waterbury with the air of the old experienced globe-trotter. "There's a third one, further up, but you can't see it for the smoke." And he went on and on, volubly airing his intimate knowledge of the great city which he visited once a year for two or three days to buy goods. He ended with a scornful, "My, but Cincinnati's a dirty place!"

Dirty it might be, but Susan loved it, dirt and all. The smoke, the grime somehow seemed part of it, one of its charms, one of the things that made it different from, and superior to, monotonous country and country town. She edged away from the Waterburys, hid in her stateroom watching the panorama through the curtained glass of her promenade deck door. She was completely carried away. The city! So, this was the city! And her dreams of travel, of new sights, new faces, were beginning to come true. She forgot herself, forgot what she had left behind, forgot what she was to face. All her power of thought and feeling was used up in absorbing these unfolding wonders. And when the June sun suddenly pierced the heavy clouds of fog and smoke, she clasped her hands and gasped, "Lovely! Oh, how lovely!"

And now the steamer was at the huge wharf-boat, in shape like the one at Sutherland, but in comparative size like the real Noah's Ark beside a toy ark. And from the whole tremendous scene rose an enormous clamor, the stentorian voice of the city. That voice is discordant and terrifying to many. To Susan, on that day, it was the most splendid burst of music. "Awake—awake!" it cried. "Awake, and *live!*" She opened her door that she might hear it better—rattle and rumble and roar, shriek of whistle, clang of bell. And the people!—Thousands on thousands hurrying hither and yon, like bees in a hive. "Awake—awake, and live!"

The noises from the saloon reminded her that the journey was ended, that she must leave the boat. And she did not know where to go—she and her bundle. She waited until she saw the Waterburys, along with the other passengers, moving up the levee. Then she issued forth—by the promenade deck door so that she would not pass the office. But at the head of the companionway, in the forward part of the deck, there the clerk stood, looking even pettier and more offensive by daylight. She thought to slip by him. But he stopped stroking his mustache and called out to her, "Haven't your friends come?"

She frowned, angry in her nervousness. "I shall get on very well," she said curtly. Then she repented, smiled politely, added, "Thank you."

"I'll put you in a carriage," he offered, hastening down the stairs to join her.

She did not know what to say or do. She walked silently beside him, he carrying her bundle. They

102

crossed the wharf-boat. A line of dilapidated looking carriages was drawn up near the end of the gangplank. The sight of them, the remembrance of what she had heard of the expensiveness of city carriages, nerved her to desperation. "Give me my things, please," she said. "I think I'll walk."

"Where do you want to go?"

The question took her breath away. With a quickness that amazed her, her lips uttered, "The Gibson House."

"Oh! That's a right smart piece. But you can take a car. I'll walk with you to the car. There's a line a couple of squares up that goes almost by the door. You know it isn't far from Fourth Street."

She was now in a flutter of terror. She went stumbling along beside him, not hearing a word of his voluble and flirtatious talk. They were in the midst of the mad rush and confusion. The noises, no longer mingled but individual, smote savagely upon her ears, startling her, making her look dazedly round as if expecting death to swoop upon her. At the corner of Fourth Street the clerk halted. He was clear out of humor with her, so dumb, so unappreciative. "There'll be a car along soon," said he sourly.

"You needn't wait," said she timidly. "Thank you again."

"You can't miss it. Good-by." And he lifted his hat—"tipped" it, rather—for he would not have wasted a full lift upon such a female. She gave a gasp of relief when he departed; then a gasp of terror—for upon the opposite corner stood the Waterburys. The globe-trotter and his wife were so dazed by the city that they did not see her, though in their helpless glancing round they looked straight at her. She hastily ran into a drug store on the corner. A young man in shirt sleeves held up by pink garters, and with oily black hair carefully parted and plastered, put down a pestle and mortar and came forward. He had kind brown eyes, but there was something wrong with the lower part of his face. Susan did not dare look to see what it was, lest he should think her unfeeling. He was behind the counter. Susan saw the soda fountain. As if by inspiration, she said, "Some chocolate soda, please."

"Ice cream?" asked the young man in a peculiar voice, like that of one who has a harelip.

"Please," said Susan. And then she saw the sign, "Ice Cream, ten cents," and wished she hadn't.

The young man mixed the soda, put in a liberal helping of ice cream, set it before her with a spoon in it, rested the knuckles of his brown hairy hands on the counter and said:

"It *is* hot."

"Yes, indeed," assented Susan. "I wonder where I could leave my bundle for a while. I'm a stranger and I want to look for a boarding house."

"You might leave it here with me," said the young man. "That's about our biggest line of trade—that and postage stamps and telephone—*and* the directory." He laughed heartily. Susan did not see why; she did not like the sound, either, for the young man's deformity of lower jaw deformed his laughter as well as his speech. However, she smiled politely and ate and drank her soda slowly.

"I'll be glad to take care of your bundle," the young man said presently. "Ever been here before?"

"No," said Susan. "That is, not since I was about four years old."

"I was four," said the young man, "when a horse stepped on my mouth in the street."

"My, how dreadful!" exclaimed Susan.

"You can see some of the scar yet," the young man assured her, and he pointed to his curiously sunken mouth. "The doctors said it was the most remarkable case of the kind on record," continued he proudly. "That was what led me into the medical line. You don't seem to have your boarding house picked."

"I was going to look in the papers."

"That's dangerous—especially for a young lady. Some of them boarding houses—well, they're no better'n they ought to be."

"I don't suppose you know of any?"

"My aunt keeps one. And she's got a vacancy, it being summer."

"I'm afraid it'd be too expensive for me," said Susan, to feel her way.

The young man was much flattered. But he said, "Oh, it ain't so toppy. I think you could make a deal with her for five per."

Susan looked inquiring.

"Five a week—room and board."

"I might stand that," said Susan reflectively. Then, deciding for complete confidence, "I'm looking for work, too."

"What line?"

"Oh, I never tried anything. I thought maybe dressmaking or millinery."

"Mighty poor season for jobs. The times are bad, anyhow." He was looking at her with kindly curiosity. "If I was you, I'd go back home—and wait."

Susan shrank within herself. "I can't do that," she said.

The young man thought awhile, then said: "If you should go to my aunt's, you can say Mr. Ellison sent you. No, that ain't me. It's the boss. You see, a respectable boarding house asks for references."

Susan colored deeply and her gaze slowly sank. "I didn't know that," she murmured.

"Don't be afraid. Aunt Kate ain't so particular —leastways, not in summer when things is slow. And I know you're quiet."

By the time the soda was finished, the young man —who said his name was Robert Wylie—had written on the back of Ellison's business card in a Spencerian hand: "Mrs. Kate Wylie, 347 West Sixth Street." He explained that Susan was to walk up two squares and take the car going west; the conductor would let her off at the right place. "You'd better leave your things here," said Mr. Wylie, holding up the card so that they could admire his penmanship together. "You may not hit it off with Aunt Kate. Don't think you've got to stay there just because of me."

"I'm sure I'll like it," Susan declared confidently. Her spirits were high; she felt that she was in a strong run of luck.

Wylie lifted her package over the counter and went to the door with her to point out the direction. "This is Fourth. The next up is Fifth. The next wide one is Sixth—and you can read it on the lamp-post, too."

"Isn't that convenient!" exclaimed Susan. "What a lovely city this is!"

"There's worse," said Mr. Wylie, not to seem vain of his native town.

They shook hands most friendly and she set out in the direction he had indicated. She was much upset by the many vehicles and the confusion, but she did her best to seem at ease and at home. She watched a girl walking ahead of her—a shopgirl who seemed well-dressed and stylish, especially about the hat and hair. Susan tried to walk like her. "I suppose I look and act greener than I really am," thought she. "But I'll keep my eyes open and catch on." And in this, as in all her thoughts and actions since leaving, she showed confidence not because she was conceited, but because she had not the remotest notion what she was actually attempting. How many of us get credit for courage as we walk unconcerned through perils, or essay and conquer great obstacles, when in truth we are not courageous but simply unaware! As a rule knowledge is power or, rather, a source of power, but there are times when ignorance is a power and knowledge a weakness. If Susan had known, she might perhaps have stayed at home and submitted and, with crushed spirit, might have sunk under the sense of shame and degradation. But she did not know; so Columbus before his sailors or Cæsar at the Rubicon among his soldiers did not seem more tranquil than she really was. Wylie, who suspected in the direction of the truth, wondered at her. "She's game, she is," he muttered again and again that morning. "What a nerve for a kid—and a lady, too!"

She found the right corner and the right car without further adventure; and the conductor assured her that he would set her down before the very door of the address on the card. It was an open car with few passengers. She took the middle of the long seat nearest the rear platform and looked about her like one in a happy dream. On and on and yet on they went. With every square they passed more people, so it seemed to her, than there were in all Sutherland.

And what huge stores! And what wonderful displays of things to wear! Where would the people be found to buy such quantities, and where would they get the money to pay? How many restaurants and saloons! Why, everybody must be eating and drinking all the time. And at each corner she looked up and down the cross streets, and there were more and ever more magnificent buildings, throngs upon throngs of people. Was there no end to it? This was Sixth Street, still Sixth Street, as she saw at the corner lamp-posts. Then there must be five more such streets between this and the river; and she could see, up the cross streets, that the city was even vaster in the direction of the hills. And there were all these cross streets! It was stupefying—overwhelming—incredible.

She began to be nervous, they were going so far. She glanced anxiously at the conductor. He was watching her interestedly, understood her glance, answered it with a reassuring nod. He called out:

"I'm looking out for you, miss. I've got you on my mind. Don't you fret."

She gave him a bright smile of relief. They were passing through a double row of what seemed to her stately residences, and there were few people on the sidewalks. The air, too, was clearer, though the walls were grimy and also the grass in the occasional tiny front yards. But the curtains at the windows looked clean and fresh, and so did the better class of people among those on the sidewalk. It delighted her to see so many well-dressed women, wearing their clothes with an air which she told herself she must acquire. She was startled by the conductor's calling out:

"Now, miss!"

She rose as he rang the bell and was ready to get

off when the car stopped, for she was eager to cause him as little trouble as possible.

"The house is right straight before you," said the conductor. "The number's in the transom."

She thanked him, descended, was on the sidewalk before Mrs. Wylie's. She looked at the house and her heart sank. She thought of the small sum in her purse; it was most unlikely that such a house as this would harbor her. For here was a grand stone stairway ascending to a deep stone portico, and within it great doors, bigger than those of the Wright mansion, the palace of Sutherland. However, she recalled the humble appearance and mode of speech of her friend the drug clerk and plucked up the courage to ascend and to ring.

A slattern, colored maid opened the door. At the first glance within, at the first whiff of the interior air, Susan felt more at ease. For she was seeing what even her bedazzled eyes recognized as cheap dowdiness, and the smell that assailed her nostrils was that of a house badly and poorly kept—the smell of cheap food and bad butter cooking, of cats, of undusted rooms, of various unrecognizable kinds of staleness. She stood in the center of the big dingy parlor, gazing round at the grimed chromos until Mrs. Wylie entered—a thin middle-aged woman with small brown eyes set wide apart, a perpetual frown, and a chin so long and so projected that she was almost jimber-jawed. While Susan explained stammeringly what she had come for, Mrs. Wylie eyed her with increasing disfavor. When Susan had finished, she unlocked her lips for the first time to say:

"The room's took."

"Oh!" cried Susan in dismay.

109

The telephone rang in the back parlor. Mrs. Wylie excused herself to answer. After a few words she closed the doors between. She was gone fully five minutes; to Susan it seemed an hour. She came back, saying:

"I've been talking to my nephew. He called up. Well, I reckon you can have the room. It ain't my custom to take in ladies as young as you. But you seem to be all right. Your parents allowed you to come?"

"I haven't any," replied Susan. "I'm here to find a place and support myself."

Mrs. Wylie continued to eye her dubiously. "Well, I have no wish to pry into your affairs. 'Mind your own business,' that's my rule." She spoke with defiance, as if the contrary were being asserted by some invisible person who might appear and gain hearing and belief. She went on: "If Mr. Ellison wants it, why I suppose it's all right. But you can't stay out later'n ten o'clock."

"I shan't go out at all of nights," said Susan eagerly.

"You *look* quiet," said Mrs. Wylie, with the air of adding that appearances were rarely other than deceptive.

"Oh, I *am* quiet," declared Susan. It puzzled her, this recurrence of the suggestion of noisiness.

"I can't allow much company—none in your room."

"There won't be any company." She blushed deeply. "That is, a—a young man from our town—he may call once. But he'll be off for the East right away."

Mrs. Wylie reflected on this, Susan the while standing uneasily, dreading lest decision would be against her. Finally Mrs. Wylie said:

"Robert says you want the five-dollar room. I'll show it to you."

They ascended two flights through increasing shabbiness. On the third floor at the rear was a room —a mere continuation of the narrow hall, partitioned off. It contained a small folding bed, a small table, a tiny bureau, a washstand hardly as large as that in the cabin on the boat, a row of hooks with a curtain of flowered chintz before them, a kitchen chair, a chromo of "Awake and Asleep," a torn and dirty rag carpet. The odor of the room, stale, damp, verging on moldy, seemed the fitting exhalation from such an assemblage of forbidding objects.

"It's a nice, comfortable room," said Mrs. Wylie aggressively. "I couldn't afford to give it and two meals for five dollars except till the first of September. After that it's eight."

"I'll be glad to stay, if you'll let me," said Susan. Mrs. Wylie's suspicion, so plain in those repellent eyes, took all the courage out of her. The great adventure seemed rapidly to be losing its charms. She could not think of herself as content or anything but sad and depressed in such surroundings as these. How much better it would be if she could live out in the open, out where it was attractive!

"I suppose you've got some baggage," said Mrs. Wylie, as if she rather expected to hear that she had not.

"I left it at the drug store," explained Susan.

"Your trunk?"

Susan started nervously at that explosive exclamation. "I—I haven't got a trunk—only a few things in a shawl strap."

"Well, I never!"

Mrs. Wylie tossed her head, clucked her tongue disgustedly against the roof of her mouth. "But I suppose if Mr. Ellison says so, why you can stay."

"Thank you," said Susan humbly. Even if it would not have been basest ingratitude to betray her friend, Mr. Wylie, still she would not have had the courage to confess the truth about Mr. Ellison and so get herself ordered into the street. "I—I think I'll go for my things."

"The custom is to pay in advance," said Mrs. Wylie sharply.

"Oh, yes—of course," stammered Susan.

She seated herself on the wooden chair and opened out her purse. She found the five among her few bills, extended it with trembling fingers toward Mrs. Wylie. At the same time she lifted her eyes. The woman's expression as she bored into the pocketbook terrified her. Never before had she seen the savage greediness that is bred in the city among the people who fight against fearful odds to maintain their respectability and to save themselves from the ever threatened drop to the despised working class.

"Thank you," said Mrs. Wylie, taking the bill as if she were conferring a favor upon Susan. "I make everybody pay promptly. The first of the week or out they go! I used to be easy and I came near going down."

"Oh, I shouldn't stay a minute if I couldn't pay," said the girl. "I'm going to look for something right away."

"Well, I don't want to discourage you, but there's a great many out of work. Still, I suppose you'll be able to wheedle some man into giving you a job. But I warn you I'm very particular about morals. If I see any signs——" Mrs. Wylie did not finish her sentence.

Any words would have been weaker than her look.

Susan colored and trembled. Not at the poisonous hint as to how money could be got to keep on paying for that room, for the hint passed wide of Susan. She was agitated by the thought: if Mrs. Wylie should learn that she was not respectable! If Mrs. Wylie should learn that she was nameless—was born in disgrace so deep that, no matter how good she might be, she would yet be classed with the wicked.

"I'm down like a thousand of brick on any woman that is at all loose with the men," continued the landlady. "I never could understand how any woman could so far forget herself." And the woman whom the men had all her life been helping to their uttermost not to "forget herself" looked sharp suspicion and envy at Susan, the lovely. Why are women of the Mrs. Wylie sort so swift to suspect? Can it be that in some secret chamber of their never assailed hearts there lurks a longing—a feeling as to what they would do if they had the chance? Mrs. Wylie continued, "I hope you have strict Christian principles?"

"I was brought up Presbyterian," said Susan anxiously. She was far from sure that in Cincinnati and by its Mrs. Wylies Presbyterian would be regarded as Christian.

"There's your kind of a church a few squares from here," was all Mrs. Wylie deigned to reply. Susan suspected a sneer at Presbyterianism in her accent.

"That'll be nice," she murmured. She was eager to escape. "I'll go for my things."

"You can walk down and take the Fourth Street car," suggested her landlady. "Then you can watch out and not miss the store. The conductors are very impudent and forgetful."

Susan escaped from the house as speedily as her flying feet would take her down the two flights. In the street once more, her spirits rose. She went south to Fourth Street, decided to walk instead of taking a car. She now found herself in much more impressive surroundings than before, and realized that Sixth Street was really one of the minor streets. The further uptown she went, the more excited she became. After the district of stately mansions with wonderful carriages driving up and away and women dressed like those in the illustrated story papers, came splendid shops and hotels, finer than Susan had believed there were anywhere in the world. And most of the people —the crowds on crowds of people!—looked prosperous and cheerful and so delightfully citified! She wondered why so many of the men stared at her. She assumed it must be something rural in her appearance—though that ought to have set the women to staring, too. But she thought little about this, so absorbed was she in seeing all the new things. She walked slowly, pausing to inspect the shop windows— the gorgeous dresses and hats and jewelry, the thousand costly things scattered in careless profusion. And the crowds! How secure she felt among these multitudes of strangers, not one of them knowing or suspecting her secret of shame! She no longer had the sense of being outcast, branded.

When she had gone so far that it seemed to her she certainly must have missed the drug store, carefully though she had inspected each corner as she went, she decided that she must stop someone of this hurrying throng and inquire the way. While she was still screwing her courage to this boldness, she espied the sign and hastened joyfully across the street. She and Wylie welcomed each other like old friends. He was delighted when he learned that she had taken the room.

"You won't mind Aunt Kate after a while," said he. "She's sour and nosey, but she's honest and respectable—and that's the main thing just now with you. And I think you'll get a job all right. Aunt Kate's got a lady friend that's head saleslady at Shillito's. She'll know of something."

Wylie was so kind and so hopeful that Susan felt already settled. As soon as customers came in, she took her parcel and went, Wylie saying, "I'll drop round after supper and see how things are getting on." She took the Sixth Street car back, and felt like an old resident. She was critical of Sixth Street now, and of the women she had been admiring there less than two hours before—critical of their manners and of their dress. The exterior of the boarding house no longer awed her. She was getting a point of view —as she proudly realized. By the time Sam came— and surely that wouldn't be many days—she would be quite transformed.

She mounted the steps and was about to ring when Mrs. Wylie herself, with stormy brow and snapping eyes, opened the door. "Go into the parlor," she jerked out from between her unpleasant-looking receding teeth.

Susan gave her a glance of frightened wonder and obeyed.

VIII

AT the threshold her bundles dropped to the floor and all color fled from her face. Before her stood her Uncle George and Sam Wright and his father. The two elderly men were glowering at her; Sam, white as his shirt and limp, was hanging his head.

"So, miss!—You've got back, eh?" cried her uncle in a tone she would not have believed could come from him.

As quickly as fear had seized her she now shook it off. "Yes, Uncle," she said calmly, meeting his angry eyes without flinching. And back came that expression of resolution—of stubbornness we call it when it is the flag of opposition to *our* will.

"What'd have become of you," demanded her uncle, "if I hadn't found out early this morning, and got after Sam here and choked the truth out of him?"

Susan gazed at Sam; but he was such a pitiful figure, so mean and frightened, that she glanced quickly back to her uncle. She said:

"But he didn't know where I was."

"Don't lie to me," cried Warham. "It won't do you any good, any more than his lying kept us from finding you. We came on the train and saw the Waterburys in the street and they'd seen you go into the drug store. We'd have caught you there if we'd been a few minutes sooner, but we drove, and got here in time. Now, tell me, Susan"—and his voice was cruelly harsh—"all about what's been going on between you and Sam."

She gazed fearlessly and was silent.

"Speak up!" commanded Sam's father.

"Yes—and no lies," said her uncle.

"I don't know what you mean," Susan at last answered—truthfully enough, yet to gain time, too.

"You can't play that game any longer," cried Warham. "You did make a fool of me, but my eyes are open. Your aunt's right about you."

"Oh, Uncle George!" said the girl, a sob in her voice.

But he gazed pitilessly—gazed at the woman he was now abhorring as the treacherous, fallen, unsexed daughter of fallen Lorella. "Speak out. Crying won't help you. What have you and this fellow been up to? You disgrace!"

Susan shrank and shivered, but answered steadfastly, "That's between him and me, Uncle."

Warham gave a snort of fury, turned to the elder Wright. "You see, Wright," cried he. "It's as my wife and I told you. Your boy's lying. We'll send the landlady out for a preacher and marry them."

"Hold on, George," objected Wright soothingly. "I agreed to that only if there'd been something wrong. I'm not satisfied yet." He turned to Susan, said in his gruff, blunt way:

"Susan, have you been loose with my boy here?"

"Loose?" said Susan wonderingly.

Sam roused himself. "Tell them it isn't so, Susan," he pleaded, and his voice was little better than a whine of terror. "Your uncle's going to kill me and my father'll kick me out."

Susan's heart grew sick as she looked at him—looked furtively, for she was ashamed to see him so abject. "If you mean did I let him kiss me," she said

117

to Mr. Wright, "why, I did. We kissed several times. But we had the right to. We were engaged."

Sam turned on his father in an agony of terror. "That isn't true!" he cried. "I swear it isn't, father. We aren't engaged. I only made love to her a little, as a fellow does to lots of girls."

Susan looked at him with wide, horrified eyes. "Sam!" she exclaimed breathlessly. "Sam!"

Sam's eyes dropped, but he managed to turn his face in her direction. The situation was too serious for him; he did not dare to indulge in such vanities as manhood or manly appearance. "That's the truth, Susan," he said sullenly. "*You* talked a lot about marrying but *I* never thought of such a thing."

"But—you said—you loved me."

"*I* didn't mean anything by it."

There fell a silence that was interrupted by Mr. Wright. "You see there's nothing in it, Warham. I'll take my boy and go."

"Not by a damn sight!" cried Warham. "He's got to marry her. Susan, did Sam promise to marry you?"

"When he got through college," replied Susan.

"I thought so! And he persuaded you to run away."

"No," said Susan. "He——"

"I say yes," stormed her uncle. "Don't lie!"

"Warham! Warham!" remonstrated Mr. Wright. "Don't browbeat the girl."

"He begged me not to go," said Susan.

"You lying fool!" shouted her uncle. Then to Wright, "If he did ask her to stay it was because he was afraid it would all come out—just as it has."

"I never promised to marry her!" whined Sam. "Honest to God, father, I never did. Honest to God,

Mr. Warham! You know that's so, Susan. It was you that did all the marrying talk."

"Yes," she said slowly. "Yes, I believe it was." She looked dazedly at the three men. "I supposed he meant marriage because—" her voice faltered, but she steadied it and went on—"because we loved each other."

"I knew it!" cried her uncle. "You hear, Wright? She admits he betrayed her."

Susan remembered the horrible part of her cousin's sex revelations. "Oh, no!" she cried. "I wouldn't have let him do that—even if he had wanted to. No—not even if we'd been married."

"You see, Warham!" cried Mr. Wright, in triumph.

"I see a liar!" was Warham's furious answer. "She's trying to defend him and make out a case for herself."

"I am telling the truth," said Susan.

Warham gazed unbelievingly at her, speechless with fury. Mr. Wright took his silk hat from the corner of the piano. "I'm satisfied they're innocent," said he. "So I'll take my boy and go."

"Not if I know it!" retorted Warham. "He's got to marry her."

"But the girl says she's pure, says he never spoke of marriage, says he begged her not to run away. Be reasonable, Warham."

"For a good Christian," sneered he at Wright, "you're mighty easily convinced by a flimsy lie. In your heart you know the boy has wronged her and that she's shielding him, just as——" There Warham checked himself; it would be anything but timely to remind Wright of the character of the girl's mother.

"I'll admit," said Mr. Wright smoothly, "that I wasn't overanxious for my boy's marriage with a girl whose mother was—unfortunate. But if your charge had been true, Warham, I'd have made the boy do her justice, she being only seventeen. Come, Sam."

Sam slunk toward the door. Warham stared fiercely at the elder Wright. "And you call yourself a Christian!" he sneered.

At the door—Sam had already disappeared—Mr. Wright paused to say, "I'm going to give Sam a discipline he'll remember. The girl's only been foolish. Don't be harsh with her."

"You damned hypocrite!" shouted Warham. "I might have known what to expect from a man who cut the wages of his hands to pay his church subscription."

But Wright was far too crafty to be drawn. He went on pushing Sam before him.

As the outer door closed behind them Mrs. Wylie appeared. "I want you both to get out of my house as quick as you can," she snapped. "My boarders'll be coming to dinner in a few minutes."

Warham took his straw hat from the floor beside the chair behind him. "I've nothing to do with this girl here. Good day, madam." And he strode out of the house, slamming the door behind him.

Mrs. Wylie looked at Susan with storming face and bosom. Susan did not see. She was gazing into space, her face blanched. "Clear out!" cried Mrs. Wylie. And she ran to the outer door and opened it. "How dare you come into a respectable house!" She wished to be so wildly angry that she would forget the five dollars which she, as a professing Christian in full church standing, would have to pay back if she remembered. "Clear out this minute!" she cried shrilly. "If you don't, I'll throw your bundle into the street and you after it."

Susan took up the bundle mechanically, slowly went out on the stoop. The door closed with a slam behind her. She descended the steps, walked a few yards up the street, paused at the edge of the curb and looked dazedly about. Her uncle stood beside her. "Now where are you going?" he said roughly.

Susan shook her head.

"I suppose," he went on, "I've got to look after you. You shan't disgrace my daughter any further."

Susan simply looked at him, her eyes unseeing, her brain swept clean of thought by the cyclone that had destroyed all her dreams and hopes. She was not horrified by his accusations; such things had little meaning for one practically in complete ignorance of sex relations. Besides, the miserable fiasco of her romantic love left her with a feeling of abasement, of degradation little different from that which overwhelms a woman who believes her virtue is her all and finds herself betrayed and abandoned. She now felt indeed the outcast, looked down upon by all the world.

"If you hadn't lied," he fumed on, "you'd have been his wife and a respectable woman."

The girl shivered.

"Instead, you're a disgrace. Everybody in Sutherland'll know you've gone the way your mother went."

"Go away," said the girl piteously. "Let me alone."

"Alone? What will become of you?" He addressed the question to himself, not to her.

"It doesn't matter," was her reply in a dreary tone. "I've been betrayed, as my mother was. It doesn't matter what——"

"I knew it!" cried Warham, with no notion of what the girl meant by the word "betrayed." "Why didn't you confess the truth while he was here and his father was ready to marry him to you? I knew you'd been loose with him, as your Aunt Fanny said."

"But I wasn't," said Susan. "I wouldn't do such a thing."

"There you go, lying again!"

"It doesn't matter," said she. "All I want is for you to go away."

"You do?" sneered he. "And then what? I've got to think of Ruthie." He snatched the bundle from her hand. "Come on! I must do all I can to keep the disgrace to my family down. As for you, you don't deserve anything but the gutter, where you'd sink if I left you. Your aunt's right. You're rotten. You were born rotten. You're your mother's own brat."

"Yes, I am," she cried. "And I'm proud of it!" She turned from him, was walking rapidly away.

"Come with me!" ordered Warham, following and seizing her by the arm.

"No," said Susan, wrenching herself free.

"Then I'll call a policeman and have you locked up."

Uncle and niece stood regarding each other, hatred and contempt in his gaze, hatred and fear in hers.

"You're a child in law—though, God knows, you're anything but a child in fact. Come along with me. You've got to. I'm going to see that you're put out of harm's way."

"You wouldn't take me back to Sutherland!" she cried.

He laughed savagely. "I guess not! You'll not show your face there again—though I've no doubt you'd be brazen enough to brass it out. No—you can't pollute my home again."

"I can't go back to Sutherland!"

"You shan't, I say. You ran off because you had disgraced yourself."

"No!" cried Susan. "No!"

"Don't lie to me! Don't speak to me. I'll see what I can do to hide this mess. Come along!"

Susan looked helplessly round the street, saw nothing, not even eager, curious faces pressed against many a window pane, saw only a desolate waste. Then she walked along beside her uncle, both of them silent, he carrying her bundle, she tightly clutching her little purse.

Perhaps the most amazing, the most stunning, of all the blows fate had thus suddenly showered upon her was this transformation of her uncle from gentleness to ferocity. But many a far older and far wiser woman than seventeen-year-old Susan has failed to understand how it is with the man who does not regard woman as a fellow human being. To such she is either an object of adoration, a quintessence of purity and innocence, or less than the dust, sheer filth. Warham's anger was no gust. He was simply the average man of small intelligence, great vanity, and abject snobbishness or terror of public opinion. There could be but one reason for the flight of Lorella's daughter—rottenness. The only point to consider now was how to save the imperiled family standing, how to protect his own daughter, whom his good nature and his wife's weakness had thus endangered. The one thing that could have appeased his hatred of Susan would have been her marriage to Sam Wright. Then he would have—not, indeed, forgiven or reinstated her—but tolerated her. It is the dominance of such ideas as his that makes for woman the slavery she discovers beneath her queenly sway if she happens to do something deeply displeasing to her masculine subject and adorer.

They went to the Central Station. The O. and M. express which connected with the train on the branch line to Sutherland would not leave until a quarter past two. It was only a few minutes past one. Warham led the way into the station restaurant; with a curt nod he indicated a seat at one of the small tables, and dropped into the opposite seat. He ordered beefsteak and fried potatoes, coffee and apple pie.

"Sit still!" he said to her roughly and rose to go out to buy a paper.

The girl sat with her hands in her lap and her eyes upon them. She looked utterly, pitifully tired. A moment and he came back to resume his seat and read the paper. When the waiter flopped down the steak and the dish of greasily fried potatoes before his plate, he stuffed the paper in his pocket, cut a slice of the steak and put it on the plate. The waiter noisily exchanged it for the empty plate before Susan. Warham cut two slices of the steak for himself, took a liberal helping of the potatoes, pushed the dish toward her.

"Do you want the coffee now, or with the pie?" asked the waiter.

"Now," said Warham.

"Coffee for the young lady, too?"

Warham scowled at her. "Coffee?" he demanded. She did not answer; she did not hear.

"Yes, she wants coffee," said Warham. "Hustle it!"

"Yes, sir." And the waiter bustled away with a great deal of motion that created a deceptive impression of speed. Warham was helping himself to steak again when the coffee came—a suspicious-looking liquid diffusing an odor of staleness reheated again and again, an under odor of metal pot not too frequently scoured.

Warham glanced at Susan's plate. She had not disturbed the knife and fork on either side of it. "Eat!" he commanded. And when she gave no sign of having heard, he repeatedly sharply, "Eat, I tell you."

She started, nervously took up the knife and fork, cut a morsel off the slice of steak. When she lifted it to her lips, she suddenly put it back in the plate. "I can't," she said.

"You've got to," ordered he. "I won't have you acting this way."

"I can't," she repeated monotonously. "I feel sick." Nature had luckily so made her that it was impossible for her to swallow when her nerves were upset or when she was tired; thus, she would not have the physical woes that aggravate and prolong mental disturbance if food is taken at times when it instantly turns to poison.

He repeated his order in a still more savage tone. She put her elbows on the table, rested her head wearily upon her hands, shook her head. He desisted.

When he had eaten all of the steak, except the fat and the gristly tail, and nearly all the potatoes, the waiter took the used dishes away and brought two generous slices of apple pie and set down one before each. With the pie went a cube of American cream or "rat-trap" cheese. Warham ate his own pie and cheese; then, as she had not touched hers, he reached for it and ate it also. Now he was watching the clock and, between liftings of laden fork to his mouth, verifying the clock's opinion of the hour by his own watch. He called for the bill, paid it, gave the waiter five cents —a concession to the tipping custom of the effete city which, judging by the waiter's expression, might as well not have been made. Still, Warham had not made it with an idea of promoting good feeling between himself and the waiter, but simply to show that he knew the city and its ways. He took up the shawl strap, said, "Come on" in the voice which he deemed worthy of the fallen creature he must, through Christian duty and worldly prudence, for the time associate with. She rose and followed him to the ticket office. He had the return half of his own ticket. When she heard him ask for a ticket to North Sutherland she shivered. She knew that her destination was his brother Zeke's farm.

From Cincinnati to North Vernon, where they were to change cars, he sat beside her without speech. At North Vernon, where they had to occupy a bench outside the squat and squalid station for nearly two hours, he sat beside her without speech. And without a single word on either side they journeyed in the poking, no-sooner-well-started-than-stopping accommodation train southbound. Several Sutherland people were aboard. He nodded surlily to those who spoke to him. He read an Indianapolis paper which he had bought at North Vernon. All the way she gazed unseeingly out over the fair June landscape of rolling or hilly fields ripening in the sun.

At North Sutherland he bade her follow him to a dilapidated barn a few yards from the railway tracks, where was displayed a homemade sign—"V. Goslin. Livery and Sale Stable." There was dickering and a final compromise on four dollars where the proprieter had demanded five and Warham had declared two fifty liberal. A surrey was hitched with two horses. Warham opened the awkward door to the rear seat and ordered Susan to jump in. She obeyed; he put the bundle on the floor beside her. He sat with the driver

—the proprietor himself. The horses set off at a round pace over the smooth turnpike. It was evening, and a beautiful coolness issued from the woods on either side. They skimmed over the long level stretches; they climbed hills, they raced down into valleys. Warham and the ragged, rawboned old proprietor kept up a kind of conversation—about crops and politics, about the ownership, value, and fertility of the farms they were passing. Susan sat quiet, motionless most of the time.

The last daylight faded; the stars came out; the road wound in and out, up and down, amid cool dark silence and mysterious fascinating shadows. The moon appeared above the tree tops straight ahead—a big moon, with a lower arc of the rim clipped off. The turnpike ended; they were making equally rapid progress over the dirt road which was in perfect condition as there had been no rain for several days. The beat of the flying hoofs was soft now; the two men's voices fell into a lower key; the moon marked out the line of the road clearly, made strange spectral minglings of light and darkness in the woods, glorified the open fields and gave the occasional groups of farm buildings an ancient beauty and dignity. The girl slept.

At nine o'clock the twenty-mile drive ended in a long, slow climb up a road so washed out, so full of holes and bowlders, that it was no road at all but simply a weather-beaten hillside. A mile of this, with the liveryman's curses—"dod rot it" and "gosh dang it" and similar modifications of profanity for Christian use and for the presence of "the sex"—ringing out at every step. Susan soon awakened, rather because the surrey was pitching so wildly than because of Goslin's denunciations. A brief level stretch and they stopped for

Warham to open the outer gate into his brother Zeke's big farm. A quarter of a mile through wheat to the tops of the wheels and they reached the second gate. A descent into a valley, a crossing of a creek, an ascent of a steep hill, and they were at the third gate—between pasture and barnyard. Now they came into view of the house, set upon a slope where a spring bubbled out. The house was white and a white picket fence cut off its lawn from the barnyard. A dog with a deep voice began to bark. They drove up to the front gate and stopped. The dog barked in a frenzy of rage, and they heard his straining and jerking at his chain. A clump of cedars brooded to the right of the house; their trunks were whitewashed up to the lowest branches. The house had a high stoop with wooden steps.

As Warham descended and hallooed, there came a fierce tugging at the front door from the inside. But the front door was not in the habit of being opened, and stoutly resisted. The assault grew more strenuous; the door gave way and a tall thin farmer appeared.

"Hello, Zeke," called George. He opened the surrey door. "Get down," he said to the girl, at the same time taking her bundle. He set it on the horse block beside the gate, took out his pocketbook and paid over the four dollars. "Good-by, Vic," said he pleasantly. "That's a good team you've got."

"Not so coarse," said Vic. "Good-by, Mr. Warham." And off he drove.

Zeke Warham had now descended the steps and was opening the front gate, which was evidently as unaccustomed to use as the front door. "Howdy, George," said he. "Ain't that Susie you've got with you?" Like

George, Zeke had had an elementary education. But he had married an ignorant woman, and had lived so long among his farm hands and tenants that he used their mode of speech.

"Yes, it's Susie," said George, shaking hands with his brother.

"Howdy, Susie," said Zeke, shaking hands with her. "I see you've got your things with you. Come to stay awhile?"

George interrupted. "Susan, go up on the porch and take your bundle."

The girl took up the shawl strap and went to the front door. She leaned upon the railing of the stoop and watched the two men standing at the gate. George was talking to his brother in a low tone. Occasionally the brother uttered an ejaculation. She could not hear; their heads were so turned that she could not see their faces. The moon made it almost as bright as day. From the pasture woods came a low, sweet chorus of night life—frogs and insects and occasionally a night bird. From the orchard to the left and the clover fields beyond came a wonderful scented breeze. She heard a step in the hall; her Aunt Sallie appeared—a comfortable, voluble woman, a hard worker and a harder eater and showing it in thin hair and wrinkled face.

"Why, Susie Lenox, ain't that you?" she exclaimed.

"Yes, Aunt," said Susan.

Her aunt kissed her, diffusing that earthy odor which is the basis of the smell of country persons. At various hours of the day this odor would be modified with the smell of cow stables, of chickens, of cooking, according to immediate occupation. But whatever other smell there was, the earthy smell persisted. And it was the smell of the house, too.

"Who's at the gate with your Uncle Zeke?" inquired Sallie. "Ain't it George?"

"Yes," said Susan.

"Why don't he come in?" She raised her voice. "George, ain't you coming in?"

"Howdy, Sallie," called George. "You take the girl in. Zeke and I'll be along."

"Some business, I reckon," said her aunt to Susan. "Come on. Have you had supper?"

"No," said Susan. She was hungry now. The splendid health of the girl that had calmed her torment of soul into a dull ache was clamoring for food—food to enable her body to carry her strong and enduring through whatever might befall.

"I'll set something out for you," said Sallie. "Come right in. You might leave your bundle here by the parlor door. We'll put you in the upstairs room."

They passed the front stairway, went back through the hall, through the big low-ceilinged living-room with its vast fireplace now covered for the warm season by a screen of flowered wallpaper. They were in the plain old dining-room with its smaller fireplace and its big old-fashioned cupboards built into the wall on either side of the projecting chimney-piece. "There ain't much," resumed Sallie. "But I reckon you kin make out."

On the gayly patterned table cover she set an array of substantial plates and glasses. From various cupboards in dining-room and adjoining kitchen she assembled a glass pitcher of sweet milk, a glass pitcher of buttermilk, a plate of cold cornbread, a platter of cold fried chicken, a dish of golden butter, a pan of cold fried potatoes, a jar of preserved crab apples and another of peach butter. Susan watched with hungry eyes. She was thinking of nothing but food now. Her aunt looked at her and smiled.

"My, but you're shootin' up!" she exclaimed, admiring the girl's tall, straight figure. "And you don't seem to get stringy and bony like so many, but keep nice and round. Do set down."

"I—I think I'll wait until Uncle George comes."

"Nothing of the kind!" She pushed a wooden chair before one of the two plates she had laid. "I see you've still got that lovely skin. And how tasty you dress! Now, do set!"

Susan seated herself.

"Pitch right in, child," urged Sallie. "How's yer aunt and her Ruth?"

"They're—they're—well, thank you."

"Do eat!"

"No," said Susan. "I'll wait for Uncle."

"Never mind your manners. I know you're starved." Then seeing that the girl would not eat, she said, "Well, I'll go fetch him."

But Susan stopped her. "Please—please don't," she entreated.

Sallie started to oppose; then, arrested by the intense, appealing expression in those violet-gray eyes, so beautifully shaded by dark lashes and brows, she kept silent, bustled aimlessly about, boiling with suddenly aroused curiosity. It was nearly half an hour by the big square wooden clock on the chimney-piece when Susan heard the steps of her two uncles. Her hunger fled; the deathly sickness surged up again. She trembled, grew ghastly in the yellow lamplight. Her hands clutched each other in her lap.

"Why, Susie!" cried her aunt. "Whatever is the matter of you!"

The girl lifted her eyes to her aunt's face—the eyes of a wounded, suffering, horribly suffering animal. She rose, rushed out of the door into the yard, flung herself down on the grass. But still she could not get the relief of tears. After a while she sat up and listened. She heard faintly the voices of her uncle and his relatives. Presently her aunt came out to her. She hid her face in her arm and waited for the new harshness to strike.

"Get up and come in, Susie." The voice was kind, was pitying—not with the pity that galls, but with the pity of one who understands and feels and is also human, the pity that soothes. At least to this woman she was not outcast.

The girl flung herself down again and sobbed— poured out upon the bosom of our mother earth all the torrents of tears that had been damming up within her. And Sallie knelt beside her and patted her now and then, with a "That's right. Cry it out, sweetie."

When tears and sobs subsided Sallie lifted her up, walked to the house with her arm round her. "Do you feel better?"

"Some," admitted Susan.

"The men folks have went. So we kin be comfortable. After you've et, you'll feel still better."

George Warham had made a notable inroad upon the food and drink. But there was an abundance left. Susan began with a hesitating sipping at a glass of milk and nibbling at one of the generous cubes of old-fashioned cornbread. Soon she was busy. It delighted Sallie to see her eat. She pressed the preserves, the chicken, the cornbread upon her. "I haven't eaten since early this morning," apologized the girl.

"That means a big hole to fill," observed Sallie. "Try this buttermilk."

But Susan could hold no more.

"I reckon you're pretty well tired out," observed Sallie.

"I'll help you straighten up," said Susan, rising.

"No. Let me take you up to bed—while the men's still outside."

Susan did not insist. They returned through the empty sitting-room and along the hall. Aunt Sallie took the bundle, and they ascended to the spare bedroom. Sallie showed her into the front room—a damp, earthy odor; a wallpaper with countless reproductions of two little brown girls in a brown swing under a brown tree; a lofty bed, white and tomb-like; some preposterous artificial flowers under glass on chimneypiece and table; three bright chromos on the walls; "God Bless Our Home" in pink, blue and yellow worsted over the door.

"I'll run down and put the things away," said her aunt. "Then I'll come back."

Susan put her bundle on the sofa, opened it, found nightgown and toilet articles on top. She looked uncertainly about, rapidly undressed, got into the nightgown. "I'll turn down the bed and lie on it until Auntie comes," she said to herself. The bed was delightfully cool; the shuck mattress made soft crackling sounds under her and gave out a soothing odor of the fields. Hardly had her head touched the pillow when she fell sound asleep. In a few minutes her aunt came hurrying in, stopped short at sight of that lovely childlike face with the lamplight full upon it. One of Susan's tapering arms was flung round her dark wavy hair. Sallie Warham smiled gently. "Bless the baby," she said half aloud. Then her smile faded and a look of sadness and pity came. "Poor child!" she murmured. "The Warham men's hard. But then all the men's hard. Poor child." And gently she kissed the girl's flushed cheek. "And she never had no mother, nor nothing." She sighed, gradually lowered the flame of the little old glass lamp, blew it out, and went noiselessly from the room, closing the door behind her.

IX

SUSAN sat up in bed suddenly, rubbing the sleep from her eyes. It was broad day, and the birds were making a mighty clamor. She gazed round, astonished that it was not her own room. Then she remembered. But it was as a child remembers; for when we have the sense of perfect physical well-being we cannot but see our misfortunes with the child's sense of unreality—and Susan had not only health but youth, was still in the child stage of the period between childhood and womanhood. She lay down again, with the feeling that so long as she could stay in that comfortable bed, with the world shut out, just so long would all be well with her. Soon, however, the restlessness of all nature under the stimulus and heat of that brilliant day communicated itself to her vigorous young body. For repose and inaction are as foreign to healthy life as death itself, of which they are the symptoms; and if ever there was an intense and vivid life, Susan had it. She got up and dressed, and leaned from the window, watching the two-horse reaper in the wheat fields across the hollow of the pasture, and listening to its faint musical whirr. The cows which had just been milked were moving sedately through the gate into the pasture, where the bull, under a tree, was placidly awaiting them. A boy, in huge straw hat and a blue cotton shirt and linsey woolsey trousers rolled high upon his brown bare legs, was escorting the herd.

Her aunt in fresh, blue, checked calico came in.

"Wouldn't you like some breakfast?" said she. And Susan read in her manner that the men were out of the way.

"No, I don't feel hungry," Susan replied.

She thought this was true; but when she was at the table she ate almost as heartily as she had the night before. As Susan ate she gazed out into the back yard of the house, where chickens of all sizes, colors and ages were peering and picking about. Through the fence of the kitchen garden she saw Lew, the farm hand, digging potatoes. There were ripening beans on tall poles, and in the farther part the forming heads of cabbages, the sprouting melon vines, the beautiful fresh green of the just springing garden corn. The window through which she was looking was framed in morning glories and hollyhocks, and over by the garden gate were on the one side a clump of elders, on the other the hardy graceful stalks of gaudily spreading sunflowers. Bees flew in and out, and one lighted upon the dish of honey in the comb that went so well with the hot biscuit.

She rose and wandered out among the chickens, to pick up little fluffy youngsters one after another, and caress them, to look in the henhouse itself, where several hens were sitting with the pensive expression that accompanies the laying of eggs. She thought of those other hens, less conventional, who ran away to lay in secret places in the weeds, to accumulate a store against the time when the setting instinct should possess them. She thought of those cannier, less docile hens and laughed. She opened a gate into the barnyard, intending to go to the barn for a look at the horses, taking in the duck pond and perhaps the pigs on the way. Her Uncle George's voice arrested her.

"Susan," he cried. "Come here."

She turned and looked wistfully at him. The same harsh, unforgiving countenance—mean with anger and petty thoughts. As she moved hesitatingly toward him he said, "You are not to go out of the yard." And he reëntered the house. What a mysterious cruel world! Could it be the same world she had lived in so happily all the years until a few days ago—the same she had always found "God's beautiful world," full of gentleness and kindness?

And why had it changed? What was this sin that after a long sleep in her mother's grave had risen to poison everyone against her? And why had it risen? It was all beyond her.

She strolled wretchedly within bounds, with a foreboding of impending evil. She watched Lew in the garden; she got her aunt to let her help with the churning—drive the dasher monotonously up and down until the butter came; then she helped work the butter, helped gather the vegetables for dinner, did everything and anything to keep herself from thinking. Toward eleven o'clock her Uncle Zeke appeared in the dining-room, called his wife from the kitchen. Susan felt that at last something was to happen. After a long time her aunt returned; there were all the evidences of weeping in her face.

"You'd better go to your room and straighten it up," she said without looking at the girl. "The things has aired long enough, I reckon. . . . And you'd better stay up there till I call you."

Susan had finished the room, was about to unpack the heavy-laden shawl strap and shake the wrinkles out of the skirts, folded away for two days now. She heard the sound of a horse's hoofs, went to the window. A

young man whom she recognized as one of her Uncle
Zeke's tenants was hitching to the horse block a well-
set-up young mare drawing a species of broad-seated
breaking sulky. He had a handsome common face, a
wavy black mustache. She remembered that his name
was Ferguson—Jeb Ferguson, and that he was working on shares what was known as "the creek-bottom
farm," which began about a mile and a half away,
straight down the pasture hollow. He glanced up at
the window, raised his black slouch hat, and nodded
with the self-conscious, self-assured grin of the desired
of women. She tried to return this salute with a
pleasant smile. He entered the gate and she heard
his boots upon the front steps.

Now away across the hollow another figure appeared
—a man on horseback coming through the wheat fields.
He was riding toward the farther gate of the pasture
at a leisurely dignified pace. She had only made out
that he had abundant whiskers when the sound of a
step upon the stairs caused her to turn. As that step
came nearer her heart beat more and more wildly. Her
wide eyes fixed upon the open door of the room. It
was her Uncle George.

"Sit down," he said as he reached the threshhold.
"I want to talk to you."

She seated herself, with hands folded in her lap. Her
head was aching from the beat of the blood in her
temples.

"Zeke and I have talked it over," said Warham.
"And we've decided that the only thing to do with you
is to get you settled. So in a few minutes now you're
going to be married."

Her lack of expression showed that she did not understand. In fact, she could only feel—feel the cruel,

contemptuous anger of that voice which all her days before had caressed her.

"We've picked out a good husband for you," Warham continued. "It's Jeb Ferguson."

Susan quivered. "I—I don't want to," she said.

"It ain't a question of what you want," retorted Warham roughly. He was twenty-four hours and a night's sleep away from his first fierce outblazing of fury—away from the influence of his wife and his daughter. If it had not been for his brother Zeke, narrow and cold, the event might have been different. But Zeke was there to keep his "sense of duty" strong. And that he might nerve himself and hide and put down any tendency to be a "soft-hearted fool"—a tendency that threatened to grow as he looked at the girl —the child—he assumed the roughest manner he could muster.

"It ain't a question of what you want," he repeated. "It's a question of what's got to be done, to save my family and you, too—from disgrace. We ain't going to have any more bastards in this family."

The word meant nothing to the girl. But the sound of it, as her uncle pronounced it, made her feel as though the blood were drying up in her veins.

"We ain't going to take any chances," pursued Warham, less roughly; for now that he had looked the situation full and frankly in the face, he had no nerve to brace himself. The necessity of what he was prepared to do and to make her do was too obvious. "Ferguson's here, and Zeke saw the preacher we sent for riding in from the main road. So I've come to tell you. If you'd like to fix up a little, why your Aunt Sallie'll be here in a minute. You want to pray God to make you a good wife. And you ought to be thankful you have sensible relations to step in and save you from yourself."

Susan tried to speak; her voice died in her throat. She made another effort. "I don't want to," she said.

"Then what do you want to do—tell me that!" exclaimed her uncle, rough again. For her manner was very moving, the more so because there was none of the usual appeal to pity and to mercy.

She was silent.

"There isn't anything else for you to do."

"I want to—to stay here."

"Do you think Zeke'd harbor you—when you're about certain to up and disgrace us as your mother did?"

"I haven't done anything wrong," said the girl dully.

"Don't you dare lie about that!"

"I've seen Ruth do the same with Artie Sinclair—and all the girls with different boys."

"You miserable girl!" cried her uncle.

"I never heard it was so dreadful to let a boy kiss you."

"Don't pretend to be innocent. You know the difference between that and what you did!"

Susan realized that when she had kissed Sam she had really loved him. Perhaps that was the fatal difference. And her mother—the sin there had been that she really loved while the man hadn't. Yes, it must be so. Ruth's explanation of these mysteries had been different; but then Ruth had also admitted that she knew little about the matter—and Susan most doubted the part that Ruth had assured her was certainly true. "I didn't know," said Susan to her uncle. "Nobody ever told me. I thought we were engaged."

"A good woman don't need to be told," retorted

140

Warham. "But I'm not going to argue with you. You've got to marry."

"I couldn't do that," said the girl. "No, I couldn't."

"You'll either take him or you go back to Sutherland and I'll have you locked up in the jail till you can be sent to the House of Correction. You can take your choice."

Susan sat looking at her slim brown hands and interlacing her long fingers. The jail! The House of Correction was dreadful enough, for though she had never seen it she had heard what it was for, what kind of boys and girls lived there. But the jail—she had seen the jail, back behind the courthouse, with its air of mystery and of horror. Not Hell itself seemed such a frightful thing as that jail.

"Well—which do you choose?" said her uncle in a sharp voice.

The girl shivered. "I don't care what happens to me," she said, and her voice was dull and sullen and hard.

"And it doesn't much matter," sneered Warham. Every time he looked at her his anger flamed again at the outrage to his love, his trust, his honor, and the impending danger of more illegitimacy. "Marrying Jeb will give you a chance to reform and be a good woman. He understands—so you needn't be afraid of what he'll find out."

"I don't care what happens to me," the girl repeated in the same monotonous voice.

Warham rose. "I'll send your Aunt Sallie," said he. "And when I call, she'll bring you down."

The girl's silence, her non-resistance—the awful expression of her still features—made him uneasy. He went to the window instead of to the door. He glanced furtively at her; but he might have glanced openly as there wasn't the least danger of meeting her eyes. "You're marrying about as well as you could have hoped to, anyhow—better, probably," he observed, in an argumentative, defensive tone. "Zeke says Jeb's about the likeliest young fellow he knows—a likelier fellow than either Zeke or I was at his age. I've given him two thousand dollars in cash. That ought to start you off well." And he went out without venturing another look at her. Her youth and helplessness, her stony misery, were again making it harder for him to hold himself to what he and the fanatic Zeke had decided to be his duty as a Christian, as a father, as a guardian. Besides, he did not dare face his wife and his daughter until the whole business was settled respectably and finally.

His sister-in-law was waiting in the next room. As soon as his descent cleared the way she hurried in. From the threshold she glanced at the girl; what she saw sent her hurrying out to recompose herself. But the instant she again saw that expression of mute and dazed despair the tears fought for release. The effort to suppress outward signs of pity made her plain fat face grotesque. She could not speak. With a corner of her apron she wiped imaginary dust from the glass bells that protected the artificial flowers. The poor child! And all for no fault of hers—and because she had been born out of wedlock. But then, the old woman reflected, was it not one of the most familiar of God's mysterious ways that people were punished most severely of all for the things that weren't their fault—for being born in shame, or in bad or low families, or sickly, or for being stupid or ugly or ignorant? She envied Zeke—his unwavering belief in religion. She

believed, but her tender heart was always leading her
into doubts.

She at last got some sort of control over her voice.
"It'll turn out for the best," she said, with her back
to Susan. "It don't make much difference nohow who
a woman marries, so long as he's steady and a good
provider. Jeb seems to be a nice feller. He's better
looking than your Uncle George was before he went
to town and married a Lenox and got sleeked up. And
Jeb ain't near so close as some. That's a lot in a
husband." And in a kind of hysteria, bred of fear
of silence just then, she rattled on, telling how this
man lay awake o' nights thinking how to skin a flea
for its hide and tallow, how that one had said only a
fool would pay over a quarter for a new hat for his
wife——

"Will it be long?" asked the girl.

"I'll go down and see," said Mrs. Warham, glad of
a real excuse for leaving the room. She began to cry
as soon as she was in the hall. Two sparrows lit upon
the window sill near Susan and screamed and pecked
at each other in a mock fight. She watched them; but
her shiver at the faint sound of her aunt's returning
step far away down the stairs showed where her attention was. When Zeke's wife entered she was standing
and said:

"Is it time?"

"Come on, honey. Now don't be afraid."

Susan advanced with a firm step, preceded her aunt
down the stairs. The black slouch hat and the straw
of dignified cut were side by side on the shiny hall table.
The parlor door was open; the rarely used showroom
gave forth an earthy, moldy odor like that of a disturbed grave. Its shutters, for the first time in per-

haps a year, were open; the mud daubers that had
built in the crevices between shutters and sills, fancying they would never be disturbed, were buzzing crossly
about their ruined homes. The four men were seated,
each with his legs crossed, and each wearing the funereal expression befitting a solemn occasion. Susan did
not lift her eyes. The profusely whiskered man seated
on the haircloth sofa smoothed his black alpaca coat,
reset the black tie deep hid by his beard, rose and
advanced with a clerical smile whose real kindliness
took somewhat from its offensive unction. "This is
the young lady, is it?" said he, reaching for Susan's
rising but listless hand. "She is indeed a *young* lady!"

The two Warham men stood, shifting uneasily from
leg to leg and rubbing their faces from time to time.
Sallie Warham was standing also, her big unhealthy
face twitching fantastically. Jeb alone was seated—
chair tilted back, hands in trousers pockets, a bucolic
grin of embarrassment giving an expression of pain
to his common features. A strained silence, then Zeke
Warham said:

"I reckon we might as well go ahead."

The preacher took a small black-bound book from
the inside pocket of his limp and dusty coat, cleared
his throat, turned over the pages. That rustling, the
creaking of his collar on his overstarched shirt band,
and the buzzing of the mud daubers round the windows
were the only sounds. The preacher found the place,
cleared his throat again.

"Mr. Ferguson——"

Jeb, tall, spare, sallow, rose awkwardly.

"——You and Miss Lenox will take your places
here——" and he indicated a position before him.

Susan was already in place; Jeb shuffled up to stand

at her left. Sallie Warham hid her face in her apron.
The preacher cleared his throat vigorously, began—
"Dearly beloved"—and so on and on. When he put
the questions to Susan and Jeb he told them what
answer was expected, and they obeyed him, Jeb muttering, Susan with a mere movement of the lips. When
he had finished—a matter of less than three minutes
—he shook hands warmly first with Susan, then with
Jeb. "Live in the fear of the Lord," he said. "That's
all that's necessary."

Sallie put down her apron. Her face was haggard
and gray. She kissed Susan tenderly, then led her from
the room. They went upstairs to the bedroom. "Do
you want to stay to dinner?" she asked in the hoarse
undertone of funeral occasions. "Or would you rather
go right away?"

"I'd rather go," said the girl.

"You set down and make yourself comfortable. I'll
hook up your shawl strap."

Susan sat by the window, her hands in her lap. The
hand with the new circlet of gold on it was uppermost.
Sallie busied herself with the bundle; abruptly she
threw her apron over her face, knelt by the bed and
sobbed and uttered inarticulate moans. The girl made
no sound, did not move, looked unseeingly at her inert
hands. A few moments and Sallie set to work again.
She soon had the bundle ready, brought Susan's hat,
put it on.

"It's so hot, I reckon you'll carry your jacket. I
ain't seen as pretty a blue dress as this—yet it's plain-
like, too." She went to the top of the stairs. "She
wants to go, Jeb," she called loudly. "You'd better
get the sulky ready."

The answer from below was the heavy thump of

Jeb's boots on the oilcloth covering of the hall floor. Susan, from the window, dully watched the young farmer unhitch the mare and lead her up in front of the gate.

"Come on, honey," said Aunt Sallie, taking up the bundle.

The girl—she seemed a child now—followed her. On the front stoop were George and his brother and the preacher. The men made room for them to pass. Sallie opened the gate; Susan went out. "You'll have to hold the bundle," said Sallie. Susan mounted to the seat, took the bundle on her knees. Jeb, who had the lines, left the mare's head and got up beside his bride.

"Good day, all," he said, nodding at the men on the stoop. "Good day, Mrs. Warham."

"Come and see us real soon," said Sallie. Her fat chin was quivering; her tired-looking, washed-out eyes gazed mournfully at the girl who was acting and looking as if she were walking in her sleep.

"Good day, all," repeated Jeb, and again he made the clucking sound.

"Good-by and God bless you," said the preacher. His nostrils were luxuriously sniffing the air which bore to them odors of cookery.

The mare set out. Susan's gaze rested immovably upon the heavy bundle in her lap. As the road was in wretched repair, Jeb's whole attention was upon his driving. At the gate between barnyard and pasture he said, "You hold the lines while I get down."

Susan's fingers closed mechanically upon the strips of leather. Jeb led the mare through the gate, closed it, resumed his seat. This time the mare went on without exacting the clucking sound. They were following

146

the rocky road along the western hillside of the pasture hollow. As they slowly made their way among the deep ruts and bowlders, from frequent moistenings of the lips and throats, noises, and twitchings of body and hands, it was evident that the young farmer was getting ready for conversation. The struggle at last broke surface with, "Zeke Warham don't waste no time road patchin'—does he?"

Susan did not answer.

Jeb studied her out of the corner of his eye, the first time a fairly good bit of roadway permitted. He could make nothing of her face except that it was about the prettiest he had ever seen. Plainly she was not eager to get acquainted; still, acquainted they must get. So he tried again:

"My sister Keziah—she keeps house for me—she'll be mighty surprised when I turn up with a wife. I didn't let on to her what I was about, nary a word."

He laughed and looked expectantly at the girl. Her expression was unchanged. Jeb again devoted himself to his driving.

"No, I didn't let on," he presently resumed. "Fact is, I wan't sure myself till I seed you at the winder." He smiled flirtatiously at her. "Then I decided to go ahead. I dunno, but I somehow kinder allow you and me'll·hit it off purty well—don't you?"

Susan tried to speak. She found that she could not —that she had nothing to say.

"You're the kind of a girl I always had my mind set on," pursued Jeb, who was an expert love-maker. "I like a smooth skin and pouty lips that looks as if they wanted to be kissed." He took the reins in one hand, put his arm round her, clumsily found her lips with his. She shrank slightly, then submitted. But Jeb somehow felt no inclination to kiss her again. After a moment he let his arm drop away from her waist and took the reins in both hands with an elaborate pretense that the bad road compelled it.

A long silence, then he tried again: "It's cool and nice under these here trees, ain't it?"

"Yes," she said.

"I ain't saw you out here for several years now. How long has it been?"

"Three summers ago."

"You must 'a' growed some. I don't seem to recollect you. You like the country?"

"Yes."

"Sho! You're just sayin' that. You want to live in town. Well, so do I. And as soon as I get things settled a little I'm goin' to take what I've got and the two thousand from your Uncle George and open up a livery stable in town."

Susan's strange eyes turned upon him. "In Sutherland?" she asked breathlessly.

"Right in Sutherland," replied he complacently. "I think I'll buy Jake Antle's place in Jefferson Street."

Susan was blanched and trembling. "Oh, no," she cried. "You mustn't do that!"

Jeb laughed. "You see if I don't. And we'll live in style, and you can keep a gal and stay dolled up all the time. Oh, I know how to treat you."

"I want to stay in the country," cried Susan. "I hate Sutherland."

"Now, don't you be afraid," soothed Jeb. "When people see you've got a husband and money they'll not be down on you no more. They'll forget all about your maw—and they won't know nothin' about the other things. You treat me right and I'll treat you right. I'm not one to rake up the past. There ain't arry bit of meanness about me!"

"But you'll let me stay here in the country?" pleaded Susan. Her imagination was torturing her with pictures of herself in Sutherland and the people craning and whispering and mocking.

"You go where I go," replied Jeb. "A woman's place is with her man. And I'll knock anybody down that looks cockeyed at you."

"Oh!" murmured Susan, sinking back against the support.

"Don't you fret, Susie," ordered Jeb, confident and patronizing. "You do what I say and everything'll be all right. That's the way to get along with me and get nice clothes—do what I say. With them that crosses me I'm mighty ugly. But you ain't a-goin' to cross me. . . . Now, about the house. I reckon I'd better send Keziah off right away. You kin cook?"

"A—a little," said Susan.

Jeb looked relieved. "Then she'd be in the way. Two women about always fights—and Keziah's got the Ferguson temper. She's afraid of me, but now and then she fergits and has a tantrum." Jeb looked at her with a smile and a frown. "Perk up a little," he more than half ordered. "I don't want Keziah jeerin' at me."

Susan made a pitiful effort to smile. He eyed it sourly, grunted, gave the mare a cut with the whip that caused her to leap forward in a gallop. "Whoa!" he yelled. "Whoa—damn you!" And he sawed cruelly at her mouth until she quieted down. A turning and they were before a shallow story-and-a-half frame house which squatted like an old roadside beggar behind a weather-beaten picket fence. The sagging shingle roof sloped abruptly; there were four little windows downstairs and two smaller upstairs. The door was in the center of the house; a weedy path led from its crooked step, between two patches of weedy grass, to the gate in the fence.

"Whoa!" shouted Jeb, with the double purpose of stopping the mare and informing the house of his arrival. Then to Susan: "You git down and I'll drive round to the barn yonder." He nodded toward a dilapidated clapboard structure, small and mean, set between a dirty lopsided straw heap and a manure heap. "Go right in and make yourself at home. Tell Keziah who you air. I'll be along, soon as I unhitch and feed the mare."

Susan was staring stupidly at the house—at her new home.

"Git down," he said sharply. "You don't act as if your hearin' or your manners was much to brag on."

He felt awkward and embarrassed with this delicately bred, lovely child-woman in the, to him, wonderfully fine and fashionable dress. To hide his nervousness and to brave it out, he took the only way he knew, the only way shy people usually know—the way of gruffness. It was not a ferocious gruffness for a man of his kind; but it seemed so to her who had been used to gentleness only, until these last few days. His grammar, his untrained voice, his rough clothes, the odor of stale sweat and farm labor he exhaled, made him horrible to her—though she only vaguely knew why she felt so wretched and why her body shrank from him.

She stepped down from the sulky, almost falling in her dizziness and blindness. Jeb touched the mare with the whip and she was alone before the house—a sweet forlorn figure, childish, utterly out of place in those surroundings. On the threshold, in faded and patched calico, stood a tall gaunt woman with a family likeness to Jeb. She had thin shiny black hair, a hard brown skin, high cheekbones and snapping black eyes. When her thin lips parted she showed on the left side of the mouth three large and glittering gold teeth that in the contrast made their gray, not too clean neighbors seem white.

"Howdy!" she called in a tone of hostility.

Susan tried in vain to respond. She stood gazing.

"What d'ye want?"

"He—he told me to go in," faltered Susan. She had no sense of reality. It was a dream—only a dream—and she would awaken in her own clean pretty pale-gray bedroom with Ruth gayly calling her to come down to breakfast.

"Who are you?" demanded Keziah—for at a glance it was the sister.

"I'm—I'm Susan Lenox."

"Oh—Zeke Warham's niece. Come right in." And Keziah looked as if she were about to bite and claw.

Susan pushed open the latchless gate, went up the short path to the doorstep. "I think I'll wait till he comes," she said.

"No. Come in and sit down, Miss Lenox." And Keziah drew a rush-bottomed rocking chair toward the doorway. Susan was looking at the interior. The lower floor of the house was divided into three small rooms. This central room was obviously the parlor—the calico-covered sofa, the center table, the two dingy chromos, and a battered cottage organ made that certain. On the floor was a rag carpet; on the walls, torn and dirty paper, with huge weather stains marking where water had leaked from the roof down the supporting beams. Keziah scowled at Susan's frank expression of repulsion for the surroundings. Susan seated herself on the edge of the chair, put her bundle beside her.

"I allow you'll stay to dinner," said Keziah.

"Yes," replied Susan.

"Then I'll go put on some more to cook."

"Oh, no—please don't—I couldn't eat anything—really, I couldn't." The girl spoke hysterically.

Just then Jeb came round the house and appeared in the doorway. He grinned and winked at Susan, looked at his sister. "Well, Keziah," said he, "what d'ye think of her?"

"She says she's going to stay to dinner," observed Keziah, trying to maintain the veneer of manners she had put on for company.

The young man laughed loudly. "That's a good one—that is!" he cried, nodding and winking at Susan. "So you ain't tole her? Well, Keziah, I've been and gone and got married. And there *she* is."

"Shut up—you fool!" said Keziah. And she looked apologetically at their guest. But the expression of Susan's face made her catch her breath. "For the Lord's sake!" she ejaculated. "She ain't married *you!*"

"Why not?" demanded Jeb. "Ain't this a free country? Ain't I as good as anybody?"

Keziah blew out her breath in a great gust and seated herself on the tattered calico cover of the sofa. Susan grew deathly white. Her hands trembled. Then she sat quiet upon the edge of the old rush-bottomed chair. There was a terrible silence, broken by Jeb's saying loudly and fiercely, "Keziah, you go get the dinner. Then you pack your duds and clear out for Uncle Bob's."

Keziah stared at the bride, rose and went to the rear door. "I'm goin' now," she answered. "The dinner's ready except for putting on the table."

Through the flimsy partitions they heard her mounting the uncarpeted stairs, hustling about upon an uncarpeted floor above, and presently descending. "I'll hoof it," she said, reappearing in the doorway. "I'll send for my things this afternoon."

Jeb, not caring to provoke the "Ferguson temper," said nothing.

"As for this here marryin'," continued Keziah, "I never allowed you'd fall so low as to take a baby, and a bastard at that."

She whirled away. Jeb flung his hat on the table, flung himself on the sofa. "Well—that's settled," said he. "You kin get the dinner. It's all in there." And he jerked his head toward the door in the partition to the left. Susan got up, moved toward the indicated door. Jeb laughed. "Don't you think you might take off your hat and stay awhile?" said he.

She removed her hat, put it on top of the bundle which she left on the floor beside the rocking chair. She went into the kitchen dining-room. It was a squalid room, its ceiling and walls smoke-stained from the cracked and never polished stove in the corner. The air was foul with the strong old onions stewing on the stove. In a skillet slices of pork were frying. On the back of the stove stood a pan of mashed potatoes and a tin coffeepot. On the stained flowered cloth which covered the table in the middle of the room had been laid coarse, cracked dishes and discolored steel knives and forks with black wooden handles. Susan, half fainting, dropped into a chair by one of the open windows. A multitude of fat flies from the stable were running and crawling everywhere, were buzzing about her head. She was aroused by Jeb's voice: "Why, what the —the damnation! You've fell asleep!"

She started up. "In a minute!" she muttered, nervously.

And somehow, with Jeb's eyes on her from the doorway, she got the evil-smelling messes from the stove into table dishes from the shelves and then on the table, where the flies descended upon them in troops of scores and hundreds. Jeb, in his shirt sleeves now, sat down and fell to. She sat opposite him, her hands in her lap. He used his knife in preference to his fork, heaping the blade high, packing the food firmly upon it with fork or fingers, then thrusting it into his mouth. He ate voraciously, smacking his lips, breathing hard, now and then eructing with frank energy and satisfaction.

"My stummick's gassy right smart this year," he observed after a huge gulp of coffee. "Some says the heavy rains last spring put gas into everything, but I dunno. Maybe it's Keziah's cooking. I hope you'll do better. Why, you ain't eatin' nothin'!"

"I'm not hungry," said Susan. Then, as he frowned suspiciously, "I had a late breakfast."

He laughed. "And the marrying, too," he suggested with a flirtatious nod and wink. "Women's always upset by them kind of things."

When he had filled himself he pushed his chair back. "I'll set with you while you wash up," said he. "But you'd better take off them Sunday duds. You'll find some calikers that belonged to maw in a box under the bed in our room." He laughed and winked at her.

"That's the one on t'other side of the settin'-room. Yes—that's our'n!" And he winked again.

The girl, ghastly white, her great eyes staring like a sleepwalker's, rose and stood resting one hand on the back of the chair to steady her.

Jeb drew a cigar from his waistcoat pocket and lighted it. "Usually," said he, "I take a pipe or a chaw. But this bein' a weddin' day——"

He laughed and winked again, rose, took her in his arms and kissed her. She made a feeble gesture of thrusting him away. Her head reeled, her stomach turned.

She got away as soon as he would release her, crossed the sitting-room and entered the tiny dingy bedroom. The windows were down and the bed had not yet been made. The odor was nauseating—the staleness left by a not too clean sleeper who abhors fresh air. Susan saw the box under the bed, knelt to draw it out. But instead she buried her face in her hands, burst into wild sobs. "Oh, God," she prayed, "stop punishing me. I didn't mean to do wrong—and I'm sure my mother didn't, either. Stop, for Thy Son's sake, amen." Now surely she would wake. God must answer that prayer. She dared not take her palms from her eyes. Suddenly she felt herself caught from behind. She gave a wild scream and sprang up.

Jeb was looking at her with eyes that filled her with a fear more awful than the fear of death. "Don't!" she cried. "Don't!"

"Never mind, hon," said he in a voice that was terrible just because it was soft. "It's only your husband. My, but you're purty!" And he seized her. She fought. He crushed her. He kissed her with great slobbering smacks and gnawed at the flesh of her neck with teeth that craved to bite.

"Oh, Mr. Ferguson, for pity's sake!" she wailed. Then she opened her mouth wide as one gasping for breath where there is no air; and pushing at him with all her strength she vented a series of maniac shrieks.

X

LATE that afternoon Jeb returned to the house after several hours of uneasy, aimless pottering about at barn and woodshed. He stumped and stamped around the kitchen, then in the sitting-room, finally he mustered the courage to look into the bedroom, from which he had slunk like a criminal three hours before. There she lay, apparently in the same position. Her waxen color and her absolute stillness added fear to his sense of guilt—a guilt against which he protested, because he felt he had simply done what God and man expected of him. He stood in the low doorway for some time, stood there peering and craning until his fear grew so great that he could no longer put off ending or confirming it.

"Sleepin'?" said he in a hoarse undertone.

She did not reply; she did not move. He could not see that she was breathing.

"It'll soon be time to git supper," he went on—not because he was thinking of supper but because he was desperately clutching for something that must draw a reply from her—if she could reply. "Want me to clean up the dinner and put the supper things on?"

She made a feeble effort to rise, sank back again. He drew an audible sigh of relief; at least she was not what her color had suggested.

In fact, she was morbidly conscious. The instant she had heard him at the outer door she had begun to shiver and shake, and not until he moved toward the bedroom door did she become quiet. Then a calm had come into her nerves and her flesh—the calm that descends upon the brave when the peril actually faces. As he stood there her eyes were closed, but the smell of him —beneath the earthy odor of his clothing the odor of the bodies of those who eat strong, coarse food— stole into her nostrils, into her nerves. Her whole body sickened and shrank—for to her now that odor meant marriage—and she would not have believed Hell contained or Heaven permitted such a thing as was marriage. She understood now why the Bible always talked of man as a vile creature born in sin.

Jeb was stealthily watching her ghastly face, her limp body. "Feelin' sickish?" he asked.

A slight movement of the head in assent.

"I kin ride over to Beecamp and fetch Doc Christie."

Another and negative shake of the head, more determined. The pale lips murmured, "No—no, thank you." She was not hating him. He existed for her only as a symbol, in this hideous dream called life, that was coiled like a snake about her and was befouling her and stinging her to death.

"Don't you bother 'bout supper," said he with gruff, shamefaced generosity. "I'll look out for myself, this onct."

He withdrew to the kitchen, where she heard him clattering dishes and pans. Daylight waned to twilight, twilight to dusk, to darkness. She did not think; she did not feel, except an occasional dull pang from some bodily bruise. Her soul, her mind, were absolutely numb. Suddenly a radiance beat upon her eyes. All in an instant, before the lifting of her eyelids, soul and body became exquisitely acute; for she thought it was he come again, with a lamp. She looked; it was the moon whose beams struck full in at the uncurtained

window and bathed her face in their mild brightness.
She closed her eyes again and presently fell asleep—
the utter relaxed sleep of a child that is worn out with
pain, when nature turns gentle nurse and sets about
healing and soothing as only nature can. When she
awoke it was with a scream. No, she was not dreaming; there was an odor in the room—his odor, with
that of a saloon added to it.

After cooking and eating supper he had taken the
jug from its concealment behind the woodbox and had
proceeded to cheer his drooped spirits. The more he
drank the better content he was with himself, with his
conduct, and the clearer became his conviction that the
girl was simply playing woman's familiar game of
dainty modesty. A proper game it was too; only a
man must not pay attention to it unless he wished his
woman to despise him. When this conviction reached
the point of action he put away the jug, washed the
glass, ate a liberal mouthful of the left-over stewed
onions, as he would not for worlds have his bride catch
him tippling. He put out the lamp and went to the
bedroom, chuckling to himself like a man about to
play a particularly clever and extremely good-humored
practical joke. His preparations for the night were,
as always, extremely simple—merely a flinging off of
his outer clothes and, in summer, his socks. From time
to time he cast an admiring amorous glance at the
lovely childlike face in the full moonlight. As he was
about to stretch himself on the bed beside her he happened to note that she was dressed as when she came.
That stylish, Sundayish dress was already too much
mussed and wrinkled. He leaned over to wake her with
a kiss. It was then that she started up with a scream.

"Oh—oh—my God!" she exclaimed, passing her hand

over her brow and staring at him with crazed, anguished eyes.

"It's jest me," said he. "Thought you'd want to git ready fur bed, like as not."

"No, thank you, no," she stammered, drawing away toward the inner side of the bed. "Please—I want to be as I am."

"Now, don't put on, sweetness," he wheedled. "You know you're married and 'ave got to git used to it."

He laid his hand on her arm. She had intended to obey, since that was the law of God and man and since in all the world there was no other place for her, nameless and outcast. But at his touch she clenched her teeth, cried:

"No—Mr. Ferguson—please—*please* let me be."

"Now, hon," he pleaded, seizing her with strong gentleness. "There ain't no call to be skittish. We're married, you know."

She wrenched herself free. He seized her again. "What's the use of puttin' on? I know all about you. You little no-name," he cursed, when her teeth sank into his hand. For an instant, at that reminder of her degradation, her indelible shame that made her of the low and the vile, she collapsed in weakness. Then with new and fierce strength she fought again. When she had exhausted herself utterly she relaxed, fell to sobbing and moaning, feebly trying to shelter her face from his gluttonous and odorous kisses. And upon the scene the moon shone in all that beauty which from time immemorial has filled the hearts of lovers with ecstasy and of devotees with prayer.

They lay quietly side by side; he fell into a profound sleep. He was full upon his back, his broad chest heaving in the gray cotton undershirt, his mouth wide open with its upper fringe of hair in disarray and agitated by his breath. Soon he began to snore, a deafening clamor that set some loose object in the dark part of the room to vibrating with a tapping sound. Susan stealthily raised herself upon her elbow, looked at him. There was neither horror nor fear in her haggard face but only eagerness to be sure he would not awaken. She, inch by inch, more softly than a cat, climbed over the low footboard, was standing on the floor. One silent step at a time, with eyes never from his face so clear in the moonlight, she made her way toward the door. The snoring stopped—and her heart stopped with it. He gasped, gurgled, gave a snort, and sat up.

"What—which——" he ejaculated. Then he saw her near the door. "Hello—whar ye goin'?"

"I thought I'd undress," she lied, calmly and smoothly.

"Oh—that's right." And he lay down.

She stood in the darkness, making now and then a faint sound suggestive of undressing. The snoring began again—soft, then deep, then the steady, uproarious intake with the fierce whistling exhalation. She went into the sitting-room, felt round in the darkness, swift and noiseless. On the sofa she found her bundle, tore it open. By feeling alone she snatched her sailor hat, a few handkerchiefs, two stockings, a collar her fingers chanced upon and a toothbrush. She darted to the front door, was outside, was gliding down the path, out through the gate into the road.

To the left would be the way she had come. She ran to the right, with never a backward glance—ran with all the speed in her lithe young body, ran with

all the energy of her fear and horror and resolve to die
rather than be taken. For a few hundred yards the
road lay between open fields. But after that it entered
a wood. And in that dimness she felt the first beginnings of a sense of freedom. Half a mile and open
fields again, with a small house on the right, a road
southeastward on the left. That would be away from
her Uncle Zeke's and also away from Sutherland, which
lay twenty miles to the southwest. When she would·
be followed Jeb would not think of this direction until
he had exhausted the other two.

She walked, she ran, she rested; she walked and ran
and walked again. The moon ascended to the zenith,
crossed the levels of the upper sky, went down in the
west; a long bar of dusky gray outlined a cloud low
upon the horizon in the northeast. She was on the
verge of collapse. Her skin, the inside of her mouth,
were hot and dry. She had to walk along at snail's
pace or her heart would begin to beat as if it were
about to burst and the blood would choke up into the
veins of her throat to suffocate her. A terrible pain
came in her side—came and went—came and stayed.
She had passed turning after turning, to the right, to
the left—crossroads leading away in all directions.
She had kept to the main road because she did not
wish to lose time, perhaps return upon her path, in
the confusion of the darkness. Now she began to look
about her at the country. It was still the hills as round
Zeke Warham's—the hills of southeastern Indiana. But
they were steeper and higher, for she was moving toward the river. There was less open ground, more
and denser undergrowth and forest. She felt that she
was in a wilderness, was safe. Night still lay too thick
upon the landscape for her to distinguish anything

but outlines. She sat down on the ruined and crumbling panel of a zigzag fence to rest and to wait for light. She listened; a profound hush. She was alone, all alone. How far had she come? She could not guess; but she knew that she had done well. She would have been amazed if she had known how well. All the years of her life, thanks to Mrs. Warham's good sense about health, she had been steadily adding to the vitality and strength that were hers by inheritance. Thus, the response to this first demand upon them had been almost inevitable. It augured well for the future, if the future should draw her into hardships. She knew she had gone far and in what was left of the night and with what was left of her strength she would put such a distance between her and them that they would never believe she had got so far, even should they seek in this direction. She was supporting her head upon her hands, her elbows upon her knees. Her eyes closed, her head nodded; she fought against the impulse, but she slept.

When she straightened up with a start it was broad day. The birds must have finished their morning song, for there was only happy, comfortable chirping in the branches above her. She rose stiffly. Her legs, her whole body, ached; and her feet were burning and blistered. But she struck out resolutely.

After she had gone halfway down a long steep hill, she had to turn back because she had left her only possessions. It was a weary climb, and her heart quaked with terror. But no one appeared, and at last she was once more at the ruins of the fence panel. There lay her sailor hat, the handkerchiefs, wrapped round the toothbrush, the collar—and two stockings, one black, the other brown. And where was her purse?

Not there, certainly. She glanced round in swift
alarm. No one. Yet she had been absolutely sure
she had taken her purse from the sitting-room table
when she came upon it, feeling about in the dark. She
had forgotten it; she was without a cent!

But she had no time to waste in self-reproaches or
forebodings. Though the stockings would be of no
use to her, she took them along because to leave them
was to leave a trail. She hastened down the hill. At
the bottom ran a deep creek—without a bridge. The
road was now a mere cowpath which only the stoutest
vehicles or a horseman would adventure. To her left
ran an even wilder trail, following the downward course
of the creek. She turned out of the road, entered the
trail. She came to a place where the bowlders over
which the creek foamed and splashed as it hurried
southeastward were big and numerous enough to make
a crossing. She took it, went slowly on down the other
bank.

There was no sign of human intrusion. Steeply on
either side rose a hill, strewn with huge bowlders, many
of them large as large houses. The sun filtered through
the foliage to make a bright pattern upon the carpet
of last year's leaves. The birds twittered and chirped;
the creek hummed its drowsy, soothing melody. She
was wretchedly weary, and Oh, so hungry! A little
further, and two of the great bowlders, tumbled down
from the steeps, had cut off part of the creek, had
formed a pool which their seamed and pitted and fern-
adorned walls hid from all observation except that of
the birds and the squirrels in the boughs.

At once she thought how refreshed she would be if
she could bathe in those cool waters. She looked
round, stepped in between the bowlders. She peered

out; she listened. She was safe; she drew back into
her little inclosure. There was a small dry shelf of
rock. She hurried off her clothes, stood a moment in
the delicious warmth of the sunshine, stepped into the
pool. She would have liked to splash about; but she
dared make no sound that could be heard above the
noise of the water. Luckily the creek was just there
rather loud, as it was expressing its extreme annoyance over the stolid impudence of the interrupting
bowlders. Here where there were no traces, no re-
minders of the human race which had cast her out and
pursued her with torture of body and soul, here in the
wilderness her spirits were going up, and her young
eyes were looking hopefully round and forward. The
up-piling horrors of those two days and their hideous
climax seemed a dream which the sun had scattered.
Hopefully! That blessed inexperience and sheer imagination of youth enabling it to hope in a large,
vague way when to hope for any definite and real thing
would be impossible.

She cleaned her tan low shoes with branches of fern
and grass, put them on. It is impossible to account
for the peculiarities of physical vanity. Probably no
one was ever born who had not physical vanity of
some kind; Susan's was her feet and ankles. Not her
eyes, nor her hair, nor her contour, nor her skin, nor
her figure, though any or all of these might well have
been her pleasure. Of them she never thought in the
way of pride or vanity. But of her feet and ankles she
was both proud and vain—in a reserved, wholly unobtrusive way, be it said, so quietly that she had passed
unsuspected. There was reason for this shy, secret
self-satisfaction, so amusing in one otherwise self-unconscious. Her feet were beautifully formed and the

curves of her instep and ankle were beautiful. She gave more attention now to the look of her shoes and of her stockings than to all the rest of this difficult woodland toilet. She then put on the sailor hat, fastened the collar to her garter, slipped the handkerchiefs into the legs of her stockings. Carrying her underclothes, ready to roll them into a ball should she meet anyone, she resumed her journey into that rocky wilderness. She was sore, she had pains that were the memories of the worst horrors of her hideous dream, but up in her strong, healthy body, up through her strong young soul, surged joy of freedom and joy of hope. Compared with what her lot had been until such a few brief days before, this lot of friendless wanderer in the wilderness was dark indeed. But she was comparing it with the monstrous dream from which it was the awakening. She was almost happy—and madly hungry.

An enormous bowlder, high above her and firmly fixed in the spine of the hill, invited as a place where she could see without being seen, could hide securely until darkness came again. She climbed to the base of it, found that she might reach the top by stepping from ledge to ledge with the aid of the trees growing so close around it that some of their boughs seemed rooted in its weather-dented cliffs. She dragged herself upward the fifty or sixty feet, glad of the difficulties because they would make any pursuer feel certain she had not gone that way. After perhaps an hour she came upon a flat surface where soil had formed, where grass and wild flowers and several little trees gave shade and a place to sleep. And from her eyrie she commanded a vast sweep of country—hills and valleys, fields, creeks, here and there lonely farmhouses, and far away to the east the glint of the river!

To the river! That was her destination. And somehow it would be kind, would take her where she would never, never dream those frightful dreams again!

She went to the side of the bowlder opposite that which she had climbed. She drew back hastily, ready to cry with vexation. It was not nearly so high or so steep; and on the slope of the hill a short distance away was set a little farmhouse, with smoke curling up from its rough stone chimmey. She dropped to all fours in the tall grass and moved cautiously toward the edge. Flat upon her breast, she worked her way to the edge and looked down. A faintly lined path led from the house through a gate in a zig-zag fence and up to the base of her fortress. The rock had so crumbled on that side that a sort of path extended clear up to the top. But her alarm quieted somewhat when she noted how the path was grass-grown.

As nearly as she could judge it was about five o'clock. So that smoke meant breakfast! Her eyes fixed hungrily upon the thin column of violet vapor mounting straight into the still morning air. When smoke rose in that fashion, she remembered, it was sure sign of clear weather. And then the thought came, "What if it had been raining!" She simply could not have got away.

As she interestedly watched the little house and its yard she saw hurrying through the burdock and dog fennel toward the base of her rock a determined looking hen. Susan laughed silently, it was so obvious that the hen was on a pressing and secret business errand. But almost immediately her attention was distracted to observing the movements of a human being she could obscurely make out through one of the windows just back of the chimney. Soon she saw that it was a woman, cleaning up a kitchen after breakfast—the early breakfast of the farmhouse in summer.

What had they had for breakfast? She sniffed the air. "I think I can smell ham and cornbread," she said aloud, and laughed, partly at the absurdity of her fancy, chiefly at the idea of such attractive food. She aggravated her hunger by letting her imagination loose upon the glorious possibilities. A stealthy fluttering brought her glance back to the point where the hen had disappeared. The hen reappeared, hastened down the path and through the weeds, and rejoined the flock in the yard with an air which seemed to say, "No, indeed, I've been right here all the time."

"Now, what was she up to?" wondered Susan, and the answer came to her. Eggs! A nest hidden somewhere near or in the base of the rock!

Could she get down to that nest without being seen from the house or from any other part of the region below? She drew back from the edge, crawled through the grass to the place where the path, if path it could be called, reached the top. She was delighted to find that it made the ascent through a wide cleft and not along the outside. She let herself down cautiously, as the footway was crumbling and rotten and slippery with grass. At the lower end of the cleft she peered out. Trees and bushes—plenty of them, a thick shield between her and the valleys. She moved slowly downward; a misstep might send her through the boughs to the hillside forty feet below. She had gone up and down several times before her hunger-sharpened eyes caught the gleam of white through the ferns growing thickly out of the moist mossy cracks which everywhere seamed the wall. She pushed the ferns aside. There was the nest, the length of her forearm into the dim seclusion of a deep hole. She felt round, found the egg that was warm. And as she drew it out she laughed softly and said half aloud: "Breakfast is ready!"

No, not quite ready. Hooking one arm round the bough of a tree that shot up from the hillside to the height of the rock and beyond, she pressed her foot firmly against the projecting root of an ancient vine of poison ivy. Thus ensconced, she had free hands; and she proceeded to remove the thin shell of the egg piece by piece. She had difficulty in restraining herself until the end. At last she put the whole egg into her mouth. And never had she tasted anything so good.

But one egg was only an appetizer. She reached in again. She did not wish to despoil the meritorious hen unnecessarily, so she held the egg up in her inclosing fingers and looked through it, as she had often seen the cook do at home. She was not sure, but the inside seemed muddy. She laid it to one side, tried another. It was clear and she ate it as she had eaten the first. She laid aside the third, the fourth, and the fifth. The sixth seemed all right—but was not. Fortunately she had not been certain enough to feel justified in putting the whole egg into her mouth before tasting it. The taste, however, was enough to make her reflect that perhaps on the whole two eggs were sufficient for breakfast, especially as there would be at least dinner and supper before she could go further. As she did not wish to risk another descent, she continued to sort out the eggs. She found four that were, or seemed to be, all right. The thirteen that looked doubtful or worse

when tested by the light she restored with the greatest
care. It was an interesting illustration of the rare
quality of consideration which at that period of her
life dominated her character.

She put the four eggs in the bosom of her blouse and
climbed up to her eyrie. All at once she felt the delicious languor of body and mind which is Nature's fore-
warning that she is about to put us to sleep, whether
we will or no. She lost all anxiety about safety, looked
hastily around for a bed. She found just the place
in a corner of the little tableland where the grass grew
tall and thick. She took from her bosom the four eggs
—her dinner and supper—and put them between the
roots of a tree with a cover of broad leaves over them
to keep them cool. She pulled grass to make a pillow,
took off her collar and laid herself down to sleep.
And that day's sun did not shine upon a prettier sight
than this soundly and sweetly sleeping girl, with her
oval face suffused by a gentle flush, with her rounded
young shoulders just moving the bosom of her gray
silk blouse, with her slim, graceful legs curled up to
the edge of her carefully smoothed blue serge skirt.
You would have said never a care, much less a sorrow,
had shadowed her dawning life. And that is what it
means to be young—and free from the curse of self-
pity, and ignorant of life's saddest truth, that future
and past are not two contrasts; one is surely bright
and the other is sober, but they are parts of a continuous fabric woven of the same threads and into the
same patterns from beginning to end.

When she awoke, beautifully rested, her eyes clear
and soft, the shadows which had been long toward the
southwest were long, though not so long toward the
southeast. She sat up and smiled; it was so fine to be

free! And her woes had not in the least shaken that serene optimism which is youth's most delightful if most dangerous possession. She crawled through the grass to the edge of the rock and looked out through the screening leaves of the dense undergrowth. There was no smoke from the chimney of the house. The woman, in a blue calico, was sitting on the back door-step knitting. Farther away, in fields here and there, a few men—not a dozen in all—were at work. From a barnyard at the far edge of the western horizon came the faint sound of a steam thresher, and she thought she could see the men at work around it, but this might have been illusion. It was a serene and lovely panorama of summer and country. Last of all her eyes sought the glimpse of distant river.

She ate two of her four eggs, put on the underclothes, which she had thoroughly washed, shook out and re-braided her hair. Then she cast about for some way to pass the time.

She explored the whole top of the rock, but that did not use up more than fifteen minutes, as it was so small that every part was visible from every other part. However, she found a great many wild flowers and gathered a huge bouquet of the audacious colors of nature's gardens, so common yet so effective. She did a little botanizing—anything to occupy her mind and keep it from the ugly visions and fears. But all too soon she had exhausted the resources of her hiding place. She looked down into the valley to the north —the valley through which she had come. She might go down there and roam; it would be something to do, and her young impatience of restraint was making her so restless that she felt she could not endure the confines of that little rock. It had seemed huge; a brief experience of freedom, a few hours between her and the night's horrors and terrors, and it had shrunk to a tiny prison cell. Surely she would run no risk in journeying through the trackless wilderness; she need not be idle, she could hasten her destiny by following the creek in its lonely wanderings, which must sooner or later bring it to the river. The river!

She was about to get the two remaining eggs and abandon her stronghold when it occurred to her that she would do well to take a last look all around. She went back to the side of the rock facing the house.

The woman had suspended knitting and was gazing intently across the hollow to the west, where the road from the north entered the landscape. Susan turned her eyes in that direction. Two horsemen at a gallop were moving southward. The girl was well screened, but instinctively she drew still further back behind the bushes—but not so far that the two on horseback, riding so eagerly, were out of her view. The road dipped into the hollow; the galloping horsemen disappeared with it. Susan shifted her gaze to the point on the brow of the hill where the road reappeared. She was quivering in every nerve. When they came into view again she would know.

The place she was watching swam before her eyes. Suddenly the two, still at a gallop, rose upon the crest of the hill. Jeb and her Uncle Zeke! Her vision cleared, her nerve steadied.

They did not draw rein until they were at the road gate of the little house. The woman rose, put down her knitting in the seat of her stiff, rush-bottomed rocker, advanced to the fence. The air was still, but Susan could not hear a sound, though she craned forward and strained her ears to the uttermost. She

shrank as if she had been struck when the three began to gaze up at the rock—to gaze, it seemed to
her, at the very spot where she was standing. Was
her screen less thick than she thought? Had they
seen—if not her, perhaps part of her dress?

Wildly her heart beat as Jeb dismounted from his
horse—the mare behind which she had made her wedding journey—and stood in the gateway, talking with
the woman and looking toward the top of the rock.
Zeke Warham turned his horse and began to ride slowly
away. He got as far as the brow of the hill, with Jeb
still in the gateway, hesitating. Then Susan heard:
"Hold on, Mr. Warham. I reckon you're right."
Warham halted his horse, Jeb remounted and joined
him. As the woman returned toward the back door-
step the two men rode at a walk down into the hollow. When they reappeared it was on the road by
which they had come. And the girl knew the pursuit
in that direction—the right direction—was over.
Trembling and with a fluttering in her breast like the
flapping of a bird's wings, she sank to the ground.
Presently she burst into a passion of tears. Without
knowing why, she tore off the wedding ring which
until then she had forgotten, and flung it out among
the treetops. A few minutes, and she dried her eyes
and stood up. The two horsemen were leaving the
landscape at the point at which they had entered it.
The girl would not have known, would have been frightened by, her own face had she seen it as she watched
them go out of her sight—out of her life. She did not
understand herself, for she was at that age when
one is no more conscious of the forces locked up within
his unexplored and untested character than the dyna-
mite cartridge is of its secrets of power and terror.

XI

S HE felt free to go now. She walked toward the
place where she had left the eggs. It was on
the side of the rock overlooking the creek. As
she knelt to remove the leaves, she heard from far below a man's voice singing. She leaned forward and
glanced down at the creek. In a moment appeared
a young man with a fishing rod and a bag slung over
his shoulder. His gray and white striped flannel
trousers were rolled to his knees. His fair skin and
the fair hair waving about his forehead were exposed
by the flapping-brimmed straw hat set upon the back
of his head. His voice, a strong and manly tenor, was
sending up those steeps a song she had never heard
before—a song in Italian. She had not seen what he
looked like when she remembered herself and hastily fell
back from view. She dropped to the grass and crawled
out toward the ledge. When she showed her face
it so happened that he was looking straight at her.

"Hello!" he shouted. "That you, Nell?"

Susan drew back, her blood in a tumult. From below, after a brief silence, came a burst of laughter.
She waited a long time, then through a shield of
bunches of grass looked again. The young man was
gone. She wished that he had resumed his song, for
she thought she had never heard one so beautiful.
Because she did not feel safe in descending until he
was well out of the way, and because she was so comfortable lying there in the afternoon sunshine watching the birds and listening to them, she continued on

there, glancing now and then at where the creek entered and where it left her range of vision, to make sure that no one else should come and catch her. Suddenly sounded a voice from somewhere behind her:

"Hey, Nell! I'm coming!"

She sprang to her feet, faced about; and Crusoe was not more agitated when he saw the print of the naked foot on his island's strand. The straw hat with the flapping brim was just lifting above the edge of the rock at the opposite side, where the path was. She could not escape; the shelf offered no hiding place. Now the young man was stepping to the level, panting loudly.

"Gee, what a climb for a hot day!" he cried. "Where are you?"

With that he was looking at Susan, less than twenty yards away and drawn up defiantly. He stared, took off his hat. He had close-cropped wavy hair and eyes as gray as Susan's own, but it was a blue-gray instead of violet. His skin was fair, too, and his expression intelligent and sympathetic. In spite of his hat, and his blue cotton shirt, and trousers rolled high on bare sunburned legs, there was nothing of the yokel about him.

"I beg your pardon," he exclaimed half humorously. "I thought it was my cousin Nell."

"No," said Susan, disarmed by his courtesy and by the frank engaging manner of it.

"I didn't mean to intrude." He showed white teeth in a broad smile. "I see from your face that this is your private domain."

"Oh, no—not at all," stammered Susan.

"Yes, I insist," replied he. "Will you let me stay

and rest a minute? I ran round the rock and climbed pretty fast."

"Yes—do," said Susan.

The young man sat on the grass near where he had appeared, and crossed his long legs. The girl, much embarrassed, looked uneasily about. "Perhaps you'd sit, too?" suggested he, after eyeing her in a friendly way that could not cause offense and somehow did not cause any great uneasiness.

Susan hesitated, went to the shadow of a little tree not far from him. He was fanning his flushed face with his hat. The collar of his shirt was open; below, where the tan ended abruptly, his skin was beautifully white. Now that she had been discovered, it was as well to be pleasant, she reasoned. "It's a fine day," she observed with a grown-up gravity that much amused him.

"Not for fishing," said he. "I caught nothing. You are a stranger in these parts?"

Susan colored and a look of terror flitted into her eyes. "Yes," she admitted. "I'm—I'm passing through."

The young man had all he could do to conceal his amusement. Susan flushed deeply again, not because she saw his expression, for she was not looking at him, but because her remark seemed to her absurd and likely to rouse suspicion.

"I suppose you came up here to see the view," said the man. He glanced round. "It *is* pretty good. You're not visiting down Brooksburg way, by any chance?"

"No," replied Susan, rather composedly and determined to change the subject. "What was that song I heard you singing?"

"Oh—you heard, did you?" laughed he. "It's the Duke's song from 'Rigoletto.' "

"That's an opera, isn't it—like 'Trovatore'?"

"Yes—an Italian opera. Same author."

"It's a beautiful song." It was evident that she longed to ask him to sing it. She felt at ease with him; he was so unaffected and simple, was one of those people who seem to be at home wherever they are.

"Do you sing?" he inquired.

"Not really," replied she.

"Neither do I. So if you'll sing to me, I'll sing to you."

Susan looked round in alarm. "Oh, dear, no—please don't," she cried.

"Why not?" he asked curiously. "There isn't a soul about."

"I know—but—really, you mustn't."

"Very well," said he, seeing that her nervousness was not at all from being asked to sing. They sat quietly, she gazing off at the horizon, he fanning himself and studying her lovely young face. He was somewhere in the neighborhood of twenty-five and a close observer would have suspected him of an unusual amount of experience, even for a good-looking, expansive youth of that age.

He broke the long silence. "I'm a newspaper man from Cincinnati. I'm on the *Commercial* there. My name's Roderick Spenser. My father's Clayton Spenser, down at Brooksburg"—he pointed to the southeast—"beyond that hill there, on the river. I'm here on my vacation." And he halted, looking at her expectantly.

It seemed to her that there was in courtesy no escape

without a return biographical sketch. She hung her head, twisted her tapering fingers in her lap, and looked childishly embarrassed and unhappy. Another long silence; again he broke it. "You'll pardon my saying so, but—you're very young, aren't you?"

"Not so—so *terribly* young. I'm almost seventeen," replied she, glancing this way and that, as if thinking of flight.

"You look like a child, yet you don't," he went on, and his frank, honest voice calmed her. "You've had some painful experience, I'd say."

She nodded, her eyes down.

A pause, then he: "Honest, now—aren't you—running away?"

She lifted her eyes to his piteously. "Please don't ask me," she said.

"I shouldn't think of it," replied he, with a gentleness in his persistence that made her feel still more like trusting him, "if it wasn't that——

"Well, this world isn't the easiest sort of a place. Lots of rough stretches in the road. I've struck several and I've always been glad when somebody has given me a lift. And I want to pass it on—if you'll let me. It's something we owe each other—don't you think?"

The words were fine enough; but it was the voice in which he said them that went to her heart. She covered her face with her hands and released her pent emotions. He took a package of tobacco and a sheaf of papers from his trousers pocket, rolled and lighted a cigarette. After a while she dried her eyes, looked at him shamefacedly. But he was all understanding and sympathy.

"Now you feel better, don't you?"

"Much," said she. And she laughed. "I guess I'm more upset than I let myself realize."

"Sorry you left home?"

"I haven't any home," answered she simply. "And I wouldn't go back alive to the place I came from."

There was a quality in the energy she put into her words that made him thoughtful. He counseled with the end of his cigarette. Finally he inquired:

"Where are you bound for?"

"I don't know exactly," confessed she, as if it were a small matter.

He shook his head. "I see you haven't the faintest notion what you're up against."

"Oh, I'll get along. I'm strong, and I can learn."

He looked at her critically and rather sadly.

"Yes—you are strong," said he. "But I wonder if you're strong enough."

"I never was sick in my life."

"I don't mean that. . . . I'm not sure I know just what I do mean."

"Is it very hard to get to Chicago?" inquired she.

"It's easier to get to Cincinnati."

She shook her head positively. "It wouldn't do for me to go there."

"Oh, you come from Cincinnati?"

"No—but I—I've been there."

"Oh, they caught you and brought you back?"

She nodded. This young man must be very smart to understand so quickly.

"How much money have you got?" he asked abruptly.

But his fear that she would think him impertinent came of an underestimate of her innocence. "I haven't

179

got any," replied she. "I forgot my purse. It had thirty dollars in it."

At once he recognized the absolute child; only utter inexperience of the world could speak of so small a sum so respectfully. "I don't understand at all," said he. "How long have you been here?"

"All day. I got here early this morning."

"And you haven't had anything to eat!"

"Oh, yes! I found some eggs. I've got two left."

Two eggs—and no money and no friends—and a woman. Yet she was facing the future hopefully! He smiled, with tears in his eyes.

"You mustn't tell anybody you saw me," she went on. "No matter what they say, don't think you ought to tell on me."

He looked at her, she at him. When he had satisfied himself he smiled most reassuringly. "I'll not," was his answer, and now she *knew* she could trust him.

She drew a breath of relief, and went on as if talking with an old friend. "I've got to get a long ways from here. As soon as it's dark I'm going."

"Where?"

"Toward the river." And her eyes lit.

"The river? What's there?"

"I don't know," said she triumphantly.

But he understood. He had the spirit of adventure himself—one could see it at a glance—the spirit that instinctively shuns yesterday and all its works and wings eagerly into tomorrow, unknown, different, new—therefore better. But this girl, this child-woman —or was she rather woman-child?—penniless, with nothing but two eggs between her and starvation, alone, without plans, without experience—

180

What would become of her? . "Aren't you—afraid?" he asked.

"Of what?" she inquired calmly.

It was the mere unconscious audacity of ignorance, yet he saw in her now—not fancied he saw, but saw—a certain strength of soul, both courage and tenacity. No, she might suffer, sink—but she would die fighting, and she would not be afraid. And he admired and envied her.

"Oh, I'll get along somehow," she assured him in the same self-reliant tone. Suddenly she felt it would no longer give her the horrors to speak of what she had been through. "I'm not very old," said she, and hers was the face of a woman now. "But I've learned a great deal."

"You are sure you are not making a mistake in—in—running away?"

"I couldn't do anything else," replied she. "I'm all alone in the world. There's no one—except——

"I hadn't done anything, and they said I had disgraced them—and they——" Her voice faltered, her eyes sank, the color flooded into her face. "They gave me to a man—and he—I had hardly seen him before—he——" She tried but could not pronounce the dreadful word.

"Married, you mean?" said the young man gently.

The girl shuddered. "Yes," she answered. "And I ran away."

So strange, so startling, so moving was the expression of her face that he could not speak for a moment. A chill crept over him as he watched her wide eyes gazing into vacancy. What vision of horror was she seeing, he wondered. To rouse her he spoke the first words he could assemble:

"When was this?"

The vision seemed slowly to fade and she looked at him in astonishment. "Why, it was last night!" she said, as if dazed by the discovery. "Only last night!"

"Last night! Then you haven't got far."

"No. But I must. I will. And I'm not afraid of anything except of being taken back."

"But you don't realize what may be—probably is—waiting for you—at the river—and beyond."

"Nothing could be so bad," said she. The words were nothing, but the tone and the expression that accompanied them somehow convinced him beyond a doubt.

"You'll let me help you?"

She debated. "You might bring me something to eat—mightn't you? The eggs'll do for supper. But there's tomorrow. I don't want to be seen till I get a long ways off."

He rose at once. "Yes, I'll bring you something to eat." He took a knockabout watch from the breast pocket of his shirt. "It's now four o'clock. I've got three miles to walk. I'll ride back and hitch the horse down the creek—a little ways down, so it won't attract attention to your place up here. I'll be back in about an hour and a half. . . . Maybe I'll think of something that'll help. Can I bring you anything else?

"No. That is—I'd like a little piece of soap."

"And a towel?" he suggested.

"I could take care of a towel," agreed she. "I'll send it back to you when I get settled."

"Good heavens!" He laughed at her simplicity. "What an honest child you are!" He put out his hand, and she took it with charming friendliness. "Good-by. I'll hurry."

"I'm so glad you caught me," said she. Then, apologetically, "I don't want to be any trouble. I hate to be troublesome. I've never let anybody wait on me."

"I don't know when I've had as much pleasure as this is giving me." And he made a bow that hid its seriousness behind a smile of good-humored raillery.

She watched him descend with a sinking heart. The rock—the world—her life, seemed empty now. He had reminded her that there were human beings with good hearts. But—perhaps if he knew, his kindness would turn also. . . . No, she decided not. Men like him, women like Aunt Sallie—they did not believe those dreadful, wicked ideas that people said God had ordained. Still—if he knew about her birth—branded outcast—he might change. She must not really hope for anything much until she was far, far away in a wholly new world where there would be a wholly new sort of people, of a kind she had never met. But she was sure they would welcome her, and give her a chance.

She returned to the tree against which she had been sitting, for there she could look at the place his big frame had pressed down in the tall grass, and could see him in it, and could recall his friendly eyes and voice, and could keep herself assured she had not been dreaming. He was a citified man, like Sam—but how different! A man with a heart like his would never marry a woman—no, never! He couldn't be a brute like that. Still, perhaps nice men married because it was supposed to be the right thing to do, and was the only way to have children without people thinking you a disgrace and slighting the children —and then marrying made brutes of them. No wonder her uncles could treat her so. They were men who had married.

Afar off she heard the manly voice singing the song from "Rigoletto." She sprang up and listened, with eyes softly shining and head a little on one side. The song ended; her heart beat fast. It was not many minutes before she, watching at the end of the path, saw him appear at the bottom of the huge cleft. And the look in his eyes, the merry smile about his expressive mouth, delighted her. "I'm so glad to see you!" she cried.

Over his shoulder was flung his fishing bag, and it bulged. "Don't be scared by the size of my pack," he called up, as he climbed. "We're going to have supper together—if you'll let me stay. Then you can take as much or as little as you like of what's left."

Arrived at the top, he halted for a long breath. They stood facing each other. "My, what a tall girl you are for your age!" said he admiringly.

She laughed up at him. "I'll be as tall as you when I get my growth."

She was so lovely that he could scarcely refrain from telling her so. It seemed to him, however, it would be taking an unfair advantage to say that sort of thing when she was in a way at his mercy. "Where shall we spread the table?" said he. "I'm hungry as the horseleech's daughter. And you—why, you must be starved. I'm afraid I didn't bring what you like. But I did the best I could. I raided the pantry, took everything that was portable."

He had set down the bag and had loosened its strings. First he took out a tablecloth. She laughed. "Gracious! How stylish we shall be!"

"I didn't bring napkins. We can use the corners

of the cloth." He had two knives, two forks, and a big spoon rolled up in the cloth, and a saltcellar. "Now, here's my triumph!" he cried, drawing from the bag a pair of roasted chickens. Next came a jar of quince jelly; next, a paper bag with cold potatoes and cold string beans in it. Then he fished out a huge square of cornbread and a loaf of salt-rising bread, a pound of butter—

"What will your folks say?" exclaimed she, in dismay.

He laughed. "They always have thought I was crazy, ever since I went to college and then to the city instead of farming." And out of the bag came a big glass jar of milk. "I forgot to bring a glass!" he apologized. Then he suspended unpacking to open the jar. "Why, you must be half-dead with thirst, up here all day with not a drop of water." And he held out the jar to her. "Drink hearty!" he cried.

The milk was rich and cold; she drank nearly a fourth of it before she could wrest the jar away from her lips. "My, but that was good!" she remarked. He had enjoyed watching her drink. "Surely you haven't got anything else in that bag?"

"Not much," replied he. "Here's a towel, wrapped round the soap. And here are three cakes of chocolate. You could live four or five days on them, if you were put to it. So whatever else you leave, don't leave them. And—Oh, yes, here's a calico slip and a sunbonnet, and a paper of pins. And that's all."

"What are they for?"

"I thought you might put them on—the slip over your dress—and you wouldn't look quite so—so out of place—if anybody should see you."

185

"What a fine idea!" cried Susan, shaking out the slip delightedly.

He was spreading the supper on the tablecloth. He carved one of the chickens, opened the jelly, placed the bread and vegetables and butter. "Now!" he cried. "Let's get busy."

And he set her an example she was not slow to follow. The sun had slipped down behind the hills of the northwest horizon. The birds were tuning for their evening song. A breeze sprang up and coquetted with the strays of her wavy dark hair. And they sat cross-legged on the grass on opposite sides of the tablecloth and joked and laughed and ate, and ate and laughed and joked until the stars began to appear in the vast paling opal of the sky. They had chosen the center of the grassy platform for their banquet; thus, from where they sat only the tops of trees and the sky were to be seen. And after they had finished she leaned on her elbow and listened while he, smoking his cigarette, told her of his life as a newspaper man in Cincinnati. The twilight faded into dusk, the dusk into a scarlet darkness.

"When the moon comes up we'll start," said he. "You can ride behind me on the horse part of the way, anyhow."

The shadow of the parting, the ending of this happiness, fell upon her. How lonely it would be when he was gone! "I haven't told you my name," she said.

"I've told you mine—Roderick Spenser—with an *s*, not a *c*."

"I remember," said she. "I'll never forget. . . . Mine's Susan Lenox."

"What was it—before——" He halted.

"Before what?" His silence set her to thinking.

"Oh!" she exclaimed, in a tone that made him curse his stupidity in reminding her. "My name's Susan Lenox—and always will be. It was my mother's name." She hesitated, decided for frankness at any cost, for his kindness forbade her to deceive him in any way. Proudly, "My mother never let any man marry her. They say she was disgraced, but I understand now. *She* wouldn't stoop to let any man marry her."

Spenser puzzled over this, but could make nothing of it. He felt that he ought not to inquire further. He saw her anxious eyes, her expression of one keyed up and waiting for a verdict. "I'd have only to look at you to know your mother was a fine woman," said he. Then, to escape from the neighborhood of the dangerous riddle, "Now, about your—your going," he began. "I've been thinking what to do."

"You'll help me?" said she, to dispel her last doubt —a very faint doubt, for his words and his way of uttering them had dispelled her real anxiety.

"Help you?" cried he heartily. "All I can. I've got a scheme to propose to you. You say you can't take the mail boat?"

"They know me. I—I'm from Sutherland."

"You trust me—don't you?"

"Indeed I do."

"Now listen to me—as if I were your brother. Will you?"

"Yes."

"I'm going to take you to Cincinnati with me. I'm going to put you in my boarding house as my sister. And I'm going to get you a position. Then—you can start in for yourself."

"But that'll be a great lot of trouble, won't it?"

"Not any more than friends of mine took for me

when I was starting out." Then, as she continued silent, "What are you thinking? I can't see your face in this starlight."

"I was thinking how good you are," she said simply.

He laughed uneasily. "I'm not often accused of that," he replied. "I'm like most people—a mixture of good and bad—and not very strong either way. I'm afraid I'm mostly impulse that winks out. But— the question is, how to get you to Cincinnati. It's simply impossible for me to go tonight. I can't take you home for the night. I don't trust my people. They'd not think I was good—or you, either. And while usually they'd be right—both ways—this is an exception." This idea of an exception seemed to amuse him. He went on, "I don't dare leave you at any farmhouse in the neighborhood. If I did, you could be traced."

"No—no," she cried, alarmed at the very suggestion. "I mustn't be seen by anybody."

"We'll go straight to the river, and I'll get a boat and row you across to Kentucky—over to Carroll- ton. There's a little hotel. I can leave you——"

"No—not Carrollton," she interrupted. "My uncle sells goods there, and they know him. And if any- thing is in the Sutherland papers about me, why, they'd know."

"Not with you in that slip and sunbonnet. I'll make up a story—about our wagon breaking down and that I've got to walk back into the hills to get another before we can go on. And—it's the only plan that's at all possible."

Obviously he was right; but she would not consent. By adroit questioning he found that her objection was dislike of being so much trouble to him. "That's too ridiculous," cried he. "Why, I wouldn't have missed this adventure for anything in the world."

His manner was convincing enough, but she did not give in until moonrise came without her having thought of any other plan. He was to be Bob Peters, she his sister Kate, and they were to hail from a farm in the Kentucky hills back of Milton. They practiced the dialect of the region and found that they could talk it well enough to pass the test of a few sentences. They packed the fishing bag; she wrapped the two eggs in paper and put them in the empty milk bottle. They descended by the path—a slow journey in the darkness of that side of the rock, as there were many dangers, including the danger of making a noise that might be heard by some restless person at the house. After half an hour they were safely at the base of the rock; they skirted it, went down to the creek, found the horse tied where he had left it. With her seated sideways behind him and holding on by an arm half round his waist, they made a merry but not very speedy advance toward the river, keeping as nearly due south as the breaks in the hills permitted. After a while he asked: "Do you ever think of the stage?"

"I've never seen a real stage play," said she. "But I want to—and I will, the first chance I get."

"I meant, did you ever think of going on the stage?"

"No." So daring a flight would have been impossible for a baby imagination in the cage of the respectable-family-in-a-small-town.

"It's one of my dreams to write plays," he went on. "Wouldn't it be queer if some day I wrote plays for you to act in?"

When one's fancy is as free as was Susan's then, it takes any direction chance may suggest. Susan's fancy instantly winged along this fascinating route. "I've given recitations at school, and in the plays we used to have they let me take the best parts—that is —until—until a year or so ago."

He noted the hesitation, had an instinct against asking why there had come a time when she no longer got good parts. "I'm sure you could learn to act," declared he. "And you'll be sure of it, too, after you've seen the people who do it."

"Oh, I don't believe I could," said she, in rebuke to her own mounting self-confidence. Then, suddenly remembering her birth-brand of shame and overwhelmed by it, "No, I can't hope to be—to be anything much. They wouldn't have—*me*."

"I know how you feel," replied he, all unaware of the real reason for this deep humility. "When I first struck town I felt that way. It seemed to me I couldn't hope ever to line up with the clever people they had there. But I soon saw there was nothing in that idea. The fact is, everywhere in the world there's a lot more things to do than people who can do them. Most of those who get to the top—where did they start? Where we're starting."

She was immensely flattered by that "we" and grateful for it. But she held to her original opinion. "There wouldn't be a chance for me," said she. "They wouldn't have me."

"Oh, I understand," said he—and he fancied he did. He laughed gayly at the idea that in the theater anyone would care who she was—what kind of past she had had—or present either, for that matter. Said he, "You needn't worry. On the stage they don't ask any questions—any questions except 'Can you act? Can you get it over? Can you get the hand?'"

Then this stage, it was the world she had dreamed of—the world where there lived a wholly new kind of people—people who could make room for her. She thrilled, and her heart beat wildly. In a strangely quiet, intense voice, she said:

"I want to try. I'm sure I'll get along there. I'll work—Oh, so hard. I'll do *anything!*"

"That's the talk," cried he. "You've got the stuff in you."

She said little the rest of the journey. Her mind was busy with the idea he had by merest accident given her. If he could have looked in upon her thoughts, he would have been amazed and not a little alarmed by the ferment he had set up.

Where they reached the river the bank was mud and thick willows, the haunt of incredible armies of mosquitoes. "It's a mystery to me," cried he, "why these fiends live in lonely places far away from blood, when they're so mad about it." After some searching he found a clear stretch of sandy gravel where she would be not too uncomfortable while he was gone for a boat. He left the horse with her and walked upstream in the direction of Brooksburg. As he had warned her that he might be gone a long time, he knew she would not be alarmed for him—and she had already proved that timidity about herself was not in her nature. But he was alarmed for her—this girl alone in that lonely darkness—with light enough to make her visible to any prowler.

About an hour after he left her he returned in a rowboat he had borrowed at the water mill. He hitched the horse in the deep shadow of the break in the bank. She got into the boat, put on the slip and the sunbonnet, put her sailor hat in the bag. They pushed off and he began the long hard row across and up-stream. The moon was high now and was still near enough to its full glory to pour a flood of beautiful light upon the broad river—the lovely Ohio at its love-liest part.

"Won't you sing?" he asked.

And without hesitation she began one of the simple familiar love songs that were all the music to which the Sutherland girls had access. She sang softly, in a deep sweet voice, sweeter even than her speaking voice. She had the sunbonnet in her lap; the moon shone full upon her face. And it seemed to him that he was in a dream; there was nowhere a suggestion of reality—not of its prose, not even of its poetry. Only in the land no waking eye has seen could such a thing be. The low sweet voice sang of love, the oars clicked rhythmically in the locks and clove the water with musical splash; the river, between its steep hills, shone in the moonlight, with a breeze like a friendly spirit moving upon its surface. He urged her, and she sang another song, and another. She sighed when she saw the red lantern on the Carrollton wharf; and he, turning his head and seeing, echoed her sigh.

"The first chance, you must sing me that song," she said.

"From 'Rigoletto'? I will. But—it tells how fickle women are—'like a feather in the wind.' . . . They aren't all like that, though—don't you think so?"

"Sometimes I think everybody's like a feather in the wind," replied she. "About love—and everything."

He laughed. "Except those people who are where there isn't any wind."

XII

FOR some time Spenser had been rowing well in toward the Kentucky shore, to avoid the swift current of the Kentucky River which rushes into the Ohio at Carrollton. A few yards below its mouth, in the quiet stretch of backwater along shore, lay the wharf-boat, little more than a landing stage. The hotel was but a hundred feet away, at the top of the steep levee. It was midnight, so everyone in the village had long been asleep. After several minutes of thunderous hammering Roderick succeeded in drawing to the door a barefooted man with a candle in his huge, knotted hand—a man of great stature, amazingly lean and long of leg, with a monstrous head thatched and fronted with coarse, yellow-brown hair. He had on a dirty cotton shirt and dirty cotton trousers—a night dress that served equally well for the day. His feet were flat and thick and were hideous with corns and bunions. Susan had early been made a critical observer of feet by the unusual symmetry of her own. She had seen few feet that were fit to be seen; but never, she thought, had she seen an exhibition so repellent.

"What t'hell——" he began. Then, discovering Susan, he growled, "Beg pardon, miss."

Roderick explained—that is, told the prearranged story. The man pointed to a grimy register on the office desk, and Roderick set down the fishing bag and wrote in a cramped, scrawly hand, "Kate Peters, Milton, Ky."

The man looked at it through his screen of hair and beard, said, "Come on, ma'am."

"Just a minute," said Roderick, and he drew "Kate" aside and said to her in a low tone: "I'll be back sometime tomorrow, and then we'll start at once. But —to provide against everything—don't be alarmed if I don't come. You'll know I couldn't help it. And wait."

Susan nodded, looking at him with trustful, grateful eyes.

"And," he went on hurriedly, "I'll leave this with you, to take care of. It's yours as much as mine."

She saw that it was a pocketbook, instinctively put her hands behind her.

"Don't be silly," he said, with good-humored impatience. "You'll probably not need it. If you do, you'll need it bad. And you'll pay me back when you get your place."

He caught one of her hands and put the pocketbook in it. As his argument was unanswerable, she did not resist further. She uttered not a word of thanks, but simply looked at him, her eyes swimming and about her mouth a quiver that meant a great deal in her. Impulsively and with flaming cheek he kissed her on the cheek. "So long, sis," he said loudly, and strode into the night.

Susan did not flush; she paled. She gazed after him with some such expression as a man lost in a cave might have as he watches the flickering out of his only light. "This way, ma'am," said the hotel man sourly, taking up the fishing bag. She started, followed him up the noisy stairs to a plain, neat country bedroom. "The price of this here's one fifty a day," said he. "We've got 'em as low as a dollar."

"I'll take a dollar one, please," said Susan.

The man hesitated. "Well," he finally snarled, "business is slack jes' now. Seein' as you're a lady, you kin have this here un fur a dollar."

"Oh, thank you—but if the price is more——"

"The other rooms ain't fit fur a lady," said the hotel man. Then he grinned a very human humorous grin that straightway made him much less repulsive. "Anyhow, them two durn boys of mine an' their cousins is asleep in 'em. I'd as lief rout out a nest of hornets. I'll leave you the candle."

As soon as he had gone Susan put out the light, ran to the window. She saw the rowboat and Spenser, a black spot far out on the river, almost gone from view to the southwest. Hastily she lighted the candle again, stood at the window and waved a white cover she snatched from the table. She thought she saw one of the oars go up and flourish, but she could not be sure. She watched until the boat vanished in the darkness at the bend. She found the soap in the bag and took a slow but thorough bath in the washbowl. Then she unbraided her hair, combed it out as well as she could with her fingers, rubbed it thoroughly with a towel and braided it again. She put on the calico slip as a nightdress, knelt down to say her prayers. But instead of prayers there came flooding into her mind memories of where she had been last night, of the horrors, of the agonies of body and soul. She rose from her knees, put out the light, stood again at the window. In after years she always looked back upon that hour as the one that definitely marked the end of girlhood, of the thoughts and beliefs which go with the sheltered life, and the beginning of womanhood, of self-reliance and of the hardiness—so near akin to hardness—the hardiness that must come into the character before a man or a woman is fit to give and take in the combat of life.

The bed was coarse, but white and clean. She fell asleep instantly and did not awaken until, after the vague, gradually louder sound of hammering on the door, she heard a female voice warning her that breakfast was "put nigh over an' done." She got up, partly drew on one stocking, then without taking it off tumbled over against the pillow and was asleep. When she came to herself again, the lay of the shadows told her it must be after twelve o'clock. She dressed, packed her serge suit in the bag with the sailor hat, smoothed out the pink calico slip and put it on. For more than a year she had worn her hair in a braid doubled upon itself and tied with a bow at the back of her neck. She decided that if she would part it, plait it in two braids and bring them round her head, she would look older. She tried this and was much pleased with the result. She thought the new style not only more grown-up, but also more becoming. The pink slip, too, seemed to her a success. It came almost to her ankles and its strings enabled her to make it look something like a dress. Carrying the pink sunbonnet, down she went in search of something to eat.

The hall was full of smoke and its air seemed greasy with the odor of frying. She found that dinner was about to be served. A girl in blue calico skirt and food-smeared, sweat-discolored blue jersey ushered her to one of the tables in the dining-room. "There's a gentleman comin'," said she. "I'll set him down with you. He won't bite, I don't reckon, and there ain't no use mussin' up two tables."

There was no protesting against two such arguments; so Susan presently had opposite her a fattish man with long oily hair and a face like that of a fallen and dissipated preacher. She recognized him at once as one of those wanderers who visit small towns with cheap shows or selling patent medicines and doing juggling tricks on the street corners in the flare of a gasoline lamp. She eyed him furtively until he caught her at it—he being about the same business himself. Thereafter she kept her eyes steadily upon the tablecloth, patched and worn thin with much washing. Soon the plate of each was encircled by the familiar arc of side dishes containing assorted and not very appetizing messes—fried steak, watery peas, stringy beans, soggy turnips, lumpy mashed potatoes, a perilous-looking chicken stew, cornbread with streaks of baking soda in it. But neither of the diners was critical, and the dinner was eaten with an enthusiasm which the best rarely inspires.

With the prunes and dried-apple pie, the stranger expanded. "Warm day, miss," he ventured.

"Yes, it is a little warm," said Susan. She ventured a direct look at him. Above the pleasant, kindly eyes there was a brow so unusually well shaped that it arrested even her young and untrained attention. Whatever the man's character or station, there could be no question as to his intelligence.

"The flies are very bothersome," continued he. "But nothing like Australia. There the flies have to be picked off, and they're big, and they bite—take a piece right out of you. The natives used to laugh at us when we were in the ring and would try to brush 'em away." The stranger had the pleasant, easy manner of one who through custom of all kinds of people and all varieties of fortune, has learned to be patient and

197

good-humored—to take the day and the hour as the seasoned gambler takes the cards that are dealt him.

Susan said nothing; but she had listened politely. The man went on amusing himself with his own conversation. "I was in the show business then. Clown was my line, but I was rotten at it—simply rotten. I'm still in the show business—different line, though. I've got a show of my own. If you're going to be in town perhaps you'll come to see us tonight. Our boat's anchored down next to the wharf. You can see it from the windows. Come, and bring your folks."

"Thank you," said Susan—she had forgotten her rôle and its accent. "But I'm afraid we'll not be here."

There was an expression in the stranger's face—a puzzled, curious expression, not impertinent, rather covert—an expression that made her uneasy. It warned her that this man saw she was not what she seemed to be, that he was trying to peer into her secret. His brown eyes were kind enough, but alarmingly keen. With only half her pie eaten, she excused herself and hastened to her room.

At the threshold she remembered the pocketbook Spenser had given her. She had left it by the fishing bag on the table. There was the bag but not the pocketbook. "I must have put it in the bag," she said aloud, and the sound and the tone of her voice frightened her. She searched the bag, then the room which had not yet been straightened up. She shook out the bed covers, looked in all the drawers, under the bed, went over the contents of the bag again. The pocketbook was gone—stolen.

She sat down on the edge of the bed, her hands in

her lap, and stared at the place where she had last
seen the pocketbook—*his* pocketbook, which he had
asked her to take care of. How could she face him!
What would he think of her, so untrustworthy! What
a return for his kindness! She felt weak—so weak
that she lay down. The food she had taken turned to
poison and her head ached fiercely. What could she
do? To speak to the proprietor would be to cause a
great commotion, to attract attention to herself—
and how would that help to bring back the stolen
pocketbook, taken perhaps by the proprietor himself?
She recalled that as she hurried through the office from
the dining-room he had a queer shifting expression,
gave her a wheedling, cringing good morning not at
all in keeping with the character he had shown the night
before. The slovenly girl came to do the room; Susan
sent her away, sat by the window gazing out over
the river and downstream. He would soon be here;
the thought made her long to fly and hide. He had
been all generosity; and this was her way of appreci-
ating it!

They sent for her to come down to supper. She refused, saying she was not feeling well. She searched
the room, the bag, again and again. She would rest
a few minutes, then up she would spring and tear
everything out. Then back to the window to sit and
stare at the river over which the evening shadows were
beginning to gather. Once, as she was sitting there,
she happened to see the gaudily painted and decorated
show boat. A man—the stranger of the dinner table
—was standing on the forward end, smoking a cigar.
She saw that he was observing her, realized he could
have seen her stirring feverishly about her room. A
woman came out of the cabin and joined him. As

soon as his attention was distracted she closed her shutters. And there she sat alone, with the hours dragging their wretched minutes slowly away.

That was one of those nights upon which anyone who has had them—and who has not?—looks back with wonder at how they ever lived, how they ever came to an end. She slept a little toward dawn—for youth and health will not let the most despairing heart suffer in sleeplessness. Her headache went, but the misery of soul which had been a maddening pain settled down into a throbbing ache. She feared he would come; she feared he would not come. The servants tried to persuade her to take breakfast. She could not have swallowed food; she would not have dared take food for which she could not pay. What would they do with her if he did not come? She searched the room again, hoping against hope, a hundred times fancying she felt the purse under some other things, each time suffering sickening disappointment.

Toward noon the servant came knocking. "A letter for you, ma'am."

Susan rushed to the door, seized the letter, tore it open, read:

When I got back to the horse and started to mount, he kicked me and broke my leg. You can go on south to the L. and N. and take a train to Cincinnati. When you find a boarding house send your address to me at the office. I'll come in a few weeks. I'd write more but I can't. Don't worry. Everything'll come out right. You are brave and sensible, and I *back you to win*.

With the unsigned letter crumpled in her hands she sat at the window with scarcely a motion until noon. She then went down to the show boat. Several people

—men and women—were on the forward end, quarreling. She looked only at her acquaintance. His face was swollen and his eyes bloodshot, but he still wore the air of easy and patient good-humor. She said, standing on the shore, "Could I speak to you a minute?"

"Certainly, ma'am," replied he, lifting his dingy straw hat with gaudy, stained band. He came down the broad plank to the shore. "Why, what's the matter?" This in a sympathetic tone.

"Will you lend me two dollars and take me along to work it out?" she asked.

He eyed her keenly. "For the hotel bill?" he inquired, the cigar tucked away in the corner of his mouth.

She nodded.

"He didn't show up?"

"He broke his leg."

"Oh!" The tone was politely sympathetic, but incredulous. He eyed her critically, thoughtfully. "Can you sing?" he finally asked.

"A little."

His hands were deep in the pockets of his baggy light trousers. He drew one of them out with a two-dollar bill in it. "Go and pay him and bring your things. We're about to push off."

"Thank you," said the girl in the same stolid way. She returned to the hotel, brought the bag down from her room, stood at the office desk.

The servant came. "Mr. Gumpus has jes' stepped out," said she.

"Here is the money for my room." And Susan laid the two-dollar bill on the register.

"Ain't you goin' to wait fur yer—yer brother?"

"He's not coming," replied the girl. "So—I'll go. Good-by."

"Good-by. It's awful, bein' took sick away from home."

"Thank you," said Susan. "Good-by."

The girl's homely, ignorant face twisted in a grin. But Susan did not see, would have been indifferent had she seen. Since she accepted the war earth and heaven had declared against her, she had ceased from the little thought she had once given to what was thought of her by those of whom she thought not at all. She went down to the show boat. The plank had been taken in. Her acquaintance was waiting for her, helped her to the deck, jumped aboard himself, and was instantly busy helping to guide the boat out into mid-stream. Susan looked back at the hotel. Mr. Gumpus was in the doorway, amusement in every line of his ugly face. Beside him stood the slovenly servant. She was crying—the more human second thought of a heart not altogether corrupted by the sordid hardness of her lot. How can faith in the human race falter when one considers how much heart it has in spite of all it suffers in the struggle upward through the dense fogs of ignorance—upward, toward the truth, toward the light of which it never ceases to dream and to hope?

Susan stood in the same place, with her bag beside her, until her acquaintance came.

"Now," said he, comfortably, as he lighted a fresh cigar, "we'll float pleasantly along. I guess you and I had better get acquainted. What is your name?"

Susan flushed. "Kate Peters is the name I gave at the hotel. That'll do, won't it?"

"Never in the world!" replied he. "You must have a good catchy name. Say—er—er——" He rolled his cigar slowly, looking thoughtfully toward the willows thick and green along the Indiana shore. "Say —well, say—Lorna—Lorna—Lorna Sackville! That's a winner. Lorna Sackville!—A stroke of genius! Don't you think so?"

"Yes," said Susan. "It doesn't matter."

"But it does," remonstrated he. "You are an artist, now, and an artist's name should always arouse pleasing and romantic anticipations. It's like the odor that heralds the dish. You must remember, my dear, that you have stepped out of the world of dull reality into the world of ideals, of dreams."

The sound of two harsh voices, one male, the other female, came from within the cabin—oaths, reproaches. Her acquaintance laughed. "That's one on me—eh? Still, what I say is true—or at least ought to be. By the way, this is the Burlingham Floating Palace of Thespians, floating temple to the histrionic art. I am Burlingham—Robert Burlingham." He smiled, extended his hand. "Glad to meet you, Miss Lorna Sackville— don't forget!"

She could not but reflect a smile so genuine, so good-humored.

"We'll go in and meet the others—your fellow stars —for this is an all-star aggregation."

Over the broad entrance to the cabin was a chintz curtain strung upon a wire. Burlingham drew this aside. Susan was looking into a room about thirty feet long, about twelve feet wide, and a scant six feet high. Across it with an aisle between were narrow wooden benches with backs. At the opposite end was a stage, with the curtain up and a portable stove oc-

cupying the center. At the stove a woman in a chemise
and underskirt, with slippers on her bare feet, was
toiling over several pots and pans with fork and spoon.
At the edge of the stage, with legs swinging, sat another woman, in a blue sailor suit neither fresh nor
notably clean but somehow coquettish. Two men in
flannel shirts were seated, one on each of the front
benches, with their backs to her.

As Burlingham went down the aisle ahead of her, he
called out: "Ladies and gentlemen, I wish to present
the latest valuable addition to our company—Miss
Lorna Sackville, the renowned ballad singer."

The two men turned lazily and stared at Susan, each
with an arm hanging over the back of the bench.

Burlingham looked at the woman bent over the stove
—a fat, middle-aged woman with thin, taffy-yellow hair
done sleekly over a big rat in front and made into
a huge coil behind with the aid of one or more false
braids. She had a fat face, a broad expanse of unpleasant-looking, elderly bosom, big, shapeless white
arms. Her contour was almost gone. Her teeth were
a curious mixture of natural, gold, and porcelain.
"Miss Anstruther—Miss Sackville," called Burlingham. "Miss Sackville, Miss Violet Anstruther."

Miss Anstruther and Susan exchanged bows—Susan's timid and frightened, Miss Anstruther's accompanied by a hostile stare and a hardening of the fat,
decaying face.

"Miss Connemora—Miss Sackville." Burlingham
was looking at the younger woman—she who sat on
the edge of the little stage. She, too, was a blond,
but her hair had taken to the chemical somewhat less
reluctantly than had Miss Anstruther's, with the result that Miss Connemora's looked golden. Her face—

of the baby type—must have been softly pretty at one time—not so very distant. Now lines were coming and the hard look that is inevitable with dyed hair. Also her once fine teeth were rapidly going off, as half a dozen gold fillings in front proclaimed. At Susan's appealing look and smile Miss Connemora nodded not unfriendly.

"Good God, Bob," said she to Burlingham with a laugh, "are you going to get the bunch of us pinched for child-stealing?"

Burlingham started to laugh, suddenly checked himself, looked uneasily and keenly at Susan. "Oh, it's all right," he said with a wave of the hand. But his tone belied his words. He puffed twice at his cigar, then introduced the men—Elbert Eshwell and Gregory Tempest—two of the kind clearly if inelegantly placed by the phrase, "greasy hamfats." Mr. Eshwell's black-dyed hair was smoothly brushed down from a central part, Mr. Tempest's iron-gray hair was greasily wild—a disarray of romantic ringlets. Eshwell was inclined to fat; Tempest was gaunt and had the hollow, burning eye that bespeaks the sentimental ass.

"Now, Miss Sackville," said Burlingham, "we'll go on the forward deck and canvass the situation. What for dinner, Vi?"

"Same old rot," retorted Miss Anstruther, wiping the sweat from her face and shoulders with a towel that served also as a dishcloth. "Pork and beans—potatoes—peach pie."

"Cheer up," said Burlingham. "After tomorrow we'll do better."

"That's been the cry ever since we started," snapped Violet.

"For God's sake, shut up, Vi," groaned Eshwell. "You're always kicking."

The cabin was not quite the full width of the broad house boat. Along the outside, between each wall and the edge, there was room for one person to pass from forward deck to rear. From the cabin roof, over the rear deck, into the water extended a big rudder oar. When Susan, following Burlingham, reached the rear deck, she saw the man at this oar—a fat, amiable-looking rascal, in linsey woolsey and a blue checked shirt open over his chest and revealing a mat of curly gray hair. Burlingham hailed him as Pat—his only known name. But Susan had only a glance for him and no ear at all for the chaffing between him and the actor-manager. She was gazing at the Indiana shore, at a tiny village snuggled among trees and ripened fields close to the water's edge. She knew it was Brooksburg. She remembered the long covered bridge which they had crossed—Spenser and she, on the horse. To the north of the town, on a knoll, stood a large red brick house trimmed with white veranda and balconies—far and away the most pretentious house in the landscape. Before the door was a horse and buggy. She could make out that there were several people on the front veranda, one of them a man in black—the doctor, no doubt. Sobs choked up into her throat. She turned quickly away that Burlingham might not see. And under her breath she said,

"Good-by, dear. Forgive me—forgive me."

XIII

A WOMAN'S worktable, a rocking chair and another with a swayback that made it fairly comfortable for lounging gave the rear deck the air of an outdoor sitting-room, which indeed it was. Burlingham, after a comprehensive glance at the panorama of summer and fruitfulness through which they were drifting, sprawled himself in the swayback chair, indicating to Susan that she was to face him in the rocker. "Sit down, my dear," said he. "And tell me you are at least eighteen and are not running away from home. You heard what Miss Connemora said."

"I'm not running away from home," replied Susan, blushing violently because she was evading as to the more important fact.

"I don't know anything about you, and I don't want to know," pursued Burlingham, alarmed by the evidences of a dangerous tendency to candor. "I've no desire to have my own past dug into, and turn about's fair play. You came to me to get an engagement. I took you. Understand?"

Susan nodded.

"You said you could sing—that is, a little."

"A very little," said the girl.

"Enough, no doubt. That has been our weak point—lack of a ballad singer. Know any ballads?—Not fancy ones. Nothing fancy! We cater to the plain people, and the plain people only like the best—that is, the simplest—the things that reach for the heart-

207

strings with ten strong fingers. You don't happen to know 'I Stood on the Bridge at Midnight'?"

"No—Ruth sings that," replied Susan, and colored violently.

Burlingham ignored the slip. " 'Blue Alsatian Mountains'?"

"Yes. But that's very old."

"Exactly. Nothing is of any use to the stage until it's very old. Audiences at theaters don't want to *hear* anything they don't already know by heart. They've come to *see*, not to hear. So it annoys them to have to try to hear. Do you understand that?"

"No," confessed Susan. "I'm sorry. But I'll think about it, and try to understand it." She thought she was showing her inability to do what was expected of her in paying back the two dollars.

"Don't bother," said Burlingham. "Pat!"

"Yes, boss," said the man at the oar, without looking or removing his pipe.

"Get your fiddle."

Pat tied the oar fast and went forward along the roof of the cabin. While he was gone Burlingham explained, "A frightful souse, Pat—almost equal to Eshwell and far the superior of Tempest or Vi—that is, of Tempest. But he's steady enough for our purposes, as a rule. He's the pilot, the orchestra, the man-of-all-work, the bill distributor. Oh, he's a wonder. Graduate of Trinity College, Dublin—yeggman —panhandler—barrel-house bum—genius, nearly. Has drunk as much booze as there is water in this river——"

Pat was back beside the handle of the oar, with a violin. Burlingham suggested to Susan that she'd better stand while she sang, "and if you've any ten-

208

dency to stage fright, remember it's your bread and
butter to get through well. You'll not bother about
your audience."

Susan found this thought a potent strengthener—
then and afterward. With surprisingly little embarrassment she stood before her good-natured, sympathetic employer, and while Pat scraped out an accompaniment sang the pathetic story of the "maiden
young and fair" and the "stranger in the spring" who
"lingered near the fountains just to hear the maiden
sing," and how he departed after winning her love,
and how "she will never see the stranger where the
fountains fall again—adé, adé, adé." Her voice
was deliciously young and had the pathetic quality
that is never absent from anything which has enduring
charm for us. Tears were in Burlingham's voice—
tears for the fate of the maiden, tears of response to
the haunting pathos of Susan's sweet contralto, tears
of joy at the acquisition of such a "number" for his
program. As her voice died away he beat his plump
hands together enthusiastically.

"She'll do—eh, Pat? She'll set the hay-tossers
crazy!"

Susan's heart was beating fast from nervousness.
She sat down. Burlingham sprang up and put his
hands on her shoulders and kissed her. He laughed at
her shrinking.

"Don't mind, my dear," he cried. "It's one of our
ways. Now, what others do you know?"

She tried to recall, and with his assistance finally
did discover that she possessed a repertoire of "good
old stale ones," consisting of "Coming Thro' the Rye,"
"Suwanee River," "Annie Laurie" and "Kathleen Ma-
vourneen." She knew many other songs, but either

Pat could not play them or Burlingham declared them "above the head of Reub the rotter."

"Those five are quite enough," said Burlingham. "Two regulars, two encores, with a third in case of emergency. After dinner Miss Anstruther and I'll fit you out with a costume. You'll make a hit at Sutherland tonight."

"Sutherland!" exclaimed Susan, suddenly pale. "I can't sing there—really, I can't."

Burlingham made a significant gesture toward Pat at the oar above them, and winked at her. "You'll not have stage fright, my dear. You'll pull through."

Susan understood that nothing more was to be said before Pat. Soon Burlingham told him to tie the oar again and retire to the cabin. "I'll stand watch," said he. "I want to talk business with Miss Sackville."

When Pat had gone, Burlingham gave her a sympathetic look. "No confidences, mind you, my dear," he warned. "All I want to know is that it isn't stage fright that's keeping you off the program at Sutherland."

"No," replied the girl. "It isn't stage fright. I'm —I'm sorry I can't begin right away to earn the money to pay you back. But—I can't."

"Not even in a velvet and spangle costume—Low neck, short sleeves, with blond wig and paint and powder? You'll not know yourself, my dear—really."

"I couldn't," said Susan. "I'd not be able to open my lips."

"Very well. That's settled." It was evident that Burlingham was deeply disappointed. "We were going to try to make a killing at Sutherland." He sighed. "However, let that pass. If you can't, you can't."

"I'm afraid you're angry with me," cried she.

"I—angry!" He laughed. "I've not been angry in ten years. I'm such a *damn*, damn fool that with all the knocks life's given me I haven't learned much. But at least I've learned not to get angry. No, I understand, my dear—and will save you for the next town below." He leaned forward and gave her hands a fatherly pat as they lay in her lap. "Don't give it a second thought," he said. "We've got the whole length of the river before us."

Susan showed her gratitude in her face better far than she could have expressed it in words. The two sat silent. When she saw his eyes upon her with that look of smiling wonder in them, she said, "You mustn't think I've done anything dreadful. I haven't—really, I haven't."

He laughed heartily. "And if you had, you'd not need to hang your head in this company, my dear. We're all people who have *lived*—and life isn't exactly a class meeting with the elders taking turns at praying and the organ wheezing out gospel hymns. No, we've all been up against it most of our lives—which means we've done the best we could oftener than we've had the chance to do what we ought." He gave her one of his keen looks, nodded: "I like you. . . . What do they tell oftenest when they're talking about how you were as a baby?"

Susan did not puzzle over the queerness of this abrupt question. She fell to searching her memory diligently for an answer. "I'm not sure, but I think they speak oftenest of how I never used to like anybody to take my hand and help me along, even when I was barely able to walk. They say I always insisted on trudging along by myself."

Burlingham nodded, slapped his knee. "I can believe

it," he cried. "I always ask everybody that question to see whether I've sized 'em up right. I rather think I hit you off to a T—as you faced me at dinner yesterday in the hotel. Speaking of dinner—let's go sit in on the one I smell."

They returned to the cabin where, to make a table, a board had been swung between the backs of the second and third benches from the front on the left side of the aisle. Thus the three men sat on the front bench with their legs thrust through between seat and back, while the three women sat in dignity and comfort on the fourth bench. Susan thought the dinner by no means justified Miss Anstruther's pessimism. It was good in itself, and the better for being in this happy-go-lucky way, in this happy-go-lucky company. Once they got started, all the grouchiness disappeared. Susan, young and optimistic and determined to be pleased, soon became accustomed to the looks of her new companions—that matter of mere exterior about which we shallow surface-skimmers make such a mighty fuss, though in the test situations of life, great and small, it amounts to precious little. They were all human beings, and the girl was unspoiled, did not think of them as failures, half-wolves, of no social position, of no standing in the respectable world. She still had much of the natural democracy of children, and she admired these new friends who knew so much more than she did, who had lived, had suffered, had come away from horrible battles covered with wounds, the scars of which they would bear into the grave— battles they had lost; yet they had not given up, but had lived on, smiling, courageous, kind of heart. It was their kind hearts that most impressed her—their kind taking in of her whom those she loved had cast

212

out—her, the unknown stranger, helpless and ignorant. And what Spenser had told her about the stage
and its people made her almost believe that they would
not cast her out, though they knew the dreadful truth
about her birth.

Tempest told a story that was "broad." While
the others laughed, Susan gazed at him with a puzzled expression. She wished to be polite, to please, to
enjoy. But what that story meant she could not
fathom. Miss Anstruther jeered at her. "Look at the
innocent," she cried.

"Shut up, Vi," retorted Miss Connemora. "It's no
use for us to try to be—anything but what we are.
Still, let the baby alone."

"Yes—let her alone," said Burlingham.

"It'll soak in soon enough," Miss Connemora went
on. "No use rubbing it in."

"What?" said Susan, thinking to show her desire
to be friendly, to be one of them.

"Dirt," said Burlingham dryly. "And don't ask
any more questions."

When the three women had cleared away the dinner
and had stowed the dishes in one of the many cubby-
holes along the sides of the cabin, the three men got
ready for a nap. Susan was delighted to see them
drop to the tops of the backs of the seats three berths
which fitted snugly into the walls when not in use. She
saw now that there were five others of the same kind,
and that there was a contrivance of wires and curtains by which each berth could be shut off to itself.
She had a thrilling sense of being in a kind of Swiss
Family Robinson storybook come to life. She unpacked
her bag, contributed the food in it to the common store,
spread out her serge suit which Miss Anstruther of-

fered to press and insisted on pressing, though Susan protested she could do it herself quite well.

"You'll want to put it on for the arrival at Sutherland," said Mabel Connemora.

"No," replied Susan nervously. "Not till tomorrow."

She saw the curious look in all their eyes at sight of that dress, so different from the calico she was wearing. Mabel took her out on the forward deck where there was an awning and a good breeze. They sat there, Mabel talking, Susan gazing rapt at land and water and at the actress, and listening as to a fairy story —for the actress had lived through many and strange experiences in the ten years since she left her father's roof in Columbia, South Carolina. Susan listened and absorbed as a dry sponge dropped into a pail of water. At her leisure she would think it all out, would understand, would learn.

"Now, tell *me* about *your*self," said Mabel when she had exhausted all the reminiscences she could recall at the moment—all that were fit for a "baby's" ears.

"I will, some time," said Susan, who was ready for the question. "But I can't—not yet."

"It seems to me you're very innocent," said Mabel, "even for a well-brought-up girl. *I* was well brought up, too. I wish to God my mother had told me a few things. But no—not a thing."

"What do you mean?" inquired Susan.

That set the actress to probing the girl's innocence —what she knew and what she did not. It had been many a day since Miss Connemora had had so much pleasure. "Well!" she finally said. "I never would have believed it—though I know these things are so. Now I'm going to teach you. Innocence may be a

214

good thing for respectable women who are going to marry and settle down with a good husband to look after them. But it won't do at all—not at all, my dear!—for a woman who works—who has to meet men in their own world and on their own terms. It's hard enough to get along, if you know. If you don't—when you're knocked down, you stay knocked down."

"Yes—I want to learn," said Susan eagerly. "I want to know—*everything!*"

"You're not going back?" Mabel pointed toward the shore, to a home on a hillside, with a woman sewing on the front steps and children racing about the yard. "Back to that sort of thing?"

"No," replied Susan. "I've got nothing to go back to."

"Nonsense!"

"Nothing," repeated Susan in the same simple, final way. "I'm an outcast."

The ready tears sprang to Mabel's dissipated but still bright eyes. Susan's unconscious pathos was so touching. "Then I'll educate you. Now don't get horrified or scandalized at me. When you feel that way, remember that Mabel Connemora didn't make the world, but God. At least, so they say—though personally I feel as if the devil had charge of things, and the only god was in us poor human creatures fighting to be decent. I tell you, men and women ain't bad—not so damn bad—excuse me; they will slip out. No, it's the things that happen to them or what they're afraid'll happen—it's those things that compel them to be bad—and get them in the way of being bad—hard to each other, and to hate and to lie and to do all sorts of things."

The show boat drifted placidly down with the cur-

rent of the broad Ohio. Now it moved toward the left
bank and now toward the right, as the current was deflected by the bends—the beautiful curves that divided
the river into a series of lovely, lake-like reaches, each
with its emerald oval of hills and rolling valleys where
harvests were ripening. And in the shadow of the
awning Susan heard from those pretty, coarse lips,
in language softened indeed but still far from refined,
about all there is to know concerning the causes and
consequences of the eternal struggle that rages round
sex. To make her tale vivid, Mabel illustrated it by
the story of her own life from girlhood to the present
hour. And she omitted no detail necessary to enforce
the lesson in life. A few days before Susan would not
have believed, would not have understood. Now she
both believed and understood. And nothing that Mabel told her—not the worst of the possibilities in the
world in which she was adventuring—burned deep
enough to penetrate beyond the wound she had already
received and to give her a fresh sensation of pain and
horror.

"You don't seem to be horrified," said Mabel.

Susan shook her head. "No," she said. "I feel—
somehow I feel better."

Mabel eyed her curiously—had a sense of a mystery of suffering which she dared not try to explore.
She said: "Better? That's queer. You don't take it
at all as I thought you would."

Said Susan: "I had about made up my mind it was
all bad. I see that maybe it isn't."

"Oh, the world isn't such a bad place—in lots of
ways. You'll get a heap of fun out of it if you don't
take things or yourself seriously. I wish to God I'd
had somebody to tell me, instead of having to spell it

out, a letter at a time. I've got just two pieces of advice to give you." And she stopped speaking and gazed away toward the shore with a look that seemed to be piercing the hills.

"Please do," urged Susan, when Mabel's long mood of abstraction tried her patience.

"Oh—yes—two pieces of advice. The first is, don't drink. There's nothing to it—and it'll play hell—excuse me—it'll spoil your looks and your health and give you a woozy head when you most need a steady one. Don't drink—that's the first advice."

"I won't," said Susan.

"Oh, yes, you will. But remember my advice all the same. The second is, don't sell your body to get a living, unless you've got to."

"I couldn't do that," said the girl.

Mabel laughed queerly. "Oh, yes, you could—and will. But remember my advice. Don't sell your body because it seems to be the easy way to make a living. I know most women get their living that way."

"Oh—no—no, indeed!" protested Susan.

"What a child you are!" laughed Mabel. "What's marriage but that? . . . Believe your Aunt Betsy, it's the poorest way to make a living that ever was invented—marriage or the other thing. Sometimes you'll be tempted to. You're pretty, and you'll find yourself up against it with no way out. You'll have to give in for a time, no doubt. The men run things in this world, and they'll compel it—one way or another. But fight back to your feet again. If I'd taken my own advice, my name would be on every dead wall in New York in letters two feet high. Instead——" She laughed, without much bitterness. "And why? All because I never learned to stand alone. I've even supported men

—to have something to lean on! How's that for a poor fool?"

There Violet Anstruther called her. She rose. "You won't take my advice," she said by way of conclusion. "Nobody'll take advice. Nobody can. We ain't made that way. But don't forget what I've said. And when you've wobbled way off maybe it'll give you something to steer back by."

Susan sat on there, deep in the deepest of those brown studies that had been characteristic of her from early childhood. Often—perhaps most often—abstraction means only mental fogginess. But Susan happened to be of those who can concentrate—can think things out. And that afternoon, oblivious of the beauty around her, even unconscious of where she was, she studied the world of reality—that world whose existence, even the part of it lying within ourselves, we all try to ignore or to evade or to deny, and get soundly punished for our folly. Taking advantage of the floods of light Mabel Connemora had let in upon her—full light where there had been a dimness that was equal to darkness—she drew from the closets of memory and examined all the incidents of her life— all that were typical or for other reasons important. One who comes for the first time into new surroundings sees more, learns more about them in a brief period than has been seen and known by those who have lived there always. After a few hours of recalling and reconstructing Susan Lenox understood Sutherland probably better than she would have understood it had she lived a long eventless life there. And is not every Sutherland the world in miniature?

She also understood her own position—why the world of respectability had cast her out as soon as she emerged from childhood—why she could not have hoped for the lot to which other girls looked forward—why she belonged with the outcasts, in a world apart—and must live her life there. She felt that she could not hope to be respected, loved, married. She must work out her destiny along other lines. She understood it all, more clearly than would have been expected of her. And it is important to note that she faced her future without repining or self-pity, without either joy or despondency. She would go on; she would do as best she could. And nothing that might befall could equal what she had suffered in the throes of the casting out.

Burlingham roused her from her long reverie. He evidently had come straight from his nap—stocking feet, shirt open at the collar, trousers sagging and face shiny with the sweat that accumulates during sleep on a hot day. "Round that bend ahead of us is Sutherland," said he, pointing forward.

Up she started in alarm.

"Now, don't get fractious," cried he cheerfully. "We'll not touch shore for an hour, at least. And nobody's allowed aboard. You can keep to the cabin. I'll see that you're not bothered."

"And—this evening?"

"You can keep to the dressing-room until the show's over and the people've gone ashore. And tomorrow morning, bright and early, we'll be off. I promised Pat a day for a drunk at Sutherland. He'll have to postpone it. I'll give him three at Jeffersonville, instead."

Susan put on her sunbonnet as soon as the show boat rounded the bend above town. Thus she felt safe in staying on deck and watching the town drift by. She did not begin to think of going into the cabin until

Pat was working the boat in toward the landing a square above the old familiar wharf-boat. "What day is this?" she asked Eshwell.

"Saturday."

Only Saturday! And last Monday—less than five days ago—she had left this town for her Cincinnati adventure. She felt as if months, years, had passed. The town seemed strange to her, and she recalled the landmarks as if she were revisiting in age the scenes of youth. How small the town seemed, after Cincinnati! And how squat! Then——

She saw the cupola of the schoolhouse. Its rooms, the playgrounds flashed before her mind's eye—the teachers she had liked—those she had feared—the face of her uncle, so kind and loving—that same face, with hate and contempt in it——

She hurried into the cabin, tears blinding her eyes, her throat choked with sobs.

The Burlingham Floating Palace of Thespians tied up against the float of Bill Phibbs's boathouse—a privilege for which Burlingham had to pay two dollars. Pat went ashore with a sack of handbills to litter through the town. Burlingham followed, to visit the offices of the two evening newspapers and by "handing them out a line of smooth talk"—the one art whereof he was master—to get free advertising. Also there were groceries to buy and odds and ends of elastic, fancy crêpe, paper muslin and the like for repairing the shabby costumes. The others remained on board, Eshwell and Tempest to guard the boat against the swarms of boys darting and swooping and chattering like a huge flock of impudent English sparrows. An additional—and the chief—reason for Burlingham's keep-

ing the two actors close was that Eshwell was a drunkard and Tempest a gambler. Neither could be trusted
where there was the least temptation. Each despised the
other's vice and despised the other for being slave to
it. Burlingham could trust Eshwell to watch Tempest,
could trust Tempest to watch Eshwell.

Susan helped Mabel with the small and early supper
—cold chicken and ham, fried potatoes and coffee.
Afterward all dressed in the cabin. Some of the curtains for dividing off the berths were drawn, out of
respect to Susan not yet broken to the ways of a mode
of life which made privacy and personal modesty impossible—and when any human custom becomes impossible, it does not take human beings long to discover that it is also foolish and useless. The women
had to provide for a change of costumes. As the dressing-room behind the stage was only a narrow space
between the back drop and the forward wall of the
cabin, dressing in it was impossible, so Mabel and Vi
put on a costume of tights, and over it a dress. Susan
was invited to remain and help. The making-up of
the faces interested her; she was amazed by the transformation of Mabel into youthful loveliness, with a
dairy maid's bloom in place of her pallid pastiness.
On the other hand, make-up seemed to bring out the
horrors of Miss Anstruther's big, fat, yet hollow face,
and to create other and worse horrors—as if in covering her face it somehow uncovered her soul. When
the two women stripped and got into their tights,
Susan with polite modesty turned away. However,
catching sight of Miss Anstruther in the mirror that
had been hung up under one of the side lamps, she was
so fascinated that she gazed furtively at her by that
indirect way.

Violet happened to see, laughed. "Look at the baby's shocked face, Mabel," she cried.

But she was mistaken. It was sheer horror that held Susan's gaze upon Violet's incredible hips and thighs, violently obtruded by the close-reefed corset. Mabel had a slender figure, the waist too short and the legs too nearly of the same girth from hip to ankle, but for all that, attractive. Susan had never before seen a woman in tights without any sort of skirt.

"You would show up well in those things," Violet said to her, "that is, for a thin woman. The men don't care much for thinness."

"Not the clodhoppers and roustabouts that come to see us," retorted Mabel. "The more a woman looks like a cow or a sow, the better they like it. They don't believe it's female unless it looks like what they're used to in the barnyard and the cattle pen."

Miss Anstruther was not in the least offended. She paraded, jauntily switching her great hips and laughing. "Jealous!" she teased. "You poor little broomstick."

Burlingham was in a white flannel suit that looked well enough in those dim lights. The make-up gave him an air of rakish youth. Eshwell had got himself into an ordinary sack suit. Tempest was in the tattered and dirty finery of a seventeenth-century courtier. The paint and black made Eshwell's face fat and comic; it gave Tempest distinction, made his hollow blazing eyes brilliant and large. All traces of habitation were effaced from the "auditorium"; the lamps were lighted, a ticket box was set up on the rear deck and an iron bar was thrown half across the rear entrance to the cabin, that only one person at a time might be able to pass. The curtain was let down—a gaudy smear of a garden scene in a French palace in the eighteenth century. Pat, the orchestra, put on a dress coat and vest and a "dickey"; the coat had white celluloid cuffs pinned in the sleeves at the wrists.

As it was still fully an hour and a half from dark, Susan hid on the stage; when it should be time for the curtain to go up she would retreat to the dressing-room. Through a peephole in the curtain she admired the auditorium; and it did look surprisingly well by lamplight, with the smutches and faded spots on its bright paint softened or concealed. "How many will it hold?" she asked Mabel, who was walking up and down, carrying her long train.

"A hundred and twenty comfortably," replied Miss Connemora. "A hundred and fifty crowded. It has held as high as thirty dollars, but we'll be lucky if we get fifteen tonight."

Susan glanced round at her. She was smoking a cigarette, handling it like a man. Susan's expression was so curious that Mabel laughed. Susan, distressed, cried: "I'm sorry if—if I was impolite."

"Oh, you couldn't be impolite," said Mabel. "You've got that to learn, too—and mighty important it is. We all smoke. Why not? We got out of cigarettes, but Bob bought a stock this afternoon."

Susan turned to the peephole. Pat, ready to take tickets, was "barking" vigorously in the direction of shore, addressing a crowd which Susan of course could not see. Whenever he paused for breath, Burlingham leaned from the box and took it up, pouring out a stream of eulogies of his show in that easy, lightly cynical voice of his. And the audience straggled in— young fellows and their girls, roughs from along the river front, farmers in town for a day's sport. Susan did not see a single familiar face, and she had supposed she knew, by sight at least, everyone in Sutherland. From fear lest she should see someone she knew, her mind changed to longing. At last she was rewarded. Down the aisle swaggered Redney King, son of the washerwoman, a big hulking bully who used to tease her by pulling her hair during recess and by kicking at her shins when they happened to be next each other in the class standing in long line against the wall of the schoolroom for recitation. From her security she smiled at Redney as representative of all she loved in the old town.

And now the four members of the company on the stage and in the dressing-room lost their ease and contemptuous indifference. They had been talking sneeringly about "yokels" and "jays" and "slum bums." They dropped all that, as there spread over them the mysterious spell of the crowd. As individuals the provincials in those seats were ridiculous; as a mass they were an audience, an object of fear and awe. Mabel was almost in tears; Violet talked rapidly, with excited gestures and nervous adjustments of various parts of her toilet. The two men paced about, Eshwell trembling, Tempest with sheer fright in his rolling eyes. They wet their dry lips with dry tongues. Each again and again asked the other anxiously how he was looking and paced away without waiting for the answer. The suspense and nervous terror took hold of Susan; she stood in the corner of the dressing-room, pressing herself close against the wall, her fingers tightly interlocked and hot and cold tremors chasing up and down her body.

Burlingham left the box and combined Pat's duties with his own—a small matter, as the audience was seated and a guard at the door was necessary only to keep the loafers on shore from rushing in free. Pat advanced to the little space reserved before the stage, sat down and fell to tuning his violin with all the noise he could make, to create the illusion of a full orchestra. Miss Anstruther appeared in one of the forward side doors of the auditorium, very dignified in her black satin (paper muslin) dress, with many and sparkling hair and neck ornaments and rings that seemed alight. She bowed to the audience, pulled a little old cottage organ from under the stage and seated herself at it.

After the overture, a pause. Susan, peeping through a hole in the drop, saw the curtain go up, drew a long breath of terror as the audience was revealed beyond the row of footlights, beyond the big, befrizzled blond head of Violet and the drink-seared face of Pat. From the rear of the auditorium came Burlingham's smooth-flowing, faintly amused voice, announcing the beginning of the performance—"a delightful feast throughout, ladies and gentlemen, amusing yet elevating, ever moral yet with none of the depressing sadness of puritanism. For, ladies and gentlemen, while we are pious, we are not puritan. The first number is a monologue, 'The Mad Prince,' by that eminent artist, Gregory Tempest. He has delivered it before vast audiences amid thunders of applause."

Susan thrilled as Tempest strode forth—Tempest transformed by the footlights and by her young imagination into a true king most wonderfully and romantically bereft of reason by the woes that had assailed him in horrid phalanxes. If anyone had pointed out to her that Tempest's awful voice was simply cheap ranting, or that her own woes had been as terrible as any that had ever visited a king, or that when people go mad it is never from grief but from insides unromantically addled by foolish eating and drinking—if anyone had attempted then and there to educate the girl, how angry it would have made her, how she would have hated that well-meaning person for spoiling her illusion!

The spell of the stage seized her with Tempest's first line, first elegant despairing gesture. It held her through Burlingham and Anstruther's "sketch" of a matrimonial quarrel, through Connemora and Eshwell's "delicious symphonic romanticism" of a lovers' quarrel and making up, through Tempest's recitation of "Lasca," dying to shield her cowboy lover from the hoofs of the stampeded herd. How the tears did stream from Susan's eyes, as Tempest wailed out those last lines:

But I wonder why I do not care for the things that are
    like the things that were?
Can it be that half my heart lies buried there, in Texas
    down by the Rio Grande?

She saw the little grave in the desert and the vast blue sky and the buzzard sailing lazily to and fro, and it seemed to her that Tempest himself had inspired such a love, had lost a sweetheart in just that way. No wonder he looked gaunt and hollow-eyed and sallow. The last part of the performance was Holy Land and comic pictures thrown from the rear on a sheet substituted for the drop. As Burlingham had to work the magic lantern from the dressing-room (while Tempest, in a kind of monk's robe, used his voice and elocutionary powers in describing the pictures, now lugubriously and now in "lighter vein"), Susan was forced to retreat to the forward deck and missed that part of the show. But she watched Burlingham shifting the slides and altering the forms of the lenses, and was in another way as much thrilled and spellbound as by the acting.

Nor did the spell vanish when, with the audience gone, they all sat down to a late supper, and made coarse jests and mocked at their own doings and at the people who had applauded. Susan did not hear. She felt proud that she was permitted in so distinguished a company. Every disagreeable impression vanished. How could she have thought these geniuses common and cheap! How had she dared apply to them the standards of the people, the dull, commonplace people, among whom she had been brought up! If she could only qualify for membership in this galaxy! The thought made her feel like a worm aspiring to be a star. Tempest, whom she had liked least, now filled her with admiration. She saw the tragedy of his life plain and sad upon his features. She could not look at him without her heart's contracting in an ache.

It was not long before Mr. Tempest, who believed himself a lady-killer, noted the ingenuous look in the young girl's face, and began to pose. And it was hardly three bites of a ham sandwich thereafter when Mabel Connemora noted Tempest's shootings of his cuffs and rumplings of his oily ringlets and rollings of his hollow eyes. And at the sight Miss Mabel's bright eyes became bad and her tongue shot satire at him. But Susan did not observe this.

After supper they went straightway to bed. Burlingham drew the curtains round the berth let down for Susan. The others indulged in no such prudery on so hot a night. They put out the lamps and got ready for bed and into it by the dim light trickling in through the big rear doorway and the two small side doorways forward. To help on the circulation of air Pat raised the stage curtain and drop, and opened the little door forward. Each sleeper had a small netting suspended over him from the ceiling; without that netting the dense swarms of savage mosquitoes would have made sleep impossible. As it was, the loud singing of these baffled thousands kept Susan awake.

After a while, to calm her brain, excited by the evening's thronging impressions and by the new—or, rather, reviewed—ambitions born of them, Susan rose and went softly out on deck, in her nightgown of calico slip. Because of the breeze the mosquitoes did not trouble her there, and she stood a long time watching the town's few faint lights—watching the stars, the thronging stars of the Milky Way—dreaming—dreaming—dreaming. Yesterday had almost faded from her, for youth lives only in tomorrow—youth in tomorrow, age in yesterday, and none of us in today which is all we really have. And she, with her wonderful health of body meaning youth as long as it lasted, she would certainly be young until she was very old—would keep her youth—her dreams—her living always in tomorrow. She was dreaming of her first real tomorrow, now. She would work hard at this wonderful profession—*her* profession!—would be humble and attentive; and surely the day must come when she too would feel upon her heart the intoxicating beat of those magic waves of applause!

Susan, more excited than ever, slipped softly into the cabin and stole into her curtained berth. Like the soughing of the storm above the whimper of the tortured leaves the stentorian snorings of two of the sleepers resounded above the noise of the mosquitoes. She had hardly extended herself in her close little bed when she heard a stealthy step, saw one of her curtains drawn aside.

"Who is it?" she whispered, unsuspiciously, for she could see only a vague form darkening the space between the parted curtains.

The answer came in a hoarse undertone: "Ye dainty little darling!" She sat up, struck out madly, screamed at the top of her lungs. The curtains fell back into place, the snoring stopped. Susan, all in a sweat and a shiver, lay quiet. Hoarse whispering; then in Burlingham's voice—stern and gruff—"Get back to your bed and let her alone, you rolling-eyed——" The sentence ended with as foul a spatter of filth as man can fling at man. Silence again, and after a few minutes the two snores resumed their bass accompaniment to the falsetto of the mosquito chorus.

Susan got a little troubled sleep, was wide awake when Violet came saying, "If you want to bathe, I'll bring you a bucket of water and you can put up your berth and do it behind your curtains."

Susan thanked her and got a most refreshing bath. When she looked out the men were on deck, Violet was getting breakfast, and Connemora was combing her short, thinning, yellow hair before a mirror hung up near one of the forward doors. In the mirror Connemora saw her, smiled and nodded.

"You can fix your hair here," said she. "I'm about done. You can use my brush."

And when Susan was busy at the mirror, Mabel lounged on a seat near by smoking a before-breakfast cigarette. "I wish to God I had your hair," said she. "I never did have such a wonderful crop of grass on the knoll, and the way it up and drops out in bunches every now and then sets me crazy. It won't be long before I'll be down to Vi's three hairs and a half. You haven't seen her without her wigs? Well, don't, if you happen to be feeling a bit off. How Burlingham can—" There she stopped, blew out a volume of smoke, grinned half amusedly, half in sympathy with the innocence she was protecting—or, rather, was initiating by cautious degrees. "Who was it raised the row last night?" she inquired.

"I don't know," said Susan, her face hid by the mass of wavy hair she was brushing forward from roots to ends.

"You don't? I guess you've got a kind of idea, though."

No answer from the girl.

"Well, it doesn't matter. It isn't your fault." Mabel smoked reflectively. "I'm not jealous of *him*—a woman never is. It's the idea of another woman's getting away with her property, whether she wants it or not— *that's* what sets her mad-spot to humming. No, I don't give a—a cigarette butt—for that greasy bum actor. But I've always got to have somebody." She laughed. "The idea of his thinking *you'd* have *him!* What peacocks men are!"

Susan understood. The fact of this sort of thing was no longer a mystery to her. But the why of the fact—that seemed more amazing than ever. Now that she had discovered that her notion of love being incorporeal was as fanciful as Santa Claus, she could not conceive why it should be at all. As she was bringing round the braids for the new coiffure she had adopted she said to Mabel:

"You—love him?"

"I?" Mabel laughed immoderately. "You can have him, if you want him."

Susan shuddered. "Oh, no," she said. "I suppose he's very nice—and really he's quite a wonderful actor. But I—I don't care for men."

Mabel laughed again—curt, bitter. "Wait," she said.

Susan shook her head, with youth's positiveness.

"What's caring got to do with it?" pursued Mabel, ignoring the headshake. "I've been about quite a bit, and I've yet to see anybody that really cared for anybody else. We care for ourselves. But a man needs a woman, and a woman needs a man. They call it loving. They might as well call eating loving. Ask Burly."

XIV

AT breakfast Tempest was precisely as usual, and so were the others. Nor was there effort or any sort of pretense in this. We understand only that to which we are accustomed; the man of peace is amazed by the veteran's nonchalance in presence of danger and horror, of wound and death. To these river wanderers, veterans in the unconventional life, where the unusual is the usual, the unexpected the expected, whatever might happen was the matter of course, to be dealt with and dismissed. Susan naturally took her cue from them. When Tempest said something to her in the course of the careless conversation round the breakfast table, she answered—and had no sense of constraint. Thus, an incident that in other surroundings would have been in some way harmful through receiving the exaggeration of undue emphasis, caused less stir than the five huge and fiery mosquito bites Eshwell had got in the night. And Susan unconsciously absorbed one of those lessons in the science and art of living that have decisive weight in shaping our destinies. For intelligent living is in large part learning to ignore the unprofitable that one may concentrate upon the profitable.

Burlingham announced that they would cast off and float down to Bethlehem. There was a chorus of protests. "Why, we ought to stay here a week!" cried Miss Anstruther. "We certainly caught on last night."

"Didn't we take in seventeen dollars?" demanded

Eshwell. "We can't do better than that anywhere."

"Who's managing this show?" asked Burlingham in his suave but effective way. "I think I know what I'm about."

He met their grumblings with the utmost good-humor and remained inflexible. Susan listened with eyes down and burning cheeks. She knew Burlingham was "leaving the best cow unmilked," as Connemora put it, because he wished to protect her. She told him so when they were alone on the forward deck a little later, as the boat was floating round the bend below Suther-land.

"Yes," he admitted. "I've great hopes from your ballads. I want to get you on." He looked round casually, saw that no one was looking, drew a pecu-liarly folded copy of the *Sutherland Courier* from his pocket. "Besides"—said he, holding out the paper— "read that."

Susan read:

George Warham, Esq., requests us to announce that he has increased the reward for information as to the where-abouts of Mrs. Susan Ferguson, his young niece, née Susan Lenox, to one thousand dollars. There are grave fears that the estimable and lovely young lady, who disappeared from her husband's farm the night of her marriage, has, doubtless in a moment of insanity, ended her life. We hope not.

Susan lifted her gaze from this paragraph, after she had read it until the words ran together in a blur. She found Burlingham looking at her. Said he: "As I told you before, I don't want to know anything. But when I read that, it occurred to me, if some of the others saw it they might think it was you—and might do a dirty trick." He sighed, with a cynical little smile. "I was tempted, myself. A thousand is quite a bunch. You don't know—not yet—how a chance to make some money—any old way—compels a man—or a woman—when money's as scarce and as useful as it is in this world. As you get along, you'll notice, my dear, that the people who get moral goose flesh at the shady doings of others are always people who haven't ever really been up against it. I don't know why I didn't——" He shrugged his shoulders. "Now, my dear, you're in on the secret of why I haven't got up in the world." He smiled cheerfully. "But I may yet. The game's far from over."

She realized that he had indeed made an enormous sacrifice for her; for, though very ignorant about money, a thousand dollars seemed a fortune. She had no words; she looked away toward the emerald shore, and her eyes filled and her lip quivered. How much goodness there was in the world—how much generosity and affection!

"I'm not sure," he went on, "that you oughtn't to go back. But it's your own business. I've a kind of feeling you know what you're about."

"No matter what happens to me," said she, "I'll never regret what I've done. I'd kill myself before I'd spend another day with the man they made me marry."

"Well—I'm not fond of dying," observed Burlingham, in the light, jovial tone that would most quickly soothe her agitation, "but I think I'd take my chances with the worms rather than with the dry rot of a backwoods farm. You may not get your meals so regular out in the world, but you certainly do live. Yes—that backwoods life, for anybody with a spark of spunk, is simply being dead and knowing it." He tore the *Courier* into six pieces, flung them over the side. "None of the others saw the paper," said he. "So—Miss Lorna Sackville is perfectly safe." He patted her on the shoulder. "And she owes me a thousand and two dollars."

"I'll pay—if you'll be patient," said the girl, taking his jest gravely.

"It's a good gamble," said he. Then he laughed. "I guess that had something to do with my virtue. There's always a practical reason—always."

But the girl was not hearing his philosophies. Once more she was overwhelmed and stupefied by the events that had dashed in, upon, and over her like swift succeeding billows that give the swimmer no pause for breath or for clearing the eyes.

"No—you're not dreaming," said Burlingham, laughing at her expression. "At least, no more than we all are. Sometimes I suspect the whole damn shooting-match is nothing but a dream. Well, it's a pretty good one—eh?"

And she agreed with him, as she thought how smoothly and agreeably they were drifting into the unknown, full of the most fascinating possibilities. How attractive this life was, how much at home she felt among these people, and if anyone should tell him about her birth or about how she had been degraded by Ferguson, it wouldn't in the least affect their feeling toward her, she was sure. "When do—do you—try me?" she asked.

"Tomorrow night, at Bethlehem—a bum little town for us. We'll stay there a couple of days. I want you to get used to appearing." He nodded at her encouragingly. "You've got stuff in you, real stuff. Don't you doubt it. Get self-confidence—conceit, if you please. Nobody arrives anywhere without it. You want to feel that you can do what you want to do. A fool's conceit is that he's it already. A sensible man's conceit is that he can be it, if he'll only work hard and in the right way. See?"

"I—I think I do," said the girl. "I'm not sure."

Burlingham smoked his cigar in silence. When he spoke, it was with eyes carefully averted. "There's another subject the spirit moves me to talk to you about. That's the one Miss Connemora opened up with you yesterday." As Susan moved uneasily, "Now, don't get scared. I'm not letting the woman business bother me much nowadays. All I think of is how to get on my feet again. I want to have a theater on Broadway before the old black-flagger overtakes my craft and makes me walk the plank and jump out into the Big Guess. So you needn't think I'm going to worry you. I'm not."

"Oh, I didn't think——"

"You ought to have, though," interrupted he. "A man like me is a rare exception. I'm a rare exception to my ordinary self, to be quite honest. It'll be best for you always to assume that every man you run across is looking for just one thing. You know what?"

Susan, the flush gone from her cheeks, nodded.

"I suppose Connemora has put you wise. But there are some things even she don't know about that subject. Now, I want you to listen to your grandfather. Remember what he says. And think it over until you understand it."

"I will," said Susan.

"In the life you've come out of, virtue in a woman's everything. She's got to be virtuous, or at least to

236

have the reputation of it—or she's nothing. You understand that?"

"Yes," said Susan. "I understand that—now."

"Very well. Now, in the life you're going into, virtue in a woman is nothing—no more than it is in a man anywhere. Do you follow me?"

"I'm not sure," said the girl. "I'll have to think about it."

"That's right. Don't misunderstand. I'm not talking for or against virtue. I'm simply talking practical life, and all I mean is that you won't get on there by your virtue, and you won't get on by your lack of virtue. Now for my advice."

Susan's look of unconscious admiration and attention was the subtlest flattery. Its frank, ingenuous showing of her implicit trust in him so impressed him with his responsibility that he hesitated before he said:

"Never forget this, and don't stop thinking about it until you understand it: Make men *as* men incidental in your life, precisely as men who amount to anything make women *as* women incidental."

Her first sensation was obviously disappointing. She had expected something far more impressive. Said she:

"I don't care anything about men."

"Be sensible! How are you to know now what you care about and what you don't?" was Burlingham's laughing rebuke. "And in the line you've taken—the stage—with your emotions always being stirred up, with your thoughts always hovering round the relations of men and women—for that's the only subject of plays and music, and with opportunity thrusting at you as it never thrusts at conventional people—you'll probably soon find you care a great deal about men.

But don't ever let your emotions hinder or hurt or
destroy you. Use them to help you. I guess I'm shoot-
ing pretty far over that young head of yours, ain't I?"

"Not so very far," said the girl. "Anyhow, I'll
remember."

"If you live big enough and long enough, you'll go
through three stages. The first is the one you're in
now. They've always taught you, without realizing it,
and so you think, that only the strong can afford to do
right. You think doing right makes the ordinary
person, like yourself, easy prey for those who do wrong.
You think that good people—if they're really good—
have to wait until they get to Heaven before they get
a chance."

"Isn't that so?"

"No. But you'll not realize it until you pass into
the second stage. There, you'll think you see that only
the strong can afford to do wrong. You'll think that
everyone, except the strong, gets it in the neck if he
or she does anything out of the way. You'll think
you're being punished for your sins, and that, if you
had behaved yourself, you'd have got on much better.
That's the stage that's coming; and what you go
through with there—how you come out of the fight—
will decide your fate—show whether or not you've got
the real stuff in you. Do you understand?"

Susan shook her head.

"I thought not. You haven't lived long enough yet.
Well, I'll finish, anyhow."

"I'll remember," said Susan. "I'll think about it
until I do understand."

"I hope so. The weather and the scenery make me
feel like philosophizing. Finally, if you come through
the second stage all right, you'll enter the third stage.

There, you'll see that you were right at first when you thought only the strong could afford to do right. And you'll see that you were right in the second stage when you thought only the strong could afford to do wrong. For you'll have learned that only the strong can afford to act at all, and that they can do right or wrong as they please *because they are strong*."

"Then you don't believe in right, at all!" exclaimed the girl, much depressed, but whether for the right or for her friend she could not have told.

"Now, who said that?" demanded he, amused. "What *did* I say? Why—if you want to do right, be strong or you'll be crushed; and if you want to do wrong, take care again to be strong—or you'll be crushed. My moral is, be strong! In this world the good weaklings and the bad weaklings had better lie low, hide in the tall grass. The strong inherit the earth." They were silent a long time, she thinking, he observing her with sad tenderness. At last he said:

"You are a nice sweet girl—well brought up. But that means badly brought up for the life you've got to lead—the life you've got to learn to lead."

"I'm beginning to see that," said the girl. Her gravity made him feel like laughing, and brought the tears to his eyes. The laughter he suppressed.

"You're going to fight your way up to what's called the triumphant class—the people on top—they have all the success, all the money, all the good times. Well, the things you've been taught—at church—in the Sunday School—in the nice story-books you've read—those things are all for the triumphant class, or for people working meekly along in 'the station to which God has appointed them' and handing over their earnings to their betters. But those nice moral things you believe in—they don't apply to people like you—fighting their way up from the meek working class to the triumphant class. You won't believe me now—won't understand thoroughly. But soon you'll see. Once you've climbed up among the successful people you can afford to indulge—in moderation—in practicing the good old moralities. Any dirty work you may need done you can hire done and pretend not to know about it. But while you're climbing, no Golden Rule and no turning of the cheek. Tooth and claw then—not sheathed but naked—not by proxy, but in your own person."

"But you're not like that," said the girl.

"The more fool I," repeated he.

She was surprised that she understood so much of what he had said—childlike wonder at her wise old heart, made wise almost in a night—a wedding night. When Burlingham lapsed into silence, laughing at himself for having talked so far over the "kiddie's" head, she sat puzzling out what he had said. The world seemed horribly vast and forbidding, and the sky, so blue and bright, seemed far, far away. She sighed profoundly. "I am so weak," she murmured. "I am so ignorant."

Burlingham nodded and winked. "Yes, but you'll grow," said he. "I back you to win."

The color poured into her cheeks, and she burst into tears. Burlingham thought he understood; for once his shrewdness went far astray. Excusably, since he could not know that he had used the same phrase that had closed Spenser's letter to her.

Late in the afternoon, when the heat had abated somewhat and they were floating pleasantly along with the washing gently a-flutter from lines on the roof of the auditorium, Burlingham put Eshwell at the rudder and with Pat and the violin rehearsed her. "The main thing, the only thing to worry about," explained he, "is beginning right." She was standing in the center of the stage, he on the floor of the auditorium beside the seated orchestra. "That means," he went on, "you've simply got to learn to come in right. We'll practice that for a while."

She went to the wings—where there was barely space for her to conceal herself by squeezing tightly against the wall. At the signal from him she walked out. As she had the utmost confidence in his kindness, and as she was always too deeply interested in what she and others were doing to be uncomfortably self-conscious, she was not embarrassed, and thought she made the crossing and took her stand very well. He nodded approvingly. "But," said he, "there's a difference between a stage walk and walking anywhere else—or standing. Nothing is natural on the stage. If it were it would look unnatural, because the stage itself is artificial and whatever is there must be in harmony with it. So everything must be done unnaturally in such a way that it *seems* natural. Just as a picture boat looks natural though it's painted on a flat surface. Now I'll illustrate."

He gave her his hand to help her jump down; then he climbed to the stage. He went to the wings and walked out. As he came he called her attention to how he poised his body, how he advanced so that there would be from the auditorium no unsightly view of crossing legs, how he arranged hands, arms, shoulders, legs, head, feet for an attitude of complete rest. He repeated his illustration again and again, Susan watching and listening with open-eyed wonder and admiration. She had never dreamed that so simple a matter could be so complex. When he got her up beside him and went through it with her, she soon became as used to the new motions as a beginner at the piano to stretching an octave. But it was only after more than an hour's practice that she moved him to say:

"That'll do for a beginning. Now, we'll sing."

She tried "Suwanee River" first and went through it fairly well, singing to him as he stood back at the rear door. He was enthusiastic—cunning Burlingham, who knew so well how to get the best out of everyone! "Mighty good—eh, Pat? Yes, mighty good. You've got something better than a great voice, my dear. You've got magnetism. The same thing that made me engage you the minute you asked me is going to make you—well, go a long ways—a *long* ways. Now, we'll try 'The Last Rose of Summer.' "

She sang even better. And this improvement continued through the other four songs of her repertoire. His confidence in her was contagious; it was so evident that he really did believe in her. And Pat, too, wagged his head in a way that made her feel good about herself. Then Burlingham called in the others whom he had sent to the forward deck. Before them the girl went all to pieces. She made her entrance badly, she sang worse. And the worse she sang, the worse she felt and the worse her next attempt was. At last, with nerves unstrung, she broke down and sobbed. Burlingham climbed up to pat her on the shoulder.

"That's the best sign yet," said he. "It shows you've got temperament. Yes—you've got the stuff in you."

He quieted her, interested her in the purely mechanical part of what she was doing. "Don't think of who you're doing it before, or of how you're doing it, but only of getting through each step and each note. If your head's full of that, you'll have no room for fright." And she was ready to try again. When she finished the last notes of "Suwanee River," there was an outburst of hearty applause. And the sound that pleased her most was Tempest's rich rhetorical "Bravo!" As a man she abhorred him; but she respected the artist. And in unconsciously drawing this distinction she gave proof of yet another quality that was to count heavily in the coming days. Artist he was not. But she thought him an artist. A girl or boy without the intelligence that can develop into flower and fruit would have seen and felt only Tempest, the odious personality.

Burlingham did not let her off until she was ready to drop with exhaustion. And after supper, when they were floating slowly on, well out of the channel where they might be run down by some passing steamer with a flint-hearted captain or pilot, she had to go at it again. She went to bed early, and she slept without a motion or a break until the odor of the cooking breakfast awakened her. When she came out, her face was bright for the first time. She was smiling, laughing, chatting, was delighted with everything and everybody. Even the thought of Roderick Spenser laid up with a broken leg recurred less often and less vividly. It seemed to her that the leg must be about well. The imagination of healthy youth is reluctant to admit ideas of gloom in any circumstances. In circumstances of excitement and adventure, such as Susan's at that time, it flatly refuses to admit them.

They were at anchor before a little town sprawled upon the fields between hills and river edge. A few loafers were chewing tobacco and inspecting the show boat from the shady side of a pile of lumber. Pat had already gone forth with the bundle of handbills; he was not only waking up the town, but touring the country in horse and buggy, was agitating the farmers —for the show boat was to stay at least two nights at Bethlehem. "And we ought to do pretty well," said Burlingham. "The wheat's about all threshed, and there's a kind of lull. The hayseeds aren't so dead tired at night. A couple of weeks ago we couldn't have got half a house by paying for it."

As the afternoon wore away and the sun disappeared behind the hills to the southwest, Susan's spirits oozed. Burlingham and the others—deliberately—paid no attention to her, acted as if no great, universe-stirring event were impending. Immediately after supper Burlingham said:

"Now, Vi, get busy and put her into her harness. Make her a work of art."

Never was there a finer display of unselfishness than in their eagerness to help her succeed, in their intense nervous anxiety lest she should not make a hit. The bad in human nature, as Mabel Connemora had said, is indeed almost entirely if not entirely the result of the cumpulsion of circumstances; the good is the natural outcropping of normal instincts, and resumes control whenever circumstances permit. These wandering players had suffered too much not to have the keenest and gentlest sympathy. Susan looked on Tempest as a wicked man; yet she could not but be touched by his almost hysterical excitment over her début, when the near approach of the hour made it impossible for his emotional temperament longer to hide its agitation. Every one of them gave or loaned her a talisman—Tempest, a bit of rabbit's foot; Anstruther, a ring that had twice saved her from drowning (at least, it had been on her finger each time); Connemora, a hunchback's tooth on a faded velvet string; Pat, a penny which happened to be of the date of her birth year (the presence of the penny was regarded by all as a most encouraging sign); Eshwell loaned her a minature silver bug he wore on his watch chain; Burlingham's contribution was a large buckeye—— "Ever since I've had that, I've never been without at least the price of a meal in my pocket."

They had got together for her a kind of evening dress, a pale blue chiffon-like drapery that left her lovely arms and shoulders bare and clung softly to the lines of her figure. They did her hair up in a graceful sweep from the brow and a simple coil behind. She looked like a woman, yet like a child dressed as a woman, too, for there was as always that exuberant vitality which made each of the hairs of her head seem individual, electric. The rouge gave her color, enhanced into splendor the brilliance of her violet-gray eyes—eyes so intensely colored and so admirably framed that they were noted by the least observant. When Anstruther had put the last touches to her toilet and paraded her to the others, there was a chorus of enthusiasm. The men no less than the women viewed her with the professional eye.

"Didn't I tell you all," cried Burlingham, as they looked her up and down like a group of connoisseurs inspecting a statue. "Wasn't I right?"

"'It is the dawn, and Juliet is the east,'" orated Tempest in rich, romantic tones.

"A damn shame to waste her on these yaps," said Eshwell.

Connemora embraced her with tearful eyes. "And

as sweet as you are lovely, you dear!" she cried. "You simply can't help winning."

The two women thought her greatest charms were her form and her feet and ankles. The men insisted that her charm of charms was her eyes. And certainly, much could be said for that view. Susan's violet-gray eyes, growing grayer when she was thoughtful, growing deeper and clearer and softer, shining violet when her emotions were touched—Susan's eyes were undoubtedly unusual even in a race in which homely eyes are the exception.

When it was her turn and she emerged into the glare of the footlights, she came to a full stop and an awful wave of weakness leaped up through legs and body to blind her eyes and crash upon her brain. She shook her head, lifted it high like a swimmer shaking off a wave. Her gaze leaped in terror across the blackness of the auditorium with its thick-strewn round white disks of human faces, sought the eyes of Burlingham standing in full view in the center of the rear doorway —where he had told her to look for him. She heard Pat playing the last of the opening chords; Burlingham lifted his hand like a leader's baton. And naturally and sweetly the notes, the words of the old darkey song of longing for home began to float out through the stillness.

She did not take her gaze from Burlingham. She sang her best, sang to please him, to show him how she appreciated what he had done for her. And when she fininshed and bowed, the outburst of applause unnerved her, sent her dizzy and almost staggering into the wings. "Splendid! Splendid!" cried Mabel, and Anstruther embraced her, and Tempest and Eshwell kissed her hands. They all joined in pushing her out again for the encore—"Blue Alsatian Mountains." She did not sing quite so steadily, but got through in good form, the tremolo of nervousness in her voice adding to the wailing pathos of the song's refrain:

Adé, adé, adé, such dreams must pass away,
But the Blue Alsatian Mountains seem to watch and wait
    alway.

The crowd clapped, stamped, whistled, shouted; but Burlingham defied it. "The lady will sing again later," he cried. "The next number on the regular program is," etc., etc. The crowd yelled; Burlingham stood firm, and up went the curtain on Eshwell and Connemora's sketch. It got no applause. Nor did any other numbers on the program. The contrast between the others and the beauty of the girl, her delicate sweetness, her vital youth, her freshness of the early morning flower, was inevitable.

The crowd could think only of her. The quality of magnetism aside, she had sung neither very well nor very badly. But had she sung badly, still her beauty would have won her the same triumph. When she came on for her second number with a cloud-like azure chiffon flung carelessly over her dark hair as a scarf, Spanish fashion, she received a stirring welcome. It frightened her, so that Pat had to begin four times before her voice faintly took up the tune. Again Burlingham's encouraging, confident gaze, flung across the gap between them like a strong rescuing hand, strengthened her to her task. This time he let the crowd have two encores—and the show was over; for the astute manager, seeing how the girl had caught on, had moved her second number to the end.

Burlingham lingered in the entrance to the auditorium to feast himself on the comments of the crowd as it passed out. When he went back he had to search for the girl, found her all in a heap in a chair at the outer edge of the forward deck. She was sobbing piteously. "Well, for God's sake!" cried he. "Is *this* the way you take it!"

She lifted her head. "Did I do very badly?" she asked.

"You swept 'em off their big hulking feet," replied he.

"When you didn't come, I thought I'd disappointed you."

"I'll bet my hand there never was such a hit made in a river show boat—and they've graduated some of the swells of the profession. We'll play here a week to crowded houses—matinées every day, too. And this is a two-night stand usually. I must find some more songs." He slapped his thigh. "The very thing!" he cried. "We'll ring in some hymns. 'Rock of Ages,' say—and 'Jesus, Lover of my Soul'—and you can get 'em off in a churchy kind of costume—something like a surplice. That'll knock 'em stiff. And Anstruther can dope out the accompaniments on that wheezer. What d'you think?"

"Whatever you want," said the girl. "Oh, I am so glad!"

"I don't see how you got through so well," said he.

"I didn't dare fail," replied Susan. "If I had, I couldn't have faced you." And by the light of the waning moon he saw the passionate gratitude of her sensitive young face.

"Oh—I've done nothing," said he, wiping the tears

from his eyes—for he had his full share of the impulsive, sentimental temperament of his profession. "Pure selfishness."

Susan gazed at him with eyes of the pure deep violet of strongest feeling. "*I* know what you did," she said in a low voice. "And—I'd die for you."

Burlingham had to use his handkerchief in dealing with his eyes now. "This business has given me hysterics," said he, with a queer attempt at a laugh. Then, after a moment, "God bless you, little girl. You wait here a moment. I'll see how supper's getting on."

He wished to go ahead of her, for he had a shrewd suspicion as to the state of mind of the rest of the company. And he was right. There they sat in the litter of peanut hulls, popcorn and fruit skins which the audience had left. On every countenance was jealous gloom.

"What's wrong?" inquired Burlingham in his cheerful, derisive way. "You are a nice bunch, you are!"

They shifted uneasily. Mabel snapped out, "Where's the infant prodigy? Is she so stuck on herself already that she won't associate with us?"

"You grown-up babies," mocked Burlingham. "I found her out there crying in darkness because she thought she'd failed. Now, you go bring her in, Conny. As for the rest of you, I'm disgusted. Here we've hit on something that'll land us in Easy Street, and you're all filled up with poison."

They were ashamed of themselves. Burlingham had brought back to them vividly the girl's simplicity and sweetness that had won their hearts, even the hearts of the women in whom jealousy of her young beauty would have been more than excusable. Anstruther began to get out the supper dishes, and Mabel slipped away toward the forward deck. "When the child comes in," pursued Burlingham, "I want to see you people looking and acting human."

"We are a lot of damn fools," admitted Eshwell. "That's why we're bum actors instead of doing well at some respectable business."

And his jealousy went the way of Violet's and Mabel's. Pat began to remember that he had shared in the triumph—where would she have been without his violin work? But Tempest remained somber. In his case better nature was having a particularly hard time of it. His vanity had got savage wounds from the hoots and the "Oh, bite it off, hamfat," which had greeted his impressive lecture on the magic lantern pictures. He eyed Burlingham glumly. He exonerated the girl, but not Burlingham. He was convinced that the manager, in a spirit of mean revenge, had put up a job on him. It simply could not be in the ordinary course that any audience, without some sly trickery of prompting from an old expert of theatrical "double-crossing," would be impatient for a mere chit of an amateur when it might listen to his rich, mellow eloquence.

Susan came shyly—and at the first glance into her face her associates despised themselves for their pettiness. It is impossible for envy and jealousy and hatred to stand before the light of such a nature as Susan's. Away from her these very human friends of hers might hate her—but in her presence they could not resist the charm of her sincerity.

Everyone's spirits went up with the supper. It was Pat who said to Burlingham, "Bob, we're going to let the pullet in on the profits equally, aren't we?"

"Sure," replied Burlingham. "Anybody kicking?"

The others protested enthusiastically—except Tempest, who shot a glance of fiery scorn at Burlıngham over a fork laden with potato salad. "Then—you're elected, Miss Sackville," said Burlingham.

Susan's puzzled eyes demanded an explanation. "Just this," said he. "We divide equally at the end of the trip all we've raked in, after the rent of the boat and expenses are taken off. You get your equal share exactly as if you started with us."

"But that wouldn't be fair," protested the girl. "I must pay what I owe you first."

"She means two dollars she borrowed of me at Carrollton," explained Burlingham. And they all laughed uproariously.

"I'll only take what's fair," said the girl.

"I vote we give it all to her," rolled cut Tempest in tragedy's tone for classic satire.

Before Mabel could hurl at him the probably coarse retort she instantly got her lips ready to make, Burlingham's cool, peace-compelling tones broke in:

"Miss Sackville's right. She must get only what's fair. She shares equally from tonight on—less two dollars."

Susan nodded delightedly. She did not know—and the others did not at the excited moment recall—that the company was to date eleven dollars less well off than when it started from the headwaters of the Ohio in early June. But Burlingham knew, and that was the cause of the quiet grin to which he treated himself.

XV

BURLINGHAM had lived too long, too actively, and too intelligently to have left any of his large, original stock of the optimism that had so often shipwrecked his career in spite of his talents and his energy. Out of the bitterness of experience he used to say, "A young optimist is a young fool. An old optimist is an old ass. A fool may learn, an ass can't." And again, "An optimist steams through the fog, taking it for granted everything's all right. A pessimist steams ahead too, but he gets ready for trouble." However, he was wise enough to keep his private misgivings and reservations from his associates; the leaders of the human race always talk optimism and think pessimism. He had told the company that Susan was sure to make a go; and after she had made a go, he announced the beginning of a season of triumph. But he was surprised when his prediction came true and they had to turn people away from the next afternoon's performance. He began to believe they really could stay a week, and hired a man to fill the streets of New Washington and other inland villages and towns of the county with a handbill headlining Susan.

The news of the lovely young ballad singer in the show boat at Bethlehem spread, as interesting news ever does, and down came the people to see and hear, and to go away exclaiming. Bethlehem, the sleepy, showed that it could wake when there was anything worth waking for. Burlingham put on the hymns in

252

the middle of the week, and even the clergy sent their families. Every morning Susan, either with Mabel or with Burlingham, or with both, took a long walk into the country. It was Burlingham, by the way, who taught her the necessity of regular and methodical long walks for the preservation of her health. When she returned there was always a crowd lounging about the landing waiting to gape at her and whisper. It was intoxicating to her, this delicious draught of the heady wine of fame; and Burlingham was not unprepared for the evidences that she thought pretty well of herself, felt that she had arrived. He laughed to himself indulgently. "Let the kiddie enjoy herself," thought he. "She needs the self-confidence now to give her a good foundation to stand on. Then when she finds out what a false alarm this jay excitement was, she'll not be swept clean away into despair."

The chief element in her happiness, he of course knew nothing about. Until this success—which she, having no basis for comparison, could not but exaggerate—she had been crushed and abused more deeply than she had dared admit to herself by her birth which made all the world scorn her and by the series of calamities climaxing in that afternoon and night of horror at Ferguson's. This success—it seemed to her to give her the right to have been born, the right to live on and hold up her head without effort after Ferguson. "I'll show them all, before I get through," she said to herself over and over again. "They'll be proud of me. Ruth will be boasting to everyone that I'm her cousin. And Sam Wright—he'll wonder that he ever dared touch such a famous, great woman." She only half believed this herself, for she had much common sense and small self-confidence. But pretending that she believed it all gave her the most delicious pleasure.

Burlingham took such frank joy in her innocent vanity—so far as he understood it and so far as she exhibited it—that the others were good-humored about it too—all the others except Tempest, whom conceit and defeat had long since soured through and through. A tithe of Susan's success would have made him unbearable, for like most human beings he had a vanity that was Atlantosaurian on starvation rations and would have filled the whole earth if it had been fed a few crumbs. Small wonder that we are ever eagerly on the alert for signs of vanity in others; we are seeking the curious comfort there is in the feeling that others have our own weakness to a more ridiculous degree. Tempest twitched to jeer openly at Susan, whose exhibition was really timid and modest and not merely excusable but justifiable. But he dared go no further than holding haughtily aloof and casting vaguely into the air ever and anon a tragic sneer. Susan would not have understood if she had seen, and did not see. She was treading the heights, her eyes upon the sky. She held grave consultation with Burlingham, with Violet, with Mabel, about improving her part. She took it all very, very seriously—and Burlingham was glad of that. "Yes, she does take herself seriously," he admitted to Anstruther. "But that won't do any harm as she's so young, and as she takes her work seriously, too. The trouble about taking oneself seriously is it stops growth. She hasn't got that form of it."

"Not yet," said Violet.

"She'll wake from her little dream, poor child, long before the fatal stage." And he heaved a sigh for his own lost illusions—those illusions that had cost him so dear.

Burlingham had intended to make at least one stop before Jeffersonville, the first large town on the way down. But Susan's capacities as a house-filler decided him for pushing straight for it. "We'll go where there's a big population to be drawn on," said he. But he did not say that in the back of his head there was forming a plan to take a small theater at Jeffersonville if the girl made a hit there.

Eshwell, to whom he was talking, looked glum. "She's going pretty good with these greenies," observed he. "But I've my doubts whether city people'll care for anything so milk-like."

Burlingham had his doubts, too; but he retorted warmly: "Don't you believe it, Eshie. City's an outside. Underneath, there's still the simple, honest, grassy-green heart of the country."

Eshwell laughed. "So you've stopped jeering at jays. You've forgotten what a lot of tightwads and petty swindlers they are. Well, I don't blame you. Now that they're giving down to us so freely, I feel better about them myself. It's a pity we can't lower the rest of the program to the level of their intellectuals."

Burlingham was not tactless enough to disturb Eshwell's consoling notion that while Susan was appreciated by these ignorant country-jakes, the rest of the company were too subtle and refined in their art. "That's a good idea," replied he. "I'll try to get together some simple slop. Perhaps a melodrama, a good hot one, would go—eh?"

After ten days the receipts began to drop. On the fifteenth day there was only a handful at the matinée, and in the evening half the benches were empty. "About milked dry," said Burlingham at the late supper. "We'll move on in the morning."

This pleased everyone. Susan saw visions of bigger triumphs; the others felt that they were going where dramatic talent, not to say genius, would be at least not entirely unappreciated. So the company was at its liveliest next morning as the mosquito-infested willows of the Bethlehem shore slowly dropped away. They had made an unusually early start, for the river would be more and more crowded as they neared the three close-set cities—Louisville, Jeffersonville, and New Albany, and the helpless little show boat must give the steamers no excuse for not seeing her. All day—a long, dreamy, summer day—they drifted lazily downstream, and, except Tempest, all grew gayer and more gay. Burlingham had announced that there were three hundred and seventy-eight dollars in the japanned tin box he kept shut up in his bag.

At dusk a tug, for three dollars, nosed them into a wharf which adjoined the thickly populated labor quarter of Jeffersonville.

Susan was awakened by a scream. Even as she opened her eyes a dark cloud, a dull suffocating terrifying pain, descended upon her. When she again became conscious, she was lying upon a mass of canvas on the levee with three strange men bending over her. She sat up, instinctively caught together the front of the nightdress she had bought in Bethlehem the second day there. Then she looked wildly from face to face.

"You're all right, ma'am," said one of the men. "Not a scratch—only stunned."

"What was it?" said the girl. "Where are they?"

As she spoke, she saw Burlingham in his nightshirt propped against a big blue oil barrel. He was staring stupidly at the ground. And now she noted the others scattered about the levee, each with a group around him or her. "What was it?" she repeated.

"A tug butted its tow of barges into you," said someone. "Crushed your boat like an eggshell."

Burlingham staggered to his feet, stared round, saw her. "Thank God!" he cried. "Anyone drowned? Anyone hurt?"

"All saved—no bones broken," someone responded.

"And the boat?"

"Gone down. Nothing left of her but splinters. The barges were full of coal and building stone."

"The box!" suddenly shouted Burlingham. "The box!"

"What kind of a box?" asked a boy with lean, dirty, and much scratched bare legs. "A little black tin box like they keep money in?"

"That's it. Where is it?"

"It's all right," said the boy. "One of your people, a black actor-looking fellow——"

"Tempest," interjected Burlingham. "Go on."

"He dressed on the wharf and he had the box."

"Where is he?"

"He said he was going for a doctor. Last I seed of him he was up to the corner yonder. He was movin' fast."

Burlingham gave a kind of groan. Susan read in his face his fear, his suspicion—the suspicion he was ashamed of himself for having. She noted vaguely that he talked with the policeman aside for a few minutes, after which the policeman went up the levee. Burling-

ham rejoined his companions and took command. The
first thing was to get dressed as well as might be from
such of the trunks as had been knocked out of the cabin
by the barge and had been picked up. They were all
dazed. Even Burlingham could not realize just what
had occurred. They called to one another more or less
humorous remarks while they were dressing behind piles
of boxes, crates, barrels and sacks in the wharf-boat.
And they laughed gayly when they assembled. Susan
made the best appearance, for her blue serge suit had
been taken out dry when she herself was lifted from the
sinking wreck; the nightgown served as a blouse.
Mabel's trunk had been saved. Violet could wear none
of her things, as they were many sizes too small, so she
appeared in a property skirt of black paper muslin, a
black velvet property basque, a pair of shoes belonging
to Tempest. Burlingham and Eshwell made a fairly
respectable showing in clothing from Tempest's trunk.
Their own trunks had gone down.

"Why, where's Tempest?" asked Eshwell.

"He'll be back in a few minutes," replied Burlingham.
"In fact, he ought to be back now." His glance happened to meet Susan's; he hastily shifted his eyes.

"Where's the box?" asked Violet.

"Tempest's taking care of it," was the manager's
answer.

"Tempest!" exclaimed Mabel. Her shrewd, dissipated eyes contracted with suspicion.

"Anybody got any money?" inquired Eshwell, as he
fished in his pockets.

No one had a cent. Eshwell searched Tempest's
trunk, found a two-dollar bill and a one wrapped round
a silver dollar and wadded in among some ragged underclothes. Susan heard Burlingham mutter "Won-

258

der how he happened to overlook that!" But no one else heard.

"Well, we might have breakfast," suggested Mabel.

They went out on the water deck of the wharf-boat, looked down at the splinters of the wreck lying in the deep yellow river. "Come on," said Burlingham, and he led the way up the levee. There was no attempt at jauntiness; they all realized now.

"How about Tempest?" said Eshwell, stopping short halfway up.

"Tempest—hell!" retorted Mabel. "Come on."

"What do you mean?" cried Violet, whose left eye was almost closed by a bruise.

"We'll not see him again. Come on."

"Bob!" shrieked Violet at Burlingham. "Do you hear that?"

"Yes," said he. "Keep calm, and come on."

"Aren't you going to *do* anything?" she screamed, seizing him by the coat tail. "You must, damn it— you must!"

"I got the policeman to telephone headquarters," said Burlingham. "What else can be done? Come on."

And a moment later the bedraggled and dejected company filed into a cheap levee restaurant. "Bring some coffee," Burlingham said to the waiter. Then to the others, "Does anybody want anything else?" No one spoke. "Coffee's all," he said to the waiter.

It came, and they drank it in silence, each one's brain busy with the disaster from the standpoint of his own resulting ruin. Susan glanced furtively at each face in turn. She could not think of her own fate, there was such despair in the faces of these others. Mabel looked like an old woman. As for Violet, every feature of her homeliness, her coarseness, her dissipated premature old age stood forth in all its horror. Susan's heart contracted and her flesh crept as she glanced quickly away. But she still saw, and it was many a week before she ceased to see whenever Violet's name came into her mind. Burlingham, too, looked old and broken. Eshwell and Pat, neither of whom had ever had the smallest taste of success, were stolid, like cornered curs taking their beating and waiting in silence for the blows to stop.

"Here, Eshie," said the manager, "take care of the three dollars." And he handed him the bills. "I'll pay for the coffee and keep the change. I'm going down to the owners of that tug and see what I can do."

When he had paid they followed him out. At the curbstone he said, "Keep together somewhere round the wharf-boat. So long." He lifted the battered hat he was wearing, smiled at Susan. "Cheer up, Miss Sackville. We'll down 'em yet!" And away he went—a strange figure, his burly frame squeezed into a dingy old frock suit from among Tempest's costumes.

A dreary two hours, the last half-hour in a drizzling rain from which the narrow eaves of the now closed and locked wharf-boat sheltered them only a little. "There he comes!" cried Susan; and sure enough, Burlingham separated from the crowd streaming along the street at the top of the levee, and began to descend the slope toward them. They concentrated on his face, hoping to get some indication of what to expect; but he never permitted his face to betray his mind. He strode up the plank and joined them.

"Tempest come?" he asked.

"Tempest!" cried Mabel. "Haven't I told you he's jumped? Don't you suppose *I* know him?"

"And you brought him into the company," raged

260

Violet. "Burlingham didn't want to take him. He looked the fool and jackass he is. Why didn't you warn us he was a rotten thief, too?"

"Wasn't it for shoplifting you served six months in Joliet?" retorted Mabel.

"You lie—you streetwalker!" screamed Violet.

"Ladies! Ladies!" said Eshwell.

"That's what *I* say," observed Pat.

"I'm no lady," replied Mabel. "I'm an actress."

"An actress—he-he!" jeered Violet. "An actress!"

"Shut up, all of you," commanded Burlingham. "I've got some money. I settled for cash."

"How much?" cried Mabel and Violet in the same breath, their quarrel not merely finished but forgotten.

"Three hundred dollars."

"For the boat and all?" demanded Eshwell. "Why, Bob——"

"They think it was for boat and all," interrupted Burlingham with his cynical smile. "They set out to bully and cheat me. They knew I couldn't get justice. So I let 'em believe I owned the boat—and I've got fifty apiece for us."

"Sixty," said Violet.

"Fifty. There are six of us."

"You don't count in this little Jonah here, do you?" cried Violet, scowling evilly at Susan.

"No—no—don't count me in," begged Susan. "I didn't lose anything."

Mabel pinched her arm. "You're right, Mr. Burlingham," said she. "Miss Sackville ought to share. We're all in the same box."

"Miss Sackville will share," said Burlingham. "There's going to be no skunking about this, as long as I'm in charge."

Eshwell and Pat sided with Violet. While the rain streamed, the five, with Susan a horrified onlooker, fought on and on about the division of the money. Their voices grew louder. They hurled the most frightful epithets at one another. Violet seized Mabel by the hair, and the men interfered, all but coming to blows themselves in the mêlée. The wharfmaster rushed from his office, drove them off to the levee. They continued to yell and curse, even Burlingham losing control of himself and releasing all there was of the tough and the blackguard in his nature. Two policemen came, calmed them with threat of arrest. At last Burlingham took from his pocket one at a time three small rolls of bills. He flung one at each of the three who were opposing his division. "Take that, you dirty curs," he said. "And be glad I'm giving you anything at all. Most managers wouldn't have come back. Come on, Miss Sackville. Come on, Mabel." And the two followed him up the levee, leaving the others counting their shares.

At the street corner they went into a general store where Burlingham bought two ninety-eight-cent umbrellas. He gave Mabel one, held the other over Susan and himself as they walked along. "Well, ladies," said he, "we begin life again. A clean slate, a fresh start —as if nothing had ever happened."

Susan looked at him to try to give him a grateful and sympathetic smile. She was surprised to see that, so far as she could judge, he had really meant the words he had spoken.

"Yes, I mean it," said he. "Always look at life as it is—as a game. With every deal, whether you win or lose, your stake grows—for your stake's your wits, and you add to 'em by learning something with each deal. What are you going to do, Mabel?"

"Get some clothes. The water wrecked mine and this rain has finished my hat."

"We'll go together," said Burlingham.

They took a car for Louisville, descended before a department store. Burlingham had to fit himself from the skin out; Mabel had underclothes, needed a hat, a dress, summer shoes. Susan needed underclothes, shoes, a hat, for she was bareheaded. They arranged to meet at the first entrance down the side street; Burlingham gave Susan and Mabel each their fifty dollars and went his way. When they met again in an hour and a half, they burst into smiles of delight. Burlingham had transformed himself into a jaunty, fashionable young middle-aged man, with an air of success achieved and prosperity assured. He had put the fine finishing touch to his transformation by getting a haircut and a shave. Mabel looked like a showy chorus girl, in a striped blue and white linen suit, a big beflowered hat, and a fluffy blouse of white chiffon. Susan had resisted Mabel's entreaties, had got a plain, sensible linen blouse of a kind that on a pinch might be washed out and worn without ironing. Her new hat was a simple blue sailor with a dark blue band that matched her dress.

"I spent thirty-six dollars," said Burlingham.

"I only spent twenty-two," declared Mabel. "And this child here only parted with seven of her dollars. I had no idea she was so thrifty."

"And now—what?" said Burlingham.

"I'm going round to see a friend of mine," replied Mabel. "She's on the stage, too. There's sure to be something doing at the summer places. Maybe I can ring Miss Sackville in. There ought to be a good living in those eyes of hers and those feet and ankles. I'm sure I can put her next to something."

"Then you can give her your address," said Burlingham.

"Why, she's going with me," cried Mabel. "You don't suppose I'd leave the child adrift?"

"No, she's going with me to a boarding house I'll find for her," said Burlingham.

Into Mabel's face flashed the expression of the suspicion such a statement would at once arouse in a mind trained as hers had been. Burlingham's look drove the expression out of her face, and suspicion at least into the background. "She's not going with your friend," said Burlingham, a hint of sternness in his voice. "That's best—isn't it?"

Miss Connemora's eyes dropped. "Yes, I guess it is," replied she. "Well—I turn down this way."

"We'll keep on and go out Chestnut Street," said Burlingham. "You can write to her—or to me—care of the General Delivery."

"That's best. You may hear from Tempest. You can write me there, too." Mabel was constrained and embarrassed. "Good-by, Miss Sackville."

Susan embraced and kissed her. Mabel began to weep. "Oh, it's all so sudden—and frightful," she said. "Do try to be good, Lorna. You can trust Bob." She looked earnestly, appealingly, at him. "Yes, I'm sure you can. And—he's right about me. Good-by." She hurried away, not before Susan had seen the tears falling from her kind, fast-fading eyes.

Susan stood looking after her. And for the first time the truth about the catastrophe came to her. She turned to Burlingham. "How brave you are!" she cried.

"Oh, what'd be the use in dropping down and howling like a dog?" replied he. "That wouldn't bring the boat back. It wouldn't get me a job."

"And you shared equally, when you lost the most of all."

They were walking on. "The boat was mine, too," said he in a dry reflective tone. "I told 'em it wasn't when we started out because I wanted to get a good share for rent and so on, without any kicking from anybody."

The loss did not appeal to her; it was the lie he had told. She felt her confidence shaking. "You didn't mean to—to——" she faltered, stopped.

"To cheat them?" suggested he. "Yes, I did. So— to sort of balance things up I divided equally all I got from the tug people. What're you looking so unhappy about?"

"I wish you hadn't told me," she said miserably. "I don't see why you did."

"Because I don't want you making me into a saint. I'm like the rest you see about in pants, cheating and lying, with or without pretending to themselves that they're honest. Don't trust anybody, my dear. The sooner you get over the habit, the sooner you'll cease to tempt people to be hypocrites. All the serious trouble I've ever got into has come through trusting or being trusted."

He looked gravely at her, burst out laughing at her perplexed, alarmed expression. "Oh, Lord, it isn't as bad as all that," said he. "The rain's stopped. Let's have breakfast. Then—a new deal—with everything to gain and nothing to lose. It's a great advantage to be in a position where you've got nothing to lose!"

XVI

BURLINGHAM found for her a comfortable room in a flat in West Chestnut Street—a respectable middle-class neighborhood with three churches in full view and the spires of two others visible over the housetops. Her landlady was Mrs. Redding, a simple-hearted, deaf old widow with bright kind eyes beaming guilelessness through steel-framed spectacles. Mrs. Redding had only recently been reduced to the necessity of letting a room. She stated her moderate price—seven dollars a week for room and board—as if she expected to be arrested for attempted extortion. "I give good meals," she hastened to add. "I do the cooking myself—and buy the best. I'm no hand for canned stuff. As for that there cold storage, it's no better'n slow poison, and not so terrible slow at that. Anything your daughter wants I'll give her."

"She's not my daughter," said Burlingham, and it was his turn to be red and flustered. "I'm simply looking after her, as she's alone in the world. I'm going to live somewhere else. But I'll come here for meals, if you're willing, ma'am."

"I—I'd have to make that extry, I'm afraid," pleaded Mrs. Redding.

"Rather!" exclaimed Burlingham. "I eat like a pair of Percherons."

"How much did you calculate to pay?" inquired the widow. Her one effort at price fixing, though entirely successful, had exhausted her courage.

Burlingham was clear out of his class in those idyllic

days of protector of innocence. He proceeded to be more than honest.

"Oh, say five a week."

"Gracious! That's too much," protested she. "I hate to charge a body for food, somehow. It don't seem to be accordin' to what God tells us. But I don't see no way out."

"I'll come for five—not a cent less," insisted Burlingham. "I want to feel free to eat as much as I like." And it was so arranged. Away he went to look up his acquaintances, while Susan sat listening to the widow and trying to convince her that she and Mr. Burlingham didn't want and couldn't possibly eat all the things she suggested as suitable for a nice supper. Susan had been learning rapidly since she joined the theatrical profession. She saw why this fine old woman was getting poorer steadily, was arranging to spend her last years in an almshouse. What a queer world it was! What a strange way for a good God to order things! The better you were, the worse off you were. No doubt it was Burlingham's lifelong goodness of heart as shown in his generosity to her, that had kept him down. It was the same way with her dead mother—she had been loving and trusting, had given generously without thought of self, with generous confidence in the man she loved—and had paid with reputation and life.

She compelled Burlingham to take what was left of her fifty dollars. "You wouldn't like to make me feel mean," was the argument she used. "I must put in what I've got—the same as you do. Now, isn't that fair?" And as he was dead broke and had been unable to borrow, he did not oppose vigorously.

She assumed that after a day or two spent in getting his bearings he would take her with him as he went looking. When she suggested it, he promptly vetoed it. "That isn't the way business is done in the profession," said he. "The star—you're the star—keeps in the background, and her manager—that's me—does the hustling."

She had every reason for believing this; but as the days passed with no results, sitting about waiting began to get upon her nerves. Mrs. Redding had the remnant of her dead husband's library, and he had been a man of broad taste in literature. But Susan, ardent reader though she was, could not often lose herself in books now. She was too impatient for realities, too anxious about them.

Burlingham remained equable, neither hopeful nor gloomy; he made her feel that he was strong, and it gave her strength. Thus she was not depressed when on the last day of their week he said: "I think we'd better push on to Cincinnati tomorrow. There's nothing here, and we've got to get placed before our cash gives out. In Cincinnati there are a dozen places to one in this snide town."

The idea of going to Cincinnati gave her a qualm of fear; but it passed away when she considered how she had dropped out of the world. "They think I'm dead," she reflected. "Anyhow, I'd never be looked for among the kind of people I'm in with now." The past with which she had broken seemed so far away and so dim to her that she could not but feel it must seem so to those who knew her in her former life. She had such a sense of her own insignificance, now that she knew something of the vastness and business of the world, that she was without a suspicion of the huge scandal and excitement her disappearance had caused in Sutherland.

To Cincinnati they went next day by the L. and N. and took two tiny rooms in the dingy old Walnut Street House, at a special rate—five dollars a week for the two, as a concession to the profession. "We'll eat in cheap restaurants and spread our capital out," said Burlingham. "I want you to get placed *right,* not just placed." He bought a box of blacking and a brush, instructed her in the subtle art of making a front—an art whereof he was past master, as Susan had long since learned. "Never let yourself look poor or act poor, until you simply have to throw up the sponge," said he. "The world judges by appearances. Put your first money and your last into clothes. And never—never—tell a hard-luck story. Always seem to be doing well and comfortably looking out for a chance to do better. The whole world runs from seedy people and whimperers."

"Am I—that way?" she asked nervously.

"Not a bit," declared he. "The day you came up to me in Carrollton I knew you were playing in the hardest kind of hard luck because of what I had happened to see and hear—and guess. But you weren't looking for pity—and that was what I liked. And it made me feel you had the stuff in you. I'd not waste breath teaching a whiner or a cheap skate. You couldn't be cheap if you tried. The reason I talk to you about these things is so you'll learn to put the artistic touches by instinct into what you do."

"You've taken too much trouble for me," said the girl.

"Don't you believe it, my dear," laughed he. "If I can do with you what I hope—I've an instinct that if I win out for you, I'll come into my own at last."

"You've taught me a lot," said she.

"I wonder," replied he. "That is, I wonder how much you've learned. Perhaps enough to keep you— not to keep from being knocked down by fate, but to get on your feet afterward. I hope so—I hope so."

They dropped coffee, bought milk by the bottle, he smuggling it to their rooms disguised as a roll of newspapers. They carried in rolls also, and cut down their restaurant meals to supper which they got for twenty-five cents apiece at a bakery restaurant in Seventh Street. There is a way of resorting to these little economies—a snobbish, self-despairing way—that makes them sordid and makes the person indulging in them sink lower and lower. But Burlingham could not have taken that way. He was the adventurer born, was a hardy seasoned campaigner who had never looked on life in the snob's way, had never felt the impulse to apologize for his defeats or to grow haughty over his successes. Susan was an apt pupil; and for the career that lay before her his instructions were invaluable. He was teaching her how to keep the craft afloat and shipshape through the worst weather that can sweep the sea of life.

"How do you make yourself look always neat and clean?" he asked.

She confessed: "I wash out my things at night and hang them on the inside of the shutters to dry. They're ready to wear again in the morning."

"Getting on!" cried he, full of admiration. "They simply can't down us, and they might as well give up trying."

"But I don't look neat," sighed she. "I can't iron."

"No—that's the devil of it," laughed he. He pulled aside his waistcoat and she saw he was wearing a dickey.

"And my cuffs are pinned in," he said. "I have to be careful about raising and lowering my arms."

"Can't I wash out some things for you?" she said, then hurried on to put it more strongly. "Yes, give them to me when we get back to the hotel."

"It does help a man to feel he's clean underneath. And we've got nothing to waste on laundries."

"I wish I hadn't spent that fifteen cents to have my heels straightened and new steels put in them." She had sat in a cobbler's while this repair to the part of her person she was most insistent upon had been effected.

He laughed. "A good investment, that," said he. "I've been noticing how you always look nice about the feet. Keep it up. The surest sign of a sloven and a failure, of a moral, mental, and physical no-good is down-at-the-heel. Always keep your heels straight, Lorna."

And never had he given her a piece of advice more to her liking. She thought she knew now why she had always been so particular about her boots and shoes, her slippers and her stockings. He had given her a new confidence in herself—in a strength within her somewhere beneath the weakness she was always seeing and feeling.

Not until she thought it out afterward did she realize what they were passing through, what frightful days of failure he was enduring. He acted like the steady-nerved gambler at life that he was. He was not one of those more or less weak losers who have to make desperate efforts to conceal a fainting heart. His heart was not fainting. He simply played calmly on, feeling that the next throw was as likely to be for as against him. She kept close to her room, walking about there

—she had never been much of a sitter—thinking, practicing the new songs he had got for her—character songs in which he trained her as well as he could without music or costume or any of the accessories. He also had an idea for a church scene, with her in a choir boy's costume, singing the most moving of the simple religious songs to organ music. She from time to time urged him to take her on the rounds with him. But he stood firm, giving always the same reason of the custom in the profession. Gradually, perhaps by some form of that curious process of infiltration that goes on between two minds long in intimate contact, the conviction came to her that the reason he alleged was not his real reason; but as she had absolute confidence in him she felt that there was some good reason or he would not keep her in the background—and that his silence about it must be respected. So she tried to hide from him how weary and heartsick inaction was making her, how hard it was for her to stay alone so many hours each day.

As he watched her closely, it soon dawned on him that something was wrong, and after a day or so he worked out the explanation. He found a remedy—the reading room of the public library where she could make herself almost content the whole day long.

He began to have a haggard look, and she saw he was sick, was keeping up his strength with whisky. "It's only this infernal summer cold I caught in the smashup," he explained. "I can't shake it, but neither can it get me down. I'd not dare fall sick. What'd become of *us?*"

She knew that "us" meant only herself. Her mind had been aging rapidly in those long periods of unbroken reflection. To develop a human being, leave him or her alone most of the time; it is too much company, too little time to digest and assimilate, that keep us thoughtless and unformed until life is half over. She astonished him by suddenly announcing one evening:

"I am a drag on you. I'm going to take a place in a store."

He affected an indignation so artistic that it ought to have been convincing. "I'm ashamed of you!" he cried. "I see you're losing your nerve."

This was ingenious, but it did not succeed. "You can't deceive me any longer," was her steady answer. "Tell me—honest—couldn't you have got something to do long ago, if it hadn't been for trying to do something for me?"

"Sure," replied he, too canny to deny the obvious. "But what has that to do with it? If I'd had a living offer, I'd have taken it. But at my age a man doesn't dare take certain kinds of places. It'd settle him for life. And I'm playing for a really big stake—and I'll win. When I get what I want for you, we'll make as much money a month as I could make a year. Trust me, my dear."

It was plausible; and her "loss of nerve" was visibly aggravating his condition—the twitching of hands and face, the terrifying brightness of his eyes, of the color in the deep hollows under his cheek bones. But she felt that she must persist. "How much money have we got?" she asked.

"Oh—a great deal—enough."

"You must play square with me," said she. "I'm not a baby, but a woman—and your partner."

"Don't worry me, child. We'll talk about it to-morrow."

"How much? You've no right to hide things from me. You—hurt me."

"Eleven dollars and eighty cents—when this bill for supper's paid and the waitress tipped."

"I'll try for a place in a store," said she.

"Don't talk that way or think that way," cried he angrily. "There's where so many people fail in life. They don't stick to their game. I wish to God I'd had sense enough to break straight for Chicago or New York. But it's too late now. What I lack is nerve— nerve to do the big, bold things my brains show me I ought."

His distress was so obvious that she let the subject drop. That night she lay awake as she had fallen into the habit of doing. But instead of purposeless, rambling thoughts, she was trying definitely to plan a search for work. Toward three in the morning she heard him tossing and muttering—for the wall between their rooms was merely plastered laths covered with paper. She tried his door; it was locked. She knocked, got no answer but incoherent ravings. She roused the office, and the night porter forced the door. Burlingham's gas was lighted; he was sitting up in bed—a haggard, disheveled, insane man, raving on and on—names of men and women she had never heard—oaths, disjointed sentences.

"Brain fever, I reckon," said the porter. "I'll call a doctor."

In a few minutes Susan was gladdened by the sight of a young man wearing the familiar pointed beard and bearing the familiar black bag. He made a careful examination, asked her many questions, finally said:

"Your father has typhoid, I fear. He must be taken to a hospital."

"But we have very little money," said Susan.

"I understand," replied the doctor, marveling at the

calmness of one so young. "The hospital I mean is free. I'll send for an ambulance."

While they were waiting beside Burlingham, whom the doctor had drugged into unconsciousness with a hypodermic, Susan said: "Can I go to the hospital and take care of him?"

"No," replied the doctor. "You can only call and inquire how he is, until he's well enough to see you."

"And how long will that be?"

"I can't say." He hadn't the courage to tell her it would be three weeks at least, perhaps six or seven.

He got leave of the ambulance surgeon for Susan to ride to the hospital, and he went along himself. As the ambulance sped through the dimly lighted streets with clanging bell and heavy pounding of the horse's hoofs on the granite pavement, Susan knelt beside Burlingham, holding one of his hot hands. She was remembering how she had said that she would die for him—and here it was he that was dying for her. And her heart was heavy with a load of guilt, the heaviest she was ever to feel in her life. She could not know how misfortune is really the lot of human beings; it seemed to her that a special curse attended her, striking down all who befriended her.

They dashed up to great open doors of the hospital. Burlingham was lifted, was carried swiftly into the receiving room. Susan with tearless eyes bent over, embraced him lingeringly, kissed his fiery brow, his wasted cheeks. One of the surgeons in white duck touched her on the arm.

"We can't delay," he said.

"No indeed," she replied, instantly drawing back.

She watched the stretcher on wheels go noiselessly down the corridor toward the elevator and when it was gone she still continued to look. "You can come at any hour to inquire," said the young doctor who had accompanied her. "Now we'll go into the office and have the slip made out."

They entered a small room, divided unequally by a barrier desk; behind it stood a lean, coffee-sallowed young man with a scrawny neck displayed to the uttermost by a standing collar scarcely taller than the band of a shirt. He directed at Susan one of those obtrusively shrewd glances which shallow people practice and affect to create the impression that they have a genius for character reading. He drew a pad of blank forms toward him, wiped a pen on the mat into which his mouse-colored hair was roached above his right temple. "Well, miss, what's the patient's name?"

"Robert Burlingham."

"Age?"

"I don't know."

"About what?"

"I—I don't know. I guess he isn't very young. But I don't know."

"Put down forty, Sim," said the doctor.

"Very well, Doctor Hamilton." Then to Susan: "Color white, I suppose. Nativity?"

Susan recalled that she had heard him speak of Liverpool as his birthplace. "English," said she.

"Profession?"

"Actor."

"Residence?"

"He hasn't any. It was sunk at Jeffersonville. We stop at the Walnut Street House."

"Walnut Street House. Was he married or single?"

"Single." Then she recalled some of the disconnected ravings. "I—I—don't know."

"Single," said the clerk. "No, I guess I'll put it widower. Next friend or relative?"

"I am."

"Daughter. First name?"

"I am not his daughter."

"Oh, niece. Full name, please."

"I am no relation—just his—his friend."

Sim the clerk looked up sharply. Hamilton reddened, glowered at him. "I understand," said Sim, leering at her. And in a tone that reeked insinuation which quite escaped her, he went on, "We'll put your name down. What is it?"

"Lorna Sackville."

"You don't look English—not at all the English style of beauty, eh—Doctor?"

"That's all, Miss Sackville," said Hamilton, with a scowl at the clerk. Susan and he went out into Twelfth Street. Hamilton from time to time stole a glance of sympathy and inquiry into the sad young face, as he and she walked eastward together. "He's a strong man and sure to pull through," said the doctor. "Are you alone at the hotel?"

"I've nobody but him in the world," replied she.

"I was about to venture to advise that you go to a boarding house," pursued the young man.

"Thank you. I'll see."

"There's one opposite the hospital—a reasonable place."

"I've got to go to work," said the girl, to herself rather than to him.

"Oh, you have a position."

Susan did not reply, and he assumed that she had.

"If you don't mind, I'd like to call and see—Mr. Burlingham. The physicians at the hospital are perfectly competent, as good as there are in the city. But I'm not very busy, and I'd be glad to go."

"We haven't any money," said the girl. "And I don't know when we shall have. I don't want to deceive you."

"I understand perfectly," said the young man, looking at her with interested but respectful eyes. "I'm poor, myself, and have just started."

"Will they treat him well, when he's got no money?"

"As well as if he paid."

"And you will go and see that everything's all right?"

"It'll be a pleasure."

Under a gas lamp he took out a card and gave it to her. She thanked him and put it in the bosom of her blouse where lay all the money they had—the eleven dollars and eighty cents. They walked to the hotel, as cars were few at that hour. He did all the talking—assurances that her "father" could not fail to get well, that typhoid wasn't anything like the serious disease it used to be, and that he probably had a light form of it. The girl listened, but her heart could not grow less heavy. As he was leaving her at the hotel door, he hesitated, then asked if she wouldn't let him call and take her to the hospital the next morning, or, rather, later that same morning. She accepted gratefully; she hoped that, if he were with her, she would be admitted to see Burlingham and could assure herself that he was well taken care of.

The night porter tried to detain her for a little chat. "Well," said he, "it's a good hospital—for you folks with money. Of course, for us poor people it's different. You couldn't hire *me* to go there."

Susan turned upon him. "Why not?" she asked.

"Oh, if a man's poor, or can't pay for nice quarters,

they treat him any old way. Yes, they're good doctors and all that. But they're like everybody else. They don't give a darn for poor people. But your uncle'll be all right there."

For the first time in her life Susan did not close her eyes in sleep.

The young doctor was so moved by her worn appearance that he impulsively said: "Have you some troubles you've said nothing about? Please don't hesitate to tell me."

"Oh, you needn't worry about me," replied she. "I simply didn't sleep—that's all. Do they treat charity patients badly at the hosiptal?"

"Certainly not," declared he earnestly. "Of course, a charity patient can't have a room to himself. But that's no disadvantage."

"How much is a room?"

"The cheapest are ten dollars a week. That includes private attendance—a little better nursing than the public patients get—perhaps. But, really—Miss Sackville——"

"He must have a room," said Susan.

"You are sure you can afford it? The difference isn't——"

"He must have a room." She held out a ten-dollar bill—ten dollars of the eleven dollars and eighty cents. "This'll pay for the first week. You fix it, won't you?"

Young Doctor Hamilton hesitatingly took the money. "You are quite, quite sure, Miss Sackville?—Quite sure you can afford this extravagance—for it is an extravagance."

"He must have the best we can afford," evaded she. She waited in the office while Hamilton went up.

When he came down after perhaps half an hour, he had an air of cheerfulness. "Everything going nicely," said he.

Susan's violet-gray eyes gazed straight into his brown eyes; and the brown eyes dropped. "You are not telling me the truth," said she.

"I'm not denying he's a very sick man," protested Hamilton.

"Is he——"

She could not pronounce the word.

"Nothing like that—believe me, nothing. He has the chances all with him."

And Susan tried to believe. "He will have a room?"

"He has a room. That's why I was so long. And I'm glad he has—for, to be perfectly honest, the attendance—not the treatment, but the attendance—is much better for private patients."

Susan was looking at the floor. Presently she drew a long breath, rose. "Well, I must be going," said she. And she went to the street, he accompanying her.

"If you're going back to the hotel," said he, "I'm walking that way."

"No, I've got to go this way," replied she, looking up Elm Street.

He saw she wished to be alone, and left her with the promise to see Burlingham again that afternoon and let her know at the hotel how he was getting on. He went east, she north. At the first corner she stopped, glanced back to make sure he was not following. From her bosom she drew four business cards. She had taken the papers from the pockets of Burlingham's clothes and from the drawer of the table in his room, to put them all together for safety; she had found these cards, the addresses of theatrical agents. As she looked at them, she remembered Burlingham's having said that Blynn—Maurice Blynn, at Vine and Ninth Streets— might give them something at one of the "over the Rhine" music halls, as a last resort. She noted the address, put away the cards and walked on, looking about for a policeman. Soon she came to a bridge over a muddy stream—a little river, she thought at first, then remembered that it must be the canal—the Rhine, as it was called, because the city's huge German population lived beyond it, keeping up the customs and even the language of the fatherland. She stood on the bridge, watching the repulsive waters from which arose the stench of sewage; watching canal boats dragged drearily by mules with harness-worn hides; followed with her melancholy eyes the course of the canal under bridge after bridge, through a lane of dirty, noisy factories pouring out from lofty chimneys immense clouds of black smoke. It ought to have been a bright summer day, but the sun shone palely through the dense clouds; a sticky, sooty moisture saturated the air, formed a skin of oily black ooze over everything exposed to it. A policeman, a big German, with stupid honest face, brutal yet kindly, came lounging along.

"I beg your pardon," said Susan, "but would you mind telling me where—" she had forgotten the address, fumbled in her bosom for the cards, showed him Blynn's card—"how I can get to this?"

The policeman nodded as he read the address. "Keep on this way, lady"—he pointed his baton south—"until you've passed four streets. At the fifth street turn east. Go one—two—three—four—five streets east. Understand?"

"Yes, thank you," said the girl with the politeness of deep gratitude.

"You'll be at Vine. You'll see the name on the street lamp. Blynn's on the southwest corner. Think you can find it?"

"I'm sure I can."

"I'm going that way," continued the policeman. "But you'd better walk ahead. If you walked with me, they'd think you was pinched—and we'd have a crowd after us." And he laughed with much shaking of his fat, tightly belted body.

Susan contrived to force a smile, though the suggestion of such a disgraceful scene made her shudder. "Thank you so much. I'm sure I'll find it." And she hastened on, eager to put distance between herself and that awkward company.

"Don't mention it, lady," the policeman called after her, tapping his baton on the rim of his helmet, as a mark of elegant courtesy.

She was not at ease until, looking back, she no longer saw the bluecoat for the intervening crowds. After several slight mistakes in the way, she descried ahead of her a large sign painted on the wall of a three-story brick building:

MAURICE BLYNN, THEATRICAL AGENT
ALL KINDS OF TALENT PLACED AND SUPPLIED

After some investigation she discovered back of the saloon which occupied the street floor a grimy and uneven wooden staircase leading to the upper stories. At the first floor she came face to face with a door on the glass of which was painted the same announcement she had read from the wall. She knocked timidly, then louder. A shrill voice came from the interior:

"The door's open. Come in."

She turned the knob and entered a small, low-ceilinged room whose general grime was streaked here and there with smears of soot. It contained a small wooden table at which sprawled a freckled and undernourished office boy, and a wooden bench where fretted a woman obviously of "the profession." She was dressed in masses of dirty white furbelows. On her head reared a big hat, above an incredible quantity of yellow hair; on the hat were badly put together plumes of badly curled ostrich feathers. Beneath her skirt was visible one of her feet; it was large and fat, was thrust into a tiny slipper with high heel ending under the arch of the foot. The face of the actress was young and pertly pretty, but worn, overpainted, overpowdered and underwashed. She eyed Susan insolently.

"Want to see the boss?" said the boy.

"If you please," murmured Susan.

"Business?"

"I'm looking for a—for a place."

The boy examined her carefully. "Appointment?"

"No, sir," replied the girl.

"Well—he'll see you, anyhow," said the boy, rising.

The mass of plumes and yellow bangs and furbelows on the bench became violently agitated. "I'm first," cried the actress.

"Oh, you sit tight, Mame," jeered the boy. He opened a solid door behind him. Through the crack Susan saw busily writing at a table desk a bald, fat man with a pasty skin and a veined and bulbous nose.

"Lady to see you," said the boy in a tone loud enough for both Susan and the actress to hear.

"Who? What name?" snapped the man, not ceasing or looking up.

"She's young, and a queen," said the boy. "Shall I show her in?"

"Yep."

The actress started up. "Mr. Blynn——" she began in a loud, threatening, elocutionary voice.

" 'Lo, Mame," said Blynn, still busy. "No time to see you. Nothing doing. So long."

"But, Mr. Blynn——"

"Bite it off, Mame," ordered the boy. "Walk in, miss."

Susan, deeply colored from sympathy with the humiliated actress and from nervousness in those forbidding and ominous surroundings, entered the private office. The boy closed the door behind her. The pen scratched on. Presently the man said:

"Well, my dear, what's your name?"

With the last word, the face lifted and Susan saw a seamed and pitted skin, small pale blue eyes showing the white, or rather the bloodshot yellow all round the iris, a heavy mouth and jaw, thick lips; the lower lip protruded and was decorated with a blue-black spot like a blood boil, as if to indicate where the incessant cigar usually rested. At first glance into Susan's sweet, young face the small eyes sparkled and danced, traveled on to the curves of her form.

"Do sit down, my dear," said he in a grotesquely wheedling voice. She took the chair close to him as it was the only one in the little room.

"What can I do for you? My, how fresh and pretty you are!"

"Mr. Burlingham——" began Susan.

"Oh—you're the girl Bob was talking about." He smiled and nodded at her. "No wonder he kept you out of sight." He inventoried her charms again with his sensual, confident glance. "Bob certainly has got good taste."

284

"He's in the hospital," said Susan desperately. "So I've come to get a place if you can find me one."

"Hospital? I'm sorry to hear that." And Mr. Blynn's tones had that accent of deep sympathy which get a man or woman without further evidence credit for being "kind-hearted whatever else he is."

"Yes, he's very ill—with typhoid," said the girl. "I must do something right away to help him."

"That's fine—fine," said Mr. Blynn in the same effective tone. "I see you're as sweet as you are pretty. Yes—that's fine—fine!" And the moisture was in the little eyes. "Well, I think I can do something for you. I *must* do something for you. Had much experience?— Professional, I mean."

Mr. Blynn laughed at his, to Susan, mysterious joke. Susan smiled faintly in polite response. He rubbed his hands and smacked his lips, the small eyes dancing. The moisture had vanished.

"Oh, yes, I can place you, if you can do anything at all," he went on. "I'd 'a' done it long ago, if Bob had let me see you. But he was too foxy. He ought to be ashamed of himself, standing in the way of your getting on, just out of jealousy. Sing or dance—or both?"

"I can sing a little, I think," said Susan.

"Now, that's modest. Ever worn tights?"

Susan shook her head, a piteous look in her violet-gray eyes.

"Oh, you'll soon get used to that. And mighty well you'll look in 'em, I'll bet, eh? Where did Bob get you? And when?" Before she could answer, he went on, "Let's see, I've got a date for this evening, but I'll put it off. And she's a peach, too. So you see what a hit you've made with me. We'll have a nice

285

little dinner at the Hotel du Rhine and talk things over."

"Couldn't I go to work right away?" asked the girl.

"Sure. I'll have you put on at Schaumer's tomorrow night——" He looked shrewdly, laughingly, at her, with contracted eyelids. "*If* everything goes well. Before I do anything for you, I have to see what you can do for me." And he nodded and smacked his lips. "Oh, we'll have a lovely little dinner!" He looked expectantly at her. "You certainly are a queen! What a dainty little hand!" He reached out one of his hands—puffy as if it had been poisoned, very white, with stubby fingers. Susan reluctantly yielded her hand to his close, mushy embrace. "No rings. That's a shame, petty——" He was talking as if to a baby.—"That'll have to be fixed—yes, it will, my little sweetie. My, how nice and fresh you are!" And his great nostrils, repulsively hairy within, deeply pitted without, sniffed as if over an odorous flower.

Susan drew her hand away. "What will they give me?" she asked.

"How greedy it is!" he wheedled. "Well, you'll get plenty—plenty."

"How much?" said the girl. "Is it a salary?"

"Of course, there's the regular salary. But that won't amount to much. You know how those things are."

"How much?"

"Oh, say a dollar a night—until you make a hit."

"Six dollars a week."

"Seven. This is a Sunday town. Sunday's the big day. You'll have Wednesday, Saturday and Sunday matinées, but they don't pay for them."

"Seven dollars a week." And the hospital wanted

ten. "Couldn't I get—about fifteen—or fourteen? I think I could do on fourteen."

"Rather! I was talking only of the salary. You'll make a good many times fifteen—if you play your cards right. It's true Schaumer draws only a beer crowd. But as soon as the word flies round that *you're* there, the boys with the boodle'll flock in. Oh, you'll wear the sparklers all right, pet."

Rather slowly it was penetrating to Susan what Mr. Blynn had in mind. "I'd—I'd rather take a regular salary," said she. "I must have ten a week for him. I can live any old way."

"Oh, come off!" cried Mr. Blynn with a wink. "What's your game? Anyhow, don't play it on me. You understand that you can't get something for nothing. It's all very well to love your friend and be true to him. But he can't expect—he'll not ask you to queer yourself. That sort of thing don't go in the profession. . . . Come now, I'm willing to set you on your feet, give you a good start, if you'll play fair with me —show appreciation. Will you or won't you?"

"You mean——" began Susan, and paused there, looking at him with grave questioning eyes.

His own eyes shifted. "Yes, I mean that. I'm a business man, not a sentimentalist. I don't want love. I've got no time for it. But when it comes to giving a girl of the right sort a square deal and a good time, why you'll find I'm as good as there is going." He reached for her hands again, his empty, flabby chin bags quivering. "I want to help Bob, and I want to help you."

She rose slowly, pushing her chair back. She understood now why Burlingham had kept her in the background, why his quest had been vain, why it had fretted him into mortal illness. "I—couldn't do that," she said. "I'm sorry, but I couldn't."

He looked at her in a puzzled way. "You belong to Bob, don't you?"

"No."

"You mean you're straight—a good girl?"

"Yes."

He was half inclined to believe her, so impressive was her quiet natural way, in favorable contrast to the noisy protests of women posing as virtuous. "Well— if that's so—why you'd better drop out of the profession—and get away from Bob Burlingham."

"Can't I have a place without—what you said?"

"Not as pretty a girl as you. And if they ain't pretty the public don't want 'em."

Susan went to the door leading into the office. "No —the other door," said Blynn hastily. He did not wish the office boy to read his defeat in Susan's countenance. He got up himself, opened the door into the hall. Susan passed out. "Think it over," said he, eyes and mouth full of longing. "Come round in a day or two, and we'll have another talk."

"Thank you," said Susan. She felt no anger against him. She felt about him as she had about Jeb Ferguson. It was not his fault; it was simply the way life was lived—part of the general misery and horror of the established order—like marriage and the rest of it.

"I'll treat you white," urged Blynn, tenderly. "I've got a soft heart—that's why I'll never get rich. Any of the others'd ask more and give less."

She looked at him with an expression that haunted him for several hours. "Thank you. Good-by," she said, and went down the narrow, rickety stairs—and out into the confused maze of streets full of strangers.

XVII

AT the hotel again, she went to Burlingham's room, gathered his belongings—his suit, his well-worn, twice-tapped shoes, his one extra suit of underclothes, a soiled shirt, two dickeys and cuffs, his whisk broom, toothbrush, a box of blacking, the blacking brush. She made the package as compact as she could —it was still a formidable bundle both for size and weight—and carried it into her room. Then she rolled into a small parcel her own possessions—two blouses, an undervest, a pair of stockings, a nightgown—reminder of Bethlehem and her brief sip at the cup of success—a few toilet articles. With the two bundles she descended to the office.

"I came to say," she said calmly to the clerk, "that we have no money to pay what we owe. Mr. Burlingham is at the hospital—very sick with typhoid. Here is a dollar and eighty cents. You can have that, but I'd like to keep it, as it's all we've got."

The clerk called the manager, and to him Susan repeated. She used almost the same words; she spoke in the same calm, monotonous way. When she finished, the manager, a small, brisk man with a large brisk beard, said:

"No. Keep the money. I'd like to ask you to stay on. But we run this place for a class of people who haven't much at best and keep wobbling back and forth across the line. If I broke my rule——"

He made a furious gesture, looked at the girl angrily—holding her responsible for his being in a posi-

tion where he must do violence to every decent instinct
—"My God, miss, I've got a wife and children to look
after. If I ran my hotel on sympathy, what'd become
of them?"

"I wouldn't take anything I couldn't pay for," said
Susan. "As soon as I earn some money——"

"Don't worry about that," interrupted the manager.
He saw now that he was dealing with one who would in
no circumstances become troublesome; he went on in
an easier tone: "You can stay till the house fills up."

"Could you give me a place to wait on table and
clean up rooms—or help cook?"

"No, I don't need anybody. The town's full of people out of work. You can't ask me to turn away——"

"Please—I didn't know," cried the girl.

"Anyhow, I couldn't give but twelve a month and
board," continued the manager. "And the work—for
a lady like you——"

A lady! She dropped her gaze in confusion. If he
knew about her birth!

"I'll do anything. I'm not a lady," said she. "But
I've got to have at least ten a week in cash."

"No such place here." The manager was glad to
find the fault of uppish ideas in this girl who was making it hard for him to be businesslike. "No such place
anywhere for a beginner."

"I must have it," said the girl.

"I don't want to discourage you, but——" He was
speaking less curtly, for her expression made him suspect why she was bent upon that particular amount.
"I hope you'll succeed. Only—don't be depressed if
you're disappointed."

She smiled gravely at him; he bowed, avoiding her
eyes. She took up her bundles and went out into Wal-

nut Street. He moved a few steps in obedience to an impulse to follow her, to give her counsel and warning, to offer to help her about the larger bundle. But he checked himself with the frown of his own not too prosperous affairs.

It was the hottest part of the day, and her way lay along unshaded streets. As she had eaten nothing since the night before, she felt faint. Her face was ghastly when she entered the office of the hospital and left Burlingham's parcel. The clerk at the desk told her that Burlingham was in the same condition—"and there'll be probably no change one way or the other for several days."

She returned to the street, wandered aimlessly about. She knew she ought to eat something, but the idea of food revolted her. She was fighting the temptation to go to the *Commercial* office, Roderick Spenser's office. She had not a suspicion that his kindness might have been impulse, long since repented of, perhaps repented of as soon as he was away from her. She felt that if she went to him he would help her. "But I mustn't do it," she said to herself. "Not after what I did." No, she must not see him until she could pay him back. Also, and deeper, there was a feeling that there was a curse upon her; had not everyone who befriended her come to grief? She must not draw anyone else into trouble, must not tangle others in the meshes of her misfortunes. She did not reason this out, of course; but the feeling was not the less strong because the reasons for it were vague in her mind. And there was nothing vague about the resolve to which she finally came—that she would fight her battle herself.

Her unheeding wanderings led her after an hour or so to a big department store. Crowds of shoppers, mussy, hot, and cross, were pushing rudely in and out of the doors. She entered, approached a well-dressed, bareheaded old gentleman, whom she rightly placed as floorwalker, inquired of him:

"Where do they ask for work?"

She had been attracted to him because his was the one face within view not suggesting temper or at least bad humor. It was more than pleasant, it was benign. He inclined toward Susan with an air that invited confidence and application for balm for a wounded spirit. The instant the nature of her inquiry penetrated through his pose to the man himself, there was a swift change to lofty disdain—the familiar attitude of workers toward fellow-workers of what they regard as a lower class. Evidently he resented her having beguiled him by the false air of young lady into wasting upon her, mere servility like himself, a display reserved exclusively for patrons. It was Susan's first experience of this snobbishness; it at once humbled her into the dust. She had been put in her place, and that place was not among people worthy of civil treatment. A girl of his own class would have flashed at him, probably would have "jawed" him. Susan meekly submitted; she was once more reminded that she was an outcast, one for whom the respectable world had no place. He made some sort of reply to her question, in the tone the usher of a fashionable church would use to a stranger obviously not in the same set as the habitués. She heard the tone, but not the words; she turned away to seek the street again. She wandered on—through the labyrinth of streets, through the crowds on crowds of strangers.

Ten dollars a week! She knew little about wages, but enough to realize the hopelessness of her quest.

Ten dollars a week—and her own keep beside. The faces of the crowds pushing past her and jostling her made her heartsick. So much sickness, and harassment, and discontent—so much unhappiness! Surely all these sad hearts ought to be kind to each other. Yet they were not; each soul went selfishly alone, thinking only of its own burden.

She walked on and on, thinking, in this disconnected way characteristic of a good intelligence that has not yet developed order and sequence, a theory of life and a purpose. It had always been her habit to walk about rather than to sit, whether indoors or out. She could think better when in motion physically. When she was so tired that she began to feel weak, she saw a shaded square, with benches under the trees. She entered, sat down to rest. She might apply to the young doctor. But, no. He was poor—and what chance was there of her ever making the money to pay back? No, she could not take alms; than alms there was no lower way of getting money. She might return to Mr. Blynn and accept his offer. The man in all his physical horror rose before her. No, she could not do that. At least, not yet. She could entertain the idea as a possibility now. She remembered her wedding—the afternoon, the night. Yes, Blynn's offer involved nothing so horrible as that—and she had lived through that. It would be cowardice, treachery, to shrink from anything that should prove necessary in doing the square thing by the man who had done so much for her. She had said she would die for Burlingham; she owed even that to him, if her death would help him. Had she then meant nothing but mere lying words of pretended gratitude? But Blynn was always there; something else might turn up, and her dollar and eighty cents would last another day or so, and the ten dollars were not due for six days. No, she would not go to Blynn; she would wait, would take his advice—"think it over."

A man was walking up and down the shaded alley, passing and repassing the bench where she sat. She observed him, saw that he was watching her. He was a young man—a very young man—of middle height, strongly built. He had crisp, short dark hair, a darkish skin, amiable blue-gray eyes, pleasing features. She decided that he was of good family, was home from some college on vacation. He was wearing a silk shirt, striped flannel trousers, a thin serge coat of an attractive shade of blue. She liked his looks, liked the way he dressed. It pleased her that such a man should be interested in her; he had a frank and friendly air, and her sad young heart was horribly lonely. She pretended not to notice him; but after a while he walked up to her, lifting his straw hat.

"Good afternoon," said he. When he showed his strong sharp teeth in an amiable smile, she thought of Sam Wright—only this man was not weak and mean looking, like her last and truest memory picture of Sam—indeed, the only one she had not lost.

"Good afternoon," replied she politely. For in spite of Burlingham's explanations and cautionings she was still the small-town girl, unsuspicious toward courtesy from strange men. Also, she longed for someone to talk with. It had been weeks since she had talked with anyone nearer than Burlingham to her own age and breeding.

"Won't you have lunch with me?" he asked. "I hate to eat alone."

She, faint from hunger, simply could not help obvious hesitation before saying, "I don't think I care for any."

"You haven't had yours—have you?"

"No."

"May I sit down?"

She moved along the bench to indicate that he might, without definitely committing herself.

He sat, took off his hat. He had a clean, fresh look about the neck that pleased her. She was weary of seeing grimy, sweaty people, and of smelling them. Also, except the young doctor, since Roderick Spenser left her at Carrolltown she had talked with no one of her own age and class—the class in which she had been brought up, the class that, after making her one of itself, had cast her out forever with its mark of shame upon her. Its mark of shame—burning and stinging again as she sat beside this young man!

"You're sad about something?" suggested he, himself nearly as embarrassed as she.

"My friend's ill. He's got typhoid."

"That is bad. But he'll get all right. They always cure typhoid, nowadays—if it's taken in time and the nursing's good. Everything depends on the nursing. I had it a couple of years ago, and pulled through easily."

Susan brightened. He spoke so confidently that the appeal to her young credulity toward good news and the hopeful, cheerful thing was irresistible. "Oh, yes —he'll be over it soon," the young man went on, "especially if he's in a hospital where they've got the facilities for taking care of sick people. Where is he?"

"In the hospital—up that way." She moved her head vaguely in the direction of the northwest.

"Oh, yes. It's a good one—for the pay patients. I suppose for the poor devils that can't pay"—he glanced with careless sympathy at the dozen or so tramps on benches nearby—"it's like all the rest of 'em—like the whole world, for that matter. It must be awful not to have money—enough to get on with, I mean. I'm talking about men." He smiled cheerfully. "With a woman—if she's pretty—it's different, of course."

The girl was so agitated that she did not notice the sly, if shy, hint in the remark and its accompanying glance. Said she:

"But it's a good hospital if you pay?"

"None better. Maybe it's good straight through. I've only heard the servants' talk—and servants are such liars. Still—I'd not want to trust myself to a hospital unless I could pay. I guess the common people have good reason for their horror of free wards. Nothing free is ever good."

The girl's face suddenly and startlingly grew almost hard, so fierce was the resolve that formed within her. The money must be got—*must!*—and would. She would try every way she could think of between now and to-morrow; then—if she failed she would go to Blynn.

The young man was saying: "You're a stranger in town?"

"I was with a theatrical company on a show boat. It sank."

His embarrassment vanished. She saw, but she did not understand that it was because he thought he had "placed" her—and that her place was where he had hoped.

"You *are* up against it!" said he. "Come have some lunch. You'll feel better."

The good sense of this was unanswerable. Susan hesitated no longer, wondered why she had hesitated at first. "Well—I guess I will." And she rose with a frank, childlike alacrity that amused him immensely.

"You don't look it, but you've been about some—haven't you?"

"Rather," replied she.

"I somehow thought you knew a thing or two."

They walked west to Race Street. They were about the same height. Her costume might have been fresher, might have suggested to an expert eye the passed-on clothes of a richer relative; but her carriage and the fine look of skin and hair and features made the defects of dress unimportant. She seemed of his class—of the class comfortable, well educated, and well-bred. If she had been more experienced, she would have seen that he was satisfied with her appearance despite the curious looking little package, and would have been flattered. As it was, her interest was absorbed in things apart from herself. He talked about the town—the amusements, the good times to be had at the over-the-Rhine beer halls, at the hilltop gardens, at the dances in the pavilion out at the Zoo. He drew a lively and charming picture, one that appealed to her healthy youth, to her unsatisfied curiosity, to her passionate desire to live the gay, free city life of which the small town reads and dreams.

"You and I can go round together, can't we? I haven't got much, but I'll not try to take your time for nothing, of course. That wouldn't be square. I'm sure you'll have no cause to complain. What do you say?"

"Maybe," replied the girl, all at once absentminded. Her brain was wildly busy with some ideas started there by his significant words, by his flirtatious glances at her, by his way of touching her whenever he could make opportunity. Evidently there was an alternative to Blynn.

"You like a good time, don't you?" said he.

"Rather!" exclaimed she, the violet eyes suddenly very violet indeed and sparkling. Her spirits had suddenly soared. She was acting like one of her age. With that blessed happy hopefulness of healthy youth, she had put aside her sorrows—not because she was frivolous but for the best of all reasons, because she was young and superbly vital. Said she: "I'm crazy about dancing—and music."

"I only needed to look at your feet—and ankles—to know that," ventured he—the "ankles" being especially audacious.

She was pleased, and in youth's foolish way tried to hide her pleasure by saying, "My feet aren't exactly small."

"I should say not!" protested he with energy. "Little feet would look like the mischief on a girl as tall as you are. Yes, we can have a lot of fun."

They went into a large restaurant with fly fans speeding. Susan thought it very grand—and it was the grandest restaurant she had ever been in. They sat down—in a delightfully cool place by a window looking out on a little plot of green with a colladium, a fountain, some oleanders in full and fragrant bloom; the young man ordered, with an ease that fascinated her, an elaborate lunch—soup, a chicken, with salad, ice cream, and fresh peaches. Susan had a menu in her hand and as he ordered she noted the prices. She was dazzled by his extravagance—dazzled and frightened—and, in a curious, vague, unnerving way, fascinated. Money—the thing she must have for Burlingham in whose case "everything depended on the nursing." In the brief time this boy and she had been together, he, without making an effort to impress, had given her the feeling that he was of the best city class, that he knew the world—the high world. Thus, she felt that she must be careful not to show her "greenness." She would have liked to protest against his extravagance, but she ventured only the timid remonstrance, "Oh, I'm not a bit hungry."

She thought she was speaking the truth, for the ideas whirling so fast that they were dim quite took away the sense of hunger. But when the food came she discovered that she was, on the contrary, ravenous —and she ate with rising spirits, with a feeling of content and hope. He had urged her to drink wine or beer, but she refused to take anything but a glass of milk; and he ended by taking milk himself. He was looking more and more boldly and ardently into her eyes, and she received his glances smilingly. She felt thoroughly at ease and at home, as if she were back once more among her own sort of people—with some element of disagreeable constraint left out.

Since she was an outcast, she need not bother about the small restraints the girls felt compelled to put upon themselves in the company of boys. Nobody respected a "bastard," as they called her when they spoke frankly. So with nothing to lose she could at least get what pleasure there was in freedom. She liked it, having this handsome, well-dressed young man making love to her in this grand restaurant where things were so good to eat and so excitingly expensive. He would not regard her as fit to associate with his respectable mother and sisters. In the castes of respectability, her place was with Jeb Ferguson! She was better off clear of the whole unjust and horrible business of re-

spectable life, clear of it and free, frankly in the outcast class. She had not realized—and she did not
realize—that association with the players of the show
boat had made any especial change in her; in fact, it
had loosened to the sloughing point the whole skin of
her conventional training—that surface skin which
seems part of the very essence of our being until something happens to force us to shed it. Crises, catastrophes, may scratch that skin, or cut clear through it;
but only the gentle, steady, everywhere-acting prying-
loose of day and night association can change it from
a skin to a loose envelope ready to be shed at any
moment.

"What are you going to do?" asked the young man,
when the acquaintance had become a friendship—which
was before the peaches and ice cream were served.

"I don't know," said the girl, with the secretive instinct of self-reliance hiding the unhappiness his abrupt
question set to throbbing again.

"Honestly, I've never met anyone that was so congenial. But maybe you don't feel that way?"

"Then again maybe I do," rejoined she, forcing a
merry smile.

His face flushed with embarrassment, but his eyes
grew more ardent as he said: "What were you looking
for, when I saw you in Garfield Place?"

"Was that Garfield Place?" she asked, in evasion.

"Yes." And he insisted, "What were you looking
for?"

"What were *you* looking for?"

"For a pretty girl." They both laughed. "And I've
found her. I'm suited if you are. . . . Don't look so
serious. You haven't answered my question."

"I'm looking for work."

300

He smiled as if it were a joke. "You mean for a place on the stage. That isn't work. *You* couldn't work. I can see that at a glance."

"Why not?"

"Oh, you haven't been brought up to that kind of life. You'd hate it in every way. And they don't pay women anything for work. My father employs a lot of them. Most of his girls live at home. That keeps the wages down, and the others have to piece out with"— he smiled—"one thing and another."

Susan sat gazing straight before her. "I've not had much experience," she finally said, thoughtfully. "I guess I don't know what I'm about."

The young man leaned toward her, his face flushing with earnestness. "You don't know how pretty you are. I wish my father wasn't so close with me. I'd not let you ever speak of work again—even on the stage. What good times we could have!"

"I must be going," said she, rising. Her whole body was alternately hot and cold. In her brain, less vague now, were the ideas Mabel Connemora had opened up for her.

"Oh, bother!" exclaimed he. "Sit down a minute. You misunderstood me. I don't mean I'm flat broke."

Susan hastily reseated herself, showing her confusion. "I wasn't thinking of that."

"Then—what were you thinking of?"

"I don't know," she replied—truthfully, for she could not have put into words anything definite about the struggle raging in her like a battle in a fog. "I often don't exactly know what I'm thinking about. I somehow can't—can't fit it together—yet."

"Do you suppose," he went on, as if she had not spoken, "do you suppose I don't understand? I know you can't afford to let me take your time for nothing. . . . Don't you like me a little?"

She looked at him with grave friendliness. "Yes." Then, seized with a terror which her habitual manner of calm concealed from him, she rose again.

"Why shouldn't it be me as well as another? . . . At least sit down till I pay the bill."

She seated herself, stared at her plate.

"*Now* what are you thinking about?" he asked.

"I don't know—exactly. Nothing much."

The waiter brought the bill. The young man merely glanced at the total, drew a small roll of money from his trousers pocket, put a five-dollar note on the tray with the bill. Susan's eyes opened wide when the waiter returned with only two quarters and a dime. She glanced furtively at the young man, to see if he, too, was not disconcerted. He waved the tray carelessly aside; the waiter said "Thank you," in a matter-of-course way, dropped the sixty cents into his pocket. The waiter's tip was by itself almost as much as she had ever seen paid out for a meal for two persons.

"Now, where shall we go?" asked the young man.

Susan did not lift her eyes. He leaned toward her, took her hand. "You're different from the sort a fellow usually finds," said he. "And I'm—I'm crazy about you. Let's go," said he.

Susan took her bundle, followed him. She glanced up the street and down. She had an impulse to say she must go away alone; it was not strong enough to frame a sentence, much less express her thought. She was seeing queer, vivid, apparently disconnected visions —Burlingham, sick unto death, on the stretcher in the hospital reception room—Blynn of the hideous face and loose, repulsive body—the contemptuous old gentle-

man in the shop—odds and ends of the things Mabel
Connemora had told her—the roll of bills the young
man had taken from his pocket when he paid—Jeb Ferguson in the climax of the horrors of that wedding day
and night. They went to Garfield Place, turned west,
paused after a block or so at a little frame house set
somewhat back from the street. The young man, who
had been as silent as she—but nervous instead of pre-
occupied—opened the gate in the picket fence.

"This is a first-class quiet place," said he, embarrassed, but trying to appear at ease.

Late in the afternoon, when they were once more in
the street, he said: "I'd ask you to go to dinner with
me, but I haven't enough money."

"I can't make you out," he went on. "You're a
queer one. You've had a look in your eyes all afternoon—well, if I hadn't been sure you were experienced,
you'd almost have frightened me away."

"Yes, I've had experience. The—the worst," said
the girl.

"You—you attract me awfully; you've got—well,
everything that's nice about a woman—and at the same
time, there's something in your eyes—— Are you very
fond of your friend?"

"He's all I've got in the world."

"I suppose it's his being sick that makes you look
and act so queer?"

"I don't know what's the matter with me," she said
slowly. "I—don't know."

"I want to see you again—soon. What's your address?"

"I haven't any. I've got to look for a place to live."

"Well, you can give me the place you did live. I'll

write you there, Lorna. You didn't ask me my name when I asked you yours. You've hardly said anything. Are you always quiet like this?"

"No—not always. At least, I haven't been."

"No. You weren't part of the time this afternoon —at the restaurant. Tell me, what are you thinking about all the time? You're very secretive. Why don't you tell me? Don't you know I like you?"

"I don't know," said the girl in a slow, dazed way. "I—don't—know."

"I wouldn't take your time for nothing," he went on, after a pause. "My father doesn't give me much money, but I think I'll have some more day after to-morrow. Can I see you then?"

"I don't know."

He laughed. "You said that before. Day after to-morrow afternoon—in the same place. No matter if it's raining. I'll be there first—at three. Will you come?"

"If I can."

She made a movement to go. But still he detained her. He colored high again, in the struggle between the impulses of his generous youth and the fear of being absurd with a girl he had picked up in the street. He looked at her searchingly, wistfully. "I know it's your life, but—I hate to think of it," he went on. "You're far too nice. I don't see how you happened to be in—in this line. Still, what else is there for a girl, when she's up against it? I've often thought of those things—and I don't feel about them as most people do. . . . I'm curious about you. You'll pardon me, won't you? I'm afraid I'll fall in love with you, if I see you often. You won't fail to come day after to-morrow?"

"If I can."

"Don't you want to see me again?"

She did not speak or lift her eyes.

"You like me, don't you?"

Still no answer.

"You don't want to be questioned?"

"No," said the girl.

"Where are you going now?"

"To the hospital."

"May I walk up there with you? I live in Clifton. I can go home that way."

"I'd rather you didn't."

"Then — good-by — till day after tomorrow at three." He put out his hand; he had to reach for hers and take it. "You're not—not angry with me?"

"No."

His eyes lingered tenderly upon her. "You are *so* sweet! You don't know how I want to kiss you. Are you sorry to go—sorry to leave me—just a little? . . . I forgot. You don't like to be questioned. Well, good-by, dear."

"Good-by," she said; and still without lifting her gaze from the ground she turned away, walked slowly westward.

She had not reached the next street to the north when she suddenly felt that if she did not sit she would drop. She lifted her eyes for an instant to glance furtively round. She saw a house with stone steps leading up to the front doors; there was a "for rent" sign in one of the close-shuttered parlor windows. She seated herself, supported the upper part of her weary body by resting her elbows on her knees. Her bundle had rolled to the sidewalk at her feet. A passing man picked it up, handed it to her, with a polite bow. She looked at him vaguely, took the bundle as if she were not sure it was hers.

"Heat been too much for you, miss?" asked the man.

She shook her head. He lingered, talking volubly— about the weather—then about how cool it was on the hilltops. "We might go up to the Bellevue," he finally suggested, "if you've nothing better to do."

"No, thank you," she said.

"I'll go anywhere you like. I've got a little money that I don't care to keep."

She shook her head.

"I don't mean anything bad," he hastened to suggest—because that would bring up the subject in discussable form.

"I can't go with you," said the girl drearily. "Don't bother me, please."

"Oh—excuse me." And the man went on.

She rose and went on toward the hospital. She no longer felt weary, and the sensation of a wound that might ache if she were not so numb passed away.

A clerk she had not seen before was at the barrier desk. "I came to ask how Mr. Burlingham is," said she.

The clerk yawned, drew a large book toward him. "Burlingham—B—Bu—Bur——" he said, half to himself, turning over the leaves. "Yes—here he is." He looked at her. "You his daughter?"

"No, I'm a friend."

"Oh—then—he died at five o'clock—an hour ago."

He looked up—saw her eyes—only her eyes. They were a deep violet now, large, shining with tragic softness—like the eyes of an angel that has lost its birthright through no fault of its own. He turned hastily away, awed, terrified, ashamed of himself.

XVIII

THE next thing she knew, she felt herself seized strongly by the arm. She gazed round in a dazed way. She was in the street—how she got there she had no idea. The grip on her arm—it was the young doctor, Hamilton. "I called you twice," explained he, "but you didn't hear."

"He is dead," said she.

Hamilton had a clear view of her face now. There was not a trace of the child left. He saw her eyes—quiet, lonely, violet stars. "You must go and rest quietly," he said with gentleness. "You are worn out."

Susan took from her bosom the twenty dollars, handed it to him. "It belongs to him," said she. "Give it to them, to bury him." And she started on.

"Where are you going?" asked the young man.

Susan stopped, looked vaguely at him. "Good-by," she said. "You've been very kind."

"You've found a boarding place?"

"Oh, I'm all right."

"You want to see him?"

"No. Then he'll always be alive to me."

"You had better keep this money. The city will take care of the funeral."

"It belongs to him. I couldn't keep it for myself. I must be going."

"Shan't I see you again?"

"I'll not trouble you."

"Let me walk with you as far as your place."

"I'm not feeling—just right. If you don't mind—please—I'd rather be alone."

"I don't mean to intrude, but——"

"I'm all right," said the girl. "Don't worry about me."

"But you are too young——"

"I've been married. . . . Thank you, but—goodby."

He could think of no further excuse for detaining her. Her manner disquieted him, yet it seemed composed and natural. Probably she had run away from a good home, was now sobered and chastened, was eager to separate herself from the mess she had got into and return to her own sort of people. It struck him as heartless that she should go away in this fashion; but on second thought, he could not associate heartlessness with her. Also, he saw how there might be something in what she had said about not wishing to have to think of her friend as dead. He stood watching her straight narrow young figure until it was lost to view in the crowd of people going home from work.

Susan went down Elm Street to Garfield Place, seated herself on one of the benches. She was within sight of the unobtrusive little house with the awnings; but she did not realize it. She had no sense of her surroundings, of the passing of time, felt no grief, no sensation of any kind. She simply sat, her little bundle in her lap, her hands folded upon it.

A man in uniform paused before her. "Closing-up time," he said, sharply but in the impartial official way. "I'm going to lock the gates."

She looked at him.

In a softer, apologetic tone, he said, "I've got to lock the gates. That's the law, miss."

She did not clearly understand, but rose and went out into Race Street. She walked slowly along, not knowing or caring where. She walked—walked—walked. Sometimes her way lay through crowded streets, again through streets deserted. Now she was stumbling over the uneven sidewalks of a poor quarter; again it was the smooth flagstones of the shopping or wholesale districts. Several times she saw the river with its multitude of boats great and small; several times she crossed the canal. Twice she turned back because the street was mounting the hills behind the city—the hills with the cars swiftly ascending and descending the inclined planes, and at the crests gayly lighted pavilions where crowds were drinking and dancing. Occasionally some man spoke to her, but desisted as she walked straight on, apparently not hearing. She rested from time to time, on a stoop or on a barrel or box left out by some shopkeeper, or leaning upon the rail of a canal bridge. She was walking with a purpose—to try to scatter the dense fog that had rolled in and enveloped her mind, and then to try to think.

She sat, or rather dropped, down from sheer fatigue, in that cool hour which precedes the dawn. It happened to be the steps of a church. She fell into a doze, was startled back to consciousness by the deep boom of the bell in the steeple; it made the stone vibrate under her. One—two—three—four! Toward the east there shone a flush of light, not yet strong enough to dim the stars. The sky above her was clear. The pall of smoke rolled away. The air felt clean and fresh, even had in it a reminiscence of the green fields whence it had come. She began to revive, like a sleeper shaking off drowsiness and the spell of a bad dream and looking forward to the new day. The fog that had swathed and stupefied her brain seemed to have lifted. At her heart there was numbness and a dull throbbing, an ache; but her mind was clear and her body felt intensely, hopelessly alive and ready, clamorously ready, for food. A movement across the narrow street attracted her attention. A cellar door was rising—thrust upward by the shoulders of a man. It fell full open with a resounding crash, the man revealed by the light from beneath—a white blouse, a white cap. Toward her wafted the delicious odor of baking bread. She rose, hesitated only an instant, crossed the street directly toward the baker who had come up to the surface for cool air.

"I am hungry," said she to him. "Can't you let me have something to eat?"

The man—he had a large, smooth, florid face—eyed her in amused astonishment. "Where'd you jump from?" he demanded.

"I was resting on the church steps over there. The smell came to me and—I couldn't stand it. I can pay."

"Oh, that's all right," said the man, with a strong German accent. "Come down." And he descended the steps, she following. It was a large and lofty cellar, paved with cement; floor, ceilings, walls, were whitened with flour. There were long clean tables for rolling the dough; big wooden bowls; farther back, the ovens and several bakers at work adding to the huge piles of loaves the huge baskets of rolls. Susan's eyes glistened; her white teeth showed in a delightful smile of hunger about to be satisfied.

"Do you want bread or rolls?" asked the German. Then without waiting for her to answer, "I guess some of the 'sweet rolls,' we call 'em, would about suit a lady."

"Yes—the sweet rolls," said the girl.

The baker fumbled about behind a lot of empty baskets, found a serving basket, filled it with small rolls—some crescent in shape, some like lady fingers, some oval, some almost like biscuit, all with pulverized sugar powdered on them thick as a frosting. He set the little basket upon an empty kneading table. "Wait yet a minute," he commanded, and bustled up a flight of stairs. He reappeared with a bottle of milk and a piece of fresh butter. He put these beside the basket of rolls, drew a stool up before them. "How's that?" asked he, his hands on his hips, his head on one side, and his big jolly face beaming upon her. "Pretty good, don't it!"

Susan was laughing with pleasure. He pointed to the place well down in the bottle of milk where the cream ended. "That's the way it should be always— not so!" said he. She nodded. Then he shook the bottle to remix the separated cream and milk. "So!" he cried. Then—"*Ach, dummer Esel!*" he muttered, striking his brow a resounding thwack with the flat of his hand. "A knife!" And he hastened to repair that omission.

Susan sat at the table, took one of the fresh rolls, spread butter upon it. The day will never come for her when she cannot distinctly remember the first bite of the little sweet buttered roll, eaten in that air perfumed with the aroma of baking bread. The milk was as fine as it promised to be—she drank it from the bottle.

The German watched her a while, then beckoned to his fellow workmen. They stood round, reveling in the joyful sight of this pretty hungry girl eating so happily and so heartily.

"The pie," whispered one workman to another.

They brought a small freshly baked peach pie, light and crisp and brown. Susan's beautiful eyes danced. "But," she said to her first friend among the bakers, "I'm afraid I can't afford it."

At this there was a loud chorus of laughter. "Eat it," said her friend.

And when she had finished her rolls and butter, she did eat it. "I never tasted a pie like that," declared she. "And I like pies and can make them too."

Once more they laughed, as if she had said the wittiest thing in the world.

As the last mouthful of the pie was disappearing, her friend said, "Another!"

"Goodness, no!" cried the girl. "I couldn't eat a bite more."

"But it's an apple pie." And he brought it, holding it on his big florid fat hand and turning it round to show her its full beauty.

She sighed regretfully. "I simply can't," she said. "How much is what I've had?"

Her friend frowned. "Vot you take me for—hey?" demanded he, with a terrible frown—so terrible he felt it to be that, fearing he had frightened her, he burst out laughing, to reassure.

"Oh, but I must pay," she pleaded. "I didn't come begging."

"Not a cent!" said her friend firmly. "I'm the boss. I won't take it."

She insisted until she saw she was hurting his feelings. Then she tried to thank him; but he would not listen to that, either. "Good-by—good-by," he said gruffly.

"I must get to work once." But she understood, and went with a light heart up into the world again. He stood waist deep in the cellar, she hesitated upon the sidewalk. "Good-by," she said, with swimming eyes. "You don't know how good you've been to me."

"All right. Luck!" He waved his hand, half turned his back on her and looked intently up the street, his eyes blinking.

She went down the street, turned the first corner, dropped on a doorstep and sobbed and cried, out of the fullness of her heart. When she rose to go on again, she felt stronger and gentler than she had felt since her troubles began with the quarrel over Sam Wright. A little further on she came upon a florist's shop in front of which a wagon was unloading the supply of flowers for the day's trade. She paused to look at the roses and carnations, the lilies and dahlias, the violets and verbenas and geraniums. The fast brightening air was scented with delicate odors. She was attracted to a small geranium with many buds and two full-blown crimson flowers.

"How much for that?" she asked a young man who seemed to be in charge.

He eyed her shrewdly. "Well, I reckon about fifteen cents," replied he.

She took from her bosom the dollar bill wrapped round the eighty cents, gave him what he had asked. "No, you needn't tie it up," said she, as he moved to take it into the store. She went back to the bakeshop. The cellar door was open, but no one was in sight. Stooping down, she called: "Mr. Baker! Mr. Baker!"

The big smooth face appeared below.

She set the plant down on the top step. "For you," she said, and hurried away.

On a passing street car she saw the sign "Eden Park." She had heard of it—of its beauties, of the wonderful museum there. She took the next car of the same line. A few minutes, and it was being drawn up the inclined plane toward the lofty hilltops. She had thought the air pure below. She was suddenly lifted through a dense vapor—the cloud that always lies over the lower part of the city. A moment, and she was above the cloud, was being carried through the wide, clean tree-lined avenue of a beautiful suburb. On either side, lawns and gardens and charming houses, a hush brooding over them. Behind these walls, in comfortable beds, amid the surroundings that come to mind with the word "home," lay many girls such as she—happy, secure, sheltered. Girls like herself. A wave of homesickness swept over her, daunting her for a little while. But she fought it down, watched what was going on around her. "I mustn't look back—I mustn't! Nothing there for me." At the main gateway of the park she descended. There indeed was the, to her, vast building containing the treasures of art; but she had not come for that. She struck into the first by-path, sought out a grassy slope thickly studded with bushes, and laid herself down. She spread her skirts carefully so as not to muss them. She put her bundle under her head.

When she awoke the moon was shining upon her face—shining from a starry sky!

She sat up, looked round in wonder. Yes—it was night again—very still, very beautiful, and warm, with the air fragrant and soft. She felt intensely awake, entirely rested—and full of hope. It was as if during that long dreamless sleep her whole being had been renewed and magically borne away from the lands of shadow and pain where it had been wandering, to a land of bright promise. Oh, youth, youth, that bears so lightly the burden of the past, that faces so confidently the mystery of the future! She listened—heard a faint sound that moved her to investigate. Peering through the dense bushes, she discovered on the grass in the shadow of the next clump, a ragged, dirty man and woman, both sound asleep and snoring gently. She watched them spellbound. The man's face was deeply shaded by his battered straw hat. But she could see the woman's face plainly—the thin, white hair, the sunken eyes and mouth, the skeleton look of old features over which the dry skin of age is tightly drawn. She gazed until the man, moving in his sleep, kicked out furiously and uttered a curse. She drew back, crawled away until she had put several clumps of bushes between her and the pair. Then she sped down and up the slopes and did not stop until she was where she could see, far below, the friendly lights of the city blinking at her through the smoky mist.

She had forgotten her bundle! She did not know how to find the place where she had left it; and, had she known, she would not have dared return. This loss, however, troubled her little. Not in vain had she dwelt with the philosopher Burlingham.

She seated herself on a bench and made herself comfortable. But she no longer needed sleep. She was awake—wide awake—in every atom of her vigorous young body. The minutes dragged. She was impatient for the dawn to give the signal for the future to roll up its curtain. She would have gone down into the city to walk about but she was now afraid the police would take her in—and that probably would mean going to a reformatory, for she could not give

a satisfactory account of herself. True, her older way
of wearing her hair and some slight but telling changes
in her dress had made her look less the child. But she
could not hope to pass for a woman full grown. The
moon set; the starlight was after a long, long time
succeeded by the dawn of waking birds, and of waking
city, too—for up from below rose an ever louder roar
like a rising storm. In her restless rovings, she came
upon a fountain; she joined the birds making a toilet in
its basin, and patterned after them—washed her face
and hands, dried them on a handkerchief she by great
good luck had put into her stocking, smoothed her
hair, her dress.

And still the sense of unreality persisted, cast its
friendly spell over this child-woman suddenly caught
up from the quietest of quiet lives and whirled into a
dizzy vortex of strange events without parallel, or
similitude even, in anything she had ever known. If
anyone had suddenly asked her who she was and she
had tried to recall, she would have felt as if trying to
remember a dream. Sutherland—a faint, faint dream,
and the show boat also. Spenser—a romantic dream—
or a first installment of a lovestory read in some stray
magazine. Burlingham—the theatrical agent—the
young man of the previous afternoon—the news of the
death that left her quite alone—all a dream, a tumbled,
jumbled dream, all passed with the night and the
awakening. In her youth and perfect health, refreshed
by the long sleep, gladdened by the bright new day, she
was as irresponsible as the merry birds chattering and
flinging the water about at the opposite side of the
fountain's basin. She was now glad she had lost her
bundle. Without it her hands were free—both hands
free to take whatever might offer next. And she was

eager to see what that would be, and hopeful about it—
no—more than hopeful, confident. Burlingham, aided
by those highly favorable surroundings of the show
boat, and of the vagabond life thereafter, had developed
in her that gambler's spirit which had enabled him to
play year after year of losing hands with unabating
courage—the spirit that animates all the brave souls
whose deeds awe the docile, conventional, craven masses
of mankind.

Leisurely as a truant she tramped back toward the
city, pausing to observe anything that chanced to
catch her eye. At the moment of her discovery of the
difference between her and most girls there had begun
a cleavage between her and the social system. And
now she felt as if she were of one race and the rest of
the world of another and hostile race. She did not
realize it, but she had taken the first great step along
the path that leads to distinction or destruction. For
the world either obeys or tramples into dust those who,
in whatever way, have a lot apart from the common.
She was free from the bonds of convention—free to
soar or to sink.

Her way toward the city lay along a slowly descending street that had been, not so very long before, a
country road. Block after block there were grassy
fields intersected by streets, as if city had attempted a
conquest of country and had abandoned it. Again the
vacant lots were disfigured with the ruins of a shanty
or by dreary dump heaps. For long stretches the way
was built up only on one side. The houses were for the
most part tenement with small and unprosperous shops
or saloons on the ground floor. Toward the foot of
the hill, where the line of tenements was continuous on
either side, she saw a sign "Restaurant" projecting

over the sidewalk. When she reached it, she paused
and looked in. A narrow window and a narrow open
door gave a full view of the tiny room with its two
rows of plain tables. Near the window was a small
counter with a case containing cakes and pies and rolls.
With back to the window sat a pretty towheaded girl
of about her own age, reading. Susan, close to the
window, saw that the book was Owen Meredith's "Lu-
cile," one of her own favorites. She could even read
the words:

The ways they are many and wide, and seldom are two
ways the same.

She entered. The girl glanced up, with eyes slowly
changing from far-away dreaminess to present and
practical—pleasant blue eyes with lashes and brows of
the same color as the thick, neatly done yellowish
hair.

"Could I get a glass of milk and a roll?" asked
Susan, a modest demand, indeed, on behalf of a growing girl's appetite twenty-four hours unsatisfied.

The blonde girl smiled, showing a clean mouth with
excellent teeth. "We sell the milk for five cents, the
rolls three for a nickel."

"Then I'll take milk and three rolls," said Susan.
"May I sit at a table? I'll not spoil it."

"Sure. Sit down. That's what the tables are for."
And the girl closed the book, putting a chromo card
in it to mark her place, and stirred about to serve the
customer. Susan took the table nearest the door, took
the seat facing the light. The girl set before her a
plate, a knife and fork, a little form of butter, a tall
glass of milk, and three small rolls in a large sau-

cer. "You're up and out early?" she said to Susan.

On one of those inexplicable impulses of frankness Susan replied: "I've been sleeping in the park."

The girl had made the remark merely to be polite and was turning away. As Susan's reply penetrated to her inattentive mind she looked sharply at her, eyes opening wonderingly. "Did you get lost? Are you a stranger in town? Why didn't you ask someone to take you in?"

The girl reflected, realized. "That's so," said she. "I never thought of it before. . . . Yes, that is so! It must be dreadful not to have any place to go." She gazed at Susan with admiring eyes. "Weren't you afraid—up in the park?"

"No," replied Susan. "I hadn't anything anybody'd want to steal."

"But some man might have——" The girl left it to Susan's imagination to finish the sentence.

"I hadn't anything to steal," repeated Susan, with a kind of cynical melancholy remotely suggestive of Mabel Connemora.

The restaurant girl retired behind the counter to reflect, while Susan began upon her meager breakfast with the deliberation of one who must coax a little to go a great ways. Presently the girl said:

"Where are you going to sleep tonight?"

"Oh, that's a long ways off," replied the apt pupil of the happy-go-lucky houseboat show. "I'll find a place, I guess."

The girl looked thoughtfully toward the street. "I was wondering," she said after a while, "what I'd do if I was to find myself out in the street, with no money and nowhere to go. . . . Are you looking for something to do?"

"Do you know of anything?" asked Susan interested at once.

"Nothing worth while. There's a box factory down on the next square. But only a girl that lives at home can work there. Pa says the day's coming when women'll be like men—work at everything and get the same wages. But it isn't so now. A girl's got to get married."

Such a strange expression came over Susan's face that the waitress looked apologetic and hastened to explain herself: "I don't much mind the idea of getting married," said she. "Only—I'm afraid I can never get the kind of a man I'd want. The boys round here leave school before the girls, so the girls are better educated. And then they feel above the boys of their own class—except those boys that're beginning to get up in the world—and those kind of boys want some girl who's above them and can help them up. It's dreadful to be above the people you know and not good enough for the people you'd like to know."

Susan was not impressed; she could not understand why the waitress spoke with so much feeling. "Well," said she, pausing before beginning on the last roll, "I don't care so long as I find something to do."

"There's another thing," complained the waitress. "If you work in a store, you can't get wages enough to live on; and you learn things, and want to live better and better all the time. It makes you miserable. And you can't marry the men who work at nice refined labor because they don't make enough to marry on. And if you work in a factory or as a servant, why all but the commonest kind of men look down on you. You may get wages enough to live on, but you can't marry or get up in the world."

"You're very ambitious, aren't you?"

"Indeed I am. I don't want to be in the working class." She was leaning over the counter now, and her blond face was expressing deep discontent and scorn. "I *hate* working people. All of them who have any sense look down on themselves and wish they could get something respectable to do."

"Oh, you don't mean that," protested Susan. "Any kind of work's respectable if it's honest."

"*You* can say that," retorted the girl. "*You* don't belong in our class. You were brought up different. You are a *lady*."

Susan shrank and grew crimson. The other girl did not see. She went on crossly:

"Upper-class people always talk about how fine it is to be an honest workingman. But that's all rot. Let 'em try it a while. And pa says it'll never be straightened out till everybody has to work."

"What—what does your father do?"

"He was a cabinetmaker. Then one of the other men tipped over a big chest and his right hand was crushed—smashed to pieces, so he wasn't able to work any more. But he's mighty smart in his brains. It's the kind you can't make any money out of. He has read most everything. The trouble with pa was he had too much heart. He wasn't mean enough to try and get ahead of the other workmen, and rise to be a boss over them, and grind them down to make money for the proprietor. So he stayed on at the bench—he was a first-class cabinetmaker. The better a man is as a workman, and the nicer he is as a man, the harder it is for him to get up. Pa was too good at his trade— and too soft-hearted. Won't you have another glass of milk?"

"No—thank you," said Susan. She was still hungry, but it alarmed her to think of taking more than ten cents from her hoard.

"Are you going to ask for work at the box factory?"

"I'm afraid they wouldn't take me. I don't know how to make boxes."

"Oh, that's nothing," assured the restaurant girl. "It's the easiest kind of work. But then an educated person can pick up most any trade in a few days, well enough to get along. They'll make you a paster, at first."

"How much does that pay?"

"He'll offer you two fifty a week, but you must make him give you three. That's right for beginners. Then, if you stay on and work hard, you'll be raised to four after six months. The highest pay's five."

"Three dollars," said Susan. "How much can I rent a room for?"

The restaurant girl looked at her pityingly. "Oh, you can't afford a room. You'll have to club in with three other girls and take a room together, and cook your meals yourselves, turn about."

Susan tried not to show how gloomy this prospect seemed. "I'll try," said she.

She paid the ten cents; her new acquaintance went with her to the door, pointed out the huge bare wooden building displaying in great letters "J. C. Matson, Paper Boxes." "You apply at the office," said the waitress. "There'll be a fat black-complected man in his shirt with his suspenders let down off his shoulders. He'll be fresh with you. He used to be a working man himself, so he hasn't any respect for working people. But he doesn't mean any harm. He isn't like a good many; he lets his girls alone."

Susan had not got far when the waitress came running after her. "Won't you come back and let me know how you made out?" she asked, a little embarrassed. "I hope you don't think I'm fresh."

"I'll be glad to come," Susan assured her. And their eyes met in a friendly glance.

"If you don't find a place to go, why not come in with me? I've got only a very little bit of a room, but it's as big and a lot cleaner than any you'll find with the factory girls."

"But I haven't any money," said Susan regretfully. "And I couldn't take anything without paying."

"You could pay two dollars and a half a week and eat in with us. We couldn't afford to give you much for that, but it'd be better than what you'd get the other way."

"But you can't afford to do that."

The restaurant girl's mind was aroused, was working fast and well. "You can help in the restaurant of evenings," she promptly replied. "I'll tell ma you're so pretty you'll draw trade. And I'll explain that you used to go to school with me—and have lost your father and mother. My name's Etta Brashear."

"Mine's—Lorna Sackville," said Susan, blushing. "I'll come after a while, and we'll talk about what to do. I may not get a place."

"Oh, you'll get it. He has hard work finding girls. Factories usually pay more than stores, because the work's more looked down on—though Lord knows it's hard to think how anything could be more looked down on than a saleslady."

"I don't see why you bother about those things. What do they matter?"

"Why, everybody bothers about them. But you

don't understand. You were born a lady, and you'll always feel you've got social standing, and people'll feel that way too."

"But I wasn't," said Susan earnestly. "Indeed, I wasn't. I was born—a—a nobody. I can't tell you, but I'm just nobody. I haven't even got a name."

Etta, as romantic as the next young girl, was only the more fascinated by the now thrillingly mysterious stranger—so pretty, so sweet, with such beautiful manners and strangely outcast no doubt from some family of "high folks." "You'll be sure to come? You won't disappoint me?"

Susan kissed Etta. Etta embraced Susan, her cheeks flushed, her eyes brilliant. "'I've taken an awful fancy to you," she said. "I haven't ever had an intimate lady friend. I don't care for the girls round here. They're so fresh and common. Ma brought me up refined; she's not like the ordinary working-class woman."

It hurt Susan deeply—why, she could not have quite explained—to hear Etta talk in this fashion. And in spite of herself her tone was less friendly as she said, "I'll come when I find out."

XIX

IN the office of the factory Susan found the man Etta described. He was seated, or, rather, was sprawled before an open and overflowing rolltop desk, his collar and cuffs off, and his coat and waistcoat also. His feet—broad, thick feet with knots at the great toe joints bulging his shoes—were hoisted upon the leaf of the desk. Susan's charms of person and manners so wrought upon him that, during the exchange of preliminary questions and answers, he slowly took down first one foot then the other, and readjusted his once muscular but now loose and pudgy body into a less loaferish posture. He was as unconscious as she of the cause and meaning of these movements. Had he awakened to what he was doing he would probably have been angered against himself and against her; and the direction of Susan Lenox's life would certainly have been changed. Those who fancy the human animal is in the custody of some conscious and predetermining destiny think with their vanity rather than with their intelligence. A careful look at any day or even hour of any life reveals the inevitable influence of sheer accidents, most of them trivial. And these accidents, often the most trivial, most powerfully determine not only the direction but also the degree and kind of force—what characteristics shall develop and what shall dwindle.

"You seem to have a nut on you," said the box manufacturer at the end of the examination. "I'll start you at three."

Susan, thus suddenly "placed" in the world and ticketed with a real value, was so profoundly excited that she could not even make a stammering attempt at expressing gratitude.

"Do your work well," continued Matson, "and you'll have a good steady job with me till you get some nice young fellow to support you. Stand the boys off. Don't let 'em touch you till you're engaged—and not much then till the preacher's said the word."

"Thank you," said Susan, trying to look grave. She was fascinated by his curious habit of scratching himself as he talked—head, ribs, arm, legs, the backs of his red hairy hands.

"Stand 'em off," pursued the box-maker, scratching his ribs and nodding his huge head vigorously. "That's the way my wife got me. It's pull Dick pull devil with the gals and the boys. And the gal that's stiff with the men gets a home, while her that ain't goes to the streets. I always gives my gals a word of good advice. And many a one I've saved. There's mighty few preachers does as much good as me. When can you go to work?"

Susan reflected. With heightened color and a slight stammer she said, "I've got something to do this afternoon, if you'll let me. Can I come in the morning?"

"Seven sharp. We take off a cent a minute up to a quarter of an hour. If you're later than that, you get docked for the day. And no excuses. I didn't climb to the top from spittoon cleaner in a saloon fifteen years ago by being an easy mark for my hands."

"I'll come at seven in the morning," said Susan.

"Do you live far?"

"I'm going to live just up the street."

"That's right. It adds ten cents a day to your

wages—the ten you'll save in carfare. Sixty cents a week!" And Matson beamed and scratched as if he felt he had done a generous act. "Who are you livin' with? Respectable, I hope."

"With Miss Brashear—I think."

"Oh, yes—Tom Brashear's gal. They're nice people. Tom's an honest fellow—used to make good money till he had his hard luck. Him and me used to work together. But he never could seem to learn that it ain't workin' for yourself but makin' others work for you that climbs a man up. I never was much as a worker. I was always thinkin' out ways of makin' people work for me. And here I am at the top. And where's Tom? Well—run along now—what's your name?"

"Lorna Sackville."

"Lorny." He burst into a loud guffaw. "Lord, what a name! Sounds like a theayter. Seven sharp, Lorny. So long."

Susan nodded with laughing eyes, thanked him and departed. She glanced up the street, saw Etta standing in the door of the restaurant. Etta did not move from her own doorway, though she was showing every sign of anxiety and impatience. "I can't leave even for a minute so near the dinner hour," she explained when Susan came, "or I'd 'a' been outside the factory. And ma's got to stick to the kitchen. I see you got a job. How much?"

"Three," replied Susan.

"He must have offered it to you," said Etta, laughing. "I thought about it after you were gone and I knew you'd take whatever he said first. Oh, I've been so scared something'd happen. I do want you as my lady friend. Was he fresh?"

"Not a bit. He was—very nice."

"Well, he ought to be nice—as pa says, getting richer and richer, and driving the girls he robs to marry men they hate or to pick up a living in the gutter."

Susan felt that she owed her benefactor a strong protest. "Maybe I'm foolish," said she, "but I'm awful glad he's got that place and can give me work."

Etta was neither convinced nor abashed. "You don't understand things in our class," replied she. "Pa says it was the kind of grateful thinking and talking you've just done that's made him poor in his old age. He says you've either got to whip or be whipped, rob or be robbed—and that the really good honest people are the fools who take the losing side. But he says, too, he'd rather be a fool and a failure than stoop to stamping on his fellow-beings and robbing them. And I guess he's right"—there Etta laughed—"though I'll admit I'd hate to be tempted with a chance to get up by stepping on somebody." She sighed. "And sometimes I can't help wishing pa had done some tramping and stamping. Why not? That's all most people are fit for—to be tramped and stamped on. Now, don't look so shocked. You don't understand. Wait till you've been at work a while."

Susan changed the subject. "I'm going to work at seven in the morning. . . . I might as well have gone today. I had a kind of an engagement I thought I was going to keep, but I've about decided I won't."

Etta watched with awe and delight the mysterious look in Susan's suddenly flushed face and abstracted eyes. After a time she ventured to interrupt with:

"You'll try living with us?"

"If you're quite sure—did you talk to your mother?"

"Mother'll be crazy about you. She wants anything that'll make me more contented. Oh, I do get so lonesome!"

Mrs. Brashear, a spare woman, much bent by monotonous work—which, however, had not bent her courage or her cheerfulness—made Susan feel at home immediately in the little flat. The tenement was of rather a superior class. But to Susan it seemed full of noisome smells, and she was offended by the halls littered with evidences of the uncleanness of the tenants. She did not then realize that the apparent superior cleanness and neatness of the better-off classes was really in large part only affected, that their secluded back doors and back ways gave them opportunity to hide their uncivilized habits from the world that saw only the front. However, once inside the Brashear flat, she had an instant rise of spirits.

"Isn't this nice?" exclaimed she as Etta showed her, at a glance from the sitting-room, the five small but scrupulously clean rooms. "I'll like it here!"

Etta reddened, glanced at her for signs of mockery, saw that she was in earnest. "I'm afraid it's better to look at than to live in," she began, then decided against saying anything discouraging. "It seems cramped to us," said she, "after the house we had till a couple of years ago. I guess we'll make out, somehow."

The family paid twenty dollars a month for the flat. The restaurant earned twelve to fifteen a week; and the son, Ashbel, stocky, powerful and stupid, had a steady job as porter at ten a week. He gave his mother seven, as he had a room to himself and an enormous appetite. He talked of getting married; if he did marry, the family finances would be in disorder. But his girl had high ideas, being the daughter of a grocer who fancied himself still an independent merchant though he was in fact the even more poorly paid selling agent of the various food products trusts. She had fixed twenty a week as the least on which she would marry; his prospects of any such raise were— luckily for his family—extremely remote; for he had nothing but physical strength to sell, and the price of physical strength alone was going down, under immigrant competition, not only in actual wages like any other form of wage labor, but also in nominal wages.

Altogether, the Brashears were in excellent shape for a tenement family, were better off than upwards of ninety per cent of the families of prosperous and typical Cincinnati. While it was true that old Tom Brashear drank, it was also true that he carefully limited himself to two dollars a week. While it was true that he could not work at his trade and apparently did little but sit round and talk—usually high above his audience—nevertheless he was the actual head of the family and its chief bread-winner. It was his savings that were invested in the restaurant; he bought the supplies and was shrewd and intelligent about that vitally important department of the business—the department whose mismanagement in domestic economy is, next to drink, the main cause of failure and pauperism, of sickness, of premature disability, of those profound discouragements that lead to despair. Also, old Brashear had the sagacity and the nagging habit that are necessary to keeping people and things up to the mark. He had ideas—practical ideas as well as ideals —far above his station. But for him the housekeeping would have been in the familiar tenement fashion of slovenliness and filth, and the family would have been neat only on Sundays, and only on the surface then. Because he had the habit of speaking of himself as useless, as done for, as a drag, as one lingering on when he ought to be dead, his family and all the neighborhood thought of him in that way. Although intelligence, indeed, virtue of every kind, is expected of tenement house people—and is needed by them beyond any other condition of humanity—they are unfortunately merely human, are tainted of all human weaknesses. They lack, for instance, discrimination. So, it never occurred to them that Tom Brashear was the sole reason why the Brashears lived better than any of the other families and yielded less to the ferocious and incessant downward pressure.

But for one thing the Brashears would have been going up in the world. That thing was old Tom's honesty. The restaurant gave good food and honest measure. Therefore, the margin of profit was narrow —too narrow. He knew what was the matter. He mocked at himself for being "such a weak fool" when everybody else with the opportunity and the intelligence was getting on by yielding to the compulsion of the iron rule of dishonesty in business. But he remained honest—therefore, remained in the working class, instead of rising among its exploiters.

"If I didn't drink, I'd kill myself," said old Tom to Susan, when he came to know her well and to feel that from her he could get not the mere blind admiration the family gave him but understanding and sympathy. "Whenever anybody in the working class has any imagination," he explained, "he either kicks his way out of it into capitalist or into criminal—or else he takes to drink. I ain't mean enough to be either a capitalist or a criminal. So, I've got to drink."

Susan only too soon began to appreciate from her own experience what he meant.

In the first few days the novelty pleased her, made her think she was going to be contented. The new friends and acquaintances, different from any she had known, the new sights, the new way of living—all this interested her, even when it shocked one or many of her senses and sensibilities. But the novelty of folding and pasting boxes, of the queer new kind of girls who worked with her, hardly survived into the second week. She saw that she was among a people where the highest known standard—the mode of life regarded by them as the acme of elegance and bliss—the best they could conceive was far, far below what she had been brought up to believe the scantest necessities of respectable and civilized living. She saw this life from the inside now— as the comfortable classes never permit themselves to see it if they can avoid. She saw that to be a contented working girl, to look forward to the prospect of being a workingman's wife, a tenement housekeeper and mother, a woman must have been born to it—and born with little brains—must have been educated for it, and for nothing else. Etta was bitterly discontented; yet after all it was a vague endurable discontent. She had simply heard of and dreamed of and from afar off —chiefly through novels and poems and the theater— had glimpsed a life that was broader, that had comfort and luxury, people with refined habits and manners. Susan had not merely heard of such a life; she had lived it—it, and no other.

Always of the thoughtful temperament, she had been rapidly developed first by Burlingham and now by Tom Brashear—had been taught not only how to think but also how to gather the things to think about.

With a few exceptions the girls at the factory were woefully unclean about their persons. Susan did not blame them; she only wondered at Etta the more, and grew to admire her—and the father who held the whole family up to the mark. For, in spite of the difficulties of getting clean, without bathtub, without any but the crudest and cheapest appliances for cleanliness, without any leisure time, Etta kept herself in perfect order. The show boat and the quarters at the hotel had been trying to Susan. But they had seemed an adventure, a temporary, passing phase, a sort of somewhat prolonged camping-out lark. Now, she was settled down, to live, apparently for the rest of her life, with none of the comforts, with few of the decencies. What Etta and her people, using all their imagination, would have pictured as the pinnacle of luxury would have been for Susan a small and imperfect part of what she had been bred to regard as "living decently." She suspected that but for Etta's example she would be yielding, at least in the matter of cleanliness, when the struggle against dirt was so unequal, was thankless. Discouragement became her frequent mood; she wondered if the time would not come when it would be her fixed habit, as it was with all but a handful of those about her.

Sometimes she and Etta walked in the quarter at the top of the hill where lived the families of prosperous merchants—establishments a little larger, a little more pretentious than her Uncle George's in Sutherland, but on the whole much like it—the houses of the solid middle class which fancies itself grandly luxurious where it is in fact merely comfortable in a crude unimaginative way. Susan was one of those who are born with the instinct and mental bent for luxurious comfort; also, she had the accompanying peculiar talent for assimilating ideas about food and dress and surroundings from books and magazines, from the study of well-dressed people in the street, from glances into luxurious interiors through windows or open doors as she passed by. She saw with even quicker and more intelligently critical eyes the new thing, the good idea, the improvement on what she already knew. Etta's excitement over these commonplace rich people amused her. She herself, on the wings of her daring young fancy, could soar into a realm of luxury, of beauty and exquisite comfort, that made these self-complacent mansions seem very ordinary indeed. It was no drag upon her fancy, but the reverse, that she was sharing a narrow bed and a narrow room in a humble and tiny tenement flat.

On one of these walks Etta confided to her the only romance of her life—therefore the real cause of her deep discontent. It was a young man from one of these houses—a flirtation lasting about a year. She assured Susan it was altogether innocent. Susan—perhaps chiefly because Etta protested so insistently about her unsullied purity—had her doubts.

"Then," said Etta, "when I saw that he didn't care anything about me—except in one way—I didn't see him any more. I—I've been sorry ever since."

Susan did not offer the hoped-for sympathy. She was silent.

"Did you ever have anything like that happen to you?" inquired Etta.

"Yes," said Susan. "Something like that."

"And what did you do?"

"I didn't want to see him any more."

"Why?"

"I don't know—exactly.

"And you like him?"

"I think I would have liked him."

"You're sorry you stopped?"

"Sometimes," replied she, hesitatingly.

She was beginning to be afraid that she would soon be sorry all the time. Every day the war within burst forth afresh. She reproached herself for her growing hatred of her life. Ought she not to be grateful that she had so much—that she was not one of a squalid quartette in a foul, vermin-infested back bedroom— infested instead of only occasionally visited—that she was not a streetwalker, diseased, prowling in all weathers, the prey of the coarse humors of contemptuous and usually drunken beasts; that she was not living where everyone about her would, by pity or out of spitefulness, tear open the wounds of that hideous brand which had been put upon her at birth? Above all, she ought to be thankful that she was not Jeb Ferguson's wife.

But her efforts to make herself resigned and contented, to kill her doubts as to the goodness of "goodness," were not successful. She had Tom Brashear's "ungrateful" nature—the nature that will not let a man or a woman stay in the class of hewers of wood and drawers of water but drives him or her out of it— and up or down.

"You're one of those that things happen to," the old cabinetmaker said to her on a September evening, as they sat on the sidewalk in front of the restaurant. The tenements had discharged their swarms into the hot street, and there was that lively panorama of dirt and disease and depravity which is fascinating—to unaccustomed eyes. "Yes," said Tom, "things'll happen to you."

"What—for instance?" she asked.

"God only knows. You'll up and do something some day. You're settin' here just to grow wings. Some day—swish!—and off you'll soar. It's a pity you was born female. Still—there's a lot of females that gets up. Come to think of it, I guess sex don't matter. It's havin' the soul—and mighty few of either sex has it."

"Oh, I'm like everybody else," said the girl with an impatient sigh. "I dream, but—it doesn't come to anything."

"No, you ain't like everybody else," retorted he, with a positive shake of his finely shaped head, thatched superbly with white hair. "You ain't afraid, for instance. That's the principal sign of a great soul, I guess."

"Oh, but I *am* afraid," cried Susan. "I've only lately found out what a coward I am."

"You think you are," said the cabinetmaker. "There's them that's afraid to do, and don't do. Then there's them that's afraid to do, but goes ahead and does anyhow. That's you. I don't know where you came from—oh, I heard Etty's accountin' for you to her ma, but that's neither here nor there. I don't know where you come from, and I don't know where you're going. But—you ain't afraid—and you have imagination—and those two signs means something doing."

Susan shook her head dejectedly; it had been a cruelly hard day at the factory and the odors from the girls working on either side of her had all but overwhelmed her.

Old Tom nodded with stronger emphasis. "You're too young, yet," he said. "And not licked into shape. But wait a while. You'll get there."

Susan hoped so, but doubted it. There was no time to work at these large problems of destiny when the daily grind was so compelling, so wearing, when the problems of bare food, clothing and shelter took all there was in her.

For example, there was the matter of clothes. She had come with only what she was wearing. She gave the Brashears every Saturday two dollars and a half of her three—and was ashamed of herself for taking so much for so little, when she learned about the cost of living and how different was the food the Brashears had from that of any other family in those quarters! As soon as she had saved four dollars from her wages —it took nearly two months—she bought the necessary materials and made herself two plain outer skirts, three blouses and three pairs of drawers. Chemises and corset covers she could not afford. She bought a pair of shoes for a dollar, two pairs of stockings for thirty cents, a corset for eighty cents, an umbrella for half a dollar, two underwaists for a quarter. She bought an untrimmed hat for thirty-five cents and trimmed it with the cleaned ribbon from her summer sailor and a left over bit of skirt material. She also made herself a jacket that had to serve as wrap too —and the materials for this took the surplus of her wages for another month. The cold weather had come, and she had to walk fast when she was in the open air not to be chilled to the bone. Her Aunt Fanny had been one of those women, not too common in America, who understand and practice genuine economy in the household—not the shabby stinginess that passes for economy but the laying out of money to the best advantage that comes only when one knows values. This training stood Susan in good stead now.

It saved her from disaster—from disintegration.

She and Etta did some washing every night, hanging the things on the fire escape to dry. In this way she was able to be clean; but in appearance she looked as poor as she was. She found a cobbler who kept her shoes in fair order for a few cents; but nothing was right about them soon—except that they were not down at the heel. She could recall how she had often wondered why the poor girls at Sutherland showed so little taste, looked so dowdy. She wondered at her own stupidity, at the narrowness of an education, such as hers had been, an education that left her ignorant of the conditions of life as it was lived by all but a lucky few of her fellow beings.

How few the lucky! What an amazing world—what a strange creation the human race! How was it possible that the lucky few, among whom she had been born and bred, should know so little, really nothing, about the lot of the vast mass of their fellows, living all around them, close up against them? "If I had only known!" she thought. And then she reflected that, if she had known, pleasure would have been impossible. She could see her bureau drawers, her closets at home. She had thought herself not any too well off. Now, how luxurious, how stuffed with shameful, wasteful unnecessaries those drawers and closets seemed!

And merely to keep herself in underclothes that were at least not in tatters she had to spend every cent over and above her board. If she had had to pay carfare—ten cents a day, sixty cents a week!—as did many of the girls who lived at home, she would have been ruined. She understood now why every girl without a family back of her, and without good prospect of marriage, was revolving the idea of becoming a streetwalker—not as a hope, but as a fear. As she learned to observe more closely, she found good reasons for suspecting that from time to time the girls who became too hard pressed relieved the tension by taking to the streets on Saturday and Sunday nights. She read in the *Commercial* one noon—Mr. Matson sometimes left his paper where she could glance through it—she read an article on working girls, how they were seduced to lives of shame—by love of *finery!* Then she read that those who did not fall were restrained by religion and innate purity. There she laughed—bitterly. Fear of disease, fear of maternity, yes. But where was this religion? Who but the dullest fools in the throes of that bare and tortured life ever thought of God? As for the purity—what about the obscene talk that made her shudder because of its sheer filthy stupidity?—what about the frank shamelessness of the efforts to lure their "steadies" into speedy matrimony by using every charm of caress and of person to inflame passion without satisfying it? She had thought she knew about the relations of the sexes when she came to live and work in that tenement quarter. Soon her knowledge had seemed ignorance beside the knowledge of the very babies.

It was a sad, sad puzzle. If one ought to be good—chaste and clean in mind and body—then, why was there the most tremendous pressure on all but a few to make them as foul as the surroundings in which they were compelled to live? If it was wiser to be good, then why were most people imprisoned in a life from which they could escape only by being bad? What was this thing comfortable people had set up as good, anyhow—and what was bad? She found no answer. How could God condemn anyone for anything they did in the torments of the hell that life revealed itself to her as being, after a few weeks of its moral, mental and physical horrors? Etta's father was right; those who realized what life really was and what it might be, those who were sensitive took to drink or went to pieces some other way, if they were gentle, and if they were cruel, committed any brutality, any crime to try to escape.

In former days Susan thought well of charity, as she had been taught. Old Tom Brashear gave her a different point of view. One day he insulted and drove from the tenement some pious charitable people who had come down from the fashionable hilltop to be good and gracious to their "less fashionable fellow-beings." After they had gone he explained his harshness to Susan:

"That's the only way you can make them slicked-up brutes feel," said he, "they're so thick in the hide and satisfied with themselves. What do they come here for! To do good! Yes—to themselves. To make themselves feel how generous and sweet they was. Well, they'd better go home and read their Russia-leather covered Bibles. They'd find out that when God wanted to really do something for man, he didn't have himself created a king, or a plutocrat, or a fat, slimy church deacon in a fashionable church. No, he had himself born a bastard in a manger."

Susan shivered, for the truth thus put sounded like sacrilege. Then a glow—a glow of pride and of hope —swept through her.

"If you ever get up into another class," went on old Tom, "don't come hangin' round the common peo-

ple you'll be livin' off of and helpin' to grind down;
stick to your own class. That's the only place anybody can do any good—any real helpin' and lovin',
man to man, and woman to woman. If you want to
help anybody that's down, pull him up into your class
first. Stick to your class. You'll find plenty to do
there."

"What, for instance?" asked Susan. She understood a little of what he had in mind, but was still
puzzled.

"Them stall-fed fakers I just threw out," the old
man went on. "They come here, actin' as if this was
the Middle Ages and the lord of the castle was doin'
a fine thing when he went down among the low peasants
who'd been made by God to work for the lords. But
this ain't the Middle Ages. What's the truth about it?"

"I don't know," confessed Susan.

"Why, the big lower class is poor because the little
upper class takes away from 'em and eats up all they
toil and slave to make. Oh, it ain't the upper class's
fault. They do it because they're ignorant more'n
because they're bad, just as what goes on down here
is ignorance more'n badness. But they do it, all the
same. And they're ignorant and need to be told. Sup-
posin' you saw a big girl out yonder in the street
beatin' her baby sister. What would you do? Would
you go and hold out little pieces of candy to the baby
and say how sorry you was for her? Or would you first
grab hold of that big sister and throw her away from
beatin' of the baby?"

"I see," said Susan.

"That's it exactly," exclaimed the old man, in triumph. "And I say to them pious charity fakers, 'Git
the hell out of here where you can't do no good. Git

back to yer own class that makes all this misery, makes it faster'n all the religion and charity in the world could help it. Git back to yer own class and work with them, and teach them and make them stop robbin' and beatin' the baby.'"

"Yes," said the girl, "you are right. I see it now. But, Mr. Brashear, they meant well."

"The hell they did," retorted the old man. "If they'd 'a' had love in their hearts, they'd have seen the truth. Love's one of the greatest teachers in the world. If they'd 'a' meant well, they'd 'a' been goin' round teachin' and preachin' and prayin' at their friends and fathers and brothers, the plutocrats. They'd never 'a' come down here, pretendin' they was doin' good, killin' one bedbug out of ten million and offerin' one pair of good pants where a hundred thousand pairs is needed. They'd better go read about themselves in their Bible—what Jesus says. He knew 'em. *He* belonged to *us*—and *they* crucified him."

The horrors of that by no means lowest tenement region, its horrors for a girl bred as Susan had been! Horrors moral, horrors mental, horrors physical— above all, the physical horrors; for, worse to her than the dull wits and the lack of education, worse than vile speech and gesture, was the hopeless battle against dirt, against the vermin that could crawl everywhere —and did. She envied the ignorant and the insensible their lack of consciousness of their own plight—like the disemboweled horse that eats tranquilly on. At first she had thought her unhappiness came from her having been used to better things, that if she had been born to this life she would have been content, gay at times. Soon she learned that laughter does not always mean mirth; that the ignorant do not lack the power to suffer simply because they lack the power to appreciate; that the diseases, the bent bodies, the harrowed faces, the drunkenness, quarreling, fighting, were safer guides to the real conditions of these people than their occasional guffaws and fits of horseplay.

A woman from the hilltop came in a carriage to see about a servant. On her way through the hall she cried out: "Gracious! Why don't these lazy creatures clean up, when soap costs so little and water nothing at all!" Susan heard, was moved to face her fiercely, but restrained herself. Of what use? How could the woman understand, if she heard, "But, you fool, where are we to get the time to clean up?— and where the courage?—and would soap enough to clean up and keep clean cost so little, when every penny means a drop of blood?"

"If they only wouldn't drink so much!" said Susan to Tom.

"What, then?" retorted he. "Why, pretty soon wages'd be cut faster than they was when street carfares went down from ten cents to five. Whenever the workin' people arrange to live cheaper and to try to save something, down goes wages. No, they might as well drink. It helps 'em bear it and winds 'em up sooner. I tell you, it ain't the workin' people's fault —it's the bosses, now. It's the system—the system. A new form of slavery, this here wage system—and it's got to go—like the slaveholder that looked so copper-riveted and Bible-backed in its day."

That idea of "the system" was beyond Susan. But not what her eyes saw, and her ears heard, and her nose smelled, and her sense of touch shrank from. No ambition and no reason for ambition. No real knowl-

edge, and no chance to get any—neither the leisure
nor the money nor the teachers. No hope, and no
reason for hope. No God—and no reason for a God.

Ideas beyond her years, beyond her comprehension,
were stirring in her brain, were making her grave and
thoughtful. She was accumulating a store of knowledge about life; she was groping for the clew to its
mystery, for the missing fact or facts which would
enable her to solve the puzzle, to see what its lessons
were for her. Sometimes her heavy heart told her that
the mystery was plain and the lesson easy—hopelessness. For of all the sadness about her, of all the tragedies so sordid and unromantic, the most tragic was
the hopelessness. It would be impossible to conceive
people worse off; it would be impossible to conceive
these people better off. They were such a multitude
that only they could save themselves—and they had
no intelligence to appreciate, no desire to impel. If
their miseries—miseries to which they had fallen heir
at birth—had made them what they were, it was also
true that they were what they were—hopeless, down to
the babies playing in the filth. An unscalable cliff;
at the top, in pleasant lands, lived the comfortable
classes; at the bottom lived the masses—and while
many came whirling down from the top, how few found
their way up!

On a Saturday night Ashbel came home with the
news that his wages had been cut to seven dollars. And
the restaurant had been paying steadily less as the
hard times grew harder and the cost of unadulterated
and wholesome food mounted higher and higher. As
the family sat silent and stupefied, old Tom looked
up from his paper, fixed his keen, mocking eyes on
Susan.

"I see, here," said he, "that *we* are so rich that they want to raise the President's salary so as he can entertain *decently*—and to build palaces at foreign courts so as our representatives'll live worthy of *us!*"

XX

ON Monday at the lunch hour—or, rather, half-hour—Susan ventured in to see the boss.

Matson had too recently sprung from the working class and was too ignorant of everything outside his business to have made radical changes in his habits. He smoked five-cent cigars instead of "two-furs"; he ate larger quantities of food, did not stint himself in beer or in treating his friends in the evenings down at Wielert's beer garden. Also he wore a somewhat better quality of clothing; but he looked precisely what he was. Like all the working class above the pauper line, he made a Sunday toilet, the chief features of which were the weekly bath and the weekly clean white shirt. Thus, it being only Monday morning, he was looking notably clean when Susan entered—and was morally wound up to a higher key than he would be as the week wore on. At sight of her his feet on the leaf of the desk wavered, then became inert; it would not do to put on manners with any of the "hands." Thanks to the bath, he was not exuding his usual odor that comes from bolting much strong, cheap food.

"Well, Lorny—what's the kick?" inquired he with his amiable grin. His rise in the world never for an instant ceased to be a source of delight to him; it—and a perfect digestion—kept him in a good humor all the time.

"I want to know," stammered Susan, "if you can't give me a little more money."

He laughed, eyeing her approvingly. Her clothing was that of the working girl; but in her face was the look never found in those born to the modern form of slavery-wage servitude. If he had been "cultured" he might have compared her to an enslaved princess, though in fact that expression of her courageous violet-gray eyes and sensitive mouth could never have been in the face of princess bred to the enslaving routine of the most conventional of conventional lives; it could come only from sheer erectness of spirit, the exclusive birthright of the sons and daughters of democracy.

"More money!" he chuckled. "You *have* got a nerve! —when factories are shutting down everywhere and working people are tramping the streets in droves."

"I do about one-fourth more than the best hands you've got," replied Susan, made audacious by necessity. "And I'll agree to throw in my lunch time."

"Let me see, how much do you get?"

"Three dollars."

"And you aren't living at home. You must have a hard time. Not much over for diamonds, eh? You want to hustle round and get married, Lorny. Looks don't last long when a gal works. But you're holdin' out better'n them that gads and dances all night."

"I help at the restaurant in the evening to piece out my board. I'm pretty tired when I get a chance to go to bed."

"I'll bet! . . . So, you want more money. I've been watchin' you. I watch all my gals—I have to, to keep weedin' out the fast ones. I won't have no bad examples in *my* place! As soon as I ketch a gal livin' beyond her wages I give her the bounce."

Susan lowered her eyes and her cheeks burned—not

because Matson was frankly discussing the frivolous subject of sex. Another girl might have affected the air of distressed modesty, but it would have been affectation, pure and simple, as in those regions all were used to hearing the frankest, vilest things—and we do not blush at what we are used to hearing. Still, the tenement female sex is as full of affectation as is the sex elsewhere. But, Susan, the curiously self-unconscious, was incapable of affectation. Her indignation arose from her sense of the hideous injustice of Matson's discharging girls for doing what his meager wages all but compelled.

"Yes, I've been watching you," he went on, "with a kind of a sort of a notion of makin' you a forelady. That'd mean six dollars a week. But you ain't fit. You've got the brains—plenty of 'em. But you wouldn't be of no use to me as forelady."

"Why not?" asked Susan. Six dollars a week! Affluence! Wealth!

Matson took his feet down, relit his cigar and swung himself into an oracular attitude.

"I'll show you. What's manufacturin'? Right down at the bottom, I mean." He looked hard at the girl. She looked receptively at him.

"Why, it's gettin' work out of the hands. New ideas is nothin'. You can steal 'em the minute the other fellow uses 'em. No, it's all in gettin' work out of the hands."

Susan's expression suggested one who sees light and wishes to see more of it. He proceeded:

"You work for me—for instance, now, if every day you make stuff there's a profit of five dollars on, I get five dollars out of you. If I can push you to make stuff there's a profit of six dollars on, I get six dollars

—a dollar more. Clear extra gain, isn't it? Now multiply a dollar by the number of hands, and you'll see what it amounts to."

"I see," said Susan, nodding thoughtfully.

"Well! How did I get up? Because as a foreman I knew how to work the hands. I knew how to get those extra dollars. And how do I keep up? Because I hire forepeople that get work out of the hands."

Susan understood. But her expression was a comment that was not missed by the shrewd Matson.

"Now, listen to me, Lorny. I want to give you a plain straight talk because I'd like to see you climb. Ever since you've been here I've been laughin' to myself over the way your forelady—she's a fox, she is! —makes you the pacemaker for the other girls. She squeezes at least twenty-five cents a day over what she used to out of each hand in your room because you're above the rest of them dirty, shiftless muttonheads."

Susan flushed at this fling at her fellow-workers.

"Dirty, shiftless muttonheads," repeated Matson. "Ain't I right? Ain't they dirty? Ain't they shiftless —so no-account that if they wasn't watched every minute they'd lay down—and let me and the factory that supports 'em go to rack and ruin? And ain't they muttonheads? Do you ever find any of 'em saying or doing a sensible thing?"

Susan could not deny. She could think of excuses —perfect excuses. But the facts were about as he brutally put it.

"Oh, I know 'em. I've dealt with 'em all my life," pursued the box manufacturer. "Now, Lorny, you ought to be a forelady. You've got to toughen up and stop bein' so polite and helpful and all that.

You'll *never* get on if you don't toughen up. Business is business. Be as sentimental as you like away from business, and after you've clum to the top. But not *in* business or while you're kickin' and scratchin' and clawin' your way up."

Susan shook her head slowly. She felt painfully young and inexperienced and unfit for the ferocious struggle called life. She felt deathly sick.

"Of course it's a hard world," said Matson with a wave of his cigar. "But did I make it?"

"No," admitted Susan, as his eyes demanded a reply.

"Sure not," said he. "And how's anybody to get up in it? Is there any other way but by kickin' and stampin', eh?"

"None that I see," conceded Susan reluctantly.

"None that is," declared he. "Them that says there's other ways either lies or don't know nothin' about the practical game. Well, then!" Matson puffed triumphantly at the cigar. "Such bein' the case—and as long as the crowd down below's got to be kicked in the face by them that's on the way up, why shouldn't I do the kickin'—which is goin' to be done anyhow—instead of gettin' kicked? Ain't that sense?"

"Yes," admitted Susan. She sighed. "Yes," she repeated.

"Well—toughen up. Meanwhile, I'll raise you, to spur the others on. I'll give you four a week." And he cut short her thanks with an "Oh, don't mention it. I'm only doin' what's square—what helps me as well as you. I want to encourage you. You don't belong down among them cattle. Toughen up, Lorny. A girl with a bank account gets the pick of the beaux." And he nodded a dismissal.

Matson. and his hands, bosses and workers, brutal,

brutalizing each other more and more as they acted and reacted upon each other. Where would it end?

She was in dire need of underclothes. Her undershirts were full of holes from the rubbing of her cheap, rough corset; her drawers and stockings were patched in several places—in fact, she could not have worn the stockings had not her skirt now been well below her shoetops. Also, her shoes, in spite of the money she had spent upon them, were about to burst round the edges of the soles. But she would not longer accept from the Brashears what she regarded as charity.

"You more than pay your share, what with the work you do," protested Mrs. Brashear. "I'll not refuse the extra dollar because I've simply got to take it. But I don't want to pertend."

The restaurant receipts began to fall with the increasing hardness of the times among the working people. Soon it was down to practically no profit at all —that is, nothing toward the rent. Tom Brashear was forced to abandon his policy of honesty, to do as all the other purveyors were doing—to buy cheap stuff and to cheapen it still further. He broke abruptly with his tradition and his past. It aged him horribly all in a few weeks—but, at least, ruin was put off. Mrs. Brashear had to draw twenty of the sixty-three dollars which were in the savings bank against sickness. Funerals would be taken care of by the burial insurance; each member of the family, including Susan, had a policy. But sickness had to have its special fund; and it was frequently drawn upon, as the Brashears knew no more than their neighbors about hygiene, and were constantly catching the colds of foolish exposure or indigestion and letting them develop into fevers, bad attacks of rheumatism, stomach trouble, backache—all regarded by them as by their neighbors as a necessary part of the routine of life. Those tenement people had no more notion of self-restraint than had the "better classes" whose self-indulgences maintain the vast army of doctors and druggists. The only thing that saved Susan from all but an occasional cold or sore throat from wet feet was eating little through being unable to accustom herself to the fare that was the best the Brashears could now afford—cheap food in cheap lard, coarse and poisonous sugar, vilely adulterated coffee, doctored meat and vegetables—the food which the poor in their ignorance buy—and for which they in their helplessness pay actually higher prices than do intelligent well-to-do people for the better qualities. And not only were the times hard, but the winter also. Snow—sleet—rain—thaw—slush—noisome, disease-laden vapor—and, of course, sickness everywhere —with occasional relief in death, relief for the one who died, relief for the living freed from just so much of the burden. The sickness on every hand appalled Susan. Surely, she said to old Brashear, the like had never been before; on the contrary, said he, the amount of illness and death was, if anything, less than usual because the hard times gave people less for eating and drinking. These ghastly creatures crawling toward the hospital or borne out on stretchers to the ambulance—these yet ghastlier creatures tottering feebly homeward, discharged as cured—these corpses of men, of women, of boys and girls, of babies—oh, how many corpses of babies!—these corpses borne away for burial, usually to the public burying ground—all these stricken ones in the battle ever waging, with curses, with hoarse loud laughter, with shrieks and moans, with dull, drawn faces and jaws set—all these stricken ones were but the ordinary losses of the battle!

"And in the churches," said old Tom Brashear, "they preach the goodness and mercy of God. And in the papers they talk about how rich and prosperous we are."

"I don't care to live! It is too horrible," cried the girl.

"Oh, you mustn't take things so to heart," counseled he. "Us that live this life can't afford to take it to heart. Leave that to them who come down here from the good houses and look on us for a minute and enjoy themselves with a little weepin' and sighin' as if it was in the theater."

"It seems worse every day," she said. "I try to fool myself, because I've got to stay and——"

"Oh, no, you haven't," interrupted he.

Susan looked at him with a startled expression. It seemed to her that the old man had seen into her secret heart where was daily raging the struggle against taking the only way out open to a girl in her circumstances. It seemed to her he was hinting that she ought to take that way.

If any such idea was in his mind, he did not dare put it into words. He simply repeated:

"You won't stay. You'll pull out."

"How?" she asked.

"Somehow. When the way opens you'll see it, and take it."

There had long since sprung up between these two a sympathy, a mutual understanding beyond any necessity of expression in words or looks. She had never had this feeling for anyone, not even for Burlingham. This feeling for each other had been like that of a

father and daughter who love each other without either
understanding the other very well or feeling the need
of a sympathetic understanding. There was a strong
resemblance between Burlingham and old Tom. Both
belonged to the familiar philosopher type. But, unlike
the actor-manager, the old cabinetmaker had lived his
philosophy, and a very gentle and tolerant philosophy
it was.

After she had looked her request for light upon what
way she was to take, they sat silent, neither looking
at the other, yet each seeing the other with the eye
of the mind. She said:

"I may not dare take it."

"You won't have no choice," replied he. "You'll
have to take it. And you'll get away from here. And
you mustn't ever come back—or look back. Forget
all this misery. Rememberin' won't do us no good.
It'd only weaken you."

"I shan't ever forget," cried the girl.

"You must," said the old man firmly. He added,
"And you will. You'll have too much else to think
about—too much that has to be attended to."

As the first of the year approached and the small
shopkeepers of the tenements, like the big ones elsewhere, were casting up the year's balances and learning
how far toward or beyond the verge of ruin the hard
times had brought them, the sound of the fire engines
—and of the ambulances—became a familiar part of
the daily and nightly noises of the district. Desperate
shopkeepers, careless of their neighbors' lives and property in fiercely striving for themselves and their families—workingmen out of a job and deep in debt—
landlords with too heavy interest falling due—all these
were trying to save themselves or to lengthen the time

the fact of ruin could be kept secret by setting fire
to their shops or their flats. The Brashears had been
burned out twice in their wandering tenement house
life; so old Tom was sleeping little; was constantly
prowling about the halls of all the tenements in that
row and into the cellars.

He told Susan the open secret of the meaning of
most of these fires. And after he had cursed the fire
fiends, he apologized for them. "It's the curse of the
system," explained he. "It's all the curse of the system. These here storekeepers and the farmers the
same way—they think they're independent, but really
they're nothin' but fooled slaves of the big blood suck-
ers for the upper class. But these here little storekeepers, they're tryin' to escape. How does a man
escape? Why, by gettin' some hands together to work
for him so that he can take it out of their wages.
When you get together enough to hire help—that's
when you pass out of slavery into the master class
—master of slaves."

Susan nodded understandingly.

"Now, how can these little storekeepers like me
get together enough to begin to hire slaves? By a hundred tricks, every one of them wicked and mean. By
skimpin' and slavin' themselves and their families, by
sellin' short weight, by sellin' rotten food, by sellin'
poison, by burnin' to get the insurance. And, at last,
if they don't die or get caught and jailed, they get
together the money to branch out and hire help, and
begin to get prosperous out of the blood of their
help. These here arson fellows—they're on the
first rung of the ladder of success. You heard
about that beautiful ladder in Sunday school, didn't
you?"

"Yes," said Susan, "that and a great many other lies about God and man."

Susan had all along had great difficulty in getting sleep because of the incessant and discordant noises of the district. The unhappy people added to their own misery by disturbing each other's rest—and no small part of the bad health everywhere prevailing was due to this inability of anybody to get proper sleep because somebody was always singing or quarreling, shouting or stamping about. But Susan, being young and as yet untroubled by the indigestion that openly or secretly preyed upon everyone else, did at last grow somewhat used to noise, did contrive to get five or six hours of broken sleep. With the epidemic of fires she was once more restless and wakeful. Every day came news of fire somewhere in the tenement districts of the city, with one or more, perhaps a dozen, roasted to death, or horribly burned. A few weeks, however, and even that peril became so familiar that she slept like the rest. There were too many actualities of discomfort, of misery, to harass her all day long every time her mind wandered from her work.

One night she was awakened by a scream. She leaped from bed to find the room filling with smoke and the street bright as day, but with a flickering evil light. Etta was screaming, Ashbel was bawling and roaring like a tortured bull. Susan, completely dazed by the uproar, seized Etta and dragged her into the hall. There were Mr. and Mrs. Brashear, he in his nightdress of drawers and undershirt, she in the short flannel petticoat and sacque in which she always slept. Ashbel burst out of his room, kicking the door down instead of turning the knob.

"Lorny," cried old Tom, "you take mother and Etty

to the escape." And he rushed at his powerful, stupid son and began to strike him in the face with his one good fist, shrieking, "Shut up, you damn fool! Shut up!"

Dragging Etta and pushing Mrs. Brashear, Susan moved toward the end of the hall where the fire escape passed their windows. All the way down, the landings were littered with bedding, pots, pans, drying clothes, fire wood, boxes, all manner of rubbish, the overflow of the crowded little flats. Over these obstructions and down the ladders were falling and stumbling men, women, children, babies, in all degrees of nudity—for many of the big families that slept in one room with windows tight shut so that the stove heat would not escape and be wasted when fuel was so dear, slept stark naked. Susan contrived to get Etta and the old woman to the street; not far behind them came Tom and Ashbel, the son's face bleeding from the blows his father had struck to quiet him.

It was a penetrating cold night, with an icy drizzle falling. The street was filled with engines, hose, all manner of ruined household effects, firemen shouting, the tenement people huddling this way and that, barefooted, nearly or quite naked, silent, stupefied. Nobody had saved anything worth while. The entire block was ablaze, was burning as if it had been saturated with coal oil.

"The owner's done this," said old Tom. "I heard he was in trouble. But though he's a church member and what they call a philanthropist, I hardly thought he'd stoop to hirin' this done. If anybody's caught, it'll be some fellow that don't know who he did it for."

About a hundred families were homeless in the street. Half a dozen patrol wagons and five ambulances were taking the people away to shelter, women and babies first. It was an hour—an hour of standing in the street, with bare feet on the ice, under the ankledeep slush—before old Tom and his wife got their turn to be taken. Then Susan and Etta and Ashbel, escorted by a policeman, set out for the station house. As they walked along, someone called out to the policeman:

"Anybody killed at the fire, officer?"

"Six jumped and was smashed," replied the policeman. "I seen three dead babies. But they won't know for several days how many it'll total."

And all her life long, whenever Susan Lenox heard the clang of a fire engine, there arose before her the memory picture of that fire, in all the horror of detail. A fire bell to her meant wretched families flung into the night, shrieks of mangled and dying, moans of babies with life oozing from their blue lips, columns of smoke ascending through icy, soaking air, and a vast glare of wicked light with flame demons leaping for joy in the measureless woe over which they were presiding. As the little party was passing the fire lines, Ashbel's foot slipped on a freezing ooze of blood and slush, and he fell sprawling upon a human body battered and trampled until it was like an overturned basket of butcher's odds and ends.

The station house was eleven long squares away. But before they started for it they were already at the lowest depth of physical wretchedness which human nerves can register; thus, they arrived simply a little more numb. The big room, heated by a huge, red-hot stove to the point where the sweat starts, was crowded with abject and pitiful human specimens. Even Susan, the most sensitive person there, gazed about with stolid eyes. The nakedness of unsightly bodies, gross with fat or wasted to emaciation, the dirtiness of limbs and torsos long, long unwashed, the foul steam from it all and from the water-soaked rags, the groans of some, the silent, staring misery of others, and, most horrible of all, the laughter of those who yielded like animals to the momentary sense of physical well-being as the heat thawed them out—these sights and sounds together made up a truly infernal picture. And, like all the tragedies of abject poverty, it was wholly devoid of that dignity which is necessary to excite the deep pity of respect, was sordid and squalid, moved the sensitive to turn away in loathing rather than to advance with brotherly sympathy and love.

Ashbel, his animal instinct roused by the sight of the stove, thrust the throng aside rudely as he pushed straight for the radiating center. Etta and Susan followed in his wake. The fierce heat soon roused them to the sense of their plight. Ashbel began to curse, Etta to weep. Susan's mind was staring, without hope but also without despair, at the walls of the trap in which they were all caught—was seeking the spot where they could begin to burrow through and escape.

Beds and covers were gathered in by the police from everywhere in that district, were ranged upon the floor of the four rooms. The men were put in the cells downstairs; the women and the children got the cots. Susan and Etta lay upon the same mattress, a horse blanket over them. Etta slept; Susan, wide awake, lived in brain and nerves the heart-breaking scenes through which she had passed numb and stolid.

About six o'clock a breakfast of coffee, milk and bread was served. It was evident that the police did not know what to do with these outcasts who had nothing and no place to go—for practically all were out of work when the blow came. Ashbel demanded shoes, pants and a coat.

"I've got to get to my job," shouted he, "or else I'll lose it. Then where in the hell'd we be!"

His blustering angered the sergeant, who finally told him if he did not quiet down he would be locked in a cell. Susan interrupted, explained the situation, got Ashbel the necessary clothes and freed Etta and herself of his worse than useless presence. At Susan's suggestion such other men as had jobs were also fitted out after a fashion and sent away. "You can take the addresses of their families if you send them anywhere during the day, and these men can come back here and find out where they've gone——" this was the plan she proposed to the captain, and he adopted it. As soon as the morning papers were about the city, aid of every kind began to pour in, with the result that before noon many of the families were better established than they had been before the fire.

Susan and Etta got some clothing, enough to keep them warm on their way through the streets to the hospital to which Brashear and his wife had been taken. Mrs. Brashear had died in the ambulance—of heart disease, the doctors said, but Susan felt it was really of the sense that to go on living was impossible. And fond of her though she was, she could not but be relieved that there was one less factor in the unsolvable problem.

"She's better off," she said to Etta in the effort to console.

But Etta needed no consolation. "Ever so much better off," she promptly assented. "Mother hasn't cared about living since we had to give up our little home and become tenement house people. And she was right."

As to Brashear, they learned that he was ill; but they did not learn until evening that he was dying of pneumonia. The two girls and Ashbel were admitted to the ward where he lay—one of a long line of sufferers in bare, clean little beds. Screens were drawn round his bed because he was dying. He had been suffering torments from the savage assaults of the pneumonia; but the pain had passed away now, so he said, though the dreadful sound of his breathing made Susan's heart flutter and her whole body quiver.

"Do you want a preacher or a priest?" asked the nurse.

"Neither," replied the old man in gasps and whispers. "If there is a God he'll never let anybody from this hell of a world into his presence. They might tell him the truth about himself."

"Oh, father, father!" pleaded Etta, and Ashbel burst into a fit of hysterical and terrified crying.

The old man turned his dying eyes on Susan. He rested a few minutes, fixing her gaze upon his with a hypnotic stare. Then he began again:

"You've got somethin' more'n a turnip on your shoulders. Listen to me. There was a man named Jesus once"—gasp—gasp—"You've heard about him, but you don't know about him"—gasp—gasp—"I'll tell you—listen. He was a low fellow—a workin' man—same trade as mine—born without a father—born in a horse trough—in a stable"—gasp—gasp—

Susan leaned forward. "Born without a father," she murmured, her eyes suddenly bright.

"That's him. Listen"—gasp—gasp—gasp—"He was a big feller—big brain—big heart—the biggest

man that ever lived"—gasp—gasp—gasp—gasp—
"And he looked at this here hell of a world from the
outside, he being an outcast and a low-down common
workingman. And he *saw*—he did——

"Yes, he saw!"—gasp—gasp—gasp—"And he said
all men were brothers—and that they'd find it out some
day. He saw that this world was put together for
the strong and the cruel—that they could win out—
and make the rest of us work for 'em for what they
chose to give—like they work a poor ignorant horse
for his feed and stall in a dirty stable——" gasp—gasp
—gasp—

"For the strong and the cruel," said Susan.

"And this feller Jesus—he set round the saloons and
such places—publicans, they called 'em"—gasp—gasp
—gasp—"And he says to all the poor ignorant slaves
and such cattle, he says, 'You're all brothers. Love
one another' "—gasp—gasp—gasp—" 'Love one another,' he says, 'and learn to help each other and stand
up for each other,' he says, 'and hate war and fightin'
and money grabbin'——' " gasp—gasp—gasp—
" 'Peace on earth,' he says, 'Know the truth, and the
truth shall make you free'—and he saw there'd be a
time"—the old man raised himself on one elbow—"Yes,
by God—there *will* be!—a time when men'll learn not
to be beasts and'll be men—*men*, little gal!"

"Men," echoed Susan, her eyes shining, her bosom
heaving.

"It ain't sense and it ain't right that everything
should be for the few—for them with brains—and that
the rest—the millions—should be tramped down just
because they ain't so cruel or so 'cute'—they and
their children tramped down in the dirt. And that
feller Jesus saw it."

"Yes—yes," cried Susan. "He saw it."

"I'll tell you what he was," said old Tom in a hoarse whisper. "He wasn't no god. He was bigger'n that —bigger'n that, little gal! He was the first *man* that ever lived. He said, 'Give the weak a chance so as they kin git strong.' He says——"

The dying man fell back exhausted. His eyes rolled wildly, closed; his mouth twitched, fell wide open; there came from his throat a sound Susan had never heard before, but she knew what it was, what it meant.

Etta and Ashbel were overwhelmed afresh by the disgrace of having their parents buried in Potter's Field—for the insurance money went for debts. They did not understand when Susan said, "I think your father'd have liked to feel that he was going to be buried there—because then he'll be with—with his Friend. You know, *He* was buried in Potter's Field." However, their grief was shortlived; there is no time in the lives of working people for such luxuries as grief—no more time than there is at sea when all are toiling to keep afloat the storm-racked sinking ship and one sailor is swept overboard. In comfortable lives a bereavement is a contrast; in the lives of the wretched it is but one more in the assailing army of woes.

Etta took a job at the box factory at three dollars a week; she and Susan and Ashbel moved into two small rooms in a flat in a tenement opposite the factory—a cheaper and therefore lower house than the one that had burned. They bought on the installment plan nine dollars' worth of furniture—the scant minimum of necessities. They calculated that, by careful saving, they could pay off the debt in a year or so —unless one or the other fell ill or lost work. "That means," said Etta, eyeing their flimsy and all but down-right worthless purchases, "that means we'll still be paying when this furniture'll be gone to pieces and fit only for kindling."

"It's the best we can do," replied Susan. "Maybe one of us'll get a better job."

"*You* could, I'm sure, if you had the clothes," said Etta. "But not in those rags."

"If I had the clothes? Where?"

"At Shillito's or one of the other department stores. They'd give us both places in one of the men's depart-ments. They like pretty girls for those places—if they're not giddy and don't waste time flirting but use flirtation to sell goods. But what's the sense in talking about it? You haven't got the clothes. A saleslady's got to be counter-dressed. She can look as bad as she pleases round the skirt and the feet. But from the waist up she has to look natty, if she wants wages."

Susan had seen these girls; she understood now why they looked as if they were the put together upper and lower halves of two different persons. She recalled that, even though they went into other business, they still retained the habit, wore toilets that were counter-built. She revolved the problem of getting one of these toilets and of securing a store job. But she soon saw it was hopeless, for the time. Every cent the three had was needed to keep from starving and freezing. Also—though she did not realize it—her young enthusiasm was steadily being sapped by the life she was leading. It may have been this rather than natural gentleness—or perhaps it was as much the one as the other—that kept Susan from taking Mat-son's advice and hardening herself into a forelady.

The ruddy glow under her skin had given place to pallor; the roundness of her form had gone, and its beauty remained only because she had a figure which not even emaciation could have deprived of lines of alluring grace. But she was no longer quite so straight, and her hair, which it was a sheer impossibility to care for, was losing its soft vitality. She was still pretty, but not the beauty she had been when she was ejected from the class in which she was bred. However, she gave the change in herself little thought; it was the rapid decline of Etta's prettiness and freshness that worried her most.

Not many weeks after the fire and the deeper plunge, she began to be annoyed by Ashbel. In his clumsy, clownish way he was making advances to her. But she easily repulsed him. Then he threatened to leave them.

She reasoned that numbskull though he was, he yet had wit enough to realize how greatly to his disadvantage any change he could make would be. She did not speak of the matter to Etta, who was, therefore, taken completely by surprise when Ashbel, after a silent supper that evening, burst out with his grievance:

"I'm going to pack up," said he. "I've found a place where I'll be treated right." He looked haughtily at Susan.

He went into his room, reappeared with his few belongings done into a bundle. "So long," said he, stalking toward the hall door, and he was gone.

An hour later they had moved; for Mrs. Quinlan was able to find two lodgers to take the rooms at once. They were established with Mrs. Cassatt, had a foul and foul-smelling bed and one-half of her back room; the other half barely contained two even dirtier and more malodorous cots, in one of which slept Mrs. Cassatt's sixteen-year-old daughter Kate, in the other her fourteen-year-old son Dan. For these new quarters and the right to cook their food on the Cassatt stove the girls agreed to pay three dollars and a half a week —which left them three dollars and a half a week for food and clothing—and for recreation and for the exercise of the virtue of thrift which the comfortable so assiduously urge upon the poor.

XXI

EACH girl now had with her at all times everything she possessed in the world—a toothbrush,
a cake of castile soap, the little money left out
of the week's wages, these three items in the pocket
of her one skirt, a cheap dark blue cloth much wrinkled and patched; a twenty-five cent felt hat, Susan's
adorned with a blue ribbon, Etta's with a bunch of
faded roses; a blue cotton blouse patched under the
arms with stuff of a different shade; an old misshapen
corset that cost forty-nine cents in a bargain sale;
a suit of gray shoddy-and-wool underwear; a pair of
fifteen-cent stockings, Susan's brown, Etta's black; a
pair of worn and torn ties, scuffed and down at the
heel, bought for a dollar and nine cents; a dirt-stained
dark blue jacket, Susan's lacking one button, Etta's
lacking three and having a patch under the right arm.

Yet they often laughed and joked with each other,
with their fellow-workers. You might have said their
hearts were light; for so eager are we to believe our
fellow-beings comfortable, a smile of poverty's face
convinces us straightway that it is as happy as we, if
not happier. There would have been to their mirth
a little more than mere surface and youthful ability
to find some jest in the most crushing tragedy if only
they could have kept themselves clean. The lack of
sufficient food was a severe trial, for both had voracious
appetites; Etta was tormented by visions of quantity,
Susan by visions of quality as well as of quantity.
But only at meal times, or when they had to omit a

meal entirely, were they keenly distressed by the food question. The cold was a still severer trial; but it was warm in the factory and it was warm in Mrs. Cassatt's flat, whose windows were never opened from closing in of winter until spring came round. The inability to keep clean was the trial of trials.

From her beginning at the box factory the physical uncleanness of the other girls had made Susan suffer keenly. And her suffering can be understood only by a clean person who has been through the same ordeal. She knew that her fellow-workers were not to blame. She even envied them the ignorance and the insensibility that enabled them to bear what, she was convinced, could never be changed. She wondered sometimes at the strength and grip of the religious belief among the girls—even, or, rather, especially, among those who had strayed from virtue into the path their priests and preachers and rabbis told them was the most sinful of all strayings. But she also saw many signs that religion was fast losing its hold. One day a Lutheran girl, Emma Schmeltz, said during a Monday morning lunch talk:

"Well, anyhow, I believe it's all a probation, and everything'll be made right hereafter. *I* believe my religion, I do. Yes, we'll be rewarded in the hereafter."

Becky—Rebecca Lichtenspiel—laughed, as did most of the girls. Said Becky:

"And there ain't no hereafter. Did you ever see a corpse? Ain't they the dead ones! Don't talk to me about no hereafter."

Everybody laughed. But this was a Monday morning conversation, high above the average of the girls' talk in intelligence and liveliness. Their minds had been stimulated by the Sunday rest from the dreary and degenerating drudgery of "honest toil."

It was the physical contacts that most preyed upon Susan. She was too gentle, too considerate to show her feelings; in her determined and successful effort to conceal them she at times went to the opposite extreme and not only endured but even courted contacts that were little short of loathsome. Tongue could not tell what she suffered through the persistent affectionateness of Letty Southard, a sweet and pretty young girl of wretchedly poor family who developed an enormous liking for her. Letty, dirty and clad in noisome undergarments beneath soiled rags and patches, was always hugging and kissing her—and not to have submitted would have been to stab poor Letty to the heart and humiliate all the other girls. So no one, not even Etta, suspected what she was going through.

From her coming to the factory in the morning, to hang her hat and jacket in the only possible place, along with the soiled and smelling and often vermin-infected wraps of the others—from early morning until she left at night she was forced into contacts to which custom never in the least blunted her. However, so long as she had a home with the Brashears there was the nightly respite. But now—

There was little water, and only a cracked and filthy basin to wash in. There was no chance to do laundry work; for their underclothes must be used as night clothes also. To wash their hair was impossible.

"Does my hair smell as bad as yours?" said Etta. "You needn't think yours is clean because it doesn't show the dirt like mine."

"Does my hair smell as bad as the rest of the girls'?" said Susan.

"Not quite," was Etta's consoling reply.

By making desperate efforts they contrived partially to wash their bodies once a week, not without interruptions of privacy—to which, however, they soon grew accustomed. In spite of efforts which were literally heroic, they could not always keep free from parasites; for the whole tenement and all persons and things in it were infected—and how could it be otherwise where no one had time or money or any effective means whatsoever to combat nature's inflexible determination to breed wherever there is a breeding spot? The last traces of civilization were slipping from the two girls; they were sinking to a state of nature.

Even personal pride, powerful in Susan and strong in Etta through Susan's example, was deserting them. They no longer minded Dan's sleeping in their room. They saw him, his father, the other members of the family in all stages of nudity and at the most private acts; and they were seen by the Cassatts in the same way. To avoid this was impossible, as impossible as to avoid the parasites swarming in the bed, in the woodwork, in cracks of ceiling, walls, floor.

The Cassatts were an example of how much the people who live in the sheltered and more or less sunny nooks owe to their shelter and how little to their own boasted superiority of mind and soul. They had been a high class artisan family until a few months before. The hard times struck them a series of quick, savage blows, such as are commonplace enough under our social system, intricate because a crude jumble of makeshifts, and easily disordered because intricate. They were swept without a breathing pause down to the bottom. Those who have always been accustomed to prosperity have no reserve of experience or courage

370

to enable them to recuperate from sudden and extreme adversity. In an amazingly short time the Cassatts had become demoralized—a familiar illustration of how civilization is merely a wafer-thin veneer over most human beings as yet. Over how many is it more? They fought after a fashion; they fought valiantly. But how would it have been possible not steadily to yield ground against such a pitiless, powerful foe as poverty? The man had taken to drink, to blunt outraged self-respect and to numb his despair before the spectacle of his family's downfall. Mrs. Cassatt was as poor a manager as the average woman in whatever walk of life, thanks to the habit of educating woman in the most slipshod fashion, if at all, in any other part of the business but sex-trickery. Thus she was helpless before the tenement conditions. She gave up, went soddenly about in rags with an incredibly greasy and usually dangling tail of hair.

"Why don't you tie up that tail, ma?" said the son Dan, who had ideas about neatness.

"What's the use?" said Mrs. Cassatt. "What's the use of *anything?*"

"Ma don't want to look stylish and stuck up," said the daughter.

Mrs. Cassatt's haunting terror was lest someone who had known them in the days of their prosperity with a decently furnished little house of their own should run into one of the family now.

Kate, the sixteen-year-old daughter, had a place as saleslady in a big shop in Fifth Street; her six dollars a week was the family's entire steady income. She had formerly possessed a good deal of finery for a girl in her position, though really not much more than the daughter of the average prosperous artisan or small shopkeeper expects, and is expected to have. Being at the shop where finery was all the talk and sight and thought from opening until closing had developed in her a greedy taste for luxury. She pilfered from the stocks of goods within her reach and exchanged her stealings for the stealings of girls who happened to be able to get things more to her liking or need. But now that the family savings-bank account was exhausted, all these pilferings had to go at once to the pawnshop. Kate grew more and more ill-tempered as the family sank. Formerly she had been noted for amiability, for her vanity easily pleased with a careless compliment from no matter whom—a jocose, half-drunken ash man, half-jeering, half-admiring from his cart set quite as satisfactory as anybody. But poverty was bringing out in her all those meanest and most selfish and most brutish instincts—those primal instincts of human nature that civilization has slowly been subjecting to the process of atrophy which has lost us such other primal attributes as, for example, prehensile toes and a covering of hair.

Foul smells and sights everywhere, and foul language; no privacy, no possibility of modesty where all must do all in the same room: vermin, parasites, bad food vilely cooked—in the midst of these and a multitude of similar ills how was it possible to maintain a human standard, even if one had by chance acquired a knowledge of what constituted a human standard? The Cassatts were sinking into the slime in which their neighbors were already wallowing. But there was this difference. For the Cassatts it was a descent; for many of their neighbors it was an ascent—for the immigrants notably, who had been worse off in their European homes; in this land not yet completely in

the grip of the capitalist or wage system they were
now getting the first notions of decency and development, the first views and hope of rising in the world.
The Cassatts, though they had always lived too near
the slime to be nauseated by it, still found it disagreeable and in spots disgusting. Their neighbors—

One of the chief reasons why these people were rising
so slowly where they were rising at all was that the
slime seemed to them natural, and to try to get clean
of it seemed rather a foolish, finicky waste of time and
effort. People who have come up—by accident, or by
their own force, or by the force of some at once shrewd
and brutal member of the family—have to be far and
long from the slums before they lose the sense that
in conforming to the decencies of life they are making
absurd effeminate concessions. When they go to buy
a toothbrush they blush and stammer.

"Look at Lorna and Etta," Mrs. Cassatt was always saying to Kate.

"Well, I see 'em," Kate would reply. "And I don't
see much."

"Ain't you ashamed of yourself!" cried the mother.
"Them two lives straight and decent. And you're
better off than they are."

"Don't preach to me, ma," sneered Kate. "When I
get ready I'll—stop making a damn fool of myself."

But the example of the two girls was not without
its effect. They, struggling on in chastity against
appalling odds, became the models, not only to Mrs.
Cassatt, but all the mothers of that row held up to
their daughters. The mothers—all of them by observation, not a few by experience—knew what the "fancy
lady's" life really meant. And they strove mightily to
keep their daughters from it. Not through religion

or moral feeling, though many pretended—perhaps fancied—that this was their reason; but through the plainest kind of practical sense—the kind that in the broad determines the actions of human beings of whatever class, however lofty the idealistic pretenses may be. These mothers knew that the profession of the pariah meant a short life and a wretched one, meant disease, lower and ever lower wages, the scale swiftly descending, meant all the miseries of respectability plus a heavy burden of miseries of its own. There were many other girls besides Susan and Etta holding up their heads—girls with prospects of matrimony, girls with fairly good wages, girls with fathers and brothers at work and able to provide a home. But Susan and Etta were peculiarly valuable as examples because they were making the fight alone and unaided.

Thus, they were watched closely. In those neighborhoods everyone knows everyone else's business down to how the last cent is got and spent. If either girl had appeared in a new pair of shoes, a new hat, a new garment of any kind, at once the report would have sped that the wearer had taken a turn in the streets. And the scandal would have been justified; for where could either have respectably got the money for the smallest and cheapest addition to her toilet? Matson, too, proudly pointed them out as giving the lie to the talk about working girls not getting living wages, to the muttering against him and his fellow employers as practically procurers for the pavement and the dive, for the charity hospital's most dreadful wards, for the Morgue's most piteous boxes and slabs.

As their strength declined, as their miseries ate in and in, the two girls ceased talking together; they used to chatter much of the time like two birds on a leafy, sunny bough. Now they walked, ate their scanty, repulsive meals, dressed, worked, all in silence. When their eyes met both glanced guiltily away, each fearing the other would discover the thought she was revolving —the thought of the streets. They slept badly—Etta sometimes, Susan every night. For a long time after she came to the tenements she had not slept well, despite her youth and the dull toil that wore her out each day. But after many months she had grown somewhat used to the noisiness—to fretting babies, to wailing children, the mixed ale parties, the quarrelings of the ill and the drunk, the incessant restlessness whereever people are huddled so close together that repose is impossible. And she had gradually acquired the habit of sleeping well—that is, well for the tenement region where no one ever gets the rest without which health is impossible. Now sleeplessness came again—hours on hours of listening to the hateful and maddening discords of densely crowded humanity, hours on hours of thinking—thinking—in the hopeless circles like those of a caged animal, treading with soft swift step round and round, nose to the iron wall, eyes gleaming with despairing pain.

One Saturday evening after a supper of scorched cornmeal which had been none too fresh when they got it at the swindling grocer's on the street floor, Etta put on the tattered, patched old skirt at which she had been toiling. "I can't make it fit to wear," said she. "It's too far gone; I think"—her eyelids fluttered—"I'll go see some of the girls."

Susan, who was darning—seated on the one chair— yes, it had once been a chair—did not look up or speak. Etta put on her hat—slowly. Then, with a stealthy glance at Susan, she moved slidingly toward the door. As she reached it Susan's hands dropped to her lap; so tense were Etta's nerves that the gesture made her startle. "Etta!" said Susan in an appealing voice.

Etta's hand dropped from the knob. "Well—what is it, Lorna?" she asked in a low, nervous tone.

"Look at me, dear."

Etta tried to obey, could not.

"Don't do it," said Susan.

"You get four, I get only three—and there's no chance of a raise. I work slower instead of faster. I'm going to be discharged soon. I'm in rags."

Etta looked at her with eyes as devoted as a dog's. "Then we'll go together," she said.

Susan, pinning on her weather-stained hat, reflected. "Very well," she said finally.

They said no more; they went out into the clear, cold winter night, out under the brilliant stars. Several handsome theater buses were passing on their way from the fashionable suburb to the theater. Etta looked at them, at the splendid horses, at the men in top hats and fur coats—clean looking, fine looking, amiable looking men—at the beautiful fur wraps of the delicate women—what complexions!—what lovely hair! —what jewels! Etta, her heart bursting, her throat choking, glanced at Susan to see whether she too was observing. But Susan's eyes were on the tenement they had just left.

"What are you looking at—so queer?" asked Etta.

"I was thinking that we'll not come back here."

Etta shivered. She admired the courage, but it terrified her. "There's something—something—awful about you, Lorna," she said. "You've changed till you're like a different person from what you were when

you came to the restaurant. Sometimes—that look in
your eyes—well, it takes my breath away."

"It takes *my* breath away, too. Come on."

At the foot of the hill they took the shortest route
for Vine Street, the highway of the city's night life.
Though they were so young and walked briskly, their
impoverished blood was not vigorous enough to produce a reaction against the sharp wind of the zero
night which nosed through their few thin garments and
bit into their bodies as if they were naked. They came
to a vast department store. Each of its great show-
windows, flooded with light, was a fascinating display
of clothing for women upon wax models—costly
jackets and cloaks of wonderful furs, white, brown,
gray, rich and glossy black; underclothes fine and soft,
with ribbons and flounces and laces; silk stockings and
graceful shoes and slippers; dresses for street, for ball,
for afternoon, dresses with form, with lines, dresses elegantly plain, dresses richly embroidered. Despite the
cold the two girls lingered, going from window to window, their freezing faces pinched and purple, their eyes
gazing hungrily.

"Now that we've tried 'em all on," said Susan with a
short and bitter laugh, "let's dress in our dirty rags
again and go."

"Oh, I couldn't imagine myself in any of those things
—could you?" cried Etta.

"Yes," answered Susan. "And better."

"You were brought up to have those things, I know."
Susan shook her head. "But I'm going to have
them."

"When?" said Etta, scenting romance. "Soon?"

"As soon as I learn," was Susan's absent, unsatisfactory reply.

Etta had gone back to her own misery and the contrasts to it. "I get mad through and through," she cried, "when I think how all those things go to some women—women that never did work and never could. And they get them because they happen to belong to rich fathers and husbands or whoever protects them. It isn't fair! It makes me crazy!"

Susan gave a disdainful shrug. "What's the use of that kind of talk!" said she. "No use at all. The thing is, *we* haven't got what we want, and we've got to *get* it —and so we've got to *learn how.*"

"I can't think of anything but the cold," said Etta. "My God, how cold I am! There isn't anything I wouldn't do to get warm. There isn't anything anybody wouldn't do to get warm, if they were as cold as this. It's all very well for warm people to talk——"

"Oh, I'm sick of all the lying and faking, anyhow. Do you believe in hell, Lorna?"

"Not in a hot one," said Susan.

Soon they struck into Vine Street, bright as day almost, and lined with beer halls, concert gardens, restaurants. Through the glass fronts crowds of men and women were visible—contented faces, well-fed bodies, food on the tables or inviting-looking drink. Along the sidewalk poured an eager throng, all the conspicuous faces in it notable for the expectancy of pleasure in the eyes.

"Isn't this different!" exclaimed Etta. "My God, how cold I am—and how warm everybody else is but us!"

The sights, the sounds of laughter, of gay music, acted upon her like an intoxicant. She tossed her head in a reckless gesture. "I don't care what becomes of me," said she. "I'm ready for anything except dirt and starvation."

Nevertheless, they hurried down Vine Street, avoiding the glances of the men and behaving as if they were two working girls in a rush to get home. As they walked, Susan, to delude herself into believing that she was not hesitating, with fainting courage talked incessantly to Etta—told her the things Mabel Connemora had explained to her—about how a woman could, and must, take care of her health, if she were not to be swept under like the great mass of the ignorant, careless women of the pariah class. Susan was astonished that she remembered all the actress had told her—remembered it easily, as if she had often thought of it, had used the knowledge habitually.

They arrived at Fountain Square, tired from the long walk. They were both relieved and depressed that nothing had happened. "We might go round the fountain and then back," suggested Susan.

They made the tour less rapidly, but still keeping their heads and their glances timidly down. They were numb with the cold now. To the sharp agony had succeeded an ache like the steady grinding pain of rheumatism.

"I want to be my own boss," said Susan.

"But we may *have* to go," pleaded Etta. "It's awful cold—and if we went, at least we'd have a warm place. If we wanted to leave, why, we couldn't be any worse off for clothes than we are."

Susan had no answer for this argument. They went several squares up Vine Street in silence and separated.

An hour later Etta went into a restaurant where the girls had agreed to meet. Her eyes searched anxiously for Susan, but did not find her. She inquired at the counter. No one had asked there for a young lady. This both relieved her and increased her nervousness; Susan had not come and gone—but would she come? Etta was so hungry that she could hold out no longer. She sat at a table near the door and took up the large sheet on which was printed the bill of fare. She was almost alone in the place, as it was between dinner and supper. She read the bill thoroughly, then ordered black bean soup, a sirloin steak and German fried potatoes. This, she had calculated, would cost altogether a dollar; undoubtedly an extravagance, but everything at that restaurant seemed dear in comparison with the prices to which she had been used, and she felt horribly empty. She ordered the soup, to stay her while the steak was broiling.

As soon as the waiter set down bread and butter she began upon it greedily. As the soup came, in walked Susan—calm and self-possessed, Etta saw at first glance. "I've been so frightened. You'll have a plate of soup?" asked Etta, trying to look and speak in unconcerned fashion.

"No, thank you," replied Susan, seating herself opposite.

"There's a steak coming—a good-sized one, the waiter said it'd be."

"Very well."

Susan spoke indifferently.

"Aren't you hungry?"

"I don't know. I'll see." Susan was gazing straight ahead. Her eyes were distinctly gray—gray and as hard as Susan Lenox's eyes could be.

"What're you thinking about?"

"I don't know," she laughed queerly.

"Was—it—dreadful?"

A pause, then: "Nothing is going to be dreadful

to me any more. It's all in the game, as Mr. Burlingham used to say."

"Burlingham—who's he?" It was Etta's first faint
clew toward that mysterious past of Susan's into which
she longed to peer.

"Oh—a man I knew. He's dead."

A long pause, Etta watching Susan's unreadable
face. At last she said:

"You don't seem a bit excited."

Susan came back to the present. "Don't I? Your
soup's getting cold."

Etta ate several spoonfuls, then said with an embarrassed attempt at a laugh, "Your eyes, Susan—they
don't look natural at all." Indeed they looked super-
natural. The last trace of gray was gone. They were
of the purest, deepest violet, luminous, mysterious, with
that awe-inspiring expression of utter aloneness. But
as Etta spoke the expression changed. The gray came
back and with it a glance of irony. She said:

"Oh—nonsense! I'm all right."

Etta was still puzzling at this when the dinner now
came—a fine, thick broiled steak, the best steak Susan
had ever seen, and the best food Etta had ever seen.
They had happened upon one of those famous Cincinnati chop houses where in plain surroundings the highest quality of plain food is served. "You *are* hungry,
aren't you, Lorna?" said Etta.

"Yes—I'm hungry," declared Susan. "Cut it—
quick."

"Draught beer or bottled?" asked the waiter.

"Bring us draught beer," said Etta. "I haven't
tasted beer since our restaurant burned."

"I never tasted it," said Susan. "But I'll try it tonight."

Etta cut two thick slices from the steak, put them on Susan's plate with some of the beautifully browned fried potatoes. "Gracious, they have good things to eat here!" she exclaimed. Then she cut two thick slices for herself, and filled her mouth. Her eyes glistened, the color came into her pale cheeks. "Isn't it *grand!*" she cried, when there was room for words to pass out.

"Grand," agreed Susan, a marvelous change of expression in her face also.

The beer came. Etta drank a quarter of the tall glass at once. Susan tasted, rather liked the fresh bitter-sweet odor and flavor. "Is it—very intoxicating?" she inquired.

"If you drink enough," said Etta. "But not one glass."

Susan took quite a drink. "I feel a lot less tired already," declared she.

"Me too," said Etta. "My, what a meal! I never had anything like this in my life. When I think what we've been through! Lorna, will it *last?*"

Instead of replying Susan began to talk of what to do next. "We must find a place to sleep, and we must buy a few things to make a better appearance."

"I don't dare spend anything yet," said Etta. "I've got only my two dollars. Not that when this meal's paid for."

"We're going to share even," said Susan. "As long as either has anything, it belongs to both."

The tears welled from Etta's eyes. "You are too good, Lorna! You mustn't be. It isn't the way to get on. Anyhow, I can't accept anything from you. You wouldn't take anything from me."

"We've got to help each other up," insisted Susan. "We share even—and let's not talk any more about it.

382

Now, what shall we get? How much ought we to lay out?"

The waiter here interrupted. "Beg pardon, young ladies," said he. "Over yonder, at the table four down, there's a couple of gents that'd like to join you."

The two men were pushing eagerly toward them, the taller and less handsome slightly in advance. He said, his eyes upon Susan, "We were lonesome, and you looked a little that way too. We're much obliged." He glanced at the waiter. "Another bottle of the same."

"I don't want anything to drink," said Susan.

"Nor I," chimed in Etta. "No, thank you."

The young man waved the waiter away with, "Get it for my friend and me, then." He smiled agreeably at Susan. "You won't mind my friend and me drinking?"

"Oh, no."

"And maybe you'll change your mind," said the shorter man to Etta. "You see, if we all drink, we'll get acquainted faster. Don't you like champagne?"

"I never tasted it," Etta confessed.

"Neither did I," admitted Susan.

"You're sure to like it," said the taller man to Susan —his friend presently addressed him as John. "Nothing equal to it for making friends. I like it for itself, and I like it for the friends it has made me."

Champagne was not one of the commonplaces of that modest chop house. So the waiter opened the bottle with much ceremony. Susan and Etta startled when the cork popped ceilingward in the way that in such places is still regarded as fashionable. They watched with interested eyes the pouring of the beautiful pale amber liquid, were fascinated when they saw how the bubbles surged upward incessantly, imprisoned joys thronging to escape. And after the first glass, the four began to have the kindliest feelings for each other. Sorrow and shame, poverty and foreboding, took wings unto themselves and flew away. The girls felt deliciously warm and contented, and thought the young men charming—a splendid change from the coarse, badly dressed youths of the tenement, with their ignorant speech and rough, misshapen hands. They were ashamed of their own hands, were painfully self-conscious whenever lifting the glass to the lips brought them into view. Etta's hands in fact were not so badly spoiled as might have been expected, considering her long years of rough work; the nails were in fairly good condition and the skin was rougher to the touch than to the sight. Susan's hands had not really been spoiled as yet. She had been proud of them and had taken care of them; still, they were not the hands of a lady, but of a working girl. The young men had gentlemen's hands—strong, evidently exercised only at sports, not at degrading and deforming toil.

The shorter and handsomer youth, who answered to the name of Fatty, for obvious but not too obvious reasons, addressed himself to Etta. John—who, it came out, was a Chicagoan, visiting Fatty—fell to Susan. The champagne made him voluble; he was soon telling all about himself—a senior at Ann Arbor, as was Fatty also; he intended to be a lawyer; he was fond of a good time; was fond of the girls—liked girls who were gay rather than respectable ones—"because with the prim girls you have to quit just as the fun ought really to begin."

After two glasses Susan, warned by a slight dizziness, stopped drinking; Etta followed her example. But the boys kept on, ordered a second bottle. "This is the fourth we've had tonight," said Fatty proudly when it came.

"Don't it make you dizzy?" asked Etta.

"Not a bit," Fatty assured her. But she noticed that his tongue now swung trippingly loose. "I'll tell you what let's do. Let's all go shopping. We can help you girls select your things."

Susan laughed. "We're going to buy about three dollars' worth. There won't be any selecting. We'll simply take the cheapest."

"Then—let's go shopping," said John, "and you two girls can help Fatty and me select clothes for you."

"That's the talk!" cried Fatty. And he summoned the waiter. "The bill," said he in the manner of a man who likes to enjoy the servility of servants.

"We hadn't paid for our supper," said Susan. "How much was it, Etta?"

"A dollar twenty-five."

"We're going to pay for that," said Fatty. "What d'ye take us for?"

"Oh, no. We must pay it," said Susan.

"Don't be foolish. Of course I'll pay."

"No," said Susan quietly, ignoring Etta's wink. And from her bosom she took a crumpled five-dollar bill.

"I should say you *were* new," laughed John. "You don't even know where to carry your money yet." And they all laughed, Susan and Etta because they felt gay and assumed the joke whatever it was must be a good one. Then John laid his hand over hers and said, "Put your money away."

Susan looked straight at him. "I can't allow it," she said. "I'm not that poor—yet."

John colored. "I beg your pardon," he said. And when the bill came he compelled Fatty to let her pay a dollar and a quarter of it out of her crumpled five. The two girls were fascinated by the large roll of bills —fives, tens, twenties—which Fatty took from his trousers pocket. They stared open-eyed when he laid a twenty on the waiter's plate along with Susan's five. And it frightened them when he, after handing Susan her change, had left only a two-dollar bill, four silver quarters and a dime. He gave the silver to the waiter.

"Was that for a tip?" asked Susan.

"Yes," said Fatty. "I always give about ten per cent of the bill unless it runs over ten dollars. In that case—a quarter a person as a rule. Of course, if the bill was very large, I'd give more." He was showing his amusement at her inquisitiveness.

"I wanted to know," explained she. "I'm very ignorant, and I've got to learn."

"That's right," said John, admiringly—with a touch of condescension. "Don't be afraid to confess ignorance."

"I'm not," replied Susan. "I used to be afraid of not being respectable—and that was all. Now, I haven't any fear at all."

"You are a queer one!" exclaimed John. "You oughtn't to be in this life."

"Where then?" asked she.

"I don't know," he confessed.

"Neither do I." Her expression suddenly was absent, with a quaint, slight smile hovering about her lips. She looked at him merrily. "You see, it's got to be something that isn't respectable."

"What *do* you mean?" demanded he.

Her answer was a laugh.

Fatty declared it too cold to chase about afoot—
"Anyhow, it's late—nearly eleven, and unless we're
quick all the stores'll be closed." The waiter called
them a carriage; its driver promised to take them to a
shop that didn't close till midnight on Saturdays. Said
Fatty, as they drove away:

"Well, I suppose, Etta, you'll say you've never been
in a carriage before."

"Oh, yes, I have," cried Etta. "Twice—at funerals."

This made everyone laugh—this and the champagne
and the air which no longer seemed cruel to the girls
but stimulating, a grateful change from the close
warmth of the room. As the boys were smoking cigarettes, they had the windows down. The faces of both
girls were flushed and lively, and their cheeks seemed already to have filled out. The four made so much noise
that the crowds on the sidewalk were looking at them
—looking smilingly, delighted by the sight of such
gayety. Susan was even gayer than Etta. She sang,
she took a puff at John's cigarette; then laughed loudly
when he seized and kissed her, laughed again as she
kissed him; and she and John fell into each other's arms
and laughed uproariously as they saw Fatty and Etta
embracing.

The driver kept his promise; eleven o'clock found
them bursting into Sternberg's over the Rhine—a
famous department store for Germans of all classes.
They had an hour, and they made good use of it. Etta
was for yielding to Fatty's generous urgings and buying right and left. But Susan would not have it. She
told the men what she and Etta would take—a simple
complete outfit, and no more. Etta wanted furs and
finery. Susan kept her to plain, serviceable things.
Only once did she yield. When Etta and Fatty begged

to be allowed a big showy hat, Susan yielded—but gave John leave to buy her only the simplest of simple hats. "You needn't tell *me* any yarns about your birth and breeding," said he in a low tone so that Etta should not hear.

But that subject did not interest Susan. "Let's forget it," said she, almost curtly. "I've cut out the past—and the future. Today's enough for me."

"And for me, too," protested he. "I hope you're having as good fun as I am."

"This is the first time I've really laughed in nearly a year," said she. "You don't know what it means to be poor and hungry and cold—worst of all, cold."

"You unhappy child," said John tenderly.

But Susan was laughing again, and making jokes about a wonderful German party dress all covered with beads and lace and ruffles and embroidery. When they reached the shoe department, Susan asked John to take Fatty away. He understood that she was ashamed of their patched and holed stockings, and hastened to obey. They were making these their last purchases when the big bell rang for the closing. "I'm glad these poor tired shopgirls and clerks are set free," said John.

It was one of those well-meaning but worthless commonplaces of word-kindness that get for their utterance perhaps exaggerated credit for "good heart." Susan, conscience-stricken, halted. "And I never once thought of them!" she exclaimed. "It just shows."

"Shows what?"

"Oh, nothing. Come on. I must forget that, for I can't be happy again till I do. I understand now why the comfortable people can be happy. They keep from knowing or they make themselves forget."

"Why not?" said John. "What's the use in being

miserable about things that can't be helped?"

"No use at all," replied the girl. She laughed. "I've forgotten."

The carriage was so filled with their bundles that they had some difficulty in making room for themselves —finally accomplished it by each girl sitting on her young man's lap. They drove to a quietly placed, scrupulously clean little hotel overlooking Lincoln Park. "We're going to take rooms here and dress," explained Fatty. "Then we'll wander out and have some supper."

By this time Susan and Etta had lost all sense of strangeness. The spirit of adventure was rampant in them as in a dreaming child. And the life they had been living—what they had seen and heard and grown accustomed to—made it easy for them to strike out at once and briskly in the new road, so different from the dreary and cruel path along which they had been plodding. They stood laughing and joking in the parlor while the boys registered; then the four went up to two small but comfortable and fascinatingly clean rooms with a large bathroom between. "Fatty and I will go down to the bar while you two dress," said John.

"Not on your life!" exclaimed Fatty. "We'll have the bar brought up to us."

But John, fortified by Susan's look of gratitude for his tactfulness, whispered to his friend—what Susan could easily guess. And Fatty said, "Oh, I never thought of it. Yes, we'll give 'em a chance. Don't be long, girls."

"Thank you," said Susan to John.

"That's all right. Take your time."

Susan locked the hall door behind the two men. She rushed to the bathroom, turned on the hot water. "Oh,

Etta!" she cried, tears in her eyes, a hysterical sob in her throat. "A bathtub again!"

Etta too was enthusiastic; but she had not that intense hysterical joy which Susan felt—a joy that can be appreciated only by a person who, clean by instinct and by lifelong habit, has been shut out from thorough cleanliness for long months of dirt and foul odors and cold. It was no easy matter to become clean again after all those months. But there was plenty of soap and brushes and towels, and at last the thing was accomplished. Then they tore open the bundles and arrayed themselves in the fresh new underclothes, in the simple attractive costumes of jacket, blouse and skirt. Susan had returned to her class, and had brought Etta with her.

"What shall we do with these?" asked Etta, pointing disdainfully with the toe of her new boot to the scatter of the garments they had cast off.

Susan looked down at it in horror. She could not believe that *she* had been wearing such stuff—that it was the clothing of all her associates of the past six months—was the kind of attire in which most of her fellow-beings went about the beautiful earth. She shuddered. "Isn't life dreadful?" she cried. And she kicked together the tattered, patched, stained trash, kicked it on to a large piece of heavy wrapping paper she had spread out upon the floor. Thus, without touching her discarded self, she got it wrapped up and bound with a strong string. She rang for the maid, gave her a quarter and pointed to the bundle. "Please take that and throw it away," she said.

When the maid was gone Etta said: "I'm mighty glad to have it out of the room."

"Out of the room?" cried Susan. "Out of my heart.

Out of my life."

They put on their hats, admired themselves in the mirror, and descended—Susan remembering halfway that they had left the lights on and going back to turn them off. The door boy summoned the two young men to the parlor. They entered and exclaimed in real amazement. For they were facing two extremely pretty young women, one dark, the other fair. The two faces were wreathed in pleased and grateful smiles.

"Don't we look nice?" demanded Etta.

"Nice!" cried Fatty. "We sure did draw a pair of first prizes—didn't we, Johnny?"

John did not reply. He was gazing at Susan. Etta had young beauty but it was of the commonplace kind. In Susan's face and carriage there was far more than beauty. "Where *did* you come from?" said John to her in an undertone. "And *where* are you going?"

"Out to supper, I hope," laughed she.

"Your eyes change—don't they? I thought they were violet. Now I see they're gray—gray as can be."

XXII

A T lunch, well toward the middle of the following afternoon, Fatty—his proper name was August Gulick—said: "John and I don't start for Ann Arbor until a week from today. That means seven clear days. A lot can be done in that time, with a little intelligent hustling. What do you say, girls? Do you stick to us?"

"As long as you'll let us," said Etta, who was delighting Gulick with her frank and wondering and grateful appreciation of his munificence. Never before had his own private opinion of himself received such a flatteringly sweeping indorsement—from anyone who happened to impress him as worth while. In the last phrase lies the explanation of her success through a policy that is always dangerous and usually a failure.

So it was settled that with the quiet little hotel as headquarters the four would spend a week in exploring Cincinnati as a pleasure ground. Gulick knew the town thoroughly. His father was a brewer whose name was on many a huge beer wagon drawn about those streets by showy Clydesdales. Also he had plenty of money; and, while Redmond—for his friend was the son of Redmond, well known as a lawyer-politician in Chicago—had nothing like so much as Gulick, still he had enough to make a passable pretense at keeping up his end. For Etta and Susan the city had meant shabby to filthy tenements, toil and weariness and sorrow. There was opened to their ravished young eyes "the city"—what reveals itself to the pleasure-seeker with

392

pocket well filled—what we usually think of when we pronounce its name, forgetting what its reality is for all but a favored few of those within its borders. It was a week of music and of laughter—music especially —music whenever they ate or drank, music to dance by, music in the beer gardens where they spent the early evenings, music at the road houses where they arrived in sleighs after the dances to have supper—unless you choose to call it breakfast. You would have said that Susan had slipped out of the tenement life as she had out of its garments, that she had retained not a trace of it even in memory. But—in those days began her habit of never passing a beggar without giving something.

Within three or four days this life brought a truly amazing transformation in the two girls. You would not have recognized in them the pale and wan and ragged outcasts of only the Saturday night before. "Aren't you happy?" said Etta to Susan, in one of the few moments they were alone. "But I don't need to ask. I didn't know you could be so gay."

"I had forgotten how to laugh," replied Susan.

"I suppose I ought to be ashamed," pursued Etta.

"Why?" inquired Susan.

"Oh, you know why. You know how people'd talk if they knew."

"What people?" said Susan. "Anyone who's willing to give you anything?"

"No," admitted Etta. "But——" There she halted.

Susan went on: "I don't propose to be bothered by the other kind. They wouldn't do anything for me if they could—except sneer and condemn."

"Still, you know it isn't right, what we're doing."

"I know it isn't cold—or hunger—or rags and dirt
—and bugs," replied Susan.

Those few words were enough to conjure even to
Etta's duller fancy the whole picture to its last detail of loathsome squalor. Into Etta's face came a
dazed expression. "Was that really *us*, Lorna?"

"No," said Susan with a certain fierceness. "It was
a dream. But we must take care not to have that
dream again."

"I'd forgotten how cold I was," said Etta; "hadn't
you?"

"No," said Susan, "I hadn't forgotten anything."

"Yes, I suppose it was all worse for you than for
me. *You* used to be a lady."

"Don't talk nonsense," said Susan.

On Saturday afternoon the four were in one of the
rooms discussing where the farewell dinner should be
held and what they would eat and drink. Etta
called Susan into the other room and shut the door
between.

"Fatty wants me to go along with him and live in
Detroit," said she, blurting it out as if confessing a
crime.

At that moment Redmond came in, and Etta left
him alone with Susan. "Well, has Etta told you?"
he asked.

"Yes," replied the girl. She looked at him—simply
a look, but the violet-gray eyes had an unusual seeming of seeing into minds and hearts, an expression
that was perhaps the more disquieting because it was
sympathetic rather than critical.

His glance shifted. He was a notably handsome
young fellow—too young for any display of character

in his face, or for any development of it beyond the amiable, free and easy lover of a jolly good time that is the type repeated over and over again among the youth of the comfortable classes that send their sons to college.

"Are you going with her?" he asked.

"No," said Susan.

Redmond's face fell. "I hoped you liked me a little better than that," said he.

"It isn't a question of you."

"But it's a question of *you* with me," he cried. "I'm in love with you, Lorna. I'm—I'm tempted to say all sorts of crazy things that I think but haven't the courage to act on." He kneeled down beside her, put his arms round her waist. "I'm crazy about you, Lorna. . . . Tell me—Were you—Had you been—before we met?"

"Yes," said Susan.

"Why don't you deny it?" he exclaimed. "Why don't you fool me, as Etta fooled Gus?"

"Etta's story is different from mine," said Susan. "She's had no experience at all, compared to me."

"I don't believe it," declared he. "I know she's been stuffing Fatty, has made him think that you led her away. But I can soon knock those silly ideas out of his silly head——"

"It's the truth," interrupted Susan, calmly.

"No matter. You could be a good woman." Impulsively, "If you'll settle down and be a good woman, I'll marry you."

Susan smiled gently. "And ruin your prospects?"

"I don't care for prospects beside you. You *are* a good woman—inside. The better I know you the less like a fast woman you are. Won't you go to work,

Lorna, and wait for me?"

Her smile had a little mockery in it now—perhaps to hide from him how deeply she was moved. "No matter what else I did, I'd not wait for you, Johnny. You'd never come. You're not a Johnny-on-the-spot."

"You think I'm weak—don't you?" he said. Then, as she did not answer, "Well, I am. But I love you, all the same."

For the first time he felt that he had touched her heart. The tears sprang to her eyes, which were not at all gray now but all violet, as was their wont when she was deeply moved. She laid her hands on his shoulders. "Oh, it's so good to be loved!" she murmured.

He put his arms around her, and for the moment she rested there, content—yes, content, as many a woman who needed love less and craved it less has been content just with being loved, when to make herself content she has had to ignore and forget the personality of the man who was doing the loving—and the kind of love it was. Said he:

"Don't you love me a little—enough to be a good woman and wait till I set up in the law?"

She let herself play with the idea, to prolong this novel feeling of content. She asked, "How long will that be?"

"I'll be admitted in two years. I'll soon have a practice. My father's got influence."

Susan looked at him sadly, slowly shook her head. "Two years—and then several years more. And I working in a factory—or behind a counter—from dawn till after dark—poor, hungry—half-naked—wearing my heart out—wearing my body away——"

She drew away from him, laughed. "I was fooling, John—about marrying. I liked to hear you say those things. I couldn't marry you if I would. I'm married already."

"*You!*"

She nodded.

"Tell me about it—won't you?"

She looked at him in astonishment, so amazing seemed the idea that she could tell anyone that experience. It would be like voluntarily showing a hideous, repulsive scar or wound, for sometimes it was scar, and sometimes open wound, and always the thing that made whatever befell her endurable by comparison.

She did not answer his appeal for her confidence but went on, "Anyhow, nothing could induce me to go to work again. You don't realize what work means—the only sort of work I can get to do. It's—it's selling both body and soul. I prefer——"

He kissed her to stop her from finishing her sentence. "Don't—please," he pleaded. "You don't understand. In this life you'll soon grow hard and coarse and lose your beauty and your health—and become a moral and physical wreck."

She reflected, the grave expression in her eyes—the expression that gave whoever saw it the feeling of dread as before impending tragedy. "Yes—I suppose so," she said. "But—— Any sooner than as a working girl living in a dirty hole in a tenement? No—not so soon. And in this life I've got a chance—if I'm careful of my health and—and don't let things touch *me*. Were you ever cold?"

But it made no impression upon him who had no conception of the cold that knows not how it is ever to get warm again. He rushed on:

"Lorna, my God!" He caught hold of her and strained her to his breast. "You are lovely and sweet! It's frightful—you in this life."

Her expression made the sobs choke up into his throat. She said quietly: "Not worse than dirt and vermin and freezing cold and long, long, dull—oh, *so* dull hours of working among human beings that don't ever wash—because they can't." She pushed him gently away. "You don't understand. You haven't been through it. Comfortable people talk like fools about those things. . . . Do you remember my hands that first evening?"

He reddened and his eyes shifted. "I'm absurdly sensitive about a woman's hands," he muttered.

She laughed at him. "Oh, I saw—how you couldn't bear to look at them—how they made you shiver. Well, the hands were nothing—*nothing!*—beside what you didn't see."

"Lorna, do you love someone else?"

His eyes demanded an honest answer, and it seemed to her his feeling for her deserved it. But she could not put the answer into words. She lowered her gaze.

"Then why——" he began impetuously. But there he halted, for he knew she would not lift the veil over herself, over her past.

"I'm very, very fond of you," she said with depressing friendliness. Then with a sweet laugh, "You ought to be glad I'm not able to take you at your word. And you will be glad soon." She sighed. "What a good time we've had!"

"If I only had a decent allowance, like Fatty!" he groaned.

"No use talking about that. It's best for us to separate—best for us both. You've been good to me—
you'll never know how good. And I can't play you a
mean trick. I wish I could be selfish enough to do it,
but I can't."

"You don't love me. That's the reason."

"Maybe it is. Yes, I guess that's why I've got the
courage to be square with you. Anyhow, John, you
can't afford to care for me. And if I cared for you,
and put off the parting—why it'd only put off what
I've got to go through with before——" She did not
finish; her eyes became dreamy.

"Before—what?" he asked.

"I don't know," she said, returning with a sigh.
"Something I see—yet don't see—in the darkness,
ahead of me."

"I can't make you out," cried he. Her expression
moved him to the same awe she inspired in Etta—a
feeling that gave both of them the sense of having
known her better, of having been more intimate with
her when they first met her than they ever had been
since or ever would be again.

When Redmond embraced and kissed her for the last
time, he was in another and less sympathetic mood, was
busy with his own wounds to vanity and perhaps to
heart. He thought her heartless—good and sweet and
friendly, but without sentiment. She refused to help
him make a scene; she refused to say she would write
to him, and asked him not to write to her. "You know
we'll probably see each other soon."

"Not till the long vacation—not till nearly
July."

"Only three months."

"Oh, if you look at it that way!" said he, piqued

399

and sullen. Girls had always been more than kind, more than eager, when he had shown interest.

Etta, leaving on a later train, was even more depressed about Susan's heart. She wept hysterically, wished Susan to do the same; but Susan stood out firmly against a scene, and would not have it that Etta was shamefully deserting her, as Etta tearfully accused herself. "You're going to be happy," she said. "And I'm not so selfish as to be wretched about it. And don't you worry a minute on my account. I'm better off in every way than I've ever been. I'll get on all right."

"I know you gave up John to help me with August. I know you mean to break off everything. Oh, Lorna, you mustn't—you mustn't."

"Don't talk nonsense," was Susan's unsatisfactory reply.

When it came down to the last embrace and the last kiss, Etta did feel through Susan's lips and close encircling arms a something that dried up her hysterical tears and filled her heart with an awful aching. It did not last long. No matter how wildly shallow waters are stirred, they soon calm and murmur placidly on again. The three who had left her would have been amazed could they have seen her a few minutes after Etta's train rolled out of the Union Station. The difference between strong natures and weak is not that the strong are free from cowardice and faint-heartedness, from doubt and foreboding, from love and affection, but that they do not stay down when they are crushed down, stagger up and on.

Susan hurried to the room they had helped her find the day before—a room in a house where no questions were asked or answered. She locked herself in and gave

way to the agonies of her loneliness. And when her grief
had exhausted her, she lay upon the bed staring at the
wall with eyes that looked as though her soul had emptied itself through them of all that makes life endurable, even of hope. For the first time in her life she
thought of suicide—not suicide the vague possibility,
not suicide the remote way of escape, but suicide the
close and intimate friend, the healer of all woes, the
solace of all griefs—suicide, the speedy, accurate solver
of the worst problem destiny can put to man.

She saw her pocketbook on the floor where she had
dropped it. "I'll wait till my money's gone," thought
she. Then she remembered Etta—how gentle and loving she was, how utterly she gave herself—for Susan
was still far from the profound knowledge of character
that enables us to disregard outward signs in measuring
actualities. "If I really weren't harder than Etta," her
thoughts ran on reproachfully, "I'd not wait until the
money went. I'd kill myself now, and have it over with."
The truth was that if the position of the two girls had
been reversed and Susan had loved Gulick as intensely
as Etta professed and believed she loved him, still Susan
would have given him up rather than have left Etta
alone. And she would have done it without any sense
of sacrifice. And it must be admitted that, whether
or not there are those who deserve credit for doing
right, certainly those who do right simply because they
cannot do otherwise—the only trustworthy people—deserve no credit for it.

She counted her money—twenty-three dollars in bills,
and some change. Redmond had given her fifty dollars
each time they had gone shopping, and had made her
keep the balance—his indirect way of adjusting the
financial side. Twenty-three dollars meant perhaps

two weeks' living. Well, she would live those two weeks decently and comfortably and then—bid life adieu unless something turned up—for back to the streets she would not go. With Etta gone, with not a friend anywhere on earth, life was not worth the price she had paid for Etta and herself to the drunken man. Her streak of good fortune in meeting Redmond had given her no illusions; from Mabel Connemora, from what she herself had heard and seen—and experienced—she knew the street woman's life, and she could not live that life for herself alone. She could talk about it to Redmond tranquilly. She could think about it in the abstract, could see how other women did it, and how those who had intelligence might well survive and lift themselves up in it. But do it she could not. So she resolved upon suicide, firmly believing in her own resolve. And she was not one to deceive herself or to shrink from anything whatsoever. Except the insane, only the young make these resolves and act upon them; for the young have not yet learned to value life, have not yet fallen under life's sinister spell that makes human beings cling more firmly and more cravenly to it as they grow older. The young must have something—some hope, however fanatic and false—to live for. They will not tarry just to live. And in that hour Susan had lost hope.

She took off her street dress and opened her **trunk** to get a wrapper and bedroom slippers. As she lifted the lid, she saw an envelope addressed "Lorna"; she remembered that Redmond had locked and strapped the trunk. She tore the end from the envelope, looked in. Some folded bills; nothing more. She sat on the floor and counted two twenties, five tens, two fives—a hundred dollars! She looked dazedly at the money—gave a cry of delight—sprang to her feet, with a change like the startling shift from night to day in the tropics.

"I can pay!" she cried. "I can pay!"

Bubbling over with smiles and with little laughs, gay as even champagne and the release from the vile prison of the slums had made her, she with eager hands took from the trunk her best clothes—the jacket and skirt of dark gray check she had bought for thirty dollars at Shillito's and had had altered to her figure and her taste; the blouse of good quality linen with rather a fancy collar; the gray leather belt with a big oxidized silver buckle; her only pair of silk stockings; the pair of high-heeled patent leather shoes—the large black hat with a gray feather curling attractively round and over its brim. The hat had cost only fourteen dollars because she had put it together herself; if she had bought it made, she would have paid not less than thirty dollars.

All these things she carefully unpacked and carefully laid out. Then she thoroughly brushed her hair and did it up in a graceful pompadour that would go well with the hat. She washed away the traces of her outburst of grief, went over her finger nails, now almost recovered from the disasters incident to the life of manual labor. She went on to complete her toilet, all with the same attention to detail—a sure indication, in one so young, of a desire to please some specific person. When she had the hat set at the satisfactory angle and the veil wound upon it and draped over her fresh young face coquettishly, she took from her slender store of gloves a fresh gray pair and, as she put them on, stood before the glass examining herself.

There was now not a trace of the tenement working girl of a week and a day before. Here was beauty in bloom, fresh and alluring from head to narrow, well-booted feet. More than a hint of a fine color sense—that vital quality, if fashion, the conventional, is to be refined and individualized into style, the rare—more than a hint of color sense showed in the harmony of the pearl gray in the big feather, the pearl gray in the collar of the blouse, and the pearl white of her skin. Susan had indeed returned to her own class. She had left it, a small-town girl with more than a suggestion of the child in eyes and mouth; she had returned to it, a young woman of the city, with that look in her face which only experience can give—experience that has resulted in growth. She locked all her possessions away in her trunk—all but her money; that she put in her stockings—seventy-five dollars well down in the right leg, the rest of the bills well down in the left leg; the two dollars or so in change was all she intrusted to the pocketbook she carried. She cast a coquettish glance down at her charmingly arrayed feet—a harmless glance of coquetry that will be condemned by those whose physical vanity happens to center elsewhere. After this glance she dropped her skirts—and was ready.

By this time dusk had fallen, and it was nearly six o'clock. As she came out of the house she glanced toward the west—the instinctive gesture of people who live in rainy climates. Her face brightened; she saw an omen in the long broad streak of reddened evening sky.

XXIII

SHE went down to Fourth Street, along it to Race, to the *Commercial* building. At the entrance to the corridor at the far side of which were elevator and stairway, she paused and considered. She turned into the business office.

"Is Mr. Roderick Spenser here?" she asked of a heavily built, gray-bearded man in the respectable black of the old-fashioned financial employee, showing the sobriety and stolidity of his character in his dress.

"He works upstairs," replied the old man, beaming approvingly upon the pretty, stylish young woman.

"Is he there now?"

"I'll telephone." He went into the rear office, presently returned with the news that Mr. Spenser had that moment left, was probably on his way down in the elevator. "And you'll catch him if you go to the office entrance right away."

Susan, the inexperienced in the city ways of men with women, did not appreciate what a tribute to her charms and to her character, as revealed in the honest, grave eyes, was the old man's unhesitating assumption that Spenser would wish to see her. She lost no time in retracing her steps. As she reached the office entrance she saw at the other end of the long hall two young men coming out of the elevator. After the habit of youth, she had rehearsed speech and manner for this meeting; but at sight of him she was straightway trembling so that she feared she would be unable to speak at all. The entrance light was dim, but as he glanced at her in passing he saw her looking at him and his hand moved toward his hat. His face had not changed—the same frank, careless expression, the same sympathetic, understanding look out of the eyes. But he was the city man in dress now—notably the city man.

"Mr. Spenser," said she shyly.

He halted; his companion went on. He lifted his hat, looked inquiringly at her—the look of the enthusiast and connoisseur on the subject of pretty women, when he finds a new specimen worthy of his attention.

"Don't you know me?"

His expression of puzzled and flirtatious politeness gradually cleared away. The lighting up of his eyes, the smile round his mouth delighted her; and she grew radiant when he exclaimed eagerly, "Why, it's the little girl of the rock again! How you've grown—in a year —less than a year!"

"Yes, I suppose I have," said she, thinking of it for the first time. Then, to show him at once what a good excuse she had for intruding again, she hastened to add, "I've come to pay you that money you loaned me."

He burst out laughing, drew her into the corridor where the light was brighter. "And you've gone back to your husband," he said—she noted the quick, sharp change in his voice.

"Why do you think that?" she said.

The way his eyes lingered upon the charming details of a toilet that indicated anything but poverty might have given her a simple explanation. He offered another.

"I can't explain. It's your different expression—a kind of experienced look."

The color flamed and flared in Susan's face.

"You are—happy?" he asked.

"I've not seen—him," evaded she. "Ever since I left Carrollton I've been wandering about."

"Wandering about?" he repeated absently, his eyes busy with her appearance.

"And now," she went on, nervous and hurried, "I'm here in town—for a while."

"Then I may come to see you?"

"I'd be glad. I'm alone in a furnished room I've taken—out near Lincoln Park."

"Alone! You don't mean you're still wandering?"

"Still wandering."

He laughed. "Well, it certainly is doing you no harm. The reverse." An embarrassed pause, then he said with returning politeness: "Maybe you'll dine with me this evening?"

She beamed. "I've been hoping you'd ask me."

"It won't be as good as the one on the rock."

"There never will be another dinner like that," declared she. "Your leg is well?"

Her question took him by surprise. In his interest and wonder as to the new mystery of this mysterious young person he had not recalled the excuses he made for dropping out of the entanglement in which his impulses had put him. The color poured into his face. "Ages ago," he replied, hurriedly. "I'd have forgotten it, if it hadn't been for you. I've never been able to get you out of my head." And as a matter of truth she had finally dislodged his cousin Nell—without lingering long or vividly herself. Young Mr. Spenser was too busy and too self-absorbed a man to bother long about any one flower in a world that was one vast field abloom with open-petaled flowers.

"Nor I you," said she, as pleased as he had expected.

and showing it with a candor that made her look almost
the child he had last seen. "You see, I owed you that
money, and I wanted to pay it."

"Oh—*that* was all!" exclaimed he, half jokingly.
"Wait here a minute." And he went to the door, looked
up and down the street, then darted across it and disappeared into the St. Nicholas Hotel. He was not
gone more than half a minute.

"I had to see Bayne and tell him," he explained when
he was with her again. "I was to have dined with him
and some others—over in the café. Instead, you and
I will dine upstairs. You won't mind my not being
dressed?"

It seemed to her he was dressed well enough for any
occasion. "I'd rather you had on the flannel trousers
rolled up to your knees," said she. "But I can imagine
them."

"What a dinner that was!" cried he. "And the ride
afterward," with an effort at ease that escaped her bedazzled eyes. "Why didn't you ever write?"

He expected her to say that she did not know his
address, and was ready with protests and excuses. But
she replied:

"I didn't have the money to pay what I owed you."
They were crossing Fourth Street and ascending the
steps to the hotel. "Then, too—afterward—when I
got to know a little more about life—I—— Oh, no
matter. Really, the money was the only reason."

But he had stopped short. In a tone so correctly
sincere that a suspicious person might perhaps have
doubted the sincerity of the man using it, he said:

"What was in your mind? What did you think?
What did you—suspect me of? For I see in that
honest, telltale face of yours that it was a suspicion."

"I didn't blame you," protested the girl, "even if it was so. I thought maybe you got to thinking it over— and—didn't want to be bothered with anyone so troublesome as I had made myself."

"How *could* you suspect *me* of such a thing?"

"Oh, I really didn't," declared she, with all the earnestness of a generous nature, for she read into his heightened color and averted eyes the feelings she herself would have had before an unjust suspicion. "It was merely an idea. And I didn't blame you—not in the least. It would have been the sensible——"

Next thing, this child-woman, this mysterious mind of mixed precocity and innocence, would be showing that she had guessed a Cousin Nell.

"You are far too modest," interrupted he with a flirtatious smile. "You didn't realize how strong an impression you made. No, I really broke my leg. Don't you suppose I knew the twenty-five in the pocketbook wouldn't carry you far?" He saw—and naturally misunderstood—her sudden change of expression as he spoke of the amount. He went on apologetically, "I intended to bring more when I came. I was afraid to put money in the note for fear it'd never be delivered, if I did. And didn't I tell you to write—and didn't I give you my address here? Would I have done that, if I hadn't meant to stand by you?"

Susan was convinced, was shamed by these smooth, plausible assertions and explanations. "Your father's house—it's a big brick, with stone trimmings, standing all alone outside the little town—isn't it?"

Spenser was again coloring deeply. "Yes," admitted he uneasily.

But Susan didn't notice. "I saw the doctor—and your family—on the veranda," she said.

He was now so nervous that she could not but observe it. "They gave out that it was only a sprain," said he, "because I told them I didn't want it known. I didn't want the people at the office to know I was going to be laid up so long. I was afraid I'd lose my job."

"I didn't hear anything about it," said she. "I only saw as I was going by on a boat."

He looked disconcerted—but not to her eyes. "Well—it's far in the past now," said he. "Let's forget—all but the fun."

"Yes—all but the fun." Then very sweetly, "But I'll never forget what I owe you. Not the money—not that, hardly at all—but what you did for me. It made me able to go on."

"Don't speak of it," cried he, flushed and shamefaced. "I didn't do half what I ought." Like most human beings he was aware of his more obvious—if less dangerous—faults and weaknesses. He liked to be called generous, but always had qualms when so called because he knew he was in fact of the familiar type classed as generous only because human beings are so artless in their judgments as to human nature that they cannot see that quick impulses quickly die. The only deep truth is that there are no generous natures but just natures—and they are rarely classed as generous because their slowly formed resolves have the air of prudence and calculation.

In the hotel she went to the dressing-room, took twenty-five dollars from the money in her stocking. As soon as they were seated in the restaurant she handed it to him.

"But this makes it you who are having me to dinner—and more," he protested.

"If you knew what a weight it's been on me, you'd not talk that way," said she.

Her tone compelled him to accept her view of the matter. He laughed and put the money in his waistcoat pocket, saying: "Then I'll still owe you a dinner."

During the past week she had been absorbing as only a young woman with a good mind and a determination to learn the business of living can absorb. The lessons before her had been the life that is lived in cities by those who have money to spend and experience in spending it; she had learned out of all proportion to opportunity. At a glance she realized that she was now in a place far superior to the Bohemian resorts which had seemed to her inexperience the best possible. From earliest childhood she had shown the delicate sense of good taste and of luxury that always goes with a practical imagination—practical as distinguished from the idealistic kind of imagination that is vague, erratic, and fond of the dreams which neither could nor should come true. And the reading she had done— the novels, the memoirs, the books of travel, the fashion and home magazines—had made deep and distinct impressions upon her, had prepared her—as they have prepared thousands of Americans in secluded towns and rural regions where luxury and even comfort are very crude indeed—for the possible rise of fortune that is the universal American dream and hope. She felt these new surroundings exquisitely—the subdued coloring, the softened lights, the thick carpets, the quiet elegance and comfort of the furniture. She noted the good manners of the well-trained waiter; she listened admiringly and memorizingly as Spenser ordered the dinner—a dinner of French good taste—small but fine oysters, a thick soup, a guinea hen *en casserole*, a fruit salad, fresh strawberry ice cream, dry champagne. She saw that Spenser knew what he was about, and she was delighted with him and proud to be with him and glad that he had tastes like her own—that is, tastes such as she proposed to learn to have. Of the men she had known or known about he seemed to her far and away the best. It isn't necessary to explain into what an attitude of mind and heart this feeling of his high superiority immediately put her—certainly not for the enlightenment of any woman.

"What are you thinking?" he asked—the question that was so often thrust at her because, when she thought intensely, there was a curiosity-compelling expression in her eyes.

"Oh—about all this," replied she. "I like this sort of thing so much. I never had it in my life, yet now that I see it I feel as if I were part of it, as if it must belong to me." Her eyes met his sympathetic gaze. "You understand, don't you?" He nodded. "And I was wondering"—she laughed, as if she expected even him to laugh at her—"I was wondering how long it would be before I should possess it. Do you think I'm crazy?"

He shook his head. "I've got that same feeling," said he. "I'm poor—don't dare do this often—have all I can manage in keeping myself decently. Yet I have a conviction that I shall—shall win. Don't think I'm dreaming of being rich—not at all. I—I don't care much about that if I did go into business. But I want all my surroundings to be right."

Her eyes gleamed. "And you'll get it. And so shall I. I know it sounds improbable and absurd for me to say that about myself. But—I know it."

"I believe you," said he. "You've got the look in

412

your face—in your eyes. . . . I've never seen anyone improve as you have in this less than a year."

She smiled as she thought in what surroundings she had apparently spent practically all that time. "If you could have seen me!" she said. "Yes, I was learning and I know it. I led a sort of double life. I——" she hesitated, gave up trying to explain. She had not the words and phrases, the clear-cut ideas, to express that inner life led by people who have real imagination. With most human beings their immediate visible surroundings determine their life; with the imaginative few their horizon is always the whole wide world.

She sighed, "But I'm ignorant. I don't know how or where to take hold."

"I can't help you there, yet," said he. "When we know each other better, then I'll know. Not that you need me to tell you. You'll find out for yourself. One always does."

She glanced round the attractive room again, then looked at him with narrowed eyelids. "Only a few hours ago I was thinking of suicide. How absurd it seems now!—I'll never do that again. At least, I've learned how to profit by a lesson. Mr. Burlingham taught me that."

"Who's he?"

"That's a long story. I don't feel like telling about it now."

But the mere suggestion had opened certain doors in her memory and crowds of sad and bitter thoughts came trooping in.

"Are you in some sort of trouble?" said he, instantly leaning toward her across the table and all aglow with the impulsive sympathy that kindles in impressionable natures as quickly as fire in dry grass. Such natures are as perfect conductors of emotion as platinum is of heat—instantly absorbing it, instantly throwing it off, to return to their normal and metallic chill—and capacity for receptiveness. "Anything you can tell me about?"

"Oh, no—nothing especial," replied she. "Just loneliness and a feeling of—of discouragement." Strongly, "Just a mood. I'm never really discouraged. Something always turns up."

"Please tell me what happened after I left you at that wretched hotel."

"I can't," she said. "At least, not now."

"There is——" He looked sympathetically at her, as if to assure her that he would understand, no matter what she might confess. "There is—someone?"

"No. I'm all alone. I'm—free." It was not in the least degree an instinct for deception that made her then convey an impression of there having been no one. She was simply obeying her innate reticence that was part of her unusual self-unconsciousness.

"And you're not worried about—about money matters?" he asked. "You see, I'm enough older and more experienced to give me excuse for asking. Besides, unless a woman has money, she doesn't find it easy to get on."

"I've enough for the present," she assured him, and the stimulus of the champagne made her look—and feel—much more self-confident than she really was. "More than I've ever had before. So I'm not worried. When anyone has been through what I have they aren't so scared about the future."

He looked the admiration he felt—and there was not a little of the enthusiasm of the champagne both in the look and in the admiration—"I see you've already learned to play the game without losing your nerve."

"I begin to hope so," said she.

"Yes—you've got the signs of success in your face. Curious about those signs. Once you learn to know them, you never miss in sizing up people."

The dinner had come. Both were hungry, and it was as good a dinner as the discussion about it between Spenser and the waiter had forecast. As they ate the well-cooked, well-served food and drank the delicately flavored champagne, mellow as the gorgeous autumn its color suggested, there diffused through them an extraordinary feeling of quiet intense happiness—happiness of mind and body. Her face took on a new and finer beauty; into his face came a tenderness that was most becoming to its rather rugged features. And he had not talked with her long before he discovered that he was facing not a child, not a child-woman, but a woman grown, one who could understand and appreciate the things men and women of experience say and do.

"I've always been expecting to hear from you every day since we separated," he said—and he was honestly believing it now. "I've had a feeling that you hadn't forgotten me. It didn't seem possible I could feel so strongly unless there was real sympathy between us."

"I came as soon as I could."

He reflected in silence a moment, then in a tone that made her heart leap and her blood tingle, he said: "You say you're free?"

"Free as air. Only—I couldn't fly far."

He hesitated on an instinct of prudence, then ventured. "Far as New York?"

"What is the railroad fare?"

"Oh, about twenty-five dollars—with sleeper."

"Yes—I can fly that far."

"Do you mean to say you've no ties of any kind?"

"None. Not one." Her eyes opened wide and her nostrils dilated. "Free!"

"You love it—don't you?"

"Don't you?"

"Above everything!" he exclaimed. "Only the free *live*."

She lifted her head higher in a graceful, attractive gesture of confidence and happiness. "Well—I am ready to live."

"I'm afraid you don't realize," he said hesitatingly. "People wouldn't understand. You've your reputation to think of, you know."

She looked straight at him. "No—not even that. I'm even free from reputation." Then, as his face saddened and his eyes glistened with sympathy, "You needn't pity me. See where it's brought me."

"You're a strong swimmer—aren't you?" he said tenderly. "But then there isn't any safe and easy crossing to the isles of freedom. It's no wonder most people don't get further than gazing and longing."

"Probably I shouldn't," confessed Susan, "if I hadn't been thrown into the water. It was a case of swim or drown."

"But most who try are drowned—nearly all the women."

"Oh, I guess there are more survive than is generally supposed. So much lying is done about that sort of thing."

"What a shrewd young lady it is! At any rate, you have reached the islands."

"But I'm not queen of them yet," she reminded him. "I'm only a poor, naked, out-of-breath castaway lying on the beach."

He laughed appreciatively. Very clever, this extremely pretty young woman. "Yes—you'll win. You'll be queen." He lifted his champagne glass and watched the little bubbles pushing gayly and swiftly upward. "So—you've cast over your reputation."

"I told you I had reached the beach naked." A reckless light in her eyes now. "Fact is, I had none to start with. Anybody has a reason for starting—or for being started. That was mine, I guess."

"I've often thought about that matter of reputation—in a man or a woman—if they're trying to make the bold, strong swim. To care about one's reputation means fear of what the world says. It's important to care about one's character—for without character no one ever got anywhere worth getting to. But it's very, very dangerous to be afraid for one's reputation. And—I hate to admit it, because I'm hopelessly conventional at bottom, but it's true —reputation—fear of what the world says—has sunk more swimmers, has wrecked more characters than it ever helped. So—the strongest and best swimmers swim naked."

Susan was looking thoughtfully at him over the rim of her glass. She took a sip of the champagne, said: "If I hadn't been quite naked, I'd have sunk—I'd have been at the bottom—with the fishes——"

"But you ought to be proud that you arrived."

"No—only glad," said she. "So—so *frightfully* glad!"

In any event, their friendship was bound to flourish; aided by that dinner and that wine it sprang up into an intimacy, a feeling of mutual trust and of sympathy at every point. Like all women she admired strength in a man above everything else. She delighted in the thick obstinate growth of his fair hair, in the breadth of the line of his eyebrows, in the aggressive thrust of his large nose and long jawbone. She saw in the way his mouth closed evidence of a will against which opposition would dash about as dangerously as an egg against a stone wall. There was no question of his having those birthmarks of success about which he talked. She saw them—saw nothing of the less obtrusive—but not less important—marks of weakness which might have enabled an expert in the reading of faces to reach some rather depressing conclusion as to the nature and the degree of that success.

Finally, he burst out with, "Yes, I've made up my mind. I'll do it! I'm going to New York. I've been fooling away the last five years here—learning a lot, but still idling—drinking—amusing myself in all kinds of ways. And about a month ago—one night, as I was rolling home toward dawn—through a driving sleet storm—do you remember a line in 'Paradise Lost'——"

"I never read it," interrupted Susan.

"Well—it's where the devils have been kicked out of Heaven and are lying in agony flat on the burning lake—and Satan rises up—and marches haughtily out among them—and calls out, 'Awake! Arise! Or forever more be damned!' That's what has happened to me several times in my life. When I was a boy, idling about the farm and wasting myself, that voice came to me—'Awake! Arise! Or forever more be damned!' And I got a move on me, and insisted on going to college. Again—at college —I became a dawdler—poker—drink—dances—all the rest of it. And suddenly that voice roared in my ears, made me jump like a rabbit when a gun goes off. And last month it came again. I went to work —finished a play I've been pottering over for three years. But somehow I couldn't find the—the—whatever I needed—to make me break away. Well—*you've* given me that. I'll resign from the *Commercial* and with all I've got in the world—three hundred dollars and a trunk full of good clothes, I'll break into Broadway."

Susan had listened with bright eyes and quickened breath, as intoxicated and as convinced as was he by his eloquence. "Isn't that splendid!" she exclaimed in a low voice. . . . .

"And you?" he said meaningly.

"I?" she replied, fearing she was misunderstanding.

"Will you go?"

"Do you want me?" she asked, low and breathlessly.

With a reluctance which suggested—but not to her —that his generosity was winning a hard-fought battle with his vanity, he replied: "I need you. I doubt if I'd dare, without you to back me up."

"I've got a trunk full of fairly good clothes and about a hundred dollars. But I haven't got any play —or any art—or any trade even. Of course, I'll go." Then she hastily added, "I'll not be a drag on you. I pay my own way."

"But you mustn't be suspicious in your independence," he warned her. "You mustn't forget that I'm older than you and more experienced and that it's far easier for a man to get money than for a woman."

"To get it without lowering himself?"

"Ah!" he exclaimed, looking strangely at her. "You mean, without bowing to some boss? Without selling his soul? I had no idea you were so much of a woman when I met you that day."

"I wasn't—then," replied she. "And I didn't know where I'd got till we began to talk this evening."

"And you're very young!"

"Oh, but I've been going to a school where they make you learn fast."

"Indeed I do need you." He touched his glass to hers. "On to Broadway!" he cried.

"Broadway!" echoed she, radiant.

"Together—eh?"

She nodded. But as she drank the toast a tear splashed into her glass. She was remembering how some mysterious instinct had restrained her from going with John Redmond, though it seemed the only sane thing to do. What if she had disobeyed that instinct! And then—through her mind in swift ghostly march—past trailed the persons and events of the days just gone—just gone, yet seeming as far away as a former life in another world. Redmond and Gulick—Etta—yes, Etta, too—all past and gone—forever gone——

"What are you thinking about?"

She shook her head and the spectral procession vanished into the glooms of memory's vistas. "Thinking? —of yesterday. I don't understand myself—how I shake off and forget what's past. Nothing seems real to me but the future."

"Not even the present?" said he with a smile.

"Not even the present," she answered with grave candor. "Nothing seems to touch me—the real me.

It's like—like looking out of the window of the train at the landscape running by. I'm a traveler passing through. I wonder if it'll always be that way. I wonder if I'll ever arrive where I'll feel that I belong."

"I think so—and soon."

But she did not respond to his confident smile. "I— I hope so," she said with sad, wistful sweetness. "Then again—aren't there some people who don't belong anywhere—aren't allowed to settle down and be happy, but have to keep going—on and on—until——"

"Until they pass out into the dark," he finished for her. "Yes." He looked at her in a wondering uneasy way. "You do suggest that kind," said he. "But," smilingly, to hide his earnestness, "I'll try to detain you."

"Please do," she said. "I don't want to go on— alone."

He dropped into silence, puzzled and in a way awed by the mystery enveloping her—a mystery of aloofness and stoniness, of complete separation from the contact of the world—the mystery that incloses all whose real life is lived deep within themselves.

XXIV

FIVE days later, on the Eastern Express, they were not so confident as they had been over the St. Nicholas champagne. As confident about the remoter future, it was that annoying little stretch near at hand which gave them secret uneasiness. There had been nothing but dreaming and sentimentalizing in those four days—and that disquietingly suggested the soldier who with an impressive flourish highly resolves to give battle, then sheathes his sword and goes away to a revel. Also, like all idlers, they had spent money— far more money than total net cash resources of less than five hundred dollars warranted.

"We've spent an awful lot of money," said Susan.

She was quick to see the faint frown, the warning that she was on dangerous ground. Said he:

"Do you regret?"

"No, indeed—no!" cried she, eager to have that cloud vanish, but honest too.

She no more than he regretted a single moment of the dreaming and love-making, a single penny of the eighty and odd dollars that had enabled them fittingly to embower their romance, to twine myrtle in their hair and to provide Cupid's torch-bowls with fragrant incense. Still—with the battle not begun, there gaped that deep, wide hollow in the war chest.

Spenser's newspaper connection got them passes over one of the cheaper lines to New York—and he tried to console himself by setting this down as a saving of forty dollars against the eighty dollars of the debit item. But he couldn't altogether forget that they would have traveled on passes, anyhow. He was not regretting that he had indulged in the extravagance of a stateroom—but he couldn't deny that it was an extravagance. However, he had only to look at her to feel that he had done altogether well in providing for her the best, and to believe that he could face with courage any fate so long as he had her at his side.

"Yes, I can face anything with you," he said. "What I feel for you is the real thing. The real thing, at last."

She had no disposition to inquire curiously into this. Her reply was a flash of a smile that was like a flash of glorious light upon the crest of a wave surging straight from her happy heart.

They were opposite each other at breakfast in the restaurant car. He delighted in her frank delight in the novelty of travel—swift and luxurious travel. He had never been East before, himself, but he had had experience of sleepers and diners; she had not, and every moment she was getting some new sensation. She especially enjoyed this sitting at breakfast with the express train rushing smoothly along through the mountains—the first mountains either had seen. At times they were so intensely happy that they laughed with tears in their eyes and touched hands across the table to get from physical contact the reassurances of reality.

"How good to eat everything is!" she exclaimed. "You'll think me very greedy, I'm afraid. But if you'd eaten the stuff I have since we dined on the rock!"

They were always going back to the rock, and neither wearied of recalling and reminding each other of the smallest details. It seemed to them that everything, even the least happening, at that sacred spot must be remembered, must be recorded indelibly in the book of their romance. "I'm glad we were happy together in such circumstances," she went on. "It was a test— wasn't it, Rod?"

"If two people don't love each other enough to be happy anywhere, they could be happy nowhere," declared he.

"So, we'll not mind being very, very careful about spending money in New York," she ventured—for she was again bringing up the subject she had been privately revolving ever since they had formed the partnership. In her wanderings with Burlingham, in her sojourn in the tenements, she had learned a great deal about the care and spending of money—had developed that instinct for forehandedness which nature has implanted in all normal women along with the maternal instinct—and as a necessary supplement to it. This instinct is more or less futile in most women because they are more or less ignorant of the realities as to wise and foolish expenditure. But it is found in the most extravagant women no less than in the most absurdly and meanly stingy.

"Of course, we must be careful," assented Rod. "But I can't let you be uncomfortable."

"Now, dear," she remonstrated, "you mustn't treat me that way. I'm better fitted for hardship than you. I'd mind it less."

He laughed; she looked so fine and delicate, with her transparent skin and her curves of figure, he felt that anything so nearly perfect could not but easily be spoiled. And there he showed how little he appreciated her iron strength, her almost exhaustless endurance.

He fancied he was the stronger because he could have crushed her in his muscular arms. But exposures, privations, dissipations that would have done for a muscularly stronger man than he would have left no trace upon her after a few days of rest and sleep.

"It's the truth," she insisted. "I could prove it, but I shan't. I don't want to remember vividly. Rod, we *must* live cheaply in New York until you sell a play and I have a place in some company."

"Yes," he conceded. "But, Susie, not too cheap. A cheap way of living makes a cheap man—gives a man a cheap outlook on life. Besides, don't forget— if the worst comes to the worst, I can always get a job on a newspaper."

She would not have let him see how uneasy this remark made her. However, she could not permit it to pass without notice. Said she a little nervously:

"But you've made up your mind to devote yourself to plays—to stand or fall by that."

He remembered how he had thrilled her and himself with brave talk about the necessity of concentrating, of selecting a goal and moving relentlessly for it, letting nothing halt him or turn him aside. For his years Rod Spenser was as wise in the philosophy of success as Burlingham or Tom Brashear. But he had done that brave and wise talking before he loved her as he now did—before he realized how love can be in itself an achievement and a possession so great that other ambitions dwarf beside it. True, away back in his facile, fickle mind, behind the region where self-excuse and somebody-else-always-to-blame reigned supreme, a something—the something that had set the marks of success so strongly upon his face—was whispering to him the real reason for his now revolving a New York newspaper job. Real reasons as distinguished from alleged reasons and imagined reasons, from the reasons self-deception invents and vanity gives out—real reasons are always interesting and worth noting. What was Rod's? Not his love for her; nothing so superior, so superhuman as that. No, it was weak and wobbly misgivings as to his own ability to get on independently, the misgivings that menace every man who has never worked for himself but has always drawn pay—the misgivings that paralyze most men and keep them wage or salary slaves all their lives. Rod was no better pleased at this sly, unwelcome revelation of his real self to himself than the next human being is in similar circumstances. The whispering was hastily suppressed; love for her, desire that she should be comfortable—those must be the real reasons. But he must be careful lest she, the sensitive, should begin to brood over a fear that she was already weakening him and would become a drag upon him—the fear that, he knew, would take shape in his own mind if things began to go badly. "You may be sure, dearest," he said, "I'll do nothing that won't help me on." He tapped his forehead with his finger. "This is a machine for making plays. Everything that's put into it will be grist for it."

She was impressed but not convinced. He had made his point about concentration too clear to her intelligence. She persisted:

"But you said if you took a place on a newspaper it would make you fight less hard."

"I say a lot of things," he interrupted laughingly. "Don't be frightened about me. What I'm most afraid of is that you'll desert me. *That* would be a real knock-out blow."

He said this smilingly; but she could not bear jokes on that one subject.

"What do you mean, Rod?"

"Now, don't look so funereal, Susie. I simply meant that I hate to think of your going on the stage—or at anything else. I want you to help *me*. Selfish, isn't it? But, dear heart, if I could feel that the plays were *ours*, that we were both concentrated on the one career —darling. To love each other, to work together—not separately but together—don't you understand?"

Her expression showed that she understood, but was not at all in sympathy. "I've got to earn my living, Rod," she objected. "I shan't care anything about what I'll be doing. I'll do it simply to keep from being a burden to you——"

"A burden, Susie! You! Why, you're my wings that enable me to fly. It's selfish, but I want all of you. Don't you think, dear, that if it were possible, it would be better for you to make us a home and hold the fort while I go out to give battle to managers—and bind up my wounds when I come back—and send me out the next day well again? Don't you think we ought to concentrate?"

The picture appealed to her. All she wanted in life now was his success. "But," she objected, "it's useless to talk of that until we get on our feet—perfectly useless."

"It's true," he admitted with a sigh.

"And until we do, we must be economical."

"What a persistent lady it is," laughed he. "I wish I were like that."

In the evening's gathering dusk the train steamed into Jersey City; and Spenser and Susan Lenox, with the adventurer's mingling hope and dread, confidence and doubt, courage and fear, followed the crowd down the long platform under the vast train shed, went through the huge thronged waiting-room and aboard the giant ferryboat which filled both with astonishment because of its size and luxuriousness.

"I am a jay!" said she. "I can hardly keep my mouth from dropping open."

"You haven't any the advantage of me," he assured her. "Are you trembling all over?"

"Yes," she admitted. "And my heart's like lead. I suppose there are thousands on thousands like us, from all over the country—who come here every day—feeling as we do."

"Let's go out on the front deck—where we can see it."

They went out on the upper front deck and, leaning against the forward gates, with their traveling bags at their feet, they stood dumb before the most astounding and most splendid scene in the civilized world. It was not quite dark yet; the air was almost July hot, as one of those prematurely warm days New York so often has in March. The sky, a soft and delicate blue shading into opal and crimson behind them, displayed a bright crescent moon as it arched over the fairyland in the dusk before them. Straight ahead, across the broad, swift, sparkling river—the broadest water Susan had ever seen—rose the mighty, the majestic city. It rose direct from the water. Endless stretches of ethereal-looking structure, reaching higher and higher, in masses like mountain ranges, in peaks, in towers and domes. And millions of lights, like fairy lamps, like resplendent jewels, gave the city a glory beyond that of the stars thronging the heavens on a clear summer night.

They looked toward the north; on and on, to the far horizon's edge stretched the broad river and the lovely city that seemed the newborn offspring of the waves; on and on, the myriad lights, in masses, in festoons, in great gleaming globes of fire from towers rising higher than Susan's and Rod's native hills. They looked to the south. There, too, rose city, mile after mile, and then beyond it the expanse of the bay; and everywhere the lights, the beautiful, soft, starlike lights, shedding a radiance as of heaven itself over the whole scene. Majesty and strength and beauty.

"I love it!" murmured the girl. "Already I love it."

"I never dreamed it was like this," said Roderick, in an awed tone.

"The City of the Stars," said she, in the caressing tone in which a lover speaks the name of the beloved.

They moved closer together and clasped hands and gazed as if they feared the whole thing—river and magic city and their own selves—would fade away and vanish forever. Susan clutched Rod in terror as she saw the vision suddenly begin to move, to advance toward her, like apparitions in a dream before they vanish. Then she exclaimed, "Why, we are moving!" The big ferryboat, swift, steady as land, noiseless, had got under way. Upon them from the direction of the distant and hidden sea blew a cool, fresh breeze. Never before had either smelled that perfume, strong and keen and clean, which comes straight from the unbreathed air of the ocean to bathe New York, to put life and hope and health into its people. Rod and Susan turned their faces southward toward this breeze, drank in great draughts of it. They saw a colossal statue, vivid as life in the dusk, in the hand at the end of the high-flung arm a torch which sent a blaze of light streaming out over land and water.

"That must be Liberty," said Roderick.

Susan slipped her arm through his. She was quivering with excitement and joy. "Rod—Rod!" she murmured. "It's the isles of freedom. Kiss me."

And he bent and kissed her, and his cheek felt the tears upon hers. He reached for her hand, with an instinct to strengthen her. But when he had it within his its firm and vital grasp sent a thrill of strength through him.

A few minutes, and they paused at the exit from the ferry house. They almost shrank back, so dazed and helpless did they feel before the staggering billows of noise that swept savagely down upon them—roar and crash, shriek and snort; the air was shuddering with it, the ground quaking. The beauty had vanished—the beauty that was not the city but a glamour to lure them into the city's grasp; now that city stood revealed as a monster about to seize and devour them.

"God!" He shouted in her ear. "Isn't this *frightful!*"

She was recovering more quickly than he. The faces she saw reassured her. They were human faces; and while they were eager and restless, as if the souls behind them sought that which never could be found, they were sane and kind faces, too. Where others of her own race lived, and lived without fear, she, too, could hope to survive. And already she, who had loved this mighty offspring of the sea and the sky at first glance, saw and felt another magic—the magic of the peopled solitude. In this vast, this endless solitude she and he would be free. They could do as they pleased, live as they pleased, without thought of the opinion of others.

Here she could forget the bestial horrors of marriage; here she would fear no scornful pointing at her birth-brand of shame. She and Rod could be poor without shame; they could make their fight in the grateful darkness of obscurity.

"Scared?" he asked.

"Not a bit," was her prompt answer. "I love it more than ever."

"Well, it frightens me a little. I feel helpless—lost in the noise and the crowd. How can I do anything here!"

"Others have. Others do."

"Yes—yes! That's so. We must take hold!" And he selected a cabman from the shouting swarm. "We want to go, with two trunks, to the Hotel St. Denis," said he.

"All right, sir! Gimme the checks, please."

Spenser was about to hand them over when Susan said in an undertone, "You haven't asked the price."

Spenser hastened to repair this important omission. "Ten dollars," replied the cabman as if ten dollars were some such trifle as ten cents.

Spenser laughed at the first experience of the famous New York habit of talking in a faint careless way of large sums of money—other people's money. "You did save us a swat," he said to Susan, and beckoned another man. The upshot of a long and arduous discussion, noisy and profane, was that they got the carriage for six dollars—a price which the policeman who had been drawn into the discussion vouched for as reasonable. Spenser knew it was too high, knew the policeman would get a dollar or so of the profit, but he was weary of the wrangle; and he would not listen to

431

Susan's suggestion that they have the trunks sent by the express company and themselves go in a street car for ten cents. At the hotel they got a large comfortable room and a bath for four dollars a day. Spenser insisted it was cheap; Susan showed her alarm—less than an hour in New York and ten dollars gone, not to speak of she did not know how much change. For Roderick had been scattering tips with what is for some mysterious reason called "a princely hand," though princes know too well the value of money and have too many extravagant tastes ever to go far in sheer throwing away.

They had dinner in the restaurant of the hotel and set out to explore the land they purposed to subdue and to possess. They walked up Broadway to Fourteenth, missed their way in the dazzle and glare of south Union Square, discovered the wandering highway again after some searching. After the long, rather quiet stretch between Union Square and Thirty-fourth Street they found themselves at the very heart of the city's night life. They gazed in wonder upon the elevated road with its trains thundering by high above them. They crossed Greeley Square and stood entranced before the spectacle—a street bright as day with electric signs of every color, shape and size; sidewalks jammed with people, most of them dressed with as much pretense to fashion as the few best in Cincinnati; one theater after another, and at Forty-second Street theaters in every direction. Surely—surely—there would be small difficulty in placing his play when there were so many theaters, all eager for plays.

They debated going to the theater, decided against it, as they were tired from the journey and the excitement of crowding new sensations. "I've never been to a real theater in my life," said Susan. "I want to be fresh the first time I go."

"Yes," cried Rod. "That's right. Tomorrow night. That *will* be an experience!" And they read the illuminated signs, inspected the show windows, and slowly strolled back toward the hotel. As they were recrossing Union Square, Spenser said, "Have you noticed how many street girls there are? We must have passed a thousand. Isn't it frightful?"

"Yes," said Susan.

"You can't imagine yourself doing such a thing," said he.

She met his eyes without flinching. "Yes," she said. "I have."

He stopped short and his expression set her bosom to heaving. But her gaze was steady upon his. "Why did you tell me!" he cried. "Oh, it isn't so—it can't be. You don't mean exactly that."

"Yes, I do," said she.

"I might have known! I might have known!" he cried—rather theatrically, though sincerely withal— for Mr. Spenser was a diligent worker with the tools of the play-making trade. "I learned who you were as soon as I got home the night I left you in Carrolton. They had been telephoning about you to the village. So I knew about you."

"About my mother?" asked she. "Is that what you mean?"

"Oh, you need not look so ashamed," said he, graciously, pityingly.

"I am not ashamed," said she. But she did not tell him that her look came from an awful fear that he was about to make her ashamed of him.

"No, I suppose you aren't," he went on, incensed by

this further evidence of her lack of a good woman's instincts. "I really ought not to blame you. You were born wrong—born with the moral sense left out."

"Yes, I suppose so," said she, wearily.

"If only you had lied to me—told me the one lie!" cried he. "Then you wouldn't have destroyed my illusion. You wouldn't have killed my love."

She grew deathly white; that was all.

"I don't mean that I don't love you still," he hurried on. "But not in the same way. That's killed forever."

He took her face between his hands. "What an exquisite face it is," he said, "soft and smooth! And what clear, honest eyes! Where is *it?* Where *is* it? It *must* be there!"

"What, Rod?"

"The—the dirt."

She did not wince, but there came into her young face a deeper pathos—and a wan, deprecating, pleading smile. She said:

"Maybe love has washed it away—if it was there. It never seemed to touch me—any more than the dirt when I had to clean up my room."

"You mustn't talk that way. Why you are perfectly calm! You don't cry or feel repentant. You don't seem to care."

"It's so—so past—and dead. I feel as if it were another person. And it was, Rod!"

He shook his head, frowning. "Let's not talk about it," he said harshly. "If only I could stop thinking about it!"

She effaced herself as far as she could, living in the same room with him. She avoided the least show of the tenderness she felt, of the longing to have her wounds soothed. She lay awake the whole night, suffering, now and then timidly and softly caressing him when she was sure that he slept. In the morning she pretended to be asleep, let him call her twice before she showed that she was awake. A furtive glance at him confirmed the impression his voice had given. Behind her pale, unrevealing face there was the agonized throb of an aching heart, but she had the confidence of her honest, utter love; he would surely soften, would surely forgive. As for herself—she had, through loving and feeling that she was loved, almost lost the sense of the unreality of past and present that made her feel quite detached and apart from the life she was leading, from the events in which she was taking part, from the persons most intimately associated with her. Now that sense of isolation, of the mere spectator or the traveler gazing from the windows of the hurrying train—that sense returned. But she fought against the feeling it gave her.

That evening they went to the theater—to see Modjeska in "Magda."

Susan had never been in a real theater. The only approach to a playhouse in Sutherland was Masonic Hall. It had a sort of stage at one end where from time to time wandering players gave poor performances of poor plays or a minstrel show or a low vaudeville. But none of the best people of Sutherland went—at least, none of the women. The notion was strong in Sutherland that the theater was of the Devil —not so strong as in the days before they began to tolerate amateur theatricals, but still vigorous enough to give Susan now, as she sat in the big, brilliant auditorium, a pleasing sense that she, an outcast, was at last comfortably at home. Usually the first sight

435

of anything one has dreamed about is pitifully disappointing. Neither nature nor life can build so splendidly as a vivid fancy. But Susan, in some sort prepared for the shortcomings of the stage, was not disappointed. From rise to fall of curtain she was so fascinated, so absolutely absorbed, that she quite forgot her surroundings, even Rod. And between the acts she could not talk for thinking. Rod, deceived by her silence, was chagrined. He had been looking forward to a great happiness for himself in seeing her happy, and much profit from the study of the viewpoint of an absolutely fresh mind. It wasn't until they were leaving the theater that he got an inkling of the true state of affairs with her.

"Let's go to supper," said he.

"If you don't mind," replied she, "I'd rather go home. I'm very tired."

"You were sound asleep this morning. So you must have slept well," said he sarcastically.

"It's the play," said she.

"*Why* didn't you like it?" he asked, irritated.

She looked at him in wonder. "Like what? The play?" She drew a long breath. "I feel as if it had almost killed me."

He understood when they were in their room and she could hardly undress before falling into a sleep so relaxed, so profound, that it made him a little uneasy. It seemed to him the exhaustion of a child worn out with the excitement of a spectacle. And her failure to go into ecstasies the next day led him further into the same error. "Modjeska is very good as *Magda*," said he, carelessly, as one talking without expecting to be understood. "But they say there's an Italian woman —Duse—who is the real thing."

Modjeska—Duse—Susan seemed indeed not to understand. "I hated her father," she said. "He didn't deserve to have such a wonderful daughter."

Spenser had begun to laugh with her first sentence. At the second he frowned, said bitterly: "I might have known! You get it all wrong. I suppose you sympathize with *Magda?*"

"I worshiped her," said Susan, her voice low and tremulous with the intensity of her feeling.

Roderick laughed bitterly. "Naturally," he said. "You can't understand."

An obvious case, thought he. She was indeed one of those instances of absolute lack of moral sense. Just as some people have the misfortune to be born without arms or without legs, so others are doomed to live bereft of a moral sense. A sweet disposition, a beautiful body, but no soul; not a stained soul, but no soul at all. And his whole mental attitude toward her changed; or, rather, it was changed by the iron compulsion of his prejudice. The only change in his physical attitude— that is, in his treatment of her—was in the direction of bolder passion, of complete casting aside of all the restraint a conventional respecter of conventional womanhood feels toward a woman whom he respects. So, naturally, Susan, eager to love and to be loved, and easily confusing the not easily distinguished spiritual and physical, was reassured. Once in a while a look or a phrase from him gave her vague uneasiness; but on the whole she felt that, in addition to clear conscience from straightforwardness, she had a further reason for being glad Chance had forced upon her the alternative of telling him or lying. She did not inquire into the realities beneath the surface of their life—neither into what he thought of her, nor into what she thought of him—thought in the bottom of her heart. She continued to fight against, to ignore, her feeling of aloneness, her feeling of impending departure.

She was aided in this by her anxiety about their finances. In his efforts to place his play he was spending what were for them large sums of money—treating this man and that to dinners, to suppers—inviting men to lunch with him at expensive Broadway restaurants. She assumed that all this was necessary; he said so, and he must know. He was equally open-handed when they were alone, insisting on ordering the more expensive dishes, on having suppers they really did not need and drink which she knew she would be better off without—and, she suspected, he also. It simply was not in him, she saw, to be careful about money. She liked it, as a trait, for to her as to all the young and the unthinking carelessness about money seems a sure, perhaps the surest, sign of generosity—when in fact the two qualities are in now way related. Character is not a collection of ignorant impulses but a solidly woven fabric of deliberate purposes. Carelessness about anything most often indicates a tendency to carelessness about everything. She admired his openhanded way of scattering; she wouldn't have admired it in herself, would have thought it dishonest and selfish. But Rod was different. *He* had the "artistic temperament," while she was a commonplace nobody, who ought to be—and was—grateful to him for allowing her to stay on and for making such use of her as he saw fit. Still, even as she admired, she saw danger, grave danger, a disturbingly short distance ahead. He described to her the difficuties he was having in getting to managers, in having his play read, and the absurdity of the reasons given for turning it down. He made light of all these; the next manager would see, would give him a big advance, would put the play on—and then, Easy Street!

But experience had already killed what little optimism there was in her temperament—and there had not been much, because George Warham was a successful man in his line, and successful men do not create or permit optimistic atmosphere even in their houses. Nor had she forgotten Burlingham's lectures on the subject with illustrations from his own spoiled career; she understood it all now—and everything else he had given her to store up in her memory that retained everything. With that philippic against optimism in mind, she felt what Spenser was rushing toward. She made such inquiries about work for herself as her inexperience and limited opportunities permitted. She asked, she begged him, to let her try to get a place. He angrily ordered her to put any such notion out of her head. After a time she nerved herself again to speak. Then he frankly showed her why he was refusing.

"No," said he peremptorily, "I couldn't trust you in those temptations. You must stay where I can guard you."

A woman who had deliberately taken to the streets —why, she thought nothing of virtue; she would be having lovers with the utmost indifference; and while she was not a liar yet—"at least I think not"—how long would that last? With virtue gone, virtue the foundation of woman's character—the rest could no more stand that a house set on sand.

"As long as you want me to love you, you've got to stay with me," he declared. "If you persist, I'll know you're simply looking for a chance to go back to your old ways."

And though she continued to think and cautiously to inquire about work she said no more to him. She spent not a penny, discouraged him from throwing money away—as much as she could without irritating him—and waited for the cataclysm. Waited not in gloom and tears but as normal healthy youth awaits any adversity not definitely scheduled for an hour close at hand. It would be far indeed from the truth to picture Susan as ever for long a melancholy figure to the eye or even wholly melancholy within. Her intelligence and her too sympathetic heart were together a strong force for sadness in her life, as they cannot but be in any life. In this world, to understand and to sympathize is to be saddened. But there was in her a force stronger than either or both. She had superb health. It made her beautiful, strong body happy; and that physical happiness brought her up quickly out of any depths—made her gay in spite of herself, caused her to enjoy even when she felt that it was "almost like hard-heartedness to be happy." She loved the sun and in this city where the sun shone almost all the days, sparkling gloriously upon the tiny salt particles filling the air and making it delicious to breathe and upon the skin—in this City of the Sun as she called it, she was gay even when she was heavy-hearted.

Thus, she was no repellent, aggravating companion to Rod as she awaited the cataclysm.

It came in the third week. He spent the entire day away from her; toward midnight he returned, flushed with liquor. She had gone to bed. "Get up and dress," said he with an irritability toward her which she had no difficulty in seeing was really directed at himself. "I'm hungry—and thirsty. We're going out for some supper."

"Come kiss me first," said she, stretching out her arms. Several times this device had shifted his purpose from spending money on the needless and expensive supper."

He laughed. "Not a kiss. We're going to have one final blow-out. I start to work tomorrow. I've taken a place on the *Herald*—on space, guaranty of twenty-five a week, good chance to average fifty or sixty."

He said this hurriedly, carelessly, gayly—guiltily. She showed then and there what a surpassing wise young woman she was, for she did not exclaim or remind him of his high resolve to do or die as a playwright. "I'll be ready in a minute," was all she said.

She dressed swiftly, he lounging on the sofa and watching her. He loved to watch her dress, she did it so gracefully, and the motions brought out latent charms of her supple figure. "You're not so surefingered tonight as usual," said he. "I never saw you make so many blunders—and you've got one stocking on wrong side out."

She smiled into the glass at him. "The skirt'll cover that. I guess I was sleepy."

"Never saw your eyes more wide-awake. What're you thinking about?"

"About supper," declared she. "I'm hungry. I didn't feel like eating alone."

"I can't be here always," said he crossly—and she knew he was suspecting what she really must be thinking.

"I wasn't complaining," replied she sweetly. "You know I understand about business."

"Yes, I know," said he, with his air of generosity that always made her feel grateful. "I always feel perfectly free about you."

"I should say!" laughed she. "You know I don't care what happens so long as you succeed." Since their talk in Broadway that first evening in New York she had instinctively never said "we."

When they were at the table at Rector's and he had taken a few more drinks, he became voluble and plausible on the subject of the trifling importance of his setback as a playwright. It was the worst possible time of year; the managers were stocked up; his play would have to be rewritten to suit some particular star; a place on a newspaper, especially such an influential paper as the *Herald*, would be of use to him in interesting managers. She listened and looked convinced, and strove to convince herself that she believed. But there was no gray in her eyes, only the deepest hue of violets.

Next day they took a suite of two rooms and a bath in a pretentious old house in West Forty-fourth Street near Long Acre Square. She insisted that she preferred another much sunnier and quieter suite with no bath but only a stationary washstand; it was to be had for ten dollars a week. But he laughed at her as too economical in her ideas, and decided for the eighteen-dollar rooms. Also he went with her to buy clothes, made her spend nearly a hundred dollars where she would have spent less than twenty-five. "I prefer to make most of my things," declared she. "And I've all the time in the world." He would not have it. In her leisure time she must read and amuse herself and keep herself up to the mark, especially physically. "I'm proud of your looks," said he. "They belong to me, don't they? Well, take care of my property, Miss."

She looked at him vaguely—a look of distance, of parting, of pain. Then she flung herself into his arms with a hysterical cry—and shut her eyes tight against the beckoning figure calling her away. "No! No!" she murmured. "I belong here—*here!*"

"What are you saying?" he asked.

"Nothing—nothing," she replied.

XXV

AT the hotel they had been Mr. and Mrs. Spenser. When they moved, he tried to devise some way round this; but it was necessary that they have his address at the office, and Mrs. Pershall with the glistening old-fashioned false teeth who kept the furnished-room house was not one in whose withered bosom it would be wise to raise a suspicion as to respectability. Only in a strenuously respectable house would he live; in the other sort, what might not untrustworthy Susan be up to? So Mr. and Mrs. Spenser they remained, and the truth was suspected by only a few of their acquaintances, was known by two or three of his intimates whom he told in those bursts of confidence to which voluble, careless men are given—and for which they in resolute self-excuse unjustly blame strong drink.

One of his favorite remarks to her—sometimes made laughingly, again ironically, again angrily, again insultingly, was in this strain:

"Your face is demure enough. But you look too damned attractive about those beautiful feet of yours to be respectable at heart—and trustable."

That matter of her untrustworthiness had become a fixed idea with him. The more he concentrated upon her physical loveliness, the more he revolved the dangers, the possibilities of unfaithfulness; for a physical infatuation is always jealous. His work on the *Herald* made close guarding out of the question. The best he could do was to pop in unexpectedly upon her from time to time, to rummage through her belongings, to check up her statements as to her goings and comings by questioning the servants and, most important of all, each day to put her through searching and skillfully planned cross-examination. She had to tell him everything she did—every little thing—and he calculated the time, to make sure she had not found half an hour or so in which to deceive him. If she had sewed, he must look at the sewing; if she had read, he must know how many pages and must hear a summary of what those pages contained. As she would not and could not deceive him in any matter, however small, she was compelled to give over a plan quietly to look for work and to fit herself for some occupation that would pay a living wage—if there were such for a beginning woman worker.

At first he was covert in this detective work, being ashamed of his own suspicions. But as he drank, as he associated again with the same sort of people who had wasted his time in Cincinnati, he rapidly became franker and more inquisitorial. And she dreaded to see the look she knew would come into his eyes, the cruel tightening of his mouth, if in her confusion and eagerness she should happen not instantly to satisfy the doubt behind each question. He tormented her; he tormented himself. She suffered from humiliation; but she suffered more because she saw how his suspicions were torturing him. And in her humility and helplessness and inexperience, she felt no sense of right to resist, no impulse to resist.

And she forced herself to look on his spasms of jealousy as the occasional storms which occur even in the best climates. She reminded herself that she was secure of his love, secure in his love; and in her sad mood she reproached herself for not being content when at bottom everything was all right. After what she had been through, to be sad because the man she loved loved her too well! It was absurd, ungrateful.

He pried into every nook and corner of her being with that ingenious and tireless persistence human beings reserve for searches for what they do not wish to find. At last he contrived to find, or to imagine he had found, something that justified his labors and vindicated his disbelief in her.

They were walking in Fifth Avenue one afternoon, at the hour when there is the greatest press of equipages whose expensively and showily dressed occupants are industriously engaged in the occupation of imagining they are doing something when in fact they are doing nothing. What a world! What a grotesque confusing of motion and progress! What fantastic delusions that one is busy when one is merely occupied! They were between Forty-sixth Street and Forty-seventh, on the west side, when a small victoria drew up at the curb and a woman descended and crossed the sidewalk before them to look at the display in a milliner's window. Susan gave her the swift, seeing glance which one woman always gives another—the glance of competitors at each other's offerings. Instead of glancing away, Susan stopped short and gazed. Forgetting Rod, she herself went up to the millinery display that she might have a fuller view of the woman who had fascinated her.

"What's the matter?" cried Spenser. "Come on. You don't want any of those hats."

But Susan insisted that she must see, made him linger until the woman returned to her carriage and drove away. She said to Rod:

"Did you see her?"

"Yes. Rather pretty—nothing to scream about."

"But her *style!*" cried Susan.

"Oh, she was nicely dressed—in a quiet way. You'll see thousands a lot more exciting after you've been about in this town a while."

"I've seen scores of beautifully dressed women here—and in Cincinnati, too," replied Susan. "But that woman—she was *perfect*. And that's a thing I've never seen before."

"I'm glad you have such quiet tastes—quiet and inexpensive."

"Inexpensive!" exclaimed Susan. "I don't dare think how much that woman's clothes cost. You only glanced at her, Rod, you didn't *look*. If you had, you'd have seen. Everything she wore was just right." Susan's eyes were brilliant. "Oh, it was wonderful! The colors—the fit—the style—the making—every big and little thing. She was a work of art, Rod! That's the first woman I've seen in my life that I through and through envied."

Rod's look was interested now. "You like that sort of thing a lot?" he inquired with affected carelessness.

"Every woman does," replied she, unsuspicious. "But I care—well, not for merely fine clothes. But for the—the kind that show what sort of person is in them." She sighed. "I wonder if I'll ever learn—and have money enough to carry out. It'll take so much—so much!" She laughed. "I've got terribly extravagant ideas. But don't be alarmed—I keep them chained up."

He was eying her unpleasantly. Suddenly she became confused. He thought it was because she was seeing and understanding his look and was frightened at his having caught her at last. In fact, it was be-

cause it all at once struck her that what she had inno-
cently and carelessly said sounded like a hint or a reproach to him. He sneered:

"So you're crazy about finery—eh?"

"Oh, Rod!" she cried. "You know I didn't mean it
that way. I long for and dream about a whole lot of
beautiful things, but nothing else in the world's in the
same class with—with what we've got."

"You needn't try to excuse yourself," said he in a
tone that silenced her.

She wished she had not seen the woman who had
thus put a cloud over their afternoon's happiness.
But long after she had forgotten his queerness about
what she said, she continued to remember that "perfect"
woman—to see every detail of her exquisite toilet, so
rare in a world where expensive-looking finery is regarded as the chief factor in the art of dress. How
much she would have to learn before she could hope to
dress like that!—learn not merely about dress but
about the whole artistic side of life. For that woman
had happened to cross Susan's vision at just the right
moment—in development and in mood—to reveal to
her clearly a world into which she had never penetrated
—a world of which she had vaguely dreamed as she
read novels of life in the lands beyond the seas, the
life of palaces and pictures and statuary, of opera and
theater, of equipages and servants and food and clothing of rare quality. She had rather thought such a
life did not exist outside of novels and dreams. What
she had seen of New York—the profuse, the gigan-
tic but also the undiscriminating—had tended to
strengthen the suspicion. But this woman proved her
mistaken.

Our great forward strides are made unconsciously,

are the results of apparently trivial, often unnoted
impulses. Susan, like all our race, had always had
vague secret dreams of ambition—so vague thus far
that she never thought of them as impelling purposes
in her life. Her first long forward stride toward changing these dreams from the vague to the definite was
when Rod, before her on the horse on the way to
Brooksburg, talked over his shoulder to her of the
stage and made her feel that it was the life for her,
the only life open to her where a woman could hope to
be judged as human being instead of as mere instrument of sex. Her second long forward movement toward sharply defined ambition dated from the sight of
the woman of the milliner's window—the woman who
epitomized to Susan the whole art side of life that
always gives its highest expression in some personal
achievement—the perfect toilet, the perfect painting
or sculpture, the perfect novel or play.

But Rod saw in her enthusiasm only evidence of a
concealed longing for the money to indulge extravagant whims. With his narrowing interest in women—
narrowed now almost to sex—his contempt for them
as to their minds and their hearts was so far advancing
that he hardly took the trouble to veil it with remnants
of courtesy. If Susan had clearly understood—even if
she had let herself understand what her increasing
knowledge might have enabled her to understand—she
would have hated him in spite of the hold gratitude
and habit had given him upon her loyal nature—and
despite the fact that she had, as far as she could see,
no alternative to living with him but the tenements or
the streets.

One day in midsummer she chanced to go into the
Hotel Astor to buy a magazine. As she had not been

there before she made a wrong turning and was forced
to cross one of the restaurants. In a far corner, half
hidden by a group of palms, she saw Rod at a small
table with a strikingly pretty woman whose expression
and dress and manner most energetically proclaimed
the actress. The woman was leaning toward him, was
touching his hand and looking into his eyes with that
show of enthusiasm which raises doubts of sincerity in
an experienced man and sets him to keeping an eye or
a hand—or both—upon his money. Real emotion, even
a professional expert at display of emotion, is rarely
so adept at exhibiting itself.

It may have been jealousy that guided her to this
swift judgment upon the character of the emotion correctly and charmingly expressing itself. If so, jealousy
was for once a trustworthy guide. She turned swiftly
and escaped unseen. The idea of trapping him, of con-
fronting him, never occurred to her. She felt ashamed
and self-reproachful that she had seen. Instead of the
anger that fires a vain woman, whether she cares about
a man or not, there came a profound humiliation. She
had in some way fallen short; she had not given him
all he needed; it must be that she hadn't it to give,
since she had given him all she had. He must not
know—he must not! For if he knew he might dislike
her, might leave her—and she dared not think what life
would be without him, her only source of companionship and affection, her only means of support. She
was puzzled that her discovery, not of his treachery
—he had so broken her spirit with his suspicions and
his insulting questions that she did not regard herself
as of the rank and dignity that has the right to exact
fidelity—but of his no longer caring enough to be content with her alone, had not stunned her with amaze-

ment. She did not realize how completely the instinct
that he was estranged from her had prepared her for
the thing that always accompanies estrangement. Between the perfect accord, that is, the never realized
ideal for a man and a woman living together, and the intolerable discord that means complete repulse there is
a vast range of states of feeling imperceptibly shading
into each other. Most couples constantly move along
this range, now toward the one extreme, now toward
the other. As human beings are not given to self-
analysis, and usually wander into grotesque error
whenever they attempt it, no couple knows precisely
where it is upon the range, until something crucial happens to compel them to know. Susan and Rod had
begun as all couples begin—with an imaginary ideal
accord based upon their ignorance of each other and
their misunderstanding of what qualities they thought
they understood in each other. The delusion of accord
vanished that first evening in New York. What remained? What came in the place? They knew no
more about that than does the next couple. They were
simply "living along." A crisis, drawing them close
together or flinging them forever apart or forcing
them to live together, he frankly as keeper and she
frankly as kept, might come any day, any hour. Again
it might never come.

After a few weeks the matter that had been out of
her mind accidentally and indirectly came to the surface in a chance remark. She said:

"Sometimes I half believe a man could be untrue to
a woman, even though he loved her."

She did not appreciate the bearings of her remark
until it was spoken. With a sensation of terror lest
the dreaded crisis might be about to burst, she felt his

quick, nervous glance. She breathed freely again when she felt his reassurance and relief as she successfully withstood.

"Certainly," he said with elaborate carelessness. "Men are a rotten, promiscuous lot. That's why it's necessary for a woman to be good and straight."

All this time his cross-examination had grown in severity. Evidently he was fearing that she might be having a recurrence of the moral disease which was fatal in womankind, though only mild indiscretion in a man, if not positively a virtue, an evidence of possessing a normal masculine nature. Her mind began curiously—sadly—to revolve the occasional presents—of money, of books, of things to wear—which he gave, always quite unexpectedly. At first unconsciously, but soon consciously, she began to associate these gifts, given always in an embarrassed, shamefaced way, with certain small but significant indications of his having strayed. And it was not long before she understood; she was receiving his expiations for his indiscretions. Like an honest man and a loyal—masculinely loyal—lover he was squaring accounts. She never read the books she owed to these twinges; it was thus that she got her aversion to Thackeray—one of his "expiations" was a set of Thackeray. The things to wear she contrived never to use. The conscience money she either spent upon him or put back into his pocket a little at a time, sure that he, the most careless of men about money, would never detect her.

His work forced him to keep irregular hours; thus she could pretend to herself that his absences were certainly because of office duty. Still, whenever he was gone overnight, she became unhappy—not the crying kind of unhappiness; to that she was little given—but the kind that lies awake and aches and with morbid vivid fancy paints the scenes suspicion suggests, and stares at them not in anger but in despair. She was always urging herself to content herself with what she was getting. She recalled and lived again the things she had forgotten while Roderick was wholly hers—the penalties of the birth brand of shame—her wedding night—the miseries of the last period of her wanderings with Burlingham—her tenement days—the dirt, the nakedness, the brutal degradation, the vermin, the savage cold. And the instant he returned, no matter how low-spirited she had been, she was at once gay, often deliriously gay—until soon his awakened suspicion as to what she had been up to in his absence quieted her. There was little forcing or pretense in this gayety; it bubbled and sparkled from the strong swift current of her healthy passionate young life which, suspended in the icy clutch of fear when he was away from her, flowed as freely as the brooks in spring as soon as she realized that she still had him.

Did she really love him? She believed she did. Was she right? Love is of many degrees—and kinds. And strange and confused beyond untangling is the mixture of motives and ideas in the mind of any human being as to any other being with whom his or her relations are many sided.

Anyone who had not been roughly seized by destiny and forced to fight desperately weaponless might have found it difficult to understand how this intelligent, high-spirited girl could be so reasonable—coarsely practical, many people would have said. A brave soul—truly brave with the unconscious courage that lives heroically without any taint of heroics—such a soul learns to accept the facts of life, to make the best of things, to be grateful for whatever sunshine may be and not to shriek and gesticulate at storm. Suffering had given this sapling of a girl the strong fiber that enables a tree to push majestically up toward the open sky. Because she did not cry out was no sign that she was not hurt; and because she did not wither and die of her wounds was only proof of her strength of soul. The weak wail and the weak succumb; the strong persist—and a world of wailers and weaklings calls them hard, insensible, coarse.

Spenser was fond of exhibiting to his men friends— to some of them—this treasure to which he always returned the more enamoured for his vagary and its opportunity of comparison. Women he would not permit. In general, he held that all women, the respectable no less than the other kind, put mischief in each other's heads and egged each other on to carry out the mischief already there in embryo. In particular, he would have felt that he was committing a gross breach of the proprieties, not to say the decencies, had he introduced a woman of Susan's origin, history and present status to the wives and sisters of his friends; and, for reasons which it was not necessary even to pretend to conceal from her, he forbade her having anything to do with the kinds of woman who would not have minded, had they known all about her. Thus, her only acquaintances, her only associates, were certain carefully selected men. He asked to dinner or to the theater or to supper at Jack's or Rector's only such men as he could trust. And trustworthy meant physically unattractive. Having small and dwindling belief in the mentality of women, and no belief whatever in mentality as a force in the relations of the sexes, he was satisfied to have about her any man, however clever, provided he was absolutely devoid of physical charm.

The friend who came oftenest was Drumley, an editorial writer who had been his chum at college and had got him the place on the *Herald*. Drumley he would have trusted alone with her on a desert island; for several reasons, all of his personal convenience, it pleased him that Susan liked Drumley and was glad of his company, no matter how often he came or how long he stayed. Drumley was an emaciated Kentucky giant with grotesquely sloping shoulders which not all the ingenious padding of his tailor could appreciably mitigate. His spare legs were bowed in the calves. His skin looked rough and tough, like sandpaper and emery board. The thought of touching his face gave one the same sensation as a too deeply cut nail. His neck was thin and long, and he wore a low collar—through that interesting passion of the vain for seeing a defect in themselves as a charm and calling attention to it. The lower part of his sallow face suggested weakness—the weakness so often seen in the faces of professional men, and explaining why they chose passive instead of active careers. His forehead was really fine, but the development of the rest of the cranium above the protuberant little ears was not altogether satisfying to a claim of mental powers.

Drumley was a good sort—not so much through positive virtue as through the timidity which too often accounts for goodness, that is, for the meek conformity which passes as goodness. He was an insatiable reader, had incredible stores of knowledge; and as he had a large vocabulary and a ready speech he could dole out of those reservoirs an agreeable treacle of commonplace philosophy or comment—thus he had an ideal equipment for editorial writing. He was absolutely without physical magnetism. The most he could ever expect from any woman was respect; and that woman would have had to be foolish enough not to realize that there is as abysmal a difference between knowledge and mentality as there is between reputation and character. Susan liked him because he knew so much. She had developed still further her innate passion for educating herself. She now wanted to know all about everything. He told her what to read, set her in the way to discovering and acquiring the art of reading—an art he was himself capable of acquiring only in its rudiments —an art the existence of which is entirely unsuspected by most persons who regard themselves and are regarded as readers. He knew the histories and biographies that are most amusing and least shallow and mendacious. He instructed her in the great playwrights and novelists and poets, and gave—as his own —the reasons for their greatness assigned by the world's foremost critical writers. He showed her what scientific books to read—those that do not bore and do not hide the simple fascinating facts about the universe under pretentious, college-professor phraseology.

He was a pedant, but his pedantry was disguised, therefore mitigated by his having associated with men of the world instead of with the pale and pompous capons of the student's closet. His favorite topic was beauty and ugliness—and his abhorrence for anyone who was not good to look at. As he talked this subject, his hearers were nervous and embarrassed. He was a drastic cure for physical vanity. If this man could so far deceive himself that he thought himself handsome, who in all the world could be sure he or she was not the victim of the same incredible delusion? It was this hallucination of physical beauty that caused Rod to regard him as the safest of the safe. For it made him pitiful and ridiculous.

At first he came only with Spenser. Afterward, Spenser used to send him to dine with Susan and to spend the evenings with her when he himself had to be —or wished to be—elsewhere. When she was with Drumley he knew she was not "up to any of her old tricks." Drumley fell in love with her; but, as in his experience the female sex was coldly chaste, he never developed even the slight hope necessary to start in a man's mind the idea of treachery to his friend about a woman. Whenever Drumley heard that a woman other than the brazenly out and out disreputables was "loose" or was inclined that way, he indignantly denied it as a libel upon the empedestaled sex. If proofs beyond dispute were furnished, he raved against the man with all the venom of the unsuccessful hating the successful for their success. He had been sought of women, of course, for he had a comfortable and secure position and money put by. But the serious women who had set snares for him for the sake of a home had not attracted him; as for the better looking and livelier women who had come a-courting with alimony in view, they had unwisely chosen the method of approach that caused him to set them down as nothing but professional loose characters. Thus his high ideal of feminine beauty and his lofty notion of his own deserts, on the one hand, and his reverence for womanly propriety, on the other hand, had kept his charms and his income unshared.

Toward the end of Spenser's first year on the *Herald* —it was early summer—he fell into a melancholy so profound and so prolonged that Susan became alarmed. She was used to his having those fits of the blues that are a part of the nervous, morbidly sensitive nature and in the unhealthfulness of an irregular and dissipated life recur at brief intervals. He spent more and more time with her, became as ardent as in their first days together, with an added desperation of passionate·clinging that touched her to the depths. She had early learned to ignore his moods, to avoid sympathy which aggravates, and to meet his blues with a vigorous counterirritant of liveliness. After watching the course of this acute attack for more than a month, she decided that at the first opportunity she would try to find out from Drumley what the cause was. Perhaps she could cure him if she were not working in the dark.

One June evening Drumley came to take her to dinner at the Casino in Central Park.

It was an excursion of which she was fond. They strolled along Seventh Avenue to the Park, entered and followed the lovely walk, quiet and green and odorous, to the Mall. They sauntered in the fading light up the broad Mall, with its roof of boughs of majestic trees, with its pale blue vistas of well-kept lawns. At the steps leading to the Casino they paused to delight in the profusely blooming wistaria and to gaze away northward into and over what seemed an endless forest with towers and cupolas of castle and fortress and cathedral rising serene and graceful here and there above the sea of green. There was the sound of tinkling fountains, the musical chink-chink of harness chains of elegant equipages; on the Mall hundreds of children were playing furiously, to enjoy to the uttermost the last few moments before being snatched away to bed—and the birds were in the same hysterical state as they got ready for their evening song. The air was saturated with the fresh odors of spring and early summer flowers. Susan, walking beside the homely Drumley, was a charming and stylish figure of girlish womanhood. The year and three months in New York had wrought the same transformations in her that are so noticeable whenever an intelligent and observant woman with taste for the luxuries is dipped in the magic city of life. She had grown, was now perhaps a shade above the medium height for women, looked even taller because of the slenderness of her arms, of her neck, of the lines of her figure. There was a deeper melancholy in her violet-gray eyes. Experience had increased the allure of her wide, beautifully curved mouth.

They took a table under the trees, with beds of blooming flowers on either hand. Drumley ordered the sort of dinner she liked, and a bottle of champagne and a bottle of fine burgundy to make his favorite drink—champagne and burgundy, half and half. He was running to poetry that evening—Keats and Swinburne. Finally, after some hesitation, he produced a poem by Dowson—"I ran across it today. It's the only thing of his worth while, I believe—and it's so fine that Swinburne must have been sore when he read it because he hadn't thought to write it himself. Its moral tone is not high, but it's so beautiful, Mrs. Susan, that I'll venture to show it to you. It comes nearer to expressing what men mean by the man sort of constancy than anything I ever read. Listen to this:

"I cried for madder music and for stronger wine,
But when the feast is finished, and the lamps expire,
Then falls thy shadow, Cynara!—the night is thine;
And I am desolate and sick of an old passion,
Yea, hungry for the lips of my desire;
I have been faithful to thee, Cynara, in my fashion."

Susan took the paper, read the four stanzas several times, handed it back to him without a word. "Don't you think it fine?" asked he, a little uneasily —he was always uneasy with a woman when the conversation touched the relations of the sexes—uneasy lest he might say or might have said something to send a shiver through her delicate modesty.

"Fine," Susan echoed absently. "And true. . . . I suppose it is the best a woman can expect—to be the one he returns to. And—isn't that enough?"

"You are very different from any woman I ever met," said Drumley. "Very different from what you were last fall—wonderfully different. But you were different then, too."

"I'd have been a strange sort of person if it weren't so. I've led a different life. I've learned—because I've had to learn."

"You've been through a great deal—suffered a great deal for one of your age?"

Susan shrugged her shoulders slightly. She had her impulses to confide, but she had yet to meet the person who seriously tempted her to yield to them. Not even Rod; no, least of all Rod.

"You are—happy?"

"Happy—and more. I'm content."

The reply was the truth, as she saw the truth. Perhaps it was also the absolute truth; for when a

460

woman has the best she has ever actually possessed, and when she knows there is nowhere else on earth for her, she is likely to be content. Their destiny of subordination has made philosophers of women.

Drumley seemed to be debating how to disclose something he had in mind. But after several glances at the sweet, delicate face of the girl, he gave it over. In the subdued light from the shaded candles on their table, she looked more child-like than he had ever seen. Perhaps her big pale-blue hat and graceful pale-blue summer dress had something to do with it, also. "How old are you?" he asked abruptly.

"Nearly nineteen."

"I feel like saying, 'So much!'—and also 'So little!' How long have you been married?"

"Why all these questions?" demanded she, smiling.

He colored with embarrassment. "I didn't mean to be impertinent," said he.

"It isn't impertinence—is it?—to ask a woman how long she's been married."

But she did not go on to tell him; instead, she pretended to have her attention distracted by a very old man and a very young girl behaving in most lover-like fashion, the girl outdoing the man in enthusiastic determination to convince. She was elegantly and badly dressed in new clothes—and she seemed as new to that kind of clothes as those particular clothes were new to her. After dinner they walked down through the Park by the way they had come; it did not look like the same scene now, with the moonlight upon it, with soft shadows everywhere and in every shadow a pair of lovers. They had nearly reached the entrance when Drumley said: "Let's sit on this bench here. I want to have a serious talk with you."

Susan seated herself and waited. He lit a cigar with the deliberation of one who is striving to gain time. The bench happened to be one of those that are divided by iron arms into individual seats. He sat with a compartment between them. The moonbeams struck across his profile as he turned it toward her; they shone full upon her face. He looked, hastily glanced away. With a gruffness as if the evening mist had got into his throat he said:

"Let's take another bench."

"Why?" objected she. "I like this beautiful light."

He rose. "Please let me have my way." And he led her to a bench across which a tree threw a deep shadow; as they sat there, neither could see the other's face except in dimmest outline. After a brief silence he began:

"You love Rod—don't you?"

She laughed happily.

"Above everything on earth?"

"Or in heaven."

"You'd do anything to have him succeed?"

"No one could prevent his succeeding. He's got it in him. It's bound to come out."

"So I'd have said—until a year ago—that is, about a year ago."

As her face turned quickly toward him, he turned profile to her. "What do you mean?" said she, quickly, almost imperiously.

"Yes—I mean *you*," replied he.

"You mean you think I'm hindering him?"

When Drumley's voice finally came, it was funereally solemn. "You are dragging him down. You are killing his ambition."

"You don't understand," she protested with painful expression. "If you did, you wouldn't say that."

"You mean because he is not true to you?"

"Isn't he?" said she, loyally trying to pretend surprise. "If that's so, you've no right to tell me—you, his friend. If it isn't, you——"

"In either case I'd be beneath contempt—unless I knew that you knew already. Oh, I've known a long time that you knew—ever since the night you looked away when he absentmindedly pulled a woman's veil and gloves out of his pocket. I've watched you since then, and I know."

"You are a very dear friend, Mr. Drumley," said she. "But you must not talk of him to me."

"I must," he replied. And he hastened to make the self-fooled hypocrite's familiar move to the safety of duty's skirts. "It would be a crime to keep silent."

She rose. "I can't listen. It may be your duty to speak. It's my duty to refuse to hear."

"He is overwhelmed with debt. He is about to lose his position. It is all because he is degraded—because he feels he is entangled in an intrigue with a woman he is ashamed to love—a woman he has struggled in vain to put out of his heart."

Susan, suddenly weak, had seated herself again. From his first words she had been prey to an internal struggle—her heart fighting against understanding things about her relations with Rod, about his feeling toward her, which she had long been contriving to hide from herself. When Drumley began she knew that the end of self-deception was at hand—if she let him speak. But the instant he had spoken, the struggle ended. If he had tried to stop she would have compelled him to go on.

"That woman is you," he continued in the same solemn measured way. "Rod will not marry you. He cannot leave you. And you are dragging him down. You are young. You don't know that passionate love is a man's worst enemy. It satisfies his ambition—why struggle when one already has attained the climax of desire? It saps his strength, takes from him the energy without which achievement is impossible. Passion dies poisoned of its own sweets. But passionate love kills—at least, it kills the man. If you did not love him, I'd not be talking to you now. But you do love him. So I say, you are killing him. . . . Don't think he has told me——"

"I know he didn't," she interrupted curtly. "He does not whine."

She hadn't a doubt of the truth of her loyal defense. And Drumley could not have raised a doubt, even if she had been seeing the expression of his face. His long practice of the modern editorial art of clearness and brevity and compact statement had enabled him to put into those few sentences more than another might have been unable to express in hours of explanation and appeal. And the ideas were not new to her. Rod had often talked them in a general way and she had thought much about them. Until now she had never seen how they applied to Rod and herself. But she was seeing and feeling it now so acutely that if she had tried to speak or to move she could not have done so.

After a long pause, Drumley said: "Do you comprehend what I mean?"

She was silent—so it was certain that she compre-
hended.

"But you don't believe? . . . He began to borrow
money almost immediately on his arrival here last
summer. He has been borrowing ever since—from
everybody and anybody. He owes now, as nearly as I
can find out, upwards of three thousand dollars."

Susan made a slight but sharp movement.

"You don't believe me?"

"Yes. Go on."

"He has it in him, I'm confident, to write plays—
strong plays. Does he ever write except ephemeral
space stuff for the paper?"

"No."

"And he never will so long as he has you to go home
to. He lives beyond his means because he will have
you in comfortable surroundings and dressed to stimulate his passion. If he would marry you, it might be
a little better—though still he would never amount to
anything as long as his love lasted—the kind of love
you inspire. But he will never marry you. I learned
that from what I know of his ideas and from what I've
observed as to your relations—not from anything he
ever said about you."

If Susan had been of the suspicious temperament, or
if she had been a few years older, the manner of this
second protest might have set her to thinking how
unlike Drumley, the inexpert in matters of love and
passion, it was to analyze thus and to form such
judgments. And thence she might have gone on to
consider that Drumley's speeches sounded strangely
like paraphrases of Spenser's eloquent outbursts when

he "got going." But she had not a suspicion. Besides, her whole being was concentrated upon the idea Drumley was trying to put into words. She asked:

"Why are you telling me?"

"Because I love him," replied Drumley with feeling. "We're about the same age, but he's been like my son ever since we struck up a friendship in the first term of Freshman year."

"Is that your only reason?"

"On my honor." And so firmly did he believe it, he bore her scrutiny as she peered into his face through the dimness.

She drew back. "Yes," she said in a low voice, half to herself. "Yes, I believe it is." There was silence for a long time, then she asked quietly:

"What do you think I ought to do?"

"Leave him—if you love him," replied Drumley. "What else can you do? . . . Stay on and complete his ruin?"

"And if I go—what?"

"Oh, you can do any one of many things. You can——"

"I mean—what about him?"

"He will be like a crazy man for a while. He'll make that a fresh excuse for keeping on as he's going now. Then he'll brace up, and I'll be watching over him, and I'll put him to work in the right direction. He can't be saved, he can't even be kept afloat as long as you are with him, or within reach. With you gone out of his life—his strength will return, his self-respect can be roused. I've seen the same thing in other cases again and again. I could tell you any number of stories of——"

"He does not care for me?"

"In *one* way, a great deal. But you're like drink, like a drug to him. It is strange that a woman such as you, devoted, single-hearted, utterly loving, should be an influence for bad. But it's true of wives also. The best wives are often the worst. The philosophers are right. A man needs tranquillity at home."

"I understand," said she. "I understand—perfectly." And her voice was unemotional, as always when she was so deeply moved that she dared not release anything lest all should be released.

She was like a seated statue. The moon had moved so that it shone upon her face. He was astonished by its placid calm. He had expected her to rave and weep, to protest and plead—before denouncing him and bidding him mind his own business. Instead, she was making it clear that after all she did not care about Roderick; probably she was wondering what would become of her, now that her love was ruined. Well, wasn't it natural? Wasn't it altogether to her credit—wasn't it additional proof that she was a fine pure woman? How could she have continued deeply to care for a man scandalously untrue, and drunk much of the time? Certainly, it was in no way her fault that Rod made her the object and the victim of the only kind of so-called love of which he was capable. No doubt one reason he was untrue to her was that she was too pure for his debauched fancy. Thus reasoned Drumley with that mingling of truth and error characteristic of those who speculate about matters of which they have small and unfixed experience.

"About yourself," he proceeded. "I have a choice of professions for you—one with a company on the road—on the southern circuit—with good prospects of advancement. I know, from what I have seen of you,

and from talks we have had, that you would do well on
the stage. But the life might offend your sensibilities.
I should hesitate to recommend it to a delicate, fine-
fibered woman like you. The other position is a clerk-
ship in a business office in Philadelphia—with an increase as soon as you learn stenography and typewrit-
ing. It is respectable. It is sheltered. It doesn't
offer anything brilliant. But except the stage and
literature, nothing brilliant offers for a woman. Literature is out of the question, I think—certainly for
the present. The stage isn't really a place for a woman
of lady-like instincts. So I should recommend the
office position."

She remained silent.

"While my main purpose in talking to you," he continued, "was to try to save him, I can honestly say
that it was hardly less my intention to save you. But
for that, I'd not have had the courage to speak. He
is on the way down. He's dragging you with him.
What future have you with him? You would go on
down and down, as low as he should sink and lower.
You've completely merged yourself in him—which
might do very well if you were his wife and a good
influence in his life or a mere negation like most wives.
But in the circumstances it means ruin to you. Don't
you see that?"

"What did you say?"

"I was talking about you—your future—your——"

"Oh, I shall do well enough." She rose. "I must be
going."

Her short, indifferent dismissal of what was his real
object in speaking—though he did not permit himself
to know it—cut him to the quick. He felt a sickening
and to him inexplicable sense of defeat and disgrace.

Because he must talk to distract his mind from himself, he began afresh by saying:

"You'll think it over?"

"I am thinking it over. . . . I wonder that———"

With the fingers of one hand she smoothed her glove on the fingers of the other—"I wonder that I didn't think of it long ago. I ought to have thought of it. I ought to have seen."

"I can't tell you how I hate to have been the———"

"Please don't say any more," she requested in a tone that made it impossible for a man so timid as he to disobey.

Neither spoke until they were in Fifty-ninth Street; then he, unable to stand the strain of a silent walk of fifteen blocks, suggested that they take the car down. She assented. In the car the stronger light enabled him to see that she was pale in a way quite different from her usual clear, healthy pallor, that there was an unfamiliar look about her mouth and her eyes—a look of strain, of repression, of resolve. These signs and the contrast of her mute motionlessness with her usual vivacity of speech and expression and gesture made him uneasy.

"I'd advise," said he, "that you reflect on it all carefully and consult with me before you do anything—if you think you ought to do anything."

She made no reply. At the door of the house he had to reach for her hand, and her answer to his good night was a vague absent echo of the word. "I've only done what I saw was my duty," said he, appealingly.

"Yes, I suppose so. I must go in."

"And you'll talk with me before you———"

The door had closed behind her; she had not known he was speaking.

When Spenser came, about two hours later, and turned on the light in their bedroom, she was in the bed, apparently asleep. He stood staring with theatric self-consciousness at himself in the glass for several minutes, then sat down before the bureau and pulled out the third drawer—where he kept collars, ties, handkerchiefs, gloves and a pistol concealed under the handkerchiefs. With the awful solemnity of the youth who takes himself—and the theater—seriously he lifted the pistol, eyed it critically, turning it this way and that as if interested in the reflections of light from the bright cylinder and barrel at different angles. He laid it noiselessly back, covered it over with the handkerchiefs, sat with his fingers resting on the edge of the drawer. Presently he moved uneasily, as a man—on the stage or in its amusing imitation called civilized life among the self-conscious classes—moves when he feels that someone is behind him in a "crucial moment."

He slowly turned round. She had shifted her position so that her face was now toward him. But her eyes were closed and her face was tranquil. Still, he hoped she had seen the little episode of the pistol, which he thought fine and impressive. With his arm on the back of the chair and supporting that resolute-looking chin of his, he stared at her face from under his thick eyebrows, so thick that although they were almost as fair as his hair they seemed dark. After a while her eyelids fluttered and lifted to disclose eyes that startled him, so intense, so sleepless were they.

"Kiss me," she said, in her usual sweet, tender way— a little shyness, much of passion's sparkle and allure. "Kiss me."

"I've often thought," said he, "what would I do

470

if I should go smash, reach the end of my string? Would I kill you before taking myself off? Or would that be cowardly?"

She had not a doubt that he meant this melodramatic twaddle. It did not seem twaddle or melodramatic to her—or, for that matter, to him. She clasped him more closely. "What's the matter, dear?" she asked, her head on his breast.

"Oh, I've had a row at the *Herald*, and have quit. But I'll get another place tomorrow."

"Of course. I wish you'd fix up that play the way Drumley suggested."

"Maybe I shall. We'll see."

"Anything else wrong?"

"Only the same old trouble. I love you too much. Too damn much," he added in a tone not intended for her ears. "Weak fool—that's what I am. Weak fool. I've got *you*, anyhow. Haven't I?"

"Yes," she said. "I'd do anything for you—anything."

"As long as I keep my eyes on you," said he, half mockingly. "I'm weak, but you're weaker. Aren't you?"

"I guess so. I don't know." And she drew a long breath, nestled into his arms, and upon his breast, with her perfumed hair drowsing his senses.

He soon slept; when he awoke, toward noon, he did not disturb her. He shaved and bathed and dressed, and was about to go out when she called him. "Oh, I thought you were asleep," said he. "I can't wait for you to get breakfast. I must get a move on."

"Still blue?"

"No, indeed." But his face was not convincing. "So long, pet."

"Aren't you going to kiss me good-by?"

He laughed tenderly, yet in bitter self-mockery too. "And waste an hour or so? Not much. What a siren you are!"

She put her hand over her face quickly.

"Now, perhaps I can risk one kiss." He bent over her; his lips touched her hair. She stretched out her hand, laid it against his cheek. "Dearest," she murmured.

"I must go."

"Just a minute. No, don't look at me. Turn your face so that I can see your profile—so!" She had turned his head with a hand that gently caressed as it pushed. "I like that view best. Yes, you are strong and brave. You will succeed! No—I'll not keep you a minute." She kissed his hand, rested her head for an instant on his lap as he sat on the edge of the bed, suddenly flung herself to the far side of the bed, with her face toward the wall.

"Go to sleep again, lazy!" cried he. "I'll try to be home about dinner-time. See that you behave today! Good lord, how hard it is to leave you! Having you makes nothing else seem worth while. Good-by!"

And he was off. She started to a sitting posture, listened to the faint sound of his descending footsteps. She darted to the window, leaned out, watched him until he rounded the corner into Broadway. Then she dropped down with elbows on the window sill and hands pressing her cheeks; she stared unseeingly at the opposite house, at a gilt cage with a canary hopping and chirping within. And once more she thought all the thoughts that had filled her mind in the sleepless hours of that night and morning. Her eyes shifted in color from pure gray to pure violet—back and forth, as emotion or thought dominated her mind. She made herself coffee in the French machine, heated the milk she brought every day from the dairy, drank her *café au lait* slowly, reading the newspaper advertisements for "help wanted—female"—a habit she had formed when she first came to New York and had never altogether dropped. When she finished her coffee she took the scissors and cut out several of the demands for help.

She bathed and dressed. She moved through the routine of life—precisely as we all do, whatever may be in our minds and hearts. She went out, crossed Long Acre and entered the shop of a dealer in women's cast-off clothes. She reappeared in the street presently with a fat, sloppy looking woman in black. She took her to the rooms, offered for sale her entire wardrobe except the dress she had on and one other, the simply trimmed sailor upon her head, the ties on her feet and one pair of boots and a few small articles. After long haggling the woman made a final price—ninety-five dollars for things, most of them almost new, which had cost upwards of seven hundred. Susan accepted the offer; she knew she could do no better. The woman departed, returned with a porter and several huge sheets of wrapping paper. The two made three bundles of the purchases; the money was paid over; they and Susan's wardrobe departed.

Next, Susan packed in the traveling bag she had brought from Cincinnati the between seasons dress of brown serge she had withheld, and some such collection of bare necessities as she had taken with her when she left George Warham's. Into the bag she put the pistol from under Spenser's handkerchiefs in the third bureau drawer. When all was ready, she sent for the maid to straighten the rooms. While the maid was at work, she wrote this note:

DEAREST—Mr. Drumley will tell you why I have gone. You will find some money under your handkerchiefs in the bureau. When you are on your feet again, I may come— if you want me. It won't be any use for you to look for me. I ought to have gone before, but I was selfish and blind. Good-by, dear love—I wasn't so bad as you always suspected. I was true to you, and for the sake of what you have been to me and done for me I couldn't be so un- grateful as not to go. Don't worry about me. I shall get on. And so will you. It's best for us both. Good-by, dear heart—I was true to you. Good-by.

She sealed this note, addressed it, fastened it over the mantel in the sitting-room where they always put notes for each other. And after she had looked in each drawer and in the closet at all his clothing, and had kissed the pillow on which his head had lain, she took her bag and went. She had left for him the ninety-five dollars and also eleven dollars of the money she had in her purse. She took with her two five-dollar bills and a dollar and forty cents in change.

The violet waned in her eyes, and in its stead came the gray of thought and action.

SUSAN LENOX:
HER FALL AND RISE

DAVID GRAHAM PHILLIPS
AS HE WORKED

David Graham Phillips

SUSAN LENOX

HER FALL AND RISE

VOLUME II

WITH A PORTRAIT
OF THE AUTHOR

D. APPLETON AND COMPANY
LONDON   NEW YORK
1928

SUSAN LENOX

I

SUSAN'S impulse was toward the stage. It had become a definite ambition with her, the stronger
because Spenser's jealousy and suspicion had
forced her to keep it a secret, to pretend to herself that
she had no thought but going on indefinitely as his
obedient and devoted mistress. The hardiest and best
growths are the growths inward—where they have sun
and air from without. She had been at the theater
several times every week, and had studied the performances at a point of view very different from that of
the audience. It was there to be amused; she was there
to learn. Spenser and such of his friends as he would
let meet her talked plays and acting most of the time.
He had forbidden her to have women friends. "Men
don't demoralize women; women demoralize each other,"
was one of his axioms. But such women as she had a
bowing acquaintance with were all on the stage—in
comic operas or musical farces. She was much alone;
that meant many hours every day which could not but
be spent by a mind like hers in reading and in thinking.
Only those who have observed the difference aloneness
makes in mental development, where there is a good
mind, can appreciate how rapidly, how broadly, Susan
expanded. She read plays more than any other kind of

literature. She did not read them casually but was always thinking how they would act. She was soon making in imagination stage scenes out of dramatic chapters in novels as she read. More and more clearly the characters of play and novel took shape and substance before the eyes of her fancy. But the stage was clearly out of the question.

While the idea of a stage career had been dominant, she had thought in other directions, also. Every Sunday, indeed almost every day, she found in the newspapers articles on the subject of work for women.

"Why do you waste time on that stuff?" said Drumley, when he discovered her taste for it.

"Oh, a woman never can tell what may happen," replied she.

"She'll never learn anything from those fool articles," answered he. "You ought to hear the people who get them up laughing about them. I see now why they are printed. It's good for circulation, catches the women—even women like you." However, she persisted in reading. But never did she find an article that contained a really practical suggestion—that is, one applying to the case of a woman who had to live on what she made at the start, who was without experience and without a family to help her. All around her had been women who were making their way; but few indeed of them—even of those regarded as successful—were getting along without outside aid of some kind. So when she read or thought or inquired about work for women, she was sometimes amused and oftener made unhappy by the truth as to the conditions, that when a common worker rises it is almost always by the helping hand of a man, and rarely indeed a generous hand—a painful and shameful truth which a society resolved at any cost to think well of itself fiercely conceals from itself and hypocritically lies about.

She felt now that there was hope in only one direction—hope of occupation that would enable her to live in physical, moral and mental decency. She must find some employment where she could as decently as might be realize upon her physical assets. The stage would be best—but the stage was impossible, at least for the time. Later on she would try for it; there was in her mind not a doubt of that, for unsuspected of any who knew her there lay, beneath her sweet and gentle exterior, beneath her appearance of having been created especially for love and laughter and sympathy, tenacity of purpose and daring of ambition that were—rarely—hinted at the surface in her moments of abstraction. However, just now the stage was impossible. Spenser would find her immediately. She must go into another part of town, must work at something that touched his life at no point.

She had often been told that her figure would be one of her chief assets as a player. And ready-made clothes fitted her with very slight alterations—showing that she had a model figure. The advertisements she had cut out were for cloak models. Within an hour after she left Forty-fourth Street, she found at Jeffries and Jonas, in Broadway a few doors below Houston, a vacancy that had not yet been filled—though as a rule all the help needed was got from the throng of applicants waiting when the store opened.

"Come up to my office," said Jeffries, who happened to be near the door as she entered. "We'll see how you shape up. We want something extra—something dainty and catchy."

He was a short thick man, with flat feet, a flat face

and an almost bald head. In his flat nostrils, in the hollows of his great forward bent ears and on the lobes were bunches of coarse, stiff gray hairs. His eyebrows bristled; his small, sly brown eyes twinkled with good nature and with sensuality. His skin had the pallor that suggests kidney trouble. His words issued from his thick mouth as if he were tasting each beforehand—and liked the flavor. He led Susan into his private office, closed the door, took a tape measure from his desk. "Now, my dear," said he, "we'll size you up—eh? You're exactly the build I like." He then proceeded to take her measurements and finally turning to her said:

"You can have the place."

"What does it pay?" she asked.

"Ten dollars, to start with. Splendid wages. *I* started on two fifty. But I forgot—you don't know the business?"

"No—nothing about it," was her innocent answer.

"Ah—well, then—nine dollars—eh?"

Susan hesitated.

"Well—ten dollars, then."

Susan accepted. It was more than she had expected to get; it was less than she could hope to live on in New York in anything approaching the manner a person of any refinement or tastes or customs of comfort regards as merely decent. She must descend again to the tenements, must resume the fight against that physical degradation which sooner or later imposes—upon those *descending* to it—a degradation of mind and heart deeper, more saturating, more putrefying than any that ever originated from within. Not so long as her figure lasted was she the worse off for not knowing a trade. Jeffries was telling the truth; she would be getting splendid wages, not merely for a beginner but for any woman of the working class. Except in rare occasional instances, wages and salaries for women were kept down below the standard of decency by woman's peculiar position—by such conditions as that most women took up work as a temporary makeshift or to piece out a family's earnings, and that almost any woman could supplement—and so many did supplement —their earnings at labor with as large or larger earnings in the stealthy shameful way. Where was there a trade that would bring a girl ten dollars a week at the start? Even if she were a semi-professional, a stenographer and typewriter, it would take expertness and long service to lift her up to such wages. Thanks to her figure—to its chancing to please old Jeffries' taste —she was better off than all but a few working women, than all but a few workingmen. She was of the labor aristocracy; and if she had been one of a family of workers she would have been counted an enviable favorite of fortune. Unfortunately, she was alone—unfortunately for herself, not at all from the standpoint of the tenement class she was now joining. Among them she would be a person who could afford the luxuries of life as life revealed itself to the tenements.

"Tomorrow morning at seven o'clock," said Jeffries.

"You are a married woman?"

"Yes."

"You have lost your husband?"

"Yes."

"I saw you'd had great grief. No insurance, I judge? Well—you will find another—maybe a rich one." And he patted her on the shoulder.

She was able to muster a grateful smile; for she felt

a rare kindness of heart under the familiar animalism to which good-looking, well-formed women who go about much unescorted soon grow accustomed. Also, experience had taught her that, as things go with girls of the working class, his treatment was courteous, considerate, chivalrous almost. With men in absolute control of all kinds of work, with women stimulating the sex appetite by openly or covertly using their charms as female to assist them in the cruel struggle for existence—what was to be expected?

Her way to the elevator took her along aisles lined with tables, hidden under masses of cloaks, jackets, dresses and materials for making them. They exuded the odors of the factory—faint yet pungent odors that brought up before her visions of huge, badly ventilated rooms, where women aged or aging swiftly were toiling hour after hour monotonously—spending half of each day in buying the right to eat and sleep unhealthily. The odors—or, rather, the visions they evoked—made her sick at heart. For the moment she came from under the spell of her peculiar trait—her power to do without whimper or vain gesture of revolt the inevitable thing, whatever it was. She paused to steady herself, half leaning against a lofty uppiling of winter cloaks. A girl, young at first glance, not nearly so young thereafter, suddenly appeared before her—a girl whose hair had the sheen of burnished brass and whose soft smooth skin was of that frog-belly whiteness which suggests an inheritance of some bleaching and blistering disease. She had small regular features, eyes that at once suggested looseness, good-natured yet mercenary too. She was dressed in the sleek, tight-fitting trying-on robe of the professional model, and her figure was superb in its firm luxuriousness.

6

"Sick?" asked the girl with real kindliness.

"No—only dizzy for the moment."

"I suppose you've had a hard day."

"It might have been easier," Susan replied, attempting a smile.

"It's no fun, looking for a job. But you've caught on?"

"Yes. He took me."

"I made a bet with myself that he would when I saw you go in." The girl laughed agreeably. "He picked you for Gideon."

"What department is that?"

The girl laughed again, with a cynical squinting of the eyes. "Oh, Gideon's our biggest customer. He buys for the largest house in Chicago."

"I'm looking for a place to live," said Susan. "Some place in this part of town."

"How much do you want to spend?"

"I'm to have ten a week. So I can't afford more than twelve or fourteen a month for rent, can I?"

"If you happen to have to live on the ten," was the reply with a sly, merry smile.

"It's all I've got."

Again the girl laughed, the good-humored mercenary eyes twinkling rakishly. "Well—you can't get much for fourteen a month."

"I don't care, so long as it's clean."

"Gee, you're reasonable, ain't you?" cried the girl. "Clean! I pay fourteen a week, and all kinds of things come through the cracks from the other apartments. You must be a stranger to little old New York—bug-town, a lady friend of mine calls it. Alone?"

"Yes."

"Um——" The girl shook her head dubiously.

"Rents are mighty steep in New York, and going up all the time. You see, the rich people that own the lands and houses here need a lot of money in their business. You've got either to take a room or part of one in with some tenement family, respectable but noisy and dirty and not at all refined, or else you've got to live in a house where everthing goes. You want to live respectable, I judge?"

"Yes."

"I knew you were refined the minute I looked at you. I think you might get a room in the house of a lady friend of mine—Mrs. Tucker, up in Clinton Place near University Place—an elegant neighborhood—that is, the north side of the street. The south side's kind o' low, on account of dagoes having moved in there. They live like vermin—but then all tenement people do."

"They've got to," said Susan.

"Yes, that's a fact. Ain't it awful? I'll write down the name and address of my lady friend. I'm Miss Mary Hinkle."

"My name is Lorna Sackville," said Susan, in response to the expectant look of Miss Hinkle.

"My, what a swell name! You've been sick, haven't you?"

"No, I'm never sick."

"Me too. My mother taught me to stop eating as soon as I felt bad, and not to eat again till I was all right."

"I do that, too," said Susan. "Is it good for the health?"

"It starves the doctors. You've never worked before?"

"Oh, yes—I've worked in a factory."

Miss Hinkle looked disappointed. Then she gave
Susan a side glance of incredulity. "I'd never 'a'
thought it. But I can see you weren't brought up to
that. I'll write the address." And she went back
through the showroom, presently to reappear with a
card which she gave Susan. "You'll find Mrs. Tucker
a perfect lady—too much a lady to get on. I tell her
she'll go to ruin—and she will."

Susan thanked Miss Hinkle and departed. A few
minutes' walk brought her to the old, high-stooped,
brown-stone where Mrs. Tucker lived. The dents,
scratches and old paint scales on the door, the dust-
streaked windows, the slovenly hang of the imitation
lace window curtains proclaimed the cheap middle-class
lodging or boarding house of the humblest grade. Respectable undoubtedly; for the fitfully prosperous of-
fenders against laws and morals insist upon better accommodations. Susan's heart sank. She saw that once
more she was clinging at the edge of the precipice.
And what hope was there that she would get back to
firm ground? Certainly not by "honest labor." Back
to the tenement! "Yes, I'm on the way back," she said
to herself. However, she pulled the loose bell-knob and
was admitted to a dingy, dusty hallway by a maid so
redolent of stale perspiration that it was noticeable
even in the hall's strong saturation of smells of cheap
cookery. The parlor furniture was rapidly going to
pieces; the chromos and prints hung crazily awry;
dust lay thick upon the center table, upon the chimney-
piece, upon the picture frames, upon the carving in
the rickety old chairs. Only by standing did Susan
avoid service as a dust rag. It was typical of the
profound discouragement that blights or blasts all but
a small area of our modern civilization—a discourage-

ment due in part to ignorance—but not at all to the cause usually assigned—to "natural shiftlessness." It is chiefly due to an unconscious instinctive feeling of the hopelessness of the average lot.

While Susan explained to Mrs. Tucker how she had come and what she could afford, she examined her with results far from disagreeable. One glance into that homely wrinkled face was enough to convince anyone of her goodness of heart—and to Susan in those days of aloneness, of uncertainty, of the feeling of hopelessness, goodness of heart seemed the supreme charm. Such a woman as a landlady, and a landlady in New York, was pathetically absurd. Even to still rather simple-minded Susan she seemed an invitation to the swindler, to the sponger with the hard-luck story, to the sinking who clutch about desperately and drag down with them everyone who permits them to get a hold.

"I've only got one room," said Mrs. Tucker. "That's not any too nice. I did rather calculate to get five a week for it, but you are the kind I like to have in the house. So if you want it I'll let it to you for fourteen a month. And I do hope you'll pay as steady as you can. There's so many in such hard lines that I have a tough time with my rent. I've got to pay my rent, you know."

"I'll go as soon as I can't pay," replied Susan. The landlady's apologetic tone made her sick at heart, as a sensitive human being must ever feel in the presence of a fellow-being doomed to disaster.

"Thank you," said Mrs. Tucker gratefully. "I do wish——" She checked herself. "No, I don't mean that. They do the best they can—and I'll botch along somehow. I look at the bright side of things."

The incurable optimism of the smile accompanying

these words moved Susan, abnormally bruised and tender of heart that morning, almost to tears. A woman with her own way to make, and always looking at the bright side!

"How long have you had this house?"

"Only five months. My husband died a year ago. I had to give up our little business six months after his death. Such a nice little stationery store, but I couldn't seem to refuse credit or to collect bills. Then I came here. This looks like losing, too. But I'm sure I'll come out all right. The Lord will provide, as the Good Book says. I don't have no trouble keeping the house full. Only they don't seem to pay. You want to see your room?"

She and Susan ascended three flights to the top story—to a closet of a room at the back. The walls were newly and brightly papered. The sloping roof of the house made one wall a ceiling also, and in this two small windows were set. The furniture was a tiny bed, white and clean as to its linen, a table, two chairs, a small washstand with a little bowl and a less pitcher, a soap dish and a mug. Along one wall ran a row of hooks. On the floor was an old and incredibly dirty carpet, mitigated by a strip of clean matting which ran from the door, between washstand and bed, to one of the windows.

Susan glanced round—a glance was enough to enable her to see all—all that was there, all that the things there implied. Back to the tenement life! She shuddered.

"It ain't much," said Mrs. Tucker. "But usually rooms like these rents for five a week."

The sun had heated the roof scorching hot; the air of this room, immediately underneath, was like that of a cellar where a furnace is in full blast. But Susan knew she was indeed in luck. "It's clean and nice here," said she to Mrs. Tucker, "and I'm much obliged to you for being so reasonable with me." And to clinch the bargain she then and there paid half a month's rent. "I'll give you the rest when my week at the store's up."

"No hurry," said Mrs. Tucker who was handling the money and looking at it with glistening grateful eyes. "Us poor folks oughtn't to be hard on each other —though, Lord knows, if we was, I reckon we'd not be quite so poor. It's them that has the streak of hard in 'em what gets on. But the Bible teaches us that's what to expect in a world of sin. I suppose you want to go now and have your trunk sent?"

"This is all I've got," said Susan, indicating her bag on the table.

Into Mrs. Tucker's face came a look of terror that made Susan realize in an instant how hard-pressed she must be. It was the kind of look that comes into the eyes of the deer brought down by the dogs when it sees the hunter coming up.

"But I've a good place," Susan hastened to say. "I get ten a week. And as I told you before, when I can't pay I'll go right away."

"I've lost so much in bad debts," explained the landlady humbly. "I don't seem to see which way to turn." Then she brightened. "It'll all come out for the best. I work hard and I try to do right by everybody."

"I'm sure it will," said Susan believingly.

Often her confidence in the moral ideals trained into her from childhood had been sorely tried. But never had she permitted herself more than a hasty, ashamed doubt that the only way to get on was to work and to practice the Golden Rule. Everyone who was prosperous attributed his prosperity to the steadfast following of that way; as for those who were not prosperous, they were either lazy or bad-hearted, or would have been even worse off had they been less faithful to the creed that was best policy as well as best for peace of mind and heart.

In trying to be as inexpensive to Spenser as she could contrive, and also because of her passion for improving herself, Susan had explored far into the almost unknown art of living, on its shamefully neglected material side. She had cultivated the habit of spending much time about her purchases of every kind—had spent time intelligently in saving money intelligently. She had gone from shop to shop, comparing values and prices. She had studied quality in food and in clothing; and thus she had discovered what enormous sums are wasted through ignorance—wasted by poor even more lavishly than by rich or well-to-do, because the shops where the poor dealt had absolutely no check on their rapacity through the occasional canny customer. She had learned the fundamental truth of the material art of living; only when a good thing happens to be cheap is a cheap thing good. Spenser, cross-examining her as to how she passed the days, found out about this education she was acquiring. It amused him. "A waste of time!" he used to say. "Pay what they ask, and don't bother your head with such petty matters." He might have suspected and accused her of being stingy had not her generosity been about the most obvious and incessant trait of her character.

She was now reduced to an income below what life can be decently maintained upon—the life of a city-dweller with normal tastes for cleanliness and healthfulness. She proceeded without delay to put her in-

valuable education into use. She must fill her mind
with the present and with the future. She must not
glance back. She must ignore her wounds—their aches,
their clamorous throbs. She took off her clothes, as
soon as Mrs. Tucker left her alone, brushed them and
hung them up, put on the thin wrapper she had brought
in her bag. The fierce heat of the little packing-case
of a room became less unendurable; also, she was saving the clothes from useless wear. She sat down at
the table and with pencil and paper planned her budget.

Of the ten dollars a week, three dollars and thirty
cents must be subtracted for rent—for shelter. This
left six dollars and seventy cents for the other two
necessaries, food and clothing—there must be no incidental expenses since there was no money to meet them.
She could not afford to provide for carfare on stormy
days; a rain coat, overshoes and umbrella, more expensive at the outset, were incomparably cheaper in the
long run. Her washing and ironing she would of course
do for herself in the evenings and on Sundays. Of the
two items which the six dollars and seventy cents must
cover, food came first in importance. How little
could she live on?

That stifling hot room! She was as wet as if she had
come undried from a bath. She had thought she could
never feel anything but love for the sun of her City
of the Sun. But this undreamed-of heat—like the cruel
caresses of a too impetuous lover—

How little could she live on?"

Dividing her total of six dollars and seventy cents by
seven, she found that she had ninety-five cents a day.
She would soon have to buy clothes, however scrupulous
care she might take of those she possessed. It was
modest indeed to estimate fifteen dollars for clothes

before October. That meant she must save fifteen dollars in the remaining three weeks of June, in July, August and September—in one hundred and ten days. She must save about fifteen cents a day. And out of that she must buy soap and tooth powder, outer and under clothes, perhaps a hat and a pair of shoes. Thus she could spend for food not more than eighty cents a day, as much less as was consistent with buying the best quality—for she had learned by bitter experience the ravages poor quality food makes in health and looks, had learned why girls of the working class go to pieces swiftly after eighteen. She must fight to keep health—sick she did not dare be. She must fight to keep looks—her figure was her income.

Eighty cents a day. The outlook was not so gloomy. A cup of cocoa in the morning—made at home of the best cocoa, the kind that did not overheat the blood and disorder the skin—it would cost her less than ten cents. She would carry lunch with her to the store. In the evening she would cook a chop or something of that kind on the gas stove she would buy. Some days she would be able to save twenty or even twenty-five cents toward clothing and the like. Whatever else happened, she was resolved never again to sink to dirt and rags. Never again!—never! She had passed through that experience once without loss of self-respect only because it was by way of education. To go through it again would be yielding ground in the fight—the fight for a destiny worth while which some latent but mighty instinct within her never permitted her to forget.

She sat at the table, with the shutters closed against the fiery light of the summer afternoon sun. That hideous unacceptable heat! With eyelids drooped—deep and dark were the circles round them—she listened to the roar of the city, a savage sound like the clamor of a multitude of famished wild beasts. A city like the City of Destruction in "Pilgrim's Progress"—a city where of all the millions, but a few thousands were moving toward or keeping in the sunlight of civilization. The rest, the swarms of the cheap boarding houses, cheap lodging houses, tenements—these myriads were squirming in darkness and squalor, ignorant and never to be less ignorant, ill fed and never to be better fed, clothed in pitiful absurd rags or shoddy vulgar attempts at finery, and never to be better clothed. She would not be of those! She would struggle on, would sink only to mount. She would work; she would try to do as nearly right as she could. And in the end she must triumph. She would get at least a good part of what her soul craved, of what her mind craved, of what her heart craved.

The heat of this tenement room! The heat to which poverty was exposed naked and bound! Would not anyone be justified in doing anything—yes, *anything*—to escape from this fiend?

II

ELLEN, the maid, slept across the hall from Susan, in a closet so dirty that no one could have risked in it any article of clothing with the least pretension to cleanness. It was no better, no worse than the lodgings of more than two hundred thousand New Yorkers. Its one narrow opening, beside the door, gave upon a shaft whose odors were so foul that she kept the window closed, preferring heat like the inside of a steaming pan to the only available "outside air." This in a civilized city where hundreds of dogs with jeweled collars slept in luxurious rooms on downiest beds and had servants to wait upon them! The morning after Susan's coming, Ellen woke her, as they had arranged, at a quarter before five. The night before, Susan had brought up from the basement a large bucket of water; for she had made up her mind to take a bath every day, at least until the cold weather set in and rendered such a luxury impossible. With this water and what she had in her little pitcher, Susan contrived to freshen herself up. She had bought a gas stove and some indispensable utensils for three dollars and seventeen cents in a Fourteenth Street store, a pound of cocoa for seventy cents and ten cents' worth of rolls—three rolls, well baked, of first quality flour and with about as good butter and other things put into the dough as one can expect in bread not made at home. These purchases had reduced her cash to forty-three cents—and she ought to buy without delay a

17

clock with an alarm attachment. And pay day—Saturday—was two days away.

She made a cup of cocoa, drank it slowly, eating one
of the rolls—all in the same methodical way like a
machine that continues to revolve after the power has
been shut off. It was then, even more than during
her first evening alone, even more than when she from
time to time startled out of troubled sleep—it was then,
as she forced down her lonely breakfast, that she most
missed Rod. When she had finished, she completed her
toilet. The final glance at herself in the little mirror
was depressing. She looked fresh for her new surroundings and for her new class. But in comparison with
what she usually looked, already there was a distinct,
an ominous falling off. "I'm glad Rod never saw me
looking like this," she said aloud drearily. Taking a
roll for lunch, she issued forth at half-past six. The
hour and three-quarters she had allowed for dressing
and breakfasting had been none too much. In the coolness and comparative quiet she went down University
Place and across Washington Square under the old
trees, all alive with song and breeze and flashes of early
morning light. She was soon in Broadway's deep canyon, was drifting absently along in the stream of cross,
mussy-looking workers pushing southward. Her heart
ached, her brain throbbed. It was horrible, this loneliness; and every one of the wounds where she had severed
the ties with Spenser was bleeding. She was astonished
to find herself before the building whose upper floors
were occupied by Jeffries and Jonas. How had she
got there? Where had she crossed Broadway?

"Good morning, Miss Sackville." It was Miss Hinkle,
just arriving. Her eyes were heavy, and there were the
crisscross lines under them that tell a story to the

expert in the different effects of different kinds of dissipation. Miss Hinkle was showing her age—and she was "no spring chicken."

Susan returned her greeting, gazing at her with the dazed eyes and puzzled smile of an awakening sleeper. "I'll show you the ropes," said Miss Hinkle, as they climbed the two flights of stairs. "You'll find the job dead easy. They're mighty nice people to work for, Mr. Jeffries especially. Not easy fruit, of course, but nice for people that have got on. You didn't sleep well?"

"Yes—I think so."

"I didn't have a chance to drop round last night. I was out with one of the buyers. How do you like Mrs. Tucker?"

"She's very good, isn't she?"

"She'll never get along. She works hard, too—but not for herself. In this world you have to look out for Number One."

They were a few minutes early; so Miss Hinkle continued the conversation while they waited for the opening of the room where Susan would be outfitted for her work. "I called you Miss Sackville," said she, "but you've been married—haven't you?"

"Yes."

"I can always tell—or at least I can see whether a woman's had experience or not. Well, I've never been regularly married, and I don't expect to, unless something pretty good offers. Think I'd marry one of these rotten little clerks?" Miss Hinkle answered her own question with a scornful sniff. "They can hardly make a living for themselves. And a man who amounts to anything, he wants a refined lady to help him on up, not a working girl. Of course, there's exceptions. But as a rule a girl in our position either

has to stay single or marry beneath her—marry some
mechanic or such like. Well, I ain't so lazy, or so
crazy about being supported, that I'd sink to be
cook and slop-carrier—and worse—for a carpenter or
a bricklayer. Going out with the buyers—the gen-
tlemanly ones—has spoiled my taste. I can't stand
a coarse man—coarse dress and hands and manners.
Can you?"

Susan turned hastily away, so that her face was
hidden from Miss Hinkle.

"I'll bet you wasn't married to a coarse man."

"I'd rather not talk about myself," said Susan with
an effort. "It's not pleasant."

Her manner of checking Miss Hinkle's friendly curiosity did not give offense; it excited the experienced
working woman's sympathy. She went on:

"Well, I feel sorry for any woman that has to
work. Of course most women do—and at worse than
anything in the stores and factories. As between being a drudge to some dirty common laborer like most
women are, and working in a factory even, give me the
factory. Yes, give me a job as a pot slinger even, low
as that is. Oh, I *hate* working people! I love refinement. Up to Murray's last night I sat there, eating
my lobster and drinking my wine, and I pretended I
was a lady—and, my, how happy I was!"

The stockroom now opened. Susan, with the help
of Miss Hinkle and the stock keeper, dressed in one of
the tight-fitting satin slips that revealed every curve
and line of her form, made every motion however
slight, every breath she drew, a gesture of sensuous-
ness. As she looked at herself in a long glass in one
of the show-parlors, her face did not reflect the admiration frankly displayed upon the faces of the two

other women. That satin slip seemed to have a moral quality, an immoral character. It made her feel naked—no, as if she were naked and being peeped at through a crack or keyhole.

"You'll soon get used to it," Miss Hinkle assured her. "And you'll learn to show off the dresses and cloaks to the best advantage." She laughed her insinuating little laugh again, amused, cynical, reckless. "You know, the buyers are men. Gee, what awful jay things we work off on them, sometimes! They can't see the dress for the figure. And you've got such a refined figure, Miss Sackville—the kind I'd be crazy about if I was a man. But I must say—" here she eyed herself in the glass complacently—"most men prefer a figure like mine. Don't they, Miss Simmons?"

The stock keeper shook her fat shoulders in a gesture of indifferent disdain. "They take whatever's handiest—that's my experience."

About half-past nine the first customer appeared— Mr. Gideon, it happened to be. He was making the rounds of the big wholesale houses in search of stock for the huge Chicago department store that paid him fifteen thousand a year and expenses. He had been contemptuous of the offerings of Jeffries and Jonas for the winter season, had praised with enthusiasm the models of their principal rival, Icklemeier, Schwartz and Company. They were undecided whether he was really thinking of deserting them or was feeling for lower prices. Mr. Jeffries bustled into the room where Susan stood waiting; his flat face quivered with excitement. "Gid's come!" he said in a hoarse whisper. "Everybody get busy. We'll try Miss Sackville on him."

And he himself assisted while they tricked out Susan in an afternoon costume of pale gray, putting on her

head a big pale gray hat with harmonizing feathers.
The model was offered in all colors and also in a modified form that permitted its use for either afternoon
or evening. Susan had received her instructions, so
when she was dressed, she was ready to sweep into
Gideon's presence with languid majesty. Jeffries'
eyes glistened as he noted her walk. "She looks as if
she really was a lady!" exclaimed he. "I wish I could
make my daughters move around on their trotters like
that."

Gideon was enthroned in an easy chair, smoking a
cigar. He was a spare man of perhaps forty-five,
with no intention of abandoning the pretensions to
youth for many a year. In dress he was as spick and
span as a tailor at the trade's annual convention. But
he had evidently been "going some" for several days;
the sour, worn, haggard face rising above his elegantly
fitting collar suggested a moth-eaten jaguar that has
been for weeks on short rations or none.

"What's the matter?" he snapped, as the door began to open. "I don't like to be kept waiting."

In swept Susan; and Jeffries, rubbing his thick
hands, said fawningly, "But I think, Mr. Gideon,
you'll say it was worth waiting for."

Gideon's angry, arrogant eyes softened at first
glimpse of Susan. "Um!" he grunted, some such
sound as the jaguar aforesaid would make when the
first chunk of food hurtled through the bars and
landed on his paws. He sat with cigar poised between
his long white fingers while Susan walked up and down
before him, displaying the dress at all angles, Jeffries
expatiating upon it the while.

"Don't talk so damn much, Jeff!" he commanded
with the insolence of a customer containing possibili-

ties of large profit. "I judge for myself. I'm not a damn fool."

"I should say not," cried Jeffries, laughing the merchant's laugh for a customer's pleasantry. "But I can't help talking about it, Gid, it's so lovely!"

Jeffries' shrewd eyes leaped for joy when Gideon got up from his chair and, under pretense of examining the garment, investigated Susan's figure. "Excuse me," said Jeffries. "I'll see that they get the other things ready." And out he went, signaling at Mary Hinkle to follow him—an unnecessary gesture, as she was already on her way to the door.

Gideon understood as well as did they why they left. "I don't think I've seen you before, my dear," said he to Susan.

"I came only this morning," replied she.

"I like to know everybody I deal with. We must get better acquainted."

"Thank you," said Susan with a grave, distant smile.

"Got a date for dinner tonight?" inquired he; and, assuming that everything would yield precedence to him, he did not wait for a reply, but went on, "Tell me your address. I'll send a cab for you at seven o'clock."

"Thank you," said Susan, "but I can't go."

Gideon smiled. "Oh, don't be shy. Of course you'll go. Ask Jeffries. He'll tell you it's all right."

"There are reasons why I'd rather not be seen in the restaurants."

"That's even better. I'll come in the cab myself and we'll go to a quiet place."

His eyes smiled insinuatingly at her. Now that she looked at him more carefully he was unusually attractive for a man of his type—had strength and intelligence in his features, had a suggestion of mastery, of one used to obedience, in his voice. His teeth were even and sound, his lips firm yet not too thin.

"Come," said he persuasively. "I'll not eat you up—" with a gay and gracious smile—"at least I'll try not to."

Susan remembered what Miss Hinkle had told her. She saw that she must either accept the invitation or give up her position. She said:

"Very well," and gave him her address.

Back came Jeffries and Miss Hinkle carrying the first of the wraps. Gideon waved them away. "You've shown 'em to me before," said he. "I don't want to see 'em again. Give me the evening gowns."

Susan withdrew, soon to appear in a dress that left her arms and neck bare. Jeffries kept her walking up and down until she was ready to drop with weariness of the monotony. Gideon tried to draw her into conversation, but she would—indeed could—go no further than direct answers to his direct questions. "Never mind," said he to her in an undertone. "I'll cheer you up this evening. I think I know how to order a dinner."

Her instant conquest of the difficult and valuable Gideon so elated Jeffries that he piled the work on her. He used her with every important buyer who came that day. The temperature was up in the high nineties; the hot moist air stood stagnant as a barnyard pool; the winter models were cruelly hot and heavy. All day long, with a pause of half an hour to eat her roll and drink a glass of water, Susan walked up and down the show parlors weighted with dresses and cloaks, furs for arctic weather. The other girls, even those doing

almost nothing, were all but prostrated. It was little
short of intolerable, this struggle to gain the "honest,
self-respecting living by honest work" that there was
so much talk about. Toward five o'clock her nerves
abruptly and completely gave way, and she fainted—
for the first time in her life. At once the whole establishment was in an uproar. Jeffries cursed himself
loudly for his shortsightedness, for his overestimating
her young strength. "She'll look like hell this evening,"
he wailed, wringing his hands like a distracted peasant
woman. "Maybe she won't be able to go out at all."

She soon came round. They brought her whiskey,
and afterward tea and sandwiches. And with the power
of quick recuperation that is the most fascinating
miracle of healthy youth, she not only showed no sign
of her breakdown but looked much better. And she
felt better. We shall some day understand why it is
that if a severe physical blow follows upon a mental
blow, recovery from the physical blow is always accompanied by a relief of the mental strain. Susan came
out of her fit of faintness and exhaustion with a different point of view—as if time had been long at work softening her grief; Spenser seemed part of the present no
longer, but of the past—a past far more remote than
yesterday.

Mary Hinkle sat with her as she drank the tea. "Did
you make a date with Gid?" inquired she. Her tone let
Susan know that the question had been prompted by
Jeffries.

"He asked me to dine with him, and I said I would."

"Have you got a nice dress—dinner dress, I mean?"

"The linen one I'm wearing is all. My other dress is
for cooler weather."

"Then I'll give you one out of stock—I mean I'll

borrow one for you. This dinner's a house affair, you know—to get Gid's order. It'll be worth thousands to them."

"There wouldn't be anything to fit me on such short notice," said Susan, casting about for an excuse for not wearing borrowed finery.

"Why, you've got a model figure. I'll pick you out a white dress—and a black and white hat. I know 'em all, and I know one that'll make you look simply lovely."

Susan did not protest. She was profoundly indifferent to what happened to her. Life seemed a show in which she had no part, and at which she sat a listless spectator. A few minutes, and in puffed Jeffries, solicitous as a fussy old bird with a new family.

"You're a lot better, ain't you?" cried he, before he had looked at her. "Oh, yes, you'll be all right. And you'll have a lovely time with Mr. Gideon. He's a perfect gentleman—knows how to treat a lady. . . . The minute I laid eyes on you I said to myself, said I, 'Jeffries, she's a mascot.' And you are, my dear. You'll get us the order. But you mustn't talk business with him, you understand?"

"Yes," said Susan, wearily.

"He's a gentleman, you know, and it don't do to mix business and social pleasures. You string him along quiet and ladylike and elegant, as if there wasn't any such things as cloaks or dresses in the world. He'll understand all right. . . . If you land the order, my dear, I'll see that you get a nice present. A nice dress —the one we're going to lend you—if he gives us a slice. The dress and twenty-five in cash, if he gives us all. How's that?"

"Thank you," said Susan. "I'll do my best."

26

"You'll land it. You'll land it. I feel as if we had it with his O. K. on it."

Susan shivered. "Don't—don't count on me too much," she said hesitatingly. "I'm not in very good spirits, I'm sorry to say."

"A little pressed for money?" Jeffries hesitated, made an effort, blurted out what was for him, the business man, a giddy generosity. "On your way out, stop at the cashier's. He'll give you this week's pay in advance." Jeffries hesitated, decided against dangerous liberality. "Not ten, you understand, but say six. You see, you won't have been with us a full week." And he hurried away, frightened by his prodigality, by these hysterical impulses that were rushing him far from the course of sound business sense. "As Jones says, I'm a generous old fool," he muttered. "My soft heart'll ruin me yet."

Jeffries sent Mary Hinkle home with Susan to carry the dress and hat, to help her make a toilet and to "start her off right." In the hour before they left the store there was offered a typical illustration of why and how "business" is able to suspend the normal moral sense and to substitute for it a highly ingenious counterfeit of supreme moral obligation to it. The hysterical Jeffries had infected the entire personnel with his excitement, with the sense that a great battle was impending and that the cause of the house, which was the cause of everyone who drew pay from it, had been intrusted to the young recruit with the fascinating figure and the sweet, sad face. And Susan's sensitive nature was soon vibrating in response to this feeling. It terrified her that she, the inexperienced, had such grave responsibility. It made her heart heavy to think of probable failure, when the house had been so good to her, had taken her in, had given her unusual wages, had made it possible for her to get a start in life, had intrusted to her its cause, its chance to retrieve a bad season and to protect its employees instead of discharging a lot of them.

"Have you got long white gloves?" asked Mary Hinkle, as they walked up Broadway, she carrying the dress and Susan the hat box.

"Only a few pairs of short ones."

"You must have long white gloves—and a pair of white stockings."

"I can't afford them."

"Oh, Jeffries told me to ask you—and to go to work and buy them if you hadn't."

They stopped at Wanamaker's. Susan was about to pay, when Mary stopped her. "If you pay," said she, "maybe you'll get your money back from the house, and maybe you won't. If I pay, they'll not make a kick on giving it back to me."

The dress Mary had selected was a simple white batiste, cut out at the neck prettily, and with the elbow sleeves that were then the fashion. "Your arms and throat are lovely," said Mary. "And your hands are mighty nice, too—that's why I'm sure you've never been a real working girl—leastways, not for a long time. When you get to the restaurant and draw off your gloves in a slow, careless, ladylike kind of way, and put your elbows on the table—my, how he will take on!" Mary looked at her with an intense but not at all malignant envy. "If you don't land high, it'll be because you're a fool. And you ain't that."

"I'm afraid I am," replied Susan. "Yes, I guess I'm what's called a fool—what probably is a fool."

"You want to look out then," warned Miss Hinkle.

"You want to go to work and get over that. Beauty don't count, unless a girl's got shrewdness. The streets are full of beauties sellin' out for a bare living. They thought they couldn't help winning, and they got left, and the plain girls who had to hustle and manage have passed them. Go to Del's or Rector's or the Waldorf or the Madrid or any of those high-toned places, and see the women with the swell clothes and jewelry! The married ones, and the other kind, both. Are they raving tearing beauties? Not often. . . . The trouble with me is I've been too good-hearted and too soft about being flattered. I was too good looking, and a small easy living came too easy. You—I'd say you were— that you had brains but were shy about using them. What's the good of having them? Might as well be a boob. Then, too, you've got to go to work and look out about being too refined. The refined, nice ones goes the lowest—if they get pushed—and this is a pushing world. You'll get pushed just as far as you'll let 'em. Take it from me. I've been down the line."

Susan's low spirits sank lower. These disagreeable truths—for observation and experience made her fear they were truths—filled her with despondency. What was the matter with life? As between the morality she had been taught and the practical morality of this world upon which she had been cast, which was the right? How "take hold"? How avert the impending disaster? What of the "good" should—*must*—she throw away? What should—*must*—she cling to?

Mary Hinkle was shocked by the poor little room. "This is no place for a lady!" cried she. "But it won't last long—not after tonight, if you play your cards halfway right."

29

"I'm very well satisfied," said Susan. "If I can only keep this!"

She felt no interest in the toilet until the dress and hat were unpacked and laid out upon the bed. At sight of them her eyes became a keen and lively gray—never violet for that kind of emotion—and there surged up the love of finery that dwells in every normal woman—and in every normal man—that is put there by a heredity dating back through the ages to the very beginning of conscious life—and does not leave them until life gives up the battle and prepares to vacate before death. Ellen, the maid, passing the door, saw and entered to add her ecstatic exclamations to the excitement. Down she ran to bring Mrs. Tucker, who no sooner beheld the glory displayed upon the humble bed than she too was in a turmoil. Susan dressed with the aid of three maids as interested and eager as ever robed a queen for coronation. Ellen brought hot water and a larger bowl. Mrs. Tucker wished to lend a highly scented toilet soap she used when she put on gala attire; but Susan insisted upon her own plain soap. They all helped her bathe; they helped her select the best underclothes from her small store. Susan would put on her own stockings; but Ellen got one foot into one of the slippers and Mrs. Tucker looked after the other foot. "Ain't they lovely?" said Ellen to Mrs. Tucker, as they knelt together at their task. "I never see such feet. Not a lump on 'em, but like feet in a picture."

"It takes a mighty good leg to look good in a white stocking," observed Mary. "But yours is so nice and long and slim that they'd stand most anything."

Mrs. Tucker and Ellen stood by with no interference save suggestion and comment, while Mary, who at one time worked for a hairdresser, did Susan's thick dark hair. Susan would permit no elaborations, much to Miss Hinkle's regret. But the three agreed that she was right when the simple sweep of the vital blue-black hair was finished in a loose and graceful knot at the back, and Susan's small, healthily pallid face looked its loveliest, with the violet-gray eyes soft and sweet and serious. Mrs. Tucker brought the hat from the bed, and Susan put it on—a large black straw of a most becoming shape with two pure white plumes curling round the crown and a third, not so long, rising gracefully from the big buckle where the three plumes met. And now came the putting on of the dress. With as much care as if they were handling a rare and fragile vase, Mary and Mrs. Tucker held the dress for Susan to step into it. Ellen kept her petticoat in place while the other two escorted the dress up Susan's form.

Then the three worked together at hooking and smoothing. Susan washed her hands again, refused to let Mrs. Tucker run and bring powder, produced from a drawer some prepared chalk and with it safeguarded her nose against shine; she tucked the powder rag into her stocking. Last of all the gloves went on and a small handkerchief was thrust into the palm of the left glove.

"How do I look?" asked Susan.

"Lovely"—"Fine"—"Just grand," exclaimed the three maids.

"I feel awfully dressed up," said she. "And it's so hot!"

"You must go right downstairs where it's cool and you won't get wilted," cried Mrs. Tucker. "Hold your skirts close on the way. The steps and walls ain't none too clean."

In the bathroom downstairs there was a long mirror built into the wall, a relic of the old house's long departed youth of grandeur. As the tenant—Mr. Jessop—was out, Mrs. Tucker led the way into it. There Susan had the first satisfactory look at herself. She knew she was a pretty woman; she would have been weak-minded had she not known it. But she was amazed at herself. A touch here and there, a sinuous shifting of the body within the garments, and the suggestion of "dressed up" vanished before the reflected eyes of her agitated assistants, who did not know what had happened but only saw the results. She hardly knew the tall beautiful woman of fashion gazing at her from the mirror. Could it be that this was her hair?—these eyes hers—and the mouth and nose—and the skin? Was this long slender figure her very own? What an astounding difference clothes did make! Never before had Susan worn anything nearly so fine. "This is the way I ought to look all the time," thought she. "And this is the way I *will* look!" Only better—much better. Already her true eye was seeing the defects, the chances for improvement—how the hat could be re-bent and re-trimmed to adapt it to her features, how the dress could be altered to make it more tasteful, more effective in subtly attracting attention to her figure.

"How much do you suppose the dress cost, Miss Hinkle?" asked Ellen—the question Mrs. Tucker had been dying to put but had refrained from putting lest it should sound unrefined.

"It costs ninety wholesale," said Miss Hinkle. "That'd mean a hundred and twenty-five—a hundred and fifty, maybe—if you was to try to buy it in a department store. And the hat—well, Lichtenstein'd ask fifty or sixty for it and never turn a hair."

"Gosh—ee?" exclaimed Ellen. "Did you ever hear the like?"

"I'm not surprised," said Mrs. Tucker, who in fact was flabbergasted. "Well—it's worth the money to them that can afford to buy it. The good Lord put everything on earth to be used, I reckon. And Miss Sackville is the build for things like that. Now it'd be foolish on me, with a stomach and sitter that won't let no skirt hang fit to look at."

The bell rang. The excitement died from Susan's face, leaving it pale and cold. A wave of nausea swept through her. Ellen peeped out, Mrs. Tucker and Miss Hinkle listening with anxious faces. "It's him!" whispered Ellen, "and there's a taxi, too."

It was decided that Ellen should go to the door, that as she opened it Susan should come carelessly from the back room and advance along the hall. And this program was carried out with the result that as Gideon said, "Is Miss Sackville here?" Miss Sackville appeared before his widening, wondering, admiring eyes. He was dressed in the extreme of fashion and costliness in good taste; while it would have been impossible for him to look distinguished, he did look what he was—a prosperous business man with prospects. He came perfumed and rustling. But he felt completely outclassed—until he reminded himself that for all her brave show of fashionable lady she was only a model while he was a fifteen-thousand-a-year man on the way to a partnership.

"Don't you think we might dine on the veranda at Sherry's?" suggested he. "It'd be cool there."

At sight of him she had nerved herself, had keyed herself up toward recklessness. She was in for it. She would put it through. No futile cowardly shrinking and whimpering! Why not try to get whatever pleasure there was a chance for? But—Sherry's—was it safe? Yes, almost any of the Fifth Avenue places—except the Waldorf, possibly—was safe enough. The circuit of Spenser and his friends lay in the more Bohemian Broadway district. He had taken her to Sherry's only once, to see as part of a New York education the Sunday night crowd of fashionable people. "If you like," said she.

Gideon beamed. He would be able to show off his prize! As they drove away Susan glanced at the front parlor windows, saw the curtains agitated, felt the three friendly, excited faces palpitating. She leaned from the cab window, waved her hand, smiled. The three faces instantly appeared and immediately hid again lest Gideon should see.

But Gideon was too busy planning conversation. He knew Miss Sackville was "as common as the rest of 'em—and an old hand at the business, no doubt." But he simply could not abruptly break through the barrier; he must squirm through gradually. "That's a swell outfit you've got on," he began.

"Yes," replied Susan with her usual candor. "Miss Hinkle borrowed it out of the stock for me to wear."

Gideon was confused. He knew how she had got the hat and dress, but he expected her to make a pretense. He couldn't understand her not doing it. Such candor—any kind of candor—wasn't in the game of men and women as women had played it in his experience. The women—all sorts of women—lied and faked at their business just as men did in the business of buying and selling goods. And her voice—and her way of speaking—they made him feel more than ever out of his class.

He must get something to drink as soon as it could be served; that would put him at his ease. Yes—a drink —that would set him up again. And a drink for her —that would bring her down from this queer new kind of high horse. "I guess she must be a top notcher— the real thing, come down in the world—and not out of the near silks. But she'll be all right after a drink. One drink of liquor makes the whole world kin." That last thought reminded him of his own cleverness and he attacked the situation afresh. But the conversation as they drove up the avenue was on the whole constrained and intermittent—chiefly about the weather. Susan was observing—and feeling—and enjoying. Up bubbled her young spirits perpetually renewed by her healthy, vital youth of body. She was seeing her beloved City of the Sun again. As they turned out of the avenue for Sherry's main entrance Susan realized that she was in Forty-fourth Street. The street where she and Spenser had lived!—had lived only yesterday. No—not yesterday—impossible! Her eyes closed and she leaned back in the cab.

Gideon was waiting to help her alight. He saw that something was wrong; it stood out obviously in her ghastly face. He feared the carriage men round the entrance would "catch on" to the fact that he was escorting a girl so unused to swell surroundings that she was ready to faint with fright. "Don't be foolish," he said sharply. Susan revived herself, descended, and with head bent low and trembling body entered the restaurant. In the agitation of getting a table and settling at it Gideon forgot for the moment her sickly pallor.

He began to order at once, not consulting her —for he prided himself on his knowledge of cookery

35

and assumed that she knew nothing about it. "Have a cocktail?" asked he. "Yes, of course you will. You need it bad and you need it quick."

She said she preferred sherry. She had intended to drink nothing, but she must have aid in conquering her faintness and overwhelming depression. Gideon took a dry martini; ordered a second for himself when the first came, and had them both down before she finished her sherry. "I've ordered champagne," said he. "I suppose you like sweet champagne. Most ladies do, but I can't stand seeing it served even."

"No—I like it very dry," said Susan.

Gideon glinted his eyes gayly at her, showed his white jaguar teeth. "So you're acquainted with fizz, are you?" He was feeling his absurd notion of inequality in her favor dissipate as the fumes of the cocktails rose straight and strong from his empty stomach to his brain. "Do you know, I've a sort of feeling that we're going to like each other a lot. I think we make a handsome couple—eh—what's your first name?"

"Lorna."

"Lorna, then. My name's Ed, but everybody calls me Gid."

As soon as the melon was served, he ordered the champagne opened. "To our better acquaintance," said he, lifting his glass toward her.

"Thank you," said she, in a suffocated voice, touching her glass to her lips.

He was too polite to speak, even in banter, of what he thought was the real cause of her politeness and silence. But he must end this state of overwhelmedness at grand surroundings. Said he:

"You're kind o' shy, aren't you, Lorna? Or is that your game?"

"I don't know. You've had a very interesting life, haven't you? Won't you tell me about it?"

"Oh—just ordinary," replied he, with a proper show of modesty. And straightway, as Susan had hoped, he launched into a minute account of himself—the familiar story of the energetic, aggressive man twisting and kicking his way up from two or three dollars a week. Susan seemed interested, but her mind refused to occupy itself with a narrative so commonplace. After Rod and his friends this boastful business man was dull and tedious. Whenever he laughed at an account of his superior craft—how he had bluffed this man, how he had euchered that one—she smiled. And so in one more case the common masculine delusion that women listen to them on the subject of themselves, with interest and admiration as profound as their own, was not impaired.

"But," he wound up, "I've stayed plain Ed Gideon. I never have let prosperity swell *my* head. And anyone that knows me'll tell you I'm a regular fool for generosity with those that come at me right. . . . I've always been a favorite with the ladies."

As he was pausing for comment from her, she said, "I can believe it." The word "generosity" kept echoing in her mind. Generosity—generosity. How much talk there was about it! Everyone was forever praising himself for his generosity, was reciting acts of the most obvious selfishness in proof. Was there any such thing in the whole world as real generosity?

"They like a generous man," pursued Gid. "I'm tight in business—I can see a dollar as far as the next man and chase it as hard and grab it as tight. But when it comes to the ladies, why, I'm open-handed. If they treat me right, I treat them right." Then, fearing that he had tactlessly raised a doubt of his invincibility, he hastily added, "But they always do treat me right."

While he had been talking on and on, Susan had been appealing to the champagne to help her quiet her aching heart. She resolutely set her thoughts to wandering among the couples at the other tables in that subdued softening light—the beautifully dressed women listening to their male companions with close attention—were they too being bored by such trash by way of talk? Were they too simply listening because it is the man who pays, because it is the man who must be conciliated and put in a good humor with himself, if dinners and dresses and jewels are to be bought? That tenement attic—that hot moist workroom—poverty—privation—"honest work's" dread rewards——

"Now, what kind of a man would you say I was?" Gideon was inquiring.

"How do you mean?" replied Susan, with the dexterity at vagueness that habitually self-veiling people acquire as an instinct.

"Why, as a man. How do I compare with the other men you've known?" And he "shot" his cuffs with a gesture of careless elegance that his cuff links might assist in the picture of the "swell dresser" he felt he was posing.

"Oh—you—you're—very different."

"I *am* different," swelled Gideon. "You see, it's this way——" And he was off again into another eulogy of himself; it carried them through the dinner and two quarts of champagne. He was much annoyed that she did not take advantage of the pointed opportunity he gave her to note the total of the bill; he was even uncertain whether she had noted that he gave the waiter a dollar. He rustled and snapped it before laying it upon the tray, but her eyes looked vague.

"Well," said he, after a comfortable pull at an expensive-looking cigar, "sixteen seventy-five is quite a lively little peel-off for a dinner for only two. But it was worth it, don't you think?"

"It was a splendid dinner," said Susan truthfully.

Gideon beamed in intoxicated good humor. "I knew you'd like it. Nothing pleases me better than to take a nice girl who isn't as well off as I am out and blow her off to a crackerjack dinner. Now, you may have thought a dollar was too much to tip the waiter?"

"A dollar is—a dollar, isn't it?" said Susan.

Gideon laughed. "I used to think so. And most men wouldn't give that much to a waiter. But I feel sorry for poor devils who don't happen to be as lucky or as brainy as I am. What do you say to a turn in the Park? We'll take a hansom, and kind of jog along. And we'll stop at the Casino and at Gabe's for a drink."

"I have to get up so early——" began Susan.

"Oh, that's all right." He slowly winked at her. "You'll not have to bump the bumps for being late to-morrow——"

He carried his liquor easily. Only in his eyes and in his ever more slippery smile that would slide about his face did he show that he had been drinking. He helped her into a hansom with a flourish and, overruling her protests, bade the driver go to the Casino. Once under way she was glad; her hot skin and her weary heart were grateful for the air blowing down the avenue from the Park's expanse of green. When Gideon attempted to put his arm around her, she moved close into the corner and went on talking so calmly about calm subjects that he did not insist. But when he had tossed down a drink of whiskey at the Casino and they resumed the drive along the moonlit, shady roads, he tried again.

"Please," said she, "don't spoil a delightful evening."

"Now look here, my dear—haven't I treated you right?"

"Indeed you have, Mr. Gideon."

"Oh, don't be so damned formal. Forget the difference between our positions. Tomorrow I'm going to place a big order with your house, if you treat me right. I'm dead stuck on you—and that's a God's fact. You've taken me clean off my feet. I'm thinking of doing a lot for you."

Susan was silent.

"What do you say to throwing up your job and coming to Chicago with me? How much do you get?"

"Ten."

"Why, *you* can't live on that."

"I've lived on less—much less."

"Do you like it?"

"Naturally not."

"You want to get on—don't you?"

"I must."

"You're down in the heart about something. Love?"

Susan was silent.

"Cut love out. Cut it out, my dear. That ain't the way to get on. Love's a good consolation prize, if you ain't going to get anywhere, and know you ain't. And it's a good first prize after you've arrived and can afford the luxuries of life. But for a man—or a woman —that's pushing up, it's sheer ruination! Cut it out!"

"I am cutting it out," said Susan. "But that takes time."

"Not if you've got sense. The way to cut anything out is—cut it out!—a quick slash—just cut. If you make a dozen little slashes, each of them hurts as much as the one big slash—and the dozen hurt twelve times as much—bleed twelve times as much—put off the cure a lot more than twelve times as long."

He had Susan's attention for the first time.

"Do you know why women don't get on?"

"Tell me," said she. "That's what I want to hear."

"Because they don't play the game under the rules. Now, what does a man do? Why, he stakes everything he's got—does whatever's necessary, don't stop at *nothing* to help him get there. God! I wish I'd 'a' had your looks and your advantages as a woman to help me. I'd be a millionaire this minute, with a house facing this Park and a yacht and all the rest of it."

Susan was listening with a mind made abnormally acute by the champagne she had freely drunk. The coarse bluntness and directness of the man did not offend her. It made what he said the more effective, producing a rude arresting effect upon her nerves. It made the man himself seem more of a person. Susan was beginning to have a kind of respect for him, to change her first opinion that he was merely a vulgar, pushing commonplace.

"Never thought of that before?"

"Yes—I've thought of it. But——" She paused.

"But—what?"

"Oh, nothing."

Never mind. Some womanish heart nonsense, I suppose. Do you see the application of what I've said to you and me?"

"Go on." She was leaning forward, her elbows on the closed doors of the hansom, her eyes gazing dreamily into the moonlit dimness of the cool woods through which they were driving.

"You don't want to stick at ten per?"

"No."

"It'll be less in a little while. Models don't last. The work's too hard."

"I can see that."

"And anyhow it means tenement house."

"Yes. Tenement house."

"Well—what then? What's your plan?"

"I haven't any."

"Haven't a plan—yet want to get on! Is that good sense? Did ever anybody get anywhere without a plan?"

"I'm willing to work. I'm going to work. I *am* working."

"Work, of course. Nobody can keep alive without working. You might as well say you're going to breathe and eat—Work don't amount to anything, for getting on. It's the kind of work—working in a certain direction—working with a plan."

"I've got a plan. But I can't begin at it just yet."

"Will it take money?"

"Some."

"Have you got it?"

"No," replied Susan. "I'll have to get it."

"As an honest working girl?" said he with good-humored irony.

Susan laughed. "It does sound ridiculous, doesn't it?" said she.

"Here's another thing that maybe you haven't counted in. Looking as you do, do you suppose men that run things'll let you get past without paying toll? Not on your life, my dear. If you was ugly, you might after several years get twenty or twenty-five by working hard—unless you lost your figure first. But the

42

men won't let a good looker rise that way. Do you follow me?"

"Yes."

"I'm not talking theory. I'm talking life. Take you and me for example. I can help you—help you a lot. In fact I can put you on your feet. And I'm willing. If you was a man and I liked you and wanted to help you, I'd make you help me, too. I'd make you do a lot of things for me—maybe some of 'em not so very nice—maybe some of 'em downright dirty. And you'd do 'em, as all young fellows, struggling up, have to. But you're a woman. So I'm willing to make easier terms. But I can't help you with you not showing any appreciation. That wouldn't be good business—would it?—to get no return but, 'Oh, thank you so much, Mr. Gideon. So sweet of you. I'll remember you in my prayers.' Would that be sensible?"

"No," said Susan.

"Well, then! If I do you a good turn, you've got to do me a good turn—not one that I don't want done, but one I do want done. Ain't I right? Do you follow me?"

"I follow you."

Some vague accent in Susan's voice made him feel dissatisfied with her response. "I hope you do," he said sharply. "What I'm saying is dresses on your back and dollars in your pocket—and getting on in the world—if you work it right."

"Getting on in the world," said Susan, pensively.

"I suppose that's a sneer."

"Oh, no. I was only thinking."

"About love being all a woman needs to make her happy, I suppose?"

"No. Love is—Well, it isn't happiness."

"Because you let it run you, instead of you running it. Eh?"

"Perhaps."

"Sure! Now, let me tell you, Lorna, dear. Comfort and luxury, money in bank, property, a good solid position—*that's* the foundation. Build on *that* and you'll build solid. Build on love and sentiment and you're building upside down. You're putting the gingerbread where the rock ought to be. Follow me?"

"I see what you mean."

He tried to find her hand. "What do you say?"

"I'll think of it."

"Well, think quick, my dear. Opportunity doesn't wait round in anybody's outside office. . . . Maybe you don't trust me—don't think I'll deliver the goods?"

"No. I think you're honest."

"You're right, I am. I do what I say I'll do. That's why I've got on. That's why I'll keep on getting on. Let's drive to a hotel."

She turned her head and looked at him for the first time since he began his discourse on making one's way in the world. Her look was calm, inquiring—would have been chilling to a man of sensibility—that is, of sensibility toward an unconquered woman.

III

AT the lunch hour the next day Mary Hinkle knocked at the garret in Clinton Place. Getting no answer, she opened the door. At the table close to the window was Susan in a nightgown, her hair in disorder as if she had begun to arrange it and had stopped halfway. Her eyes turned listlessly in Mary's direction—dull eyes, gray, heavily circled.

"You didn't answer, Miss Sackville. So I thought I'd come in and leave a note," explained Mary. Her glance was avoiding Susan's.

"Come for the dress and hat?" said Susan. "There they are." And she indicated the undisturbed bed whereon hat and dress were carelessly flung.

"My, but it's hot in this room!" exclaimed Mary. "You must move up to my place. There's a room and bath vacant—only seven per."

Susan seemed not to hear. She was looking dully at her hands upon the table before her.

"Mr. Jeffries sent me to ask you how you were. He was worried because you didn't come. Mr. Gideon telephoned down the order a while ago. Mr. Jeffries says you are to keep the dress and hat."

"No," said Susan. "Take them away with you."

"Aren't you coming down this afternoon?"

"No," replied Susan. "I've quit."

"Quit?" cried Miss Hinkle. Her expression gradually shifted from astonishment to pleased understanding. "Oh, I see! You've got something better."

"No. But I'll find something."

45

Mary studied the situation, using Susan's expressionless face as a guide. After a time she seemed to get from it a clew. With the air of friendly experience bent on aiding helpless inexperience she pushed aside the dress and made room for herself on the bed. "Don't be a fool, Miss Sackville," said she. "If you don't like that sort of thing—you know what I mean—why, you can live six months—maybe a year—on the reputation of what you've done and their hope that you'll weaken down and do it again. That'll give you time to look round and find something else. For pity's sake, don't turn yourself loose without a job. You got your place so easy that you think you can get one any old time. There's where you're wrong. Believe me, you played in luck—and luck don't come round often. I know what I'm talking about. So I say, don't be a fool!"

"I am a fool," said Susan.

"Well—get over it. And don't waste any time about it, either."

"I can't go back," said Susan stolidly. "I can't face them."

"Face who?" cried Mary. "Business is business. Everybody understands that. All the people down there are crazy about you now. You got the house a hundred-thousand-dollar order. You don't *suppose* anybody in business bothers about how an order's got—do you?"

"It's the way *I* feel—not the way *they* feel."

"Don't be a fool, Miss Sackville."

Susan listened with a smile that barely disturbed the stolid calm of her features. "I'm not going back," she said.

Mary Hinkle was silenced by the quiet finality of her voice. Studying that delicate face, she felt, behind its pallid impassiveness, behind the refusal to return, a reason she could not comprehend. She dimly realized that she would respect it if she could understand it; for she suspected it had its origin somewhere in Susan's "refined ladylike nature." She knew that once in a while among the women she was acquainted with there did happen one who preferred death in any form of misery to leading a lax life—and indisputable facts had convinced her that not always were these women "just stupid ignorant fools." She herself possessed no such refinement of nerves or whatever it was. She had been brought up in a loose family and in a loose neighborhood. She was in the habit of making all sorts of pretenses, because that was the custom, while being candid about such matters was regarded as bad form. She was not fooled by these pretenses in other girls, though they often did fool each other. In Susan, she instinctively felt, it was not pretense. It was something or other else—it was a dangerous reality. She liked Susan; in her intelligence and physical charm were the possibilities of getting far up in the world; it seemed a pity that she was thus handicapped. Still, perhaps Susan would stumble upon some worth while man who, attempting to possess her without marriage and failing, would pay the heavy price. There was always that chance—a small chance, smaller even than finding by loose living a worth while man who would marry you because you happened exactly to suit him—to give him enough only to make him feel that he wanted more. Still, Susan was unusually attractive, and luck sometimes did come a poor person's way—sometimes.

"I'm overdue back," said Mary. "You want me to tell 'em that?"

"Yes."

"You'll have hard work finding a job at anything like as much as ten per. I've got two trades, and I couldn't at either one."

"I don't expect to find it."

"Then what are you going to do?"

"Take what I can get—until I've been made hard enough—or strong enough—or whatever it is—to stop being a fool."

This indication of latent good sense relieved Miss Hinkle. "I'll tell 'em you may be down tomorrow. Think it over for another day."

Susan shook her head. "They'll have to get somebody else."

"After you've had something to eat, you'll feel different."

And Miss Hinkle nodded brightly and departed. Susan resumed her seat at the bare wobbly little table, resumed her listless attitude. She did not move until Ellen came in, holding out a note and saying, "A boy from your store brung this—here."

"Thank you," said Susan, taking the note. In it she found a twenty-dollar bill and a five. On the sheet of paper round it was scrawled:

Take the day off. Here's your commission. We'll raise your pay in a few weeks.   L. L. J.

So Mary Hinkle had told them either that she was quitting or that she was thinking of quitting, and they wished her to stay, had used the means they believed she could not resist. In a dreary way this amused her. As if she cared whether or not life was kept in this worthless body of hers, in her tired heart, in her disgusted mind! Then she dropped back into listlessness.

When she was aroused again it was by Gideon, completely filling the small doorway. "Hello, my dear!" cried he cheerfully. "Mind my smoking?"

Susan slowly turned her head toward him, surveyed him with an expression but one removed from the blank look she would have had if there had been no one before her.

"I'm feeling fine today," pursued Gideon, advancing a step and so bringing himself about halfway to the table. "Had a couple of pick-me-ups and a fat breakfast. How are you?"

"I'm always well."

"Thought you seemed a little seedy. You'll be mighty glad to get out of this hole. Gosh! It's hot. Don't see how you stand it. I'm a law-abiding citizen but I must say I'd turn criminal before I'd put up with this."

In the underworld from which Gideon had sprung—the underworld where welters the overwhelming mass of the human race—there are three main types. There are the hopeless and spiritless—the mass—who welter passively on, breeding and dying. There are the spirited who also possess both shrewdness and calculation; the push upward by hook and by crook, always mindful of the futility of the struggle of the petty criminal of the slums against the police and the law; they arrive and found the aristocracies of the future. The third is the criminal class. It is also made up of the spirited —but the spirited who, having little shrewdness and no calculation—that is, no ability to foresee and measure consequences—wage clumsy war upon society and pay the penalty of their fatuity in lives of wretchedness even more wretched than the common lot. Gideon belonged to the second class—the class that pushes upward without getting into jail; he was a fair representative of this type, neither its best nor its worst, but about midway of its range between arrogant, all-dominating plutocrat and shystering merchant or lawyer or politician who barely escapes the criminal class.

"You don't ask me to sit down, dearie," he went on facetiously. "But I'm not so mad that I won't do it."

He took the seat Miss Hinkle had cleared on the bed. His glance wandered disgustedly from object to object in the crowded yet bare attic. He caught a whiff of the odor from across the hall—from the fresh-air shaft —and hastily gave several puffs at his cigar to saturate his surroundings with its perfume. Susan acted as if she were alone in the room. She had not even drawn together her nightgown.

"I phoned your store about you," resumed Gideon. "They said you hadn't showed up—wouldn't till tomorrow. So I came round here and your landlady sent me up. I want to take you for a drive this afternoon. We can dine up to Claremont or farther, if you like."

"No, thanks," said Susan. "I can't go."

"Upty-tupty!" cried Gideon. "What's the lady so sour about?"

"I'm not sour."

"Then why won't you go?"

"I can't."

"But we'll have a chance to talk over what I'm going to do for you."

"You've kept your word," said Susan.

"That was only part. Besides, I'd have given your house the order, anyhow."

Susan's eyes suddenly lighted up. "You would?" she cried.

"Well—a part of it. Not so much, of course. But I never let pleasure interfere with business. Nobody that does ever gets very far."

Her expression made him hasten to explain—without being conscious why. "I said—*part* of the order, my dear. They owe to you about half of what they'll make off me. . . . What's that money on the table? Your commission?"

"Yes."

"Twenty-five? Um!" Gideon laughed. "Well, I suppose it's as generous as I'd be, in the same circumstances. Encourage your employees, but don't swell-head 'em—that's the good rule. I've seen many a promising young chap ruined by a raise of pay. . . . Now, about you and me." Gideon took a roll of bills from his trousers pocket, counted off five twenties, tossed them on the table. "There!"

One of the bills in falling touched Susan's hand. She jerked the hand away as if the bill had been afire. She took all five of them, folded them, held them out to him. "The house has paid me," said she.

"That's honest," said he, nodding approvingly. "I like it. But in your case it don't apply."

These two, thus facing a practical situation, revealed an important, overlooked truth about human morals. Humanity divides broadly into three classes: the arrived; those who will never arrive and will never try; those in a state of flux, attempting and either failing or succeeding. The arrived and the inert together preach, and to a certain extent practice an idealistic system of morality that interferes with them in no way. It does not interfere with the arrived because they have no need to infringe it, except for amusement; it does not interfere with the inert, but rather helps them to

bear their lot by giving them a cheering notion that
their insignificance is due to their goodness. This
idealistic system receives the homage of lip service from
the third and struggling section of mankind, but no
more, for in practice it would hamper them at every
turn in their efforts to fight their way up. Susan was,
at that stage of her career, a candidate for membership
in the struggling class. Her heart was set firmly
against the unwritten, unspoken, even unwhispered code
of practical morality which dominates the struggling
class. But life had at least taught her the folly of
intolerance. So when Gideon talked in terms of that
practical morality, she listened without offense; and
she talked to him in terms of it because to talk the
idealistic morality in which she had been bred and before which she bowed the knee in sincere belief would
have been simply to excite his laughter at her innocence
and his contempt for her folly.

"I feel that I've been paid," said she. "I did it for
the house—because I owed it to them."

"Only for the house?" said he, with insinuating tenderness. He took and pressed the fingers extended
with the money in them.

"Only for the house," she repeated, a hard note in
her voice. And her fingers slipped away, leaving the
money in his hand. "At least, I suppose it must have
been for the house," she added, reflectively, talking to
herself aloud. "Why did I do it? I don't know. I
don't know. They say one always has a reason for
what one does. But I often can't find any reason for
things I do—that, for instance. I simply did it because
it seemed to me not to matter much what *I* did with
myself, and they wanted the order so badly." Then
she happened to become conscious of his presence and

to see a look of uneasiness, self-complacence, as if he were thinking that he quite understood this puzzle. She disconcerted him with what vain men call a cruel snub. "But whatever the reason, it certainly couldn't have been you," said she.

"Now, look here, Lorna," protested Gideon, the beginnings of anger in his tone. "That's not the way to talk if you want to get on."

She eyed him with an expression which would have raised a suspicion that he was repulsive in a man less self-confident, less indifferent to what the human beings he used for pleasure or profit thought of him.

"To say nothing of what I can do for you, there's the matter of future orders. I order twice a year—in big lots always."

"I've quit down there."

"Oh! Somebody else has given you something good —eh? *That's* why you're cocky."

"No."

"Then why've you quit?"

"I wish you could tell me. I don't understand. But —I've done it."

Gideon puzzled with this a moment, decided that it was beyond him and unimportant, anyhow. He blew out a cloud of smoke, stretched his legs and took up the main subject. "I was about to say, I've got a place for you. I'd like to take you to Chicago."

"So you look on me as your mistress?" And never in all her life had her eyes been so gray—the gray of cruelest irony.

"Now what's the use discussing those things? You know the world. You're a sensible woman."

Susan made closer and more secure the large loose coil of her hair, rose and leaned against the table.

"You don't understand. You couldn't. I'm not one of those respectable women, like many wives, who belong to men. And I'm not one of the other kind who also throw in their souls with their bodies for good measure. Do *you* think you had *me?*" She laughed with maddening gentle mockery, went on: "I don't hate you. I don't despise you even. You mean well. But the sight of you makes me sick. So I want to forget you as soon as I can—and that will be soon after you get out of my sight."

Her blazing eyes startled him. Her voice, not lifted above its usual quiet tones, enraged him. "You—you!" he cried. "You must be crazy, to talk to *me* like that!"

She nodded. "Yes—crazy," said she with the same quiet intensity. "For I know what kind of a beast you are—a clean, good-natured beast, but still a beast. And how could you understand?"

He had got upon his feet. He looked as if he were going to strike her.

She made a slight gesture toward the door. He felt at a hopeless disadvantage with her—with this woman who did not raise her voice, did not need to raise it to express the uttermost of any passion. His jagged teeth gleamed through his mustache; his shrewd little eyes snapped like an angry rat's. He fumbled about through the steam of his insane rage for adequate results—in vain. He rushed from the room and bolted downstairs.

Within an hour Susan was out, looking for work. There could be no turning back now. Until she went with Gideon it had been as if her dead were still unburied and in the house. Now——

Never again could she even indulge in dreams of

going to Rod. That part of her life was finished with all the finality of the closed grave. Grief—yes. But the same sort of grief as when a loved one, after a long and painful illness, finds relief in death. Her love for Rod had been stricken of a mortal illness the night of their arrival in New York. After lingering for a year between life and death, after a long death agony, it had expired. The end came—these matters of the exact moment of inevitable events are unimportant but have a certain melancholy interest—the end came when she made choice where there was no choice, in the cab with Gideon.

For better or for worse she was free. She was ready to begin her career.

IV

AFTER a few days, when she was viewing her situation in a calmer, more normal mood with the practical feminine eye, she regretted that she had refused Gideon's money. She was proud of that within herself which had impelled and compelled her to refuse it; but she wished she had it. Taking it, she felt, would have added nothing to her humiliation in her own sight; and for what he thought of her, one way or the other, she cared not a pin. It is one of the familiar curiosities of human inconsistency which is at bottom so completely consistent, that she did not regret having refused his far more valuable offer to aid her.

She did not regret even during those few next days of disheartening search for work. We often read how purpose can be so powerful that it compels. No doubt if Susan's purpose had been to get temporary relief—or, perhaps, had it been to get permanent relief by weaving a sex spell—she would in that desperate mood have been able to compel. Unfortunately she was not seeking to be a pauper or a parasite; she was trying to find steady employment at living wages—that is, at wages above the market value for female—and for most male—labor. And that sort of purpose cannot compel.

Our civilization overflows with charity—which is simply willingness to hand back to labor as generous gracious alms a small part of the loot from the just wages of labor. But of real help—just wages for honest labor—there is little, for real help would disarrange the system, would abolish the upper classes.

She had some faint hopes in the direction of millinery and dressmaking, the things for which she felt she had distinct talent. She was soon disabused. There was nothing for her, and could be nothing until after several years of doubtful apprenticeship in the trades to which any female person seeking employment to piece out an income instinctively turned first and offered herself at the employer's own price. Day after day, from the first moment of the industrial day until its end, she hunted—wearily, yet unweariedly—with resolve living on after the death of hope. She answered advertisements; despite the obviously sensible warnings of the working girls she talked with she even consulted and took lists from the religious and charitable organizations, patronized by those whose enthusiasm about honest work had never been cooled by doing or trying to do any of it, and managed by those who, beginning as workers, had made all haste to escape from it into positions where they could live by talking about it and lying about it—saying the things comfortable people subscribe to philanthropies to hear.

There was work, plenty of it. But not at decent wages, and not leading to wages that could be earned without viciously wronging those under her in an executive position. But even in those cases the prospect of promotion was vague and remote, with illness and failing strength and poor food, worse clothing and lodgings, as certainties straightway. At some places she was refused with the first glance at her. No good-looking girls wanted; even though they behaved themselves and attracted customers, the customers lost sight of matters of merchandise in the all-absorbing matter of sex. In offices a good-looking girl upset discipline, caused the place to degenerate into a deer-haunt in the mating season. No place did she find offering more than four dollars a week, except where the dress requirements made the nominally higher wages even less. Everywhere women's wages were based upon the assumption that women either lived at home or made the principal part of their incomes by prostitution, disguised or frank. In fact, all wages—even the wages of men—except in a few trades—were too small for an independent support. There had to be a family— and the whole family had to work—and even then the joint income was not enough for decency. She had no family or friends to help her—at least, no friends except those as poor as herself, and she could not commit the crime of adding to their miseries.

She had less than ten dollars left. She must get to work at once—and what she earned must supply her with all. A note came from Jeffries—a curt request that she call—curt to disguise the eagerness to have her back. She tore it up. She did not even debate the matter. It was one of her significant qualities that she never had the inclination, apparently lacked the power, to turn back once she had turned away. Mary Hinkle came, urged her. Susan listened in silence, merely shook her head for answer, changed the subject.

In the entrance to the lofts of a tall Broadway building she saw a placard: "Experienced hands at fancy ready-to-wear hat trimming wanted." She climbed three steep flights and was in a large, low-ceilinged room where perhaps seventy-five girls were at work. She paused in the doorway long enough to observe the kind of work—a purely mechanical process of stitching a few trimmings in exactly the same way

58

upon a cheap hat frame. Then she went to an open window in a glass partition and asked employment of a young Jew with an incredibly long nose thrusting from the midst of a pimply face which seemed merely its too small base.

"Experienced?" asked the young man.

"I can do what those girls are doing."

With intelligent eyes he glanced at her face, then let his glance rove contemptuously over the room full of workers. "I should hope so," said he. "Forty cents a dozen. Want to try it?"

"When may I go to work?"

"Right away. Write your name here."

Susan signed her name to what she saw at a glance was some sort of contract. She knew it contained nothing to her advantage, much to her disadvantage. But she did not care. She had to have work—something, anything that would stop the waste of her slender capital. And within fifteen minutes she was seated in the midst of the sweating, almost nauseatingly odorous women of all ages, was toiling away at the simple task of making an ugly hat frame still more ugly by the addition of a bit of tawdry cotton ribbon, a buckle, and a bunch of absurdly artificial flowers. She was soon able to calculate roughly what she could make in six days. She thought she could do two dozen of the hats a day; and twelve dozen hats at forty cents the dozen would mean four dollars and eighty cents a week!

Four dollars and eighty cents! Less than she had planned to set aside for food alone, out of her ten dollars as a model.

Next her on the right sat a middle-aged woman, grossly fat, repulsively shapeless, piteously homely— one of those luckless human beings who are foredoomed

from the outset never to know any of the great joys
of life—the joys that come through our power to
attract our fellow-beings. As this woman stitched
away, squinting through the steel-framed spectacles
set upon her snub nose, Susan saw that she had not
even good health to mitigate her lot, for her color was
pasty and on her dirty skin lay blotches of dull red.
Except a very young girl here and there all the women
had poor or bad skins. And Susan was not made disdainful by the odor which is far worse than that of any
lower animal, however dirty, because the human animal
must wear clothing. She had lived in wretchedness in
a tenement; she knew that this odor was an inevitable
part of tenement life when one has neither the time nor
the means to be clean. Poor food, foul air, broken sleep
—bad health, disease, unsightly faces, repulsive
bodies!

No wonder the common people looked almost like another race in contrast with their brothers and sisters
of the comfortable classes. Another race! The race
into which she would soon be reborn under the black
magic of poverty! As she glanced and reflected on
what she saw, viewed it in the light of her experience,
her fingers slackened, and she could speed them up only
in spurts.

"If I stay here," thought she, "in a few weeks I shall
be like these others. No matter how hard I may fight,
I'll be dragged down." As impossible to escape the
common lot as for a swimmer alone in midocean to keep
up indefinitely; whether long or brief, the struggle
could have but the one end—to be sunk in, merged in,
the ocean.

It took no great amount of vanity for her to realize
that she was in every way the superior of all those

around her—in every way except one. What did she lack? Why was it that with her superior intelligence, her superior skill both of mind and of body, she could be thus dragged down and held far below her natural level? Why could she not lift herself up among the sort of people with whom she belonged—or even make a beginning toward lifting herself up? Why could she not take hold? What did she lack? What must she acquire—or what get rid of?

At lunch time she walked with the ugly woman up and down the first side street above the building in which the factory was located. She ate a roll she bought from a pushcart man, the woman munched an apple with her few remnants of teeth. "Most of the girls is always kicking," said the woman. "But I'm mighty satisfied. I get enough to eat and to wear, and I've got a bed to sleep in—and what else is there in life for anybody, rich or poor?"

"There's something to be said for that," replied Susan, marveling to find in this piteous creature the only case of thorough content she had ever seen.

"I make my four to five per," continued the woman. "And I've got only myself. Thank God, I was never fool enough to marry. It's marrying that drags us poor people down and makes us miserable. Some says to me, 'Ain't you lonesome?' And I says to them, says I, 'Why, I'm used to being alone. I don't want anything else.' If they was all like me, they'd not be fightin' and drinkin' and makin' bad worse. The bosses always likes to give me work. They say I'm a model worker, and I'm proud to say they're right. I'm mighty grateful to the bosses that provide for the like of us. What'd we do without 'em? That's what I'd like to know."

She had pitied this woman because she could never hope to experience any of the great joys of life. What a waste of pity, she now thought. She had overlooked the joy of joys—delusions. This woman was secure for life against unhappiness.

A few days, and Susan was herself regarded as a model worker. She turned out hats so rapidly that the forewoman, urged on by Mr. Himberg, the proprietor, began to nag at the other girls. And presently a notice of general reduction to thirty-five cents a dozen was posted. There had been a union; it had won a strike two years before—and then had been broken up by shrewd employing of detectives who had got themselves elected officers. With the union out of the way, there was no check upon the bosses in their natural and lawful effort to get that profit which is the most high god of our civilization. A few of the youngest and most spirited girls—those from families containing several workers—indignantly quit. A few others murmured, but stayed on. The mass dumbly accepted the extra twist in the screw of the mighty press that was slowly squeezing them to death. Neither to them nor to Susan herself did it happen to occur that she was the cause of the general increase of hardship and misery. However, to have blamed her would have been as foolish and as unjust as to blame any other individual. The system ordained it all. Oppression and oppressed were both equally its helpless instruments. No wonder all the vast beneficent discoveries of science that ought to have made the whole human race healthy, long-lived and prosperous, are barely able to save the race from swift decay and destruction under the ravages of this modern system of labor worse than slavery—for under slavery the slave, being property whose loss could not be made good without expense, was protected in life and in health.

Susan soon discovered that she had miscalculated her earning power. She had been deceived by her swiftness in the first days, before the monotony of her task had begun to wear her down. Her first week's earnings were only four dollars and thirty cents. This in her freshness, and in the busiest season when wages were at the highest point.

In the room next hers—the same, perhaps a little dingier—lived a man. Like herself he had no trade—that is, none protected by a powerful union and by the still more powerful—in fact, the only powerful shield—requirements of health and strength and a certain grade of intelligence that together act rigidly to exclude most men and so to keep wages from dropping to the neighborhood of the line of pauperism. He was the most industrious and, in his small way, the most resourceful of men. He was insurance agent, toilet soap agent, piano tuner, giver of piano lessons, seller of pianos and of music on commission. He worked fourteen and sixteen hours a day. He made nominally about twelve to fifteen a week. Actually—because of the poverty of his customers and his too sympathetic nature—he made five to six a week—the most any working person could hope for unless in one of the few favored trades. Barely enough to keep body and soul together. And why should capital that needs so much for fine houses and wines and servants and automobiles and culture and charity and the other luxuries —why should capital pay more when so many were competing for the privilege of being allowed to work?

She gave up her room at Mrs. Tucker's—after she had spent several evenings walking the streets and ob-

serving and thinking about the miseries of the fast
women of the only class she could hope to enter. "A
woman," she decided, "can't even earn a decent living
that way unless she has the money to make the right
sort of a start. 'To him that hath shall be given;
from him that hath not shall be taken away even that
which he hath.' Gideon was my chance—and I threw
it away."

Still, she did not regret. Of all the horrors the
most repellent seemed to her to be dependence upon
some one man who could take it away at his whim.

She disregarded the advice of the other girls and
made the rounds of the religious and charitable homes
for working girls. She believed she could endure perhaps better than could girls with more false pride, with
more awe of snobbish conventionalities—at least she
could try to endure—the superciliousness, the patronizing airs, the petty restraints and oppressions, the
nauseating smugness, the constant prying and peeping,
the hypocritical lectures, the heavy doses of smug
morality. She felt that she could bear with almost
any annoyances and humiliations to be in clean surroundings and to get food that was at least not so
rotten that the eye could see it and the nose smell it.
But she found all the homes full, with long waiting
lists, filled for the most part, so the working girls said,
with professional objects of charity. Thus she had
no opportunity to judge for herself whether there was
any truth in the prejudice of the girls against these
few and feeble attempts to mitigate the miseries of a
vast and ever vaster multitude of girls. Adding together all the accommodations offered by all the homes
of every description, there was a total that might possibly have provided for the homeless girls of a dozen

factories or sweatshops—and the number of homeless girls was more than a quarter of a million, was increasing at the rate of more than a hundred a day.

Charity is so trifling a force that it can, and should be, disregarded. It serves no *good* useful service. It enables comfortable people to delude themselves that all that can be done is being done to mitigate the misfortunes which the poor bring upon themselves. It obscures the truth that modern civilization has been perverted into a huge manufacturing of decrepitude and disease, of poverty and prostitution. The reason we talk so much and listen so eagerly when our magnificent benevolences are the subject is that we do not wish to be disturbed—and that we dearly love the tickling sensation in our vanity of generosity.

Susan was compelled to the common lot—the lot that will be the common lot as long as there are people to be made, by taking advantage of human necessities, to force men and women and children to degrade themselves into machines as wage-slaves. At two dollars a week, double what her income justified—she rented a room in a tenement flat in Bleecker street. It was a closet of a room whose thin, dirt-adorned walls were no protection against sound or vermin, not giving even privacy from prying eyes. She might have done a little better had she been willing to share room and bed with one or more girls, but not enough better to compensate for what that would have meant.

The young Jew with the nose so impossible that it elevated his countenance from commonplace ugliness to weird distinction had taken a friendly fancy to her. He was Julius Bam, nephew of the proprietor. In her third week he offered her the forewoman's place. "You've got a few brains in your head," said he. "Miss

Tuohy's a boob. Take the job and you'll push up. We'll start you at five per."

Susan thanked him but declined. "What's the use of my taking a job I couldn't keep more than a day or two?" explained she. "I haven't it in me to boss people."

"Then you've got to get it, or you're done for," said he. "Nobody ever gets anywhere until he's making others work for him."

It was the advice she had got from Matson, the paper box manufacturer in Cincinnati. It was the lesson she found in all prosperity on every hand. Make others work for you—and the harder you made them work the more prosperous you were—provided, of course, you kept all or nearly all the profits of their harder toil. Obvious common sense. But how could she goad these unfortunates, force their clumsy fingers to move faster, make their long and weary day longer and wearier—with nothing for them as the result but duller brain, clumsier fingers, more wretched bodies? She realized why those above lost all patience with them, treated them with contempt. Only as one of them could any intelligent, energetic human being have any sympathy for them, stupid and incompetent from birth, made ever more and more stupid and incapable by the degrading lives they led. She could scarcely conceal her repulsion for their dirty bodies, their stained and rotting clothing saturated with stale sweat, their coarse flesh reeking coarse food smells. She could not listen to their conversation, so vulgar, so inane. Yet she felt herself—for the time—one of them, and her heart bled for them. And while she knew that only their dullness of wit and ignorance kept them from climbing up and stamping and trampling full as savagely and cruelly as did those on top, still the fact remained that they were not stamping and trampling.

As she was turning in some work, Miss Tuohy said abruptly: "You don't belong here. You ought to go back."

Susan started, and her heart beat wildly. She was going to lose her job!

The forelady saw, and instantly understood. "I don't mean that," she said. "You can stay as long as you like—as long as your health lasts. But isn't there somebody somewhere—*anybody*—you can go to and ask them to help you out of this?"

"No—there's no one," said she.

"That can't be true," insisted the forelady. "Everybody has somebody."

To confide is one of the all but universal longings—perhaps needs—of human nature. Susan's honest, sympathetic eyes, her look and her habit of reticence, were always attracting confidences from such unexpected sources as hard, forbidding Miss Tuohy. Susan was not much surprised when Miss Tuohy went on to say:

"I was spoiled when I was still a kid—by getting to know well a man who was above my class. I had tastes that way, and he appealed to them. After him I couldn't marry the sort of man that wanted me. Then my looks went—like a flash—it often happens that way with us Irish girls. But I can get on. I know how to deal with these people—and *you* never could learn. You'd treat 'em like ladies and they'd treat you as easy fruit. Yes, I get along all right, and I'm happy—away from here."

Susan's sympathetic glance of inquiry gave the

necessary encouragement. "It's a baby," Miss Tuohy explained—and Susan knew it was for the baby's sake that this good heart had hardened itself to the dirty work of forelady. Her eyes shifted as she said, "A child of my sister's—dead in Ireland. How I do love that baby——"

They were interrupted and it so happened that the confidence was never resumed and finished. But Miss Tuohy had made her point with Susan— had set her to thinking less indefinitely. "I *must* take hold!" Susan kept saying to herself. The phrase was always echoing in her brain. But how? —*how?* And to that question she could find no answer.

Every morning she bought a one-cent paper whose big circulation was in large part due to its want ads—its daily section of closely printed columns of advertisements of help wanted and situations wanted. Susan read the columns diligently. At first they acted upon her like an intoxicant, filling her not merely with hope but with confident belief that soon she would be in a situation where the pay was good and the work agreeable, or at least not disagreeable. But after a few weeks she ceased from reading.

Why? Because she answered the advertisements, scores of them, more than a hundred, before she saw through the trick and gave up. She found that throughout New York all the attractive or even tolerable places were filled by girls helped by their families or in other ways, girls working at less than living wages because they did not have to rely upon their wages for their support. And those help wanted advertisements were simply appeals for more girls of that sort—for cheaper girls; or they were inserted by employment agencies, masquerading in the newspaper as employers and lying in wait to swindle working girls by getting a fee in exchange for a false promise of good work at high wages; or they were the nets flung out by crafty employers who speeded and starved their slaves, and wished to recruit fresh relays to replace those that had quit in exhaustion or in despair.

"Why do you always read the want ads?" she said to Lany Ricardo, who spent all her spare time at those advertisements in two papers she bought and one she borrowed every day. "Did you ever get anything good, or hear of anybody that did?"

"Oh, my, no," replied Lany with a laugh. "I read for the same reason that all the rest do. It's a kind of dope. You read and then you dream about the places—how grand they are and how well off you'll be. But nobody'd be fool enough to answer one of 'em unless she was out of a job and had to get another and didn't care how rotten it was. No, it's just dope —like buyin' policy numbers or lottery tickets. You know you won't git a prize, but you have a lot of fun dreaming about it."

As Susan walked up and down at the lunch hour, she talked with workers, both men and women, in all sorts of employment. Some were doing a little better than she; others—the most—were worse off chiefly because her education, her developed intelligence, enabled her to ward off savage blows—such as illness from rotten food—against which their ignorance made them defenseless. Whenever she heard a story of someone's getting on, how grotesquely different it was from the stories she used to get out of the Sunday school library and dream over! These almost actualities of getting on had nothing in them about honesty and virtue. According to them it was always some sort of meanness or trickery; and the particular meanness or tricks were, in these practical schools of success in session at each lunch hour, related in detail as lessons in how to get on. If the success under discussion was a woman's, it was always how her boss or employer had "got stuck on her" and had given her an easier job with good pay so that she could wear clothes more agreeable to his eyes and to his touch. Now and then it was a wonderful dazzling success—some girl had got her rich employer so "dead crazy" about her that he had taken her away from work altogether and had set her up in a flat with a servant and a "swell trap"; there was even talk of marriage.

Was it true? Were the Sunday school books through and through lies—ridiculous, misleading lies, wicked lies—wicked because they hid the shameful truth that ought to be proclaimed from the housetops? Susan was not sure. Perhaps envy twisted somewhat these tales of rare occasional successes told by the workers to each other. But certain it was that, wherever she had the opportunity to see for herself, success came only by hardness of heart, by tricks and cheats. Certain it was also that the general belief among the workers was that success could be got in those ways only—and this belief made the falsehood, if it was a falsehood, or the partial truth, if it was a twisted truth, full as poisonous as if it had been true throughout. Also, if the thing were not true, how came it that everyone in practical life believed it to be so—how came it that everyone who talked in praise of honesty

and virtue looked, as he talked, as if he were canting
and half expected to be laughed at?

All about her as badly off as she, or worse off. Yet
none so unhappy as she—not even the worse off. In
fact, the worse off as the better off were not so deeply
wretched. Because they had never in all their lives
known the decencies of life—clean lodgings, clean clothing, food fit to eat, leisure and the means of enjoying
leisure. And Susan had known all these things. When
she realized why her companions in misery, so feeble in
self-restraint, were able to endure patiently and for
the most part even cheerfully, how careful she was
never to say or to suggest anything that might put
ideas of what life might be, of what it was for the
comfortable few, into the minds of these girls who
never had known and could only be made wretched by
knowing! How fortunate for them, she thought, that
they had gone to schools where they met only their
own kind! How fortunate that the devouring monster
of industry had snatched them away from school before
their minds had been awakened to the realities of life!
How fortunate that their imaginations were too dull
and too heavy to be touched by the sights of luxury
they saw in the streets or by what they read in the
newspapers and in the cheap novels! To them, as she
soon realized, their world seemed the only world, and
the world that lived in comfort seemed a vague unreality, as must seem whatever does not come into our
own experience.

One lunch hour an apostle of discontent preaching
some kind of politics or other held forth on the corner
above the shop. Susan paused to listen. She had
heard only a few words when she was incensed to the
depths of her heart against him. He ought to be

stopped by the police, this scoundrel trying to make these people unhappy by awakening them to the misery and degradation of their lot! He looked like an honest, earnest man. No doubt he fancied that he was in some way doing good. These people who were always trying to do the poor good—they ought all to be suppressed! If someone could tell them how to cease to be poor, that would indeed be good. But such a thing would be impossible. In Sutherland, where the best off hadn't so painfully much more than the worst off, and where everybody but the idle and the drunken, and even they most of the time, had enough to eat, and a decent place to sleep, and some kind of Sunday clothes—in Sutherland the poverty was less than in Cincinnati, infinitely less than in this vast and incredibly rich New York where in certain districts wealth, enormous wealth, was piled up and up. So evidently the presence of riches did not help poverty but seemed to increase it. No, the disease was miserable, thought Susan. For most of the human race, disease and bad food and vile beds in dingy holes and days of fierce, poorly paid toil—that was the law of this hell of a world. And to escape from that hideous tyranny, you must be hard, you must trample, you must rob, you must cease to be human.

The apostle of discontent insisted that the law could be changed, that the tyranny could be abolished. She listened, but he did not convince her. He sounded vague and dreamy—as fantastically false in his new way as she had found the Sunday school books to be. She passed on.

She continued to pay out a cent each day for the newspaper. She no longer bothered with the want ads. Pipe dreaming did not attract her; she was too fiercely bent upon escape, actual escape, to waste time in dreaming of ways of escape that she never could realize. She read the paper because, if she could not live in the world but was battered down in its dark and foul and crowded cellar, she at least wished to know what was going on up in the light and air. She found every day news of great doings, of wonderful rises, of rich rewards for industry and thrift, of abounding prosperity and of opportunity fairly forcing itself into acceptance. But all this applied only to the few so strangely and so luckily chosen, while the mass was rejected. For that mass, from earliest childhood until death, there was only toil in squalor—squalid food, squalid clothing, squalid shelter. And when she read one day—in an obscure paragraph in her newspaper—that the income of the average American family was less than twelve dollars a week—less than two dollars and a half a week for each individual—she realized that what she was seeing and living was not New York and Cincinnati, but was the common lot, country wide, no doubt world wide.

"*Must* take hold!" her mind cried incessantly to her shrinking heart. "Somehow—anyhow—take hold!—must—must—*must!*"

Those tenement houses! Those tenement streets! Everywhere wandering through the crowds the lonely old women—holding up to the girls the mirror of time and saying: "Look at my misery! Look at my disease-blasted body. Look at my toil-bent form and toil-wrecked hands. Look at my masses of wrinkles, at my rags, at my leaky and rotten shoes. Think of my aloneness—not a friend—feared and cast off by my relatives because they are afraid they will have to give me food and lodgings. Look at me—think of my life—and know that I am *you* as you will be a few years

73

from now whether you work as a slave to the machine or as a slave to the passions of one or of many men. I am *you*. Not one in a hundred thousand escape my fate—except by death."

"Somehow—anyhow—I must take hold," cried Susan to her swooning heart.

When her capital had dwindled to three dollars Mrs. Tucker appeared. Her face was so beaming bright that Susan, despite her being clad in garments on which a pawnshop would advance nothing, fancied she had come with good news.

"Now that I'm rid of that there house," said she, "I'll begin to perk up. I ain't got nothing left to worry me. I'm ready for whatever blessings the dear Master'll provide. My pastor tells me I'm the finest example of Christian fortitude he ever saw. But"—and Mrs. Tucker spoke with genuine modesty—"I tell him I don't deserve no credit for leaning on the Lord. If I can trust Him in death, why not in life?"

"You've got a place? The church has——"

"Bless you, no," cried Mrs. Tucker. "Would I burden 'em with myself, when there's so many that has to be looked after? No, I go direct to the Lord."

"What are you going to do? What place have you got?"

"None as yet. But He'll provide something—something better'n I deserve."

Susan had to turn away, to hide her pity—and her disappointment. Not only was she not to be helped, but also she must help another. "You might get a job at the hat factory," said she.

Mrs. Tucker was delighted. "I knew it!" she cried. "Don't you see how He looks after me?"

Susan persuaded Miss Tuohy to take Mrs. Tucker

on. She could truthfully recommend the old woman as a hard worker. They moved into a room in a tenement in South Fifth Avenue. Susan read in the paper about a model tenement and went to try for what was described as real luxury in comfort and cleanliness. She found that sort of tenements filled with middle-class families on their way down in the world and making their last stand against rising rents and rising prices. The model tenement rents were far, far beyond her ability to pay. She might as well think of moving to the Waldorf. She and Mrs. Tucker had to be content with a dark room on the fifth floor, opening on a damp air shaft whose odor was so foul that in comparison the Clinton Place shaft was as the pure breath of the open sky. For this shelter—more than one-half the free and proud citizens of prosperous America dwelling in cities occupy its like, or worse—they paid three dollars a week—a dollar and a half apiece. They washed their underclothing at night, slept while it was drying. And Susan, who could not bring herself to imitate the other girls and wear a blouse of dark color that was not to be washed, rose at four to do the necessary ironing. They did their own cooking. It was no longer possible for Susan to buy quality and content herself with small quantity. However small the quantity of food she could get along on, it must be of poor quality—for good quality was beyond her means.

It maddened her to see the better class of working girls. Their fairly good clothing, their evidences of some comfort at home, seemed to mock at her as a poor fool who was being beaten down because she had not wit enough to get on. She knew these girls were either supporting themselves in part by prostitution or were held up by their families, by the pooling of the earnings of several persons. Left to themselves, to their own earnings at work, they would be no better off than she, or at best so little better off that the difference was unimportant. If to live decently in New York took an income of fifteen dollars a week, what did it matter whether one got five or ten or twelve? Any wages below fifteen meant a steady downward drag —meant exposure to the dirt and poison of poverty tenements—meant the steady decline of the power of resistance, the steady oozing away of self-respect, of the courage and hope that give the power to rise. To have less than the fifteen dollars absolutely necessary for decent surroundings, decent clothing, decent food —that meant one was drowning. What matter whether the death of the soul was quick, or slow, whether the waters of destruction were twenty feet deep or twenty thousand?

Mrs. Reardon, the servant woman on the top floor, was evicted and Susan and Mrs. Tucker took her in. She protested that she could sleep on the floor, that she had done so a large part of her life—that she preferred it to most beds. But Susan made her up a kind of bed in the corner. They would not let her pay anything. She had rheumatism horribly, some kind of lung trouble, and the almost universal and repulsive catarrh that preys upon working people. Her hair had dwindled to a meager wisp. This she wound into a hard little knot and fastened with an imitation tortoise-shell comb, huge, high, and broken, set with large pieces of glass cut like diamonds. Her teeth were all gone and her cheeks almost met in her mouth.

One day, when Mrs. Tucker and Mrs. Reardon were exchanging eulogies upon the goodness of God to them, Susan shocked them by harshly ordering them to be silent. "If God hears you," she said, "He'll think you're mocking Him. Anyhow, I can't stand any more of it. Hereafter do your talking of that kind when I'm not here."

Another day Mrs. Reardon told about her sister. The sister had worked in a factory where some sort of poison that had a rotting effect on the human body was used in the manufacture. Like a series of others the sister caught the disease. But instead of rotting out a spot, a few fingers, or part of the face, it had eaten away the whole of her lower jaw so that she had to prepare her food for swallowing by first pressing it with her fingers against her upper teeth. Used as Susan was to hearing horrors in this region where disease and accident preyed upon every family, she fled from the room and walked shuddering about the streets —the streets with their incessant march past of blighted and blasted, of maimed and crippled and worm-eaten. Until that day Susan had been about as unobservant of the obvious things as is the rest of the race. On that day she for the first time noticed the crowd in the street, with mind alert to signs of the ravages of accident and disease. Hardly a sound body, hardly one that was not piteously and hideously marked.

When she returned—and she did not stay out long— Mrs. Tucker was alone. Said she:

"Mrs. Reardon says the rotten jaw was sent on her sister as a punishment for marrying a Protestant, she being a Catholic. How ignorant some people is! Of course, the good Lord sent the judgment on her for being a Catholic at all."

"Mrs. Tucker," said Susan, "did you ever hear of Nero?"

"He burned up Rome—and he burned up the Christian martyrs," said Mrs. Tucker. "I had a good schooling. Besides, sermons is highly educating."

"Well," said Susan, "if I had a choice of living under Nero or of living under that God you and Mrs. Reardon talk about, I'd take Nero and be thankful and happy."

Mrs. Tucker would have fled if she could have afforded it. As it was all she ventured was a sigh and lips moving in prayer.

On a Friday in late October, at the lunch hour, Susan was walking up and down the sunny side of Broadway. It was the first distinctly cool day of the autumn; there had been a heavy downpour of rain all morning, but the New York sun that is ever struggling to shine and is successful on all but an occasional day was tearing up and scattering the clouds with the aid of a sharp north wind blowing down the deep canyon. She was wearing her summer dress still—old and dingy but clean. That look of neatness about the feet—that charm of a well-shaped foot and a well-turned ankle properly set off—had disappeared—with her the surest sign of the extreme of desperate poverty. Her shoes were much scuffed, were even slightly down at the heel; her sailor hat would have looked only the worse had it had a fresh ribbon on its crown. This first hint of winter had stung her fast numbing faculties into unusual activity. She was remembering the misery of the cold in Cincinnati—the misery that had driven her into prostitution as a drunken driver's lash makes the frenzied horse rush he cares not where in his desire to escape. This wind of Broadway—this first warning of winter—it was hissing in her ears: "Take hold! Winter is coming! Take hold!"

Summer and winter—fiery heat and brutal cold.

Like the devils in the poem, the poor—the masses, all
but a few of the human race—were hurried from fire
to ice, to vary their torment and to make it always
exquisite.

To shelter herself for a moment she paused at a spot
that happened to be protected to the south by a projecting sidewalk sign. She was facing, with only a
tantalizing sheet of glass between, a display of winter
underclothes on wax figures. To show them off more
effectively the sides and the back of the window were
mirrors. Susan's gaze traveled past the figures to a
person she saw standing at full length before her.
"Who is that pale, stooped girl?" she thought. "How
dreary and sad she looks! How hard she is fighting to
make her clothes look decent, when they aren't! She
must be something like me—only much worse off." And
then she realized that she was gazing at her own image,
was pitying her own self. The room she and Mrs.
Tucker and the old scrubwoman occupied was so dark,
even with its one little gas jet lighted, that she was able
to get only a faint look at herself in the little cracked
and water-marked mirror over its filthy washstand—
filthy because the dirt was so ground in that only
floods of water and bars of soap could have cleaned
down to its original surface. She was having a clear
look at herself for the first time in three months.

She shrank in horror, yet gazed on fascinated. Why,
her physical charm had gone—gone, leaving hardly a
trace! Those dull, hollow eyes—that thin and almost
ghastly face—the emaciated form—the once attratcive
hair now looking poor and stringy because it could not
be washed properly—above all, the sad, bitter expression about the mouth. Those pale lips! Her lips had
been from childhood one of her conspicuous and most

tempting beauties; and as the sex side of her nature had developed they had bloomed into wonderful freshness and vividness of form and color. Now——

Those pale, pale lips! They seemed to form a sort of climax of tragedy to the melancholy of her face. She gazed on and on. She noted every detail. How she had fallen! Indeed, a fallen woman! These others had been born to the conditions that were destroying her; they were no worse off, in many cases better off. But she, born to comfort and custom of intelligent educated associations and associates——

A fallen woman!

Honest work! Even if it were true that this honest work was a sort of probation through which one rose to better things—even if this were true, could it be denied that only a few at best could rise, that the most —including all the sensitive, and most of the children— must wallow on, must perish? Oh, the lies, the lies about honest work!

Rosa Mohr, a girl of her own age who worked in the same room, joined her. "Admiring yourself?" she said laughing. "Well, I don't blame you. You *are* pretty."

Susan at first thought Rosa was mocking her. But the tone and expression were sincere.

"It won't last long," Rosa went on. "I wasn't so bad myself when I quit the high school and took a job because father lost his business and his health. He got in the way of one of those trusts. So of course they handed it to him good and hard. But he wasn't a squealer. He always said they'd done only what he'd been doing himself if he'd had the chance. I always think of what papa used to say when I hear people carrying on about how wicked this or that somebody else is."

"Are you going to stay on—at this life?" asked Susan, still looking at her own image.

"I guess so. What else is there? . . . I've got a steady. We'll get married as soon as he has a raise to twelve per. But I'll not be any better off. My beau's too stupid ever to make much. If you see me ten years from now I'll probably be a fat, sloppy old thing, warming a window sill or slouching about in dirty rags."

"Isn't there any way to—to escape?"

"It does look as though there ought to be—doesn't it? But I've thought and thought, and *I* can't see it —and I'm pretty near straight Jew. They say things are better than they used to be, and I guess they are. But not enough better to help me any. Perhaps my children—*if* I'm fool enough to have any—perhaps they'll get a chance. . . . But I wouldn't gamble on it."

Susan was still looking at her rags—at her pale lips—was avoiding meeting her own eyes. "Why not try the streets?"

"Nothing in it," said Rosa, practically.

The two girls stood facing each other, each looking past the other into the wind-swept canyon of Broadway—the majestic vista of lofty buildings, symbols of wealth and luxury so abundant that it flaunted itself, overflowed in gaudy extravagance. Finally Susan said:

"Do you ever think of killing yourself?"

"I thought I would," replied the other girl. "But I guess I wouldn't have. Everybody knows there's no hope, yet they keep on hopin'. And I've got pretty good health yet, and once in a while I have some fun. You ought to go to dances—and drink.

You wouldn't be blue *all* the time, then."

"If it wasn't for the sun," said Susan.

"The sun?" inquired Rosa.

"Where I came from," explained Susan, "it rained a great deal, and the sky was covered so much of the time. But here in New York there is so much sun. I love the sun. I get desperate—then out comes the sun, and I say to myself, 'Well, I guess I can go on a while longer, with the sun to help me.'"

"I hadn't thought of it," said Rosa, "but the sun is a help."

That indefatigable New York sun! It was like Susan's own courage. It fought the clouds whenever clouds dared to appear and contest its right to shine upon the City of the Sun, and hardly a day was so stormy that for a moment at least the sun did not burst through for a look at its beloved.

For weeks Susan had eaten almost nothing. During her previous sojourn in the slums—the slums of Cincinnati, though they were not classed as slums—the food had seemed revolting. But she was less discriminating then. The only food she could afford now—the food that is the best obtainable for a majority of the inhabitants of any city—was simply impossible for her. She ate only when she could endure no longer. This starvation no doubt saved her from illness; but at the same time it drained her strength. Her vitality had been going down, a little each day—lower and lower. The poverty which had infuriated her at first was now acting upon her like a soothing poison. The reason she had not risen to revolt was this slow and subtle poison that explains the inertia of the tenement poor from babyhood. To be spirited one must have health or a nervous system diseased in some of the ways that cause constant irritation. The disease called poverty is not an irritant, but an anesthetic. If Susan had been born to that life, her naturally vivacious temperament would have made her gay in unconscious wretchedness; as it was, she knew her own misery and suffered from it keenly—at times hideously—yet was rapidly losing the power to revolt.

Perhaps it was the wind—yes, it must have been the wind with its threat of winter—that roused her sluggish blood, that whipped thought into action. Anything—anything would be right, if it promised escape. Right—wrong! Hypocritical words for comfortable people!

That Friday night, after her supper of half-cooked corn meal and tea, she went instantly to work at washing out clothes. Mrs. Tucker spent the evening gossiping with the janitress, came in about midnight. As usual she was full to the brim with news of misery—of jobs lost, abandoned wives, of abused children, of poisoning from rotten "fresh" food or from "embalmed" stuff in cans, of sickness and yet more sickness, of maiming accidents, of death—news that is the commonplace of tenement life. She loved to tell these tales with all the harrowing particulars and to find in each some evidence of the goodness of God to herself. Often Susan could let her run on and on without listening. But not that night. She resisted the impulse to bid her be silent, left the room and stood at the hall window. When she returned Mrs. Tucker was in bed, was snoring in a tranquility that was the reverse of contagious. With her habitual cheerfulness she had adapted herself to her changed condition without fretting. She had become as rugged and as dirty as her neighbors; she so wrought upon Susan's sensibilities, blunted though they were, that the girl would have been unable to sleep in the same bed if she had not always been tired to exhaustion when she lay down. But for that matter only exhaustion could have kept her asleep in that vermin-infested hole. Even the fiercest swarms of the insects that flew or ran or crawled and bit, even the filthy mice squeaking as they played upon the covers or ran over the faces of the sleepers, did not often rouse her.

While Mrs. Tucker snored, Susan worked on, getting every piece of at all fit clothing in her meager wardrobe into the best possible condition. She did not once glance at the face of the noisy sleeper—a face homely enough in Mrs. Tucker's waking hours, hideous now with the mouth open and a few scattered rotten teeth exposed and the dark yellow-blue of the unhealthy gums and tongue.

At dawn Mrs. Tucker awoke with a snort and a start. She rubbed her eyes with her dirty and twisted and wrinkled fingers—the nails were worn and broken, turned up as if warped at the edges, blackened with dirt and bruisings. "Why, are you up already?" she said to Susan.

"I've not been to bed," replied the girl.

The woman stretched herself, sat up, thrust her thick, stockinged legs over the side of the bed. She slept in all her clothing but her skirt, waist, and shoes. She kneeled down upon the bare, sprung, and slanting floor, said a prayer, arose with a beaming face. "It's nice and warm in the room. How I do dread the winter, the cold weather—though no doubt we'll make out all right! Everything always does turn out well for me. The Lord takes care of me. I must make me a cup of tea."

"I've made it," said Susan.

The tea was frightful stuff—not tea at all, but cheap adulterants colored poisonously. Everything they got was of the same quality; yet the prices they paid for the tiny quantities they were able to buy at any one time were at a rate that would have bought the finest quality at the most expensive grocery in New York.

"Wonder why Mrs. Reardon don't come?" said Mrs. Tucker. Mrs. Reardon had as her only work a one-night job at scrubbing. "She ought to have come an hour ago."

"Her rheumatism was bad when she started," said Susan. "I guess she worked slow."

When Mrs. Tucker had finished her second cup she put on her shoes, overskirt and waist, made a few passes at her hair. She was ready to go to work.

Susan looked at her, murmured: "An honest, God-fearing working woman!"

"Huh?" said Mrs. Tucker.

"Nothing," replied Susan who would not have permitted her to hear. It would be cruel to put such ideas before one doomed beyond hope.

Susan was utterly tired, but even the strong craving for a stimulant could not draw that tea past her lips. She ate a piece of dry bread, washed her face, neck, and hands. It was time to start for the factory.

That day—Saturday—was a half-holiday. Susan drew her week's earnings—four dollars and ten cents—

and came home. Mrs. Tucker, who had drawn—
"thanks to the Lord"—three dollars and a quarter,
was with her. The janitress halted them as they passed
and told them that Mrs. Reardon was dead. She
looked like another scrubwoman, living down the street,
who was known always to carry a sum of money in
her dress pocket, the banks being untrustworthy. Mrs.
Reardon, passing along in the dusk of the early morning, had been hit on the head with a blackjack. The
one blow had killed her.

Violence, tragedy of all kinds, were too commonplace
in that neighborhood to cause more than a slight ripple.
An old scrubwoman would have had to die in some
peculiarly awful way to receive the flattery of agitating
an agitated street. Mrs. Reardon had died what was
really almost a natural death. So the faint disturbance of the terrors of life had long since disappeared.
The body was at the Morgue, of course.

"We'll go up, right away," said Mrs. Tucker.

"I've something to do that can't be put off," replied Susan.

"I don't like for anyone as young as you to be so
hard," reproached Mrs. Tucker.

"Is it hard," said Susan, "to see that death isn't
nearly so terrible as life? She's safe and at peace.
I've got to *live*."

Mrs. Tucker, eager for an emotional and religious
opportunity, hastened away. Susan went at her wardrobe—ironing, darning, fixing buttonholes, hooks and
eyes. She drew a bucket of water from the tap in the
hall and proceeded to wash her hair with soap; she
rinsed it, dried it as well as she could with their one
small, thin towel, left it hanging free for the air to
finish the job.

86

It had rained all the night before—the second heavy rain in two months. But at dawn the rain had ceased, and the clouds had fled before the sun that rules almost undisputed nine months of the year and wars valiantly to rule the other three months—not altogether in vain. A few golden strays found their way into that cave-like room and had been helping her wonderfully. She bathed herself and scrubbed herself from head to foot. She manicured her nails, got her hands and feet into fairly good condition. She put on her best under-clothes, her one remaining pair of undarned stockings, the pair of ties she had been saving against an emerg-ency. And once more she had the charm upon which she most prided herself—the charm of an attractive look about the feet and ankles. She then took up the dark-blue hat frame—one of a lot of "seconds"—she had bought for thirty-five cents at a bargain sale, trimmed it with a broad dark-blue ribbon for which she had paid sixty cents. She was well pleased—and justly so—with the result. The trimmed hat might well have cost ten or fifteen dollars—for the largest part of the price of a woman's hat is usually the taste of the arrangement of the trimming.

By this time her hair was dry. She did it up with a care she had not had time to give it in many a week. She put on the dark-blue serge skirt of the between-seasons dress she had brought with her from Forty-fourth Street; she had not worn it at all. With the feeble aid of the mirror that distorted her image into grotesqueness, she put on her hat with the care that important detail of a woman's toilet always de-serves.

She completed her toilet with her one good and un-worn blouse—plain white, the yoke gracefully pointed

87

—and with a blue neck piece she had been saving. She made a bundle of all her clothing that was fit for anything—including the unworn batiste dress Jeffries and Jonas had given her. And into it she put the pistol she had brought away from Forty-fourth Street. She made a separate bundle of the Jeffries and Jonas hat with its valuable plumes. With the two bundles she descended and went to a pawnshop in Houston Street, to which she had made several visits.

A dirty-looking man with a short beard fluffy and thick like a yellow hen's tail lurked behind the counter in the dark little shop. She put her bundles on the counter, opened them. "How much can I get for these things?" she asked.

The man examined every piece minutely. "There's really nothing here but the summer dress and the hat," said he. "And they're out of style. I can't give you more than four dollars for the lot—and one for the pistol which is good but old style now. Five dollars. How'll you have it?"

Susan folded the things and tied up the bundles. "Sorry to have troubled you," she said, taking one in either hand.

"How much did you expect to get, lady?" asked the pawnbroker.

"Twenty-five dollars."

He laughed, turned toward the back of the shop. As she reached the door he called from his desk at which he seemed about to seat himself, "I might squeeze you out ten dollars."

"The plumes on the hat will sell for thirty dollars," said Susan. "You know as well as I do that ostrich feathers have gone up."

The man slowly advanced. "I hate to see a customer

88

go away unsatisfied," said he. "I'll give you twenty dollars."

"Not a cent less than twenty-five. At the next place I'll ask thirty—and get it."

"I never can stand out against a lady. Give me the stuff."

Susan put it on the counter again. Said she:

"I don't blame you for trying to do me. You're right to try to buy your way out of hell."

The pawnbroker reflected, could not understand this subtlety, went behind his counter. He produced a key from his pocket, unlocked a drawer underneath and took out a large tin box. With another key from another pocket he unlocked this, threw back the lid revealing a disorder of papers. From the depths he fished a paper bag. This contained a roll of bills. He gave Susan a twenty and a five, both covered with dirt so thickly that she could scarcely make out the denominations.

"You'll have to give me cleaner money than this," said she.

"You are a fine lady," grumbled he. But he found cleaner bills.

She turned to her room. At sight of her Mrs. Tucker burst out laughing with delight. "My, but you do look like old times!" cried she. "How neat and tasty you are! I suppose it's no need to ask if you're going to church?"

"No," said Susan. "I've got nothing to give, and I don't beg."

"Well, I ain't going there myself, lately—somehow. They got so they weren't very cordial—or maybe it was me thinking that way because I wasn't dressed up like. Still I do wish you was more religious. But you'll come to it, for you're naturally a good girl. And when you do, the Lord'll give you a more contented heart. Not that you complain. I never knew anybody, especially a young person, that took things so quiet. . . . It can't be you're going to a dance?"

"No," said Susan. "I'm going to leave—go back uptown."

Mrs. Tucker plumped down upon the bed. "Leave for good?" she gasped.

"I've got Nelly Lemayer to take my place here, if you want her," said Susan. "Here is my share of the rent for next week and half a dollar for the extra gas I've burned last night and today."

"And Mrs. Reardon gone, too!" sobbed Mrs. Tucker, suddenly remembering the old scrubwoman whom both had forgotten. "And up to that there Morgue they wouldn't let me see her except where the light was so poor that I couldn't rightly swear it was her. How brutal everybody is to the poor! If they didn't have the Lord, what would become of them! And you leaving me all alone!"

The sobs rose into hysteria. Susan stood impassive. She had seen again and again how faint the breeze that would throw those shallow waters into commotion and how soon they were tranquil again. It was by observing Mrs. Tucker that she first learned an important unrecognized truth about human nature—that amiable, easily sympathetic and habitually good-humored people are invariably hard of heart. In this parting she had no sense of loss, none of the melancholy that often oppresses us when we separate from someone to whom we are indifferent yet feel bound by the tie of misfortunes borne together. Mrs. Tucker, fallen into the habits of their surroundings, was for her simply part

of them. And she was glad she was leaving them—
forever, she hoped. *Christian,* fleeing the City of Destruction, had no sterner mandate to flight than her
instinct was suddenly urging upon her.

When Mrs. Tucker saw that her tears were not appreciated, she decided that they were unnecessary. She
dried her eyes and said:

"Anyhow, I reckon Mrs. Reardon's taking-off was a
mercy."

"She's better dead," said Susan. She had abhorred
the old woman, even as she pitied and sheltered her.
She had a way of fawning and cringing and flattering
—no doubt in well meaning attempt to show gratitude
—but it was unendurable to Susan. And now that she
was dead and gone, there was no call for further
pretenses.

"You ain't going right away?" said Mrs. Tucker.

"Yes," said Susan.

"You ought to stay to supper."

Supper! That revolting food! "No, I must go
right away," replied Susan.

"Well, you'll come to see me. And maybe you'll be
back with us. You might go farther and do worse.
On my way from the morgue I dropped in to see a lady
friend on the East Side. I guess the good Lord has
abandoned the East Side, there being nothing there but
Catholics and Jews, and no true religion. It's dreadful the way things is over there—the girls are taking
to the streets in droves. My lady friend was telling
me that some of the mothers is sending their little girls
out streetwalking, and some's even taking out them
that's too young to be trusted to go alone. And no
money in it, at that. And food and clothing prices
going up and up. Meat and vegetables two and three

times what they was a few years ago. And rents!"
Mrs. Tucker threw up her hands.

"I must be going," said Susan. "Good-by."

She put out her hand, but Mrs. Tucker insisted on
kissing her. She crossed Washington Square, beautiful in the soft evening light, and went up Fifth Avenue. She felt that she was breathing the air of a different world as she walked along the broad clean sidewalk with the handsome old houses on either side, with
carriages and automobiles speeding past, with clean,
happy-faced, well dressed human beings in sight everywhere. It was like coming out of the dank darkness
of Dismal Swamp into smiling fields with a pure, star-
spangled sky above. She was free—free! It might be
for but a moment; still it was freedom, infinitely sweet
because of past slavery and because of the fear of
slavery closing in again. She had abandoned the old
toilet articles. She had only the clothes she was wearing, the thirty-one dollars divided between her stockings, and the two-dollar bill stuffed into the palm of
her left glove.

She had walked but a few hundred feet. She had
advanced into a region no more prosperous to the eye
than that she had been working in every day. Yet she
had changed her world—because she had changed her
point of view. The strata that form society lie in
roughly parallel lines one above the other. The flow
of all forms of the currents of life is horizontally along
these strata, never vertically from one stratum to another. These strata, lying apparently in contact, one
upon another, are in fact abysmally separated. There
is not—and in the nature of things never can be—any
genuine human sympathy between any two strata. We
sympathize in our own stratum, or class; toward other

strata—other classes—our attitude is necessarily a looking up or a looking down. Susan, a bit of flotsam, ascending, descending, ascending across the social layers—belonging nowhere—having attachments, not sympathies, a real settled lot nowhere—Susan was once more upward bound.

At the corner of Fourteenth Street there was a shop with large mirrors in the show windows. She paused to examine herself. She found she had no reason to be disturbed about her appearance. Her dress and hat looked well; her hair was satisfactory; the sharp air had brought some life to the pallor of her cheeks, and the release from the slums had restored some of the light to her eyes. "Why did I stay there so long?" she demanded of herself. Then, "How have I suddenly got the courage to leave?" She had no answer to either question. Nor did she care for an answer. She was not even especially interested in what was about to happen to her.

The moment she found herself above Twenty-third Street and in the old familiar surroundings, she felt an irresistible longing to hear about Rod Spenser. She was like one who has been on a far journey, leaving behind him everything that has been life to him; he dismisses it all because he must, until he finds himself again in his own country, in his old surroundings. She went into the Hoffman House and at the public telephone got the *Herald* office. "Is Mr. Drumley there?"

"No," was the reply. "He's gone to Europe."

"Did Mr. Spenser go with him?"

"Mr. Spenser isn't here—hasn't been for a long time. He's abroad too. Who is this?"

"Thank you," said Susan, hanging up the receiver. She drew a deep breath of relief.

She left the hotel by the women's entrance in Broadway. It was six o'clock. The sky was clear—a typical New York sky with air that intoxicated blowing from it—air of the sea—air of the depths of heaven. A crescent moon glittered above the Diana on the Garden tower. It was Saturday night and Broadway was thronged—with men eager to spend in pleasure part of the week's wages or salary they had just drawn; with women sparkling-eyed and odorous of perfumes and eager to help the men. The air was sharp—was the ocean air of New York at its delicious best. And the slim, slightly stooped girl with the earnest violet-gray eyes and the sad bitter mouth from whose lips the once brilliant color had now fled was ready for whatever might come. She paused at the corner, and gazed up brilliantly lighted Broadway.

"Now!" she said half aloud and, like an expert swimmer adventuring the rapids, she advanced into the swift-moving crowd of the highway of New York's gayety.

V

AT the corner of Twenty-sixth Street a man put himself squarely across her path. She was attracted by the twinkle in his good-natured eyes. He was a youngish man, had the stoutness of indulgence in a fondness for eating and drinking—but the stoutness was still well within the bounds of decency. His clothing bore out the suggestion of his self-assured way of stopping her—the suggestion of a confidence-giving prosperity.

"You look as if you needed a drink, too," said he. "How about it, lady with the lovely feet?"

For the first time in her life she was feeling on an equality with man. She gave him the same candidly measuring glance that man gives man. She saw good-nature, audacity without impudence—at least not the common sort of impudence. She smiled merrily, glad of the chance to show her delight that she was once more back in civilization after the long sojourn in the prison workshops where it is manufactured. She said:

"A drink? Thank you—yes."

"That's a superior quality of smile you've got there," said he. "That, and those nice slim feet of yours ought to win for you anywhere. Let's go to the Martin."

"Down University Place?"

The stout young man pointed his slender cane across the street. "You must have been away."

"Yes," said the girl. "I've been—dead."

"I'd like to try that myself—if I could be sure of

95

coming to life in little old New York." And he looked round with laughing eyes as if the lights, the crowds, the champagne-like air intoxicated him.

At the first break in the thunderous torrent of traffic they crossed Broadway and went in at the Twenty-sixth Street entrance. The restaurant, to the left, was empty. Its little tables were ready, however, for the throng of diners soon to come. Susan had difficulty in restraining herself. She was almost delirious with delight. She was agitated almost to tears by the freshness, the sparkle in the glow of the red-shaded candles, in the colors and odors of the flowers decorating every table. While she had been down there all this had been up here—waiting for her! Why had she stayed down there? But then, why had she gone? What folly, what madness! To suffer such horrors for no reason —beyond some vague, clinging remnant of a superstition—or had it been just plain insanity? "Yes, I've been crazy—out of my head. The break with—Rod— upset my mind."

Her companion took her into the café to the right. He seated her on one of the leather benches not far from the door, seated himself in a chair opposite; there was a narrow marble-topped table between them. On Susan's right sat a too conspicuously dressed but somehow important looking actress; on her left, a shopkeeper's fat wife. Opposite each woman sat the sort of man one would expect to find with her. The face of the actress's man interested her. It was a long pale face, the mouth weary, in the eyes a strange hot fire of intense enthusiasm. He was young—and old— and neither. Evidently he had lived every minute of every year of his perhaps forty years. He was wearing a quiet suit of blue and his necktie was of a darker

96

shade of the same color. His clothes were draped upon his good figure with a certain fascinating distinction. He was smoking an unusually long and thick cigarette. The slender strong white hand he raised and lowered was the hand of an artist. He might be a bad man, a very bad man—his face had an expression of freedom, of experience, that made such an idea as conventionality in connection with him ridiculous. But however bad he might be, Susan felt sure it would be an artistic kind of badness, without vulgarity. He might have reached the stage at which morality ceases to be a conviction, a matter of conscience, and becomes a matter of preference, of tastes—and he surely had good taste in conduct no less than in dress and manner. The woman with him evidently wished to convince him that she loved him, to convince those about her that they were lovers; the man evidently knew exactly what she had in mind—for he was polite, attentive, indifferent, and—Susan suspected—secretly amused.

Susan's escort leaned toward her and said in a low tone, "The two at the next table—the woman's Mary Rigsdall, the actress, and the man's Brent, the fellow who writes plays." Then in a less cautious tone, "What are you drinking?"

"What are *you* drinking?" asked Susan, still covertly watching Brent.

"You are going to dine with me?"

"I've no engagement."

"Then let's have Martinis—and I'll go get a table and order dinner while the waiter's bringing them."

When Susan was alone, she gazed round the crowded café, at the scores of interesting faces—thrillingly interesting to her after her long sojourn among countenances merely expressing crude elemental appetites if anything at all beyond toil, anxiety, privation, and bad health. These were the faces of the triumphant class—of those who had wealth or were getting it, fame or were striving for it, of those born to or acquiring position of some sort among the few thousands who lord it over the millions. These were the people among whom she belonged. Why was she having such a savage struggle to attain it? Then, all in an instant the truth she had been so long groping for in vain flung itself at her. None of these women, none of the women of the prosperous classes would be there but for the assistance and protection of the men. She marveled at her stupidity in not having seen the obvious thing clearly long ago. The successful women won their success by disposing of their persons to advantage—by getting the favor of some man of ability. Therefore, she, a woman, must adopt that same policy if she was to have a chance at the things worth while in life. She must make the best bargain—or series of bargains—she could. And as her necessities were pressing she must lose no time. She understood now the instinct that had forced her to fly from South Fifth Avenue, that had overruled her hesitation and had compelled her to accept the good-natured, prosperous man's invitation. . . . There was no other way open to her. She must not evade that fact; she must accept it. Other ways there might be—for other women. But not for her, the outcast without friends or family, the woman alone, with no one to lean upon or to give her anything except in exchange for what she had to offer that was marketable. She must make the bargain she could, not waste time in the folly of awaiting a bargain to her liking. Since she was living in the world and wished to continue to live there, she must accept the world's terms.

To be sad or angry either one because the world did not offer her as attractive terms as it apparently offered many other women—the happy and respected wives and mothers of the prosperous classes, for instance—to rail against that was silly and stupid, was unworthy of her intelligence. She would do as best she could, and move along, keeping her eyes open; and perhaps some day a chance for much better terms might offer—for the best—for such terms as that famous actress there had got. She looked at Mary Rigsdall. An expression in her interesting face—the latent rather than the surface expression—set Susan to wondering whether, if she knew Rigsdall's *whole* story—or any woman's whole story—she might not see that the world was not bargaining so hardly with her, after all. Or any man's whole story. There her eyes shifted to Rigsdall's companion, the famous playwright of whom she had so often heard Rod and his friends talk.

She was startled to find that his gaze was upon her —an all-seeing look that penetrated to the very core of her being. He either did not note or cared nothing about her color of embarrassment. He regarded her steadily until, so she felt, he had seen precisely what she was, had become intimately acquainted with her. Then he looked away. It chagrined her that his eyes did not again turn in her direction; she felt that he had catalogued her as not worth while. She listened to the conversation of the two. The woman did the talking, and her subject was herself—her ability as an actress, her conception of some part she either was about to play or was hoping to play. Susan, too young to have acquired more than the rudiments of the difficult art of character study, even had she had especial talent for it—which she had not—Susan decided that the famous Rigsdall was as shallow and vain as Rod had said all stage people were.

The waiter brought the cocktails and her stout young companion came back, beaming at the thought of the dinner he had painstakingly ordered. As he reached the table he jerked his head in self-approval. "It'll be a good one," said he. "Saturday night dinner—and after—means a lot to me. I work hard all week. Saturday nights I cut loose. Sundays I sleep and get ready to scramble again on Monday for the dollars." He seated himself, leaned toward her with elevated glass. "What name?" inquired he.

"Susan."

"That's a good old-fashioned name. Makes me see the hollyhocks, and the hens scratching for worms. Mine's Howland. Billy Howland. I came from Maryland . . . and I'm mighty glad I did. I wouldn't be from anywhere else for worlds, and I wouldn't be there for worlds. Where do you hail from?"

"The West," said Susan.

"Well, the men in your particular corner out yonder must be a pretty poor lot to have let you leave. I spotted you for mine the minute I saw you—Susan. I hope you're not as quiet as your name. Another cocktail?"

"Thanks."

"Like to drink?"

"I'm going to do more of it hereafter."

"Been laying low for a while—eh?"

"Very low," said Susan. Her eyes were sparkling now; the cocktail had begun to stir her long languid blood.

"Live with your family?"

"I haven't any. I'm free."

"On the stage?"

"I'm thinking of going on."

"And meanwhile?"

"Meanwhile—whatever comes." Susan laughed.

"Hope you're going to do a lot of that laughing," said he. "It's the best I've heard—such a quiet, gay sound. I sure do have the best luck. Until five years ago there was nothing doing for Billy—hall bedroom —Wheeling stogies—one shirt and two pairs of cuffs a week—not enough to buy a lady an ice-cream soda. All at once—bang! The hoodoo busted, and everything that arrived was for William C. Howland. Better get aboard."

"Here I am."

"Hold on tight. I pay no attention to the speed laws, and round the corners on two wheels. Do you like good things to eat?"

"I haven't eaten for six months."

"You must have been out home. Ah!—There's the man to tell us dinner's ready."

They finished the second cocktail. Susan was pleased to note that Brent was again looking at her; and she thought—though she suspected it might be the cocktail—that there was a question in his look—a question about her which he had been unable to answer to his satisfaction. When she and Howland were at one of the small tables against the wall in the restaurant, she said to him:

"You know Mr. Brent?"

"The play man? Lord, no. I'm a plain business dub. He wouldn't bother with me. You like that sort of man?"

"I want to get on the stage, if I can," was Susan's diplomatic reply.

"Well—let's have dinner first. I've ordered champagne, but if you prefer something else——"

"Champagne is what I want. I hope it's very dry."

Howland's eyes gazed tenderly at her. "I do like a woman who knows the difference between champagne and carbonated sirup. I think you and I've got a lot of tastes in common. I like eating—so do you. I like drinking—so do you. I like a good time—so do you. You're a little bit thin for my taste, but you'll fatten up. I wonder what makes your lips so pale."

"I'd hate to remind myself by telling you," said Susan.

The restaurant was filling. Most of the men and women were in evening dress. Each arriving woman brought with her a new exhibition of extravagance in costume, diffused a new variety of powerful perfume. The orchestra in the balcony was playing waltzes and the liveliest Hungarian music and the most sensuous strains from Italy and France and Spain. And before her was food!—food again!—not horrible stuff unfit for beasts, worse than was fed to beasts, but human food—good things, well cooked and well served. To have seen her, to have seen the expression of her eyes, without knowing her history and without having lived as she had lived, would have been to think her a glutton. Her spirits giddied toward the ecstatic. She began to talk—commenting on the people about her— the one subject she could venture with her companion. As she talked and drank, he ate and drank, stuffing and gorging himself, but with a frankness of gluttony that delighted her. She found she could not eat much, but she liked to see eating; she who had so long been seeing only poverty, bolting wretched food and drinking the vilest kinds of whiskey and beer, of alleged coffee and tea—she reveled in Howland's exhibition. She must learn to live altogether in her senses, never to think except about an appetite. Where could she find a better teacher? . . . They drank two quarts of champagne, and with the coffee she took *crème de menthe* and he brandy. And as the sensuous temperament that springs from intense vitality reasserted itself, the opportunity before her lost all its repellent features, became the bright, vivid countenance of lusty youth, irradiating the joy of living.

"I hear there's a lively ball up at Terrace Garden," said he. "Want to go?"

"That'll be fine!" cried she.

She saw it would have taken nearly all the money she possessed to have paid that bill. About four weeks' wages for one dinner! Thousands of families living for two weeks on what she and he had consumed in two hours! She reached for her half empty champagne glass, emptied it. She must forget all those things! "I've played the fool once. I've learned my lesson. Surely I'll never do it again." As she drank, her eyes chanced upon the clock. Half-past ten. Mrs. Tucker had probably just fallen asleep. And Mrs. Reardon was going out to scrub—going out limping and groaning with rheumatism. No, Mrs. Reardon was lying up at the morgue dead, her one chance to live lost forever. Dead! Yet better off than Mrs. Tucker lying alive.

The ball proved as lively as they hoped. A select company from the Tenderloin was attending, and the regulars were all of the gayest crowd among the sons and daughters of artisans and small merchants up and down the East Side. Not a few of the women were extremely pretty. All, or almost all, were young, and those who on inspection proved to be older than eighteen or twenty were acting younger than the youngest. Everyone had been drinking freely, and continued to drink. The orchestra played continuously. The air was giddy with laughter and song. Couples hugged and kissed in corners, and finally openly on the dancing floor. For a while Susan and Howland danced together. But soon they made friends with the crowd and danced with whoever was nearest. Toward three in the morning it flashed upon her that she had not even seen him for many a dance. She looked round—searched for him—got a blond-bearded man in evening dress to assist her.

"The last seen of your stout friend," this man finally reported, "he was driving away in a cab with a large lady from Broadway. He was asleep, but I guess she wasn't."

A sober thought winked into her whirling brain—he had warned her to hold on tight, and she had lost her head—and her opportunity. A bad start—a foolishly bad start. But out winked the glimpse of sobriety and Susan laughed. "That's the last I'll ever see of *him*," said she.

This seemed to give Blond-Beard no regrets. Said he: "Let's you and I have a little supper. I'd call it breakfast, only then we couldn't have champagne."

And they had supper—six at the table, all uproarious, Susan with difficulty restrained from a skirt dance on the table up and down among the dishes and bottles. It was nearly five o'clock when she and Blond-Beard helped each other toward a cab.

Late that afternoon she established herself in a room with a bath in West Twenty-ninth Street not far from

Broadway. The exterior of the house was dingy and
down-at-the-heel. But the interior was new and scrupulously clean. Several other young women lived there
alone also, none quite so well installed as Susan, who
had the only private bath and was paying twelve dollars a week. The landlady, frizzled and peroxide, explained—without adding anything to what she already
knew—that she could have "privileges," but cautioned
her against noise. "I can't stand for it," said she.
"First offense—out you go. This house is for ladies,
and only gentlemen that know how to conduct themselves as a gentleman should with a lady are allowed
to come here."

Susan paid a week in advance, reducing to thirty-one
dollars her capital which Blond-Beard had increased to
forty-three. The young lady who lived at the other
end of the hall smiled at her, when both happened to
glance from their open doors at the same time. Susan
invited her to call and she immediately advanced along
the hall in the blue silk kimono she was wearing over
her nightgown.

"My name is Ida Driscoll," said she, showing a
double row of charming white teeth—her chief positive
claim to beauty.

She was short, was plump about the shoulders but
slender in the hips. Her reddish brown hair was neatly
done over a big rat, and was so spread that its thinness
was hidden well enough to deceive masculine eyes. Nor
would a man have observed that one of her white round
shoulders was full two inches higher than the other.
Her skin was good, her features small and irregular,
her eyes shrewd but kindly.

"My name's"—Susan hesitated—"Lorna Sackville."

"I guess Lorna and Ida'll be enough for us to bother

to remember," laughed Miss Driscoll. "The rest's liable
to change. You've just come, haven't you?"

"About an hour ago. I've got only a toothbrush, a
comb, a washrag and a cake of soap. I bought them
on my way here."

"Baggage lost—eh?" said Ida, amused.

"No," admitted Susan. "I'm beginning an entire
new deal."

"I'll lend you a nightgown. I'm too short for my
other things to fit you."

"Oh, I can get along. What's good for a headache?
I'm nearly crazy with it."

"Wine?"

"Yes."

"Wait a minute." Ida, with bedroom slippers clattering, hurried back to her room, returned with a bottle
of bromo seltzer and in the bathroom fixed Susan a
dose. "You'll feel all right in half an hour or so. Gee,
but you're swell—with your own bathroom."

Susan shrugged her shoulders and laughed.

Ida shook her head gravely. "You ought to save
your money. I do."

"Later—perhaps. Just now—I *must* have a fling."

Ida seemed to understand. She went on to say: "I
was in millinery. But in this town there's nothing in
anything unless you have capital or a backer. I got
tired of working for five per, with ten or fifteen as the
top notch. So I quit, kissed my folks up in Harlem
good-by and came down to look about. As soon as I've
saved enough I'm going to start a business. That'll
be about a couple of years—maybe sooner, if I find an
angel."

"I'm thinking of the stage."

"Cut it out!" cried Ida. "It's on the bum."

"Seems to me the men's tastes even for what they want at home are getting louder and louder all the time. They hate anything that looks slow."

To change the subject Susan invited Ida to dine with her.

"What's the use of your spending money in a restaurant?" objected Ida. "You eat with me in my room. I always cook myself something when I ain't asked out by some one of my gentleman friends. I can cook you a chop and warm up a can of French peas and some dandy tea biscuits I bought yesterday."

Susan accepted the invitation, promising that when she was established she would reciprocate. As it was about six, they arranged to have the dinner at seven, Susan to dress in the meantime. The headache had now gone, even to that last heaviness which seems to be an ominous threat of a return. When she was alone, she threw off her clothes, filled the big bathtub with water as hot as she could stand it. Into this she gently lowered herself until she was able to relax and recline without discomfort. Then she stood up and with the soap and washrag gave herself the most thorough scrubbing of her life. Time after time she soaped and rubbed and scrubbed, and dipped herself in the hot water. When she felt that she had restored her body to somewhere near her ideal of cleanliness, she let the water run out and refilled the tub with even hotter water. In this she lay luxuriously, reveling in the magnificent sensations of warmth and utter cleanliness. Her eyes closed; a delicious languor stole over her and through her, soothing every nerve. She slept.

She was awakened by Ida, who had entered after knocking and calling at the outer door in vain. Susan slowly opened her eyes, gazed at Ida with a soft dreamy smile. "You don't know what this means. It seems to me I was never quite so comfortable or so happy in my life."

"It's a shame to disturb you," said Ida. "But dinner's ready. Don't stop to dress first. I'll bring you a kimono."

Susan turned on the cold water, and the bath rapidly changed from warm to icy. When she had indulged in the sense of cold as delightful in its way as the sense of warmth, she rubbed her glowing skin with a rough towel until she was rose-red from head to foot. Then she put on stockings, shoes and the pink kimono Ida had brought, and ran along the hall to dinner. As she entered Ida's room, Ida exclaimed, "How sweet and pretty you do look! You sure ought to make a hit!"

"I feel like a human being for the first time in—it seems years—ages—to me."

"You've got a swell color—except your lips. Have they always been pale like that?"

"No."

"I thought not. It don't seem to fit in with your style. You ought to touch 'em up. You look too serious and innocent, anyhow. They make a rouge now that'll stick through everything—eating, drinking—anything."

Susan regarded herself critically in the glass. "I'll see," she said.

The odor of the cooking chops thrilled Susan like music. She drew a chair up to the table, sat in happy-go-lucky fashion, and attacked the chop, the hot biscuit, and the peas, with an enthusiasm that inspired Ida to imitation. "You know how to cook a chop," she said to Ida. "And anybody who can cook a chop right can cook. Cooking's like playing the piano. If you can do the simple things perfectly, you're ready to do anything."

"Wait till I have a flat of my own," said Ida. "I'll show you what eating means. And I'll have it, too, before very long. Maybe we'll live together. I was to a fortune teller's yesterday. That's the only way I waste money. I go to fortune tellers nearly every day. But then all the girls do. You get your money's worth in excitement and hope, whether there's anything in it or not. Well, the fortune teller she said I was to meet a dark, slender person who was to change the whole course of my life—that all my troubles would roll away —and that if any more came, they'd roll away, too. My, but she did give me a swell fortune, and only fifty cents! I'll take you to her."

Ida made black coffee and the two girls, profoundly contented, drank it and talked with that buoyant cheerfulness which bubbles up in youth on the slightest pretext. In this case the pretext was anything but slight, for both girls had health as well as youth, had that freedom from harassing responsibility which is the chief charm of every form of unconventional life. And Susan was still in the first flush of the joy of escape from the noisome prison whose poisons had been corroding her, soul and body. No, poison is not a just comparison; what poison in civilization parallels, or even approaches, in squalor, in vileness of food and air, in wretchedness of shelter and clothing, the tenement life that is really the typical life of the city? From time to time Susan, suffused with the happiness that is too deep for laughter, too deep for tears even, gazed round like a dreamer at those cheerful comfortable surroundings and drew a long breath—stealthily, as if she feared she would awaken and be again in South Fifth

Avenue, of rags and filth, of hideous toil without hope.

"You'd better save your money to put in the millinery business with me," Ida advised. "I can show you
how to make a lot."

Susan threw her arms round Ida and kissed her.
"Don't bother about me," she said. "I've got to act
in my own foolish, stupid way. I'm like a child going
to school. I've got to learn a certain amount before
I'm ready to do whatever it is I'm going to do. And
until I learn it, I can't do much of anything. I thought
I had learned in the last few months. I see I haven't."

"Do listen to sense, Lorna," pleaded Ida. "If you
wait till the last minute, you'll get left. The time to
get the money's when you have money. And I've a feeling that you're not particularly flush."

"I'll do the best I can. And I can't move till I'm
ready."

Susan, silent, her thoughts flowing like a mill race,
helped Ida with the dishes. Then they dressed and
went together for a walk. It being Sunday evening, the
streets were quiet. They sauntered up Fifth Avenue
as far as Fifty-ninth Street and back.

They returned home at half-past nine without adventure. Toward midnight one of Ida's regulars called and
Susan was free to go to bed. She slept hardly at all.
Ever before her mind hovered a nameless, shapeless horror. And when she slept she dreamed of her wedding
night, woke herself screaming, "Please, Mr. Ferguson—
please!"

Meanwhile she continued to search for work—work
that would enable her to live *decently*, wages less degrading than the wages of shame. In a newspaper she
read an advertisement of a theatrical agency. Adver-

tisements of all kinds read well; those of theatrical
agencies read—like the fairy tales that they were.
However, she found in this particular offering of dazzling careers and salaries a peculiar phrasing that decided her to break the rule she had made after having
investigated scores of this sort of offers.

Rod was abroad; anyhow, enough time had elapsed.
One of the most impressive features of the effect of
New York—meaning by "New York" only that small
but significant portion of the four millions that thinks
—at least, after a fashion, and acts, instead of being
mere passive tools of whatever happens to turn up—
the most familiar notable effect of this New York is
the speedy distinction in the newcomer of those illusions and delusions about life and about human nature,
about good and evil, that are for so many people the
most precious and the only endurable and beautiful thing
in the world. New York, destroyer of delusions and
cherished hypocrisies and pretenses, therefore makes the
broadly intelligent of its citizens hardy, makes the
others hard—and between the hardy and hard, between
sense and cynicism, yawns a gulf like that between Absa-
lom and Dives. Susan, a New Yorker now, had got
the habit—in thought, at least—of seeing things with
somewhat less distortion from the actual. She no
longer exaggerated the importance of the Rod-Susan
episode. She saw that in New York, where life is
crowded with events, everything in one's life, except
death, becomes incident, becomes episode, where in regions offering less to think about each rare happening
took on an aspect of vast importance. The Rod-Susan
love adventure, she now saw, was not what it would have
seemed—therefore, would have been—in Sutherland,
but was mere episode of a New York life, giving its

light and shade to a certain small part of the long, variedly patterned fabric of her life, and of his, not determining the whole. She saw that it was simply like a bend in the river, giving a new turn to current and course but not changing the river itself, and soon left far behind and succeeded by other bends giving each its equal or greater turn to the stream.

Rod had passed from her life, and she from his life. Thus she was free to begin her real career—the stage— if she could. She went to the suite of offices tenanted by Mr. Josiah Ransome. She was ushered in to Ransome himself, instead of halting with underlings. She owed this favor to advantages which her lack of vanity and of self-consciousness prevented her from surmising. Ransome—smooth, curly, comfortable looking—received her with a delicate blending of the paternal and the gallant. After he had inspected her exterior with flattering attentiveness and had investigated her qualifications with a thoroughness that was convincing of sincerity he said:

"Most satisfactory! I can make you an exceptional assurance. If you register with me, I can guarantee you not less than twenty-five a week."

Susan hesitated long and asked many questions before she finally—with reluctance—paid the five dollars. She felt ashamed of her distrust, but might perhaps have persisted in it had not Mr. Ransome said:

"I don't blame you for hesitating, my dear young lady. And if I could I'd put you on my list without payment. But you can see how unbusinesslike that would be. I am a substantial, old-established concern. You—no doubt you are perfectly reliable. But I have been fooled so many times. I must not let myself forget that after all I know nothing about you."

As soon as Susan had paid he gave her a list of vaudeville and musical comedy houses where girls were wanted. "You can't fail to suit one of them," said he. "If not, come back here and get your money."

After two weary days of canvassing she went back to Ransome. He was just leaving. But he smiled genially, opened his desk and seated himself. "At your service," he said. "What luck?"

"None," replied Susan. " I couldn't live on the wages they offered at the musical comedy places, even if I could get placed."

"And the vaudeville people?"

"When I said I could only sing and not dance, they looked discouraged. When I said I had no costumes they turned me down."

"Excellent!" cried Ransome. "You mustn't be so easily beaten. You must take dancing lessons—perhaps a few singing lessons, too. And you must get some costumes."

"But that means several hundred dollars."

"Three or four hundred," said Ransome airily. "A matter of a few weeks."

"But I haven't anything like that," said Susan. "I haven't so much as——"

"I comprehend perfectly," interrupted Ransome. She interested him, this unusual looking girl, with her attractive mingling of youth and experience. Her charm that tempted people to give her at once the frankest confidences, moved him to go out of his way to help her. "You haven't the money," he went on. "You must have it. So—I promised to place you, and I will. I don't usually go so far in assisting my clients. It's not often necessary—and where it's necessary it's usually imprudent. However—I'll give you the address of a flat where there is a lady—a trustworthy, square sort, despite her—her profession. She will put you in the way of getting on a sound financial basis."

Ransome spoke in a matter-of-fact tone, like a man stating a simple business proposition. Susan understood. She rose. Her expression was neither shock nor indignation; but it was none the less a negative.

To her amazement he held out a five-dollar bill. "Here's your fee back." He laughed at her expression. "Oh, I'm not a robber," said he. "I only wish I could serve you. I didn't think you were so—" his eyes twinkled—"so unreasonable, let us say. Among those who don't know anything about life there's an impression that my sort of people are in the business of dragging women down. Perhaps one of us occasionally does as bad—about a millionth part as bad—as the average employer of labor who skims his profits from the lifeblood of his employees. But as a rule we folks merely take those that are falling and help them to light easy—or even to get up again."

Susan felt ashamed to take her money. But he pressed it on her. "You'll need it," said he. "I know how it is with a girl alone and trying to get a start. Perhaps later on you'll be more in the mood where I can help you."

"Perhaps," said Susan.

"But I hope not. It'll take uncommon luck to pull you through—and I hope you'll have it."

"Thank you," said Susan. He took her hand, pressed it friendlily—and she felt that he was a man with real good in him, more good than many who would have shrunk from him in horror.

She was waiting for a thrust from fate. But fate, disappointing as usual, would not thrust. It seemed bent on the malicious pleasure of compelling her to degrade herself deliberately and with calculation, like a woman marrying for support a man who refuses to permit her to decorate with any artificial floral concealments of faked-up sentiment the sordid truth as to what she is about. She searched within herself in vain for the scruple or sentiment or timidity or whatever it was that held her back from the course that was plainly inevitable. She had got down to the naked fundamentals of decency and indecency that are deep hidden by, and for most of us under, hypocrisies of conventionality. She had found out that a decent woman was one who respected her body and her soul, that an indecent woman was one who did not, and that marriage rites or the absence of them, the absence of financial or equivalent consideration, or its presence, or its extent or its form, were all irrelevant non-essentials. Yet—she hesitated, knowing the while that she was risking a greater degradation, and a stupid and fatal folly to boot, by shrinking from the best course open to her—unless it were better to take a dose of poison and end it all. She probably would have done that had she not been so utterly healthy, therefore overflowing with passionate love of life. Except in fiction suicide and health do not go together, however superhumanly sensitive the sore beset hero or heroine. Susan was sensitive enough; whenever she did things incompatible with our false and hypocritical and unscientific notions of sensitiveness, allowances should be made for her because of her superb and dauntless health. If her physical condition had been morbid, her conduct might have been, would have been, very different.

She was still hesitating when Saturday night came round again—swiftly despite long disheartening days, and wakeful awful nights. In the morning her rent would be due. She had a dollar and forty-five cents.

After dinner alone—a pretense at dinner—she wandered the streets of the old Tenderloin until midnight. An icy rain was falling. Rains such as this—any rains except showers—were rare in the City of the Sun. That rain by itself was enough to make her downhearted. She walked with head down and umbrella close to her shoulders. No one spoke to her. She returned dripping; she had all but ruined her one dress. She went to bed, but not to sleep. About nine—early for that house—she rose, drank a cup of coffee and ate part of a roll. Her little stove and such other things as could not be taken along she rolled into a bundle, marked it, "For Ida." On a scrap of paper she wrote this note:

Don't think I'm ungrateful, please. I'm going without saying good-by because I'm afraid if I saw you, you'd be generous enough to put up for me, and I'd be weak enough to accept. And if I did that, I'd never be able to get strong or even to hold my head up. So—good-by. I'll learn sooner or later—learn how to live. I hope it won't be too long—and that the teacher won't be too hard on me.

Yes, I'll learn, and I'll buy fine hats at your grand millinery store yet. Don't forget me altogether.

She tucked this note into the bundle and laid it against the door behind which Ida and one of her regulars were sleeping peacefully. The odor of Ida's powerful perfume came through the cracks in the door; Susan drew it eagerly into her nostrils, sobbed softly, turned away. It was one of the perfumes classed as immoral; to Susan it was the aroma of a friendship as noble, as disinterested, as generous, as human sympathy had ever breathed upon human woe. With her few personal possessions in a package she descended the stairs unnoticed, went out into the rain. At the corner of Sixth Avenue she paused, looked up and down the street. It was almost deserted. Now and then a streetwalker, roused early by a lover with perhaps a family waiting for him, hurried by, looking piteous in the daylight which showed up false and dyed hair, the layers of paint, the sad tawdriness of battered finery from the cheapest bargain troughs.

Susan went slowly up Sixth Avenue. Two blocks, and she saw a girl enter the side door of a saloon across the way. She crossed the street, pushed in at the same door, went on to a small sitting-room with blinds drawn, with round tables, on every table a match stand. It was one of those places where streetwalkers rest their weary legs between strolls, and sit for company on rainy or snowy nights, and take shy men for sociability-breeding drinks and for the preliminary bargaining. The air of the room was strong with stale liquor and tobacco, the lingering aroma of the night's vanished revels. In the far corner sat the girl she had followed; a glass of raw whiskey and another of water stood on the table before her. Susan seated herself near the door and when the swollen-faced, surly bartender came, ordered whiskey. She poured herself a drink— filled the glass to the brim. She drank it in two gulps, set the empty glass down. She shivered like an animal as it is hit in the head with a poleax. The mechanism of life staggered, hesitated, went on with a sudden leaping acceleration of pace. Susan tapped her glass against the matchstand. The bartender came.

"Another," said she.

The man stared at her. "The—hell!" he ejaculated. "You must be afraid o' catchin' cold. Or maybe you're lookin' for the menagerie?"

Susan laughed and so did the girl in the corner. "Won't you have a drink with me?" asked Susan.

"That's very kind of you," replied the girl, in the manner of one eager to show that she, too, is a perfect lady in every respect, used to the ways of the best society. She moved to a chair at Susan's table.

She and Susan inventoried each other. Susan saw a mere child—hardly eighteen—possibly not seventeen —but much worn by drink and irregular living—evidently one of those who rush into the fast woman's life with the idea that it is a career of gayety—and do not find out their error until looks and health are gone. Susan drank her second drink in three gulps, several minutes apart.

The bartender served the third drink and Susan paid for them, the other girl insisting on paying for the one she was having when Susan came. Susan's head was whirling. Her spirits were spiraling up and up. Her pale lips were wreathed in a reckless smile. She felt courageous for adventure—any adventure. Her capital had now sunk to three quarters and a five-cent piece. They issued forth, talking without saying anything, laughing without knowing or caring why. Life was a joke—a coarse, broad joke—but amusing if one drank enough to blunt any refinement of sensibility. And what was sensibility but a kind of snobbishness? And what more absurd than snobbishness in an outcast?

"That's good whiskey they had, back there," said Susan.

"Good? Yes—if you don't care what you say."

"If you don't want to care what you say or do," explained Susan.

"Oh, all booze is good for that," said the girl.

VI

THEY went through to Broadway and there stood waiting for a car, each under her own umbrella. "Holy Gee!" cried Susan's new acquaintance. "Ain't this rain a soaker?"

It was coming in sheets, bent and torn and driven horizontally by the wind. The umbrella, sheltering the head somewhat, gave a wholly false impression of protection. Both girls were soon sopping wet. But they were more than cheerful about it; the whiskey made them indifferent to external ills as they warmed themselves by its bright fire. At that time a famous and much envied, admired and respected "captain of industry," having looted the street-car systems, was preparing to loot them over again by the familiar trickery of the receivership and the reorganization. The masses of the people were too ignorant to know what was going on; the classes were too busy, each man of each of them, about his own personal schemes for graft of one kind and another. Thus, the street-car service was a joke and a disgrace. However, after four or five minutes a north-bound car appeared.

"But it won't stop," cried Susan. "It's jammed."

"That's why it will stop," replied her new acquaintance. "You don't suppose a New York conductor'd miss a chance to put his passengers more on the bum than ever?"

She was right, at least as to the main point; and the conductor with much free handling of their waists and shoulders added them to the dripping, straining press of passengers, enduring the discomforts the captain of industry put upon them with more patience than cattle would have exhibited in like circumstances. All the way up Broadway the new acquaintance enlivened herself and Susan and the men they were squeezed in among by her loud gay sallies which her young prettiness made seem witty. And certainly she did have an amazing and amusing acquaintance with the slang at the moment current. The worn look had vanished, her rounded girlhood freshness had returned. As for Susan, you would hardly have recognized her as the same person who had issued from the house in Twenty-ninth Street less than an hour before. Indeed, it was not the same person. Drink nervifies every character; here it transformed, suppressing the characteristics that seemed, perhaps were, essential in her normal state, and causing to bloom in sudden audacity of color and form the passions and gayeties at other times subdued by her intelligence and her sensitiveness. Her brilliant glance moved about the car full as boldly as her companion's. But there was this difference: Her companion gazed straight into the eyes of the men; Susan's glance shot past above or just below their eyes.

"You forgot your package—back in the saloon!" said the girl.

"Then I didn't forget much," laughed Susan. It appealed to her, the idea of entering the new life empty-handed.

The hotel was one that must have been of the first class in its day—not a distant day, for the expansion of New York in craving for showy luxury has been as sudden as the miraculous upward thrust of a steel sky-scraper. It had now sunk to relying upon the trade of those who came in off Broadway for a few minutes. It was dingy and dirty; the walls and plastering were peeling; the servants were slovenly and fresh. The girl nodded to the evil-looking man behind the desk, who said:

"Hello, Miss Maud. Just in time. The boys were sending out for some others."

"They've got a nerve!" laughed Maud. And she led Susan down a rather long corridor to a door with the letter B upon it. Maud explained: "This is the swellest suite in the house—parlor, bedroom, bath." She flung open the door, disclosing a sitting-room in disorder with two young men partly dressed, seated at a small table on which were bottles, siphons, matches, remains of sandwiches, boxes of cigarettes—a chaotic jumble of implements to dissipation giving forth a powerful, stale odor. Maud burst into a stream of picturesque profanity which set the two men to laughing. Susan had paused on the threshold. The shock of this scene had for the moment arrested the triumphant march of the alcohol through blood and nerve and brain.

"Oh, bite it off!" cried the darker of the two men to Maud, "and have a drink. Ain't you ashamed to speak so free before your innocent young lady friend?" He grinned at Susan. "What Sunday School do you hail from?" inquired he.

The other young man was also looking at Susan; and it was an arresting and somewhat compelling gaze. She saw that he was tall and well set up. As he was dressed only in trousers and a pale blue silk undershirt, the strength of his shoulders, back and arms was in full evidence. His figure was like that of the wonderful young prize-fighters she had admired at moving picture

shows to which Drumley had taken her. He had a
singularly handsome face, blond, yet remotely suggesting Italian. He smiled at Susan and she thought she
had never seen teeth more beautiful—pearl-white, regular, even. His eyes were large and sensuous; smiling
though they were, Susan was ill at ease—for in them
there shone the same untamed, uncontrolled ferocity
that one sees in the eyes of a wild beast. His youth, his
good looks, his charm made the sinister savagery hinted
in the smile the more disconcerting. He poured whiskey from a bottle into each of the two tall glasses, filled
them up with selzer, extended one toward Susan.

The young man said, "Your name's Queenie, mine's
Freddie."

"Now, I'm going to stand behind you. I've got a
pull with the organization. I'm one of Finnegan's
lieutenants. Some day—when I'm older and have
served my apprenticeship—I'll pull off something
good. Meanwhile—I manage to live. I always have
managed it—and I never did a stroke of real work
since I was a kid—and never shall. God was mighty
good to me when he put a few brains in this nut of
mine."

An extraordinary man, certainly—and in what a
strange way!

"Yes," said he presently, looking at her with his
gentle, friendly smile. "We'll be partners."

Her reply to his restatement of the partnership
was:

"No, thank you. I want nothing to do with it."

"You're dead slow," said he, with mild and patient
persuasion.

"I'll look out for myself," persisted she.

"Bless the baby!" exclaimed he, immensely amused.

He let her reflect a while. Then he went on:

"You don't understand about fellows like Jim and me—though Jim's a small potato beside me, as you'll soon find out. Suppose you didn't obey orders—just as I do what Finnegan tells me—just as Finnegan does what the big shout down below says? Suppose you didn't obey—what then?"

"I don't know," confessed Susan.

"Well, it's time you learned. We'll say, you act stubborn. You say good-by to me and start out. Do you think I'm wicked enough to let you make a fool of yourself? Well, I'm not. You won't get outside the door before your good angel here will get busy. I'll be telephoning to a fly cop of this district. And what'll he do? Why, about the time you are halfway down the block, he'll pinch you. He'll take you to the station house. And in Police Court tomorrow the Judge'll give you a week on the Island."

Susan shivered. She instinctively glanced toward the window. The rain was still falling, changing the City of the Sun into a city of desolation. It looked as though it would never see the sun again—and her life looked that way, also.

The more intelligent a trapped animal is, the less resistance it offers, once it realizes. Helpless—absolutely helpless. No money—no friends. No escape but death. The sun was shining. Outside lay the vast world; across the street on a flagpole fluttered the banner of freedom. Freedom! Was there any such thing anywhere? Perhaps if one had plenty of money —or powerful friends. But not for her, any more than for the masses whose fate of squalid and stupid slavery she was trying to escape. Not for her; so long as she was helpless she would simply move from one land of slavery to another. Helpless! To struggle would not be courageous, but merely absurd.

She took the quarters he directed—a plain clean room two flights up at seven dollars a week, in a furnished room house on West Forty-third Street near Eighth Avenue. She was but a few blocks from where she and Rod had lived. New York illustrates in the isolated lives of its never isolated inhabitants how little relationship there is between space and actualities of distance. Wherever on earth there are as many as two human beings, one may see an instance of the truth. That an infinity of spiritual solitude can stretch uncrossable even between two locked in each other's loving arms! But New York's solitudes, its separations, extend to the surface things. Susan had no sense of the apparent nearness of her former abode. Her life again lay in the same streets; but there again came the sense of strangeness which only one who has lived in New York could appreciate. The streets were the same; but to her they seemed as the streets of another city, because she was now seeing in them none of the things she used to see, was seeing instead kinds of people, aspects of human beings, modes of feeling and acting and existing of which she used to have not the faintest knowledge. There were as many worlds as kinds of people. Thus, though we all talk to each other as if about the same world, each of us is thinking of his own kind of world, the only one he sees. And that is why there can never be sympathy and understanding among the children of men until there is some approach to resemblance in their various lots; for the lot determines the man.

"On Mr. Palmer's recommendation," said she; "I'll

give you two days to pay. My terms are in advance. But Mr. Palmer's a dear friend of mine."

She was a short woman, with a monstrous bust and almost no hips. Her thin hair was dyed and frizzled, and her voice sounded as if it found its way out of her fat lips after a long struggle to pass through the fat of her throat and chest. Her second chin lay upon her bosom in a soft swollen bag that seemed to be suspended from her ears. Her eyes were hard and evil, of a brownish gray. She affected suavity and elaborate politeness; but if the least thing disturbed her, she became red and coarse of voice and vile of language. The vile language and the nature of her business and her private life aside, she would have compared favorably with anyone in the class of those who deal—as merchants, as landlords, as boarding-house keepers—with the desperately different classes of uncertain income.

After the talk with Maud about the realities of life as it is lived by several hundred thousand of the inhabitants of Manhattan Island, Susan had not the least disposition to test by defiance the truth of Freddie Palmer's plain statement as to his powers. And at half-past seven Maud came. At once she inspected Susan's face.

"Might be a bit worse," she said.

Susan began letting down her hair.

"What are you doing that for?" cried Maud impatiently. "We're late now and——"

"I don't like the way my hair's done," cried Susan.

"Why, it was all right—real swell—good as a hairdresser could have done."

But Susan went on at her task. Ever since she came East she had worn it in a braid looped at the

back of her head. She proceeded to change this rad-
ically. With Maud forgetting to be impatient in admiration of her swift fingers she made a coiffure much
more elaborate—wide waves out from her temples and
a big round loose knot behind. She was well content
with the result—especially when she got her veil on and
it was assisting in the change.

"What do you think?" she said to Maud when she
was ready.

"My, but you look different!" exclaimed Maud. "A
lot dressier—and sportier. More—more Broadway."

"That's it—Broadway," said Susan. She had always avoided looking like Broadway. Now, she would
take the opposite tack. Not loud toilets—for they
would defeat her purpose. Not loud—just common.

"But," added Maud, "you do look swell about the
feet. Where *do* you get your shoes? No, I guess
it's the feet."

While Susan, later on in the back of a saloon, was
having two more drinks Maud talked about Freddie.
She seemed to know little about him, though he was
evidently one of the conspicuous figures. He had
started in the lower East Side—had been leader of one
of those gangs that infest tenement districts—the
young men who refuse to submit to the common lot of
stupid and badly paid toil and try to fight their
way out by the quick method of violence instead
of the slower but surer methods of robbing the poor
through a store of some kind. These gangs
were thieves, blackmailers, kidnappers of young girls
for houses of prostitution, repeaters. Most of them
graduated into habitual jailbirds, a few—the clev-
erest—became saloonkeepers and politicians and

high-class professional gamblers and race track men.

Freddie, Maud explained, was not much over twenty-five, yet was already well up toward the place where successful gang leaders crossed over into the respectable class—that is, grafted in "big figures." He was a great reader, said Maud, and had taken courses at some college. "They say he and his gang used to kill somebody nearly every night. Then he got a lot of money out of one of his jobs—some say it was a bank robbery and some say they killed a miner who was drunk with a big roll on him. Anyhow, Freddie got next to Finnegan—he's worth several millions that he made out of policy shops and poolrooms, and contracts and such political things. So he's in right—and he's got the brains. He's a good one for working out schemes for making people work hard and bring him their money. And everybody's afraid of him because he won't stop at nothing and is too slick to get caught."

Maud broke off abruptly and rose, warned by the glazed look in Susan's eyes.

"How many girls has Freddie got?"

"Search me. Not many that he'd speak to himself. Jim's his wardman—does his collecting for him. Freddie's above most of the men in this business. The others are about like Jim—tough straight through, but Freddie's a kind of a pullman. The other men—even Jim—hate him for being such a snare and being able to hide it that he's in such a low business. They'd have done him up long ago, if they could. But he's too wise for them. That's why they have to do what he says. I tell you, you're in right, for sure. You'll have Freddie eating out of your hand, if you play a cool hand."

VII

EACH morning she awoke in a state of depression so horrible that she wondered why she could not bring herself to plan suicide.

Once a young doctor said to her:

"What a heart action you have got! Let me listen to that again."

"Is it all wrong?" asked Susan, as he pressed his ear against her chest.

"You ask that as if you rather hoped it was."

"I do—and I don't."

"Well," said he, after listening for a third time, "you'll never die of heart trouble. I never heard a heart with such a grand action—like a big, powerful pump, built to last forever. You're never ill, are you?"

"Not thus far."

"And you'll have a hard time making yourself ill. Health? Why, your health must be perfect. Let me see." And he proceeded to thump and press upon her chest with an expertness that proclaimed the student of medicine. He was all interest and enthusiasm, took a pencil, and, spreading a sheet upon her chest over her heart, drew its outlines. "There!" he cried.

"What is it?" asked Susan. "I don't understand."

The young man drew a second and much smaller heart within the outline of hers. "This," he explained, "is about the size of an ordinary heart. You can see for yourself that yours is fully one-fourth bigger than the normal."

"What of it?" said Susan.

"Why, health and strength—and vitality—courage —hope—all one-fourth above the ordinary allowance. Yes, more than a fourth. I envy you. You ought to live long, stay young until you're very old—and get pretty much anything you please. You don't belong to this life. Some accident, I guess. Every once in a while I run across a case something like yours. You'll go back where you belong. This is a dip, not a drop."

"You sound like a fortune-teller." She was smiling mockingly. But in truth she had never in all her life heard words that thrilled her so, that heartened her so.

"I am. A scientific fortune-teller. And what that kind says comes true, barring accidents. No, nothing can stop you but death—unless you're far less intelligent than you look. Oh, yes—death and one other thing."

"Drink." And he looked shrewdly at her.

But drink she must. And each day, as soon as she dressed and was out in the street, she began to drink, and kept it up until she had driven off the depression and had got herself into the mood of recklessness in which she found a certain sardonic pleasure in outraging her own sensibilities. There is a stage in a drinking career when the man or the woman becomes depraved and ugly as soon as the liquor takes effect. But she was far from this advanced stage. Her disposition was, if anything, more sweet and generous when she was under the influence of liquor. The whiskey—she almost always drank whiskey—seemed to act directly and only upon the nerves that ached and throbbed when she was sober, the nerves that made the life she was leading seem loathsome beyond the power of habit to accustom. With these nerves stupefied, her natural gayety asserted itself, and a fondness for quiet and subtle mockery—her indulgence in it did not make her popular with vain men sufficiently acute to catch her meaning.

By observation and practice she was soon able to measure the exact amount of liquor that was necessary to produce the proper state of intoxication at the hour for going "on duty." That gayety of hers was of the surface only. Behind it her real self remained indifferent or somber or sardonic, according to her mood of the day. And she had the sense of being in the grasp of a hideous, fascinating nightmare, of being dragged through some dreadful probation from which she would presently emerge to ascend to the position she would have earned by her desperate fortitude. The past—unreal. The present—a waking dream. But the future—ah, the future!

He has not candidly explored far beneath the surface of things who does not know the strange allure, charm even, that many loathsome things possess. And drink is peculiarly fitted to bring out this perverse quality—drink that blurs all the conventionalities, even those built up into moral ideas by centuries and ages of unbroken custom. The human animal, for all its pretenses of inflexibility, is almost infinitely adaptable—that is why it has risen in several million years of evolution from about the humblest rank in the mammalian family to overlordship of the universe. Still, it is doubtful if, without drink to help her, a girl of Susan's intelligence and temperament would have been apt to endure. She would probably have chosen the alternative—death. Hundreds, perhaps thousands, of girls, at least her equals in sensibility, are caught in the same calamity every year, tens of thousands, ever more and more as our civilization transforms under the pressure of industrialism, are caught in the similar calamities of soul-destroying toil. And only the few survive who have perfect health and abounding vitality. Susan's iron strength enabled her to live; but it was drink that enabled her to endure. Beyond question one of the greatest blessings that could now be conferred upon the race would be to cure it of the drink evil. But at the same time, if drink were taken away before the causes of drink were removed, there would be an appalling increase in suicide—in insanity, in the general total of human misery. For while drink retards the growth of intelligent effort to end the stupidities in the social system, does it not also help men and women to bear the consequences of those stupidities? Our crude and undeveloped new civilization, strapping men and women and children to the machines and squeezing all the energy out of them, all the capacity for vital life, casts them aside as soon as they are useless but long before they are dead. How unutterably wretched they would be without drink to give them illusions!

Susan grew fond of cigarettes, fond of whiskey; to the rest she after a few weeks became numb—no new or strange phenomenon in a world where people with a cancer or other hideous running sore or some gross and frightful deformity of fat or excrescence are seen laughing, joining freely and comfortably in the company of the unafflicted. In her affliction Susan at least saw only those affected like herself—and that helped not a little, helped the whiskey to confuse and distort her outlook upon life.

The old Cartesian formula—"I think, therefore, I am"—would come nearer to expressing a truth, were it reversed—"I am, therefore, I think." Our characters are compressed, and our thoughts bent by our environment. And most of us are unconscious of our slavery because our environment remains unchanged from birth until death, and so seems the whole universe to us.

In spite of her life, in spite of all she did to disguise herself, there persisted in her face—even when she was dazed or giddied or stupefied with drink—the expression of the woman on the right side of the line. Whether it was something in her character, whether it was not rather due to superiority of breeding and intelligence, would be difficult to say. However, there was the *different* look that irritated many of the other girls, interfered with her business and made her feel a hypocrite. She heard so much about the paleness of her lips that she decided to end that comment by using paint—the durable kind Ida had recommended. When her lips flamed carmine, a strange and striking effect resulted. The sad sweet pensiveness of her eyes—the pallor of her clear skin—then, that splash of bright red, artificial, bold, defiant—the contrast of the combination seemed somehow to tell the story of her life—her past no less than her present. And when her beauty began to come back—for, hard though her life was, it was a life of good food, of plenty of sleep, of much open air; so it put no such strain upon her as had the life of the factory and the tenement—when her beauty came back, the effect of that contrast of scarlet splash against the sad purity of pallid cheeks and violet-gray eyes became a mark of individuality, of distinction. It was not long before Susan would have as soon thought of issuing forth with her body uncovered as with her lips unrouged.

She turned away from men who sought her a second time. She was difficult to find, she went on "duty" only enough days each week to earn a low average of what was expected from the girls by their protectors. Yet she got many unexpected presents—and so had money to lend to the other girls, who soon learned how "easy" she was.

Maud, sometimes at her own prompting, sometimes prompted by Jim, who was prompted by Freddie— warned her every few days that she was skating on the thinnest of ice. But she went her way. Not until she accompanied a girl to an opium joint to discover whether dope had the merits claimed for it as a deadener of pain and a producer of happiness—not until then did Freddie come in person.

"I hear," said he, "that you come into the hotel drunk."

"I must drink," said Susan.

"You must *stop* drink," retorted he, amiable in his terrible way. "If you don't, I'll have you pinched and sent up. That'll bring you to your senses."

"I must drink," said Susan.

"Then I must have you pinched," said he, with his mocking laugh. "Don't be a fool," he went on.

She had laughed as he spoke.

Freddie nodded approval. "You're getting broken in. Don't take yourself so seriously. After all, what are you doing? Why, learning to live like a man."

She found this new point of view interesting—and true, too. Like a man—like all men, except possibly a few—not enough exceptions to change the rule. Like a man; getting herself hardened up to the point where she could take part in the cruel struggle on equal terms with the men. It wasn't their difference of body any more than it was their difference of dress that handicapped women; it was the idea behind skirt and sex— and she was getting rid of that. . . .

The theory was admirable; but it helped her not at all in practice. She continued to keep to the darkness, to wait in the deep doorways, so far as she could in her "business hours," and to repulse advances in the daytime or in public places—and to drink. She did not go again to the opium joint, and she resisted the nightly offers of girls and their "gentlemen friends" to try cocaine in its various forms. "Dope," she saw, was the medicine of despair. And she was far from despair. Had she not youth? Had she not health and intelligence and good looks? Some day she would have finished her apprenticeship. Then—the career!

Freddie let her alone for nearly a month, though she was earning less than fifty dollars a week—which meant only thirty for him. He had never "collected" from her directly, but always through Jim; and she had now learned enough of the methods of the system of which she was one of the thousands of slaves to appreciate that she was treated by Jim with unique consideration. Not only by the surly and brutal Jim, but also by the police, who oppressed in petty ways wherever they dared because they hated Freddie's system, which took away from them a part of the graft they regarded as rightfully theirs.

Yes, rightfully theirs. And anyone disposed to be critical of police morality—or of Freddie Palmer morality—in this matter of graft would do well to pause and consider the source of his own income before he waxes too eloquent and too virtuous. Graft is one of those general words that mean everything and nothing. What is graft and what is honest income? Just where shall we draw the line between rightful exploitation of our fellow-beings through their necessities and their ignorance of their helplessness, and wrongful ex-

ploitation? Do attempts to draw that line resolve
down to making virtuous whatever I may appropriate
and vicious whatever is appropriated in ways other
than mine? And if so, are not the police and the
Palmers entitled to their day in the moral court no less
than the tariff-baron and market-cornerer, the herder
and driver of wage slaves, the retail artists in cold
storage filth, short weight and shoddy goods? However, "we must draw the line somewhere" or there will
be no such thing as morality under our social system.
So why not draw it at anything the other fellow does
to make money. In adopting this simple rule, we not
only preserve the moralities from destruction, but also
establish our own virtue and the other fellow's villainy.
Truly, never is the human race so delightfully, so
unconsciously, amusing as when it discusses right and
wrong.

When she saw Freddie again, he was far from
sober. He showed it by his way of beginning. Said
he:

"I've got to hand you a line of rough talk, Queenie.
I want you to promise me you'll take a brace."

No answer.

"You won't promise?"

"No—because I don't intend to. I'm doing the best
I can."

"You think I'm a good thing. You think I'll take
anything off you, because I'm stuck on you—and appreciate that you ain't on the same level with the rest
of these heifers. Well—I'll not let any woman con
me. I never have. I never will. And I'll make you
realize that you're not square with me. I'll let you
get a taste of life as it is when a girl hasn't got a
friend with a pull."

"As you please," said Susan indifferently. "I don't in the least care what happens to me."

"We'll see about that," cried he, enraged. "I'll give you a week to brace up in."

The look he shot at her by way of finish to his sentence was menacing enough. But she was not disturbed; these signs of anger tended to confirm her in her sense of security from him. For it was wholly unlike the Freddie Palmer the rest of the world knew, to act in this irresolute and stormy way. She knew that Palmer, in his fashion, cared for her—better still, liked her—liked to talk with her, liked to show—and to develop—the aspiring side of his interesting, unusual nature for her benefit.

A week passed, during which she did not see him. But she heard that he was losing on both the cards and the horses, and was drinking wildly. A week—ten days—then——

One night, as she came out of a saloon a block or so down Seventh Avenue from Forty-second, a fly cop seized her by the arm.

"Come along," said he, roughly. "You're drinking and soliciting. I've got to clear the streets of some of these tarts. It's got so decent people can't move without falling over 'em."

Susan had not lived in the tenement districts where the ignorance and the helplessness and the lack of a voice that can make itself heard among the ruling classes make the sway of the police absolute and therefore tyrannical—she had not lived there without getting something of that dread and horror of the police which to people of the upper classes seems childish or evidence of secret criminal hankerings. And this nervousness had latterly been increased to terror by what she had learned from her fellow-outcasts—the hideous tales of oppression, of robbery, of bodily and moral degradation. But all this terror had been purely fanciful, as any emotion not of experience proves to be when experience evokes the reality. At that touch, at the sound of those rough words—at that *reality* of the terror she had imagined from the days when she went to work at Matson's and to live with the Brashears, she straightway lost consciousness. When her senses returned she was in a cell, lying on a wooden bench.

There must have been some sort of wild struggle; for her clothes were muddy, her hat was crushed into shapelessness, her veil was so torn that she had difficulty in arranging it to act as any sort of concealment. Though she had no mirror at which to discover the consolation, she need have had no fear of being recognized, so distorted were all her features by the frightful paroxysms of grief that swept and ravaged her body that night. She fainted again when they led her out to put her in the wagon.

She fainted a third time when she heard her name—"Queenie Brown"—bellowed out by the court officer. They shook her into consciousness, led her to the court-room. She was conscious of a stifling heat, of a curious crowd staring at her with eyes which seemed to bore red hot holes into her flesh. As she stood before the judge, with head limp upon her bosom, she heard in her ear a rough voice bawling, "You're discharged. The judge says don't come here again." And she was pushed through an iron gate. She walked unsteadily up the aisle, between two masses of those burning-eyed human monsters. She felt the cold outside air like a vast drench of icy water flung upon her. If it had been raining, she might have gone toward the river.

But than that day New York had never been more radiantly the City of the Sun. How she got home she never knew, but late in the afternoon she realized that she was in her own room.

Hour after hour she lay upon the bed, body and mind inert. Helpless—no escape—no courage to live —yet no wish to die. How much longer would it last? Surely the waking from this dream must come soon.

About noon the next day Freddie came. "I let you off easy," said he. "Have you been drinking again?"

"No," she muttered.

He watched her with baffled, longing eyes. "What is it," he muttered, "that's so damn peculiar about you?"

It was the question every shrewd, observant person who saw her put to himself in one way or another; and there was excellent reason why this should have been.

Life has a certain set of molds—lawyer, financier, gambler, preacher, fashionable woman, prostitute, domestic woman, laborer, clerk, and so on through a not extensive list of familiar types with which we all soon become acquainted. And to one or another of these patterns life fits each of us as we grow up. Not one in ten thousand glances into human faces is arrested because it has lit upon a personality that cannot be immediately located, measured, accounted for. The reason for this sterility of variety which soon makes the world rather monotonous to the seeing eye is that few of us are born with any considerable amount of personality, and what little we have is speedily suppressed by a system of training which is throughout based upon an abhorrence of originality. We obey the law of nature—and nature so abhors variety that, when-

ever a variation from a type happens, she tries to kill
it, and, that failing, reproduces it a myriad times to
make it a type. When an original man or woman
appears and all the strenuous effort to suppress him
or her fails, straightway spring up a thousand imitators and copiers, and the individuality is lost in the
school, the fashion, the craze. We have not the courage to be ourselves, even where there is anything in us
that might be developed into something distinctive
enough to win us the rank of real identity. Individuality—distinction—where it does exist, almost never
shows until experience brings it out—just as up to a
certain stage the embryo of any animal is like that of
every other animal, though there is latent in it the
most positive assertion of race and sex, of family, type,
and so on.

Susan had from childhood possessed certain qualities of physical beauty, of spiritedness, of facility in
mind and body—the not uncommon characteristic of
the child that is the flower of passionate love. But now
there was beginning to show in her a radical difference
from the rest of the crowd pouring through the streets
of the city. It made the quicker observers in the passing throng turn the head for a second and wondering
glance. Most of them assumed they had been stirred
by her superiority of face and figure. But striking
faces and figures of the various comely types are frequent in the streets of New York and of several other
American cities. The truth was that they were interested by her expression—an elusive expression telling
of a soul that was being moved to its depths by experience which usually finds and molds mere passive material. This expression was as evident in her mouth
as in her eyes, in her profile as in her full face. And

as she sat there on the edge of the bed twisting up her thick dark hair, it was this expression that disconcerted Freddie Palmer, for the first time in all his contemptuous dealings with the female sex. In his eyes was a ferocious desire to seize her and try to conquer and to possess.

She had become almost unconscious of his presence. He startled her by suddenly crying, "Oh, you go to hell!" and flinging from the room, crashing the door shut behind him.

Susan's first horror of the men she met—men of all classes—was rapidly modified into an inconsistent, therefore characteristically human, mingling of horror and tolerance. Nobody, nothing, was either good or bad, but all veered like weathercocks in the shifting wind. She decided that people were steadily good only where their lot happened to be cast in a place in which the good wind held steadily, and that those who were usually bad simply had the misfortune to have to live where the prevailing winds were bad.

For instance, there was the handsome, well educated, well mannered young prize-fighter, Ned Ballou, who was Estelle's "friend." Ballou, big and gentle and as incapable of bad humor as of constancy or of honesty about money matters, fought under the name of Joe Geary, and was known as Upper Cut Joe because usually, in the third round, never later than the fifth, he gave the knockout to his opponent by a cruelly swift and savage uppercut. He had educated himself marvelously well. But he had been brought up among thieves and had by some curious freak never learned to know what a moral sense was, which is one—and a not unattractive—step deeper down than those who know what a moral sense is but never use it. At supper in Gaffney's he related to Susan and Estelle how he had won his greatest victory—the victory of Terry the Cyclone, that had lifted him up into the class of secure money-makers. He told how he always tried to "rattle" his opponent by talking to him, by pouring out in an undertone a stream of gibes, jeers, insults. The afternoon of the fight Terry's first-born had died, but the money for the funeral expenses, and to save the wife from the horrors and dangers of the free wards had to be earned. Joe Geary knew that he must win this fight or drop into the working or the criminal class. Terry was a "hard one"; so circumstances compelled those desperate measures which great men, from financiers and generals down to prize-fighters, do not shrink from—else they would not be great, but small.

As soon as he was facing Terry in the ring Joe—so he related with pride in his cleverness—began to "guy"—"Well, you Irish fake—so the kid's dead—eh?" and so on. And Terry, insane with grief and fury, fought wild—and Joe became a champion.

As she listened, Susan grew cold with horror and with hate. Estelle said:

"Tell the rest of it, Joe."

"Oh, that was nothing," replied he.

When he strolled away to talk with some friends Estelle told "the rest" that was "nothing." The championship secure, Joe had paid all Terry's bills, had supported Terry and his wife for a year, had relapsed into old habits and "pulled off a job" of safe-cracking because, the prize-fighting happening to pay poorly, he would have had a default on the payments for a month or so. He was caught, did a year on the Island before his "pull" could get him out. And all the time

141

he was in the "pen" he so arranged it with his friends that the invalid Terry and his invalid wife did not suffer. And all this he had done not because he had a sense of owing Terry, but because he was of the "set" in which it is the custom to help anybody who happens to need it, and aid begun becomes an obligation to "see it through."

It was an extreme case of the moral chaos about her —the chaos she had begun to discover when she caught her aunt and Ruth conspiring to take Sam away from her.

What a world! If only these shifting, usually evil winds of circumstance could be made to blow good!

A few evenings after the arrest, Maud came for Susan, persuaded her to go out. They dined at about the only good restaurant where unescorted women were served after nightfall. Afterward they went "on duty." It was fine overhead, and the air was cold and bracing—one of those marvelous New York winter nights which have the tonic of both sea and mountains and an exhilaration, in addition, from the intense bright-burning life of the mighty city. For more than a week there had been a steady downpour of snow, sleet, and finally rain.

They went into the back room of a saloon where perhaps half a dozen women were already seated, some of them gray with the cold against which their thin showy garments were no protection. Susan and Maud sat at a table in a corner; Maud broke her rule and drank whiskey with Susan. After they had taken perhaps half a dozen drinks, Maud grew really confidential. She always, even in her soberest moments, seemed to be telling everything she knew; but Susan had learned that there were in her many deep secrets, some of which not even liquor could unlock.

"I'm going to tell you something," she now said to Susan. "You must promise not to give me away."

"Don't tell me," replied Susan. She was used to being flattered—or victimized, according to the point of view—with confidences. She assumed Maud was about to confess some secret about her own self, as she had the almost universal habit of never thinking of anyone else. "Don't tell me," said she. "I'm tired of being used to air awful secrets. It makes me feel like a tenement wash line."

"This is about you," said Maud. "If it's ever found out that I put your wise, Jim'll have me killed. Yes—killed."

Susan, reckless by this time, laughed. "Oh, trash!" she said.

"No trash at all," insisted Maud. "When you know this town through and through you'll know that murder's something that can be arranged as easy as buying a drink. What risk is there in making one of *us* 'disappear'? None in the world. I always feel that Jim'll have me killed some day—unless I go crazy sometime and kill him. He's stuck on me—or, at least, he's jealous of me—and if he ever found out I had a lover—somebody—anybody that didn't pay—why, it'd be all up with me. Little Maud would go on the grill."

She ordered and slowly drank another whiskey before she recalled what she had set out to confide. By way of a fresh start she said, "What do you think of Freddie?"

"I don't know," replied Susan. And it was the truth. Her instinctive belief in a modified kind of fatalism made her judgments of people—even of those who caused her to suffer—singularly free from per-

143

sonal bitterness. Freddie, a mere instrument of destiny, had his good side, his human side, she knew. At his worst he was no worse than the others. And aside from his queer magnetism, there was a certain force in him that compelled her admiration; at least he was not one of the petty instruments of destiny. He had in him the same quality she felt gestating within herself. "I don't know what to think," she repeated.

Maud had been reflecting while Susan was casting about, as she had many a time before, for her real opinion of her master who was in turn the slave of Finnegan, who was in his turn the slave of somebody higher up, she didn't exactly know who—or why—or the why of any of it—or the why of the grotesque savage purposeless doings of destiny in general. Maud now burst out:

"I don't care. I'm going to put you wise if I die for it."

"Don't," said Susan. "I don't want to know."

"But I've *got* to tell you. Do you know what Freddie's going to do?"

Susan smiled disdainfully. "I don't care. You mustn't tell me—when you've been drinking this way."

"Finnegan's police judge is a man named Bennett. As soon as Bennett comes back to Jefferson Market Police Court, Freddie's going to have you sent up for three months."

Susan's glass was on the way to her lips. She set it down again. The drunken old wreck of an entertainer at the piano in the corner was bellowing out his favorite song—"I Am the King of the Vikings." Susan began to hum the air.

"It's gospel," cried Maud, thinking Susan did not believe her. "He's a queer one, is Freddie. They're all afraid of him. You'd think he was a coward, the way he bullies women and that. But somehow he ain't —not a bit. He'll be a big man in the organization some day, they all say. He never lets up till he gets square. And he thinks you're not square—after all he's done for you."

"Perhaps not—as he looks at it," said Susan.

"And Jim says he's crazy in love with you, and that he wants to put you where other men can't see you and where maybe he can get over caring about you. That's the real reason. He's a queer devil. But then all men are—though none quite like Freddie."

"So I'm to go to the Island for three months," said Susan reflectively.

"You don't seem to care. It's plain you never was there. . . . And you've got to go. There's no way out of it—unless you skip to another city. And if you did you never could come back here. Freddie'd see that you got yours as soon as you landed."

Susan sat looking at her glass. Maud watched her in astonishment. "You're as queer as Freddie," said she at length. "I never feel as if I was acquainted with you—not really. I never had a lady friend like that before. You don't seem to be a bit excited about what Freddie's going to do. Are you in love with him?"

Susan lifted strange, smiling eyes to Maud's curious gaze. "I—in *love*—with a *man*," she said slowly. And then she laughed.

"Don't laugh that way," cried Maud. "It gives me the creeps. What are you going to do?"

"What can I do?"

"Nothing."

"Then if there's nothing to do, I'll do nothing."

"Go to the Island for three months?"

Susan shrugged her shoulders. "I haven't gone yet." She rose. "It's too stuffy and smelly in here," said she. "Let's move out."

"No. I'll wait. I promised to meet a gentleman friend here. You'll not tell that I tipped you off?"

"You'd not have told me if you hadn't known I wouldn't."

"That's so. But—why don't you make it up with Freddie?"

"I couldn't do that."

"He's dead in love. I'm sure you could."

Again Susan's eyes became strange. "I'm sure I couldn't. Good night." She got as far as the door, came back. "Thank you for telling me."

"Oh, that's all right," murmured the girl. She was embarrassed by Susan's manner. She was frightened by Susan's eyes. "You ain't going to——" There she halted.

"What?"

"To jump off? Kill yourself?"

"Hardly," said Susan. "I've got a lot to do before I die."

She went directly home. Palmer was there.

She went to the bureau, unlocked the top drawer and took a bill she had there. She locked the drawer, tossed the key into an open box of hairpins. She moved toward the door.

"Where are you going?" asked he, still staring at the ceiling.

"What's the use of telling you? You'd not understand."

"Perhaps I would. I'm one-fourth Italian—and

146

they understand everything. . . . You're fond of reading, aren't you?"

"It passes the time."

"While I was waiting for you I glanced at your
new books—Emerson—Dickens—Zola." He was looking toward the row of paper backs that filled almost
the whole length of the mantel. "I must read them.
I always like your books. You spend nearly as much
time reading as I do—and you don't need it, for you've
got a good education. What do you read for? To
amuse yourself?"

"No."

"To get away from yourself?"

"No."

"Then why?" persisted he.

"To find out about myself."

He thought a moment, turned his face toward her.
"You *are* clever!" he said admiringly. "What's your
game?"

"My game?"

"What are you aiming for? You've got too much
sense not to be aiming for something."

She looked at him; the expression that marked her
as a person peculiar and apart was glowing in her
eyes like a bed of red-hot coals covered with ashes.

"What?" he repeated.

"To get strong," replied she. "Women are born
weak and bred weaker. I've got to get over being a
woman. For there isn't any place in this world for a
woman except under the shelter of some man. And I
don't want that." The underlying strength of her
features abruptly came into view. "And I won't have
it," she added.

He laughed. "But the men'll never let *you* be anything but a woman."

"We'll see," said she, smiling. The strong look had vanished into the soft contour of her beautiful youth.

"Personally, I like you better when you've been drinking," he went on. "You're sad when you're sober. As you drink you liven up."

"When I get over being sad if I'm sober, when I learn to take things as they come, just like a man—a strong man, then I'll be——" She stopped.

"Be what?"

"Ready."

"Ready for what?"

"How do I know?"

He swung himself to a sitting position. "Meanwhile, you're coming to live with me. I've been fighting against it, but I give up. I need you. You're the one I've been looking for. Pack your traps. I'll call a cab and we'll go over to my flat. Then we'll go to Rector's and celebrate."

She shook her head. "I'm sorry, but I can't."

"Why not?"

"I told you. There's something in me that won't let me."

An hour later, when he was asleep, she changed to her plainest dress. Leaving her discarded blouse on the bed beside him where she had flung it down after tearing it off, she turned out the light, darted down stairs and into the street. At Times Square she took the Subway for the Bowery. To change one's world, one need not travel far in New York; the ocean is not so wide as is the gap between the Tenderloin and the lower East Side.

148

VIII

SHE had thought of escape daily, hourly almost, for nearly five months. She had advanced not an inch toward it; but she never for an instant lost hope. She believed in her destiny, felt with all the strength of her health and vitality that she had not yet found her place in the world, that she would find it, and that it would be high. Now—she was compelled to escape, and this with only seventeen dollars and in the little time that would elapse before Palmer returned to consciousness and started in pursuit, bent upon cruel and complete revenge. She changed to an express train at the Grand Central Subway station, left the express on impulse at Fourteenth Street, took a local to Astor Place, there ascended to the street.

She was far indeed from the Tenderloin, in a region not visited by the people she knew. As for Freddie, he never went below Fourteenth Street, hated the lower East Side, avoided anyone from that region of his early days, now shrouded in a mystery that would not be dispelled with his consent. Freddie would not think of searching for her there; and soon he would believe she was dead—drowned, and at the bottom of river or bay. As she stepped from the exit of the underground, she saw in the square before her, under the Sunset Cox statue, a Salvation Army corps holding a meeting. She heard a cry from the center of the crowd:

"The wages of sin is death!"

She drifted into the fringe of the crowd and glanced at the little group of exhorters and musicians. The

woman who was preaching had taken the life of the
streets as her text. Well fed and well clad and certain
of a clean room to sleep in—certain of a good living,
she was painting the moral horrors of the street life.

"The wages of sin is death!" she shouted.

She caught Susan's eye, saw the cynical-bitter smile
round her lips. For Susan had the feeling that, unsuspected by the upper classes, animates the masses as
to clergy and charity workers of all kinds—much the
same feeling one would have toward the robber's mes-
senger who came bringing from his master as a loving
gift some worthless trifle from the stolen goods. Not
from clergy, not from charity worker, not from the life
of the poor as they take what is given them with hypocritical cringe and tear of thanks, will the upper classes
get the truth as to what is thought of them by the
masses in this day of awakening intelligence and slow
heaving of crusts so long firm that they have come to
be regarded as bed-rock of social foundation.

Cried the woman, in response to Susan's satirical
look:

"You mock at that, my lovely young sister. Your
lips are painted, and they sneer. But you know I'm
right—yes, you show in your eyes that you know it
in your aching heart! The wages of sin is *death!*
Isn't that so, sister?"

Susan shook her head.

"Speak the truth, sister! God is watching you. The
wages of sin is *death!*"

"The wages of weakness is death," retorted Susan.
"But—the wages of sin—well, it's sometimes a house
in Fifth Avenue."

And then she shrank away before the approving
laughter of the little crowd and hurried across into

Eighth Street. In the deep shadow of the front of
Cooper Union she paused, as the meaning of her own
impulsive words came to her. The wages of sin! And
what was sin, the supreme sin, but weakness? It was
exactly as Burlingham had explained. He had said
that, whether for good or for evil, really to live one
must be strong. Strong!

What a good teacher he had been—one of the rare
kind that not only said things interestingly but also
said them so that you never forgot. How badly she
had learned!

She strolled on through Eighth Street, across Third
Avenue and into Second Avenue. It was ten o'clock.
The effects of the liquor she had drunk had worn away.
In so much wandering she had acquired the habit of
closing up an episode of life as a traveler puts behind
him the railway journey at its end. She was less than
half an hour from her life in the Tenderloin; it was as
completely in her past as it would ever be. The cards
had once more been shuffled; a new deal was on.

A new deal. What? To fly to another city—that
meant another Palmer, or the miseries of the unprotected woman of the streets, or slavery to the madman
of what the French with cruel irony call a *maison de
joie*. To return to work——

No—not work—never again.

A new deal! And a new deal meant at least even
chance for good luck.

As she drifted down the west side of Second Avenue,
her thoughts so absorbed her that she was oblivious of
the slushy sidewalk, even of the crossings where one
had to pick one's way as through a shallow creek with
stepping stones here and there. There were many
women alone, as in every other avenue and every fre-

quented cross street throughout the city—women made eager to desperation by the long stretch of impossible weather. Every passing man was hailed, sometimes boldly, sometimes softly. Again and again that grotesque phrase, "Let's go have a good time," fell upon the ears. After several blocks, when her absent-mindedness had got her legs wet to the knees in the shallow shiny slush, she was roused by the sound of music—an orchestra playing and playing well a lively Hungarian dance. She was standing before the winter garden from which the sounds came. As she opened the door she was greeted by a rush of warm air pleasantly scented with fresh tobacco smoke, the odors of spiced drinks and of food, pastry predominating. Some of the tables were covered ready for those who would wish to eat; but many of them were for the drinkers. The large, low-ceilinged room was comfortably filled. There were but a few women and they seemed to be wives or sweethearts. Susan was about to retreat when a waiter —one of those Austrians whose heads end abruptly an inch or so above the eyebrows and whose chins soon shade off into neck—advanced smilingly with a polite, "We serve ladies without escorts."

She chose a table that had several other vacant tables round it. On the recommendation of the waiter she ordered a "burning devil"; he assured her she would find it delicious and the very thing for a cold slushy night. At the far end of the room on a low platform sat the orchestra. A man in an evening suit many sizes too large for him sang in a strong, not disagreeable tenor a German song that drew loud applause at the end of each stanza. The "burning devil" came—an almost black mixture in a large heavy glass. The waiter touched a match to it, and it was at once wreathed in pale flickering flames that hovered like butterflies, now rising as if to float away, now lightly descending to flit over the surface of the liquid or to dance along the edge of the glass.

"What shall I do with it?" said Susan.

"Wait till it goes out," said the waiter. "Then drink, as you would anything else." And he was off to attend to the wants of a group of card players a few feet away.

Susan touched her finger to the glass, when the flame suddenly vanished. She found it was not too hot to drink, touched her lips to it. The taste, sweetish, suggestive of coffee and of brandy and of burnt sugar, was agreeable. She slowly sipped it, delighting in the sensation of warmth, of comfort, of well being that speedily diffused through her. The waiter came to receive her thanks for his advice. She said to him:

"Do you have women sing, too?"

"Oh, yes—when we can find a good-looker with a voice. Our customers know music."

"I wonder if I could get a trial?"

The waiter was interested at once. "Perhaps. You sing?"

"I have sung on the stage."

"I'll ask the boss."

He went to the counter near the door where stood a short thick-set Jew of the East European snub-nosed type in earnest conversation with a seated blonde woman. She showed that skill at clinging to youth which among the lower middle and lower classes pretty clearly indicates at least some experience at the fast life. For only in the upper and upper middle class does a respectable woman venture thus to advertise so suspcious a guest within as a desire to be agreeable in the sight of men. Susan watched the waiter as he spoke to the proprietor, saw the proprietor's impatient shake of the head, sent out a wave of gratitude from her heart when her waiter friend persisted, compelled the proprietor to look toward her. She affected an air of unconsciousness; in fact, she was posing as if before a camera. Her heart leaped when out of the corner of her eye she saw the proprietor coming with the waiter. The two paused at her table, and the proprietor said in a sharp, impatient voice:

"Well, lady—what is it?"

"I want a trial as a singer."

The proprietor was scanning her features and her figure which was well displayed by the tight-fitting jacket. The result seemed satisfactory, for in a voice oily with the softening influence of feminine charm upon male, he said:

"You've had experience?"

"Yes—a lot of it. But I haven't sung in about two years."

"Sing German?"

"Only ballads in English. But I can learn anything."

"English'll do—*if* you can *sing*. What costume do you wear?" And the proprietor seated himself and motioned the waiter away.

"I have no costume. As I told you, I've not been singing lately."

"We've got one that might fit—a short blue silk skirt—low neck and blue stockings. Slippers too, but they might be tight—I forget the number."

"I did wear threes. But I've done a great deal of walking. I wear a five now." Susan thrust out a foot

154

and ankle, for she knew that despite the overshoe they were good to look at.

The proprietor nodded approvingly and there was the note of personal interest in his voice as he said: "They can try your voice tomorrow morning. Come at ten o'clock."

"If you decide to try me, what pay will I get?"

The proprietor smiled slyly. "Oh, we don't pay anything to the singers. That man who sang—he gets his board here. He works in a factory as a bookkeeper in the daytime. Lots of theatrical and musical people come here. If a man or a girl can do any stunt worth while, there's a chance."

"I'd have to have something more than board," said Susan.

The proprietor frowned down at his stubby fingers whose black and cracked nails were drumming on the table. "Well—I might give you a bed. There's a place I could put one in my daughter's room. She sings and dances over at Louis Blanc's garden in Third Avenue. Yes, I could put you there. But—no privileges, you understand."

"Certainly. . . . I'll decide tomorrow. Maybe you'll not want me."

"I suppose there isn't any work I could do in the daytime?"

"Not here."

"Perhaps——"

"Not nowhere, so far as I know. That is, work you'd care to do. The factories and stores is hard on a woman, and she don't get much. And besides they ain't very classy to my notion. Of course, if a woman ain't got looks or sense or any tone to her, if she's satisfied to live in a bum tenement and marry some dub that can't make nothing, why, that's different. But you look like a woman that had been used to something and wanted to get somewhere. I wouldn't have let *my* daughter go into no such low, foolish life."

She had intended to ask about a place to stop for the night. She now decided that the suggestion that she was homeless might possibly impair her chances. After some further conversation—the proprietor repeating what he had already said, and repeating it in about the same language—she paid the waiter fifteen cents for the drink and a tip of five cents out of the change she had in her purse, and departed. It had clouded over, and a misty, dismal rain was trickling through the saturated air to add to the messiness of the churn of cold slush. Susan went on down Second Avenue. On a corner near its lower end she saw a Raines Law hotel with awnings, indicating that it was not merely a blind to give a saloon a hotel license but was actually open for business. She went into the "family" entrance of the saloon, was alone in a small clean sitting-room with a sliding window between it and the bar. A tough but not unpleasant young face appeared at the window. It was the bartender.

"Evening, cutie," said he. "What'll you have?"

"Some rye whiskey," replied Susan. "May I smoke a cigarette here?"

"Sure, go as far as you like. Ten-cent whiskey—or fifteen?"

"Fifteen—unless it's out of the same bottle as the ten."

"Call it ten—seeing as you are a lady. I've got a soft heart for you ladies. I've got a wife in the business, myself."

When he came in at the door with the drink, a young man followed him—a good-looking, darkish youth, well dressed in a ready made suit of the best sort. At second glance Susan saw that he was at least partly of Jewish blood, enough to elevate his face above the rather dull type which predominates among clerks and merchants of the Christian races. He had small, shifty eyes, an attractive smile, a manner of assurance bordering on insolence. He dropped into a chair at Susan's table with a, "You don't mind having a drink on me."

As Susan had no money to spare, she acquiesced. She said to the bartender, "I want to get a room here—a plain room. How much?"

"Maybe this gent'll help you out," said the bartender with a grin and a wink. "He's got money to burn—and burns it."

The bartender withdrew. The young man struck a match and held it for her to light the cigarette she took from her purse. Then he lit one himself. "Next time try one of mine," said he. "I get 'em of a fellow that makes for the swellest uptown houses. But I get 'em ten cents a package instead of forty. I haven't seen you down here before. What a good skin you've got! It's been a long time since I've seen a skin as fine as that, except on a baby now and then. And that shape of yours is all right, too. I suppose it's the real goods?"

Susan shrugged her shoulders. "Why not?" asked she carelessly.

She did not look forward with pleasure to being alone. The man was clean and well dressed, and had an unusual amount of personal charm that softened his impertinence of manner. Evidently he had the habit

of success with women. She much preferred him sitting
with her to her own depressing society. So she accepted his invitation. She took one of his cigarettes,
and it was as good as he had said. He rattled on,
mingling frank coarse compliments with talk about
"the business" from a standpoint so practical that she
began to suspect he was somehow in it himself. He
clearly belonged to those more intelligent children of
the upper class tenement people, the children who are
too bright and too well educated to become working--
men and working women like their parents; they refuse
to do any kind of manual labor, as it could never in
the most favorable circumstances pay well enough to
give them the higher comforts they crave, the expensive
comforts which every merchant is insistently and tempt-
ingly thrusting at a public for the most part too poor
to buy; so these cleverer children of the working class
develop into shyster lawyers, politicians, sports, prostitutes, unless chance throws into their way some respectable means of getting money. Vaguely she wondered—without caring to question or guess what particular form of activity this young man had taken in
avoiding monotonous work at small pay.

After her second drink came she found that she did
not want it. She felt tired and sleepy and wished to
get her wet stockings off and to dry her skirt which,
for all her careful holding up, had not escaped the
fate of whatever was exposed to that abominable night.
"I'm going along with you," said the young man
as she rose. "Here's to our better acquaintance."

"Thanks, but I want to be alone," replied she af-
fably. And, not to seem unappreciative of his courtesy, she took a small drink from her glass. It tasted
very queer. She glanced suspiciously at the young

man. Her legs grew suddenly and strangely heavy; her heart began to beat violently, and a black fog seemed to be closing in upon her eyes. Through it she saw the youth grinning sardonically. And instantly she knew. "What a fool I am!" she thought.

She had been trapped by another form of the slave system. This man was a recruiting sergeant for houses of prostitution—was one of the "cadets." They search the tenement districts for good-looking girls and young women. They hang about the street corners, flirting. They attend the balls where go the young people of the lower middle class and upper lower class. They learn to make love seductively; they understand how to tempt a girl's longing for finery, for an easier life, her dream of a husband above her class in looks and in earning power. And for each recruit "broken in" and hardened to the point of willingness to go into a sporting house, they get from the proprietor ten to twenty-five dollars according to her youth and beauty. Susan knew all about the system, had heard stories of it from the lips of girls who had been embarked through it—embarked a little sooner than they would have embarked under the lash of want, or of that other and almost equally compelling brute, desire for the comforts and luxuries that mean decent living. Susan knew; yet here she was, because of an unguarded moment, and because of a sense of security through experience— here she was, succumbing to knockout drops as easily as the most innocent child lured away from its mother's door to get a saucer of ice cream! She tried to rise, to scream, though she knew any such effort was futile.

With a gasp and a sigh her head fell forward and she was unconscious.

She awakened in a small, rather dingy room. She was lying on the bed. Beyond the foot of the bed stood a man, his back to her.

With a groan Susan lifted herself to a sitting position, drew the spread about her—a gesture of instinct rather than of conscious modesty. "They drugged me and brought me here," said she. "I want you to help me get out."

"Good Lord!" cried the man, instantly all a-quiver with nervousness. "I'm a married man. I don't want to get mixed up in this." And out of the room he bolted, closing the door behind him.

Susan smiled at herself satirically. After all her experience, to make this silly appeal—she who knew men! "I must be getting feeble-minded," thought she. Then——

Her clothes! With a glance she swept the little room. No closet! Her own clothes gone! On the chair beside the bed a fast-house parlor dress of pink cotton silk, and a kind of abbreviated chemise. The stockings on her legs were not her own, but were of pink cotton, silk finished. A pair of pink satin slippers stood on the floor beside the two galvanized iron wash basins.

A few minutes later in came the madam. Susan, exhausted, sick, lay inert in the middle of the bed. She fixed her gaze upon the eyes looking through the hideous mask of paint and powder partially concealing the madam's face.

"Well, are you going to be a good girl now?" said the madam.

Susan interrupted her with a laugh. "Oh, come off," said she. "I'll not stand for that. I'll go back to Jim Finnegan."

The old woman's eyes pounced for her face instantly. "Do you know Finnegan?"

"I'm his girl," said Susan carelessly.

The madam gave a kind of howl. "You're Finnegan's girl, and he'll make trouble for me."

"He's got a nasty streak in him," said Susan drowsily. She laughed, yawned. "Put out the light."

"No, I won't put out the light," shrieked the madam. "I'm going to telephone Jim Finnegan to come and get you."

Susan started up angrily, as if she were half-crazed by drink.

"Do get dressed, dear," wheedled the madam, handing her her own clothing again.

Susan dressed with the utmost deliberation, the madam urging her to make haste. After some argument, Susan yielded to the madam's pleadings and contented herself with the twenty dollars. The madam herself escorted Susan down to the outside door and slathered her with sweetness and politeness. The rain had stopped again. Susan went up Second Avenue slowly. Two blocks from the dive from which she had escaped, she sank down on a stoop and fainted.

IX

THE dash of cold rain drops upon her face and the chill of moisture soaking through her clothing revived her. Throughout the whole range of life, whenever we resist we suffer. As Susan dragged her aching, cold wet body up from that stoop, it seemed to her that each time she resisted the penalty grew heavier. Could she have been more wretched had she remained in that dive? From her first rebellion that drove her out of her uncle's house had she ever bettered herself by resisting? She had gone from bad to worse, from worse to worst.

Worst? "This *must* be the worst!" she thought. "Surely there can be no lower depth than where I am now." And then she shuddered and her soul reeled. Had she not thought this at each shelf of the precipice down which she had been falling? "Has it a bottom? Is there no bottom?"

Wet through, tired through, she put up her umbrella and forced herself feebly along. "Where am I going? Why do I not kill myself? What is it that drives me on and on?"

There came no direct answer to that last question. But up from those deep vast reservoirs of vitality that seemed sufficient whatever the drain upon them—up from those reservoirs welled strength and that unfaltering will to live which breathes upon the corpse of hope and quickens it. And she had a sense of an invisible being, a power that had her in charge, a destiny, walking beside her, holding up her drooping strength, compelling her toward some goal hidden in the fog and the storm.

At Eighth Street she turned west; at Third Avenue she paused, waiting for chance to direct her. Was it not like the maliciousness of fate that in the city whose rarely interrupted reign of joyous sunshine made her call it the city of the Sun her critical turn of chance should have fallen in foul weather? Evidently fate was resolved on a thorough test of her endurance. In the open square, near the Peter Cooper statue, stood a huge all-night lunch wagon. She moved toward it, for she suddenly felt hungry. It was drawn to the curb; a short flight of ladder steps led to an interior attractive to sight and smell. She halted at the foot of the steps and looked in. The only occupant was the man in charge. In a white coat he was leaning upon the counter, reading a newspaper which lay flat upon it. His bent head was extensively and roughly thatched with black hair so thick that to draw a comb through it would have been all but impossible. As Susan let down her umbrella and began to ascend, he lifted his head and gave her a full view of a humorous young face, bushy of eyebrows and mustache and darkly stained by his beard, close shaven though it was. He looked like a Spaniard or an Italian, but he was a black Irishman, one of the West coasters who recall in their eyes and coloring the wrecking of the Armada.

"Good morning, lady," said he. "Breakfast or supper?"

"Both," replied Susan. "I'm starved."

The air was gratefully warm in the little restaurant on wheels. The dominant odor was of hot coffee; but that aroma was carried to a still higher delight by a suggestion of pastry. "The best thing I've got," said the restaurant man, "is hot corn beef hash. It's so good I hate to let any of it go. You can have griddle cakes, too—and coffee, of course."

"Very well," said Susan.

She was ascending upon a wave of reaction from the events of the night. Her headache had gone. The rain beating upon the roof seemed musical to her now, in this warm shelter with its certainty of the food she craved.

The young man was busy at the shiny, compact stove; the odors of the good things she was presently to have grew stronger and stronger, stimulating her hunger, bringing joy to her heart and a smile to her eyes. She wondered at herself. After what she had passed through, how could she feel thus happy— yes, positively happy? It seemed to her this was an indication of a lack in her somewhere—of seriousness, of sensibility, of she knew not what. She ought to be ashamed of that lack. But she was not ashamed. She was shedding her troubles like a child—or like a philosopher.

"Do you like hash?" inquired the restaurant man over his shoulder.

"Just as you're making it," said she. "Dry but not too dry. Brown but not too brown."

"You don't think you'd like a poached egg on top of it?"

"Exactly what I want!"

"It isn't everybody that can poach an egg," said the restaurant man. "And it isn't every egg that can be poached. Now, my eggs are the real thing. And I can poach 'em so you'd think they was done with one of them poaching machines. I don't have 'em with the yellow on a slab of white. I do it so that the white's all round the yellow, like in the shell. And I keep 'em tender, too. Did you say one egg or a pair?"

"Two," said Susan.

The dishes were thick, but clean and whole. The hash—"dry but not too dry, brown but not too brown" —was artistically arranged on its platter, and the two eggs that adorned its top were precisely as he had promised. The coffee, boiled with the milk, was real coffee, too. When the restaurant man had set these things before her, as she sat expectant on a stool, he viewed his handiwork with admiring eyes.

"Delmonico couldn't beat it," said he. "No, nor Oscar, neither. That'll take the tired look out of your face, lady, and bring the beauty back."

Susan ate slowly, listening to the music of the beating rain. It was like an oasis, a restful halt between two stretches of desert journey; she wished to make it as long as possible. Only those who live exposed to life's buffetings ever learn to enjoy to the full the great little pleasures of life—the halcyon pauses in the storms —the few bright rays through the break in the clouds, the joy of food after hunger, of a bath after days of privation, of a jest or a smiling face or a kind word or deed after darkness and bitterness and contempt. She saw the restaurant man's eyes on her, a curious expression in them.

"What's the matter?" she inquired.

"I was thinking," said he, "how miserable you must have been to be so happy now."

"Oh, I guess none of us has any too easy a time," said she.

"But it's mighty hard on women. I used to think different, before I had bad luck and got down to tending this lunch wagon. But now I understand about a lot of things. It's all very well for comfortable people to talk about what a man or a woman ought to do and oughtn't to do. But let 'em be slammed up against it. They'd sing a different song—wouldn't they?"

"Quite different," said Susan.

The man waved a griddle spoon. "I tell you, we do what we've got to do. Yes—the thieves and—and—all of us. Some's used for foundations and some for roofing and some for inside fancy work and some for outside wall. And some's used for the rubbish heap. But all's used. They do what they've got to do. I was a great hand at worrying what I was going to be used for. But I don't bother about it any more." He began to pour the griddle cake dough. "I think I'll get there, though," said he doggedly, as if he expected to be derided for vanity.

"You will," said Susan.

"I'm twenty-nine. But I've been being got ready for something. They don't chip away at a stone as they have at me without intending to make some use of it."

"No, indeed," said the girl, hope and faith welling up in her own heart.

"And what's more, I've stood the chipping. I ain't become rubbish; I'm still a good stone. That's promising, ain't it?"

"It's a sure sign," declared Susan. Sure for herself, no less than for him.

The restaurant man took from under the counter several well-worn schoolbooks. He held them up, looked at Susan and winked. "Good business—eh?"

She laughed and nodded. He put the books back under the counter, finished the cakes and served them. As he gave her more butter he said:

"It ain't the best butter—not by a long shot. But

it's good—as good as you get on the average farm—or better. Did you ever eat the best butter?"

"I don't know. I've had some that was very good."

"Eighty cents a pound?"

"Mercy, no," exclaimed Susan.

"Awful price, isn't it? But worth the money—yes, sir! Some time when you've got a little change to spare, go get half a pound at one of the swell groceries or dairies. And the best milk, too. Twelve cents a quart. Wait till I get money. I'll show 'em how to live. I was born in a tenement. Never had nothing. Rags to wear, and food one notch above a garbage barrel."

"I know," said Susan.

"But even as a boy I wanted the high-class things. It's wanting the best that makes a man push his way up."

Another customer came—a keeper of a butcher shop, on his way to market. Susan finished the cakes, paid the forty cents and prepared to depart. "I'm looking for a hotel," said she to the restaurant man, "one where they'll take me in at this time, but one that's safe—not a dive."

"Right across the square there's a Salvation Army shelter—very good—clean. I don't know of any other place for a lady."

"There's a hotel on the next corner," put in the butcher, suspending the violent smacking and sipping which attended his taking rolls and coffee. "It ain't neither the one thing nor the other. It's clean and cheap, and they'll let you behave if you want to."

"That's all I ask," said the girl. "Thank you." And she departed, after an exchange of friendly glances with the restaurant man. "I feel lots better," said she.

"It was a good breakfast," replied he.

"That was only part. Good luck!"

"Same to you, lady. Call again. Try my chops."

At the corner the butcher had indicated Susan found the usual Raines Law hotel, adjunct to a saloon and open to all comers, however "transient." But she took the butcher's word for it, engaged a dollar-and-a-half room from the half-asleep clerk, was shown to it by a colored bellboy who did not bother to wake up. It was a nice little room with barely space enough for a bed, a bureau, a stationary washstand, a chair and a small radiator. As she undressed by the light of a sad gray dawn, she examined her dress to see how far it needed repair and how far it might be repaired. She had worn away from Forty-third Street her cheapest dress because it happened to be of an inconspicuous blue. It was one of those suits that look fairly well at a glance on the wax figure in the department store window, that lose their bloom as quickly as a country bride, and at the fourth or fifth wearing begin to make frank and sweeping confession of the cheapness of every bit of the material and labor that went into them. These suits are typical of all that poverty compels upon the poor, all that they in their ignorance and inexperience of values accept without complaint, fancying they are getting money's worth and never dreaming they are more extravagant than the most prodigal of the rich. However, as their poverty gives them no choice, their ignorance saves them from futilities of angry discontent. Susan had bought this dress because she had to have another dress and could not afford to spend more than twelve dollars, and it had been marked down from twenty-five. She had worn it in fair weather and had contrived to keep it looking pretty well. But this rain had finished it quite. Thereafter, until she could get another dress, she must expect to be classed as poor and seedy—therefore, on the way toward deeper poverty—therefore, an object of pity and of prey. If she went into a shop, she would be treated insultingly by the shopgirls, despising her as a poor creature like themselves. If a man approached her, he would calculate upon getting her very cheap because a girl in such a costume could not have been in the habit of receiving any great sum. And if she went with him, he would treat her with far less consideration than if she had been about the same business in smarter attire.

She spread the dress on bureau and chair, smoothing it, wiping the mud stains from it. She washed out her stockings at the stationary stand, got them as dry as her remarkably strong hands could wring them, hung them on a rung of the chair near the hot little radiator. She cleaned her boots and overshoes with an old newspaper she found in a drawer, and wet at the washstand. She took her hat to pieces and made it over into something that looked almost fresh enough to be new. Then, ready for bed, she got the office of the hotel on the telephone and left a call for half-past nine o'clock —three hours and a half away. When she was throwing up the window, she glanced into the street.

The rain had once more ceased. Through the gray dimness the men and women, boys and girls, on the way to the factories and shops for the day's work, were streaming past in funereal procession. Some of the young ones were lively. But the mass was sullen and dreary. Bodies wrecked or rapidly wrecking by ignorance of hygiene, by the foul air and foul food of the tenements, by the monotonous toil of factory and shop —mindless toil—toil that took away mind and put in its place a distaste for all improvement—toil of the factories that distorted the body and enveloped the soul in sodden stupidity—toil of the shops that meant breathing bad air all day long, meant stooped shoulders and varicose veins in the legs and the arches of the insteps broken down, meant dull eyes, bad skin, female complaints, meant the breeding of desires for the luxury the shops display, the breeding of envy and servility toward those able to buy these luxuries.

Susan lingered, fascinated by this exhibit of the price to the many of civilization for the few. Work? Never! Not any more than she would. "Work" in a dive! Work—either branch of it, factory and shop or dive—meant the sale of all the body and all the soul; her profession—at least as she practiced it—meant that perhaps she could buy with part of body and part of soul the privilege of keeping the rest of both for her own self. If she had stayed on at work from the beginning in Cincinnati, where would she be now? Living in some stinking tenement hole, with hope dead. And how would she be looking? As dull of eye as the rest, as pasty and mottled of skin, as ready for any chance disease. Work? Never! Never! "Not at anything that'd degrade me more than this life. Yes—more." And she lifted her head defiantly. To her hunger Life was thus far offering only a plate of rotten apples; it was difficult to choose among them—but there was choice.

She was awakened by the telephone bell; and it kept on ringing until she got up and spoke to the office through the sender. Never had she so craved sleep; and her mental and physical contentment of three hours and a half before had been succeeded by headache, a general soreness, a horrible attack of the blues. She grew somewhat better, however, as she washed first in hot water, then in cold at the stationary stand which was quite as efficient if not so luxurious as a bathtub. She dressed in a rush, but not so hurriedly that she failed to make the best toilet the circumstances permitted. Her hair went up unusually well; the dress did not look so badly as she had feared it would. "As it's a nasty day," she reflected, "it won't do me so much damage. My hat and my boots will make them give me the benefit of the doubt and think I'm saving my good clothes."

She passed through the office at five minutes to ten. When she reached Lange's winter garden, its clock said ten minutes past ten, but she knew it must be fast. Only one of the four musicians had arrived—the man who played the drums, cymbals, triangle and xylophone —a fat, discouraged old man who knew how easily he could be replaced. Neither Lange nor his wife had come; her original friend, the Austrian waiter, was wiping off tables and cleaning match stands. He welcomed her with a smile of delight that showed how few teeth remained in the front of his mouth and how deeply yellow they were. But Susan saw only his eyes —and the kind heart that looked through them.

"Maybe you haven't had breakfast already?" he suggested.

"I'm not hungry, thank you."

"Perhaps some coffee—yes?"

Susan thought the coffee would make her feel better. So he brought it—Vienna fashion—an open china pot full of strong, deliciously aromatic black coffee, a jug of milk with whipped white of egg on top, a basket of small sweet rolls powdered with sugar and caraway seed. She ate one of the rolls, drank the coffee. Before she had finished, the waiter stood beaming before her and said:

"A cigarette—yes?"

"Oh, no," replied Susan, a little sadly.

"But yes," urged he. "It isn't against the rules. The boss's wife smokes. Many ladies who come here do—real ladies. It is the custom in Europe. Why not?" And he produced a box of cigarettes and put it on the table. Susan lit one of them and once more with supreme physical content came a cheerfulness that put color and sprightliness into the flowers of hope. And the sun had won its battle with the storm; the storm was in retreat. Sunshine was streaming in at the windows, into her heart. The waiter paused in his work now and then to enjoy himself in contemplating the charming picture she made. She was thinking of what the wagon restaurant man had said. Yes, Life had been chipping away at her; but she had remained good stone, had not become rubbish.

About half-past ten Lange came down from his flat which was overhead. He inspected her by daylight and finding that his electric light impressions were not delusion was highly pleased with her. He refused to allow her to pay for the coffee. "Johann!" he called, and the leader of the orchestra approached and made a respectful bow to his employer. He had a solemn pompous air and the usual pompadour. He and Susan plunged into the music question, found that the only song they both knew was Tosti's "Good Bye."

"That'll do to try," said Lange. "Begin!"

And after a little tuning and voice testing, Susan sang the "Good Bye" with full orchestra accompaniment. It was not good; it was not even pretty good; but it was not bad. "You'll do all right," said Lange.

"You can stay. Now, you and Johann fix up some songs and get ready for tonight." And he turned away to buy supplies for restaurant and bar.

Johann, deeply sentimental by nature, was much pleased with Susan's contralto. "You do not know how to sing," said he. "You sing in your throat and you've got all the faults of parlor singers. But the voice is there—and much expressiveness—much temperament. Also, you have intelligence—and that will make a very little voice go a great way."

Before proceeding any further with the rehearsal, he took Susan up to a shop where sheet music was sold and they selected three simple songs: "Gipsy Queen," "Star of My Life" and "Love in Dreams." They were to try "Gipsy Queen" that night, with "Good Bye" and, if the applause should compel, "Suwanee River."

When they were back at the restaurant Susan seated herself in a quiet corner and proceeded to learn the words of the song and to get some notion of the tune.

She had lunch with Mr. and Mrs. Lange and Katy, whose hair was very golden indeed and whose voice and manner proclaimed the Bowery and its vaudeville stage. She began by being grand with Susan, but had far too good a heart and far too sensible a nature to keep up long. It takes more vanity, more solemn stupidity and more leisure than plain people have time for, to maintain the force of fake dignity. Before lunch was over it was Katy and Lorna; and Katy was distressed that her duties at the theater made it impossible for her to stay and help Lorna with the song.

At the afternoon rehearsal Susan distinguished herself. To permit business in the restaurant and the rehearsal at the same time, there was a curtain to divide the big room into two unequal parts. When Susan sang her song through for the first time complete, the men smoking and drinking on the other side of the curtain burst into applause. Johann shook hands with Susan, shook hands again, kissed her hand, patted her shoulder. But in the evening things did not go so well.

Susan, badly frightened, got away from the orchestra, lagged when it speeded to catch up with her. She made a pretty and engaging figure in the costume, low in the neck and ending at the knees. Her face and shoulders, her arms and legs, the lines of her slender, rounded body made a success. But they barely saved her from being laughed at. When she finished, there was no applause—so no necessity for an encore. She ran upstairs, and, with nerves all a-quiver, hid herself in the little room she and Katy were to share. Until she failed she did not realize how much she had staked upon this venture. But now she knew; and it seemed to her that her only future was the streets. Again her chance had come; again she had thrown it away. If there were anything in her—anything but mere vain hopes—that could not have occurred. In her plight anyone with a spark of the divinity that achieves success would have scored. "I belong in the streets," said she. Before dinner she had gone out and had bought a ninety-five cent night-dress and some toilet articles. These she now bundled together again. She changed to her street dress; she stole down the stairs.

She was out at the side door, she was flying through the side street toward the Bowery. "Hi!" shouted someone behind her. "Where you going?" And overtaking her came her staunch friend Albert, the waiter. Feeling that she must need sympathy and encouragement, he had slipped away from his duties to go up to her. He had reached the hall in time to see what she was about and had darted bareheaded after her.

"Where you going?" he repeated, excitedly.

A crowd began to gather. "Oh, good-by," she cried. "I'm getting out before I'm told to go—that's all. I made a failure. Thank you, Albert." She put out her hand; she was still moving and looking in the direction of the Bowery.

"Now you mustn't be foolish," said he, holding on tightly to her hand. "The boss says it's all right. Tomorrow you do better."

"I'd never dare try again."

"Tomorrow makes everything all right. You mustn't act like a baby. The first time Katy tried, they yelled her off the stage. Now she gets eleven a week. Come back right away with me. The boss'd be mad if you won't. You ain't acting right, Miss Lorna. I didn't think you was such a fool."

He had her attention now. Unmindful of the little crowd they had gathered, they stood there discussing until to save Albert from pneumonia she returned with him. He saw her started up the stairs, then ventured to take his eye off her long enough to put his head into the winter garden and send a waiter for Lange. He stood guard until Lange came and was on his way to her.

The next evening, a Saturday, before a crowded house she sang well, as well as she had ever sung in her life—sang well enough to give her beauty of face and figure, her sweetness, her charm the opportunity to win a success. She had to come back and sing "Suwanee River." She had to come for a second encore; and, flushed with her victory over her timidity, she sang Tosti's sad cry of everlasting farewell with all the tenderness there was in her. That song exactly fitted her passionate, melancholy voice; its words harmonized with the deep sadness that was her real self, that is the real self of every sensitive soul this world has ever tried with its exquisite torments for flesh and spirit. The tears that cannot be shed were in her voice, in her face, as she stood there, with her violet-gray eyes straining into vacancy. But the men and the women shed tears; and when she moved, breaking the spell of silence, they not only applauded, they cheered.

The news quickly spread that at Lange's there was a girl singer worth hearing and still more worth looking at. And Lange had his opportunity to arrive.

But several things stood in his way, things a man of far more intelligence would have found it hard to overcome.

Like nearly all saloon-keepers, he was serf to a brewery; and the particular brewery whose beer his mortgage compelled him to push did not make a beer that could be pushed. People complained that it had a disagreeably bitter aftertaste. In the second place, Mrs. Lange was a born sitter. She had married to rest—and she was resting. She was always piled upon a chair. Thus, she was not an aid but a hindrance, an encourager of the help in laziness and slovenliness. Again, the cooking was distinctly bad; the only really good thing the house served was coffee, and that was good only in the mornings. Finally, Lange was a saver by nature and not a spreader. He could hold tightly to any money he closed his stubby fingers upon; he did not know how to plant money and make it grow, but only how to hoard.

Thus it came to pass that, after the first spurt, the business fell back to about where it had been before

Susan came. Albert, the Austrian waiter, explained to Susan why it was that her popularity did the house apparently so little good—explained with truth where she suspected kind-hearted plotting, that she had arrested its latterly swift-downward slide. She was glad to hear what he had to say, as it was most pleasant to her vanity; but she could not get over the depression of the central fact—she was not making the sort of business to justify asking Lange for more than board and lodging; she was not in the way of making the money that was each day more necessary, as her little store dwindled.

The question of getting money to live on is usually dismissed in a princely way by writers about human life. It is in reality, except with the few rich, the ever-present question—as ever-present as the necessity of breathing—and it is not, like breathing, a matter settled automatically. It dominates thought; it determines action. To leave it out of account ever, in writing a human history, is to misrepresent and distort as utterly as would a portrait painter who neglected to give his subject eyes, or a head, even. With the overwhelming mass of us, money is at all times all our lives long the paramount question—for to be without it is destruction worse than death, and we are almost all perilously near to being without it. Thus, airily to pass judgment upon men and women as to their doings in getting money for necessaries, for what the compulsion of custom and habit has made necessaries to them—airily to judge them for their doings in such dire straits is like sitting calmly on shore and criticizing the conduct of passengers and sailors in a storm-beset sinking ship. It is one of the favorite pastimes of the comfortable classes; it makes an excellent impression as to one's virtue upon one's audience; it gives us a pleasing sense of superior delicacy and humor. But it is none the less mean and ridiculous. Instead of condemnation, the world needs to bestir itself to remove the stupid and cruel creatures that make evil conduct necessary; for can anyone, not a prig, say that the small part of the human race that does well does so because it is naturally better than the large part that does ill?

Spring was slow in opening. Susan's one dress was in a deplorable state. The lining hung in rags. The never good material was stretched out of shape, was frayed and worn gray in spots, was beyond being made up as presentable by the most careful pressing and cleaning. She had been forced to buy a hat, shoes, underclothes. She had only three dollars and a few cents left, and she simply did not dare lay it all out in dress materials. Yet, less than all would not be enough; all would not be enough.

Lange had from time to time more than hinted at the opportunities she was having as a public singer in his hall. But Susan, for all her experience, had remained one of those upon whom such opportunities must be thrust if they are to be accepted.

So long as she had food and shelter, she could not make advances; she could not even go so far as passive acquiescence. She knew she was again violating the fundamental canon of success; whatever one's business, do it thoroughly if at all. But she could not overcome her temperament which had at this feeble and false opportunity at once resented itself. She knew perfectly that therein was the whole cause of her failure to make the success she ought to have made when she came up from the tenements, and again when she fell into the clutches of Freddie Palmer. But it is one thing to know; it is another thing to do. Susan ignored the attempts of the men; she pretended not to understand Lange when they set him on to intercede with her for them. She saw that she was once more drifting to disaster—and that she had not long to drift. She was exasperated against herself; she was disgusted with herself. But she drifted on.

Growing seedier looking every day, she waited, defying the plain teachings of experience. She even thought seriously of going to work. But the situation in that direction remained unchanged. She was seeing things, the reasons for things, more clearly now, as experience developed her mind. She felt that to get on in respectability she ought to have been either more or less educated. If she had been used from birth to conditions but a step removed from savagery, she might have been content with what offered, might even have felt that she was rising. Or if she had been bred to a good trade, and educated only to the point where her small earnings could have satisfied her desires, then she might have got along in respectability. But she had been bred a "lady"; a Chinese woman whose feet have been bound from babyhood until her fifteenth or sixteenth year—how long it would be, after her feet were freed, before she could learn to walk at all!—and would she ever be able to learn to walk well?

What is luxury for one is squalor for another; what is elevation for one degrades another. In respectability she could not earn what was barest necessity for her—what she was now getting at Lange's—decent shelter, passable food. Ejected from her own class that shelters its women and brings them up in unfitness for the unsheltered life, she was dropping

as all such women must and do drop—was going
down, down, down—striking on this ledge and that,
and rebounding to resume her ever downward course.

She saw her own plight only too vividly. Those
whose outward and inward lives are wide apart get a
strong sense of dual personality. It was thus with
Susan. There were times when she could not believe
in the reality of her external life.

She often glanced through the columns on columns,
pages on pages of "want ads" in the papers—not with
the idea of answering them, for she had served her
apprenticeship at that, but simply to force herself to
realize vividly just how matters stood with her. Those
columns and pages of closely printed offerings of work!
Dreary tasks, all of them—tasks devoid of interest, of
personal sense of usefulness, tasks simply to keep degrading soul in degenerating body, tasks performed in
filthy factories, in foul-smelling workrooms and shops,
in unhealthful surroundings. And this, throughout
civilization, was the "honest work" so praised—by all
who don't do it, but live pleasantly by making others
do it. Wasn't there something in the ideas of Etta's
father, old Tom Brashear? Couldn't sensible, really
loving people devise some way of making most tasks
less repulsive, of lessening the burdens of those tasks
that couldn't be anything but repulsive? Was this
stupid system, so cruel, so crushing, and producing at
the top such absurd results as flashy, insolent autos
and silly palaces and overfed, overdressed women, and
dogs in jeweled collars, and babies of wealth brought
up by low menials—was this system really the best?

"If they'd stop canting about 'honest work' they
might begin to get somewhere."

In the effort to prevent her downward drop from

beginning again she searched all the occupations open to her. She could not find one that would not have meant only the most visionary prospect of some slight remote advancement, and the certain and speedy destruction of what she now realized was her chief asset and hope—her personal appearance. And she resolved that she would not even endanger it ever again. The largest part of the little capital she took away from Forty-third Street had gone to a dentist who put in several fillings of her back teeth. She had learned to value every charm—hair, teeth, eyes, skin, figure, hands. She watched over them all, because she felt that when her day finally came—and come it would, she never allowed long to doubt—she must be ready to enter fully into her own. Her day! The day when fate should change the life of her outward self would be compelled to live, would bring it into harmony with the life of inward self—the self she could control. Her day! It would never come to her in these surroundings. She must go and seek it.

SHE was like one who has fallen bleeding and broken into a cave; who after a time gathers himself together and crawls toward a faint and far distant gleam of light; who suddenly sees the light no more and at the same instant lurches forward and down into a deeper chasm.

Occasionally sheer exhaustion of nerves made it impossible for her to drink herself again into apathy before the effects of the last doses of the poison had worn off. In these intervals of partial awakening—she never permitted them to lengthen out, as such sensation as she had was of one falling—falling—through empty space—with whirling brain and strange sounds in the ears and strange distorted sights or hallucinations before the eyes—falling down—down—whither?—to how great a depth?—or was there no bottom, but simply presently a plunging on down into the black of death's bottomless oblivion?

Drink—always drink. Yet in every other way she took care of her health—a strange mingling of prudence and subtle hope with recklessness and frank despair. All her refinement, baffled in the moral ways, concentrated upon the physical. She would be neat and well dressed; she would not let herself be seized of the diseases on the pariah in those regions—the diseases through dirt and ignorance and indifference.

In the regions she now frequented recklessness was the keynote. There was the hilarity of the doomed; there was the cynical or stolid indifference to heat or cold, to rain or shine, to rags, to filth, to jail, to ejection for nonpayment of rent, to insult of word or blow. The fire engines—the ambulance—the patrol wagon—the city dead wagon—these were all ever passing and repassing through those swarming streets. It was the vastest, the most populous tenement area of the city. Its inhabitants represented the common lot —for it is the common lot of the overwhelming mass of mankind to live near to nakedness, to shelterlessness, to starvation, without ever being quite naked or quite roofless or quite starved. The masses are eager for the necessities; the classes are eager for the comforts and luxuries. The masses are ignorant; the classes are intelligent—or, at least, shrewd. The unconscious and inevitable exploitation of the masses by the classes automatically and of necessity stops just short of the catastrophe point—for the masses must have enough to give them the strength to work and reproduce. To go down through the social system as had Susan from her original place well up among the classes is like descending from the beautiful dining room of the palace where the meat is served in taste and refinement upon costly dishes by well mannered servants to attractively dressed people—descending along the various stages of the preparation of the meat, at each stage less of refinement and more of coarseness, until one at last arrives at the slaughter pen. The shambles, stinking and reeking blood and filth! The shambles, with hideous groan or shriek, or more hideous silent look of agony! The shambles of society where the beauty and grace and charm of civilization are created out of noisome sweat and savage toil, out of the health and strength of men and women and children, out of their ground up bodies, out of their ground up souls. Susan knew those regions well. She had no theories about them, no resentment against the fortunate classes, no notion that any other or better system might be possible, any other or better life for the masses. She simply accepted life as she found it, lived it as best she could.

Throughout the masses of mankind life is sustained by illusions—illusions of a better lot tomorrow, illusions of a heaven beyond a grave, where the nightmare, life in the body, will end and the reality, life in the spirit, will begin. She could not join the throngs moving toward church and synagogue to indulge in their dream that the present was a dream from which death would be a joyful awakening. She alternately pitied and envied them. She had her own dream that this dream, the present, would end in a joyful awakening to success and freedom and light and beauty. She admitted to herself that the dream was probably an illusion, like that of the pious throngs. But she was as unreasonably tenacious of her dream as they were of theirs. She dreamed it because she was a human being—and to be human means to hope, and to hope means to dream of a brighter future here or hereafter, or both here and hereafter. The earth is peopled with dreamers; she was but one of them. The last thought of despair as the black earth closes is a hope, perhaps the most colossal of hope's delusions, that there will be escape in the grave.

There is the time when we hope and know it and believe in it. There is the time when we hope and know it but have ceased to believe in it. There is the time when we hope, believing that we have altogether ceased to hope. That time had come for Susan. She seemed to think about the present. She moved about like a sleepwalker.

What women did she know—what men? She only
dimly remembered from day to day—from hour to
hour. Blurred faces passed before her, blurred voices
sounded in her ears, blurred personalities touched hers.
It was like the jostling of a huge crowd in night streets.
A vague sense of buffetings—of rude contacts—of momentary sensations of pain, of shame, of disgust, all
blunted and soon forgotten.

In estimating suffering, physical or mental, to fail
to take into account a more important factor—the
merciful paralysis or partial paralysis of any center
of sensibility—that is insistently assaulted.

She no longer had headaches or nausea after drinking deeply. And where formerly it had taken many
stiff doses of liquor to get her into the state of recklessness or of indifference, she was now able to put herself into the mood in which life was endurable with two
or three drinks, often with only one. The most marked
change was that never by any chance did she become
gay; the sky over her life was steadily gray—gray or
black, to gray again—never lighter.

How far she had fallen! But swift descent or gradual,
she had adapted herself—had, in fact, learned by much
experience of disaster to mitigate the calamities, to
have something to keep a certain deep-lying self of selfs
intact—unaffected by what she had been forced to
undergo. It seemed to her that if she could get the
chance—or could cure herself of the blindness which
was always preventing her from seeing and seizing the
chance that doubtless offered again and again—she
could shed the surface her mode of life had formed
over her and would find underneath a new real surface,
stronger, sightly, better able to bear—like the skin
that forms beneath the healing wound.

In these tenements, as in all tenements of all degrees, she and the others of her class were fiercely resented by the heads of families where there was any hope left to impel a striving upward. She had the best furnished room in the tenement. She was the best dressed woman—a marked and instantly recognizable figure because of her neat and finer clothes. Her profession kept alive and active the instincts for care of the person that either did not exist or were momentary and feeble in the respectable women. The slovenliness, the scurrilousness of even the wives and daughters of the well-to-do and the rich of that region would not have been tolerated in any but the lowest strata of her profession, hardly even in those sought by men of the laboring class. Also, the deep horror of disease, which her intelligence never for an instant permitted to relax its hold, made her particular and careful when in other circumstances drink might have reduced her to squalor. She spent all her leisure time—for she no longer read—in the care of her person.

She was watched with frightened, yet longing and curious, eyes by all the girls who were at work. The mothers hated her; many of them spat upon the ground after she had passed.

To speak of the conditions there as a product of civilization is to show ignorance of the history of our race, is to fancy that we are civilized today, when in fact we are—historically—in a turbulent and painful period of transition from a better yesterday toward a tomorrow in which life will be worth living as it never has been before in all the ages of duration. In this today of movement toward civilization which began with the discovery of iron and will end when we shall have discovered how to use for the benefit of all the

main forces of nature—in this today of agitation incident to journeying, we are in some respects better off,
in other respects worse off, than the race was ten or
fifteen thousand years ago. We have lost much of the
freedom that was ours before the rise of governments
and ruling classes: we have gained much—not so much
as the ignorant and the unthinking and the unedu-
cated imagine, but still much. In the end we—which
means the masses of us—will gain infinitely. But
gain or loss has not been in so-called morality. There
is not a virtue that has not existed from time ages
before record. Not a vice which is shallowly called
"effete" or the "product of overcivilization," but originated before man was man.

To speak of the conditions in which Susan Lenox
now lived as savagery is to misuse the word. Every
transitional stage is accompanied by a disintegration.
Savagery was a settled state in which every man and
every woman had his or her fixed position, settled duties and rights. With the downfall of savagery, with
the beginning of the journey toward that hope of tomorrow, civilization, everything in the relations of men
with men and men with women, became unsettled.
Such social systems as the world has known since have
all been makeshift and temporary—like our social systems of today, like the moral and extinct codes rising
and sinking in power over a vast multitude of emi-
grants moving from a distant abandoned home toward
a distant promised land and forced to live as best they
can in the interval. In the historic day's journey of
perhaps fifteen thousand years our present time is but
a brief second. In that second there has come a breaking up of the makeshift organization which long
served the working multitudes fairly well. The result

is an anarchy in which the strong oppress the weak, in which the masses are being crushed by the burdens imposed upon them by the classes. And in that particular part of the human race en route into which fate had flung Susan Lenox conditions not of savagery but of primitive chaos were prevailing. A large part of the population lived off the unhappy workers by prostitution, by thieving, by petty swindling, by politics, by the various devices in coarse, crude and small imitation of the devices employed by the ruling classes. And these petty parasites imitated the big parasites in their ways of spending their dubiously got gains. To have a "good time" was the ideal here as in idle Fifth Avenue; and the notions of a "good time" in vogue in the two opposite quarters differed in degree rather than in kind.

Nothing to think about but the appetites and their vices. Nothing to hope for but the next carouse. Susan had brought down with her from above one desire unknown to her associates and neighbors—the desire to forget. If she could only forget! If the poison would not wear off at times!

She could not quite forget. And to be unable to forget is to remember—and to remember is to long—and to long is to hope.

Several times she heard of Freddie Palmer. Twice she chanced upon his name in the newspaper—an incidental reference to him in connection with local politics. The other times were when men talking together in the drinking places frequented by both sexes spoke of him as a minor power in the organization. Each time she got a sense of her remoteness, of her security. Once she passed in Grand Street a detective she had often seen with him in Considine's at Broadway and

Forty-second. The "bull" looked sharply at her. Her heart stood still. But he went on without recognizing her. The sharp glance had been simply that official expression of see-all and know-all which is mere formality, part of the official livery, otherwise meaningless. However, it is not to that detective's discredit that he failed to recognize her. She had adapted herself to her changed surroundings.

Because she was of a different and higher class, and because she picked and chose her company, even when drink had beclouded her senses and instinct alone remained on drowsy guard, she prospered despite her indifference. For that region had its aristocracy of rich merchants, tenement-owners, politicians whose sons, close imitators of the uptown aristocracies in manners and dress, spent money freely in the amusements that attract nearly all young men everywhere. Susan made almost as much as she could have made in the more renowned quarters of the town. And presently she was able to move into a tenement which, except for two workingmen's families of a better class, was given over entirely to fast women. It was much better kept, much cleaner, much better furnished than the tenements for workers chiefly; they could not afford decencies, much less luxuries. All that sort of thing was, for the neighborhood, concentrated in the saloons, the dance halls, the fast houses and the fast flats.

Her walks in Grand Street and the Bowery, repelling and capricious though she was with her alternating moods of cold moroseness and sardonic and mocking gayety, were bringing her in a good sum of money for that region. Sometimes as much as twenty dollars a week, rarely less than twelve or fifteen. And despite her drinking and her freehandedness with her fellow-professionals less fortunate and with the street beggars and for tenement charities, she had in her stockings a capital of thirty-one dollars.

She avoided the tough places, the hang-outs of the gangs. She rarely went alone into the streets at night —and the afternoons were, luckily, best for business as well as for safety. She made no friends and therefore no enemies. Without meaning to do so and without realizing that she did so, she held herself aloof without haughtiness through sense of loneliness, not at all through sense of superiority. Had it not been for her scarlet lips, a far more marked sign in that region than anywhere uptown, she would have passed in the street for a more or less respectable woman—not thoroughly respectable; she was too well dressed, too intelligently cared for to seem the good working girl.

On one of the few nights when she lingered in the little back room of the saloon a few doors away at the corner, as she entered the dark passageway of the tenement, strong fingers closed upon her throat and she was borne to the floor. She knew at once that she was in the clutch of one of those terrors of tenement women, the lobbygows—men who live by lying in wait in the darkness to seize and rob the lonely, friendless woman. She struggled—and she was anything but weak. But not a sound could escape from her tight-pressed throat.

One of the workingmen, returning drunk from the meeting of the union, in the corner saloon, stumbled over her, gave her a kick in his anger. This roused her; she uttered a faint cry.

"Never mind me," said Susan. "I was only stunned."

190

"Oh, I thought it was the booze."

"No—a lobbygow."

"How much did he get?"

"About thirty-five."

"The hell he did! Want me to call a cop?"

"No," replied Susan, who was on her feet again. "What's the use?"

"I'll help you upstairs."

"No, thank you," said she. Not that she did not need help.

She went upstairs, the man waiting below until she should be safe—and out of the way. She staggered into her room, tottered to the bed, fell upon it. A girl named Clara, who lived across the hall, was sitting in a rocking-chair reading a Bertha Clay novel and smoking a cigarette. She glanced up, was arrested by the strange look in Susan's eyes.

"Hello—been hitting the pipe, I see," said she. "Down in Gussie's room?"

"No. A lobbygow," said Susan.

"Did he get much?"

"About thirty-five."

"I'll bet it was Gussie's fellow. I've suspected him," cried Clara.

The greater the catastrophe, the longer the time before it is fully realized. Susan's loss of the money that represented so much of savage if momentary horror, and so much of unconscious hope—this calamity did not overwhelm her for several days. Then she yielded for the first time to the lure of opium. She had listened longingly to the descriptions of the delights as girls and men told; for practically all of them smoked —or took cocaine. But to Clara's or Gussie's invitations to join the happy band of dreamers, she had always replied, "Not yet. I'm saving that." Now, however, she felt that the time had come. Hope in this world she had none. Before the black adventure, why not try the world of blissful unreality to which it gave entrance? Why leave life until she had exhausted all it put within her reach?

She went to Gussie's room at midnight and flung herself down in a wrapper upon a couch opposite a sallow, delicate young man. His great dark eyes were gazing unseeingly at her, were perhaps using her as an outline sketch from which his imagination could picture a beauty of loveliness beyond human. Gussie taught her how to prepare the little ball of opium, how to put it on the pipe and draw in its fumes. Her system was so well prepared for it by the poisons she had drunk that she had satisfactory results from the outset. And she entered upon the happiest period of her life thus far. All the hideousness of her profession disappeared under the gorgeous draperies of the imagination. Opium's magic transformed the vile, the obscene, into the lofty, the romantic, the exalted. The world she had been accustomed to regard as real ceased to be even the blur the poisonous liquors had made of it, became a vague, distant thing seen in a dream. Her opium world became the vivid reality.

The life she had been leading had made her extremely thin, had hardened and dulled her eyes, had given her that sad, shuddering expression of the face upon which have beaten a thousand mercenary and lustful kisses. The opium soon changed all this. Her skin, always tending toward pallor, became of the dead amber-white of old ivory. Her thinness took on an ethereal transparency that gave charm even to her slight stoop. Her face became dreamy, exalted, rapt;

and her violet-gray eyes looked from it like the vents of poetical fires burning without ceasing upon an altar to the god of dreams. Never had she been so beautiful; never had she been so happy—not with the coarser happiness of dancing eye and laughing lip, but with the ecstasy of soul that is like the shimmers of a tranquil sea quivering rhythmically under the caresses of moonlight.

In her descent she had now reached that long narrow shelf along which she would walk so long as health and looks should last—unless some accident should topple her off on the one side into suicide or on the other side into the criminal prostitute class. And such accidents were likely to happen. Still there was a fair chance of her keeping her balance until loss of looks and loss of health—the end of the shelf—should drop her abruptly to the very bottom. She could guess what was there. Every day she saw about the streets, most wretched and most forlorn of its wretched and forlorn things, the solitary old women, bent and twisted, wrapped in rotting rags, picking papers and tobacco from the gutters and burrowing in garbage barrels, seeking somehow to get the drink or the dope that changed hell into heaven for them.

Despite liquor and opium and the degradations of the street-woman's life she walked that narrow ledge with curious steadiness. She was unconscious of the cause. Indeed, self-consciousness had never been one of her traits. The cause is interesting.

In our egotism, in our shame of what we ignorantly regard as the lowliness of our origin we are always seeking alleged lofty spiritual explanations of our doings, and overlook the actual, quite simple, real reason. One of the strongest factors in Susan's holding

herself together in face of overwhelming odds, was the
nearly seventeen years of early training her Aunt
Fanny Warham had given her in orderly and systematic ways—a place for everything and everything in
its place; a time for everything and everything at its
time, neatness, scrupulous cleanliness, no neglecting of
any of the small, yet large, matters that conserve the
body. Susan had not been so apt a pupil of Fanny
Warham's as was Ruth, because Susan had not Ruth's
nature of the old-maidish, cut-and-dried conventional.
But during the whole fundamentally formative period
of her life Susan Lenox had been trained to order and
system, and they had become part of her being, beyond
the power of drink and opium and prostitution to dis-
integrate them until the general break-up should come.
In all her wanderings every man or woman or girl she
had met who was not rapidly breaking up, but was
offering more or less resistance to the assaults of bad
habits, was one who like herself had acquired in childhood strong good habits to oppose the bad habits and
to fight them with. An enemy must be met with his
own weapons or stronger. The strongest weapons that
can be given a human animal for combating the de-
structive forces of the struggle for existence are not
good sentiments or good principles or even pious or
moral practices—for, bad habits can make short work
of all these—but are good habits in the practical, material matters of life. They operate automatically
every day; they apply to all the multitude of small,
semi-unconscious actions of the daily routine. They
preserve the *morale*. And not morality but morals is
the warp of character—the part which, once destroyed
or even frayed, cannot be restored.

Susan, unconsciously and tenaciously practicing her

early training in order and system whenever she could and wherever she could, had an enormous advantage over the mass of the girls, both respectable and fast. And while their evidence was always toward "going to pieces" her tendency was always to repair and to put off the break-up.

One June evening she was looking through the better class of dance halls and drinking resorts for Clara, to get her to go up to Gussie's for a smoke. She opened a door she had never happened to enter before—a dingy door with the glass frosted. Just inside there was a fetid little bar; view of the rest of the room was cut off by a screen from behind which came the sound of a tuneless old piano. She knew Clara would not be in such a den, but out of curiosity she glanced round the screen. She was seeing a low-ceilinged room, the walls almost dripping with the dirt of many and many a hard year. In a corner was the piano, battered, about to fall to pieces, its ancient and horrid voice cracked by the liquor which had been poured into it by facetious drunkards. At the keyboard sat an old hunchback, broken-jawed, dressed in slimy rags. His filthy fingers were pounding out a waltz.

Susan stood rooted to the threshold of that scene. She leaned against the wall, her throat contracting in a fit of nausea. She grew cold all over; her teeth chattered. She tried in vain to tear her gaze from the spectacle; some invisible power seemed to be holding her head in a vise, thrusting her struggling eyelids violently open.

There were several men, dead drunk, asleep in old wooden chairs against the wall. One of these men was so near her that she could have touched him. His clothing was such an assortment of rags slimy and greasy as one sometimes sees upon the top of a filled garbage barrel to add its horrors of odor of long un-washed humanity to the stenches from vegetable decay. His wreck of a hard hat had fallen from his head as it dropped forward in drunken sleep. Something in the shape of the head made her concentrate upon this man. She gave a sharp cry, stretched out her hand, touched the man's shoulder.

"Rod!" she cried. "Rod!"

The head slowly lifted, and the bleary, blowsy wreck of Roderick Spenser's handsome face was turned stupid-ly toward her. Into his gray eyes slowly came a gleam of recognition. Then she saw the red of shame burst into his hollow cheeks, and the head quickly drooped.

She shook him. "Rod! It's *you!*"

"Get the hell out," he mumbled. "I want to sleep."

"You know me," she said. "I see the color in your face. Oh, Rod—you needn't be ashamed before *me.*"

She felt him quiver under her fingers pressing upon his shoulder. But he pretended to snore.

"Rod," she pleaded, "I want you to come along with me. I can't do you any harm now."

The hunchback had stopped playing. The old women were crowding round Spenser and her, were peering at them, with eyes eager and ears a-cock for romance—for nowhere on this earth do the stars shine so sweetly as down between the precipices of shame to the black floor of the slum's abyss. Spenser, stooped and shaking, rose abruptly, thrust Susan aside with a sweep of the arm that made her reel, bolted into the street. She recovered her balance and amid hoarse croakings of "That's right, honey! Don't give him up!" followed the shambling, swaying figure. He was too utterly drunk to go far; soon down he sank, a heap of rags and filth, against a stoop.

She bent over him, saw he was beyond rousing, straightened and looked about her. Two honest looking young Jews stopped. "Won't you help me get him home?" she said to them.

"Sure!" replied they in chorus. And, with no outward sign of the disgust they must have felt at the contact, they lifted up the sot, in such fantastic contrast to Susan's clean and even stylish appearance, and bore him along, trying to make him seem less the helpless whiskey-soaked dead weight. They dragged him up the two flights of stairs and, as she pushed back the door, deposited him on the floor. She assured them they could do nothing more, thanked them, and they departed. Clara appeared in her doorway.

"Lorna!" she cried. "*What* have you got there? How'd it get in?"

Clara, looking at Spenser's face now, saw those signs which not the hardest of the world's hard uses can cut or tear away. "Oh!" she said, in a tone of sympathy. "He *is* down, isn't he? But he'll pull round all right."

She went into her room to take off her street clothes and to get herself into garments as suitable as she possessed for one of those noisome tasks that are done a dozen times a day by the bath nurses in the receiving department of a charity hospital. When she returned, Susan too was in her chemise and ready to begin the search for the man, if man there was left deep buried in that muck.

In a short time they had cleansed him thoroughly.

"Who is he?" asked Clara.

"A man I used to know," said Susan.

"What're you going to do with him?"

"I don't know," confessed Susan.

She was not a little uneasy at the thought of his
awakening. Would he despise her more than ever now
—fly from her back to his filth? Would he let her try
to help him? And she looked at the face which had
been, in that other life so long, long ago, dearer to her
than any face her eyes had ever rested upon; a sob
started deep down within her, found its slow and painful way upward, shaking her whole body and coming
from between her clenched teeth in a groan. She forgot
all she had suffered from Rod—forgot the truth about
him which she had slowly puzzled out after she left him
and as experience enabled her to understand actions
she had not understood at the time. She forgot it all.
That past—that far, dear, dead past! Again she was
a simple, innocent girl upon the high rock, eating that
wonderful dinner. Again the evening light faded, stars
and moon came out, and she felt the first sweet stirring
of love for him. She could hear his voice, the light,
clear, entrancing melody of the Duke's song—

> La Donna è mobile
> Qua penna al vento—

She burst into tears—tears that drenched her soul
as the rain drenches the blasted desert and makes the
things that could live in beauty stir deep in its bosom.
And Clara, sobbing in sympathy, kissed her and stole
away, softly closing the door. "If a man die, shall he
live again?" asked the old Arabian philosopher. If a
woman die, shall she live again? . . . Shall not that
which dies in weakness live again in strength? . . .
Looking at him, as he lay there sleeping so quietly, her
being surged with the heaving of high longings and

hopes. If *they* could only live again! Here they were, together, at the lowest depth, at the rock bottom of life. If they could build on that rock, build upon the very foundation of the world, then would they indeed build in strength! Then, nothing could destroy—nothing! . . . If they could live again! If they could build!

She had something to live for—something to fight for. Into her eyes came a new light; into her soul came peace and strength. Something to live for—someone to redeem.

XI

SHE fell asleep, her head resting upon her hand, her elbow on the arm of the chair. She awoke with a shiver; she opened her eyes to find him gazing at her. The eyes of both shifted instantly. "Wouldn't you like some whiskey?" she asked.

"Thanks," replied he, and his unchanged voice reminded her vividly of his old self, obscured by the beard and by the dissipated look.

She took the bottle from its concealment in the locked washstand drawer, poured him out a large drink. When she came back where he could see the whiskey in the glass, his eyes glistened and he raised himself first on his elbow, then to a sitting position. His shaking hand reached out eagerly and his expectant lips quivered. He gulped the whiskey down.

"Thank you," he said, gazing longingly at the bottle as he held the empty glass toward her.

"More?"

"I *would* like a little more," said he gratefully.

Again she poured him a large drink, and again he gulped it down. "That's strong stuff," said he. "But then they sell strong stuff in this part of town. The other kind tastes weak to me now."

He dropped back against the pillows. She poured herself a drink. Halfway to her lips the glass halted. "I've got to stop that," thought she, "if I'm going to do anything for him or for myself." And she poured the whiskey back and put the bottle away. The whole incident took less than five seconds. It did not occur that she was essaying and achieving the heroic, that she had in that instant revealed her right to her dream of a career high above the common lot.

"Don't *you* drink?" said he.

"I've decided to cut it out," replied she carelessly. "There's nothing in it."

"I couldn't live without it—and wouldn't."

"It *is* a comfort when one's on the way down," said she. "But I'm going to try the other direction—for a change."

She held a box of cigarettes toward him. He took one, then she; she held the lighted match for him, lit her own cigarette, let the flame of the match burn on, she absently watching it.

"Look out! You'll burn yourself!" cried he.

She started, threw the match into the slop jar. "How do you feel?" inquired she.

"Like the devil," he answered. "But then I haven't known what it was to feel any other way for several months—except when I couldn't feel at all." A long silence, both smoking, he thinking, she furtively watching him. "You haven't changed so much," he finally said. "At least, not on the outside."

"More on the outside than on the inside," said she. "The inside doesn't change much. There I'm almost as I was that day on the big rock. And I guess you are, too—aren't you?"

"The devil I am! I've grown hard and bitter."

"That's all outside," declared she. "That's the shell —like the scab that stays over the sore spot till it heals."

"Sore spot? I'm nothing but sore spots. I've been treated like a dog."

And he proceeded to talk about the only subject that

interested him—himself. He spoke in a defensive way, as if replying to something she had said or thought. "I've not got down in the world without damn good excuse. I wrote several plays, and they were tried out of town. But we never could get into New York. I think Brent was jealous of me, and his influence kept me from a hearing. I know it sounds conceited, but I'm sure I'm right."

"Brent?" said she, in a queer voice. "Oh, I think you must be mistaken. He doesn't look like a man who could do petty mean things. No, I'm sure he's not petty."

"Do you know him?" cried Spenser, in an irritated tone.

"No. But—someone pointed him out to me once—a long time ago—one night in the Martin. And then— you'll remember—there used to be a great deal of talk about him when we lived in Forty-third Street. You admired him tremendously."

"Well, he's responsible," said Spenser, sullenly. "The men on top are always trampling down those who are trying to climb up. He had it in for me. One of my friends who thought he was a decent chap gave him my best play to read. He returned it with some phrases about its showing talent—one of those phrases that don't mean a damn thing. And a few weeks ago—" Spenser raised himself excitedly— "the thieving hound produced a play that was a clean steal from mine. I'd be laughed at if I protested or sued. But I *know*, curse him!"

He fell back shaking so violently that his cigarette dropped to the sheet. Susan picked it up, handed it to him. He eyed her with angry suspicion. "You don't believe me, do you?" he demanded.

"I don't know anything about it," replied she. "Anyhow, what does it matter? The man I met on that show boat—the Mr. Burlingham I've often talked about —he used to say that the dog that stopped to lick his scratches never caught up with the prey."

He flung himself angrily in the bed. "You never did have any heart—any sympathy. But who has? Even Drumley went back on me—let 'em put a roast of my last play in the *Herald*—a telegraphed roast from New Haven—said it was a dead failure. And who wrote it? Why, some newspaper correspondent in the pay of the *Syndicate*—and that means Brent. And of course it was a dead failure. So—I gave up—and here I am. . . . "Give me my clothes," he ordered, waving his fists in a fierce, feeble gesture.

"They were torn all to pieces. I threw them away. I'll get you some more in the morning."

He dropped back again, a scowl upon his face. "I've got no money—not a damn cent. I did half a day's work on the docks and made enough to quiet me last night." He raised himself. "I can work again. Give me my clothes!"

"They're gone," said Susan. "They were completely used up."

This brought back apparently anything but dim memory of what his plight had been. "How'd I happen to get so clean?"

"Clara and I washed you off a little. You had fallen down."

He lay silent a few minutes, then said in a hesitating, ashamed tone, "My troubles have made me a boor. I beg your pardon. You've been tremendously kind to me."

"Oh, it wasn't much. Don't you feel sleepy?"

"Not a bit." He dragged himself from the bed. "But *you* do. I must go."

She laughed in the friendliest way. "You can't. You haven't any clothes."

He passed his hand over his face and coughed violently, she holding his head and supporting his emaciated shoulders. After several minutes of coughing and gagging, gasping and groaning and spitting, he was relieved by the spasm and lay down again. When he got his breath, he said—with rest between words—"I'd ask you to send for the ambulance, but if the doctors catch me, they'll lock me away. I've got consumption. Oh, I'll soon be out of it."

Susan sat silent. She did not dare look at him lest he should see the pity and horror in her eyes.

"They'll find a cure for it," pursued he. "But not till the day after I'm gone. That is the way my luck runs. Still, I don't see why I should care to stay—and I don't! Have you any more of that whiskey?"

Susan brought out the bottle again, gave him the last of the whiskey—a large drink. He sat up, sipping it to make it last. He noted the long row of books on the shelf fastened along the wall beside the bed, the books and magazines on the table. Said he:

"As fond of reading as ever, I see?"

"Fonder," said she. "I takes me out of myself."

"I suppose you read the sort of stuff you really like, now—not the things you used to read to make old Drumley think you were cultured and intellectual."

"No—the same sort," replied she, unruffled by his contemptuous, unjust fling. "Trash bores me."

"Come to think of it, I guess you did have pretty good taste in books."

But he was interested in himself, like all invalids;

and, like them, he fancied his own intense interest could not but be shared by everyone. He talked on and on of himself, after the manner of failures—told of his wrongs, of how friends had betrayed him, of the jealousies and enmities his talents had provoked. Susan was used to these hard-luck stories, was used to analyzing them. With the aid of what she had worked out as to his character after she left him, she had no difficulty in seeing that he was deceiving himself, was excusing himself. But after all she had lived through, after all she had discovered about human frailty, especially in herself, she was not able to criticize, much less condemn, anybody. Her doubts merely set her to wondering whether he might not also be self-deceived as to his disease.

"Why do you think you've got consumption?" asked she.

"I was examined at the free dispensary up in Second Avenue the other day. I've suspected what was the matter for several months. They told me I was right."

"But the doctors are always making mistakes. I'd not give up if I were you."

"Do you suppose I would if I had anything to live for?"

"I was thinking about that a while ago—while you were asleep."

"Oh, I'm all in. That's a cinch."

"So am I," said she. "And as we've nothing to lose and no hope, why, trying to do something won't make us any worse off. . . . We've both struck the bottom. We can't go any lower." She leaned forward and, with her earnest eyes fixed upon him, said, "Rod—why not try—together?"

He closed his eyes.

"I'm afraid I can't be of much use to you," she went on. "But you can help me. And helping me will make you help yourself. I can't get up alone. I've tried. No doubt it's my fault. I guess I'm one of those women that aren't hard enough or self-confident enough to do what's necessary unless I've got some man to make me do it. Perhaps I'd get the—the strength or whatever it is, when I was much older. But by that time—in my case—I guess it'd be too late. Won't you help me, Rod?"

He turned his head away, without opening his eyes.

"You've helped me many times—beginning with the first day we met."

"Don't," he said. "I went back on you. I did sprain my ankle, but I could have come."

"That wasn't anything," replied she. "You had already done a thousand times more than you needed to do."

His hand wandered along the cover in her direction. She touched it. Their hands clasped.

"I lied about where I got the money yesterday. I didn't work. I begged. Three of us—from the saloon they call the Owl's Chute—two Yale men—one of them had been a judge—and I. We've been begging for a week. We were going out on the road in a few days— to rob. Then—I saw you—in that old women's dance hall—the Venusberg, they call it."

"You've come down here for me, Rod. You'll take me back? You'll save me from the Venusberg?"

"I couldn't save anybody. Susie, at bottom I'm N. G. I always was—and I knew it. Weak—vain. But you! If you hadn't been a woman—and such a sweet, considerate one—you'd have never got down here."

"Such a fool," corrected Susan. "But, once I get up,

I'll not be so again. I'll fight under the rules, instead of acting in the silly way they teach us as children."

"Don't say those hard things, Susie!"

"Aren't they true?"

"Yes, but I can't bear to hear them from a woman. . . . I told you that you hadn't changed. But after I'd looked at you a while I saw that you have. You've got a terrible look in your eyes—wonderful and terrible. You had something of that look as a child—the first time I saw you."

"The day after my marriage," said the girl, turning her face away.

"It was there then," he went on. "But now—it's—it's heartbreaking, Susie—when your face is in repose."

"I've gone through a fire that has burned up every bit of me that can burn," said she. "I've been wondering if what's left isn't strong enough to do something with. I believe so—if you'll help me."

"Help you? I—help anybody? Don't mock me, Susie."

"I don't know about anybody else," said she sweetly and gently, "but I do know about me."

"No use—too late. I've lost my nerve." He began to sob. "It's because I'm unstrung," explained he. "Don't think I'm a poor contemptible fool of a whiner. . . . Yes, I *am* a whiner! Susie, I ought to have been the woman and you the man. Weak—weak—weak!"

She turned the gas low, bent over him, kissed his brow, caressed him. "Let's do the best we can," she murmured.

He put his arm round her. "I wonder if there *is* any hope," he said. "No—there couldn't be."

"Let's not hope," pleaded she. "Let's just do the best we can."

"What—for instance?"

"You know the theater people. You might write a little play—a sketch—and you and I could act it in one of the ten-cent houses."

"That's not a bad idea!" exclaimed he. "A little comedy—about fifteen or twenty minutes." And he cast about for a plot, found the beginnings of one— the ancient but ever acceptable commonplace of a jealous quarrel between two lovers—"I'll lay the scene in Fifth Avenue—there's nothing low life likes so much as high life." He sketched, she suggested. They planned until broad day, then fell asleep, she half sitting up, his head pillowed upon her lap.

She was awakened by a sense of a parching and suffocating heat. She started up with the idea of fire in her drowsy mind. But a glance at him revealed the real cause. His face was fiery red, and from his lips came rambling sentences, muttered, whispered, that indicated the delirium of a high fever. She had first seen it when she and the night porter broke into Burlingham's room in the Walnut Street House, in Cincinnati. She had seen it many a time since; for, while she herself had never been ill, she had been surrounded by illness all the time, and the commonest form of it was one of these fevers, outraged nature's frenzied rise against the ever denser swarms of enemies from without which the slums sent to attack her. Susan ran across the hall and roused Clara, who would watch while she went for a doctor. "You'd better get Einstein in Grand Street," Clara advised.

"Why not Sacci?" asked Susan.

"Our doctor doesn't know anything but the one thing —and he doesn't like to take other kinds of cases. No, get Einstein. . . . You know, he's like all of them—he won't come unless you pay in advance."

"How much?" asked Susan.

"Three dollars. I'll lend you if——"

"No—I've got it." She had eleven dollars and sixty cents in the world.

Einstein pronounced it a case of typhoid. "You must get him to the hospital at once."

Susan and Clara looked at each other in terror. To them, as to the masses everywhere, the hospital meant almost certain death; for they assumed—and they had heard again and again accusations which warranted it —that the public hospital doctors and nurses treated their patients with neglect always, with downright inhumanity often. Not a day passed without their hearing some story of hospital outrage upon poverty, without their seeing someone—usually some child—who was paying a heavy penalty for having been in the charity wards.

Einstein understood their expression. "Nonsense!" said he gruffly. "You girls look too sensible to believe those silly lies."

Susan looked at him steadily. His eyes shifted. "Of course, the pay service *is* better," said he in a strikingly different tone.

"How much would it be at a pay hospital?" asked Susan.

"Twenty-five a week including my services," said Doctor Einstein. "But you can't afford that."

"Will he get the best treatment for that?"

"The very best. As good as if he were Rockefeller or the big chap uptown."

"In advance, I suppose?"

"Would we ever get our money out of people if we

didn't get it in advance? We've got to live just the same as any other class."

"I understand," said the girl. "I don't blame you. I don't blame anybody for anything." She said to Clara, "Can you lend me twenty?"

"Sure. Come in and get it." When she and Susan were in the hall beyond Einstein's hearing, she went on: "I've got the twenty and you're welcome to it. But— Lorna—hadn't you better———"

"In the same sort of a case, what'd *you* do?" interrupted Susan.

Clara laughed. "Oh—of course." And she gave Susan a roll of much soiled bills—a five, the rest ones and twos.

"I can get the ambulance to take him free," said Einstein. "That'll save you five for a carriage."

She accepted this offer. And when the ambulance went, with Spenser burning and raving in the tightly wrapped blankets, Susan followed in a street car to see with her own eyes that he was properly installed. It was arranged that she could visit him at any hour and stay as long as she liked.

She returned to the tenement, to find the sentiment of the entire neighborhood changed toward her. Not loss of money, not loss of work, not dispossession nor fire nor death is the supreme calamity among the poor, but sickness. It is their most frequent visitor—sickness in all its many frightful forms—rheumatism and consumption, cancer and typhoid and the rest of the monsters. Yet never do the poor grow accustomed or hardened. And at the sight of the ambulance the neighborhood had been instantly stirred. When the reason for its coming got about, Susan became the object of universal sympathy and respect. She was not sending her friend to be neglected and killed at a charity hospital; she was paying twenty-five a week that he might have a chance for life—twenty-five dollars a week!

Rafferty, who kept the saloon at the corner and was chief lieutenant to O'Frayne, the District Leader, sent for her and handed her a twenty. "That may help some," said he.

Susan hesitated—gave it back. Thank you," said she, "and perhaps later I'll have to get it from you. But I don't want to get into debt. I already owe twenty."

"This ain't debt," explained Rafferty. "Take it and forget it."

"I couldn't do that," said the girl. "But maybe you'll lend it to me, if I need it in a week or so?"

"Sure," said the puzzled saloon man—liquor store man, he preferred to be called, or politician. "Any amount you want."

As she went away he looked after her, saying to his barkeeper: "What do you think of that, Terry? I offered her a twenty and she sidestepped."

"She's a nice girl," said Rafferty, sauntering away. He was a broad, tolerant and good-humored man; he made allowances for an employee whose brother was in for murder.

Susan had little time to spend at the hospital. She must now earn fifty dollars a week—nearly double the amount she had been averaging. She must pay the twenty-five dollars for Spenser, the ten dollars for her lodgings. Then there was the seven dollars which must be handed to the police captain's "wardman" in the darkness of some entry every Thursday night. She had been paying the patrolman three dollars a week to keep him in a good humor, and two dollars to the janitor's wife; she might risk cutting out these items for the time, as both janitor's wife and policeman were sympathetic. But on the closest figuring, fifty a week would barely meet her absolute necessities—would give her but seven a week for food and other expenses and nothing toward repaying Clara.

Fifty dollars a week! She might have a better chance to make it could she go back to the Broadway-Fifth Avenue district. But however vague other impressions from the life about her might have been, there had been branded into her a deep and terrible fear of the police—an omnipotence as cruel as destiny itself—indeed, the visible form of that sinister god at present. Once in the pariah class, once with a "police record," and a man or woman would have to scale the steeps of respectability up to a far loftier height than Susan ever dreamed of again reaching, before that malign and relentless power would abandon its tyranny. She did not dare risk adventuring a part of town where she had no "pull" and where, even should she by chance escape arrest, Freddie Palmer would hear of her; would certainly revenge himself by having her arrested and made an example of. In the Grand Street district she must stay, and she must "stop the nonsense" and "play the game"—must be businesslike.

She went to see the "wardman," O'Ryan, who under the guise of being a plains clothes man or detective, collected and turned in to the captain, who took his "bit" and passed up the rest, all the money levied upon saloons, dives, procuresses, dealers in unlawful goods of any kind from opium and cocaine to girls for "hock shops."

O'Ryan was a huge brute of a man, his great hard face bearing the scars of battles against pistol, knife, bludgeon and fist. He was a sour and savage brute, hated and feared by everyone for his tyrannies over the helpless poor and the helpless outcast class. He had primitive masculine notions as to feminine virtue, intact despite the latter day general disposition to concede toleration and even a certain respectability to prostitutes. But by some chance which she and the other girls did not understand he treated Susan with the utmost consideration, made the gangs appreciate that if they annoyed her or tried to drag her into the net of tribute in which they had enmeshed most of the girls worth while, he would regard it as a personal defiance to himself.

Susan waited in the back room of the saloon nearest O'Ryan's lodgings and sent a boy to ask him to come. The boy came back with the astonishing message that she was to come to O'Ryan's flat. Susan was so doubtful that she paused to ask the janitress about it.

"It's all right," said the janitress. "Since his wife died three years ago him and his baby lives alone. There's his old mother but she's gone out. He's always at home when he ain't on duty. He takes care of the baby himself, though it howls all the time something awful."

Susan ascended, found the big policeman in his shirt sleeves, trying to soothe the most hideous monstrosity she had ever seen—a misshapen, hairy animal looking like a monkey, like a rat, like a half dozen repulsive animals, and not at all like a human being. The thing was clawing and growling and grinding its teeth. At sight of Susan it fixed malevolent eyes on her and began to snap its teeth at her.

"Don't mind him," said O'Ryan. "He's only acting up queer."

Susan sat not daring to look at the thing lest she should show her aversion, and not knowing how to state her business when the thing was so clamorous, so fiendishly uproariously. After a time O'Ryan succeeded in quieting it. He seemed to think some explanation was necessary. He began abruptly, his gaze tenderly on the awful creature, his child, lying quiet now in his arms:

"My wife—she died some time ago—died when the baby here was born."

"You spend a good deal of time with it," said Susan.

"All I can spare from my job. I'm afraid to trust him to anybody, he being kind of different. Then, too, I *like* to take care of him. You see, it's all I've got to remember *her* by. I'm kind o' tryin' to do what *she'd* want did." His lips quivered. He looked at his monstrous child. "Yes I *like* settin' here, thinkin'—and takin' care of him.'

This brute of a slave driver, this cruel tyrant over the poor and the helpless—yet, thus tender and gentle —thus capable of the enormous sacrifice of a great, pure love!

"*You've* got a way of lookin' out of the eyes that's like her," he went on—and Susan had the secret of his strange forbearance toward her. "I suppose you've come about being let off on the assessment?"

Already he knew the whole story of Rod and the hospital. "Yes—that's why I'm bothering you," said she.

"You needn't pay but five-fifty. I can only let you off a dollar and a half—my bit and the captain's. We pass the rest on up—and we don't dare let you off."

"Oh, I can make the money," Susan said hastily. "Thank you, Mr. O'Ryan, but I don't want to get anyone into trouble."

"We've got the right to knock off one dollar and a half," said O'Ryan. "But if we let you off the other, the word would get up to—to wherever the graft goes— and they'd send down along the line, to have merry hell raised with us. The whole thing's done systematic, and they won't take no excuses, won't allow no breaks in the system nowhere. You can see for yourself— it'd go to smash if they did."

"Somebody must get a lot of money," said Susan.

"Oh, it's dribbled out—and as you go higher up, I don't suppose them that gets it knows where it comes from. The whole world's nothing but graft, anyhow. Sorry I can't let you off."

The thing in his lap had recovered strength for a fresh fit of malevolence. It was tearing at its hairy, hideous face with its claws and was howling and shriek- ing, the big father gently trying to soothe it—for *her* sake. Susan got away quickly. She halted in the deserted hall and gave way to a spasm of dry sobbing —an overflow of all the emotions that had been accu- mulating within her. In this world of noxious and re- pulsive weeds, what sudden startling upshooting of what beautiful flowers! Flowers where you would ex- pect to find the most noisome weeds of all, and vilest weeds where you would expect to find flowers. What a world!

However—the fifty a week must be got—and she must be businesslike.

Most of the girls who took to the streets came direct from the tenements of New York, of the foreign cities or of the factory towns of New England. And the world over, tenement house life is an excellent school for the life of the streets. It prevents modesty from developing; it familiarizes the eye, the ear, the nerves, to all that is brutal; it takes away from a girl every feeling that might act as a restraining influence except fear—fear of maternity, of disease, of prison. Thus, practically all the other girls had the advantage over Susan. Soon after they definitely abandoned respectability and appeared in the streets frankly members of the profession, they became bold and rapacious. They had an instinctive feeling that their business was as reputable as any other, more reputable than many held in high repute, that it would be most reputable if it paid better and were less uncertain. They respected themselves for all things, talk to the contrary in the search for the sympathy and pity most human beings crave. They despised the men as utterly as the men despised them. They bargained as shamelessly as the men. Even those who did not steal still felt that stealing was justifiable; for, in the streets the sex impulse shows stripped of all disguise, shows as a brutal male appetite, and the female feels that her yielding to it entitles her to all she can compel and cozen and crib. Susan had been unfitted for her profession—as for all active, unsheltered life—by her early training. The point of view given us in our childhood remains our point of view as to all the essentials of life to the end. Reason, experience, the influence of contact with many phases of the world, may change us seemingly, but the under-instinct remains unchanged. Thus, Susan had never lost, and never would lose her original repugnance; not even drink had ever given her the courage to approach men or to bargain with them. Her shame was a false shame, like most of the shame in the world— a lack of courage, not a lack of desire—and, however we may pretend, there can be no virtue in abstinence merely through cowardice. Still, if there be merit in

shrinking, even when the cruelest necessities were goad-
ing, that merit was hers in full measure. As a matter
of reason and sense, she admitted that the girls who
respected themselves and practiced their profession
like merchants of other kinds were right, were doing
what she ought to do. Anyhow, it was absurd to practice a profession half-heartedly. To play your game,
whatever it might be, for all there was in it—that was
the obvious first principle of success. Yet—she remained laggard and squeamish.

What she had been unable to do for herself, to save
herself from squalor, from hunger, from cold, she was
now able to do for the sake of another—to help the
man who had enabled her to escape from that marriage,
more hideous than anything she had endured since, or
ever could be called upon to endure—to save him from
certain neglect and probable death in the "charity"
hospital. Not by merely tolerating the not too impossible men who joined her without sign from her, and
not by merely accepting what they gave, could fifty
dollars a week be made. She must dress herself in
franker avowal of her profession, must look as expensive as her limited stock of clothing, supplemented
by her own taste, would permit. She must flirt, must
bargain, must ask for presents, must make herself
agreeable, must resort to the crude female arts—which,
however, are subtle enough to convince the self-en-
chanted male even in face of the discouraging fact of
the mercenary arrangement. She must crush down her
repugnance, must be active, not simply passive—must
get the extra dollars by stimulating male appetites,
instead of simply permitting them to satisfy themselves. She must seem rather the eager mistress than
the reluctant and impatient wife.

And she did abruptly change her manner. There was in her, as her life had shown, a power of endurance, an ability to sacrifice herself in order to do the thing that seemed necessary, and to do it without shuffling or whining. Whatever else her career had done for her, it undoubtedly had strengthened this part of her nature. And now the result of her training showed. With her superior intelligence for the first time free to make the best of her opportunities, she abruptly became equal to the most consummate of her sisters in that long line of her sister-panders to male appetites which extends from the bought wife or mistress or fiancée of the rich grandee down all the social ranks to the wife or street girl cozening for a tipsy day-laborer's earnings on a Saturday night and the work girl teasing her "steady company" toward matrimony on the park bench or in the dark entry of the tenement.

She was able to pay Clara back in less than ten days. In Spenser's second week at the hospital she had him moved to better quarters and better attendance at thirty dollars a week.

And when Roderick should be well, and the sketch written—an an engagement got—Ah, then! Life indeed—life, at last! Was it this hope that gave her the strength to fight down and conquer the craving for opium? Or was it the necessity of keeping her wits and of saving every cent? Or was it because the opium habit, like the drink habit, like every other habit, is a matter of a temperament far more than it is a matter of an appetite—and that she had the appetite but not the temperament? No doubt this had its part in the quick and complete victory. At any rate, fight and conquer she did. The strongest interest always wins. She had an interest stronger than love of opium

—an interest that substituted itself for opium and for drink and supplanted them. Life indeed—life, at last!

In his third week Rod began to round toward health. Einstein observed from the nurse's charts that Susan's visits were having an unfavorably exciting effect. He showed her the readings of temperature and pulse, and forbade her to stay longer than five minutes at each of her two daily visits. Also, she must not bring up any topic beyond the sickroom itself. One day Spenser greeted her with, "I'll feel better, now that I've got this off my mind." He held out to her a letter. "Take that to George Fitzalan. He's an old friend of mine—one I've done a lot for and never asked any favors of. He may be able to give you something fairly good, right away."

Susan glanced penetratingly at him, saw he had been brooding over the source of the money that was being spent upon him. "Very well," said she, "I'll go as soon as I can."

"Go this afternoon," said he with an invalid's fretfulness. "And when you come this evening you can tell me how you got on."

"Very well. This afternoon. But you know, Rod, there's not a ghost of a chance."

"I tell you Fitzalan's my friend. He's got some gratitude. He'll *do* something."

"I don't want you to get into a mood where you'll be awfully depressed if I should fail."

"But you'll not fail."

It was evident that Spenser, untaught by experience and flattered into exaggerating his importance by the solicitude and deference of doctors and nurses to a paying invalid, had restored to favor his ancient enemy—optimism, the certain destroyer of any man who does not shake it off. She went away, depressed and worried. When she should come back with the only possible news, what would be the effect upon him—and he still in a critical stage? As the afternoon must be given to business, she decided to go straight uptown, hoping to catch Fitzalan before he went out to lunch. And twenty minutes after making this decision she was sitting in the anteroom of a suite of theatrical offices in the Empire Theater building. The girl in attendance had, as usual, all the airs little people assume when they are in close, if menial, relations with a person who, being important to them, therefore fills their whole small horizon. She deigned to take in Susan's name and the letter. Susan seated herself at the long table and with the seeming of calmness that always veiled her in her hours of greatest agitation, turned over the pages of the theatrical journals and magazines spread about in quantity.

After perhaps ten silent and uninterrupted minutes a man hurried in from the outside hall, strode toward the frosted glass door marked "Private." With his hand reaching for the knob he halted, made an impatient gesture, plumped himself down at the long table—at its distant opposite end. With a sweep of the arm he cleared a space wherein he proceeded to spread papers from his pocket and to scribble upon them furiously. When Susan happened to glance at him, his head was bent so low and his straw hat was tilted so far forward that she could not see his face. She observed that he was dressed attractively in an extremely light summer suit of homespun; his hands were large and strong and ruddy—the hands of an artist, in good health. Her glance returned to the magazine. After a few minutes she looked up. She was startled to find that the man was giving her a curious, searching inspection—and that he was Brent, the playwright—the same fascinating face, keen, cynical, amused—the same seeing eyes, that, in the Café Martin long ago, had made her feel as if she were being read to her most secret thought. She dropped her glance.

His voice made her start. "It's been a long time since I've seen you," he was saying.

She looked up, not believing it possible he was addressing her. But his gaze was upon her. Thus, she had not been mistaken in thinking she had seen recognition in his eyes. "Yes," she said, with a faint smile.

"A longer time for you than for me," said he.

"A good deal has happened to me," she admitted.

"Are you on the stage?"

"No. Not yet."

The girl entered by way of the private door. "Miss Lenox—this way, please." She saw Brent, became instantly all smiles and bows. "Oh—Mr. Fitzalan doesn't know you're here, Mr. Brent," she cried. Then, to Susan, "Wait a minute."

She was about to reënter the private office when Brent stopped her with, "Let Miss Lenox go in first. I don't wish to see Mr. Fitzalan yet." And he stood up, took off his hat, bowed gravely to Susan, said, "I'm glad to have seen you again."

Susan, with some color forced into her old-ivory skin by nervousness and amazement, went into the presence of Fitzalan. As the now obsequious girl closed the door behind her, she found herself facing a youngish man with a remnant of hair that was little more than fuzz on the top of his head. His features were sharp, aggressive, rather hard. He might have sat

for the typical successful American young man of forty
—so much younger in New York than is forty elsewhere
in the United States—and so much older. He looked
at Susan with a pleasant sympathetic smile.

"So," said he, "you're taking care of poor Spenser,
are you? Tell him I'll try to run down to see him. I
wish I could do something for him—something worth
while, I mean. But—his request——

"Really, I've nothing of the kind. I couldn't possibly place you—at least, not at present—perhaps,
later on——"

"I understand," interrupted Susan. "He's very ill.
It would help him greatly if you would write him a
few lines, saying you'll give me a place at the first
vacancy, but that it may not be soon. I'll not trouble
you again. I want the letter simply to carry him over
the crisis."

Fitzalan hesitated, rubbed his fuzzy crown with his
jeweled hand. "Tell him that," he said, finally. "I'm
rather careful about writing letters. . . . Yes, say to
him what you suggested, as if it was from me."

"The letter will make all the difference between his
believing and not believing," urged Susan. "He has
great admiration and liking for you—thinks you would
do anything for him."

Fitzalan frowned; she saw that her insistence had
roused—or, rather, had strengthened—suspicion.
"Really—you must excuse me. What I've heard about
him the past year has not——

"But, no matter, I can't do it. You'll let me know
how he's getting on? Good day." And he gave her
that polite yet positive nod of dismissal which is a
necessary part of the equipment of men of affairs,
constantly beset as they are and ever engaged in the

battle to save their chief asset, time, from being wasted.

Susan looked at him—a straight glance from gray eyes, a slight smile hovering about her scarlet lips. He reddened, fussed with the papers before him on the desk from which he had not risen. She opened the door, closed it behind her. Brent was seated with his back full to her and was busy with his scribbling. She passed him, went on to the outer door. She was waiting for his voice; she knew it would come.

"Miss Lenox!"

As she turned he was advancing. His figure, tall and slim and straight, had the ease of movement which proclaims the man who has been everywhere and so is at home anywhere. He held out a card. "I wish to see you on business. You can come at three this afternoon?"

"Yes," said Susan.

"Thanks," said he, bowing and returning to the table. She went on into the hall, the card between her fingers. At the elevator, she stood staring at the name —Robert Brent—as if it were an inscription in a forgotten language. She was so absorbed, so dazed that she did not ring the bell. The car happened to stop at that floor; she entered as if it were dark. And, in the street, she wandered many blocks down Broadway before she realized where she was.

She left the elevated and walked eastward through Grand Street. She was filled with a new and profound dissatisfaction. She felt like one awakening from a hypnotic trance. The surroundings, inanimate and animate, that had become endurable through custom abruptly resumed their original aspect of squalor and ugliness of repulsion and tragedy. A stranger—the ordinary, unobservant, feebly imaginative person, going along those streets would have seen nothing but tawdriness and poverty. Susan, experienced, imaginative, saw *all*—saw what another would have seen only after it was pointed out, and even then but dimly. And that day her vision was no longer staled and deadened by familiarity, but with vision fresh and with nerves acute. The men—the women—and, saddest, most tragic of all, the children! When she entered her room her reawakened sensitiveness, the keener for its long repose, for the enormous unconscious absorption of impressions of the life about her—this morbid sensitiveness of the soul a-clash with its environment reached its climax. As she threw open the door, she shrank back before the odor—the powerful, sensual, sweet odor of chypre so effective in covering the bad smells that came up from other flats and from the noisome back yards. The room itself was neat and clean and plain, with not a few evidences of her personal taste—in the blending of colors, in the selection of framed photographs on the walls. The one she especially liked was the largest—a nude woman lying at full length, her head supported by her arm, her face gazing straight out of the picture, upon it a baffling expression—of sadness, of cynicism, of amusement perhaps, of experience, yet of innocence. It hung upon the wall opposite the door. When she saw this picture in the department store, she felt at once a sympathy between that woman and herself, felt she was for the first time seeing another soul like her own, one that would have understood her strange sense of innocence in the midst of her own defiled and depraved self—a core of unsullied nature. Everyone else in the world would have mocked at this notion of a something within—a true self to which all that seemed to be her own self was as external as her clothing; this woman of the photograph would understand. So, there she hung—Susan's one prized possession.

The question of dressing for this interview with Brent was most important. Susan gave it much thought before she began to dress, changed her mind again and again in the course of dressing. Through all her vicissitudes she had never lost her interest in the art of dress or her skill at it—and despite the unfavorable surroundings she had steadily improved; any woman anywhere would instantly have recognized her as one of those few favored and envied women who know how to get together a toilet. She finally chose the simplest of the half dozen summer dresses she had made for herself—a plain white lawn, with a short skirt. It gave her an appearance of extreme youth, despite her height and the slight stoop in her shoulders —a mere drooping that harmonized touchingly with the young yet weary expression of her face. To go with the dress she had a large hat of black rough straw with a very little white trimming on it. With this large black hat bewitchingly set upon her gracefully-done dark wavy hair, her sad, dreamy eyes, her pallid skin, her sweet-bitter mouth with its rouged lips seemed to her to show at their best. She felt that nothing was quite so effective for her skin as a white dress. In other colors—though she did not realize— the woman of bought kisses showed more distinctly— never brazenly as in most of the girls, but still unmistakably. In white she took on a glamour of melancholy ⸺and the human countenance is capable of no expression so universally appealing as the look of melancholy that suggests the sadness underlying all life, the pain that pays for pleasure, the pain that pays and gets no pleasure, the sorrow of the passing of all things, the

faint foreshadow of the doom awaiting us all. She
washed the rouge from her lips, studied the effect in
the glass. "No," she said aloud, "without it I feel like
a hypocrite—and I don't look half so well." And she
put the rouge on again—the scarlet dash drawn startlingly across her strange, pallid face.

XII

AT three that afternoon she stood in the vestibule of Brent's small house in Park Avenue overlooking the oblong of green between East Thirty-seventh Street and East Thirty-eighth. A most reputable looking Englishman in evening dress opened the door; from her reading and her theater-going she knew that this was a butler. He bowed her in. The entire lower floor was given to an entrance hall, done in plain black walnut, almost lofty of ceiling, and with a grand stairway leading to the upper part of the house. There was a huge fireplace to the right; a mirror filled the entire back wall; a broad low seat ran all round the room. In one corner, an enormous urn of dark pottery; in another corner, a suit of armor, the helmet, the breastplate and the gauntlets set with gold of ancient lackluster.

The butler left her there and ascended the polished but dead-finished stairway noiselessly. Susan had never before been in so grand a room. The best private house she had ever seen was Wright's in Sutherland; and while everybody else in Sutherland thought it magnificent, she had felt that there was something wrong, what she had not known. The grandiose New York hotels and restaurants were more showy and more pretentious far than this interior of Brent's. But her unerring instinct of those born with good taste knew at first view of them that they were simply costly; there were beautiful things in them, fine carvings and paintings and tapestries, but personality was lacking. And

without personality there can be no unity; without
unity there can be no harmony—and without harmony,
no beauty.

Looking round her now, she had her first deep
draught of esthetic delight in interior decoration.
She loved this quiet dignity, this large simplicity—
nothing that obtruded, nothing that jarred, everything
on the same scale of dark coloring and large size.
She admired the way the mirror, without pretense of
being anything but a mirror, enhanced the spacious-
ness of the room and doubled the pleasure it gave by
offering another and different view of it.

Last of all Susan caught sight of herself—a slim,
slightly stooped figure, its white dress and its big black
hat with white trimmings making it stand out strongly
against the rather somber background. In a curiously
impersonal way her own sad, wistful face interested her.
A human being's face is a summary of his career. No
man can realize at a thought what he is, can epitomize
in just proportion what has been made of him by experience of the multitude of moments of which life is
composed. But in some moods and in some lights we
do get such an all-comprehending view of ourselves in
looking at our own faces. As she had instinctively felt,
there was a world of meaning in the contrast between
her pensive brow above melancholy eyes and the blood-
red line of her rouged lips.

The butler descended. "Mr. Brent is in his library,
on the fourth floor," said he. "Will you kindly step
this way, ma'am?"

Instead of indicating the stairway, he went to the
panel next the chimney piece. She saw that it was a
hidden door admitting to an elevator. She entered;
the door closed; the elevator ascended rapidly. When

it came to a stop the door opened and she was facing Brent.

"Thank you for coming," said he, with almost formal courtesy.

For all her sudden shyness, she cast a quick but seeing look round. It was an overcast day; the soft floods of liquid light—the beautiful light of her beloved City of the Sun—poured into the big room through an enormous window of clear glass which formed the entire north wall. Round the other walls from floor almost to lofty ceiling were books in solid rows; not books with ornamental bindings, but books for use, books that had been and were being used. By way of furniture there were an immense lounge, wide and long and deep, facing the left chimney piece, an immense table desk facing the north light, three great chairs with tall backs, one behind the table, one near the end of the table, the third in the corner farthest from the window; a grand piano, open, with music upon its rack, and a long carved seat at its keyboard. The huge window had a broad sill upon which was built a generous window garden fresh and lively with bright flowers. The woodwork, the ceiling, the furniture were of mahogany. The master of this splendid simplicity was dressed in a blue house suit of some summer material like linen. He was smoking a cigarette, and offered her one from the great carved wood box filled with them on the table desk.

"Thanks," said she. And when she had lighted it and was seated facing him as he sat at his desk, she felt almost at her ease. After all, while his gaze was penetrating, it was also understanding; we do not mind being unmasked if the unmasker at once hails us as brother. Brent's eyes seemed to say to her, "Human!

—like me." She smoked and let her gaze wander from her books to window garden, from window garden to piano.

"You play?" said he.

"A very little. Enough for accompaniments to simple songs."

"You sing?"

"Simple songs. I've had but a few lessons from a small-town teacher."

"Let me hear."

She went to the piano, laid her cigarette in a tray ready beside the music rack. She gave him the "Gipsy Queen," which she liked because it expressed her own passion of revolt against restraints of every conventional kind and her love for the open air and open sky. He somehow took away all feeling of embarrassment; she felt so strongly that he understood and was big enough not to have it anywhere in him to laugh at anything sincere. When she finished she resumed her cigarette and returned to the chair near his.

"It's as I thought," said he. "Your voice can be trained—to speak, I mean. I don't know as to its singing value. . . . Have you good health?"

"I never have even colds. Yes, I'm strong."

"You'll need it."

"I have needed it," said she. Into her face came the sad, bitter expression with its curious relief of a faint cynical smile.

He leaned back in his chair and looked at her through a cloud of smoke. She saw that his eyes were not gray, as she had thought, but brown, a hazel brown with points of light sparkling in the irises and taking away all the suggestion of weakness and sentimentality that

230

makes pure brown eyes unsatisfactory in a man. He said slowly:

"When I saw you—in the Martin—you were on the way down. You went, I see."

She nodded. "I'm still there."

"You like it? You wish to stay?"

She shook her head smilingly. "No, but I can stay if it's necessary. I've discovered that I've got the health and the nerves for anything."

"That's a great discovery. . . . Well, you'll soon be on your way up. . . . Do you wish to know why I spoke to you this morning?—Why I remembered you?"

"Why?"

"Because of the expression of your eyes—when your face is in repose."

She felt no shyness—and no sense of necessity of responding to a compliment, for his tone forbade any thought of flattery. She lowered her gaze to conceal the thoughts his words brought—the memories of the things that had caused her eyes to look as Rod and now Brent said.

"Such an expression," the playwright went on, "must mean character. I am sick and tired of the vanity of these actresses who can act just enough never to be able to learn to act well. I'm going to try an experiment with you. I've tried it several times but— No matter. I'm not discouraged. I never give up. . . . Can you stand being alone?"

"I spend most of my time alone. I prefer it."

"I thought so. Yes—you'll do. Only the few who can stand being alone ever get anywhere. Everything worth while is done alone. The big battle—it isn't fought in the field, but by the man sitting alone in his tent, working it all out. The bridge—the tunnel

through the great mountains—the railway—the huge
business enterprise—all done by the man alone, thinking, plotting to the last detail. It's the same way
with the novel, the picture, the statue, the play—writing it, acting it—all done by someone alone, shut in
with his imagination and his tools. I saw that you were
one of the lonely ones. All you need is a chance. You'd
surely get it, sooner or later. Perhaps I can bring
it a little sooner. . . . How much do you need to
live on?"

"I must have fifty dollars a week—if I go on at—
as I am now. If you wish to take all my time—then,
forty."

He smiled in a puzzled way.

"The police," she explained. "I need ten——"

"Certainly—certainly," cried he. "I understand—
perfectly. How stupid of me! I'll want all your time.
So it's to be forty dollars a week. When can you begin?"

Susan reflected. "I can't go into anything that'll
mean a long time," she said. "I'm waiting for a man
—a friend of mine—to get well. Then we're going to
do something together."

Brent made an impatient gesture. "An actor? Well,
I suppose I can get him something to do. But I don't
want you to be under the influence of any of these
absurd creatures who think they know what acting
is—when they merely know how to dress themselves
in different suits of clothes, and strut themselves about
the stage. They'd rather die than give up their own
feeble, foolish little identities. I'll see that your actor
friend is taken care of, but you must keep away from
him—for the time at least."

"He's all I've got. He's an old friend."

232

"You—care for him?"

"I used to. And lately I found him again—after we had been separated a long time. We're going to help each other up."

"Oh—he's down and out—eh? Why?"

"Drink—and hard luck."

"Not hard luck. That helps a man. It has helped you. It has made you what you are."

"What am I?" asked Susan.

Brent smiled mysteriously. "That's what we're going to find out," said he. "There's no human being who has ever had a future unless he or she had a past —and the severer the past the more splendid the future."

Susan was attending with all her senses. This man was putting into words her own inarticulate instincts.

"A past," he went on in his sharp, dogmatic way, "either breaks or makes. You go into the crucible a mere ore, a possibility. You come out slag or steel." He was standing now, looking down at her with quizzical eyes. "You're about due to leave the pot," said he.

"And I've hopes that you're steel. If not——" He shrugged his shoulders—"You'll have had forty a week for your time, and I'll have gained useful experience."

Susan gazed at him as if she doubted her eyes and ears.

"What do you want me to do?" she presently inquired.

"Learn the art of acting—which consists of two parts. First, you must learn to act—thousands of the profession do that. Second, you must learn not to act—and so far I know there aren't a dozen in the whole world who've got that far along. I've written

a play I think well of. I want to have it done properly—it, and several other plays I intend to write.
I'm going to give you a chance to become famous—
better still, great."

Susan looked at him incredulously. "Do you know
who I am?" she asked at last.

"Certainly."

Her eyes lowered, the faintest tinge of red changed
the amber-white pallor of her cheeks, her bosom rose
and fell quickly.

"I don't mean," he went on, "that I know any of
the details of your experience. I only know the results
as they are written in your face. The details are unimportant. When I say I know who you are, I mean
I know that you are a woman who has suffered, whose
heart has been broken by suffering, but not her spirit.
Of where you came from or how you've lived, I know
nothing. And it's none of my business—no more than
it's the public's business where *I* came from and how
I've learned to write plays."

Well, whether he was guessing any part of the truth
or all of it, certainly what she had said about the police and now this sweeping statement of his attitude
toward her freed her of the necessity of disclosing
herself. She eagerly tried to dismiss the thoughts that
had been making her most uneasy. She said:

"You think I can learn to act?"

"That, of course," replied he. "Any intelligent person can learn to act—and also most persons who have
no more intelligence in their heads than they have in
their feet. I'll guarantee you some sort of career.
What I'm interested to find out is whether you can
learn *not* to act. I believe you can. But——" He
laughed in self-mockery. "I've made several absurd

mistakes in that direction. . . . You have led a life in which most women become the cheapest sort of liars —worse liars even than is the usual respectable person, because they haven't the restraint of fearing loss of reputation. Why is it you have not become a liar?"

Susan laughed. "I'm sure I don't know. Perhaps because lying is such a tax on the memory. May I have another cigarette?"

He held the match for her. "You don't paint—except your lips," he went on, "though you have no color. And you don't wear cheap finery. And while you use a strong scent, it's not one of the cheap and nasty kind—it's sensual without being slimy. And you don't use the kind of words one always hears in your circle."

Susan looked immensely relieved. "Then you *do* know who I am!" she cried.

"You didn't suppose I thought you fresh from a fashionable boarding school, did you? I'd hardly look there for an actress who could act. You've got experience—experience—experience—written all over your face—sadly, satirically, scornfully, gayly, bitterly. And what I want is experience—not merely having been through things, but having been through them understandingly. You'll help me in my experiment?"

He looked astonished, then irritated, when the girl, instead of accepting eagerly, drew back in her chair and seemed to be debating. His irritation showed still more plainly when she finally said:

"That depends on him. And he—he thinks you don't like him."

"What's his name?" said Brent in his abrupt, intense fashion. "What's his name?"

"Spenser—Roderick Spenser."

Brent looked vague.

"He used to be on the *Herald*. He writes plays."

"Oh—yes. I remember. He's a weak fool."

Susan abruptly straightened, an ominous look in eyes and brow.

Brent made an impatient gesture. "Beg pardon. Why be sensitive about him? Obviously because you know I'm right. I said fool, not ass. He's clever, but ridiculously vain. I don't dislike him. I don't care anything about him—or about anybody else in the world. No man does who amounts to anything. With a career it's as Jesus said—leave father and mother, husband and wife—land, ox—everything—and follow it."

"What for?" said Susan.

"To save your soul! To be a somebody; to be strong. To be able to give to anybody and everybody —whatever they need. To be happy."

"Are you happy?"

"No," he admitted. "But I'm growing in that direction. . . . Don't waste yourself on Stevens—I beg pardon, Spenser. You're bigger than that. He's a small man with large dreams—a hopeless misfit. Small dreams for small men; large dreams for—" he laughed —"you and me—our sort."

Susan echoed his laugh, but faint-heartedly. "I've watched your name in the papers," she said, sincerely unconscious of flattery. "I've seen you grow more and more famous. But—if there had been anything in me, would I have gone down and down?"

"How old are you?"

"About twenty-one."

"Only twenty-one—and that look in your face! Magnificent! I don't believe I'm to be disappointed this time. You ask why you've gone down! You haven't. You've gone *through*."

"Down," she insisted, sadly.

"Nonsense! The soot'll rub off the steel."

She lifted her head eagerly. Her own secret thought put into words.

"No secret longing for social position?" said he.

"None. Even if I would, I couldn't."

"That's one heavy handicap out of the way. But I'll not let myself begin to hope until I find out whether you've got incurable and unteachable vanity. If you have—then, no hope. If you haven't—there's a fighting chance."

"You forget my compact," Susan reminded him.

"Oh—the lover—Spenser."

Brent reflected, strolled to the big window, his hands deep in his pockets. Susan took advantage of his back to give way to her own feelings of utter amazement and incredulity. She certainly was not dreaming. And the man gazing out at the window was certainly flesh and blood—a great man, if voluble and eccentric. Perhaps to act and speak as one pleased was one of the signs of greatness, one of its perquisites. Was he amusing himself with her? Was he perchance taken with her physically, and employing these extraordinary methods as ways of approach? She had seen many peculiarities of sex-approach in men—some grotesque, many terrible, all beyond comprehension. Was this another such?

He wheeled suddenly, surprised her eyes upon him. He burst out laughing, and she felt that he had read her thoughts. However, he merely said:

"Have you anything to suggest—about Spenser?"

"I can't even tell him of your offer now. He's very ill—and sensitive about you."

"About me? How ridiculous! I'm always coming across men I don't know who are full of venom toward me. I suppose he thinks I crowded him. No matter. You're sure you're not fancying yourself in love with him?"

"No, I am not in love with him. He has changed —and so have I."

He smiled at her. "Especially in the last hour?" he suggested.

"I had changed before that. I had been changing right along. But I didn't realize it fully until you talked with me—no, until after you gave me your card this morning."

"You saw a chance—a hope—eh?"

She nodded.

"And at once became all nerves and courage. . . . As to Spenser—I'll have some play carpenter sent to collaborate with him and set him up in the play business. You know it's a business as well as an art. And the chromos sell better than the oil paintings—except the finest ones. It's my chromos that have earned me the means and the leisure to try oils."

"He'd never consent. He's very proud."

"Vain, you mean. Pride will consent to anything as a means to an end. It's vanity that's squeamish and haughty. He needn't know."

"But I couldn't discuss any change with him until he's much better."

"I'll send the play carpenter to him—get Fitzalan to send one of his carpenters." Brent smiled. "You don't think *he'll* hang back because of the compact, do you?"

Susan flushed painfully. "No," she admitted in a low voice.

Brent was still smiling at her, and the smile was cynical. But his tone soothed where his words would have wounded, as he went on: "A man of his sort—an average, 'there-are-two-kinds-of-women, good-and-bad' sort of man—has but one use for a woman of your sort."

"I know that," said Susan.

"Do you mind it?"

"Not much. I'd not mind it at all if I felt that I was somebody."

Brent put his hand on her shoulder. "You'll do, Miss Lenox," he said with quiet heartiness. "You may not be so big a somebody as you and I would like. But you'll count as one, all right."

She looked at him with intense appeal in her eyes. "Why?" she said earnestly. "*Why* do you do this?"

He smiled gravely down at her—as gravely as Brent could smile—with the quizzical suggestion never absent from his handsome face, so full of life and intelligence. "I've been observing your uneasiness," said he. "Now listen. It would be impossible for you to judge me, to understand me. You are young, and as yet, small. I am forty, and have lived twenty-five of my forty years intensely. So, don't fall into the error of shallow people, and size me up by your own foolish little standards. Do you see what I mean?"

Susan's candid face revealed her guilt. "Yes," said she, rather humbly.

"I see you do understand," said he. "And that's a good sign. Most people, hearing what I said, would have disregarded it as merely my vanity, would have gone on with their silly judging, would have set me down as a conceited ass who, by some accident, had got a reputation. But to proceed—I have not chosen you on impulse. Long and patient study has made me able to judge character by the face, as a horse dealer can judge horses by looking at them. I don't need to read every line of a book to know whether it's wise or foolish, worth while or not. I don't need to know a human being for years or for hours or for minutes even, before I can measure certain things. I measured you. It's like astronomy. An astronomer wants to get the orbit of a star. He takes its position twice —and from the two observations he can calculate the orbit to the inch. I've got three observations of your orbit. Enough—and to spare."

"I shan't misunderstand again," said Susan.

"One thing more," insisted Brent. "In our relations, we are to be not man and woman, but master and pupil. I shan't waste your time with any—other matters."

It was Susan's turn to laugh. "That's your polite way of warning me not to waste any of your time with—other matters."

"Precisely," conceded he. "A man in my position— a man in any sort of position, for that matter—is much annoyed by women trying to use their sex with him. I wished to make it clear at the outset that——"

"That I could gain nothing by neglecting the trade of actress for the trade of woman," interrupted Susan. "I understand perfectly."

He put out his hand. "I see that at least we'll get on together. I'll have Fitzalan send the carpenter to your friend at once."

"Today!" exclaimed Susan, in surprise and delight.

"Why not?" He arranged paper and pen. "Sit

here and write Spenser's address, and your own. Your salary begins with today. I'll have my secretary mail you a check. And as soon as I can see you again, I'll send you a telegram. Meanwhile—" He rummaged among a lot of paper-bound plays on the table— "Here's 'Cavalleria Rusticana.' Read it with a view to yourself as either *Santuzza* or *Lola*. Study her first entrance—what you would do with it. Don't be frightened. I expect nothing from you—nothing whatever. I'm glad you know nothing about acting. You'll have the less to unlearn."

They had been moving toward the elevator. He shook hands again, and, after adjusting the mechanism for the descent, closed the door. As it was closing she saw in his expression that his mind had already dismissed her for some one of the many other matters that crowded his life.

XIII

THE Susan Lenox who left Delancey Street at half past two that afternoon to call upon Robert Brent was not the Susan Lenox who returned to Delancey Street at half-past five. A man is wandering, lost in a cave, is groping this way and that in absolute darkness, with flagging hope and fainting strength—has reached the point where he wonders at his own folly in keeping on moving—is persuading himself that the sensible thing would be to lie down and give up. He sees a gleam of light. Is it a reality? Is it an illusion—one more of the illusions that have lured him on and on? He does not know; but instantly a fire sweeps through him, warming his dying strength into vigor.

So it was with Susan.

The pariah class—the real pariah class—does not consist of merely the women formally put beyond the pale for violations of conventional morality and the men with the brand of thief or gambler upon them. Our social, our industrial system has made it far vaster. It includes almost the whole population—all those who sell body or brain or soul in an uncertain market for uncertain hire, to gain the day's food and clothing, the night's shelter. This vast mass floats hither and yon on the tides and currents of destiny. Now it halts, resting sluggishly in a dead calm; again it moves, sometimes slowly, sometimes under the lash of tempest. But it is ever the same vast inertia, with no particle of it possessing an aim beyond keeping afloat and alive.

Susan had been an atom, a spray of weed, in this Sargasso Sea.

If you observe a huge, unwieldy crowd so closely packed that nothing can be done with it and it can do nothing with itself, you will note three different types. There are the entirely inert—and they make up most of the crowd. They do not resist; they helplessly move this way and that as the chance waves of motion prompt. Of this type is the overwhelming majority of the human race. Here and there in the mass you will see examples of a second type. These are individuals who are restive and resentful under the sense of helplessness and impotence. They struggle now gently, now furiously. They thrust backward or forward or to one side. They thresh about. But nothing comes of their efforts beyond a brief agitation, soon dying away in ripples. The inertia of the mass and their own lack of purpose conquer them. Occasionally one of these grows so angry and so violent that the surrounding inertia quickens into purpose—the purpose of making an end of this agitation which is serving only to increase the general discomfort. And the agitator is trampled down, disappears, perhaps silently, perhaps with groan or shriek. Continue to look at this crowd, so pitiful, so terrible, such a melancholy waste of incalculable power—continue to observe and you may chance upon an example of the third type. You are likely at first to confuse the third type with the second, for they seem to be much alike. Here and there, of the resentful strugglers, will be one whose resentment is intelligent. He struggles, but it is not aimless struggle. He has seen or suspected in a definite direction a point where he would be more or less free, perhaps entirely free. He realizes how he is hemmed in, realizes how difficult, how dangerous, will be his endeavor to get to that point. And he proceeds to try to minimize or overcome the difficulties, the dangers. He struggles now gently, now earnestly, now violently—but always toward his fixed objective. He is driven back, to one side, is almost overwhelmed. He causes commotions that threaten to engulf him, and must pause or retreat until they have calmed. You may have to watch him long before you discover that, where other strugglers have been aimless, he aims and resolves. And little by little he gains, makes progress toward his goal—and once in a long while one such reaches that goal. It is triumph, success.

Susan, young, inexperienced, dazed; now too despondent, now too hopeful; now too gentle and again too infuriated—Susan had been alternating between inertia and purposeless struggle. Brent had given her the thing she lacked—had given her a definite, concrete, tangible purpose. He had shown her the place where, if she should arrive, she might be free of that hideous slavery of the miserable mass; and he had inspired her with the hope that she could reach it.

And that was the Susan Lenox who came back to the little room in Delancey Street at half-past five.

Curiously, while she was thinking much about Brent, she was thinking even more about Burlingham—about their long talks on the show boat and in their wanderings in Louisville and Cincinnati. His philosophy, his teachings—the wisdom he had, but was unable to apply—began to come back to her. It was not strange that she should remember it, for she had admired him intensely and had listened to his every word, and she was then at the time when the memory takes its clearest and strongest impressions. The strangeness lay in the suddenness with which Burlingham, so long dead, suddenly came to life, changed from a sad and tender memory to a vivid possibility, advising her, helping her, urging her on.

Clara, dressed to go to dinner with her lover, was waiting to arrange about their meeting to make together the usual rounds in the evening. "I've got an hour before I'm due at the hospital," said Susan. "Let's go down to Kelly's for a drink."

While they were going and as they sat in the clean little back room of Kelly's well ordered and select corner saloon, Clara gave her all the news she had gathered in an afternoon of visits among their acquaintances—how, because of a neighborhood complaint, there was to be a fake raid on Gussie's opium joint at midnight; that Mazie had caught a frightful fever; and that Nettie was dying in Gouverneur of the stab in the stomach her lover had given her at a ball three nights before; that the police had raised the tariff for sporting houses, and would collect seventy-five and a hundred a month protection money where the charge had been twenty-five and fifty—the plea was that the reformers, just elected and hoping for one term only, were compelling a larger fund from vice than the old steady year-in-and-year-out ruling crowd. "And they may raise *us* to fifteen a week," said Clara, "though I doubt it. They'll not cut off their nose to spite their face. If they raised the rate for the streets they'd drive two-thirds of the girls back to the factories and sweat shops. You're not listening, Lorna. What's up?"

"Nothing."

"Your fellow's not had a relapse?"

"No—nothing."

"Need some money? I can lend you ten. I did have twenty, but I gave Sallie and that little Jew girl who's her side partner ten for the bail bondsman. They got pinched last night for not paying up to the police. They've gone crazy about that prize-fighter—at least, he thinks he is—that Joe O'Mara, and they're giving him every cent they make. It's funny about Sallie. She keeps straight on Sunday—no money'll tempt her—I've seen it tried. Do you want the ten?"

"No. I've got plenty."

"We must look in at that Jolly Rovers' ball tonight. There'll be a lot of fellows with money there. We can sure pull off something pretty good. Anyhow, we'll have fun. But you don't care for the dances. Well, they are a waste of time. And because the men pay for a few bum drinks and dance with a girl, they don't want to give up anything more. How's she to live, I want to know?"

"Would you like to get out of this, Clara?" interrupted Susan, coming out of her absent-mindedness.

"Would I! But what's the use of talking?"

"I mean, go on the stage," said Susan.

"I wouldn't mind, if I could get in right. Everything in this world depends on getting in right. I was born four flights up in a tenement, and I've been in wrong ever since."

"I was in wrong from the beginning, too," said Susan, thoughtfully. "In wrong—that's it exactly." Clara's eyes again became eager with the hope of a peep into the mystery of Susan's origin. But Susan went on, "Yes, I've always been in wrong. Always."

"Oh, no," declared Clara. "You've got education —and manners—and ladylike instincts. I'm at home here. I was never so well off in my life. I'm, you might say, on my way up in the world. Most of us girls are—like the fellow that ain't got nothing to eat or no place to sleep and gets into jail—he's better off, ain't he? But you—you don't belong here at all."

"I belong anywhere — and everywhere — and no- where," said Susan. "Yes, I belong here. I've got a chance uptown. If it pans out, I'll let you in."

Clara looked at her wistfully. Clara had a wicked temper when she was in liquor, and had the ordinary human proneness to lying, to mischievous gossip, and to utter laziness. The life she led, compelling cleanli- ness and neatness and a certain amount of thrift un- der penalty of instant ruin, had done her much good in saving her from going to pieces and becoming the ordinary sloven and drag on the energies of some man. "Lorna," she now said, "I do believe you like me a little."

"More than that," Susan assured her. "You've saved me from being hard-hearted. I must go to the hospital. So long!"

"How about this evening?" asked Clara.

"I'm staying in. I've got something to do."

"Well—I may be home early—unless I go to the ball."

Susan was refused admittance at the hospital. Spen- ser, they said, had received a caller, had taxed his strength enough for the day. Nor would it be worth while to return in the morning. The same caller was coming again. Spenser had said she was to come in the afternoon. She received this cheerfully, yet not without a certain sense of hurt—which, however, did not last long.

When she was admitted to Spenser the following afternoon, she faced him guiltily—for the thoughts Brent had set to bubbling and boiling in her. And her guilt showed in the tone of her greeting, in the reluctance and forced intensity of her kiss and embrace. She had compressed into the five most receptive years of a human being's life an experience that was, for one of her intelligence and education, equal to many times five years of ordinary life. And this experience had developed her instinct for concealing her deep feelings into a fixed habit. But it had not made her a liar—had not robbed her of her fundamental courage and self-respect which made her shrink in disdain from deceiving anyone who seemed to her to have the right to frankness. Spenser, she felt as always, had that right—this, though he had not been frank with her; still, that was a matter for his own conscience and did not affect her conscience as to what was courageous and honorable toward him. So, had he been observing, he must have seen that something was wrong. But he was far too excited about his own affairs to note her.

"My luck's turned!" cried he, after kissing her with enthusiasm. "Fitzalan has sent Jack Sperry to me, and we're to collaborate on a play. I told you Fitz was the real thing."

Susan turned hastily away to hide her telltale face. "Who's Sperry?" asked she, to gain time for self-control.

"Oh, he's a play-smith—and a bear at it. He has

knocked together half a dozen successes. He'll supply the trade experience that I lack, and Fitzalan will be sure to put on our piece."

"You're a lot better—aren't you?"

"Better? I'm almost well."

He certainly had made a sudden stride toward health. By way of doing something progressive he had had a shave, and that had restored the look of youth to his face—or, rather, had uncovered it. A strong, handsome face it was—much handsomer than Brent's—and with the subtle, moral weakness of optimistic vanity well concealed. Yes, much handsomer than Brent's, which wasn't really handsome at all—yet was superbly handsomer, also—the handsomeness that comes from being through and through a somebody. She saw again why she had cared for Rod so deeply; but she also saw why she could not care again, at least not in that same absorbed, self-effacing way. Physical attraction—yes. And a certain remnant of the feeling of comradeship, too. But never again utter belief, worshipful admiration — or any other degree of belief or admiration beyond the mild and critical. She herself had grown. Also, Brent's penetrating and just analysis of Spenser had put clearly before her precisely what he was — precisely what she herself had been vaguely thinking of him.

As he talked on and on of Sperry's visit and the new projects, she listened, looking at his character in the light Brent had turned upon it—Brent who had in a few brief moments turned such floods of light upon so many things she had been seeing dimly or not at all. Moderate prosperity and moderate adversity bring out the best there is in a man; the extreme of either brings out his worst. The actual man is the best there is in him, and not the worst, but it is one of the tragedies of life that those who have once seen his worst ever afterward have sense of it chiefly, and cannot return to the feeling they had for him when his worst was undreamed of. "I'm not in love with Brent," thought Susan. "But having known him, I can't ever any more care for Rod. He seems small beside Brent—and he *is* small."

Spenser in his optimistic dreaming aloud had reached a point where it was necessary to assign Susan a rôle in his dazzling career. "You'll not have to go on the stage," said he. "I'll look out for you. By next week Sperry and I will have got together a scenario for the play and when Sperry reads it to Fitzalan we'll get an advance of at least five hundred. So you and I will take a nice room and bath uptown—as a starter—and we'll be happy again—happier than before."

"No, I'm going to support myself," said Susan promptly.

"Trash!" cried Spenser, smiling tenderly at her. "Do you suppose I'd allow you to mix up in stage life? You've forgotten how jealous I am of you. You don't know what I've suffered since I've been here sick, brooding over what you're doing, to——"

She laid her fingers on his lips. "What's the use of fretting about anything that has to be?" said she, smilingly. "I'm going to support myself. You may as well make up your mind to it."

"Plenty of time to argue that out," said he, and his tone forecast his verdict on the arguing. And he changed the subject by saying, "I see you still cling to your fad of looking fascinating about the feet. That was one of the reasons I never could trust you. A girl with as charming feet and ankles as you have, and so much pride in getting them up well, simply cannot be trustworthy." He laughed. "No, you were made to be taken care of, my dear."

She did not press the matter. She had taken her stand; that was enough for the present. After an hour with him, she went home to get herself something to eat on her gas stove. Spenser's confidence in the future did not move her even to the extent of laying out half a dollar on a restaurant dinner. Women have the habit of believing in the optimistic outpourings of egotistical men, and often hasten men along the road to ruin by proclaiming this belief and acting upon it. But not intelligent women of experience; that sort of woman, by checking optimistic husbands, fathers, sons, lovers, has even put off ruin—sometimes until death has had the chance to save the optimist from the inevitable consequence of his folly. When she finished her chop and vegetable, instead of lighting a cigarette and lingering over a cup of black coffee she quickly straightened up and began upon the play Brent had given her. She had read it several times the night before, and again and again during the day. But not until now did she feel sufficiently calmed down from her agitations of thought and emotion to attack the play understandingly.

Thanks to defective education the most enlightened of us go through life much like a dim-sighted man who has no spectacles. Almost the whole of the wonderful panorama of the universe is unseen by us, or, if seen, is but partially understood or absurdly misunderstood. When it comes to the subtler things, the things of

science and art, rarely indeed is there anyone who
has the necessary training to get more than the crudest, most imperfect pleasure from them. What little
training we have is so limping that it spoils the charm
of mystery with which savage ignorance invests the
universe from blade of grass to star, and does not
put in place of that broken charm the profounder and
loftier joy of understanding. To take for illustration
the most widely diffused of all the higher arts and
sciences, reading: How many so-called "educated"
people can read understandingly even a novel, the form
of literature designed to make the least demand upon
the mind? People say they have read, but, when questioned, they show that they have got merely a glim-
mering of the real action, the faintest hint of style
and characterization, have perhaps noted some stray
epigram which they quote with evidently faulty grasp
of its meaning.

When the thing read is a play, almost no one can
get from it a coherent notion of what it is about. Most
of us have nothing that can justly be called imagination; our early training at home and at school killed
in the shoot that finest plant of the mind's garden. So
there is no ability to fill in the picture which the dramatic author draws in outline. Susan had not seen
"Cavalleria Rusticana" either as play or as opera.
But when she and Spenser were together in Forty-
fourth Street, she had read plays and had dreamed over
them; the talk had been almost altogether of plays—
of writing plays, of constructing scenes, of productions,
of acting, of all the many aspects of the theater.
Spenser read scenes to her, got her to help him with
criticism, and she was present when he went over his
work with Drumley, Riggs, Townsend and the others.

Thus, reading a play was no untried art to her. She read "Cavalleria" through slowly, taking about an hour to it. She saw now why Brent had given it to her as the primer lesson—the simple, elemental story of a peasant girl's ruin under promise of marriage; of her lover's wearying of one who had only crude physical charm; of his being attracted by a young married woman, gay as well as pretty, offering the security in intrigue that an unmarried woman could not offer. Such a play is at once the easiest and the hardest to act—the easiest because every audience understands it perfectly and supplies unconsciously almost any defect in the acting; the hardest because any actor with the education necessary to acting well finds it next to impossible to divest himself or herself of the sophistications of education and get back to the elemental animal.

Santuzza or *Lola?* Susan debated. *Santuzza* was the big and easy part; *Lola*, the smaller part, was of the kind that is usually neglected. But Susan saw possibilities in the character of the woman who won *Turiddu* away—the triumphant woman. The two women represented the two kinds of love—the love that is serious, the love that is light. And experience had taught her why it is that human nature soon tires of intensity, turns to frivolity. She felt that, if she could act, she would try to show that not *Turiddu's* fickleness nor his contempt of the woman who had yielded, but *Santuzza's* sad intensity and *Lola's* butterfly gayety had cost *Santuzza* her lover and her lover his life. So, it was not *Santuzza's* but *Lola's* first entrance that she studied.

In the next morning's mail, under cover addressed "Miss Susan Lenox, care of Miss Lorna Sackville," as she had written it for Brent, came the promised check for forty dollars. It was signed John P. Garvey, Secretary, and was inclosed with a note bearing the same signature:

DEAR MADAM:

Herewith I send you a check for forty dollars for the first week's salary under your arrangement with Mr. Brent. No receipt is necessary. Until further notice a check for the same amount will be mailed you each Thursday. Unless you receive notice to the contrary, please call as before, at three o'clock next Wednesday.

It made her nervous to think of those five days before she should see Brent. He had assured her he would expect nothing from her; but she felt she must be able to show him that she had not been wasting her time—his time, the time for which he was paying nearly six dollars a day. She must work every waking hour, except the two hours each day at the hospital. She recalled what Brent had said about the advantage of being contented alone—and how everything worth doing must be done in solitude. She had never thought about her own feelings as to company and solitude, as it was not her habit to think about herself. But now she realized how solitary she had been, and how it had bred in her habits of thinking and reading—and how valuable these habits would be to her in her work. There was Rod, for example. He hated being alone, must have someone around even when he was writing; and he had no taste for order or system. She understood why it was so hard for him to stick at anything, to put anything through to the finish. With her fondness for being alone, with her passion for reading and thinking about what she read, surely she ought

soon to begin to accomplish something—if there was
any ability in her.

She found Rod in higher spirits. Several ideas for
his play had come to him; he already saw it acted, successful, drawing crowded houses, bringing him in anywhere from five hundred to a thousand a week. She was
not troubled hunting for things to talk about with
him—she, who could think of but one thing and that a
secret from him. He talked his play, a steady stream
with not a seeing glance at her or a question about
her. She watched the little clock at the side of the
bed. At the end of an hour to the minute, she interrupted him in the middle of a sentence. "I must
go now," said she, rising.

"Sit down," he cried. "You can stay all day. The
doctor says it will do me good to have you to talk
with. And Sperry isn't coming until tomorrow."

"I can't do it," said she. "I must go."

He misunderstood her avoiding glance. "Now,
Susie—sit down there," commanded he. "We've got
plenty of money. You—you needn't bother about it
any more."

"We're not settled yet," said she. "Until we are,
I'd not dare take the risk." She was subtly adroit by
chance, not by design.

"Risk!" exclaimed he angrily. "There's no risk.
I've as good as got the advance money. Sit down."

She hesitated. "Don't be angry," pleaded she in a
voice that faltered. "But I must go."

Into his eyes came the gleam of distrust and jealousy. "Look at me," he ordered.

With some difficulty she forced her eyes to meet
his.

"Have you got a lover?"

"No."

"Then where do you get the money we're living on?"

He counted on her being too humiliated to answer in words. Instead of the hanging head and burning cheeks he saw clear, steady eyes, heard a calm, gentle and dignified voice say:

"In the streets."

His eyes dropped and a look of abject shame made his face pitiable. "Good Heavens," he muttered. "How low we are!"

"We've been doing the best we could," said she simply.

"Isn't there any decency anywhere in you?" he flashed out, eagerly seizing the chance to forget his own shame in contemplating her greater degradation.

She looked out of the window. There was something terrible in the calmness of her profile. She finally said in an even, pensive voice:

"You have been intimate with a great many women, Rod. But you have never got acquainted with a single one."

He laughed good-humoredly. "Oh, yes, I have. I've learned that 'every woman is at heart a rake,' as Mr. Jingle Pope says."

She looked at him again, her face now curiously lighted by her slow faint smile. "Perhaps they showed you only what they thought you'd be able to appreciate," she suggested.

He took this as evidence of her being jealous of him. "Tell me, Susan, did you leave me—in Forty-fourth Street—because you thought or heard I wasn't true to you?"

"What did Drumley tell you?"

"I asked him, as you said in your note. He told me he knew no reason."

So Drumley had decided it was best Rod should not know why she left. Well, perhaps—probably—Drumley was right. But there was no reason why he shouldn't know the truth now. "I left," said she, "because I saw we were bad for each other."

This amused him. She saw that he did not believe. It wounded her, but she smiled carelessly. Her smile encouraged him to say: "I couldn't quite make up my mind whether the reason was jealousy or because you had the soul of a shameless woman. You see, I know human nature, and I know that a woman who once crosses the line never crosses back. I'll always have to watch you, my dear. But somehow I like it. I guess you have—you and I have—a rotten streak in us. We were brought up too strictly. That always makes one either too firm or too loose. I used to think I liked good women. But I don't. They bore me. That shows I'm rotten."

"Or that your idea of what's good is—is mistaken."

"You don't pretend that *you* haven't done wrong?" cried Rod.

"I might have done worse," replied she. "I might have wronged others. No, Rod, I can't honestly say I've ever felt wicked."

"Why, what brought you here?"

She reflected a moment, then smiled. "Two things brought me down," said she. "In the first place, I wasn't raised right. I was raised as a lady instead of as a human being. So I didn't know how to meet the conditions of life. In the second place—" her smile returned, broadened— "I was too—too what's called 'good.' "

"Pity about you!" mocked he.

"Being what's called good is all very well if you're independent or if you've got a husband or a father to do life's dirty work for you—or, perhaps, if you happen to be in some profession like preaching or teaching —though I don't believe the so-called 'goodness' would let you get very far even as a preacher. In most lines, to practice what we're taught as children would be to go to the bottom like a stone. You know this is a hard world, Rod. It's full of men and women fighting desperately for food and clothes and a roof to cover them—fighting each other. And to get on you've got to have the courage and the indifference to your fellow beings that'll enable you to do it."

"There's a lot of truth in that," admitted Spenser. "If I'd not been such a 'good fellow,' as they call it— a fellow everybody liked—if I'd been like Brent, for instance—Brent, who never would have any friends, who never would do anything for anybody but himself, who hadn't a thought except for his career—why, I'd be where he is."

It was at the tip of Susan's tongue to say, "Yes— strong—able to help others—able to do things worth while." But she did not speak.

Rod went on: "I'm not going to be a fool any longer. I'm going to be too busy to have friends or to help people or to do anything but push my own interests."

Susan, indifferent to being thus wholly misunderstood, was again moving toward the door. "I'll be back this evening, as usual," said she.

Spenser's face became hard and lowering: "You're going to stay here now, or you're not coming back," said he. "You can take your choice. Do you want me to know you've got the soul of a streetwalker?"

She stood at the foot of the bed, gazing at the wall above his head. "I must earn our expenses until we're safe," said she, once more telling a literal truth that was yet a complete deception.

"Why do you fret me?" exclaimed he. "Do you want me to be sick again?"

"Suppose you didn't get the advance right away," urged she.

"I tell you I shall get it! And I won't have you— do as you are doing. If you go, you go for keeps."

She seated herself. "Do you want me to read or take dictation?"

His face expressed the satisfaction small people find in small successes at asserting authority. "Don't be angry," said he. "I'm acting for your good. I'm saving you from yourself."

"I'm not angry," replied she, her strange eyes resting upon him.

He shifted uncomfortably. "Now what does that look mean?" he demanded with an uneasy laugh.

She smiled, shrugged her shoulders.

Sperry—small and thin, a weather-beaten, wooden face suggesting Mr. Punch, sly keen eyes, theater in every tone and gesture—Sperry pushed the scenario hastily to completion and was so successful with Fitzalan that on Sunday afternoon he brought two hundred and fifty dollars, Spenser's half of the advance money.

"Didn't I tell you!" said Spenser to Susan, in triumph. "We'll move at once. Go pack your traps and put them in a carriage, and by the time you're back here Sperry and the nurses will have me ready."

It was about three when Susan got to her room.
"Why, you're packing up!" cried Clara, when she
came in a little later.

Clara dropped into a chair and began to weep. "I'll
miss you something fierce!" sobbed she. "You're the
only friend in the world I give a damn for, or that
gives a damn for me. I wish to God I was like you.
You don't need anybody."

"Oh, yes, I do, dear," cried Susan.

"But, I mean, you don't lean on anybody. I don't
mean you're hard-hearted—for you ain't. You've
pulled me and a dozen other girls out of the hole lots
of times. But you're independent. Can't you take me
along? I can drop that bum across the hall. I don't
give a hoot for him. But a girl's got to make believe
she cares for somebody or she'll blow her brains out."

"I can't take you along, but I'm going to come for
you as soon as I'm on my feet," said Susan. "I've got
to get up myself first. I've learned at least that much."

"Oh, you'll forget all about *me*."

"No," said Susan.

And Clara knew that she would not. Moaned Clara,
"I'm not fit to go. I'm only a common streetwalker.
You belong up there. You're going back to your own.
But I belong here. I wish to God I was like most of
the people down here, and didn't have any sense. No
wonder you used to drink so! I'm getting that way,
too. The only people that don't hit the booze hard
down here are the muttonheads who don't know nothing
and can't learn nothing. . . . I used to be contented.
But somehow, being with you so much has made me
dissatisfied."

"That means you're on your way up," said Susan,
busy with her packing.

"It would, if I had sense enough. Oh, it's torment to have sense enough to see, and not sense enough to do!"

"I'll come for you soon," said Susan. "You're going up with me."

Clara watched her for some time in silence. "You're sure you're going to win?" said she, at last.

"Sure," replied Susan.

"Oh, you can't be as sure as that."

"Yes, but I can," laughed she. "I'm done with foolishness. I've made up my mind to get up in the world."

"Do you mean to say you've got any respect for yourself?" said Clara. "*I* haven't. And I don't see how any girl in our line can have."

"I thought I hadn't," was Susan's reply, "until I talked with—with someone I met the other day. If you slipped and fell in the mud—or were thrown into it—you wouldn't say, 'I'm dirty, through and through, I can never get clean again'—would you?"

"But that's different," objected Clara.

"Not a bit," declared Susan. "If you look around this world, you'll see that everybody who ever moved about at all has slipped and fallen in the mud—or has been pushed in."

"Mostly pushed in."

"Mostly pushed in," assented Susan. "And those that have good sense get up as soon as they can, and wash as much of the mud off as'll come off—maybe all —and go on. The fools—they worry about the mud. But not I—not any more! . . . And not you, my dear —when I get you uptown."

Clara was now looking on Susan's departure as a dawn of good luck for herself. She took a headache powder, telephoned for a carriage, and helped carry down the two big packages that contained all Susan's possessions worth moving. And they kissed each other good-by with smiling faces. Susan did not give Clara, the loose-tongued, her new address; nor did Clara, conscious of her own weakness, ask for it.

"Don't put yourself out about me," cried Clara in farewell. "Get a good tight grip yourself, first."

"That's advice I need," answered Susan. "Good-by. Soon—*soon!*"

The carriage had to move slowly through those narrow tenement streets, so thronged were they with the people swarmed from hot little rooms into the open to try to get a little air that did not threaten to burn and choke as it entered the lungs. Susan's nostrils were filled with the stenches of animal and vegetable decay—stenches descending in heavy clouds from the open windows of the flats and from the fire escapes crowded with all manner of rubbish; stenches from the rotting, brimful garbage cans; stenches from the groceries and butcher shops and bakeries where the poorest qualities of food were exposed to the contamination of swarms of disgusting fat flies, of mangy, vermin-harassed children and cats and dogs; stenches from the never washed human bodies, clad in filthy garments and drawn out of shape by disease and toil. Sore eyes, scrofula, withered arm or leg, sagged shoulder, hip out of joint—There, crawling along the sidewalk, was the boy whose legs had been cut off by the street car; and the stumps were horribly ulcered. And there at the basement window drooled and cackled the fat idiot girl whose mother sacrificed everything always to dress her freshly in pink. What a world!—where a few people—such a very few!—lived in health and comfort and cleanliness—and the millions lived in disease and squalor, ignorant, untouched of civilization save to wear its cast-off clothes and to eat its castaway food and to live in its dark noisome cellars!—And to toil unceasingly to make for others the good things of which they had none themselves! It made her heart-sick—the sadder because nothing could be done about it. Stay and help? As well stay to put out a conflagration barehanded and alone.

As the carriage reached wider Second Avenue, the horses broke into a trot. Susan drew a long breath of the purer air—then shuddered as she saw the corner where the dive into which the cadet had lured her flaunted its telltale awnings. Lower still her spirits sank when she was passing, a few blocks further on, the music hall. There, too, she had had a chance, had let hope blaze high. And she was going forward—into —the region where she had been a slave to Freddie Palmer—no, to the system of which he was a slave no less than she——

"I *must* be strong! I *must!*" Susan said to herself, and there was desperation in the gleam of her eyes, in the set of her chin. "This time I will fight! And I feel at last that I can."

But her spirits soared no more that day.

XIV

SPERRY had chosen for "Mr. and Mrs. Spenser" the second floor rear of a house on the south side of West Forty-fifth Street a few doors off Sixth Avenue. It was furnished as a sitting-room— elegant in red plush, with oil paintings on the walls, a fringed red silk-plush dado fastened to the mantelpiece with bright brass-headed tacks, elaborate imitation lace throws on the sofa and chairs, and an imposing piece that might have been a cabinet organ or a pianola or a roll-top desk but was in fact a comfortable folding bed. There was a marble stationary washstand behind the hand-embroidered screen in the corner, near one of the two windows. Through a deep clothes closet was a small but satisfactory bathroom.

"And it's warm in winter," said Mrs. Norris, the landlady, to Susan. "Don't you hate a cold bathroom?"

Susan declared that she did.

"There's only one thing I hate worse," said Mrs. Norris, "and that's cold coffee."

She had one of those large faces which look bald because the frame of hair does not begin until unusually far back. At fifty, when her hair would be thin, Mrs. Norris would be homely; but at thirty she was handsome in a bold, strong way. Her hair was always carefully done, her good figure beautifully corseted. It was said she was not married to Mr. Norris—because New York likes to believe that people are living together without being married, because Mr. Norris came and went irregularly, and because Mrs. Norris was so particular about her toilet—and everyone knows that when a woman has the man with whom she's satisfied securely fastened, she shows her content or her virtuous indifference to other men—or her laziness —by neglecting her hair and her hips and dressing in any old thing any which way. Whatever the truth as to Mrs. Norris's domestic life, she carried herself strictly and insisted upon keeping her house as respectable as can reasonably be expected in a large city. That is, everyone in it was quiet, was of steady and sedate habit, was backed by references. Not until Sperry had thoroughly qualified as a responsible person did Mrs. Norris accept his assurances as to the Spensers and consent to receive them. Downtown the apartment houses that admit persons of loose character are usually more expensive because that class of tenants have more and expect more than ordinary working people. Uptown the custom is the reverse; to get into a respectable house you must pay more. The Spensers had to pay fourteen a week for their quarters—and they were getting a real bargain, Mrs. Norris having a weakness for literature and art where they were respectable and paid regularly.

"What's left of the two hundred and fifty will not last long," said Spenser to Susan, when they were established and alone. "But we'll have another five hundred as soon as the play's done, and that'll be in less than a month. We're to begin tomorrow. In less than two months the play'll be on and the royalties will be coming in. I wonder how much I owe the doctor and the hospital."

"That's settled," said Susan.

He glanced at her with a frown. "How much was it? You had no right to pay!"

"You couldn't have got either doctor or room without payment in advance." She spoke tranquilly, with a quiet assurance of manner that was new in her, the nervous and sensitive about causing displeasure in others. She added, "Don't be cross, Rod. You know it's only pretense."

"Don't you believe anybody has any decency?" demanded he.

"It depends on what you mean by decency," replied she. "But why talk of the past? Let's forget it."

"I would that I could!" exclaimed he.

She laughed at his heroics. "Put that in your play," said she. "But this isn't the melodrama of the stage. It's the farce comedy of life."

"How you have changed! Has all the sweetness, all the womanliness, gone out of your character?"

She showed how little she was impressed. "I've learned to take terrible things—really terrible things—without making a fuss—or feeling like making a fuss. You can't expect me to get excited over mere—staginess. They're fond of fake emotions up in this part of town. But down where I've been so long the real horrors come too thick and fast for there to be any time to fake."

He continued to frown, presently came out of a deep study to say, "Susie, I see I've got to have a serious talk with you."

"Wait till you're well, my dear," said she. "I'm afraid I'll not be very sympathetic with your seriousness."

"No—today. I'm not an invalid. And our relations worry me, whenever I think of them."

He observed her as she sat with hands loosely clasped in her lap; there was an inscrutable look upon her delicate face, upon the clear-cut features so attractively framed by her thick dark hair, brown in some lights, black in others.

"Well?" said she.

"To begin, I want you to stop rouging your lips. It's the only sign of—of what you were. I'd a little rather you didn't smoke. But as respectable women smoke nowadays, why I don't seriously object. And when you get more clothes, get quieter ones. Not that you dress loudly or in bad taste——"

"Thank you," murmured Susan.

"What did you say?"

"I didn't mean to interrupt. Go on."

"I admire the way you dress, but it makes me jealous. I want you to have nice clothes for the house. I like things that show your neck and suggest your form. But I don't want you attracting men's eyes and their loose thoughts, in the street. . . . And I don't want you to look so damnably alluring about the feet. That's your best trick—and your worst. Why are you smiling—in that fashion?"

"You talk to me as if I were your wife."

He gazed at her with an expression that was as affectionate as it was generous—and it was most generous. "Well, you may be some day—if you keep straight. And I think you will."

The artificial red of her lips greatly helped to make her sweetly smiling face the perfection of gentle irony. "And you?" said she.

"You know perfectly well it's different about a man."

"I know nothing of the sort," replied she. "Among

267

certain kinds of people that is the rule. But I'm not
of those kinds. I'm trying to make my way in the
world, exactly like a man. So I've got to be free from
the rules that may be all very well for ladies. A
woman can't fight with her hands tied, any more than
a man can—and you know what happens to the men
who allow themselves to be tied; they're poor down-
trodden creatures working hard at small pay for the
men who fight with their hands free."

"I've taken you out of the unprotected woman
class, my dear," he reminded her. "You're mine, now,
and you're going back where you belong."

"Back to the cage it's taken me so long to learn to
do without?" She shook her head. "No, Rod—I
couldn't possibly do it—not if I wanted to. . . .
You've got several false ideas about me. You'll have
to get rid of them, if we're to get along."

"For instance?"

"In the first place, don't delude yourself with the
notion that I'd marry you. I don't know whether the
man I was forced to marry is dead or whether he's
got a divorce. I don't care. No matter how free
I was I shouldn't marry you."

He smiled complacently. She noted it without irritation. Truly, small indeed is the heat of any kind
that can be got from the warmed-up ashes of a burnt-
out passion. She went easily on:

"You have nothing to offer me—neither love nor
money. And a woman—unless she's a poor excuse—
insists on one or the other. You and I fancied we loved
each other for a while. We don't fool ourselves in
that way now. At least I don't, though I believe you
do imagine I'm in love with you."

"You wouldn't be here if you weren't."

"Put that out of your head, Rod. It'll only breed trouble. I don't like to say these things to you, but you compel me to. I learned long ago how foolish it is to put off unpleasant things that will have to be faced in the end. The longer they're put off the worse the final reckoning is. Most of my troubles have come through my being too weak or good-natured—or whatever it was—to act as my good sense told me. I'm not going to make that mistake any more. And I'm going to start the new deal with absolute frankness with you. I am not in love with you."

"I know you better than you know yourself," said he.

"For a little while after I found you again I did have a return of the old feeling—or something like it. But it soon passed. I couldn't love you. I know you too well."

He struggled hard with his temper, as his vanity lashed at it. She saw, struggled with her old sensitiveness about inflicting even necessary pain upon others, went on:

"I simply like you, Rod—and that's all. We're well acquainted. You're physically attractive to me—not wildly so, but enough—more than any other man— probably more than most husbands are to their wives —or most wives to their husbands. So as long as you treat me well and don't wander off to other women, I'm more than willing to stay on here."

"Really!" said he, in an intensely sarcastic tone. "Really!"

"Now—keep your temper," she warned. "Didn't I keep mine when you were handing me that impertinent talk about how I should dress and the rest of it? No —let me finish. In the second place and in conclusion, my dear Rod, I'm not going to live off you. I'll pay my half of the room. I'll pay for my own clothes—and rouge for my lips. I'll buy and cook what we eat in the room; you'll pay when we go to a restaurant. I believe that's all."

"Are you quite sure?" inquired he with much satire.

"Yes, I think so. Except—if you don't like my terms, I'm ready to leave at once."

"And go back to the streets, I suppose?" jeered he.

"If it were necessary—yes. So long as I've got my youth and my health, I'll do precisely as I please. I've no craving for respectability—not the slightest. I—I——" She tried to speak of her birth, that secret shame of which she was ashamed. She had been thinking that Brent's big fine way of looking at things had cured her of this bitterness. She found that it had not—as yet. So she went on, "I'd prefer your friendship to your ill will—much prefer it, as you're the only person I can look to for what a man can do for a woman, and as I like you. But if I have to take tyranny along with the friendship—" she looked at him quietly and her tones were almost tender, almost appealing—"then, it's good-by, Rod."

She had silenced him, for he saw in her eyes, much more gray than violet though the suggestion of violet was there, that she meant precisely what she said. He was astonished, almost dazed by the change in her. This woman grown was not the Susie who had left him. No—and yet——

She had left him, hadn't she? That showed a character completely hidden from him, perhaps the character he was now seeing. He asked—and there was no sarcasm and a great deal of uneasiness in his tone:

"How do you expect to make a living?"

"I've got a place at forty dollars a week."

"Forty dollars a week! You!" He scowled savagely at her. "There's only one thing anyone would pay you forty a week for."

"That's what I'd have said," rejoined she. "But it seems not to be true. My luck may not last, but while it lasts, I'll have forty a week."

"I don't believe you," said he, with the angry bluntness of jealousy.

"Then you want me to go?" inquired she, with a certain melancholy but without any weakness.

He ignored her question. He demanded:

"Who's giving it to you?"

"Brent."

Spenser leaned from the bed toward her in his excitement. "*Robert* Brent?" he cried.

"Yes. I'm to have a part in one of his plays."

Spenser laughed harshly. "What rot! You're his mistress."

"It wouldn't be strange for you to think I'd accept that position for so little, but you must know a man of his sort wouldn't have so cheap a mistress."

"It's simply absurd."

"He is to train me himself."

"You never told me you knew him."

"I don't."

"Who got you the job?"

"He saw me in Fitzalan's office the day you sent me there. He asked me to call, and when I went he made me the offer."

"Absolute rot. What reason did he give?"

"He said I looked as if I had the temperament he was in search of."

"You must take me for a fool."

"Why should I lie to you?"

"God knows. Why do women lie to men all the time? For the pleasure of fooling them."

"Oh, no. To get money, Rod—the best reason in the world, it being rather hard for a woman to make money by working for it."

"The man's in love with you!"

"I wish he were," said Susan, laughing. "I'd not be here, my dear—you may be sure of that. And I'd not content myself with forty a week. Oh, you don't know what tastes I've got! Wait till I turn myself loose."

"Well—you can—in a few months," said Spenser. Even as he had been protesting his disbelief in her story, his manner toward her had been growing more respectful—a change that at once hurt and amused her with its cynical suggestions, and also pleased her, giving her a confidence-breeding sense of a new value in herself. Rod went on, with a kind of shamefaced mingling of jest and earnest:

"You stick by me, Susie, old girl, and the time'll come when I'll be able to give you more than Brent."

"I hope so," said Susan.

He eyed her sharply. "I feel like a fool believing such a fairy story as you've been telling me. Yet I do."

"That's good," laughed she. "Now I can stay. If you hadn't believed me, I'd have had to go. And I don't want to do that—not yet."

His eyes flinched. "Not yet? What does that mean?"

"It means I'm content to stay, at present. Who can answer for tomorrow?" Her eyes lit up mockingly. "For instance—you. Today you think you're

272

going to be true to me—don't you? Yet tomorrow—
or as soon as you get strength and street clothes, I may
catch you in some restaurant telling some girl she's the
one you've been getting ready for."

He laughed, but not heartily. Sperry came, and
Susan went to buy at a department store a complete
outfit for Rod, who still had only nightshirts. As she
had often bought for him in the old days, she felt she
would have no difficulty in fitting him nearly enough,
with her accurate eye supplementing the measurements
she had taken. When she got back home two hours and
a half later, bringing her purchases in a cab, Sperry
had gone and Rod was asleep. She sat in the bathroom, with the gas lighted, and worked at "Cavalleria"
until she heard him calling. He had awakened in high
good-humor.

"That was an awful raking you gave me before
Sperry came," began he. "But it did me good. A
man gets so in the habit of ordering women about that
it becomes second nature to him. You've made it clear
to me that I've even less control over you than you
have over me. So, dear, I'm going to be humble and
try to give satisfaction, as servants say."

"You'd better," laughed Susan. "At least, until
you get on your feet again."

"You say we don't love each other," Rod went on,
a becoming brightness in his strong face. "Well—
maybe so. But—we suit each other—don't we?"

"That's why I want to stay," said Susan, sitting on
the bed and laying her hand caressingly upon his. "I
could stand it to go, for I've been trained to stand anything—everything. But I'd hate it."

He put his arm round her, drew her against his
breast. "Aren't you happy here?" he murmured.

"Happier than any place else in the world," replied she softly.

After a while she got a small dinner for their two selves on the gas stove she had brought with her and had set up in the bathroom. As they ate, she cross-legged on the bed opposite him, they beamed contentedly at each other. "Do you remember the dinner we had at the St. Nicholas in Cincinnati?" asked she.

"It wasn't as good as this," declared he. "Not nearly so well cooked. You could make a fortune as a cook. But then you do everything well."

"Even to rouging my lips?"

"Oh, forget it!" laughed he. "I'm an ass. There's a wonderful fascination in the contrast between the dash of scarlet and the pallor of that clear, lovely skin of yours."

Her eyes danced. "You are getting well!" she exclaimed. "I'm sorry I bought you clothes. I'll be uneasy every time you're out."

"You can trust me. I see I've got to hustle to keep my job with you. Well, thank God, your friend Brent's old enough to be your father."

"Is he?" cried Susan. "Do you know, I never thought of his age."

"Yes, he's forty at least—more. Are you sure he isn't after *you*, Susie?"

"He warned me that if I annoyed him in that way he'd discharge me."

"Do you like him?"

"I—don't—know," was Susan's slow, reflective answer. "I'm—afraid of him—a little."

Both became silent. Finally Rod said, with an impatient shake of the head, "Let's not think of him."

"Let's try on your new clothes," cried Susan.

And when the dishes were cleared away they had a grand time trying on the things she had bought. It was amazing how near she had come to fitting him. "You ought to feel flattered," said she. "Only a labor of love could have turned out so well."

He turned abruptly from admiring his new suit in the glass and caught her in his arms. "You do love me—you do!" he cried. "No woman would have done all you've done for me, if she didn't."

For answer, Susan kissed him passionately; and as her body trembled with the sudden upheaval of emotions long dormant or indulged only in debased, hateful ways, she burst into tears. She knew, even in that moment of passion, that she did not love him; but not love itself can move the heart more deeply than gratitude—and her bruised heart was so grateful for his words and tones and gestures of affection!

Wednesday afternoon, on the way to Brent's house, she glanced up at the clock in the corner tower of the Grand Central Station. It lacked five minutes of three. She walked slowly, timed herself so accurately that, as the butler opened the door, a cathedral chime hidden somewhere in the upper interior boomed the hour musically. The man took her direct to the elevator, and when it stopped at the top floor, Brent himself opened the door, as before. He was dismissing a short fat man whom Susan placed as a manager, and a tall, slim, and most fashionably dressed woman with a beautiful insincere face—anyone would have at once declared her an actress, probably a star. The woman gave Susan a searching, feminine look which changed swiftly to superciliousness. Both the man and the woman were loath to go, evidently had not finished what they had come to say. But Brent, in his abrupt but courteous way, said:

"Tomorrow at four, then. As you see, my next appointment has begun." And he had them in the elevator with the door closed. He turned upon Susan the gaze that seemed to take in everything. "You are in better spirits, I see," said he.

"I'm sorry to have interrupted," said she. "I could have waited."

"But *I* couldn't," replied he. "Some day you'll discover that your time is valuable, and that to waste it is far sillier than if you were to walk along throwing your money into the gutter. Time ought to be used like money—spent generously but intelligently." He talked rapidly on, with his manner as full of unexpressed and inexpressible intensity as the voice of the violin, with his frank egotism that had no suggestion of vanity or conceit. "Because I systematize my time, I'm never in a hurry, never at a loss for time to give to whatever I wish. I didn't refuse to keep you waiting for your sake but for my own. Now the next hour belongs to you and me—and we'll forget about time— as, if we were dining in a restaurant, we'd not think of the bill till it was presented. What did you do with the play?"

Susan could only look at him helplessly.

He laughed, handed her a cigarette, rose to light a match for her. "Settle yourself comfortably," said he, "and say what's in your head."

With hands deep in the trousers of his house suit, he paced up and down the long room, the cigarette loose between his lips. Whenever she saw his front face she was reassured; but whenever she saw his profile, her nerves trembled—for in the profile there was an expression of almost ferocious resolution, of tragic sadness, of the sternness that spares not. The full face was kind, if keen; was sympathetic—was the man as nature had made him. The profile was the great man—the man his career had made. And Susan knew that the profile was master.

"Which part did you like—*Santuzza* or *Lola?*"

"*Lola*," replied she.

He paused, looked at her quickly. Why?"

"Oh, I don't sympathize with the woman—or the man—who's deserted. I pity, but I can't help seeing it's her or his own fault. *Lola* explains why. Wouldn't you rather laugh than cry? *Santuzza* may have been attractive in the moments of passion, but how she must have bored *Turiddu* the rest of the time! She was so intense, so serious—so vain and selfish."

"Vain and selfish? That's interesting." He walked up and down several times, then turned on her abruptly. "Well—go on," he said. "I'm waiting to hear why she was vain and selfish."

"Isn't it vain for a woman to think a man ought to be crazy about her all the time because he once has been? Isn't it selfish for her to want him to be true to her because it gives *her* pleasure, even though she knows it doesn't give *him* pleasure?"

"Men and women are all vain and selfish in love," said he.

"But the women are meaner than the men," replied she, "because they're more ignorant and narrow-minded."

He was regarding her with an expression that made her uneasy. "But that isn't in the play—none of it," said he.

"Well, it ought to be," replied she. "*Santuzza* is the

old-fashioned conventional heroine. I used to like them—until I had lived a little, myself. She isn't true to life. But in *Lola*——"

"Yes—what about *Lola?*" he demanded.

"Oh, she wasn't a heroine, either. She was just human—taking happiness when it offered. And her gayety—and her capriciousness. A man will always break away from a solemn, intense woman to get that sort of sunshine."

"Yes—yes—go on," said Brent.

"And her sour, serious, solemn husband explains why wives are untrue to their husbands. At least, it seems so to me."

He was walking up and down again. Every trace of indolence, of relaxation, was gone from his gait and from his features. His mind was evidently working like an engine at full speed. Suddenly he halted. "You've given me a big idea," said he. "I'll throw away the play I was working on. I'll do your play."

Susan laughed—pleased, yet a little afraid he was kinder than she deserved. "What I said was only common sense—what my experience has taught me."

"That's all that genius is, my dear," replied he. "As soon as we're born, our eyes are operated on so that we shall never see anything as it is. The geniuses are those who either escape the operation or are reëndowed with true sight by experience." He nodded approvingly at her. "You're going to be a person—or, rather, you're going to show you're a person. But that comes later. You thought of *Lola* as your part?"

"I tried to. But I don't know anything about acting—except what I've seen and the talk I've heard."

"As I said the other day, that means you've little to learn. Now—as to *Lola's* entrance."

278

"Oh, I thought of a lot of things to do—to show that she, too, loved *Turiddu* and that she had as much right to love—and to be loved—as *Santuzza* had. *Santuzza* had had her chance, and had failed."

Brent was highly amused. "You seem to forget that *Lola* was a married woman—and that if *Santuzza* didn't get a husband she'd be the mother of a fatherless child."

Never had he seen in her face such a charm of sweet melancholy as at that moment. "I suppose the way I was born and the life I've led make me think less of those things than most people do," replied she. "I was talking about natural hearts—what people think in-side—the way they act when they have courage."

"When they have courage," Brent repeated reflect-ively. "But who has courage?"

"A great many people are compelled to have it," said she.

"I never had it until I got enough money to be inde-pendent."

"I never had it," said Susan, "until I had no money."

He leaned against the big table, folded his arms on his chest, looked at her with eyes that made her feel absolutely at ease with him. Said he:

"You have known what it was to have no money—none?"

Susan nodded. "And no friends—no place to sleep —worse off than *Robinson Crusoe* when the waves threw him on the island. I had to—to suck my own blood to keep alive."

"You smile as you say that," said he.

"If I hadn't learned to smile over such things," she answered, "I'd have been dead long ago."

He seated himself opposite her. He asked:

"Why didn't you kill yourself?"

"I was afraid."

"Of the hereafter?"

"Oh no. Of missing the coming true of my dreams about life."

"Love?"

"That—and more. Just love wouldn't satisfy me. I want to see the world—to know the world—and to be somebody. I want to try *everything*."

She laughed gayly—a sudden fascinating vanishing of the melancholy of eyes and mouth, a sudden flashing out of young beauty. "I've been down about as deep as one can go. I want to explore in the other direction."

"Yes—yes," said Brent, absently. "You must see it all."

He remained for some time in a profound reverie, she as unconscious of the passing of time as he—for if he had his thoughts, she had his face to study. Try as she would, she could not associate the idea of age with him—any age. He seemed simply a grown man. And the more closely she studied him the greater her awe became. He knew so much; he understood so well. She could not imagine him swept away by any of the petty emotions—the vanities, the jealousies, the small rages, the small passions and loves that made up the petty days of the small creatures who inhabit the world and call it theirs. Could he fall in love? Had he been in love? Yes—he must have been in love—many times —for many women must have taken trouble to please a man so well worth while, and he must have passed from one woman to another as his whims or his tastes changed. Could he ever care about her—as a woman? Did he think her worn out as a physical woman? Or would he realize that body is nothing by itself; that unless the soul enters it, it is cold and meaningless and worthless—like the electric bulb when the filament is dark and the beautiful, hot, brilliant and intensely living current is not in it? Could she love him? Could she ever feel equal and at ease, through and through, with a man so superior?

"You'd better study the part of *Lola*—learn the lines," said he, when he had finished his reflecting. "Then—this day week at the same hour—we will begin. We will work all afternoon—we will dine together—go to some theater where I can illustrate what I mean. Beginning with next Wednesday that will be the program every day until further notice."

"Until you see whether you can do anything with me or not?"

"Just so. You are living with Spenser?"

"Yes." Susan could have wished his tone less matter-of-fact.

"How is he getting on?"

"He and Sperry are doing a play for Fitzalan."

"Really? That's good. He has talent. If he'll learn of Sperry and talk less and work more, and steadily, he'll make a lot of money. You are not tied to him in any way?"

"No—not now that he's prospering. Except, of course, that I'm fond of him."

He shrugged his shoulders. "Oh, everybody must have somebody. You've not seen this house. I'll show it to you, as we've still fifteen minutes."

A luxurious house it was—filled with things curious and, some of them, beautiful—things gathered in excursions through Europe, Susan assumed. The only absolutely simple room was his bedroom, big and bare and so arranged that he could sleep practically out of doors. She saw servants—two men besides the butler, several women. But the house was a bachelor's house, with not a trace of feminine influence. And evidently he cared nothing about it but lived entirely in that wonderful world which so awed Susan—the world he had created within himself, the world of which she had alluring glimpses through his eyes, through his tones and gestures even. Small people strive to make, and do make, impression of themselves by laboring to show what they know and think. But the person of the larger kind makes no such effort. In everything Brent said and did and wore, in all his movements, gestures, expressions, there was the unmistakable hallmark of the man worth while. The social life has banished simplicity from even the most savage tribe. Indeed, savages, filled with superstitions, their every movement the result of some notion of proper ceremonial, are the most complex of all the human kind. The effort toward simplicity is not a movement back to nature, for there savage and lower animal are completely enslaved by custom and instinct; it is a movement upward toward the freedom of thought and action of which our best intelligence has given us a conception and for which it has given us a longing. Never had Susan met so simple a man; and never had she seen one so far from all the silly ostentations of rudeness, of unattractive dress, of eccentric or coarse speech wherewith the cheap sort of man strives to proclaim himself individual and free.

With her instinct for recognizing the best at first sight, Susan at once understood. And she was like one who has been stumbling about searching for the right road, and has it suddenly shown to him. She fairly darted along this right road. She was immediately busy, noting the mistakes in her own ideas of manners and dress, of good and bad taste. She realized how much she had to learn. But this did not discourage her. For she realized at the same time that she could learn—and his obvious belief in her as a possibility was most encouraging.

When he bade her good-by at the front door and it closed behind her, she was all at once so tired that it seemed to her she would then and there sink down through sheer fatigue and fall asleep. For no physical exercise so quickly and utterly exhausts as real brain exercise—thinking, studying, learning with all the concentrated intensity of a thoroughbred in the last quarter of the mile race.

XV

SPENSER had time and thought for his play only. He no longer tormented himself with jealousy of the abilities and income and fame of Brent and the other successful writers for the stage; was not he about to equal them, probably to surpass them? As a rule, none of the mean emotions is able to thrive—unless it has the noxious vapors from disappointment and failure to feed upon. Spenser, in spirits and in hope again, was content with himself. Jealousy of Brent about Susan had been born of dissatisfaction with himself as a failure and envy of Brent as a success; it died with that dissatisfaction and that envy. His vanity assured him that while there might be—possibly—ways in which he was not without rivals, certainly where women were concerned he simply could not be equaled; the woman he wanted he could have—and he could hold her as long as he wished. The idea that Susan would give a sentimental thought to a man "old enough to be her father"—Brent was forty-one—was too preposterous to present itself to his mind. She loved the handsome, fascinating, youthful Roderick Spenser; she would soon be crazy about him.

Rarely does it occur to a man to wonder what a woman is thinking. During courtship very young men attribute intellect and qualities of mystery and awe to the woman they love. But after men get an insight into the mind of woman and discover how trivial are the matters that of necessity usually engage it, they become skeptical about feminine mentality; they would

284

as soon think of speculating on what profundities fill
the brain of the kitten playing with a ball as of seeking
a solution of the mystery behind a woman's fits of abstraction. However, there was in Susan's face, especially in her eyes, an expression so unusual, so arresting
that Spenser, self-centered and convinced of woman's
intellectual deficiency though he was, did sometimes
inquire what she was thinking about. He asked this
question at breakfast the morning after that second
visit to Brent.

"Was I thinking?" she countered.

"You certainly were not listening. You haven't a
notion what I was talking about."

"About your play."

"Of course. You know I talk nothing else," laughed
he. "I must bore you horribly."

"No, indeed," protested she.

"No, I suppose not. You're not bored because you
don't listen."

He was cheerful about it. He talked merely to arrange his thoughts, not because he expected Susan to
understand matters far above one whom nature had
fashioned and experience had trained to minister satis-
fyingly to the physical and sentimental needs of man.
He assumed that she was as worshipful before his
intellect as in the old days. He would have been even
more amazed than enraged had he known that she regarded his play as mediocre claptrap, false to life, fit
only for the unthinking, sloppily sentimental crowd
that could not see the truth about even their own
lives, their own thoughts and actions.

"There you go again!" cried he, a few minutes later.
"What *are* you thinking about? I forgot to ask how
you got on with Brent. Poor chap—he's had several

failures in the past year. He must be horribly cut up. They say he's written out. What does he think he's trying to get at with you?"

"Acting, as I told you," replied Susan. She felt ashamed for him, making this pitiable exhibition of patronizing a great man.

"Sperry tells me he has had that twist in his brain for a long time—that he has tried out a dozen girls or more—drops them after a few weeks or months. He has a regular system about it—runs away abroad, stops the pay after a month or so."

"Well, the forty a week's clear gain while it lasts," said Susan. She tried to speak lightly. But she felt hurt and uncomfortable. There had crept into her mind one of those disagreeable ideas that skurry into some dusky corner to hide, and reappear from time to time making every fit of the blues so much the sadder and aggravating despondency toward despair.

"Oh, I didn't mean to suggest that *you* wouldn't succeed," Spenser hastened to apologize with more or less real kindliness. "Sperry says Brent has some good ideas about acting. So, you'll learn something—maybe enough to enable me to put you in a good position—if Brent gets tired and if you still want to be independent, as you call it."

"I hope so," said Susan absently.

Spenser was no more absorbed in his career than she in hers; only, she realized how useless it would be to try to talk it to him—that he would not give her so much as ears in an attitude of polite attention. If he could have looked into her head that morning and seen what thoughts were distracting her from hearing about the great play, he would have been more amused and disgusted than ever with feminine frivolity of mind and incapacity in serious matters. For, it so happened that at the moment Susan was concentrating on a new dress. He would have laughed in the face of anyone saying to him that this new dress was for Susan in the pursuit of her scheme of life quite as weighty a matter, quite as worthy of the most careful attention, as was his play for him. Yet that would have been the literal truth. Primarily man's appeal is to the ear, woman's to the eye—the reason, by the way, why the theater—preëminently the place to *see*—tends to be dominated by woman.

Susan had made up her mind not only that she would rapidly improve herself in every way, but also how she would go about the improving. She saw that, for a woman at least, dress is as much the prime essential as an arresting show window for a dealer in articles that display well. She knew she was far from the goal of which she dreamed—the position where she would no longer be a woman primarily but a personage. Dress would not merely increase her physical attractiveness; it would achieve the far more important end of gaining her a large measure of consideration. She felt that Brent, even Brent, dealer in actualities and not to be fooled by pretenses, would in spite of himself change his opinion of her if she went to him dressed less like a middle class working girl, more like the woman of the upper classes. At best, using all the advantages she had, she felt there was small enough chance of her holding his interest; for she could not make herself believe that he was not deceiving himself about her. However, to strengthen herself in every way with him was obviously the wisest effort she could make. So, she must have a new dress for the next meeting, one which would make him better pleased to take her out to dinner. True, if she came in rags, he would not be disturbed—for he had nothing of the snob in him. But at the same time, if she came dressed like a woman of his own class, he would be impressed. "He's a man, if he is a genius," reasoned she.

Vital though the matter was, she calculated that she did not dare spend more than twenty-five dollars on this toilet. She must put by some of her forty a week; Brent might give her up at any time, and she must not be in the position of having to choose immediately between submitting to the slavery of the kept woman as Spenser's dependent and submitting to the costly and dangerous and repulsive freedom of the woman of the streets. Thus, to lay out twenty-five dollars on a single costume was a wild extravagance. She thought it over from every point of view; she decided that she must take the risk.

Late in the afternoon she walked for an hour in Fifth Avenue. After some hesitation she ventured into the waiting- and dressing-rooms of several fashionable hotels. She was in search of ideas for the dress, which must be in the prevailing fashion. She had far too good sense and good taste to attempt to be wholly original in dress; she knew that the woman who understands her business does not try to create a fashion but uses the changing and capricious fashion as the means to express a constant and consistent style of her own. She appreciated her limitations in such matters —how far she as yet was from the knowledge necessary to forming a permanent and self-expressive style. She was prepared to be most cautious in giving play to an individual taste so imperfectly educated as hers had necessarily been.

She felt that she had the natural instinct for the

best and could recognize it on sight—an instinct without which no one can go a step forward in any of the arts. She had long since learned to discriminate among the vast masses of offering, most of them tasteless or commonplace, to select the rare and few things that have merit. Thus, she had always stood out in the tawdrily or drearily or fussily dressed throngs, had been a pleasure to the eyes even of those who did not know why they were pleased. On that momentous day, she finally saw a woman dressed in admirable taste who was wearing a costume simple enough for her to venture to think of copying the main points. She walked several blocks a few yards behind this woman, then hurried ahead of her, turned and walked toward her to inspect the front of the dress. She repeated this several times between the St. Regis and Sherry's. The woman soon realized, as women always do, what the girl in the shirtwaist and short skirt was about. But she happened to be a good-natured person, and smiled pleasantly at Susan, and got in return a smile she probably did not soon forget.

The next morning Susan went shopping. She had it in mind to get the materials for a costume of a certain delicate shade of violet. A dress of that shade, and a big hat trimmed in tulle to match or to harmonize, with a bunch of silk violets fastened in the tulle in a certain way.

Susan knew she had good looks, knew what was becoming to her darkly and softly fringed violet eyes, pallid skin, to her rather tall figure, slender, not voluptuous yet suggesting voluptuousness. She could see herself in that violet costume. But when she began to look at materials she hesitated. The violet would be beautiful; but it was not a wise investment for a girl with few clothes, with but one best dress. She did not give it up definitely, however, until she came upon a sixteen-yard remnant of soft gray China crêpe. Gray was a really serviceable color for the best dress of a girl of small means. And this remnant, certainly enough for a dress, could be had for ten dollars, where violet China crêpe of the shade she wanted would cost her a dollar a yard. She took the remnant.

She went to the millinery department and bought a large hat frame. It was of a good shape and she saw how it could be bent to suit her face. She paid fifty cents for this, and two dollars and seventy cents for four yards of gray tulle. She found that silk flowers were beyond her means; so she took a bunch of presentable looking violets of the cheaper kind at two dollars and a half. She happened to pass a counter whereon were displayed bargains in big buckles and similar odds and ends of steel and enamel. She fairly pounced upon a handsome gray buckle with violet enamel, which cost but eighty-nine cents. For a pair of gray suède ties she paid two dollars; for a pair of gray silk stockings, ninety cents. These matters, with some gray silk net for the collar, gray silk for a belt, linings and the like, made her total bill twenty-three dollars and sixty-seven cents. She returned home content and studied "Cavalleria" until her purchases arrived.

Spenser was out now, was working all day and in the evenings at Sperry's office high up in the Times Building. So, Susan had freedom for her dressmaking operations. To get them off her mind that she might work uninterruptedly at learning *Lola's* part in "Cavalleria," she toiled all Saturday, far into Sunday morning, was astir before Spenser waked, finished the dress soon after breakfast and the hat by the middle of the afternoon. When Spenser returned from Sperry's office to take her to dinner, she was arrayed. For the first time he saw her in fashionable attire and it was really fashionable, for despite all her disadvantages she, who had real and rare capacity for learning, had educated herself well in the chief business of woman the man-catcher in her years in New York.

He stood rooted to the threshold. It would have justified a vanity less vigorous than Susan or any other normal human being possessed, to excite such a look as was in his eyes. He drew a long breath by way of breaking the spell over speech.

"You are *beautiful!*" he exclaimed.

And his eyes traveled from the bewitching hat, set upon her head coquettishly yet without audacity, to the soft crêpe dress, its round collar showing her perfect throat, its graceful lines subtly revealing her alluring figure, to the feet that men always admired, whatever else of beauty or charm they might fail to realize.

"How you have grown!" he ejaculated. Then, "How did you do it?"

"By all but breaking myself."

"It's worth whatever it cost. If I had a dress suit, we'd go to Sherry's or the Waldorf. I'm willing to go, without the dress suit."

"No. I've got everything ready for dinner at home."

"Then, why on earth did you dress? To give me a treat?"

"Oh, I hate to go out in a dress I've never worn. And a woman has to wear a hat a good many times before she knows how."

"What a lot of fuss you women do make about clothes."

"You seem to like it, all the same."

"Of course. But it's a trifle."

"It has got many women a good provider for life. And not paying attention to dress or not knowing how has made most of the old maids. Are those things trifles?"

Spenser laughed and shifted his ground without any sense of having been pressed to do so. "Men are fools where women are concerned."

"Or women are wise where men are concerned."

"I guess they do know their business—some of them," he confessed. "Still, it's a silly business, you must admit."

"Nothing is silly that's successful," said Susan.

"Depends on what you mean by success," argued he.

"Success is getting what you want."

"Provided one wants what's worth while," said he.

"And what's worth while?" rejoined she. "Why, whatever one happens to want."

To avoid any possible mischance to the *grande toilette* he served the dinner and did the dangerous part of the clearing up. They went to the theater, Rod enjoying even more than she the very considerable admiration she got. When she was putting the dress away carefully that night, Rod inquired when he was to be treated again.

"Oh—I don't know," replied she. "Not soon."

She was too wise to tell him that the dress would not be worn again until Brent was to see it. The hat she took out of the closet from time to time and experimented with it, reshaping the brim, studying the different effects of different angles. It delighted Spenser to catch her at this "foolishness"; he felt so superior, and with his incurable delusion of the shallow that dress is an end, not merely a means, he felt more confident than ever of being able to hold her when he should have the money to buy her what her frivolous and feminine nature evidently craved beyond all else in the world. But——

When he bought a ready-to-wear evening suit, he made more stir about it than had Susan about her costume—this, when dress to him was altogether an end in itself and not a shrewd and useful means. He spent more time in admiring himself in it before the mirror, and looked at it, and at himself in it, with far more admiration and no criticism at all. Susan noted this —and after the manner of women who are wise or indifferent—or both—she made no comment.

At the studio floor of Brent's house the door of the elevator was opened for Susan by a small young man with a notably large head, bald and bulging. His big smooth face had the expression of extreme amiability that usually goes with weakness and timidity. "I am Mr. Brent's secretary, Mr. Garvey," he explained. And Susan—made as accurate as quick in her judgments of character by the opportunities and the necessities of her experience—saw that she had before her one of those nice feeble folk who either get the shelter of some strong personality as a bird hides from the storm in the thick branches of a great tree or are tossed and torn and ruined by life and exist miserably until rescued by death. She knew the type well; it had been the dominant type in her surroundings ever since she left Sutherland. Indeed, is it not the dominant type in the whole ill-equipped, sore-tried human race? And does it not usually fail of recognition because so many of us who are in fact weak, look—and feel—strong because we are sheltered by inherited money or by powerful friends or relatives or by chance lodgment in a nook unvisited of the high winds of life in the open? Susan liked Garvey at once; they exchanged smiles and were friends.

She glanced round the room. At the huge open window Brent, his back to her, was talking earnestly to a big hatchet-faced man with a black beard. Even as Susan glanced Brent closed the interview; with an emphatic gesture of fist into palm he exclaimed, "And that's final. Good-by." The two men came toward her, both bowed, the hatchet-faced man entered the elevator and was gone. Brent extended his hand with a smile.

"You evidently didn't come to work today," said he with a careless, fleeting glance at the *grande toilette*. "But we are prepared against such tricks. Garvey, take her down to the rear dressing-room and have the maid lay her out a simple costume." To Susan, "Be as quick as you can." And he seated himself at his desk and was reading and signing letters.

Susan, crestfallen, followed Garvey down the stair-way. She had confidently expected that he would show some appreciation of her toilette. She knew she had never in her life looked so well. In the long glass in the dressing-room, while Garvey was gone to send the maid, she inspected herself again. Yes—never anything like so well. And Brent had noted her appearance only to condemn it. She was always telling herself that she wished him to regard her as a working woman, a pupil in stagecraft. But now that she had proof that he did so regard her, she was depressed, resentful. However, this did not last long. While she was changing to linen skirt and shirtwaist, she began to laugh at herself. How absurd she had been, thinking to impress this man who had known so many beautiful women, who must have been satiated long ago with beauty—she thinking to create a sensation in such a man, with a simple little costume of her own crude devising. She reappeared in the studio, laughter in her eyes and upon her lips. Brent apparently did not glance at her; yet he said, "What's amusing you?"

She confessed all, on one of her frequent impulses to candor—those impulses characteristic both of weak natures unable to exercise self-restraint and of strong natures, indifferent to petty criticism and misunderstanding, and absent from vain mediocrity, which always has itself—that is, appearances—on its mind. She described in amusing detail how she had planned and got together the costume—how foolish his reception of it had made her feel. "I've no doubt you guessed what was in my head," concluded she. "You see everything."

"I did notice that you were looking unusually well, and that you felt considerably set up over it," said he. "But why not? Vanity's an excellent thing. Like everything else it's got to be used, not misused. It can help us to learn instead of preventing."

"I had an excuse for dressing up," she reminded him. "You said we were to dine together. I thought you wouldn't want there to be too much contrast between us. Next time I'll be more sensible."

"Dress as you like—for the present," said he. "You can always change here. Later on dress will be one of the main things, of course. But not now. Have you learned the part?"

And they began. She saw at the far end of the room a platform about the height of a stage. He explained that Garvey, with the book of the play, would take the other parts in *Lola's* scenes, and sent them both to the stage. "Don't be nervous," Garvey said to her in an undertone. "He doesn't expect anything of you. This is simply to get started." But she could not suppress the trembling in her legs and arms, the hysterical contractions of her throat. However, she did contrive to go through the part—Garvey prompting. She knew she was ridiculous; she could not carry out a single one of the ideas of "business" which had come to her as she studied; she was awkward, inarticulate, panic-stricken.

"Rotten!" exclaimed Brent, when she had finished. "Couldn't be worse—therefore, couldn't be better."

She dropped to a chair and sobbed hysterically.

"That's right—cry it out," said Brent. "Leave us alone, Garvey."

Brent walked up and down smoking until she lifted her head and glanced at him with a pathetic smile. "Take a cigarette," he suggested. "We'll talk it over. Now, we've got something to talk about."

She found relief from her embarrassment in the cigarette. "You can laugh at me now," she said. "I shan't mind. In fact, I didn't mind, though I thought I did. If I had, I'd not have let you see me cry."

"Don't think I'm discouraged," said Brent. "The reverse. You showed that you have nerve—a very different matter from impudence. Impudence fails when it's most needed. Nerve makes one hang on, regardless. In such a panic as yours was, the average girl would have funked absolutely. You stuck it out. Now, you and I will try *Lola's* first entrance. No, don't throw away your cigarette. *Lola* might well come in smoking a cigarette."

She did better. What Burlingham had once thoroughly drilled into her now stood her in good stead, and Brent's sympathy and enthusiasm gave her the stimulating sense that he and she were working together. They spent the afternoon on the one thing—*Lola* coming on, singing her gay song, her halt at sight of *Santuzza* and *Turiddu*, her look at *Santuzza*, at *Turiddu*, her greeting for each. They tried it twenty different ways. They discussed what would have been in the minds of all three. They built up "business" for *Lola*, and for the two others to increase the significance of *Lola's* actions.

"As I've already told you," said he, "anyone with a voice and a movable body can learn to act. There's no question about your becoming a good actress. But it'll be some time before I can tell whether you can be what I hope—an actress who shows no sign that she's acting."

Susan showed the alarm she felt. "I'm afraid you'll find at the end that you've been wasting your time," said she.

"Put it straight out of your head," replied he. "I never waste time. To live is to learn. Already you've given me a new play—don't forget that. In a month I'll have it ready for us to use. Besides, in teaching you I teach myself. Hungry?"

"No—that is, yes. I hadn't thought of it, but I'm starved."

"This sort of thing gives one an appetite like a field hand." He accompanied her to the door of the rear dressing-room on the floor below. "Go down to the reception room when you're ready," said he, as he left her to go on to his own suite to change his clothes. "I'll be there."

The maid came immediately, drew a bath for her,

afterward helped her to dress. It was Susan's first experience with a maid, her first realization how much time and trouble one saves oneself if free from the routine, menial things. And then and there a maid was set down upon her secret list of the luxurious comforts to which she would treat herself—*when?* The craving for luxury is always a part, usually a powerful part, of an ambitious temperament. Ambition is simply a variously manifested and variously directed impulse toward improvement—a discomfort so keen that it compels effort to change to a position less uncomfortable. There had never been a time when luxury had not attracted her. At the slightest opportunity she had always pushed out for luxuries—for better food, better clothing, more agreeable surroundings. Even in her worst hours of discouragement she had not really relaxed in the struggle against rags and dirt. And when moral horror had been blunted by custom and drink, physical horror had remained acute. For, human nature being a development upward through the physical to the spiritual, when a process of degeneration sets in, the topmost layers, the spiritual, wear away first—then those in which the spiritual is a larger ingredient than the material—then those in which the material is the larger—and last of all those that are purely material. As life educated her, as her intelligence and her knowledge grew, her appreciation of luxury had grown apace—and her desire for it. With most human beings, the imagination is a heavy bird of feeble wing; it flies low, seeing only the things of the earth. When they describe heaven, it has houses of marble and streets of gold. Their pretense to sight of higher things is either sheer pretense or sight at second hand. Susan was of the few whose fancy can soar. She saw the earthy things; she saw the things of the upper regions also. And she saw the lower region from the altitudes of the higher—and in their perspective.

As she and Brent stood together on the sidewalk before his house, about to enter his big limousine, his smile told her that he had read her thought—her desire for such an automobile as her very own. "I can't help it," said she. "It's my nature to want these things."

"And to want them intelligently," said he. "Everybody wants, but only the few want intelligently—and they get. The three worst things in the world are sickness, poverty and obscurity. Your splendid health safeguards you against sickness. Your looks and your brains can carry you far away from the other two. Your one danger is of yielding to the temptation to become the wife or the mistress of some rich man. The prospect of several years of heart-breaking hard work isn't wildly attractive at twenty-two."

"You don't know me," said Susan—but the boast was uttered under her breath.

The auto rushed up to Delmonico's entrance, came to a halt abruptly yet gently. The attentiveness of the personnel, the staring and whispering of the people in the palm room showed how well known Brent was. There were several women—handsome women of what is called the New York type, though it certainly does not represent the average New York woman, who is poorly dressed in flimsy ready-made clothes and has the mottled skin that indicates bad food and too little sleep. These handsome women were dressed beautifully as well as expensively, in models got in—not from— Paris. One of them smiled sweetly at Brent, who responded, so Susan thought, rather formally. She felt dowdy in her home-made dress. All her pride in it vanished; she saw only its defects. And the gracefully careless manner of these women—the manners of those who feel sure of themselves—made her feel "green" and out of place. She was disgusted with the folly that had caused her to thrill with pleasure when his order to his chauffeur at his door told her she was actually to be taken to one of the restaurants in which she had wished to exhibit herself with him. She heartily wished she had insisted on going where she would have been as well dressed and as much at home as anyone there.

She lifted her eyes, to distract her mind from these depressing sensations. Brent was looking at her with that amused, mocking yet sympathetic expression which was most characteristic of him. She blushed furiously.

He laughed. "No, I'm not ashamed of your home-made dress," said he. "I don't care what is thought of me by people who don't give me any money. And, anyhow, you are easily the most unusual looking and the most tastefully dressed woman here. The rest of these women are doomed for life to commonplace obscurity. You——

"We'll see your name in letters of fire on the Broadway temples of fame."

"I know you're half laughing at me," said Susan. "But I feel a little better."

"Then I'm accomplishing my object. Let's not think about ourselves. That makes life narrow. Let's keep the thoughts on our work—on the big splendid dreams that come to us and invite us to labor and to dare."

And as they lingered over the satisfactory dinner he had ordered, they talked of acting—of the different rôles of "Cavalleria" as types of fundamental instincts

and actions—of how best to express those meanings—
how to fill out the skeletons of the dramatist into personalities actual and vivid. Susan forgot where she
was, forgot to be reserved with him. In her and Rod's
happiest days she had never been free from the constraint of his and her own sense of his great superiority.
With Brent, such trifles of the petty personal disappeared. And she talked more naturally than she had
since a girl at her uncle's at Sutherland. She was
amazed by the fountain that had suddenly gushed forth
in her mind at the conjuring of Brent's sympathy. She
did not recognize herself in this person so open to ideas,
so eager to learn, so clear in the expression of her
thoughts. Not since the Burlingham days had she
spent so long a time with a man in absolute unconsciousness of sex.

They were interrupted by the intrusion of a fashionable young man with the expression of assurance
which comes from the possession of wealth and the
knowledge that money will buy practically everything and everybody. Brent received him so coldly
that, after a smooth sentence or two, he took himself
off stammering and in confusion. "I suppose," said
Brent when he was gone, "that young ass hoped I
would introduce him to you and invite him to sit. But
you'll be tempted often enough in the next few years
by rich men without my helping to put temptation in
your way."

"I've never been troubled thus far," laughed Susan.

"But you will, now. You have developed to the
point where everyone will soon be seeing what it took
expert eyes to see heretofore."

"If I am tempted," said Susan, "do you think I'll
be able to resist?"

"I don't know," confessed Brent. "You have a strong sense of honesty, and that'll keep you at work with me for a while. Then——

"If you have it in you to be great, you'll go on. If you're merely the ordinary woman, a little more intelligent, you'll probably—sell out. All the advice I have to offer is, don't sell cheap. As you're not hampered by respectability or by inexperience, you needn't." He reflected a moment, then added, "And if you ever do decide that you don't care to go on with a career, tell me frankly. I may be able to help you in the other direction."

"Thank you," said Susan, her strange eyes fixed upon him.

"Why do you put so much gratitude in your tone and in your eyes?" asked he.

"I didn't put it there," she answered. "It—just came. And I was grateful because—well, I'm human, you know, and it was good to feel—that—that——"

"Go on," said he, as she hesitated.

"I'm afraid you'll misunderstand."

"What does it matter, if I do?"

"Well—you've acted toward me as if I were a mere machine that you were experimenting with."

"And so you are."

"I understand that. But when you offered to help me, if I happened to want to do something different from what you want me to do, it made me feel that you thought of me as a human being, too."

The expression of his unseeing eyes puzzled her. She became much embarrassed when he said, "Are you dissatisfied with Spenser? Do you want to change lovers? Are you revolving me as a possibility?"

"I haven't forgotten what you said," she protested.

"But a few words from me wouldn't change you from a woman into a sexless ambition."

An expression of wistful sadness crept into the violet-gray eyes, in contrast to the bravely smiling lips. She was thinking of her birth that had condemned her to that farmer Ferguson, full as much as of the life of the streets, when she said:

"I know that a man like you wouldn't care for a woman of my sort."

"If I were you," said he gently, "I'd not say those things about myself. Saying them encourages you to think them. And thinking them gives you a false point of view. You must learn to appreciate that you're not a sheltered woman, with reputation for virtue as your one asset, the thing that'll enable you to get some man to undertake your support. You are dealing with the world as a man deals with it. You must demand and insist that the world deal with you on that basis."

There came a wonderful look of courage and hope into the eyes of Lorella's daughter.

"And the world will," he went on. "At least, the only part of it that's important to you."

"Do you *really* believe that way?" asked Susan, earnestly.

"It doesn't in the least matter whether I do or not," laughed he. "Don't bother about what I think —what anyone thinks—of you. The point here, as always, is that you believe it, yourself. There's no reason why a woman who is making a career should not be virtuous. She will probably not get far if she isn't more or less so. Dissipation doesn't help man or woman, especially the ruinous dissipation of license in passion. On the other hand, no woman can ever hope to make a career who persists in narrowing and cheapening herself with the notion that her virtue is her all. She'll not amount to much as a worker in the fields of action."

Susan reflected, sighed. "It's very, very hard to get rid of one's sex."

"It's impossible," declared he. "Don't try. But don't let it worry you, either."

"Everyone can't be as strong as you are—so absorbed in a career that they care for nothing else."

This amused him. With forearms on the edge of the table he turned his cigarette slowly round between his fingers, watching the smoke curl up from it. She observed that there was more than a light sprinkle of gray in his thick, carefully brushed hair. She was filled with curiosity as to the thoughts just then in that marvelous brain of his; nor did it lessen her curiosity to know that never would those thoughts be revealed to her. What women had he loved? What women had loved him? What follies had he committed? From how many sources he must have gathered his knowledge of human nature—of woman nature! And no doubt he was still gathering. What woman was it now?

When he lifted his glance from the cigarette, it was to call the waiter and get the bill. "I've a supper engagement," he said, "and it's nearly eleven o'clock."

"Eleven o'clock!" she exclaimed.

"Time does fly—doesn't it—when a man and a woman, each an unexplored mystery to the other, are dining alone and talking about themselves."

"It was my fault," said Susan.

His quizzical eyes looked into hers—uncomfortably far.

She flushed. "You make me feel guiltier than I am," she protested, under cover of laughing glance and tone of raillery.

"Guilty? Of what?"

"You think I've been trying to—to 'encourage' you," replied she frankly.

"And why shouldn't you, if you feel so inclined?" laughed he. "That doesn't compel me to be—encouraged."

"Honestly I haven't," said she, the contents of seriousness still in the gay wrapper of raillery. "At least not any more than——"

"You know, a woman feels bound to 'encourage' a man who piques her by seeming—difficult."

"Naturally, you'd not have objected to baptizing the new hat and dress with my heart's blood." She could not have helped laughing with him. "Unfortunately for you—or rather for the new toilette—my poor heart was bled dry long, long ago. I'm a busy man, too—busy and a little tired."

"I deserve it all," said she. "I've brought it on myself. And I'm not a bit sorry I started the subject. I've found out you're quite human—and that'll help me to work better."

They separated with the smiling faces of those who have added an evening altogether pleasant to memory's store of the past's happy hours—that roomy storehouse which is all too empty even where the life has been what is counted happy. He insisted on sending her home in his auto, himself taking a taxi to the Players' where the supper was given. The moment she was alone for the short ride home, her gayety evaporated like a delicious but unstable perfume.

Why? Perhaps it was the sight of the girls on the

stroll. Had she really been one of them?—and only a
few days ago? Impossible! Not she—not the real
self . . . and perhaps she would be back there with
them before long. No—never, never, in any circumstances! . . . She had said, "Never!" the first time
she escaped from the tenements, yet she had gone back
. . . were any of those girls strolling along—were,
again, any of them Freddie Palmer's? At the thought
she shivered and quailed. She had not thought of him,
except casually, in many months. What if he should
see her, should still feel vengeful—he who never forgot
or forgave—who would dare anything! And she would
be defenseless against him. . . . She remembered what
she had last read about him in the newspaper. He
had risen in the world, was no longer in the criminal
class apparently, had moved to the class of semi-crimi-
nal wholly respectable contractor-politician. No, he
had long since forgotten her, vindictive Italian though
he was.

The auto set her down at home. Her tremors about
Freddie departed; but the depression remained. She
felt physically as if she had been sitting all evening in
a stuffy room with a dull company after a heavy, badly
selected dinner. She fell easy prey to one of those fits
of the blues to which all imaginative young people are
at least occasional victims, and by which those cursed
and hampered with the optimistic temperament are
haunted and harassed and all but or quite undone.
She had a sense of failure, of having made a bad impression. She feared he, recalling and reinspecting
what she had said, would get the idea that she was
not in earnest, was merely looking for a lover—for a
chance to lead a life of luxurious irresponsibility.
Would it not be natural for him, who knew women well,

to assume from her mistakenly candid remarks, that she was like the rest of the women, both the respectable and the free? Why should he believe in her, when she did not altogether believe in herself but suspected herself of a secret hankering after something more immediate, more easy and more secure than the stage career? The longer she thought of it the clearer it seemed to her to be that she had once more fallen victim to too much hope, too much optimism, too much and too ready belief in her fellow-beings—she who had suffered so much from these follies, and had tried so hard to school herself against them.

She fought this mood of depression—fought alone, for Spenser did not notice and she would not annoy him. She slept little that night; she felt that she could not hope for peace until she had seen Brent again.

XVI

TOWARD half-past ten the next day, a few minutes after Rod left for the theater, she was
in the bathroom cleaning the coffee machine.
There came a knock at the door of the sitting-room
bedroom. Into such disorder had her mood of depression worried her nerves that she dropped the coffee
machine into the washbowl and jumped as if she were
seeing a ghost. Several dire calamities took vague
shape in her mind, then the image of Freddie Palmer,
smiling sweetly, cruelly. She wavered only a moment,
went to the door, and after a brief hesitation that still
further depressed her about herself she opened it.
The maid—a good-natured sloven who had become devoted to Susan because she gave her liberal fees and
made her no extra work—was standing there, in an
attitude of suppressed excitement. Susan laughed, for
this maid was a born agitator, a person who is always
trying to find a thrill or to put a thrill into the most
trivial event.

"What is it now, Annie?" Susan asked.

"Mr. Spenser—he's gone, hasn't he?"

"Yes—a quarter of an hour ago."

Annie drew a breath of deep relief. "I was sure he
had went," said she, producing from under her apron
a note. "I saw it was in a gentleman's writing, so I
didn't come up with it till he was out of the way,
though the boy brought it a little after nine."

"Oh, bother!" exclaimed Susan, taking the note.

"Well, Mrs. Spenser, I've had my lesson," replied

Annie, apologetic but firm. "When I first came to New York, green as the grass that grows along the edge of the spring, what does I do but go to work and take up a note to a lady when her husband was there! Next thing I knew he went to work and hauled her round the floor by the hair and skinned out—yes, beat it for good. And my madam says to me, 'Annie, you're fired. Never give a note to a lady when her gent is by or to a gent when his lady's by. That's the first rule of life in gay New York.' And you can bet I never have since—nor never will."

Susan had glanced at the address on the note, had recognized the handwriting of Brent's secretary. Her heart had straightway sunk as if the foreboding of calamity had been realized. As she stood there uncertainly, Annie seized the opportunity to run on and on. Susan now said absently, "Thank you. Very well," and closed the door. It was a minute or so before she tore open the envelope with an impatient gesture and read:

DEAR MRS. SPENSER:

Mr. Brent requests me to ask you not to come until further notice. It may be sometime before he will be free to resume.

Yours truly,

JOHN C. GARVEY.

It was a fair specimen of Garvey's official style, with which she had become acquainted—the style of the secretary who has learned by experience not to use frills or flourishes but to convey his message in the fewest and clearest words. Had it been a skillfully worded insult Susan, in this mood of depression and distorted mental vision, could not have received it differently.

She dropped to a chair at the table and stared at the five lines of neat handwriting until her eyes became circled and her face almost haggard. Precisely as Rod had described! After a long, long time she crumpled the paper and let it fall into the waste-basket. Then she walked up and down the room—presently drifted into the bathroom and resumed cleaning the coffee machine. Every few moments she would pause in the task—and in her dressing afterwards—would be seized by the fear, the horror of again being thrust into that hideous underworld. What was between her and it, to save her from being flung back into its degradation? Two men on neither of whom she could rely. Brent might drop her at any time—perhaps had already dropped her. As for Rod—vain, capricious, faithless, certain to become an unendurable tyrant if he got her in his power— Rod was even less of a necessity than Brent. What a dangerous situation was hers! How slender her chances of escape from another catastrophe. She leaned against wall or table and was shaken by violent fits of shuddering. She felt herself slipping—slipping. It was all she could do to refrain from crying out. In those moments, no trace of the self-possessed Susan the world always saw. Her fancy went mad and ran wild. She quivered under the actuality of coarse contacts— Mrs. Tucker in bed with her—the men who had bought her body for an hour—the vermin of the tenements— the brutal hands of policemen.

Then with an exclamation of impatience or of anger she would shake herself together and go resolutely on —only again to relapse. "Because I so suddenly cut off the liquor and the opium," she said. It was the obvious and the complete explanation. But her heart was like lead, and her sky like ink. This note, the

day after having tried her out as a possibility for
the stage and as a woman. She stared down at the
crumpled note in the waste-basket. That note—it was
herself. He had crumpled her up and thrown her into
the waste-basket, where she no doubt belonged.

It was nearly noon before she, dressed with unconscious care, stood in the street doorway looking about
uncertainly as if she did not know which way to turn.
She finally moved in the direction of the theater where
Rod's play was rehearsing. She had gone to none of
the rehearsals because Rod had requested it. "I want
you to see it as a total surprise the first night," explained he. "That'll give you more pleasure, and also
it will make your criticism more valuable to us." And
she had acquiesced, not displeased to have all her time
for her own affairs. But now she, dazed, stunned almost, convinced that it was all over for her with Brent,
instinctively turned to Rod to get human help—not to
ask for it, but in the hope that somehow he would divine
and would say or do something that would make the
way ahead a little less forbidding—something that
would hearten her for the few first steps, anyhow. She
turned back several times—now, because she feared Rod
wouldn't like her coming; again because her experience
—enlightened good sense——told her that Rod would
—could—not help her, that her sole reliance was herself. But in the end, driven by one of those spasms of
terror lest the underworld should be about to engulf
her again, she stood at the stage door.

As she was about to negotiate the surly looking man
on guard within, Sperry came rushing down the long
dark passageway. He was brushing past her when he
saw who it was. "Too late!" he cried. "Rehearsal's
over."

"I didn't come to the rehearsal," explained Susan. "I thought perhaps Rod would be going to lunch."

"So he is. Go straight back. You'll find him on the stage. I'll join you if you'll wait a minute or so." And Sperry hurried on into the street.

Susan advanced along the passageway cautiously as it was but one remove from pitch dark. Perhaps fifty feet, and she came to a cross passage. As she hesitated, a door at the far end of it opened and she caught a glimpse of Spenser and a woman. Susan, ashamed at having caught him, frightened lest she should be found where she had no business to be, fled back along the main passage and jerked open the street door. She ran squarely into Sperry.

"I—I beg your pardon," stammered he. "I was in such a rush—I ought to have been thinking where I was going. Did I hurt you?" This last most anxiously. "I'm so sorry——"

"It's nothing—nothing," laughed Susan. "You are the one that's hurt."

And in fact she had knocked Sperry breathless. "You don't look anything like so strong," gasped he.

"Oh, my appearance is deceptive—in a lot of ways."

For instance, he could have got from her face just then no hint of the agony of fear torturing her—fear of the drop into the underworld.

"Find Rod?" asked he.

"He wasn't on the stage. So—I came out again."

"Wait here," said Sperry. "I'll hunt him up."

"Oh, no—please don't. I stopped on impulse. I'll not bother him." She smiled mischievously. "I might be interrupting."

Sperry promptly reddened. She had no difficulty in

reading what was in his mind—that her remark had reminded him of Rod's "affair," and he was cursing
himself for having been so stupid as to forget it for
the moment and put his partner in danger of detection.

"I—I guess he's gone," stammered Sperry. "Lord,
but that was a knock you gave me! Better come to
lunch with me."

Susan hesitated, a wistful, forlorn look in her eyes.
"Do you really want me?" asked she.

"Come right along," said Sperry in a tone that left
no doubt of his sincerity. "We'll go to the Knickerbocker and have something good to eat."

"Oh, no—a quieter place," urged Susan.

Sperry laughed. "You mean less expensive. There's
one of the great big differences between you and the
make-believe ladies one bumps into in this part of town.
You don't like to be troublesome or expensive. But
we'll go to the Knickerbocker. I feel 'way down today,
and I intended to treat myself. You don't look any too
gay-hearted yourself."

"I'll admit I don't like the way the cards are running," said Susan. "But—they'll run better—sooner
or later."

"Sure!" cried Sperry. "You needn't worry about
the play. That's all right. How I envy women!"

"Why?"

"Oh—you have Rod between you and the fight.
While I—I've got to look out for myself."

"So have I," said Susan. "So has everyone, for
that matter."

"Believe me, Mrs. Spenser," cried Sperry, earnestly,
"you can count on Rod. No matter what——"

"Please!" protested Susan. "I count on nobody. I
learned long ago not to lean."

"Well, leaning isn't exactly a safe position," Sperry admitted. "There never was a perfectly reliable crutch. Tell me your troubles."

Susan smilingly shook her head. "That'd be leaning. . . . No, thank you. I've got to think it out for myself. I believe I had arranged for a career for myself. It seems to have gone to pieces. That's all. Something else will turn up—after lunch."

"Not a doubt in the world," replied he confidently. "Meanwhile—there's Rod."

Susan's laugh of raillery made him blush guiltily. "Yes," said she, "there's Rod." She laughed again, merrily. "There's Rod—but where is there?"

"You're the only woman in the world he has any real liking for," said Sperry, earnest and sincere. "Don't you ever doubt that, Mrs. Spenser."

When they were seated in the café and he had ordered, he excused himself and Susan saw him make his way to a table where sat Fitzalan and another man who looked as if he too had to do with the stage. It was apparent that Fitzalan was excited about something; his lips, his arms, his head were in incessant motion. Susan noted that he had picked up many of Brent's mannerisms; she had got the habit of noting this imitativeness in men—and in women, too—from having seen in the old days how Rod took on the tricks of speech, manner, expression, thought even, of whatever man he happened at the time to be admiring. May it not have been this trait of Rod's that gave her the clue to his character, when she was thinking him over, after the separation?

Sperry was gone nearly ten minutes. He came, full of apologies. "Fitz held on to me while he roasted Brent. You've heard of Brent, of course?"

"Yes," said Susan.

"Fitz has been seeing him off. And he says it's——"

Susan glanced quickly at him. "Off?" she said.

"To Europe."

Susan had paused in removing her left glove. Rod's description of Brent's way of sidestepping—Rod's description to the last detail. Her hands fluttered uncertainly—fluttering fingers like a flock of birds flushed and confused by the bang of a gun.

"And Fitz says——"

"For Europe," said Susan. She was drawing her fingers slowly one by one from the fingers of her glove.

"Yes. He sailed, it seems, on impulse—barely time to climb aboard. Fitz always lays everything to a woman. He says Brent has been mixed up for a year or so with—— Oh, it doesn't matter. I oughtn't to repeat those things. I don't believe 'em—on principle. Every man—or woman—who amounts to anything has scandal talked about him or her all the time. Good Lord! If Robert Brent bothered with half the affairs that are credited to him, he'd have no time or strength —not to speak of brains—to do plays."

"I guess even the busiest man manages to fit a woman in somehow," observed Susan. "A woman or so."

Sperry laughed. "I guess yes," said he. "But as to Brent, most of the scandal about him is due to a fad of his—hunting for an undeveloped female genius who——"

"I've heard of that," interrupted Susan. "The service is dreadfully slow here. How long is it since you ordered?"

"Twenty minutes—and here comes our waiter." And then, being one of those who must finish whatever they have begun, he went on. "Well, it's true Brent does pick up and drop a good many ladies of one kind and another. And naturally, every one of them is good-looking and clever or he'd not start in. But—you may laugh at me if you like—I think he's strictly business with all of them. He'd have got into trouble if he hadn't been. And Fitz admits this one woman— she's a society woman—is the only one there's any real basis for talk about in connection with Brent."

Susan had several times lifted a spoonful of soup to her lips and had every time lowered it untasted.

"And Brent's mighty decent to those he tries and has to give up. I know of one woman he carried on his pay roll for nearly two years——"

"Let's drop Mr. Brent," cried Susan. "Tell me about—about the play."

"Rod must be giving you an overdose of that."

"I've not seen much of him lately. How was the rehearsal?"

"Fair—fair." And Sperry forgot Brent and talked on and on about the play, not checking himself until the coffee was served. He had not observed that Susan was eating nothing. Neither had he observed that she was not listening; but there was excuse for this oversight, as she had set her expression at absorbed attention before withdrawing within herself to think—and to suffer. She came to the surface again when Sperry, complaining of the way the leading lady was doing her part, said: "No wonder Brent drops one after another. Women aren't worth much as workers. Their real mind's always occupied with the search for a man to support 'em."

"Not always," cried Susan, quivering with sudden pain. "Oh, no, Mr. Sperry—not always."

"Yes—there are exceptions," said Sperry, not noting

how he had wounded her. "But—well, I never happened to run across one."

"Can you blame them?" mocked Susan. She was ashamed that she had been stung into crying out.

"To be honest—no," said Sperry. "I suspect I'd throw up the sponge and sell out if I had anything a lady with cash wanted to buy. I only *suspect* myself."

She was struggling with the re-aroused insane terror of a fall back to the depths whence she had once more just come—and she felt that, if she fell again, it would mean the very end of hope. It must have been instinct or accident, for it certainly was not any prompting from her calm expression, that moved him to say:

"Now, tell me *your* troubles. I've told you mine . . . You surely must have some?"

Susan forced a successful smile of raillery. "None to speak of," evaded she.

When she reached home there was a telegram—from Brent:

Compelled to sail suddenly. Shall be back in a few weeks. Don't mind this annoying interruption. R. B.

A very few minutes after she read these words, she was at work on the play. But—a very few minutes thereafter she was sitting with the play in her lap, eyes gazing into the black and menacing future. The misgivings of the night before had been fed and fattened into despairing certainties by the events of the day. The sun was shining, never more brightly; but it was not the light of her City of the Sun. She stayed in all afternoon and all evening. During those hours before she put out the light and shut herself away in the dark a score of Susans, every one different from every other, had been seen upon the little theater of that lodging house parlor-bedroom. There had been a hopeful Susan, a sad but resolved Susan, a strong Susan, a weak Susan; there had been Susans who could not have shed a tear; there had been Susans who shed many tears—some of them Susans all bitterness, others Susans all humility and self-reproach. Any spectator would have been puzzled by this shifting of personality. Susan herself was completely confused. She sought for her real self among this multitude so contradictory. Each successive one seemed the reality; yet none persisted. When we look in at our own souls, it is like looking into a many-sided room lined with mirrors. We see reflections—re-reflections—views at all angles—but we cannot distinguish the soul itself among all these counterfeits, all real yet all false because partial.

"What shall I do? What can I do? What will I do?"—that was her last cry as the day ended. And it was her first cry as her weary brain awakened for the new day.

At the end of the week came the regular check with a note from Garvey—less machine-like, more human. He apologized for not having called, said one thing and another had prevented, and now illness of a near relative compelled him to leave town for a few days, but as soon as he came back he would immediately call. It seemed to Susan that there could be but one reason why he should call—the reason that would make a timid, soft-hearted man such as he put off a personal interview as long as he could find excuses. She flushed hot with rage and shame as she reflected on her position. Garvey pitying her! She straightway sat down and wrote:

Dear Mr. Garvey: Do not send me any more checks until Mr. Brent comes back and I have seen him. I am in doubt whether I shall be able to go on with the work he and I had arranged.

She signed this "Susan Lenox" and dispatched it. At once she felt better in spite of the fact that she had, with characteristic and fatal folly, her good sense warned her, cut herself off from all the income in sight or in prospect. She had debated sending back the check, but had decided that if she did she might give the impression of pique or anger. No, she would give him every chance to withdraw from a bargain with which he was not content; and he would get the idea that it was she who was ending the arrangement, would therefore feel no sense of responsibility for her. She would save her pride; she would spare his feelings. She was taking counsel of Burlingham these days—was recalling the lesson he had taught her, was getting his aid in deciding her course. Burlingham protested vehemently against this sending back of the check; but she let her pride, her aversion to being an object of pity, overrule him.

A few days more, and she was so desperate, so harassed that she altogether lost confidence in her own judgment. While outwardly she seemed to be the same as always with Rod, she had a feeling of utter alienation. Still, there was no one else to whom she could turn. Should she put the facts before him and ask his opinion? Her intelligence said no; her heart said perhaps. While she was hesitating, he decided for her. One morning at breakfast he stopped talking about himself long enough to ask carelessly:

"About you and Brent—he's gone away. What are you doing?"

"Nothing," said she.

"Going to take that business up again, when he comes back?"

"I don't know."

"I wouldn't count on it, if I were you. . . . You're so sensitive that I've hesitated to say anything. But I think that chap was looking for trouble, and when he found you were already engaged, why, he made up his mind to drop it."

"Do you think so?" said Susan indifferently. "More coffee?"

"Yes—a little. If my play's as good as your coffee— That's enough, thanks. . . . Do you still draw your—your——"

His tone as he cast about for a fit word made her flush scarlet. "No—I stopped it until we begin work again."

He did not conceal his thorough satisfaction. "That's right!" he cried. "The only cloud on our happiness is gone. You know, a man doesn't like that sort of thing."

"I know," said Susan drily.

And she understood why that very night he for the first time asked her to supper after the rehearsal with Sperry and Constance Francklyn, the leading lady, with whom he was having one of those affairs which as he declared to Sperry were "absolutely necessary to a man of genius to keep him freshened up—to keep the fire burning brightly." He had carefully coached Miss Francklyn to play the part of unsuspected "understudy"—Susan saw that before they had been seated in Jack's ten minutes. And she also saw that he was himself resolved to conduct himself "like a gentleman." But after he had taken two or three highballs, Susan was forced to engage deeply in conversation with the exasperated and alarmed Sperry to avoid seeing how madly Rod and Constance were flirting. She, however, did contrive to see nothing—at least, the other three were convinced that she had not seen. When they were back in their rooms, Rod—where through pretense or through sidetracked amorousness or from simple intoxication—became more demonstrative than he had been for a long time.

"No, there's nobody like you," he declared. "Even if I wandered I'd always come back to you."

"Really?" said Susan with careless irony. "That's good. No, I can unhook my blouse."

"I do believe you're growing cold."

"I don't feel like being messed with tonight."

"Oh, very well," said he sulkily. Then, forgetting his ill humor after a few minutes of watching her graceful movements and gestures as she took off her dress and made her beautiful hair ready for the night, he burst out in a very different tone: "You don't know how glad I am that you're dependent on me again. You'll not be difficult any more."

A moment's silence, then Susan, with a queer little laugh, "Men don't in the least mind—do they?"

"Mind what?"

"Being loved for money." There was a world of sarcasm in her accent on that word loved.

"Oh, nonsense. You don't understand yourself," declared he with large confidence. "Women never grow up. They're like babies—and babies, you know, love the person that feeds them."

"And dogs—and cats—and birds—and all the lower orders." She took a book and sat in a wrapper under the light.

"Come to bed—please, dear," pleaded he.

"No, I'll read a while."

And she held the book before her until he was asleep. Then she sat a long time, her elbows on her knees, her chin supported by her hands, her gaze fixed upon his face—the face of the man who was her master now. She must please him, must accept what treatment he saw fit to give, must rein in her ambitions to suit the uncertain gait and staying power of his ability to achieve. She could not leave him; he could leave her when he might feel so inclined. Her master—capricious, tyrannical, a drunkard. Her sole reliance—and the first condition of his protection was that she should not try to do for herself. A dependent, condemned to become even more dependent.

XVII

SHE now spent a large part of every day in wandering, like a derelict, drifting aimlessly this way or that, up into the Park or along Fifth Avenue. She gazed intently into shop windows, apparently inspecting carefully all the articles on display; but she passed on, unconscious of having seen anything. If she sat at home with a book she rarely turned a page, though her gaze was fastened upon the print as if she were absorbingly interested.

What was she feeling? The coarse contacts of street life and tenement life—the choice between monstrous defilements from human beings and monstrous defilements from filth and vermin. What was she seeing? The old women of the slums—the forlorn, aloof figures of shattered health and looks—creeping along the gutters, dancing in the barrel houses, sleeping on the floor in some vile hole in the wall—sleeping the sleep from which one awakes bitten by mice and bugs, and swarming with lice.

She had entire confidence in Brent's judgment. Brent must have discovered that she was without talent for the stage—for if he had thought she had the least talent, would he not in his kindness have arranged or offered some sort of place in some theater or other? Since she had no stage talent—then—what should she do? What *could* she do? And so her mind wandered as aimlessly as her wandering steps. And never before had the sweet melancholy of her eyes been so moving.

But, though she did not realize it, there was a

highly significant difference between this mood of profound discouragement and all the other similar moods that had accompanied and accelerated her downward plunges. Every time theretofore, she had been cowed by the crushing mandate of destiny—had made no struggle against it beyond the futile threshings about of aimless youth. This time she lost neither strength nor courage. She was no longer a child; she was no longer mere human flotsam and jetsam. She did not know which way to turn; but she did know, with all the certainty of a dauntless will, that she would turn some way—and that it would not be a way leading back to the marshes and caves of the underworld. She wandered—she wandered aimlessly; but not for an instant did she cease to keep watch for the right direction— the direction that would be the best available in the circumstances. She did not know or greatly care which way it led, so long as it did not lead back whence she had come.

In all her excursions she had—not consciously but by instinct—kept away from her old beat. Indeed, except in the company of Spenser or Sperry she had never ventured into the neighborhood of Long Acre. But one day she was deflected by chance at the Forty-second Street corner of Fifth Avenue and drifted westward, pausing at each book stall to stare at the titles of the bargain offerings in literature. As she stood at one of these stalls near Sixth Avenue, she became conscious that two men were pressing against her, one on either side. She moved back and started on her way. One of the men was standing before her. She lifted her eyes, was looking into the cruel smiling eyes of a man with a big black mustache and the jaws of a prize-fighter. His smile broadened.

"I thought it was you, Queenie," said he. "Delighted to see you."

She recognized him as a fly cop who had been one of Freddie Palmer's handy men. She fell back a step and the other man—she knew him instantly as also a policeman—lined up beside him of the black mustache. Both men were laughing.

"We've been on the lookout for you a long time, Queenie," said the other. "There's a friend of yours that wants to see you mighty bad."

Susan glanced from one to the other, her face pale but calm, in contrast to her heart where was all the fear and horror of the police which long and savage experience had bred. She turned away without speaking and started toward Sixth Avenue.

"Now, what d'ye think of that?" said Black Mustache to his "side kick." "I thought she was too much of a lady to cut an old friend. Guess we'd better run her in, Pete."

"That's right," assented Pete. "Then we can keep her safe till F. P. can get the hooks on her."

Black Mustache laughed, laid his hand on her arm. "You'll come along quietly," said he. "You don't want to make a scene. You always was a perfect lady."

She drew her arm away. "I am a married woman— living with my husband."

Black Mustache laughed. "Think of that, Pete! And she soliciting us. That'll be good news for your loving husband. Come along, Queenie. Your record's against you. Everybody'll know you've dropped back to your old ways."

"I am going to my husband," said she quietly. "You had better not annoy me."

Pete looked uneasy, but Black Mustache's sinister

face became more resolute. "If you wanted to live respectable, why did you solicit us two? Come along— or do you want me and Pete to take you by the arms?"

"Very well," said she. "I'll go." She knew the police, knew that Palmer's lieutenant would act as he said —and she also knew what her "record" would do toward carrying through the plot.

She walked in the direction of the station house, the two plain clothes men dropping a few feet behind and rejoining her only when they reached the steps between the two green lamps. In this way they avoided collecting a crowd at their heels. As she advanced to the desk, the sergeant yawning over the blotter glanced up.

"Bless my soul!" cried he, all interest at once. "If it ain't F. P.'s Queenie!"

"And up to her old tricks, sergeant," said Black Mustache. "She solicited me and Pete."

Susan was looking the sergeant straight in the eyes. "I am a married woman," said she. "I live with my husband. I was looking at some books in Forty-second Street when these two came up and arrested me."

The sergeant quailed, glanced at Pete who was guiltily hanging his head—glanced at Black Mustache. There he got the support he was seeking. "What's your husband's name?" demanded Black Mustache roughly. "What's your address?"

And Rod's play coming on the next night but one! She shrank, collected herself. "I am not going to drag him into this, if I can help it," said she. "I give you a chance to keep yourselves out of trouble." She was gazing calmly at the sergeant again. "You know these men are not telling the truth. You know they've brought me here because of Freddie Palmer. My husband knows all about my past. He will stand by me. But I wish to spare him."

The sergeant's uncertain manner alarmed Black Mustache. "She's putting up a good bluff," scoffed he. "The truth is she ain't got no husband. She'd not have solicited us if she was living decent."

"You hear what the officer says," said the sergeant, taking the tone of great kindness. "You'll have to give your name and address—and I'll leave it to the judge to decide between you and the officers." He took up his pen. "What's your name?"

Susan, weak and trembling, was clutching the iron rail before the desk—the rail worn smooth by the nervous hands of ten thousand of the social system's sick or crippled victims.

"Come—what's your name?" jeered Black Mustache.

Susan did not answer.

"Put her down Queenie Brown," cried he, triumphantly.

The sergeant wrote. Then he said: "Age?"

No answer from Susan. Black Mustache answered for her: "About twenty-two now."

"She don't look it," said the sergeant, almost at ease once more. "But brunettes stands the racket better'n blondes. Native parents?"

No answer.

"Native. You don't look Irish or Dutch or Dago— though you might have a dash of the Spinnitch or the Frog-eaters. Ever arrested before?"

No answer from the girl, standing rigid at the bar. Black Mustache said:

"At least oncet, to my knowledge. I run her in myself."

"Oh, she's got a record?" exclaimed the sergeant, now wholly at ease. "Why the hell didn't you say so?"

"I thought you remembered. You took her pedigree."

"I do recollect now," said the sergeant. "Take my advice, Queenie, and drop that bluff about the officers lying. Swallow your medicine—plead guilty—and you'll get off with a fine. If you lie about the police, the judge'll soak it to you. It happens to be a good judge—a friend of Freddie's." Then to the policemen: "Take her along to court, boys, and get back here as soon as you can."

"I want her locked up," objected Black Mustache. "I want F. P. to see her. I've got to hunt for him."

"Can't do it," said the sergeant. "If she makes a yell about police oppression, our holding on to her would look bad. No, put her through."

Susan now straightened herself and spoke. "I shan't make any complaint," said she. "Anything rather than court. I can't stand that. Keep me here."

"Not on your life!" cried the sergeant. "That's a trick. She'd have a good case against us."

"F. P.'ll raise the devil if——" began Black Mustache.

"Then hunt him up right away. To court she's got to go. I don't want to get broke."

The two men fell afoul each other with curse and abuse. They were in no way embarrassed by the presence of Susan. Her "record" made her of no account either as a woman or as a witness. Soon each was so well pleased with the verbal wounds he had dealt the other that their anger evaporated. The upshot of the hideous controversy was that Black Mustache said:

"You take her to court, Pete. I'll hunt up F. P. Keep her till the last."

In after days she could recall starting for the street car with the officer, Pete; then memory was a blank until she was sitting in a stuffy room with a prison odor —the anteroom to the court. She and Pete were alone. He was walking nervously up and down pulling his little fair mustache. It must have been that she had retained throughout the impassive features which, however stormy it was within, gave her an air of strength and calm. Otherwise Pete would not presently have halted before her to say in a low, agitated voice:

"If you can make trouble for us, don't do it. I've got a wife, and three babies—one come only last week —and my old mother paralyzed. You know how it is with us fellows—that we've got to do what them higher up says or be broke."

Susan made no reply.

"And F. P.—he's right up next the big fellows nowadays. What he says goes. You can see for yourself how much chance against him there'd be for a common low-down cop."

She was still silent, not through anger as he imagined but because she had no sense of the reality of what was happening. The officer, who had lost his nerve, looked at her a moment, in his animal eyes a humble pleading look; then he gave a groan and turned away. "Oh, hell!" he muttered.

Again her memory ceased to record until—the door swung open; she shivered, thinking it was the summons to court. Instead, there stood Freddie Palmer. The instant she looked into his face she became as calm and strong as her impassive expression had been falsely making her seem. Behind him was Black Mustache, his face ghastly, sullen, cowed. Palmer made a jerky motion of head and arm. Pete went; and the door closed and she was alone with him.

"I've seen the Judge and you're free," said Freddie.

She stood and began to adjust her hat and veil.

"I'll have those filthy curs kicked off the force."

She was looking tranquilly at him.

"You don't believe me? You think I ordered it done?"

She shrugged her shoulders. "No matter," she said. "It's undone now. I'm much obliged. It's more than I expected."

"You don't believe me—and I don't blame you. You think I'm making some sort of grandstand play."

"You haven't changed—at least not much."

"I'll admit, when you left I was wild and did tell 'em to take you in as soon as they found you. But that was a long time ago. And I never meant them to disturb a woman who was living respectably with her husband. There may have been—yes, there was a time when I'd have done that—and worse. But not any more. You say I haven't changed. Well, you're wrong. In some ways I have. I'm climbing up, as I always told you I would—and as a man gets up he sees things differently. At least, he acts differently. I don't do *that* kind of dirty work, any more."

"I'm glad to hear it," murmured Susan for lack of anything else to say.

He was as handsome as ever, she saw—had the same charm of manner—a charm owing not a little of its potency to the impression he made of the man who would dare as far as any man, and then go on to dare a step farther—the step from which all but the rare, utterly unafraid man shrinks. His look at her could not but appeal to her vanity as woman, and to her woman's craving for being loved; at the same time it agitated her with specters of the days of her slavery to him. He said:

"*You*'ve changed—a lot. And all to the good. The only sign is rouge on your lips and that isn't really a sign nowadays. But then you never did look the professional—and you weren't."

His eyes were appealingly tender as he gazed at her sweet, pensive face, with its violet-gray eyes full of mystery and sorrow and longing. And the clear pallor of her skin, and the slender yet voluptuous lines of her form suggested a pale, beautiful rose, most delicate of flowers yet about the hardiest.

"So—you've married and settled down?"

"No," replied Susan. "Neither the one nor the other."

"Why, you told——"

"I'm supposed to be a married woman."

"Why didn't you give your name and address at the police station?" said he. "They'd have let you go at once."

"Yes, I know," replied she. "But the newspapers would probably have published it. So—I couldn't. As it is I've been worrying for fear I'd be recognized, and the man would get a write-up."

"That was square," said he. "Yes, it'd have been a dirty trick to drag him in."

It was the matter-of-course to both of them that she should have protected her "friend." She had simply obeyed about the most stringent and least often violated article in the moral code of the world of outcasts. If Freddie's worst enemy in that world had murdered him, Freddie would have used his last breath in shielding him from the common foe, the law.

"If you're not married to him, you're free," said Freddie with a sudden new kind of interest in her.

"I told you I should always be free."

They remained facing each other a moment. When she moved to go, he said:

"I see you've still got your taste in dress—only more so."

She smiled faintly, glanced at his clothing. He was dressed with real fashion. He looked Fifth Avenue at its best, and his expression bore out the appearance of the well-bred man of fortune. "I can return the compliment," said she. "And you too have improved."

At a glance all the old fear of him had gone beyond the possibility of return. For she instantly realized that, like all those who give up war upon society and come in and surrender, he was enormously agitated about his new status, was impressed by the conventionalities to a degree that made him almost weak and mildly absurd. He was saying:

"I was brought up badly—badly for the game, I mean. But I'm doing better, and I shall do still better. I can't abolish the system. I can't stand out against it —and live. So, I'm yielding—in my own foolish fashion."

"You don't lay up against me the—the—you know what I mean?"

The question surprised her, so far as it aroused any emotion. She answered indifferently:

"I don't lay anything up against anybody. What's the use? I guess we all do the best we can—the best the system'll let us."

And she was speaking the exact truth. She did not

reason out the causes of a state of mind so alien to the experiences of the comfortable classes that they could not understand it, would therefore see in it hardness of heart. In fact, the heart has nothing to do with this attitude in those who are exposed to the full force of the cruel buffetings of the storms that incessantly sweep the wild and wintry sea of active life. They lose the sense of the personal. Where they yield to anger and revenge upon the instrument the blow fate has used it to inflict, the resentment is momentary. The mood of personal vengeance is characteristic of stupid people leading uneventful lives—of comfortable classes, of remote rural districts. She again moved to go, this time putting out her hand with a smile. He said, with an awkwardness most significant in one so supple of mind and manner:

"I want to talk to you. I've got something to propose—something that'll interest you. Will you give me—say, about an hour?"

She debated, then smiled. "You will have me arrested if I refuse?"

He flushed scarlet. "You're giving me what's coming to me," said he. "The reason—one reason—I've got on so well is that I've never been a liar."

"No—you never were that."

"You, too. It's always a sign of bravery, and bravery's the one thing I respect. Yes, what I said I'd do always I did. That's the only way to get on in politics—and the crookeder the politics the more careful a man has to be about acting on the level. I can borrow a hundred thousand dollars without signing a paper—and that's more than the crooks in Wall Street can do—the biggest and best of them. So, when I told you how things were with me about you, I was on the level."

"I know it," said Susan. "Where shall we go? I can't ask you to come home with me."

"We might go to tea somewhere——"

Susan laughed outright. Tea! Freddie Palmer proposing tea! What a changed hooligan—how ridiculously changed! The other Freddie Palmer—the real one—the fascinating repelling mixture of all the barbaric virtues and vices must still be there. But how carefully hidden—and what strong provocation would be needed to bring that savage to the surface again. The Italian in him, that was carrying him so far so cleverly, enabled him instantly to understand her amusement. He echoed her laugh. Said he:

"You've no idea the kind of people I'm traveling with —not political swells, but the real thing. What do you say to the Brevoort?"

She hesitated.

"You needn't be worried about being seen with me, no matter how high you're flying," he hastened to say. "I always did keep myself in good condition for the rise. Nothing's known about me—or ever will be."

The girl was smiling at him again. "I wasn't thinking of those things," said she. "I've never been to the Brevoort."

"It's quiet and respectable."

Susan's eyes twinkled. "I'm glad it's respectable," said she.

As they walked through West Ninth Street she noted that there was more of a physical change in him than she had seen at first glance. He was less athletic, heavier of form and his face was fuller. "You don't

334

keep in as good condition as you used," said she.

"It's those infernal automobiles," cried he. "They're death to figure—to health, for that matter. But I've got the habit, and I don't suppose I'll ever break myself of it. I've taken on twenty pounds in the past year and I've got myself so upset that the doctor has ordered me abroad to take a cure. Then there's champagne. I can't let that alone, either, though I know it's plain poison."

And when they were in the restaurant of the Brevoort he insisted on ordering champagne—and left her for a moment to telephone for his automobile. It amused her to see a man so masterful thus pettily enslaved. She laughed at him, and he again denounced himself as a weak fool. "Money and luxury are too much for me. They are for everybody. I'm not as strong willed as I used to be," he said. "And it makes me uneasy. That's another reason for my proposition."

"Well—let' hear it," said she. "I happen to be in a position where I'm fond of hearing propositions—even if I have no intention of accepting."

She was watching him narrowly. The Freddie Palmer he was showing to her was a surprising but perfectly logical development of a side of his character with which she had been familiar in the old days; she was watching for that other side—the sinister and cruel side. "But first," he went on, "I must tell you a little about myself. You know about my family."

"I remember," said Susan.

"Well, honestly, do you wonder that I was what I used to be?"

"No," she answered. "I wonder that you are what you *seem* to be."

"What I come pretty near being," cried he. "The part that's more or less put on today is going to be the real thing tomorrow. That's the way it is with life—you put on a thing, and gradually learn to wear it. And—I want you to help me."

There fell silence between them, he gazing at his glass of champagne, turning it round and round between his long white fingers and watching the bubbles throng riotously up from the bottom. "Yes," he said thoughtfully, "I want you to help me. I've been waiting for you. I knew you'd turn up again." He laughed. "I've been true to you in a way—a man's way. I've hunted the town for women who suggested you—a poor sort of makeshift—but—I had to do something."

"What were you going to tell me?"

Her tone was businesslike. He did not resent it, but straightway acquiesced. "I'll plunge right in. I've been, as you know, a bad one—bad all my life. I was born bad. You know about my mother and father. One of my sisters died in a disreputable resort. The other—well, the last I heard of her, she was doing time in an English pen. I've got a brother—he's a degenerate. Well! I made up my mind to get the thing that is necessary."

"Respectability," said Susan.

"Respectability—exactly. So I set out to improve my brains. I went to night school and read and studied. And I didn't stay a private in the gang of toughs. I had the brains to be leader, but the leader's got to be a fighter too. I took up boxing and made good in the ring. I got to be leader. Then I pushed my way up where I thought out the dirty work for the others to do, and I stayed under cover and made 'em bring the big share of the profits to me. And they did it because I had the brains to think out jobs that paid well and that could be pulled off without getting pinched—at least, not always getting pinched."

Palmer sipped his champagne, looked at her to see if she was appreciative. "I thought you'd understand," said he. "I needn't go into details. You remember about the women?"

"Yes, I remember," said Susan. "That was one step in the ladder up?"

"It got me the money to make my first play for respectability. I couldn't have got it any other way. I had extravagant tastes—and the leader has to be always giving up to help this fellow and that out of the hole. And I never did have luck with the cards and the horses."

"Why did you want to be respectable?" she asked.

"Because that's the best graft," explained he. "It means the best money, and the most influence. The coyotes that raid the sheepfold don't get the big share—though they may get a good deal. No, it's the shepherds and the owners that pull off the most. I've been leader of coyotes. I'm graduating into shepherd and proprietor."

"I see," said Susan. "You make it beautifully clear."   •

He bowed and smiled. "Thank you, kindly. Then, I'll go on. I'm deep in the contracting business now. I've got a pot of money put away. I've cut out the cards—except a little gentlemen's game now and then, to help me on with the right kind of people. Horses, the same way. I've got my political pull copper-riveted. It's as good with the Republicans as with Democrats, and as good with the reform crowd as with either. My next move is to cut loose from the gang. I've put a lot of lieutenants between me and them, instead of dealing with them direct. I'm putting in several more—fellows I'm not ashamed to be seen with in Delmonico's."

"What's become of Jim?" asked Susan.

"Dead—a kike shot him all to pieces in a joint in Seventh Avenue about a month ago. As I was saying, how do these big multi-millionaires do the trick? They don't tell somebody to go steal what they happen to want. They tell somebody they want it, and that somebody else tells somebody else to get it, and that somebody else passes the word along until it reaches the poor devils who must steal it or lose their jobs. I studied it all out, and I've framed up my game the same way. Nowadays, every dollar that comes to me has been thoroughly cleaned long before it drops into my pocket. But you're wondering where *you* come in."

"Women are only interested in what's coming to them," said Susan.

"Sensible men are the same way. The men who aren't—they work for wages and salaries. If you're going to live off of other people, as women and the rich do, you've got to stand steady, day and night, for Number One. And now, here's where *you* come in. You've no objection to being respectable?"

"I've no objection to not being disreputable."

"That's the right way to put it," he promptly agreed. "Respectable, you know, doesn't mean anything but appearances. People who are really respectable, who let it strike in, instead of keeping it on the outside where it belongs—they soon get poor and drop down and out."

Palmer's revelation of himself and of a philosophy which life as it had revealed itself to her was incessantly urging her to adopt so grappled her attention that she altogether forgot herself. A man on his way to the scaffold who suddenly sees and feels a cataclysm rocking the world about him forgets his own plight. Unconsciously he was epitomizing, unconsciously she was learning, the whole story of the progress of the race upward from beast toward intellect—the brutal and bloody building of the highway from the caves of darkness toward the peaks of light. The source from which springs, and ever has sprung, the cruelty of man toward man is the struggle of the ambition of the few who see and insist upon better conditions, with the inertia and incompetence of the many who have little sight and less imagination. Ambition must use the inert mass—must persuade it, if possible, must compel it by trick or force if persuasion fails. But Palmer and Susan Lenox were, naturally, not seeing the thing in the broad but only as it applied to themselves.

"I've read a whole lot of history and biography," Freddie went on, "and I've thought about what I read and about what's going on around me. I tell you the world's full of cant. The people who get there don't act on what is always preached. The preaching isn't all lies—at least, I think not. But it doesn't fit the facts a man or a woman has got to meet."

"I realized that long ago," said Susan.

"There's a saying that you can't touch pitch without being defiled. Well—you can't build without touching pitch—at least not in a world where money's king and where those with brains have to live off of those without brains by making 'em work and showing 'em what to work at. It's a hell of a world, but *I* didn't get it up."

"And we've got to live in it," said she, "and get out of it the things we want and need."

"That's the talk!" cried Palmer. "I see you're 'on.' Now—to make a long story short—you and I can get what we want. We can help each other. You were better born than I am—you've had a better training in manners and dress and all the classy sort of things. I've got the money—and brains enough to learn with—and I can help you in various ways. So—I propose that we go up together."

"We've got—pasts," said Susan.

"Who hasn't that amounts to anything? Mighty few. No one that's made his own pile, I'll bet you. I'm in a position to do favors for people—the people we'd need. And I'll get in a position to do more and more. As long as they can make something out of us —or hope to—do you suppose they'll nose into our pasts and root things up that'd injure them as much as us?"

"It would be an interesting game, wouldn't it?" said Susan.

She was reflectively observing the handsome, earnest face before her—an incarnation of intelligent ambition, a Freddie Palmer who was somehow divesting himself of himself—was growing up—away from the rotten soil that had nourished him—up into the air—was growing strongly—yes, splendidly!

"And we've got everything to gain and nothing to lose," pursued he. "We'd not be adventurers, you see. Adventurers are people who haven't any money and are looking round to try to steal it. We'd have money. So, we'd be building solid, right on the rock." The handsome young man—the strongest, the most intelligent, the most purposeful she had ever met, except possibly Brent—looked at her with an admiring tenderness that moved her, the forlorn derelict adrift on the vast, lonely, treacherous sea. "The reason I've waited for you to invite you in on this scheme is that I tried you out and I found that you belong to the mighty few people who do what they say they'll do, good bargain or bad. It'd never occur to you to shuffle out of trying to keep your word."

"It hasn't—so far," said Susan.

"Well—that's the only sort of thing worth talking about as morality. Believe me, for I've been through the whole game from chimney pots to cellar floor."

"There's another thing, too," said the girl.

"What's that?"

"Not to injure anyone else."

Palmer shook his head positively. "It's believing that and acting on it that has kept you down in spite of your brains and looks."

"That I shall never do," said the girl. "It may be weakness—I guess it is weakness. But—I draw the line there."

"But I'm not proposing that you injure anyone— or proposing to do it myself. As I said, I've got up where I can afford to be good and kind and all that. And I'm willing to jump you up over the stretch of the climb that can't be crossed without being—well, anything but good and kind."

She was reflecting.

"You'll never get over that stretch by yourself. It'll always turn you back."

"Just what do you propose?" she asked.

It gave her pleasure to see the keen delight her

question, with its implication of hope, aroused in him.
Said he:

"That we go to Europe together and stay over there
several years—as long as you like—as long as it's
necessary. Stay till our pasts have disappeared—
work ourselves in with the right sort of people. You
say you're not married?"

"Not to the man I'm with."

"To somebody else?"

"I don't know. I was."

"Well—that'll be looked into and straightened out.
And then we'll quietly marry."

Susan laughed. "You're too fast," said she. "I'll
admit I'm interested. I've been looking for a road—
one that doesn't lead toward where we've come from.
And this is the first road that has offered. But I
haven't agreed to go in with you yet—haven't even
begun to think it over. And if I did agree—which I
probably won't—why, still I'd not be willing to marry.
That's a serious matter. I'd want to be very, very
sure I was satisfied."

Palmer nodded, with a return of the look of admiration. "I understand. You don't promise until you
intend to stick, and once you've promised all hell
couldn't change you."

"Another thing—very unfortunate, too. It looks to
me as if I'd be dependent on you for money."

Freddie's eyes wavered. "Oh, we'd never quarrel
about that," said he with an attempt at careless confidence.

"No," replied she quietly. "For the best of reasons.
I'd not consider going into any arrangement where
I'd be dependent on a man for money. I've had my
experience. I've learned my lesson. If I lived with

342

you several years in the sort of style you've suggested —no, not several years but a few months—you'd have me absolutely at your mercy. You'd thought of that, hadn't you?"

His smile was confession.

"I'd develop tastes for luxuries and they'd become necessities." Susan shook her head. "No—that would be foolish—very foolish."

He was watching her so keenly that his expression was covert suspicion. "What do you suggest?" he asked.

"Not what you suspect," replied she, amused. "I'm not making a play for a gift of a fortune. I haven't anything to suggest."

There was a long silence, he turning his glass slowly and from time to time taking a little of the champagne thoughtfully. She observed him with a quizzical expression. It was apparent to her that he was debating whether he would be making a fool of himself if he offered her an independence outright. Finally she said:

"Don't worry, Freddie. I'd not take it, even if you screwed yourself up to the point of offering it."

He glanced up quickly and guiltily. "Why not?" he said. "You'd be practically my wife. I can trust you. You've had experience, so you can't blame me for hesitating. Money puts the devil in anybody who gets it—man or woman. But I'll trust you—" he laughed—"since I've got to."

"No. The most I'd take would be a salary. I'd be a sort of companion."

"Anything you like," cried he. This last suspicion born of a life of intimate dealings with his fellow-beings took flight. "It'd have to be a big salary because you'd have to dress and act the part. What do you say? Is it a go?"

"Oh, I can't decide now."

"When?"

She reflected. "I can tell you in a week."

He hesitated, said, "All right—a week."

She rose to go. "I've warned you the chances are against my accepting."

"That's because you haven't looked the ground over," replied he, rising.

"Where shall I send you word?"

"I've an apartment at Sherry's now."

"Then—a week from today."

She put out her hand. He took it, and she marveled as she felt a tremor in that steady hand of his. But his voice was resolutely careless as he said, "So long. Don't forget how much I want or need you. And if you do forget that, think of the advantages— seeing the world with plenty of money—and all the rest of it. Where'll you get such another chance? You'll not be fool enough to refuse."

She smiled, said as she went, "You may remember I used to be something of a fool."

"But that was some time ago. You've learned a lot since then—surely."

"We'll see. I've become—I think—a good deal of a—of a New Yorker."

"That means frank about doing what the rest of the world does under a stack of lies. It's a lovely world, isn't it?"

"If I had made it," laughed Susan, "I'd not own up to the fact."

She laughed; but she was seeing the old women of the slums—was seeing them as one sees in the magic

mirror the vision of one's future self. And on the way
home she said to herself, "It was a good thing that I
was arrested today. It reminded me. It warned me.
But for it, I might have gone on to make a fool of
myself." And she recalled how it had been one of
Burlingham's favorite maxims that everything is for
the best, for those who know how to use it.

XVIII

S HE wrote Garvey asking an appointment. The reply should have come the next day or the next day but one at the farthest; for Garvey had been trained by Brent to the supreme courtesy of promptness. It did not come until the fourth day; before she opened it Susan knew about what she would read—the stupidly obvious attempt to put off facing her—the cowardice of a kind-hearted, weak fellow. She really had her answer—was left without a doubt for hope to perch upon. But she wrote again, insisting so sharply that he came the following day. His large, tell-tale face was a restatement of what she had read in his delay and between the lines of his note. He was effusively friendly with a sort of mortuary suggestion, like one bearing condolences, that tickled her sense of humor, far though her heart was from mirth.

"Something has happened," began she, "that makes it necessary for me to know when Mr. Brent is coming back."

"Really, Mrs. Spenser——"

"Miss Lenox," she corrected.

"Yes—Miss Lenox, I beg your pardon. But really —in my position—I know nothing of Mr. Brent's plans—and if I did, I'd not be at liberty to speak of them. I have written him what you wrote me about the check—and—and—that is all."

"Mr. Garvey, is he ever—has he——" Susan, desperate, burst out with more than she intended to say: "I care nothing about it, one way or the other. If

346

Mr. Brent is politely hinting that I won't do, I've a right to know it. I have a chance at something else. Can't you tell me?"

"I don't know anything about it—honestly I don't, Miss Lenox," cried he, sweating profusely.

"You put an accent on the 'know,'" said Susan. "You suspect that I'm right, don't you?"

"I've no ground for suspecting—that is—no, I haven't. He said nothing to me—nothing. But he never does. He's very peculiar and uncertain . . . and I don't understand him at all."

"Isn't this his usual way with the failures—his way of letting them down easily?"

Susan's manner was certainly light and cheerful, an assurance that he need have no fear of hysterics or despair or any sort of scene trying to a soft heart. But Garvey could take but the one view of the favor or disfavor of the god of his universe. He looked at her like a dog that is getting a whipping from a friend. "Now, Miss Lenox, you've no right to put me in this painful——"

"That's true," said Susan, done since she had got what she sought. "I shan't say another word. When Mr. Brent comes back, will you tell him I sent for you to ask you to thank him for me—and say to him that I found something else for which I hope I'm better suited?"

"I'm so glad," said Garvey, hysterically. "I'm delighted. And I'm sure he will be, too. For I'm sure he liked you, personally—and I must say I was surprised when he went. But I must not say that sort of thing. Indeed, I know nothing, Miss Lenox—I assure you——"

"And please tell him," interrupted Susan, "that I'd

347

have written him myself, only I don't want to bother him."

"Oh, no——no, indeed. Not that, Miss Lenox. I'm so sorry. But I'm only the secretary. I can't say anything."

It was some time before Susan could get rid of him, though he was eager to be gone. He hung in the doorway, ejaculating disconnectedly, dropping and picking up his hat, perspiring profusely, shaking hands again and again, and so exciting her pity for his misery of the good-hearted weak that she was for the moment forgetful of her own plight. Long before he went, he had greatly increased her already strong belief in Brent's generosity of character——for, thought she, he'd have got another secretary if he hadn't been too kind to turn adrift so helpless and foolish a creature. Well ——he should have no trouble in getting rid of her.

She was seeing little of Spenser and they were saying almost nothing to each other. When he came at night, always very late, she was in bed and pretended sleep. When he awoke, she got breakfast in silence; they read the newspapers as they ate. And he could not spare the time to come to dinner. As the decisive moment drew near, his fears dried up his confident volubility. He changed his mind and insisted on her coming to the theater for the final rehearsals. But "Shattered Lives" was not the sort of play she cared for, and she was wearied by the profane and tedious wranglings of the stage director and the authors, by the stupidity of the actors who had to be told every little intonation and gesture again and again. The agitation, the labor seemed grotesquely out of proportion to the triviality of the matter at issue. At the first night she sat in a box from which Spenser, in a high fever and twitching with nervousness, watched the play, gliding out just before the lights were turned up for the intermission. The play went better than she had expected, and the enthusiasm of the audience convinced her that it was a success before the fall of the curtain on the second act. With the applause that greeted the chief climax—the end of the third act—Spenser, Sperry and Fitzalan were convinced. All three responded to curtain calls. Susan had never seen Spenser so handsome, and she admired the calmness and the cleverness of his brief speech of thanks. That line of footlights between them gave her a new point of view on him, made her realize how being so close to his weaknesses had obscured for her his strong qualities—for, unfortunately, while a man's public life is determined wholly by his strong qualities, his intimate life depends wholly on his weaknesses. She was as fond of him as she had ever been; but it was impossible for her to feel any thrill approaching love. Why? She looked at his fine face and manly figure; she recalled how many good qualities he had. Why had she ceased to love him? She thought perhaps some mystery of physical lack of sympathy was in part responsible; then there was the fact that she could not trust him. With many women, trust is not necessary to love; on the contrary, distrust inflames love. It happened not to be so with Susan Lenox. "I do not love him. I can never love him again. And when he uses his power over me, I shall begin to dislike him." The lost illusion! The dead love! If she could call it back to life! But no—there it lay, coffined, the gray of death upon its features. Her heart ached.

After the play Fitzalan took the authors and the leading lady, Constance Francklyn, and Miss Lenox to supper in a private room at Rector's. This was Miss

Francklyn's first trial in a leading part. She had small ability as an actress, having never risen beyond the primer stage of mere posing and declamation in which so many players are halted by their vanity—the universal human vanity that is content with small triumphs, or with purely imaginary triumphs. But she had a notable figure of the lank, serpentine kind and a bad, sensual face that harmonized with it. Especially in artificial light she had an uncanny allure of the elemental, the wild animal in the jungle. With every disposition and effort to use her physical charms to further herself she would not have been still struggling at twenty-eight, had she had so much as a thimbleful of intelligence.

"Several times," said Sperry to Susan as they crossed Long Acre together on the way to Rector's, "yes, at least half a dozen times to my knowledge, Constance had had success right in her hands. And every time she has gone crazy about some cheap actor or sport and has thrown it away."

"But she'll get on now," said Susan.

"Perhaps," was Sperry's doubting reply. "Of course, she's got no brains. But it doesn't take brains to act—that is, to act well enough for cheap machine-made plays like this. And nowadays playwrights have learned that it's useless to try to get actors who can act. They try to write parts that are actor-proof."

"You don't like your play?" said Susan.

"Like it? I love it. Isn't it going to bring me in a pot of money? But as a play"—Sperry laughed. "I know Spenser thinks it's great, but—there's only one of us who can write plays, and that's Brent. It takes a clever man to write a clever play. But it takes a genius to write a clever play that'll draw the damn fools who buy theater seats. And Robert Brent now and then does the trick. How are you getting on with your ambition for a career?"

Susan glanced nervously at him. The question, coming upon the heels of talk about Brent, filled her with alarm lest Rod had broken his promise and had betrayed her confidence. But Sperry's expression showed that she was probably mistaken.

"My ambition?" said she. "Oh—I've given it up."

"The thought of work was too much for you—eh?"

Susan shrugged her shoulders.

A sardonic grin flitted over Sperry's Punch-like face. "The more I see of women, the less I think of 'em," said he. "But I suppose the men'd be lazy and worthless too, if nature had given 'em anything that'd sell or rent. . . . Somehow I'm disappointed in *you*, though."

That ended the conversation until they were sitting down at the table. Then Sperry said:

"Are you offended by my frankness a while ago?"

"No," replied Susan. "The contrary. Some day your saying that may help me."

"It's quite true, there's something about you—a look—a manner—it makes one feel you could do things if you tried."

"I'm afraid that 'something' is a fraud," said she. No doubt it was that something that had misled Brent —that had always deceived her about herself. No, she must not think herself a self-deceived dreamer. Even if it was so, still she must not think it. She must say to herself over and over again "Brent or no Brent, I shall get on—I shall get on" until she had silenced the last disheartening doubt.

Miss Francklyn, with Fitzalan on her left and Spenser on her right, was seated opposite Susan. About the time the third bottle was being emptied the attempts of Spenser and Constance to conceal from her their doings became absurd. Long before the supper was over there had been thrust at her all manner of proofs that Spenser was again untrue, that he was whirling madly in one of those cyclonic infatuations which soon wore him out and left him to return contritely to her. Sperry admired Susan's manners as displayed in her unruffled serenity—an admiration which she did not in the least deserve. She was in fact as deeply interested as she seemed in his discussion of plays and acting, illustrated by Brent's latest production. By the time the party broke up, Susan had in spite of herself collected a formidable array of incriminating evidence, including the stealing of one of Constance's jeweled show garters by Spenser under cover of the tablecloth and a swift kiss in the hall when Constance went out for a moment and Spenser presently suspended his drunken praises of himself as a dramatist, and appointed himself a committee to see what had become of her.

At the door of the restaurant, Spenser said:

"Susan, you and Miss Francklyn take a taxicab. She'll drop you at our place on her way home. Fitz and Sperry and I want one more drink."

"Not for me," said Sperry savagely, with a scowl at Constance. But Fitzalan, whose arm Susan had seen Rod press, remained silent.

"Come on, my dear," cried Miss Francklyn, smiling sweet insolent treachery into Susan's face.

Susan smiled sweetly back at her. As she was leaving the taxicab in Forty-fifth Street, she said:

"Send Rod home by noon, won't you? And don't tell him I know."

Miss Francklyn, who had been drinking greedily, began to cry. Susan laughed. "Don't be a silly," she urged. "If I'm not upset, why should you be? And how could I blame you two for getting crazy about each other? I wouldn't spoil it for worlds. I want to help it on."

"Don't you love him—really?" cried Constance, face and voice full of the most thrilling theatricalism.

"I'm very fond of him," replied Susan. "We're old, old friends. But as to love—I'm where you'll be a few months from now."

Miss Francklyn dried her eyes. "Isn't it the devil!" she exclaimed. "Why *can't* it last?"

"Why, indeed," said Susan. "Good night—and don't forget to send him by twelve o'clock." And she hurried up the steps without waiting for a reply.

She felt that the time for action had again come—that critical moment which she had so often in the past seen come and had let pass unheeded. He was in love with another woman; he was prosperous, assured of a good income for a long time, though he wrote no more successes. No need to consider him. For herself, then—what? Clearly, there could be no future for her with Rod. Clearly, she must go.

Must go—must take the only road that offered. Up before her—as in every mood of deep depression—rose the vision of the old women of the slums—the solitary, bent, broken forms, clad in rags, feet wrapped in rags —shuffling along in the gutters, peering and poking among filth, among garbage, to get together stuff to sell for the price of a drink. The old women of the tenements, the old women of the gutters, the old women drunk and dancing as the lecherous-eyed hunchback played the piano.

She must not this time wait and hesitate and hope; this time she must take the road that offered—and since it must be taken she must advance along it as if of all possible roads it was the only one she would have freely chosen.

Yet after she had written and sent off the note to Palmer, a deep sadness enveloped her—a grief, not for Rod, but for the association, the intimacy, their life together, its sorrows and storms perhaps more than the pleasures and the joys. When she left him before, she had gone sustained by the feeling that she was doing it for him, was doing a duty. Now, she was going merely to save herself, to further herself. Life, life in that great and hard school of practical living, New York, had given her the necessary hardiness to go, aided by Rod's unfaithfulness and growing uncongeniality. But not while she lived could she ever learn to be hard. She would do what she must—she was no longer a fool. But she could not help sighing and crying a little as she did it.

It was not many minutes after noon when Spenser came. He looked so sheepish and uncomfortable that Susan thought Constance had told him. But his opening sentence of apology was:

"I took too many nightcaps and Fitz had to lug me home with him."

"Really?" said Susan. "How disappointed Constance must have been!"

Spenser was not a good liar. His face twisted and twitched so that Susan laughed outright. "Why, you look like a caught married man," cried she. "You forget we're both free."

354

"Whatever put that crazy notion in your head—about Miss Francklyn?" demanded he.

"When you take me or anyone for that big a fool, Rod, you only show how foolish you yourself are," said she with the utmost good humor. "The best way to find out how much sense a person has is to see what kind of lies he thinks'll deceive another person."

"Now—don't get jealous, Susie," soothed he. "You know how a man is."

The tone was correctly contrite, but Susan felt underneath the confidence that he would be forgiven—the confidence of the egotist giddied by a triumph. Said she:

"Don't you think mine's a strange way of acting jealous?"

"But you're a strange woman."

Susan looked at him thoughtfully. "Yes, I suppose I am," said she. "And you'll think me stranger when I tell you what I'm going to do."

He started up in a panic. And the fear in his eyes pleased her, at the same time that it made her wince.

She nodded slowly. "Yes, Rod—I'm leaving."

"I'll drop Constance," cried he. "I'll have her put out of the company."

"No—go on with her till you've got enough—or she has."

"I've got enough, this minute," declared he with convincing energy and passion. "You must know, dearest, that to me Constance—all the women I've ever seen—aren't worth your little finger. You're all that they are, and a whole lot more besides." He seized her in his arms. "You wouldn't leave me—you couldn't! You understand how men are—how they get these fits of craziness about a pair of eyes or a figure or some trick of voice or manner. But that doesn't affect the man's heart. I love you, Susan. I adore you."

She did not let him see how sincerely he had touched her. Her eyes were of their deepest violet, but he had never learned that sign. She smiled mockingly; the fingers that caressed his hair were trembling. "We've tided each other over, Rod. The play's a success. You're all right again—and so am I. Now's the time to part."

"Is it Brent, Susie?"

"I quit him last week."

"There's no one else. You're going because of Constance!"

She did not deny. "You're free—and so am I," said she practically. "I'm going. So—let's part sensibly. Don't make a silly scene."

She knew how to deal with him—how to control him through his vanity. He drew away from her, chilled and sullen. "If you can live through it, I guess I can," said he. "You're making a damn fool of yourself—leaving a man that's fond of you—and leaving when he's successful."

"I always was a fool, you know," said she. She had decided against explaining to him and so opening up endless and vain argument. It was enough that she saw it was impossible to build upon or with him, saw the necessity of trying elsewhere—unless she would risk—no, invite—finding herself after a few months, or years, back among the drift, back in the underworld.

He gazed at her as she stood smiling gently at him—smiling to help her hide the ache at her heart, the terror before the vision of the old women of the tenement gutters, earning the wages, not of sin, not of vice, not of stupidity, but of indecision, of overhopefulness—of

356

weakness. Here was the kind of smile that hurts worse than tears, that takes the place of tears and sobs and moans. But he who had never understood her did not understand her now. Her smile infuriated his vanity. "You can *laugh!*" he sneered. "Well—go to the filth where you belong! You were born for it." And he flung out of the room, went noisily down the stairs. She heard the front door's distant slam; it seemed to drop her into a chair. She sat there all crouched together until the clock on the mantel struck two. This roused her hastily to gather into her trunk such of her belongings as she had not already packed. She sent for a cab. The man of all work carried down the trunk and put it on the box. Dressed in a simple blue costume as if for traveling, she entered the cab and gave the order to drive to the Grand Central Station.

At the corner she changed the order and was presently entering the Beaux Arts restaurant where she had asked Freddie to meet her. He was there, smoking calmly and waiting. At sight of her he rose. "You'll have lunch?" said he.

"No, thanks."

"A small bottle of champagne?"

"Yes—I'm rather tired."

He ordered the champagne. "And," said he, "it'll be the real thing—which mighty few New Yorkers get —even at the best places." When it came he sent the waiter away and filled the glasses himself. He touched the brim of his glass to the bottom of hers. "To the new deal," said he.

She smiled and nodded, and emptied the glass. Suddenly it came to her why she felt so differently toward him. She saw the subtle, yet radical change that always transforms a man of force of character when his position in the world notably changes. This man before her, so slightly different in physical characteristics from the man she had fled, was wholly different in expression.

"When shall we sail?" asked he. "Tomorrow?"

"First—there's the question of money," said she.

He was much amused. "Still worrying about your independence."

"No," replied she. "I've been thinking it out, and I don't feel any anxiety about that. I've changed my scheme of life. I'm going to be sensible and practice what life has taught me. It seems there's only one way for a woman to get up. Through some man."

Freddie nodded. "By marriage or otherwise, but always through a man."

"So I've discovered," continued she. "So, I'm going to play the game. And I think I can win now. With the aid of what I'll learn and with the chances I'll have, I can keep my feeling of independence. You see, if you and I don't get on well together, I'll be able to look out for myself. Something'll turn up."

"Or—*somebody*—eh?"

"Or somebody."

"That's candid."

"Don't you want me to be candid? But even if you don't, I've got to be."

"Yes—truth—especially disagreeable truth—is your long suit," said he. "Not that I'm kicking. I'm glad you went straight at the money question. We can settle it and never think of it again. And neither of us will be plotting to take advantage of the other, or fretting for fear the other is plotting. Sometimes I think nearly all the trouble in this world comes through failure to have a clear understanding about money matters."

Susan nodded. Said she thoughtfully, "I guess that's why I came—one of the main reasons. You are wonderfully sensible and decent about money."

"And the other chap isn't?"

"Oh, yes—and no. He likes to make a woman feel dependent. He thinks—but that doesn't matter. He's all right."

"Now—for our understanding with each other," said Palmer. "You can have whatever you want. The other day you said you wanted some sort of a salary. But if you've changed——"

"No—that's what I want."

"So much a year?"

"So much a week," replied she. "I want to feel, and I want you to feel, that we can call it off at any time on seven days' notice."

"But that isn't what I want," said he—and she, watching him closely if furtively, saw the strong lines deepen round his mouth.

She hesitated. She was seeing the old woman's dance hall, was hearing the piano as the hunchback played and the old horrors reeled about, making their palsy rhythmic. She was seeing this, yet she dared. "Then you don't want me," said she, so quietly that he could not have suspected her agitation. Never had her habit of concealing her emotion been so useful to her.

He sat frowning at his glass—debating. Finally he said:

"I explained the other day what I was aiming for. Such an arrangement as you suggest wouldn't help. You see that?"

"It's all I can do—at present," replied she firmly.

And she was now ready to stand or fall by that decision. She had always accepted the other previous terms— or whatever terms fate offered. Result—each time, disaster. She must make no more fatal blunders. This time, her own terms or not at all.

He was silent a long time. She knew she had convinced him that her terms were final. So, his delay could only mean that he was debating whether to accept or to go his way and leave her to go hers. At last he laughed and said:

"You've become a true New Yorker. You know how to drive a hard bargain." He looked at her admiringly. "You certainly have got courage. I happen to know a lot about your affairs. I've ways of finding out things. And I know you'd not be here if you hadn't broken with the other fellow first. So, if I turned your proposition down you'd be up against it—wouldn't you?"

"Yes," said she. "But—I won't in any circumstances tie myself. I must be free."

"You're right," said he. "And I'll risk your sticking. I'm a good gambler."

"If I were bound, but didn't want to stay, would I be of much use?"

"Of no use. You can quit on seven minutes' notice, instead of seven days."

"And you, also," said she.

Laughingly they shook hands. She began to like him in a new and more promising way. Here was a man, who at least was cast in a big mold. Nothing small and cheap about him—and Brent had made small cheap men forever intolerable to her. Yes, here was a man of the big sort; and a big man couldn't possibly be a bad man. No matter how many bad things he might do, he would still be himself, at least, a scorner of the pettiness and sneakiness and cowardice inseparable from villainy.

"And now," said he, "let's settle the last detail. How much a week? How would five hundred strike you?"

"That's more than twelve times the largest salary I ever got. It's many times as much as I made in the——"

"No matter," he hastily interposed. "It's the least you can hold down the job on. You've got to spend money—for clothes and so on."

"Two hundred is the most I can take," said she. "It's the outside limit."

He insisted, but she remained firm. "I will not accustom myself to much more than I see any prospect of getting elsewhere," explained she. "Perhaps later on I'll ask for an increase—later on, when I see how things are going and what my prospects elsewhere would be. But I must begin modestly."

"Well, let it go at two hundred for the present. I'll deposit a year's salary in a bank, and you can draw against it. Is that satisfactory? You don't want me to hand you two hundred dollars every Saturday, do you?"

"No. That would get on my nerves," said she.

"Now—it's all settled. When shall we sail?"

"There's a girl I've got to lcok up before I go."

"Maud? You needn't bother about her. She's married to a piker from up the state—a shoe manufacturer. She's got a baby, and is fat enough to make two or three like what she used to be."

"No, not Maud. One you don't know."

"I hoped we could sail tomorrow. Why not take a taxi and go after her now?"

"It may be a long search."

"She's a——?" He did not need to finish his sentence in order to make himself understood.

Susan nodded.

"Oh, let her——"

"I promised," interrupted she.

"Then—of course." Freddie drew from his trousers pocket a huge roll of bills. Susan smiled at this proof that he still retained the universal habit of gamblers, politicians and similar loose characters of large income, precariously derived. He counted off three hundreds and four fifties and held them out to her. "Let me in on it," said he.

Susan took the money without hesitation. She was used to these careless generosities of the men of that class—generosities passing with them and with the unthinking for evidences of goodness of heart, when in fact no generosity has any significance whatever beyond selfish vanity unless it is a sacrifice of necessities —real necessities.

"I don't think I'll need money," said she. "But I may."

"You've got a trunk and a bag on the cab outside," he went on. "I've told them at Sherry's that I'm to be married."

Susan flushed. She hastily lowered her eyes. But she need not have feared lest he should suspect the cause of the blush . . . a strange, absurd resentment of the idea that she could be married to Freddie Palmer. Live with him—yes. But marry—now that it was thus squarely presented to her, she found it unthinkable. She did not pause to analyze this feeling, indeed could not have analyzed it, had she tried. It was, however, a most interesting illustration of how she had been educated at last to look upon questions of sex as a man looks on them. She was like the man who openly takes a mistress whom he in no circumstances would elevate to the position of wife.

"So," he proceeded, "you might as well move in at Sherry's."

"No," objected she. "Let's not begin the new deal until we sail."

The wisdom of this was obvious. "Then we'll take your things over to the Manhattan Hotel," said he. "And we'll start the search from there."

But after registering at the Manhattan as Susan Lenox, she started out alone. She would not let him look in upon any part of her life which she could keep veiled.

XIX

SHE left the taxicab at the corner of Grand Street and the Bowery, and plunged into her former haunts afoot. Once again she had it forced upon her how meaningless in the life history are the words "time" and "space." She was now hardly any distance, as measurements go, from her present world, and she had lived here only a yesterday or so ago. Yet what an infinity yawned between! At the Delancey Street apartment house there was already a new janitress, and the kinds of shops on the ground floor had changed. Only after two hours of going up and down stairs, of knocking at doors, of questioning and cross-questioning, did she discover that Clara had moved to Allen Street, to the tenement in which Susan herself had for a few weeks lived—those vague, besotted weeks of despair.

When we go out into the streets with bereavement in mind, we see nothing but people dressed in mourning. And a similar thing occurs, whatever the emotion that oppresses us. It would not have been strange if Susan, on the way to Allen Street afoot, had seen only women of the streets, for they swarm in every great thoroughfare of our industrial cities. They used to come out only at night. But with the passing of the feeling against them that existed when they were a rare, unfamiliar, mysteriously terrible minor feature of life, they issue forth boldly by day, like all the other classes, making a living as best they can. But on that day Susan felt as if she were seeing only the broken down and cast-out creatures of the class—the old women, old in body rather than in years, picking in the gutters, fumbling in the garbage barrels, poking and peering everywhere for odds and ends that might pile up into the price of a glass of the poison sold in the barrel houses. The old women—the hideous, lonely old women —and the diseased, crippled children, worse off than the cats and the dogs, for cat and dog were not compelled to wear filth-soaked rags. Prosperous, civilized New York!

A group of these children were playing some rough game, in imitation of their elders, that was causing several to howl with pain. She heard a woman, being shown about by a settlement worker or some such person, say:

"Really, not at all badly dressed—for street games. I must confess I don't see signs of the misery they talk so much about."

A wave of fury passed through Susan. She felt like striking the woman full in her vain, supercilious, patronizing face—striking her and saying: "You smug liar! What if you had to wear such clothes on that fat, overfed body of yours! You'd realize then how filthy they are!"

She gazed in horror at the Allen Street house. Was it possible that *she* had lived there? In the filthy doorway sat a child eating a dill pickle—a scrawny, ragged little girl with much of her hair eaten out by the mange. She recalled this little girl as the formerly pretty and lively youngster, the daughter of the janitress. She went past the child without disturbing her, knocked at the janitress' door. It presently opened, disclosing in a small and foul room four prematurely old women, all in the family way, two with babies in arms. One of these was the janitress. Though she was not a Jewess, she was wearing one of the wigs assumed by orthodox Jewish women when they marry. She stared at Susan with not a sign of recognition.

"I am looking for Miss Clara," said Susan.

The janitress debated, shifted her baby from one arm to the other, glanced inquiringly at the other women. They shook their heads; she looked at Susan and shook her head. "There ain't a Clara," said she. "Perhaps she's took another name?"

"Perhaps," conceded Susan. And she described Clara and the various dresses she had had. At the account of one with flounces on the skirts and lace puffs in the sleeves, the youngest of the women showed a gleam of intelligence. "You mean the girl with the cancer of the breast," said she.

Susan remembered. She could not articulate; she nodded.

"Oh, yes," said the janitress. "She had the third floor back, and was always kicking because Mrs. Pfister kept a guinea pig for her rheumatism and the smell came through."

"Has she gone?" asked Susan.

"Couple of weeks."

"Where?"

The janitress shrugged her shoulders. The other women shrugged their shoulders. Said the janitress:

"Her feller stopped coming. The cancer got awful bad. I've saw a good many—they're quite plentiful down this way. I never see a worse'n hers. She didn't have no money. Up to the hospital they tried a new cure on her that made her gallopin' worse. The day before I was going to have to go to work and put her out—she left."

"Can't you give me any idea?" urged Susan.

"She didn't take her things," said the janitress meaningly. "Not a stitch."

"The—the river?"

The janitress shrugged her shoulders. "She always said she would, and I guess——"

Again the fat, stooped shoulders lifted and lowered. "She was most crazy with pain."

There was a moment's silence, then Susan murmured, "Thank you," and went back to the hall. The house was exhaling a frightful stench—the odor of cheap kerosene, of things that passed there for food, of animals human and lower, of death and decay. On her way out she dropped a dollar into the lap of the little girl with the mange. A parrot was shrieking from an upper window. On the topmost fire escape was a row of geraniums blooming sturdily. Her taxicab had moved up the street, pushed out of place by a hearse— a white hearse, with polished mountings, the horses caparisoned in white netting, and tossing white plumes. A baby's funeral—this mockery of a ride in state after a brief life of squalor. It was summer, and the babies were dying like lambs in the shambles. In winter the grown people were slaughtered; in summer the children. Across the street, a few doors up, the city dead wagon was taking away another body—in a plain pine box—to the Potter's Field where find their way for the final rest one in every ten of the people of the rich and splendid city of New York.

Susan hurried into her cab. "Drive fast," she said.

When she came back to sense of her surroundings she was flying up wide and airy Fifth Avenue with gorgeous sunshine bathing its palaces, with wealth and fashion and ease all about her. Her dear City of the Sun! But it hurt her now, was hateful to look upon.

She closed her eyes; her life in the slums, her life when she was sharing the lot that is really the lot of the human race as a race, passed before her—its sights and sounds and odors, its hideous heat, its still more hideous cold, its contacts and associations, its dirt and disease and degradation. And through the roar of the city there came to her a sound, faint yet intense—like the still, small voice the prophet heard—but not the voice of God, rather the voice of the multitude of aching hearts, aching in hopeless poverty—hearts of men, of women, of children——

The children! The multitudes of children with hearts that no sooner begin to beat than they begin to ache. She opened her eyes to shut out these sights and that sound of heartache.

She gazed round, drew a long breath of relief. She had almost been afraid to look round lest she should find that her escape had been only a dream. And now the road she had chosen—or, rather, the only road she could take—the road with Freddie Palmer—seemed attractive, even dazzling. What she could not like, she would ignore—and how easily she, after her experience, could do that! What she could not ignore she would tolerate—would compel herself to like.

Poor Clara!—Happy Clara!—better off in the dregs of the river than she had ever been in the dregs of New York. She shuddered. Then, as so often, the sense of the grotesque thrust in, as out of place as jester in cap and bells at a bier—and she smiled sardonically. "Why," thought she, "in being squeamish about Freddie I'm showing that I'm more respectable than the respectable women. There's hardly one of them that doesn't swallow worse doses with less excuse or no excuse at all—and without so much as a wry face."

XX

IN the ten days on the Atlantic and the Mediterranean Mr. and Mrs. Palmer, as the passenger list declared them, planned the early stages of their campaign. They must keep to themselves, must make no acquaintances, no social entanglements of any kind, until they had effected the exterior transformation which was to be the first stride—and a very long one, they felt—toward the conquest of the world.that commands all the other worlds. Several men aboard knew Palmer slightly—knew him vaguely as a big politician and contractor. They had a hazy notion that he was reputed to have been a thug and a grafter. But New Yorkers have few prejudices except against guilelessness and failure. They are well aware that the wisest of the wise Hebrew race was never more sagacious than when he observed that "he who hasteth to be rich shall not be innocent." They are too well used to unsavory pasts to bother much about that kind of odor; and where in the civilized world—or in that which is not civilized—is there an odor from reputation —or character—whose edge is not taken off by the strong, sweet, hypnotic perfume of money? Also, Palmer's appearance gave the lie direct to any scandal about him. It could not be—it simply could not be— that a man of such splendid physical build, a man with a countenance so handsome, had ever been a low, wicked fellow! Does not the devil always at once exhibit his hoofs, horns, tail and malevolent smile, that all men may know who and what he is? A frank, manly

369

young leader of men—that was the writing on his countenance. And his Italian blood put into his good looks
an ancient and aristocratic delicacy that made it incredible that he was of low origin. He spoke good
English, he dressed quietly; he did not eat with his
knife; he did not retire behind a napkin to pick his
teeth, but attended to them openly, if necessity compelled—and splendid teeth they were, set in a wide,
clean mouth, notably attractive for a man's. No,
Freddie Palmer's past would not give him any trouble
whatever; in a few years it would be forgotten, would
be romanced about as the heroic struggles of a typical
American rising from poverty.

"Thank God," said Freddie, "I had sense enough not
to get a jail smell on me!"

Susan colored painfully—and Palmer, the sensitive,
colored also. But he had the tact that does not try
to repair a blunder by making a worse one; he pretended not to see Susan's crimson flush.

Her past would not be an easy matter—if it should
ever rise to face her publicly. Therefore it must not
rise till Freddie and she were within the walls of the
world they purposed to enter by stealth, and had got
themselves well intrenched. Then she would be Susan
Lenox of Sutherland, Indiana, who had come to New
York to study for the stage and, after many trials
from all of which she had emerged with unspotted virtue, whatever vicious calumny might in envy say, had
captured the heart and the name of the handsome, rich
young contractor. There would be nasty rumors,
dreadful stories, perhaps. But in these loose and cynical days, with the women more and more audacious and
independent, with the universal craving for luxury beyond the reach of laboriously earned incomes, with mar-

riage decaying in city life among the better classes—
in these easy-going days, who was not suspected, hinted
about, attacked? And the very atrociousness of the
stories would prevent their being believed. One glance
at Susan would be enough to make doubters laugh at
their doubts.

The familiar types of fast women of all degrees come
from the poorest kinds of farms and from the tenements. In America, practically not until the panics
and collapses of recent years which have tumbled another and better section of the middle class into the
abyss of the underworld—not until then did there appear in the city streets and houses of ill repute any
considerable number of girls from good early surroundings. Before that time, the clamor for luxury—the
luxury that civilization makes as much a necessity as
food—had been satisfied more or less by the incomes of
the middle class; and any girl of that class, with physical charm and shrewdness enough to gain a living as
outcast woman, was either supported at home or got
a husband able to give her at least enough of what her
tastes craved to keep her in the ranks of the reputable.
Thus Susan's beauty of refinement, her speech and manner of the lady, made absurd any suggestion that she
could ever have been a fallen woman. The crimson
splash of her rouged lips did not suggest the *cocotte*,
but the lady with a dash of gayety in her temperament.
This, because of the sweet, sensitive seriousness of her
small, pallid face with its earnest violet-gray eyes and
its frame of abundant dark hair, simply and gracefully
arranged. She was of the advance guard of a type
which the swift downfall of the middle class, the increasing intelligence and restlessness and love of luxury
among women, and the decay of formal religion with its

exactions of chastity as woman's one diamond-fine jewel, are now making familiar in every city. The demand for the luxurious comfort which the educated regard as merely decent existence is far outstripping the demand for, and the education of, women in lucrative occupations other than prostitution.

Luckily Susan had not been arrested under her own name; there existed no court record which could be brought forward as proof by some nosing newspaper.

Susan herself marveled that there was not more trace of her underworld experience in her face and in her mind. She could not account for it. Yet the matter was simple enough to one viewing it from the outside. It is what we think, what we feel about ourselves, that makes up our expression of body and soul. And never in her lowest hour had her soul struck its flag and surrendered to the idea that she was a fallen creature. She had a temperament that estimated her acts not as right and wrong but as necessity. Men, all the rest of the world, might regard her as nothing but sex symbol; she regarded herself as an intelligence. And the filth slipped from her and could not soak in to change the texture of her being. She had no more the feeling or air of the *cocotte* than has the married woman who lives with her husband for a living. Her expression, her way of looking at her fellow beings and of meeting their looks, was that of the woman of the world who is for whatever reason above that slavery to opinion, that fear of being thought bold or forward which causes women of the usual run to be sensitive about staring or being stared at. Sometimes—in *cocottes*, in stage women, in fashionable women—this expression is self-conscious, or supercilious. It was not so with Susan, for she had little self-consciousness and no snobbishness at all. It merely gave the charm of worldly experience and expertness to a beauty which, without it, might have been too melancholy.

Susan, become by sheer compulsion philosopher about the vagaries of fate, did not fret over possible future dangers. She dismissed them and put all her intelligence and energy to the business in hand—to learning and to helping Palmer learn the ways of that world which includes all worlds.

Toward the end of the voyage she said to him:

"About my salary—or allowance—or whatever it is —— I've been thinking things over. I've made up my mind to save some money. My only chance is that salary. Have you any objection to my saving it—as much of it as I can?"

He laughed. "Tuck away anything and everything you can lay your hands on," said he. "I'm not one of those fools who try to hold women by being close and small with them. I'd not want you about if you were of the sort that could be held that way."

"No—I'll put by only from my salary," said she. "I admit I've no right to do that. But I've become sensible enough to realize that I mustn't ever risk being out again with no money. It has got on my mind so that I'd not be able to think of much else for worrying —unless I had at least a little."

"Do you want me to make you independent?"

"No," replied she. "Whatever you gave me I'd have to give back if we separated."

"*That* isn't the way to get on, my dear," said he.

"It's the best I can do—as yet," replied she. "And it's quite an advance on what I was. Yes, I *am* learning—slowly."

"Save all your salary, then," said Freddie. "When

you buy anything charge it, and I'll attend to the bill."

Her expression told him that he had never made a shrewder move in his life. He knew he had made himself secure against losing her; for he knew what a force gratitude was in her character.

Her mind was now free—free for the educational business in hand. She appreciated that he had less to learn than she. Civilization, the science and art of living, of extracting all possible good from the few swift years of life, has been—since the downfall of woman from hardship, ten or fifteen thousand years ago—the creation of the man almost entirely. Until recently among the higher races such small development of the intelligence of woman as her seclusion and servitude permitted was sporadic and exotic. Nothing intelligent was expected of her—and it is only under the compulsion of peremptory demand that any human being ever is roused from the natural sluggishness. But civilization, created *by* man, was created *for* woman. Woman has to learn how to be the civilized being which man has ordained that she shall be—how to use for man's comfort and pleasure the ingenuities and the graces he has invented.

It is easy for a man to pick up the habits, tastes, manners and dress of male citizens of the world, if he has as keen eyes and as discriminating taste as had Palmer, clever descendant of the supple Italian. But to become a female citizen of the world is not so easy. For Susan to learn to be an example of the highest civilization, from her inmost thoughts to the outermost penumbra of her surroundings—that would be for her a labor of love, but still a labor. As her vanity was of the kind that centers on the advantages she actually had, instead of being the more familiar kind

374

that centers upon non-existent charms of mind and person, her task was possible of accomplishment—for those who are sincerely willing to learn, who sincerely know wherein they lack, can learn, can be taught. As she had given these matters of civilization intelligent thought she knew where to begin—at the humble, material foundation, despised and neglected by those who talk most loudly about civilization, art, culture, and so on. They aspire to the clouds and the stars at once—and arrive nowhere except in talk and pretense and flaunting of ill-fitting borrowed plumage. They flap their gaudy artificial wings; there is motion, but no ascent. Susan wished to build—and build solidly. She began with the so-called trifles.

When they had been at Naples a week Palmer said: "Don't you think we'd better push on to Paris?"

"I can't go before Saturday," replied she. "I've got several fittings yet."

"It's pretty dull here for me—with you spending so much time in the shops. I suppose the women's shops are good"—hesitatingly—"but I've heard those in Paris are better."

"The shops here are rotten. Italian women have no taste in dress. And the Paris shops are the best in the world."

"Then let's clear out," cried he. "I'm bored to death. But I didn't like to say anything, you seemed so busy."

"I am busy. And—can you stand it three days more?"

"But you'll only have to throw away the stuff you buy here. Why buy so much?"

"I'm not buying much. Two ready-to-wear Paris dresses—models they call them—and two hats."

Palmer looked alarmed. "Why, at that rate," protested he, "it'll take you all winter to get together your winter clothes, and no time left to wear 'em."

"You don't understand," said she. "If you want to be treated right in a shop—be shown the best things —have your orders attended to, you've got to come looking as if you knew what the best is. I'm getting ready to make a good first impression on the dressmakers and milliners in Paris."

"Oh, you'll have the money, and that'll make 'em step round."

"Don't you believe it," replied she. "All the money in the world won't get you *fashionable* clothes at the most fashionable place. It'll only get you *costly* clothes."

"Maybe that's so for women's things. It isn't for men's."

"I'm not sure of that. When we get to Paris, we'll see. But certainly it's true for women. If I went to the places in the rue de la Paix dressed as I am now, it'd take several years to convince them that I knew what I wanted and wouldn't be satisfied with anything but the latest and best. So I'm having these miserable dressmakers fit those dresses on me until they're absolutely perfect. It's wearing me out, but I'll be glad I did it."

Palmer had profound respect for her as a woman who knew what she was about. So he settled himself patiently and passed the time investigating the famous Neapolitan political machine with the aid of an interpreter guide whom he hired by the day. He was enthusiastic over the dresses and the hats when Susan at last had them at the hotel and showed herself to him in them. They certainly did work an amazing change in her. They were the first real Paris models she had ever worn.

"Maybe it's because I never thought much about women's clothes before," said Freddie, "but those things seem to be the best ever. How they do show up your complexion and your figure! And I hadn't any idea your hair was as grand as all that. I'm a little afraid of you. We've got to get acquainted all over again. These clothes of mine look pretty poor, don't they? Yet I paid all kinds of money for 'em at the best place in Fifth Avenue."

He examined her from all points of view, going round and round her, getting her to walk up and down to give him the full effect of her slender yet voluptuous figure in that beautifully fitted coat and skirt. He felt that his dreams were beginning to come true.

"We'll do the trick!" cried he. "Don't you think about money when you're buying clothes. It's a joy to give up for clothes for you. You make 'em look like something."

"Wait till I've shopped a few weeks in Paris," said Susan.

"Let's start tonight," cried he. "I'll telegraph to the Ritz for rooms."

When she began to dress in her old clothes for the journey, he protested. "Throw all these things away," he urged. "Wear one of the new dresses and hats."

"But they're not exactly suitable for traveling."

"People'll think you lost your baggage. I don't want ever to see you again looking any way except as you ought to look."

"No, I must take care of those clothes," said she firmly. "It'll be weeks before I can get anything in Paris, and I must keep up a good front."

He continued to argue with her until it occurred to him that as his own clothes were not what they should be, he and she would look much better matched if she dressed as she wished. He had not been so much in jest as he thought when he said to her that they would have to get acquainted all over again. Those new clothes of hers brought out startlingly—so clearly that even his vanity was made uneasy—the subtle yet profound difference of class between them. He had always felt this difference, and in the old days it had given him many a savage impulse to degrade her, to put her beneath him as a punishment for his feeling that she was above him. Now he had his ambition too close at heart to wish to rob her of her chief distinction; he was disturbed about it, though, and looked forward to Paris with uneasiness.

"You must help me get my things," said he.

"I'd be glad to," said she. "And you must be frank with me, and tell me where I fall short of the best of the women we see."

He laughed. The idea that he could help her seemed fantastic. He could not understand it—how this girl who had been brought up in a jay town away out West, who had never had what might be called a real chance to get in the know in New York, could so quickly pass him who had been born and bred in New York, had spent the last ten years in cultivating style and all the other luxurious tastes. He did not like to linger on this puzzle; the more he worked at it, the farther away from him Susan seemed to get. Yet the puzzle would not let him drop it.

They came in at the Gare de Lyon in the middle of a beautiful October afternoon. Usually, from late September or earlier until May or later, Paris has about the vilest climate that curses a civilized city. It is one of the bitterest ironies of fate that a people so passionately fond of the sun, of the outdoors, should be doomed for two-thirds of the year to live under leaden, icily leaking skies with rarely a ray of real sunshine. And nothing so well illustrates the exuberant vitality, the dauntless spirit of the French people, as the way they have built in preparation for the enjoyment of every bit of the light and warmth of any chance ray of sunshine. That year it so fell that the winter rains did not close in until late, and Paris reveled in a long autumn of almost New York perfection. Susan and Palmer drove to the Ritz through Paris, the lovely, the gay.

"This is the real thing—isn't it?" said he, thrilled into speech by that spectacle so inspiring to all who have the joy of life in their veins—the Place de l'Opéra late on a bright afternoon.

"It's the first thing I've ever seen that was equal to what I had dreamed about it," replied she.

They had chosen the Ritz as their campaign headquarters because they had learned that it was the most fashionable hotel in Paris—which meant in the world. There were hotels more grand, the interpreter-guide at Naples had said; there were hotels more exclusive. There were even hotels more comfortable. "But for fashion," said he, "it is the summit. There you see the most beautiful ladies, most beautifully dressed. There you see the elegant world at tea and at dinner."

At first glance they were somewhat disappointed in the quiet, unostentatious general rooms. The suite assigned them—at a hundred and twenty francs a day —was comfortable, was the most comfortable assem-

blage of rooms either had ever seen. But there was
nothing imposing. This impression did not last long,
however. They had been misled by their American
passion for looks. They soon discovered that the guide
at Naples had told the literal truth. They went down
for tea in the garden, which was filled as the day was
summer warm. Neither spoke as they sat under a
striped awning umbrella, she with tea untasted before
her, he with a glass of whiskey and soda he did not lift
from the little table. Their eyes and their thoughts
were too busy for speech; one cannot talk when one
is thinking. About them were people of the world of
which neither had before had any but a distant glimpse.
They heard English, American, French, Italian. They
saw men and women with that air which no one can
define yet everyone knows on sight—the assurance without impertinence, the politeness without formality, the
simplicity that is more complex than the most elaborate
ornamentation of dress or speech or manner. Susan
and Freddie lingered until the departure of the last
couple—a plainly dressed man whose clothes on inspection revealed marvels of fineness and harmonious
color; a quietly dressed woman whose costume from
tip of plume to tip of suède slipper was a revelation of
how fine a fine art the toilet can be made.

"Well—we're right in it, for sure," said Freddie,
dropping to a sofa in their suite and lighting a cigarette.

"Yes," said Susan, with a sigh. "In it—but not
of it."

"I almost lost my nerve as I sat there. And for
the life of me I can't tell why."

"Those people know how," replied Susan. "Well—
what they've learned we can learn."

"Sure," said he energetically. "It's going to take a lot of practice—a lot of time. But I'm game." His expression, its suggestion of helplessness and appeal, was a clear confession of a feeling that she was his superior.

"We're both of us ignorant," she hastened to say. "But when we get our bearings—in a day or two—we'll be all right."

"Let's have dinner up here in the sitting-room. I haven't got the nerve to face that gang again to-day."

"Nonsense!" laughed she. "We mustn't give way to our feelings—not for a minute. There'll be a lot of people as badly off as we are. I saw some this afternoon—and from the way the waiters treated them, I know they had money or something. Put on your evening suit, and you'll be all right. I'm the one that hasn't anything to wear. But I've got to go and study the styles. I must begin to learn what to wear and now to wear it. We've come to the right place, Freddie. Cheer up!"

He felt better when he was in evening clothes which made him handsome indeed, bringing out all his refinement of feature and coloring. He was almost cheerful when Susan came into the sitting-room in the pale gray of her two new toilettes. It might be, as she insisted, that she was not dressed properly for fashionable dining; but there would be no more delicate, no more lady-like loveliness. He quite recovered his nerve when they faced the company that had terrified him in prospect. He saw many commonplace looking people, not a few who were downright dowdy. And presently he had the satisfaction of realizing that not only Susan but he also was getting admiring attention. He no longer floundered panicstricken; his feet touched bottom and he felt foolish about his sensations of a few minutes before.

After all, the world over, dining in a restaurant is nothing but dining in a restaurant. The waiter and the head waiter spoke English, were gracefully, tactfully, polite; and as he ordered he found his self-confidence returning with the surging rush of a turned tide on a low shore. The food was wonderful, and the champagne, "English taste," was the best he had ever drunk. Halfway through dinner both he and Susan were in the happiest frame of mind. The other people were drink· ing too, were emerging from caste into humanness. Women gazed languorously and longingly at the handsome young American; men sent stealthy or open smiles of adoration at Susan whenever Freddie's eyes were safely averted. But Susan was more careful than a woman of the world to which she aspired would have been; she ignored the glances and without difficulty assumed the air of wife.

"I don't believe we'll have any trouble getting acquainted with these people," said Freddie.

"We don't want to, yet," replied she.

"Oh, I feel we'll soon be ready for them," said he.

"Yes—that," said she. "But that amounts to nothing. This isn't to be merely a matter of clothes and acquaintances—at least, not with me."

"What then?" inquired he.

"Oh—we'll see as we get our bearings." She could not have put into words the plans she was forming—plans for educating and in every way developing him and herself. She was not sure at what she was aiming, but only of the direction. She had no idea how far she could go herself—or how far he would consent to go. The wise course was just to work along from day to day—keeping the direction.

"All right. I'll do as you say. You've got this game sized up better than I."

Is there any other people that works as hard as do the Parisians? Other peoples work with their bodies; but the Parisians, all classes and masses too, press both mind and body into service. Other peoples, if they think at all, think how to avoid work; the Parisians think incessantly, always, how to provide themselves with more to do. Other peoples drink to stupefy themselves lest peradventure in a leisure moment they might be seized of a thought; Parisians drink to stimulate themselves, to try to think more rapidly, to attract ideas that might not enter and engage a sober and therefore somewhat sluggish brain. Other peoples meet a new idea as if it were a mortal foe; the Parisians as if it were a longlost friend. Other peoples are agitated chiefly, each man or woman, about themselves; the Parisians are full of their work, their surroundings, bother little about themselves except as means to what they regard as the end and aim of life—to make the world each moment as different as possible from what it was the moment before, to transform the crass and sordid universe of things with the magic of ideas. Being intelligent, they prefer good to evil; but they have God's own horror of that which is neither good nor evil, and spew it out of their mouths.

At the moment of the arrival of Susan and Palmer the world that labors at amusing itself was pausing in Paris on its way from the pleasures of sea and mountains to the pleasures of the Riviera and Egypt. And as the weather held fine, day after day the streets, the cafés, the restaurants, offered the young adventurers an incessant dazzling panorama of all they had come abroad to seek. A week passed before Susan permitted herself to enter any of the shops where she intended to buy dresses, hats and the other and lesser paraphernalia of the woman of fashion.

"I mustn't go until I've seen," said she. "I'd yield to the temptation to buy and would regret it."

And Freddie, seeing her point, restrained his impatience for making radical changes in himself and in her. The fourth day of their stay at Paris he realized that he would buy, and would wish to buy, none of the things that had tempted him the first and second days. Secure in the obscurity of the crowd of strangers, he was losing his extreme nervousness about himself. That sort of emotion is most characteristic of Americans and gets them the reputation for profound snobbishness. In fact, it is not snobbishness at all. In no country on earth is ignorance in such universal disrepute as in America. The American, eager to learn, eager to be abreast of the foremost, is terrified into embarrassment and awe when he finds himself in surroundings where are things that he feels he ought to know about —while a stupid fellow, in such circumstances, is calmly content with himself, wholly unaware of his own deficiencies.

Susan let full two weeks pass before she, with much hesitation, gave her first order toward the outfit on which Palmer insisted upon her spending not less than five thousand dollars. Palmer had been going to the shops with her. She warned him it would make prices higher if she appeared with a prosperous looking man; but he wanted occupation and everything concerning her fascinated him now. His ignorance of the details of feminine dress was giving place rapidly to a knowledge which he thought profound—and it was profound, for a man. She would not permit him to go with her to order, however, or to fittings. All she would tell him in advance about this first dress was that it was for evening wear and that its color was green. "But not a greeny green," said she.

"I understand. A green something like the tint in your skin at the nape of your neck."

"Perhaps," admitted she. "Yes."

"We'll go to the opera the evening it comes home. I'll have my new evening outfit from Charvet's by that time."

It was about ten days after this conversation that she told him she had had a final fitting, had ordered the dress sent home. He was instantly all excitement and rushed away to engage a good box for the opera. With her assistance he had got evening clothes that sent through his whole being a glow of self-confidence —for he knew that in those clothes, he looked what he was striving to be. They were to dine at seven. He dressed early and went into their sitting-room. He was afraid he would spoil his pleasure of complete surprise by catching a glimpse of the *grande toilette* before it was finished. At a quarter past seven Susan put her head into the sitting-room—only her head. At sight of his anxious face, his tense manner, she burst out laughing. It seemed, and was, grotesque that one so imperturbable of surface should be so upset.

"Can you stand the strain another quarter of an hour?" said she.

"Don't hurry," he urged. "Take all the time you want. Do the thing up right." He rose and came toward her with one hand behind him. "You said the dress was green, didn't you?"

"Yes."

"Well—here's something you may be able to fit in somewhere." And he brought the concealed hand into view and held a jewel box toward her.

She reached a bare arm through the crack in the door and took it. The box, the arm, the head disappeared. Presently there was a low cry of delight that thrilled him. The face reappeared. "Oh— Freddie!" she exclaimed, radiant. "You must have spent a fortune on them."

"No. Twelve thousand—that's all. It was a bargain. Go on dressing. We'll talk about it afterward." And he gently pushed her head back—getting a kiss in the palm of his hand—and drew the door to.

Ten minutes later the door opened part way again. "Brace yourself," she called laughingly. "I'm coming."

A breathless pause and the door swung wide. He stared with eyes amazed and bewitched. There is no more describing the effects of a harmonious combination of exquisite dress and exquisite woman than there is reproducing in words the magic and the thrill of sunrise or sunset, of moonlight's fanciful amorous play, or of starry sky. As the girl stood there, her eyes starlike with excitement, her lips crimson and sensuous against the clear old-ivory pallor of her small face in its frame of glorious dark hair, it seemed to him that her soul, more beautiful counterpart of herself, had come from its dwelling place within and was hovering about her body like an aureole. Round her lovely throat was the string of emeralds. Her shoulders were bare and also her bosom, over nearly half its soft, girlish swell. And draped in light and clinging grace about her slender, sensuous form was the most wonder-

ful garment he had ever seen. The great French de-
signers of dresses and hats and materials have a genius
for taking an idea—a pure poetical abstraction—and
materializing it, making it visible and tangible without destroying its spirituality. This dress of Susan's
did not suggest matter any more than the bar of music
suggests the rosined string that has given birth to it.
She was carrying the train and a pair of long gloves
in one hand. The skirt, thus drawn back, revealed her
slim, narrow foot, a slender slipper of pale green satin,
a charming instep with a rosiness shimmering through
the gossamer web of pale green silk, the outline of a
long, slender leg whose perfection was guaranteed by
the beauty of her bare arm.

His expression changed slowly from bedazzlement to
the nearest approach to the old slumbrous, smiling
wickedness she had seen since they started. And her
sensitive instinct understood; it was the menace of an
insane jealousy, sprung from fear—fear of losing her.
The look vanished, and once again he was Freddie
Palmer the delighted, the generous and almost romantically considerate, because everything was going
as he wished.

"No wonder I went crazy about you," he said.

"Then you're not disappointed?"

He came to her, unclasped the emeralds, stood off
and viewed her again. "No—you mustn't wear them,"
said he.

"Oh!" she cried, protesting. "They're the best of
all."

"Not tonight," said he. "They look cheap. They
spoil the effect of your neck and shoulders. Another
time, when you're not quite so wonderful, but not tonight."

As she could not see herself as he saw her, she pleaded
for the jewels. She loved jewels and these were the
first she had ever had, except two modest little
birthday rings she had left in Sutherland. But he led
her to the long mirror and convinced her that he was
right. When they descended to the dining-room, they
caused a stir. It does not take much to make fashionable people stare; but it does take something to
make a whole room full of them quiet so far toward
silence that the discreet and refined handling of dishes
in a restaurant like the Ritz sounds like a vulgar clat-
ter. Susan and Palmer congratulated themselves that
they had been at the hotel long enough to become ac-
climated and so could act as if they were unconscious
of the sensation they were creating. When they finished
dinner, they found all the little tables in the long
corridor between the restaurant and the entrance taken
by people lingering over coffee to get another and closer
view. And the men who looked at her sweet dreaming
violet-gray eyes said she was innocent; those who looked
at her crimson lips said she was gay; those who saw
both eyes and lips said she was innocent—as yet. A
few very dim-sighted, and very wise, retained their
reason sufficiently to say that nothing could be told
about a woman from her looks—especially an American woman. She put on the magnificent cloak, white
silk, ermine lined, which he had seen at Paquin's and
had insisted on buying. And they were off for the
opera in the aristocratic looking auto he was taking
by the week.

She had a second triumph at the opera—was the
center that drew all glasses the instant the lights went
up for the intermission. There were a few minutes
when her head was quite turned, when it seemed to her

that she had arrived very near to the highest goal of human ambition—said goal being the one achieved and so self-complacently occupied by these luxurious, fashionable people who were paying her the tribute of interest and admiration. Were not these people at the top of the heap? Was she not among them, of them, by right of excellence in the things that made them, distinguished them?

Ambition, drunk and heavy with luxury, flies sluggishly and low. And her ambition was—for the moment—in danger of that fate.

During the last intermission the door of their box opened. At once Palmer sprang up and advanced with beaming face and extended hand to welcome the caller.

"Hello, Brent, I *am* glad to see you! I want to introduce you to Mrs. Palmer"—that name pronounced with the unconscious pride of the possessor of *the* jewel.

Brent bowed. Susan forced a smile.

"We," Palmer hastened on, "are on a sort of postponed honeymoon. I didn't announce the marriage—didn't want to have my friends out of pocket for presents. Besides, they'd have sent us stuff fit only to furnish out a saloon or a hotel—and we'd have had to use it or hurt their feelings. My wife's a Western girl—from Indiana. She came on to study for the stage. But"—he laughed delightedly—"I persuaded her to change her mind."

"You are from the West?" said Brent in the formal tone one uses in addressing a new acquaintance. "So am I. But that's more years ago than you could count. I live in New York—when I don't live here—or in the Riviera."

The moment had passed when Susan could, without

creating an impossible scene, admit and compel Brent to admit that they knew each other. What did it matter? Was it not best to ignore the past? Probably Brent had done this deliberately, assuming that she was beginning a new life with a clean slate.

"Been here long?" said Brent to Palmer.

As he and Palmer talked, she contrasted the two men. Palmer was much the younger, much the handsomer. Yet in the comparison Brent had the advantage. He looked as if he amounted to a great deal, as if he had lived and had understood life as the other man could not. The physical difference between them was somewhat the difference between look of lion and look of tiger. Brent looked strong; Palmer, dangerous. She could not imagine either man failing of a purpose he had set his heart upon. She could not imagine Brent reaching for it in any but an open, direct, daring way. She knew that the descendant of the supple Italians, the graduate of the street schools of stealth and fraud, would not care to have anything unless he got it by skill at subtlety. She noted their dress. Brent was wearing his clothes in that elegantly careless way which it was one of Freddie's dreams— one of the vain ones—to attain. Brent's voice was much more virile, was almost harsh, and in pronouncing some words made the nerves tingle with a sensation of mingled irritation and pleasure. Freddie's voice was manly enough, but soft and dangerous, suggestive of hidden danger. She compared the two men, as she knew them. She wondered how they would seem to a complete stranger. Palmer, she thought, would be able to attract almost any woman he might want; it seemed to her that a woman Brent wanted would feel rather helpless before the onset he would make.

It irritated her, this untimely intrusion of Brent who had the curious quality of making all other men seem less in the comparison. Not that he assumed anything, or forced comparisons; on the contrary, no man could have insisted less upon himself. Not that he compelled or caused the transfer of all interest to himself. Simply that, with him there, she felt less hopeful of Palmer, less confident of his ability to become what he seemed—and go beyond it. There are occasional men who have this same quality that Susan was just then feeling in Brent—men whom women never love yet who make it impossible for them to begin to love or to continue to love the other men within their range.

She was not glad to see him. She did not conceal it. Yet she knew that he would linger—and that she would not oppose. She would have liked to say to him: "You lost belief in me and dropped me. I have begun to make a life for myself. Let me alone. Do not upset me—do not force me to see what I must not see if I am to be happy. Go away, and give me a chance." But we do not say these frank, childlike things except in moments of closest intimacy—and certainly there was no suggestion of intimacy, no invitation to it, but the reverse, in the man facing her at the front of the box.

"Then you are to be in Paris some time?" said Brent, addressing her.

"I think so," said Susan.

"Sure," cried Palmer. "This is the town the world revolves round. I felt like singing 'Home, Sweet Home' as we drove from the station."

"I like it better than any place on earth," said Brent. "Better even than New York. I've never been quite able to forgive New York for some of the things it made me suffer before it gave me what I wanted."

"I, too," said Freddie. "My wife can't understand that. She doesn't know the side of life we know. I'm going to smoke a cigarette. I'll leave you here, old man, to entertain her."

When he disappeared, Susan looked out over the house with an expression of apparent abstraction. Brent—she was conscious—studied her with those seeing eyes—hazel eyes with not a bit of the sentimentality and weakness of brown in them. "You and Palmer know no one here?"

"Not a soul."

"I'll be glad to introduce some of my acquaintances to you—French people of the artistic set. They speak English. And you'll soon be learning French."

"I intend to learn as soon as I've finished my fall shopping."

"You are not coming back to America?"

"Not for a long time."

"Then you will find my friends useful."

She turned her eyes upon his. "You are very kind," said she. "But I'd rather—we'd rather—not meet anyone—just yet."

His eyes met hers calmly. It was impossible to tell whether he understood or not. After a few seconds he glanced out over the house. "That is a beautiful dress," said he. "You have real taste, if you'll permit me to say so. I was one of those who were struck dumb with admiration at the Ritz tonight."

"It's the first grand dress I ever possessed," said she.

"You love dresses—and jewels—and luxury?"

"As a starving man loves food."

"Then you are happy?"

"Perfectly so—for the first time in my life."

"It is a kind of ecstasy—isn't it? I remember how it was with me. I had always been poor—I worked my way through prep school and college. And I wanted *all* the luxuries. The more I had to endure—the worse food and clothing and lodgings—the madder I became about them, until I couldn't think of anything but getting the money to buy them. When I got it, I gorged myself. . . . It's a pity the starving man can't keep on loving food—keep on being always starving and always having his hunger satisfied."

"Ah, but he can."

He smiled mysteriously. "You think so, now. Wait till you are gorged."

She laughed. "You don't know! I could never get enough—never!"

His smile became even more mysterious. As he looked away, his profile presented itself to her view—an outline of sheer strength, of tragic sadness—the profile of those who have dreamed and dared and suffered. But the smile, saying no to her confident assertion, still lingered.

"Never!" she repeated. She must compel that smile to take away its disquieting negation, its relentless prophecy of the end of her happiness. She must convince him that he had come back in vain, that he could not disturb her.

"You don't suggest to me the woman who can be content with just people and just things. You will always insist on luxury. But you will demand more." He looked at her again. "And you will get it," he added, in a tone that sent a wave through her nerves.

Her glance fell. Palmer came in, bringing an odor of cologne and of fresh cigarette fumes. Brent rose.

Palmer laid a detaining hand on his shoulder. "Do stay on, Brent, and go to supper with us."

"I was about to ask you to supper with me. Have you been to the Abbaye?"

"No. We haven't got round to that yet. Is it lively?"

"And the food's the best in Paris. You'll come?"

Brent was looking at Susan. Palmer, not yet educated in the smaller—and important—refinements of politeness, did not wait for her reply or think that she should be consulted. "Certainly," said he. "On condition that you dine with us tomorrow night."

"Very well," agreed Brent. And he excused himself to take leave of his friends. "Just tell your chauffeur to go to the Abbaye—he'll know," he said as he bowed over Susan's hand. "I'll be waiting. I wish to be there ahead and make sure of a table."

As the door of the box closed upon him Freddie burst out with that enthusiasm we feel for one who is in a position to render us good service and is showing a disposition to do so. "I've known him for years," said he, "and he's the real thing. He used to spend a lot of time in a saloon I used to keep in Allen Street."

"Allen Street?" ejaculated Susan, shivering.

"I was twenty-two then. He used to want to study types, as he called it. And I gathered in types for him—though really my place was for the swell crooks and their ladies. How long ago that seems—and how far away!"

"Another life," said Susan.

"That's a fact. This is my second time on earth. *Our* second time. I tell you it's fighting for a foothold that makes men and women the wretches they are. Nowadays, I couldn't hurt a fly—could you? But then you never were cruel. That's why you stayed down so long."

Susan smiled into the darkness of the auditorium—the curtain was up, and they were talking in undertones. She said, as she smiled:

"I'll never go down and stay down for that reason again."

Her tone arrested his attention; but he could make nothing of it or of her expression, though her face was clear enough in the reflection from the footlights.

"Anyhow, Brent and I are old pals," continued he, "though we haven't seen so much of each other since he made a hit with the plays. He always used to predict I'd get to the top and be respectable. Now that it's come true, he'll help me. He'll introduce us, if we work it right."

"But we don't want that yet," protested Susan.

"You're ready and so am I," declared Palmer in the tone she knew had the full strength of his will back of it.

Faint angry hissing from the stalls silenced them, but as soon as they were in the auto Susan resumed. "I have told Mr. Brent we don't want to meet his friends yet."

"Now what the hell did you do that for?" demanded Freddie. It was the first time she had crossed him; it was the first time he had been reminiscent of the Freddie she used to know.

"Because," said she evenly, "I will not meet people under false pretenses."

"What rot!"

"I will not do it," replied she in the same quiet way.

He assumed that she meant only one of the false pretenses—the one that seemed the least to her. He said:

"Then we'll draw up and sign a marriage contract

and date it a couple of years ago, before the new marriage law was passed to save rich men's drunken sons from common law wives."

"I am already married," said Susan. "To a farmer out in Indiana."

Freddie laughed. "Well, I'll be damned! You! You!" He looked at her ermine-lined cloak and laughed again. "An Indiana farmer!" Then he suddenly sobered. "Come to think of it," said he, "that's the first thing you ever told me about your past."

"Or anybody else," said Susan. Her body was quivering, for we remember the past events with the sensations they made upon us at the time. She could smell that little room in the farmhouse. Allen Street and all the rest of her life in the underworld had for her something of the vagueness of dreams—not only now but also while she was living that life. But not Ferguson, not the night when her innocent soul was ravished as a wolf rips up and munches a bleating lamb. No vagueness of dreams about that, but a reality to make her shudder and reel whenever she thought of it—a reality vivider now that she was a woman grown in experiences and understanding.

"He's probably dead—or divorced you long ago."

"I do not know."

"I can find out—without stirring things up. What was his name?"

"Ferguson."

"What was his first name?"

She tried to recall. "I think—it was Jim. Yes, it was Jim." She fancied she could hear the voice of that ferocious sister snapping out that name in the miserable little coop of a general room in that hot, foul, farm cottage.

"Where did he live?"

"His farm was at the edge of Zeke Warham's place —not far from Beecamp, in Jefferson County."

She lapsed into silence, seemed to be watching the gay night streets of the Montmartre district—the cafés, the music halls, the sidewalk shows, the throngs of people every man and woman of them with his or her own individual variation upon the fascinating, covertly terrible face of the Paris mob. "What are you thinking about?" he asked, when a remark brought no answer.

"The past," said she. "And the future."

"Well—we'll find out in a few days that your farmer's got no claim on you—and we'll attend to that marriage contract and everything'll be all right."

"Do you want to marry me?" she asked, turning on him suddenly.

"We're as good as married already," replied he. "Your tone sounds as if *you* didn't want to marry *me*." And he laughed at the absurdity of such an idea.

"I don't know whether I do or not," said she slowly.

He laid a gentle strong hand on her knee. Gentle though it was, she felt its strength through the thickness of her cloak. "When the time comes," said he in the soft voice with the menace hidden in it, "you'll know whether you do or don't. You'll know you *do*— Queenie."

The auto was at the curb before the Abbaye. And on the steps, in furs and a top hat, stood the tall, experienced looking, cynical looking playwright. Susan's eyes met his, he lifted his hat, formal, polite.

"I'll bet he's got the best table in the place," said Palmer, before opening the door, "and I'll bet it cost him a bunch."

XXI

BRENT had an apartment in the rue de Rivoli, near the Hotel Meurice and high enough to command the whole Tuileries garden. From his balcony he could see to the east the ancient courts of the Louvre, to the south the varied, harmonious façades of the Quay d'Orsay with the domes and spires of the Left Bank behind, to the west the Obélisque, the long broad reaches of the Champs Elysées with the Arc de Triomphe at the boundary of the horizon. On that balcony, with the tides of traffic far below, one had a sense of being at the heart of the world, past, present, and to come. Brent liked to feel at home wherever he was; it enabled him to go tranquilly to work within a few minutes after his arrival, no matter how far he had journeyed or how long he had been away. So he regarded it as an economy, an essential to good work, to keep up the house in New York, a villa in Petite Afrique, with the Mediterranean washing its garden wall, this apartment at Paris; and a telegram a week in advance would reserve him the same quarters in the quietest part of hotels at Luzerne, at St. Moritz and at Biarritz.

Susan admired, as he explained his scheme of life to her and Palmer when they visited his apartment. Always profound tranquillity in the midst of intense activity. He could shut his door and be as in a desert; he could open it, and the most interesting of the sensations created by the actions and reactions of the whole human race were straightway beating upon his senses.

As she listened, she looked about, her eyes taking in impressions to be studied at leisure. These quarters of his in Paris were fundamentally different from those in New York, were the expression of a different side of his personality. It was plain that he loved them, that they came nearer to expressing his real—that is, his inmost—self.

"Though I work harder in Paris than in New York," he explained, "I have more leisure because it is all one kind of work—writing—at which I'm never interrupted. So I have time to make surroundings for myself. No one has time for surroundings in New York."

She observed that of the scores of pictures on the walls, tables, shelves of the three rooms they were shown, every one was a face—faces of all nationalities, all ages, all conditions—faces happy and faces tragic, faces homely, faces beautiful, faces irradiating the fascination of those abnormal developments of character, good and bad, which give the composite countenance of the human race its distinction, as the characteristics themselves give it intensities of light and shade. She saw angels, beautiful and ugly, devils beautiful and ugly.

When she began to notice this peculiarity of those rooms, she was simply interested. What an amazing collection! How much time and thought it must have taken! How he must have searched—and what an instinct he had for finding the unusual, the significant! As she sat there and then strolled about and then sat again, her interest rose into a feverish excitement. It was as if the ghosts of all these personalities, not one of them commonplace, were moving through the rooms, were pressing upon her. She understood why Brent had them there—that they were as necessary to him as cadavers and skeletons and physiological charts to an anatomist. But they oppressed, suffocated her; she went out on the balcony and watched the effects of the light from the setting sun upon and around the enormously magnified Arc.

"You don't like my rooms," said Brent.

"They fascinate me," replied she. "But I'd have to get used to these friends of yours. You made their acquaintance one or a few at a time. It's very upsetting, being introduced to all at once."

She felt Brent's gaze upon her—that unfathomable look which made her uneasy, yet was somehow satisfying, too. He said, after a while, "Palmer is to give me his photograph. Will you give me yours?" He was smiling. "Both of you belong in my gallery."

"Of course she will," said Palmer, coming out on the balcony and standing beside her. "I want her to have some taken right away—in the evening dress she wore to the Opera last week. And she must have her portrait painted."

"When we are settled," said Susan. "I've no time for anything now but shopping."

They had come to inspect the apartment above Brent's, and had decided to take it; Susan saw possibilities of making it over into the sort of environment of which she had dreamed. In novels the descriptions of interiors, which weary most readers, interested her more than story or characters. In her days of abject poverty she used these word paintings to construct for herself a room, suites of rooms, a whole house, to replace, when her physical eyes closed and her eyes of fancy opened wide, the squalid and nauseous cell to which poverty condemned her. In the streets she would sometimes pause before a shop window display of interior furnishings; a beautiful table or chair, a design in wall or floor covering had caught her eyes, had set her to dreaming—dreaming on and on—she in dingy skirt and leaky shoes. Now—the chance to realize her dreams had come. Palmer had got acquainted with some high-class sports, American, French and English, at an American bar in the rue Volney. He was spending his afternoons and some of his evenings with them —in the evenings winning large sums from them at cards at which he was now as lucky as at everything else. Palmer, pleased by Brent's manner toward Susan— formal politeness, indifference to sex—was glad to have him go about with her. Also Palmer was one of those men who not merely imagine they read human nature but actually can read it. He *knew* he could trust Susan. And it had been his habit—as it is the habit of all successful men—to trust human beings, each one up to his capacity for resisting temptation to treachery.

"Brent doesn't care for women—as women," said he. "He never did. Don't you think he's queer?"

"He's different," replied Susan. "He doesn't care much for people—to have them as intimates. I understand why. Love and friendship bore one—or fail one —and are unsatisfactory—and disturbing. But if one centers one's life about things—books, pictures, art, a career—why, one is never bored or betrayed. He has solved the secret of happiness, I think."

"Do you think a woman could fall in love with him?" he asked, with an air of the accidental and casual.

"If you mean, could I fall in love with him," said she, "I should say no. I think it would either amuse or annoy him to find that a woman cared about him."

"Amuse him most of all," said Palmer. "He knows

the ladies—that they love us men for what we can give them."

"Did you ever hear of anyone, man or woman, who cared about a person who couldn't give them anything?"

Freddie's laugh was admission that he thought her right. "The way to get on in politics," observed he, "is to show men that it's to their best interest to support you. And that's the way to get on in everything else—including love."

Susan knew that this was the truth about life, as it appeared to her also. But she could not divest herself of the human aversion to hearing the cold, practical truth. She wanted sugar coating on the pill, even though she knew the sugar made the medicine much less effective, often neutralized it altogether. Thus Palmer's brutally frank cynicism got upon her nerves, whereas Brent's equally frank cynicism attracted her because it was not brutal. Both men saw that life was a coarse practical joke. Palmer put the stress on the coarseness, Brent upon the humor.

Brent recommended and introduced to her a friend of his, a young French Jew named Gourdain, an architect on the way up to celebrity. "You will like his ideas and he will like yours," said Brent.

She had acquiesced in his insistent friendship for Palmer and her, but she had not lowered by an inch the barrier of her reserve toward him. His speech and actions at all times, whether Palmer was there or not, suggested that he respected the barrier, regarded it as even higher and thicker than it was. Nevertheless she felt that he really regarded the barrier as non-existent. She said:

"But I've never told you my ideas."

"I can guess what they are. Your surroundings will simply be an extension of your dress."

She would not have let him see—she would not have admitted to herself—how profoundly the subtle compliment pleased her.

Because a man's or a woman's intimate personal taste is good it by no means follows that he or she will build or decorate or furnish a house well. In matters of taste, the greater does not necessarily include the less, nor does the less imply the greater. Perhaps Susan would have shown she did not deserve Brent's compliment, would have failed ignominiously in that first essay of hers, had she not found a Gourdain, sympathetic, able to put into the concrete the rather vague ideas she had evolved in her dreaming. An architect is like a milliner or a dressmaker. He supplies the model, product of his own individual taste. The person who employs him must remold that form into an expression of his own personality—for people who deliberately live in surroundings that are not part of themselves are on the same low level with those who utter only borrowed ideas. That is the object and the aim of civilization—to encourage and to compel each individual to be frankly himself—herself. That is the profound meaning of freedom. The world owes more to bad morals and to bad taste that are spontaneous than to all the docile conformity to the standards of morals and of taste, however good. Truth—which simply means an increase of harmony, a decrease of discord, between the internal man and his environment—truth is a product, usually a byproduct, of a ferment of action.

Gourdain—chiefly, no doubt, because Susan's beauty of face and figure and dress fascinated him—was more eager to bring out her individuality than to show off his own talents. He took endless pains with her, taught her the technical knowledge and vocabulary that would enable her to express herself, then carried out her ideas religiously. "You are right, *mon ami*," said he to Brent. "She is an orchid, and of a rare species. She has a glorious imagination, like a bird of paradise balancing itself into an azure sky, with every plume raining color and brilliancy."

"Somewhat exaggerated," was Susan's pleased, laughing comment when Brent told her.

"Somewhat," said Brent. "But my friend Gourdain is stark mad about women's dressing well. That lilac dress you had on yesterday did for him. He *was* your servant; he *is* your slave."

Abruptly—for no apparent cause, as was often the case—Susan had that sickening sense of the unreality of her luxurious present, of being about to awaken in Vine Street with Etta—or in the filthy bed with old Mrs. Tucker. Absently she glanced down at her foot, holding it out as if for inspection. She saw Brent's look of amusement at her seeming vanity.

"I was looking to see if my shoes were leaky," she explained.

A subtle change came over his face. He understood instantly.

"Have you ever been—cold?" she asked, looking at him strangely.

"One cold February—cold and damp—I had no underclothes—and no overcoat."

"And dirty beds—filthy rooms—filthy people?"

"A ten-cent lodging house with a tramp for bedfellow."

They were looking at each other, with the perfect understanding and sympathy that can come only to two people of the same fiber who have braved the same storms. Each glanced hastily away.

Her enthusiasm for doing the apartment was due full as much to the fact that it gave her definitely directed occupation as to its congeniality. That early training of hers from Aunt Fanny Warham had made it forever impossible for her in any circumstances to become the typical luxuriously sheltered woman, whether legally or illegally kept—the lie-abed woman, the woman who dresses only to go out and show off, the woman who wastes her life in petty, piffling trifles —without purpose, without order or system, without morals or personal self-respect. She had never lost the systematic instinct—the instinct to use time instead of wasting it—that Fanny Warham had implanted in her during the years that determine character. Not for a moment, even without distinctly definite aim, was she in danger of the creeping paralysis that is epidemic among the rich, enfeebling and slowing down mental and physical activity. She had a regular life; she read, she walked in the Bois; she made the best of each day. And when this definite thing to accomplish offered, she did not have to learn how to work before she could begin the work itself.

All this was nothing new to Gourdain. He was born and bred in a country where intelligent discipline is the rule and the lack of it the rare exception—among all classes—even among the women of the well-to-do classes.

The finished apartment was a disappointment to Palmer. Its effects were too quiet, too restrained. Within certain small limits, those of the man of unusual intelligence but no marked originality, he had excellent taste—or, perhaps, excellent ability to recognize good taste. But in the large he yearned for the grandiose. He loved the gaudy with which the rich surround themselves because good taste forbids them to talk of their wealth and such surroundings do the talking for them and do it more effectively. He would have preferred even a vulgar glitter to the unobtrusiveness of those rooms. But he knew that Susan was right, and he was a very human arrant coward about admitting that he had bad taste.

"This is beautiful—exquisite," said he, with feigned enthusiasm. "I'm afraid, though, it'll be above their heads."

"What do you mean?" inquired Susan.

Palmer felt her restrained irritation, hastened to explain. "I mean the people who'll come here. They won't appreciate it. You have to look twice to appreciate this—and people, the best of 'em, look only once and a mighty blind look it is."

But Susan was not deceived. "You must tell me what changes you want," said she. Her momentary irritation had vanished. Since Freddie was paying, Freddie must have what suited him.

"Oh, I've got nothing to suggest. Now that I've been studying it out, I wouldn't allow you to make any changes. It does grow on one, doesn't it, Brent?"

"It will be the talk of Paris," replied Brent.

The playwright's tone settled the matter for Palmer. He was content. Said he:

"Thank God she hasn't put in any of those dirty old tapestry rags—and the banged up, broken furniture and the patched crockery."

At the same time she had produced an effect of long tenancy. There was nothing that glittered, nothing with the offensive sheen of the brand new. There was in that delicately toned atmosphere one suggestion which gave the same impression as the artificial crimson of her lips in contrast with the pallor of her skin and the sweet thoughtful melancholy of her eyes. This suggestion came from an all-pervading odor of a heavy, languorously sweet, sensuous perfume—the same that Susan herself used. She had it made at a perfumer's in the faubourg St. Honoré by mixing in a certain proportion several of the heaviest and most clinging of the familiar perfumes.

"You don't like my perfume?" she said to Brent one day.

He was in the library, was inspecting her *selections* of books. Instead of answering her question, he said:

"How did you find out so much about books? How did you find time to read so many?"

"One always finds time for what one likes."

"Not always," said he. "I had a hard stretch once—just after I struck New York. I was a waiter for two months. Working people don't find time for reading—and such things."

"That was one reason why I gave up work," said she.

"That—and the dirt—and the poor wages—and the hopelessness—and a few other reasons," said he.

"Why don't you like the perfume I use?"

"Why do you say that?"

"You made a queer face as you came into the drawing-room."

"Do *you* like it?"

"What a queer question!" she said. "No other man would have asked it."

"The obvious," said he, shrugging his shoulders. "I couldn't help knowing you didn't like it."

"Then why should I use it?"

His glance drifted slowly away from hers. He lit a cigarette with much attention to detail.

"Why should I use perfume I don't like?" persisted she.

"What's the use of going into that?" said he.

"But I do like it—in a way," she went on after a pause. "It is—it seems to me—the odor of myself."

"Yes—it is," he admitted.

She laughed. "Yet you made a wry face."

"I did."

"At the odor?"

"At the odor."

"Do you think I ought to change to another perfume?"

"You know I do not. It's the odor of your soul. It is different at different times—sometimes inspiringly sweet as the incense of heaven, as my metaphoric friend Gourdain would say—sometimes as deadly sweet as the odors of the drugs men take to drag them to hell—sometimes repulsively sweet, making one heart sick for pure, clean smell-less air yet without the courage to seek it. Your perfume is many things, but always—always strong and tenacious and individual."

A flush had overspread the pallor of her skin; her long dark lashes hid her eyes.

"You have never been in love," he went on.

"So you told me once before." It was the first time either had referred to their New York acquaintance.

"You did not believe me then. But you do now?"

"For me there is no such thing as love," replied she. "I understand affection—I have felt it. I understand passion. It is a strong force in my life—perhaps the strongest."

"No," said he, quiet but positive.

"Perhaps not," replied she carelessly, and went on, with her more than manlike candor, and in her manner of saying the most startling things in the calmest way:

"I understand what is called love—feebleness looking up to strength or strength pitying feebleness. I understand because I've felt both those things. But love—two equal people united perfectly, merged into a third person who is neither yet is both—that I have not felt. I've dreamed it. I've imagined it—in some moments of passion. But"—she laughed and shrugged her shoulders and waved the hand with the cigarette between its fingers—"I have not felt it and I shall not feel it. I remain I." She paused, considered, added, "And I prefer that."

"You are strong," said he, absent and reflective. "Yes, you are strong."

"I don't know," replied she. "Sometimes I think so. Again——" She shook her head doubtfully.

"You would be dead if you were not. As strong in soul as in body."

"Probably," admitted she. "Anyhow, I am sure I shall always be—alone. I shall visit—I shall linger on my threshold and talk. Perhaps I shall wander in perfumed gardens and dream of comradeship. But I shall return *chez moi*."

He rose—sighed—laughed—at her and at himself. "Don't delay too long," said he.

"Delay?"

"Your career."

"My career? Why, I am in the full swing of it. I'm at work in the only profession I'm fit for."

"The profession of woman?"

"Yes—the profession of female."

He winced—and at this sign, if she did not ask

herself what pleased her, she did not ask herself why. He said sharply, "I don't like that."

"But *you* have only to *hear* it. Think of poor me who have to *live* it."

"Have to? No," said he.

"Surely you're not suggesting that I drop back into the laboring classes! No, thank you. If you knew, you'd not say anything so stupid."

"I do know, and I was not suggesting that. Under this capitalistic system the whole working class is degraded. They call what they do 'work,' but that word ought to be reserved for what a man does when he exercises mind and body usefully. What the working class is condemned to by capitalism is not work but toil."

"The toil of a slave," said Susan.

"It's shallow twaddle or sheer cant to talk about the dignity and beauty of labor under this system," he went on. "It is ugly and degrading. The fools or hypocrites who talk that way ought to be forced to join the gangs of slaves at their tasks in factory and mine and shop, in the fields and the streets. And even the easier and better paid tasks, even what the capitalists themselves do—those things aren't dignified and beautiful. Capitalism divides all men—except those of one class—the class to which I luckily belong—divides all other men into three unlovely classes—slave owners, slave drivers and slaves. But you're not interested in those questions."

"In wage slavery? No. I wish to forget about it. Any alternative to being a wage slave—or a slave driver—or a slave owner. Any alternative."

"You don't appreciate your own good fortune," said he. "Most human beings—all but a very few—have to be in the slave classes, in one way or another. They have to submit to the repulsive drudgery, with no advancement except to slave driver. As for women— if they have to work, what can they do but sell themselves into slavery to the machines, to the capitalists? But you—you needn't do that. Nature endowed you with talent—unusual talent, I believe. How lucky you are! How superior to the great mass of your fellow beings who must slave or starve, because they have no talent!"

"Talent?—I?" said Susan. "For what, pray?"

"For the stage."

She looked amused. "You evidently don't think me vain—or you'd not venture that jest."

"For the stage," he repeated.

"Thanks," said she drily, "but I'll not appeal from your verdict."

"My verdict? What do you mean?"

"I prefer to talk of something else," said she coldly, offended by his unaccountable disregard of her feelings.

"This is bewildering," said he. And his manner certainly fitted the words.

"That I should have understood? Perhaps I shouldn't—at least, not so quickly—if I hadn't heard how often you have been disappointed, and how hard it has been for you to get rid of some of those you tried and found wanting."

"Believe me—I was not disappointed in you." He spoke earnestly, apparently with sincerity. "The contrary. Your throwing it all up was one of the shocks of my life."

She laughed mockingly—to hide her sensitiveness.

"One of the shocks of my life," he repeated.

She was looking at him curiously—wondering why he was thus uncandid.

"It puzzled me," he went on. "I've been lingering on here, trying to solve the puzzle. And the more I've seen of you the less I understand. Why did you do it? How could *you* do it?"

He was walking up and down the room in a characteristic pose—hands clasped behind his back as if to keep them quiet, body erect, head powerfully thrust forward. He halted abruptly and wheeled to face her. "Do you mean to tell me you didn't get tired of work and drop it for—" he waved his arm to indicate her luxurious surroundings—"for this?"

No sign of her agitation showed at the surface. But she felt she was not concealing herself from him.

He resumed his march, presently to halt and wheel again upon her. But before he could speak, she stopped him.

"I don't wish to hear any more," said she, the strange look in her eyes. It was all she could do to hide the wild burst of emotion that had followed her discovery. Then she had not been without a chance for a real career! She might have been free, might have belonged to herself——

"It is not too late," cried he. "That's why I'm here."

"It is too late," she said.

"It is not too late," repeated he, harshly, in his way that swept aside opposition. "I shall get you back." Triumphantly, "The puzzle is solved!"

She faced him with a look of defiant negation. "That ocean I crossed—it's as narrow as the East River into which I thought of throwing myself many a time—it's as narrow as the East River beside the ocean between what I am and what I was. And I'll never go back. Never!"

She repeated the "never" quietly, under her breath. His eyes looked as if they, without missing an essential detail, had swept the whole of that to which she would never go back. He said:

"Go back? No, indeed. Who's asking you to go back? Not I. I'm not *asking* you to go anywhere. I'm simply saying that you will—*must*—go forward. If you were in love, perhaps not. But you aren't in love. I know from experience how men and women care for each other—how they form these relationships. They find each other convenient and comfortable. But they care only for themselves. Especially young people. One must live quite a while to discover that thinking about oneself is living in a stuffy little cage with only a little light, through slats in the top that give no view. . . . It's an unnatural life for you. It can't last. You—centering upon yourself—upon comfort and convenience. Absurd!"

"I have chosen," said she.

"No—you can't do it," he went on, as if she had not spoken. "*You* can't spend your life at dresses and millinery, at chattering about art, at thinking about eating and drinking—at being passively amused—at attending to your hair and skin and figure. You may think so, but in reality you are getting ready for *me* . . . for your career. You are simply educating yourself. I shall have you back."

She held the cigarette to her lips, inhaled the smoke deeply, exhaled it slowly.

"I will tell you why," he went on, as if he were answering a protest. "Every one of us has an individuality of some sort. And in spite of everything and anything, except death or hopeless disease, that individuality will insist upon expressing itself."

"Mine is expressing itself," said she with a light smile—the smile of a light woman.

"You can't rest in this present life of yours. Your individuality is too strong. It will have its way— and for all your mocking smiling, you know I am right. I understand how you were tempted into it——"

She opened her lips—changed her mind and stopped her lips with her cigarette.

"I don't blame you—and it was just as well. This life has taught you—will teach you—will advance you in your career. . . . Tell me, what gave you the idea that I was disappointed?"

She tossed her cigarette into the big ash tray. "As I told you, it is too late." She rose and looked at him with a strange, sweet smile. "I've got any quantity of faults," said she. "But there's one I haven't got. I don't whine."

"You don't whine," assented he, "and you don't lie— and you don't shirk. Men and women have been canonized for less. I understand that for some reason you can't talk about——"

"Then why do you continue to press me?" said she, a little coldly.

He accepted the rebuke with a bow. "Nevertheless," said he, with raillery to carry off his persistence, "I shall get you. If not sooner, then when the specter of an obscure—perhaps poor—old age begins to agitate the rich hangings of youth's banquet hall."

"That'll be a good many years yet," mocked she. And from her lovely young face flashed the radiant defiance of her perfect youth and health.

"Years that pass quickly," retorted he, unmoved.

She was still radiant, still smiling, but once more she was seeing the hideous old women of the tenements. Into her nostrils stole the stench of the foul den in which she had slept with Mrs. Tucker and Mrs. Reardon—and she was hearing the hunchback of the dive playing for the drunken dancing old cronies, with their tin cups of whiskey.

No danger of that now? How little she was saving of her salary from Palmer! She could not "work" men —she simply could not. She would never put by enough to be independent and every day her tastes for luxury had firmer hold upon her. No danger? As much danger as ever—a danger postponed but certain to threaten some day—and then, a fall from a greater height—a certain fall. She was hearing the battered, shattered piano of the dive.

"For pity's sake—Mrs. Palmer!" cried Brent, in a low voice.

She started. The beautiful room, the environment of luxury and taste and comfort came back.

Gourdain interrupted and then Palmer.

The four went to the Café Anglais for dinner. Brent announced that he was going to the Riviera soon to join a party of friends. "I wish you would visit me later," said he, with a glance that included them all and rested, as courtesy required, upon Susan. "There's room in my villa—barely room."

"We've not really settled here," said Susan. "And we've taken up French seriously."

"The weather's frightful," said Palmer, with a meaning glance at her. "I think we ought to go."

But her expression showed that she had no intention of going, no sympathy with Palmer's desire to use this excellent, easy ladder of Brent's offering to make the ascent into secure respectability.

"Next winter, then," said Brent, who was observing her. "Or—in the early spring, perhaps."

"Oh, we may change our minds and come," Palmer suggested eagerly. "I'm going to try to persuade my wife."

"Come if you can," said Brent cordially. "I'll have no one stopping with me."

When they were alone, Palmer sent his valet away and fussed about impatiently until Susan's maid had unhooked her dress and had got her ready for bed. As the maid began the long process of giving her hair a thorough brushing, he said, "Please let her go, Susan. I want to tell you something."

"She does not know a word of English."

"But these French are so clever that they understand perfectly with their eyes."

Susan sent the maid to bed and sat in a dressing gown brushing her hair. It was long enough to reach to the middle of her back and to cover her bosom. It was very thick and wavy. Now that the scarlet was washed from her lips for the night, her eyes shone soft and clear with no relief for their almost tragic melancholy. He was looking at her in profile. Her expression was stern as well as sad—the soul of a woman who has suffered and has been made strong, if not hard.

"I got a letter from my lawyers today," he began. "It was about that marriage. I'll read."

At the word "marriage," she halted the regular stroke of the brush. Her eyes gazed into the mirror of the dressing table—through her reflection deep into her life, deep into the vistas of memory. As he unfolded the letter, she leaned back in the low chair, let her hands drop to her lap.

"'As the inclosed documents show,'" he read, "'we have learned and have legally verified that Jeb—not James—Ferguson divorced his wife Susan Lenox about a year after their marriage, on the ground of desertion; and two years later he fell through the floor of an old bridge near Brooksburg and was killed.'"

The old bridge—she was feeling its loose flooring sag and shift under the cautious hoofs of the horse. She was seeing Rod Spenser on the horse, behind him a girl, hardly more than a child—under the starry sky —exchanging confidences—talking of their futures.

"So, you see, you are free," said Palmer. "I went round to an American lawyer's office this afternoon, and borrowed an old legal form book. And I've copied out this form——"

She was hardly conscious of his laying papers on the table before her.

"It's valid, as I've fixed things. The lawyer gave me some paper. It has a watermark five years old. I've dated back two years—quite enough. So when we've signed, the marriage never could be contested— not even by ourselves."

He took the papers from the table, laid them in her lap. She started. "What were you saying?" she asked. "What's this?"

"What were you thinking about?" said he.

"I wasn't thinking," she answered, with her slow sweet smile of self-concealment. "I was feeling—living —the past. I was watching the procession."

He nodded understandingly. "That's a kind of time-wasting that can easily be overdone."

"Easily," she agreed. "Still, there's the lesson. I

have to remind myself of it often—always, when there's anything that has to be decided."

"I've written out two of the forms," said he. "We sign both. You keep one, I the other. Why not sign now?"

She read the form—the agreement to take each other as lawful husband and wife and to regard the contract as in all respects binding and legal.

"Do you understand it?" laughed he—nervously, for her manner was disquieting.

"Perfectly."

"You stared at the paper as if it were a puzzle."

"It is," said she.

"Come into the library and we'll sign and have it over with."

She laid the papers on the dressing table, took up her brush, drew it slowly over her hair several times.

"Wake up," cried he, good humoredly. "Come on into the library." And he went to the threshold.

She continued brushing her hair. "I can't sign," said she. There was the complete absence of emotion that caused her to be misunderstood always by those who did not know her peculiarities. No one could have suspected the vision of the old women of the dive before her eyes, the sound of the hunchback's piano in her ears, the smell of foul liquors and foul bodies and foul breaths in her nostrils. Yet she repeated:

"No—I can't sign."

He returned to his chair, seated himself, a slight cloud on his brow, a wicked smile on his lips. "Now what the devil!" said he gently, a jeer in his quiet voice. "What's all this about?"

"I can't marry you," said she. "I wish to live on as we are."

"But if we do that we can't get up where we want to go."

"I don't wish to know anyone but interesting men of the sort that does things—and women of my own sort. Those people have no interest in conventionalities."

"That's not the crowd we set out to conquer," said he. "You seem to have forgotten."

"It's you who have forgotten," replied she.

"Yes—yes—I know," he hastened to say. "I wasn't accusing you of breaking your agreement. You've lived up to it—and more. But, Susan, the people you care about don't especially interest me. Brent—yes. He's a man of the world as well as one of the artistic chaps. But the others—they're beyond me. I admit it's all fine, and I'm glad you go in for it. But the only crowd that's congenial to me is the crowd that we've got to be married to get in with."

She saw his point—saw it more clearly than did he. To him the world of fashion and luxurious amusement seemed the only world worth while. He accepted the scheme of things as he found it, had the conventional ambitions—to make in succession the familiar goals of the conventional human success—power, wealth, social position. It was impossible for him to get any other idea of a successful life, of ambitions worthy a man's labor. It was evidence of the excellence of his mind that he was able to tolerate the idea of the possibility of there being another mode of success worth while.

"I'm helping you in your ambitions—in doing what you think is worth while," said he. "Don't you think you owe it to me to help me in mine?"

He saw the slight change of expression that told him how deeply he had touched her.

"If I don't go in for the high society game," he went on, "I'll have nothing to do. I'll be adrift—gambling, drinking, yawning about and going to pieces. A man's got to have something to work for—and he can't work unless it seems to him worth doing."

She was staring into the mirror, her elbows on the table, her chin upon her interlaced fingers. It would be difficult to say how much of his gentleness to her was due to her physical charm for him, and how much to his respect for her mind and her character. He himself would have said that his weakness was altogether the result of the spell her physical charm cast over him. But it is probable that the other element was the stronger.

"You'll not be selfish, Susan?" urged he. "You'll give me a square deal."

"Yes—I see that it does look selfish," said she. "A little while ago I'd not have been able to see any deeper than the looks of it. Freddie, there are some things no one has a right to ask of another, and no one has a right to grant."

The ugliness of his character was becoming less easy to control. This girl whom he had picked up, practically out of the gutter, and had heaped generosities upon, was trying his patience too far. But he said, rather amiably:

"Certainly I'm not asking any such thing of you in asking you to become a respectable married woman, the wife of a rich man."

"Yes—you are, Freddie," replied she gently. "If I married you, I'd be signing an agreement to lead your life, to give up my own—an agreement to become a sort of woman I've no desire to be and no interest in being; to give up trying to become the only sort of woman I

think is worth while. When we were discussing my coming with you, you made this same proposal in another
form. I refused it then. And I refuse it now. It's
harder to refuse now, but I'm stronger."

"Stronger, thanks to the money you've got from me
—the money and the rest of it," sneered he.

"Haven't I earned all I've got?" said she, so calmly
that he did not realize how the charge of ingratitude,
unjust though it was, had struck into her.

"You have changed!" said he. "You're getting as
hard as the rest of us. So it's all a matter of money,
of give and take—is it? None of the generosity and
sentiment you used to be full of? You've simply been
using me."

"It can be put that way," replied she. "And no
doubt you honestly see it that way. But I've got to
see my own interest and my own right, Freddie. I've
learned at last that I mustn't trust to anyone else to
look after them for me."

"Are you riding for a fall—Queenie?"

At "Queenie" she smiled faintly. "I'm riding the
way I always have," answered she. "It has carried
me down. But—it has brought me up again." She
looked at him with eyes that appealed, without yielding. "And I'll ride that way to the end—up or down,"
said she. "I can't help it."

"Then you want to break with me?" he asked—and
he began to look dangerous.

"No," replied she. "I want to go on as we are. . . .
I'll not be interfering in your social ambitions, in any
way. Over here it'll help you to have a mistress
who—" she saw her image in the glass, threw him an
arch glance—"who isn't altogether unattractive—won't
it? And if you found you could go higher by marrying

some woman of the grand world—why, you'd be free
to do it."

He had a way of looking at her that gave her—and
himself—the sense of a delirious embrace. He looked
at her so, now. He said:

"You take advantage of my being crazy about you
—*damn* you!"

"Heaven knows," laughed she, "I need every advantage I can find."

He touched her—the lightest kind of touch. It carried the sense of embrace in his look still more giddily
upward. "Queenie!" he said softly.

She smiled at him through half closed eyes that with
a gentle and shy frankness confessed the secret of his
attraction for her. There was, however, more of
strength than of passion in her face as a whole. Said
she:

"We're getting on well—as we are—aren't we? I
can meet the most amusing and interesting people—
my sort of people. You can go with the people and to
the places you like—and you'll not be bound. If you
should take a notion to marry some woman with a big
position—you'd not have to regret being tied to—
Queenie."

"But—I want you—I want you," said he. "I've got
to have you."

"As long as you like," said she. "But on terms I
can accept—always on terms I can accept. Never on
any others—never! I can't help it. I can yield everything but that."

Where she was concerned he was the primitive man
only. The higher his passion rose, the stronger became
his desire for absolute possession. When she spoke of
terms—of the limitations upon his possession of her—

she transformed his passion into fury. He eyed her wickedly, abruptly demanded:

"When did you decide to make this kick-up?"

"I don't know. Simply—when you asked me to sign, I found I couldn't."

"You don't expect *me* to believe that."

"It's the truth." She resumed brushing her hair.

"Look at me!"

She turned her face toward him, met his gaze.

"Have you fallen in love with that young Jew?"

"Gourdain? No."

"Have you a crazy notion that your looks'll get you a better husband? A big fortune or a title?"

"I haven't thought about a husband. Haven't I told you I wish to be free?"

"But that doesn't mean anything."

"It might," said she absently.

"How?"

"I don't know. If one is always free—one is ready for—whatever comes. Anyhow, I must be free—no matter what it costs."

"I see you're bent on dropping back into the dirt I picked you out of."

"Even that," she said. "I must be free."

"Haven't you any desire to be respectable—decent?"

"I guess not," confessed she. "What is there in that direction for me?"

"A woman doesn't stay young and good-looking long."

"No." She smiled faintly. "But does she get old and ugly any slower for being married?"

He rose and stood over her, looked smiling danger down at her. She leaned back in her chair to meet his eyes without constraint. "You're trying to play me a trick," said he. "But you're not going to get away with the goods. I'm astonished that you are so rotten ungrateful."

"Because I'm not for sale?"

"Queenie balking at selling herself," he jeered. "And what's the least you ever did sell for?"

"A half-dollar, I think. No—two drinks of whiskey one cold night. But what I sold was no more myself than—than the coat I'd pawned and drunk up before I did it."

The plain calm way in which she said this made it so terrible that he winced and turned away. "We have seen hell—haven't we?" he muttered. He turned toward her with genuine passion of feeling. "Susan," he cried, "don't be a fool. Let's push our luck, now that things are coming our way. We need each other —we want to stay together—don't we?"

"*I* want to stay. I'm happy."

"Then—let's put the record straight."

"Let's keep it straight," replied she earnestly. "Don't ask me to go where I don't belong. For I can't, Freddie—honestly, I can't."

A pause. Then, "You will!" said he, not in blustering fury, but in that cool and smiling malevolence which had made him the terror of his associates from his boyhood days among the petty thieves and pickpockets of Grand Street. He laid his hand gently on her shoulder. "You hear me. I say you will."

She looked straight at him. "Not if you kill me," she said. She rose to face him at his own height. "I've bought my freedom with my body and with my heart and with my soul. It's all I've got. I shall keep it."

He measured her strength with an expert eye. He knew that he was beaten. He laughed lightly and went into his dressing-room.

XXII

THEY met the next morning with no sign in the manner of either that there had been a drawn battle, that there was an armed truce. She knew that he, like herself, was thinking of nothing else. But until he had devised some way of certainly conquering her he would wait, and watch, and pretend that he was satisfied with matters as they were. The longer she reflected the less uneasy she became—as to immediate danger. In Paris the methods of violence he might have been tempted to try in New York were out of the question. What remained? He must realize that threats to expose her would be futile; also, he must feel vulnerable, himself, to that kind of attack—a feeling that would act as a restraint, even though he might appreciate that she was the sort of person who could not in any circumstances resort to it. He had not upon her a single one of the holds a husband has upon a wife. True, he could break with her. But she must appreciate how easy it would now be for her in this capital of the idle rich to find some other man glad to "protect" a woman so expert at gratifying man's vanity of being known as the proprietor of a beautiful and fashionable woman. She had discovered how, in the aristocracy of European wealth, an admired mistress was as much a necessary part of the grandeur of great nobles, great financiers, great manufacturers, or merchants, as wife, as heir, as palace, as equipage, as chef, as train of secretaries and courtiers. She knew how deeply it would cut, to find himself without his show piece that made him the envied of men and the desired of women. Also, she knew that she had an even stronger hold upon him—that she appealed to him as no other woman ever had, that she had become for him a tenacious habit. She was not afraid that he would break with her. But she could not feel secure; in former days she had seen too far into the mazes of that Italian mind of his, she knew too well how patient, how relentless, how unforgetting he was. She would have taken murder into account as more than a possibility but for his intense and intelligent selfishness; he would not risk his life or his liberty; he would not deprive himself of his keenest pleasure. He was resourceful; but in the circumstances what resources were there for him to draw upon?

When he began to press upon her more money than ever, and to buy her costly jewelry, she felt still further reassured. Evidently he had been unable to think out any practicable scheme; evidently he was, for the time, taking the course of appeal to her generous instincts, of making her more and more dependent upon his liberality.

Well—was he not right? Love might fail; passion might wane; conscience, aiding self-interest with its usual servility, might overcome the instincts of gratitude. But what power could overcome the loyalty resting upon money interest? No power but that of a longer purse than his. As she was not in the mood to make pretenses about herself to herself, she smiled at this cynical self-measuring. "But I shan't despise myself for being so material," said she to herself, "until I find a *genuine* case of a woman, respectable or otherwise, who has known poverty and escaped from it, and has then voluntarily given up wealth to go back to it.

I should not stay on with him if he were distasteful to me. And that's more than most women can honestly say. Perhaps even I should not stay on if it were not for a silly, weak feeling of obligation—but I can't be sure of that." She had seen too much of men and women preening upon noble disinterested motives when in fact their real motives were the most calculatingly selfish; she preferred doing herself less than justice rather than more.

She had fifty-five thousand francs on deposit at Munroe's—all her very own. She had almost two hundred thousand francs' worth of jewels, which she would be justified in keeping—at least, she hoped she would think so—should there come a break with Freddie. Yet in spite of this substantial prosperity—or was it because of this prosperity?—she abruptly began again to be haunted by the old visions, by warnings of the dangers that beset any human being who has not that paying trade or profession which makes him or her independent—gives him or her the only unassailable independence.

The end with Freddie might be far away. But end, she saw, there would be—the day when he would somehow get her in his power and so would drive her to leave him. For she could not again become a slave. Extreme youth, utter inexperience, no knowledge of real freedom—these had enabled her to endure in former days. But she was wholly different now. She could not sink back. Steadily she was growing less and less able to take orders from anyone. This full-grown passion for freedom, this intolerance of the least restraint—how dangerous, if she should find herself in a position where she would have to put up with the caprices of some man or drop down and down!

What real, secure support had she? None. Her building was without solid foundations. Her struggle with Freddie was a revelation and a warning. There were days when, driving about in her luxurious car, she could do nothing but search among the crowds in the streets for the lonely old women in rags, picking and peering along the refuse of the cafés—weazened, warped figures swathed in rags, creeping along, mumbling to themselves, lips folded in and in over toothless gums.

One day Brent saw again the look she often could not keep from her face when that vision of the dance hall in the slums was horrifying her. He said impulsively:

"What is it? Tell me—what is it, Susan?"

It was the first and the last time he ever called her by her only personal name. He flushed deeply. To cover his confusion—and her own—she said in her most frivolous way:

"I was thinking that if I am ever rich I shall have more pairs of shoes and stockings and take care of more orphans than anyone else in the world."

"A purpose! At last a purpose!" laughed he. "Now you will go to work."

Through Gourdain she got a French teacher—and her first woman friend.

The young widow he recommended, a Madame Clélie Délière, was the most attractive woman she had ever known. She had all the best French characteristics—a good heart, a lively mind, was imaginative yet sensible, had good taste in all things. Like most of the attractive French women, she was not beautiful, but had that which is of far greater importance—charm. She knew not a word of English, and it was perhaps Susan's chief incentive toward working hard at French that she could not really be friends with this fascinating person until she learned to speak her language. Palmer —partly by nature, partly through early experience in the polyglot tenement district of New York—had more aptitude for language than had Susan. But he had been lazy about acquiring French in a city where English is spoken almost universally. With the coming of young Madame Délière to live in the apartment, he became interested.

It was not a month after her coming when you might have seen at one of the fashionable gay restaurants any evening a party of four—Gourdain was the fourth —talking French almost volubly. Palmer's accent was better than Susan's. She could not—and felt she never could—get the accent of the trans-Alleghany region out of her voice—and so long as that remained she would not speak good French. "But don't let that trouble you," said Clélie. "Your voice is your greatest charm. It is so honest and so human. Of the Americans I have met, I have liked only those with that same tone in their voices."

"But *I* haven't that accent," said Freddie with raillery.

Madame Clélie laughed. "No—and I do not like you," retorted she. "No one ever did. You do not wish to be liked. You wish to be feared." Her lively brown eyes sparkled and the big white teeth in her generous mouth glistened. "You wish to be feared— and you *are* feared, Monsieur Freddie."

"It takes a clever woman to know how to flatter with the truth," said he. "Everybody always has been afraid of me—and is—except, of course, my wife."

He was always talking of "my wife" now. The sub-

ject so completely possessed his mind that he aired it
unconsciously. When she was not around he boasted
of "my wife's" skill in the art of dress, of "my wife's"
taste, of "my wife's" shrewdness in getting her money's
worth. When she was there, he was using the favorite
phrase—"my wife" this—"my wife" that—"my wife"
the other—until it so got on her nerves that she began
to wait for it and to wince whenever it came—never a
wait of many minutes. At first she thought he was
doing this deliberately, either to annoy her or in pur-
suance of some secret deep design. But she soon saw
that he was not aware of his inability to keep off the
subject or of his obsession for that phrase represent-
ing the thing he was intensely wishing and willing—
"chiefly," she thought, "because it is something he
cannot have." She was amazed at his display of such
a weakness. It gave her the chance to learn an important truth about human nature—that self-indulgence soon destroys the strongest nature—and she was
witness to how rapidly an inflexible will disintegrates if
incessantly applied to an impossibility. When a strong
arrogant man, unbalanced by long and successful self-
indulgence, hurls himself at an obstruction, either the
obstruction yields or the man is destroyed.

One morning early in February, as she was descending from her auto in front of the apartment house, she
saw Brent in the doorway. Never had he looked so
young or so well. His color was fine, his face had
become almost boyish; upon his skin and in his eyes was
that gloss of perfect health which until these latter
days of scientific hygiene was rarely seen after twenty-
five in a woman or after thirty in a man. She gathered
in all, to the smallest detail—such as the color of his

shirt—with a single quick glance. She knew that he had seen her before she saw him—that he had been observing her. Her happiest friendliest smile made her small face bewitching as she advanced with outstretched hand.

"When did you come?" she asked.

"About an hour ago."

"From the Riviera?"

"No, indeed. From St. Moritz—and skating and skiing and tobogganing. I rather hoped I looked it. Doing those things in that air—it's being born again."

"I felt well till I saw you," said she. "Now I feel dingy and half sick."

He laughed, his glance sweeping her from hat to boots. Certainly his eyes could not have found a more entrancing sight. She was wearing a beautiful dress of golden brown cloth, sable hat, short coat and muff, brown suède boots laced high upon her long slender calves. And when she had descended from the perfect little limousine made to order for her, he had seen a ravishing flutter of lingerie of pale violet silk. The sharp air had brought no color to her cheeks to interfere with the abrupt and fascinating contrast of their pallor with the long crimson bow of her mouth. But her skin seemed transparent and had the clearness of health itself. Everything about her, every least detail, was of Parisian perfection.

"Probably there are not in the world," said he, "so many as a dozen women so well put together as you are. No, not half a dozen. Few women carry the art of dress to the point of genius."

"I see they had only frumps at St. Moritz this season," laughed she.

But he would not be turned aside. "Most of the well dressed women stop short with being simply frivolous in spending so much time at less than perfection—like the army of poets who write pretty good verse, or the swarm of singers who sing pretty well. I've heard of you many times this winter. You are the talk of Paris."

She laughed with frank delight. It was indeed a pleasure to discover that her pains had not been in vain.

"It is always the outsider who comes to the great city to show it its own resources," he went on. "I knew you were going to do this. Still happy?"

"Oh, yes."

But he had taken her by surprise. A faint shadow flitted across her face. "Not so happy, I see."

"You see too much. Won't you lunch with us? We'll have it in about half an hour."

He accepted promptly and they went up together. His glance traveled round the drawing-room; and she knew he had noted all the changes she had made on better acquaintance with her surroundings and wider knowledge of interior furnishing. She saw that he approved, and it increased her good humor. "Are you hurrying through Paris on your way to somewhere else?" she asked.

"No, I stop here—I think—until I sail for America."

"And that will be soon?"

"Perhaps not until July. I have no plans. I've finished a play a woman suggested to me some time ago. And I'm waiting."

A gleam of understanding came into her eyes. There was controlled interest in her voice as she inquired:

"When is it to be produced?"

"When the woman who suggested it is ready to act in it."

"Do I by any chance know her?"

"You used to know her. You will know her again."

She shook her head slowly, a pensive smile hovering about her eyes and lips. "No—not again. I have—changed."

"We do not change," said he. "We move, but we do not change. You are the same character you were when you came into the world. And what you were then, that you will be when the curtain falls on the climax of your last act. Your circumstances will change—and your clothes—and your face, hair, figure —but not *you*."

"Do you believe that?"

"I *know* it."

She nodded slowly, the violet-gray eyes pensive. "Birds in the strong wind—that's what we are. Driven this way or that—or quite beaten down. But the wind doesn't change sparrow to eagle—or eagle to gull— does it?"

She had removed her coat and was seated on an oval lounge gazing into the open fire. He was standing before it, looking taller and stronger than ever, in a gray lounging suit. A cigarette depended loosely from the corner of his mouth. He said abruptly:

"How are you getting on with your acting?"

She glanced in surprise.

"Gourdain," Brent explained. "He had to talk to somebody about how wonderful you are. So he took to writing me—two huge letters a week—all about you."

"I'm fond of him. And he's fond of Clélie. She's my——"

"I know all," he interrupted. "The tie between them is their fondness for you. Tell me about the acting."

"Oh—Clélie and I have been going to the theater every few days—to help me with French. She is mad about acting, and there's nothing I like better."

"Also, *you* simply have to have occupation."

She nodded. "I wasn't brought up to fit me for an idler. When I was a child I was taught to keep busy—not at nothing, but at something. Freddie's a lot better at it than I."

"Naturally," said Brent. "You had a home, with order and a system—an old-fashioned American home. He—well, he hadn't."

"Clélie and I go at our make-believe acting quite seriously. We have to—if we're to fool ourselves that it's an occupation."

"Why this anxiety to prove to me that you're not really serious?"

Susan laughed mockingly for answer, and went on:

"You should see us do the two wives in 'L'Enigme'—or mother and daughter in that diary scene in 'L'Autre Danger'!"

"I must. . . . When are you going to resume your career?"

She rose, strolled toward an open door at one end of the salon, closed it—strolled toward the door into the hall, glanced out, returned without having closed it. She then said:

"Could I study here in Paris?"

Triumph gleamed in his eyes. "Yes. Boudrin—a splendid teacher—speaks English. He—and I—can teach you."

"Tell me what I'd have to do."

434

"We would coach you for a small part in some play that's to be produced here."

"In French?"

"I'll have an American girl written into a farce. Enough to get you used to the stage—to give you practice in what he'll teach you—the trade side of the art."

"And then?"

"And then we shall spend the summer learning your part in my play. Two or three weeks of company rehearsals in New York in September. In October—your name out over the Long Acre Theater in letters of fire."

"Could that be done?"

"Even if you had little talent, less intelligence, and no experience. Properly taught, the trade part of every art is easy. Teachers make it hard partly because they're dull, chiefly because there'd be small money for them if they taught quickly, and only the essentials. No, journeyman acting's no harder to learn than bricklaying or carpentering. And in America—everywhere in the world but a few theaters in Paris and Vienna—there is nothing seen but journeyman acting. The art is in its infancy as an art. It even has not yet been emancipated from the swaddling clothes of declamation. Yes, you can do well by the autumn. And if you develop what I think you have in you, you can leap with one bound into fame. In America or England, mind you—because there the acting is all poor to 'pretty good'."

"You are sure it could be done? No—I don't mean that. I mean, is there really a chance—any chance—for me to make my own living? A real living?"

"I guarantee," said Brent.

She changed from seriousness to a mocking kind of gayety—that is, to a seriousness so profound that she would not show it. And she said:

"You see I simply must banish my old women—and that hunchback and his piano. They get on my nerves."

He smiled humorously at her. But behind the smile his gaze—grave, sympathetic—pierced into her soul, seeking the meaning he knew she would never put into words.

At the sound of voices in the hall she said:

"We'll talk of this again."

At lunch that day she, for the first time in many a week, listened without irritation while Freddie poured forth his unending praise of "my wife." As Brent knew them intimately, Freddie felt free to expatiate upon all the details of domestic economy that chanced to be his theme, with the exquisite lunch as a text. He told Brent how Susan had made a study of that branch of the art of living; how she had explored the unrivaled Parisian markets and groceries and shops that dealt in specialties; how she had developed their breakfasts, dinners, and lunches to works of art. It is impossible for anyone, however stupid, to stop long in Paris without beginning to idealize the material side of life—for the French, who build solidly, first idealize food, clothing, and shelter, before going on to take up the higher side of life—as a sane man builds his foundation before his first story, and so on, putting the observation tower on last of all, instead of making an ass of himself trying to hang his tower to the stars. Our idealization goes forward haltingly and hypocritically because we try to build from the stars down, instead of from the ground up. The place to seek the ideal is in the homely, the commonplace, and the necessary. An ideal that does not spring deep-rooted from the soil of practical life may be a topic for a sermon or a novel or for idle conversation among silly and pretentious people. But what use has it in a world that must *live*, and must be taught to live?

Freddie was unaware that he was describing a further development of Susan—a course she was taking in the university of experience—she who had passed through its common school, its high school, its college. To him her clever housekeeping offered simply another instance of her cleverness in general. His discourse was in bad taste. But its bad taste was tolerable because he was interesting—food, like sex, being one of those universal subjects that command and hold the attention of all mankind. He rose to no mean height of eloquence in describing their dinner of the evening before—the game soup that brought to him visions of a hunting excursion he had once made into the wilds of Canada; the way the *barbue* was cooked and served; the incredible duck—and the salad! Clélie interrupted to describe that salad as like a breath of summer air from fields and limpid brooks. He declared that the cheese—which Susan had found in a shop in the Marché St. Honoré—was more wonderful than the most wonderful *petit Suisse*. "And the coffee!" he exclaimed. "But you'll see in a few minutes. We have *coffee* here."

"*Quelle histoire!*" exclaimed Brent, when Freddie had concluded. And he looked at Susan with the ironic, quizzical gleam in his eyes.

She colored. "I am learning to live," said she. "That's what we're on earth for—isn't it?"

"To learn to live—and then, to live," replied he.

She laughed. "Ah, that comes a little later."

"Not much later," rejoined he, "or there's no time left for it."

It was Freddie who, after lunch, urged Susan and Clélie to "show Brent what you can do at acting."

"Yes—by all means," said Brent with enthusiasm.

And they gave—in one end of the salon which was well suited for it—the scene between mother and daughter over the stolen diary, in "L'Autre Danger." Brent said little when they finished, so little that Palmer was visibly annoyed. But Susan, who was acquainted with his modes of expression, felt a deep glow of satisfaction. She had no delusions about her attempts; she understood perfectly that they were simply crude attempts. She knew she had done well—for her—and she knew he appreciated her improvement.

"That would have gone fine—with costumes and scenery—eh?" demanded Freddie of Brent.

"Yes," said Brent absently. "Yes—that is—Yes."

Freddie was dissatisfied with this lack of enthusiasm. He went on insistently:

"I think she ought to go on the stage—she and Madame Clélie, too."

"Yes," said Brent, between inquiry and reflection.

"What do *you* think?"

"I don't think she ought," replied Brent. "I think she *must*." He turned to Susan. "Would you like it?"

Susan hesitated. Freddie said—rather lamely, "Of course she would. For my part, I wish she would."

"Then I will," said Susan quietly.

Palmer looked astounded. He had not dreamed she would assent. He knew her tones—knew that the particular tone meant finality. "You're joking," cried he, with an uneasy laugh. "Why, you wouldn't stand the work for a week. It's hard work—isn't it, Brent?"

"About the hardest," said Brent. "And she's got practically everything still to learn."

"Shall we try, Clélie?" said Susan.

Young Madame Délière was pale with eagerness. "Ah—but that would be worth while!" cried she.

"Then it's settled," said Susan. To Brent: "We'll make the arrangements at once—today."

Freddie was looking at her with a dazed expression. His glance presently drifted from her face to the fire, to rest there thoughtfully as he smoked his cigar. He took no part in the conversation that followed. Presently he left the room without excusing himself. When Clélie seated herself at the piano to wander vaguely from one piece of music to another, Brent joined Susan at the fire and said in English:

"Palmer is furious."

"I saw," said she.

"I am afraid. For—I know him."

She looked calmly at him. "But I am not."

"Then you do not know him."

The strangest smile flitted across her face.

After a pause Brent said: "Are you married to him?"

Again the calm steady look. Then: "That is none of your business."

"I thought you were not," said Brent, as if she had answered his question with a clear negative. He added, "You know I'd not have asked if it had been 'none of my business.'"

"What do you mean?"

"If you had been his wife, I could not have gone on. I've all the reverence for a home of the man who has never had one. I'd not take part in a home-breaking. But—since you are free——"

"I shall never be anything else but free. It's because I wish to make sure of my freedom that I'm going into this."

Palmer appeared in the doorway.

That night the four and Gourdain dined together, went to the theater and afterward to supper at the Café de Paris. Gourdain and young Madame Délière formed an interesting, unusually attractive exhibit of the parasitism that is as inevitable to the rich as fleas to a dog. Gourdain was a superior man, Clélie a superior woman. There was nothing of the sycophant, or even of the courtier, about either. Yet they already had in their faces that subtle indication of the dependent that is found in all professional people who habitually work for and associate with the rich only. They had no sense of dependence; they were not dependents, for they gave more than value received. Yet so corrupting is the atmosphere about rich people that Gourdain, who had other rich clients, no less than Clélie who got her whole living from Palmer, was at a glance in the flea class and not in the dog class. Brent looked for signs of the same thing in Susan's face. The signs should have been there; but they were not. "Not yet," thought he. "And never will be now."

Palmer's abstraction and constraint were in sharp contrast to the gayety of the others. Susan drank almost nothing. Her spirits were soaring so high that she did not dare stimulate them with champagne. The Café de Paris is one of the places where the respectable go to watch *les autres* and to catch a real gayety by contagion of a gayety that is mechanical and altogether as unreal as play-acting. There is something fantastic about the official temples of Venus; the pleasure-makers are so serious under their masks and the pleasure-getters so quaintly dazzled and deluded. That is, Venus's temples are like those of so many other religions in reverence among men—disbelief and solemn humbuggery at the altar; belief that would rather die than be undeceived, in the pews. Palmer scarcely took his eyes from Susan's face. It amused and pleased her to see how uneasy this made Brent—and how her own laughter and jests aggravated his uneasiness to the point where he was almost showing it. She glanced round that brilliant room filled with men and women, each of them carrying underneath the placidity of stiff evening shirt or the scantiness of audacious evening gown the most fascinating emotions and secrets—love and hate and jealousy, cold and monstrous habits and desires, ruin impending or stealthily advancing, fortune giddying to a gorgeous climax, disease and shame and fear—yet only signs of love and laughter and lightness of heart visible. And she wondered whether at any other table there was gathered so curious an assemblage of pasts and presents and futures as at the one over which Freddie Palmer was presiding somberly. . . . Then her thoughts took another turn. She fell to noting how each man was accompanied by a woman —a gorgeously dressed woman, a woman revealing, proclaiming, in every line, in every movement, that she was thus elaborately and beautifully toiletted to please man, to appeal to his senses, to gain his gracious approval. It was the world in miniature; it was an illustration of the position of woman—of her own position. Favorite; pet. Not the equal of man, but an appetizer, a dessert. She glanced at herself in the glass, mocked

her own radiant beauty of face and form and dress.
Not really a full human being; merely a decoration.
No more; and no worse off than most of the women
everywhere, the favorites licensed or unlicensed of law
and religion. But just as badly off, and just as in-
secure. Free! No rest, no full breath until freedom
had been won! At any cost, by straight way or devious
—free!

"Let's go home," said she abruptly. "I've had
enough of this."

She was in a dressing gown, all ready for bed and
reading, when Palmer came into her sitting-room. She
was smoking, her gaze upon her book. Her thick dark
hair was braided close to her small head. There was
delicate lace on her nightgown, showing above the
wadded satin collar of the dressing gown. He dropped
heavily into a chair.

If anyone had told me a year ago that a skirt
could make a damn fool of me," said he bitterly,
"I'd have laughed in his face. Yet—here I am!
How nicely I did drop into your trap today—about
the acting!"

"Trap?"

"Oh, I admit I built and baited and set it, myself—
ass that I was! But it was your trap—yours and
Brent's, all the same. . . . A skirt—and not a clean
one, at that."

She lowered the book to her lap, took the cigarette
from between her lips, looked at him. "Why not be
reasonable, Freddie?" said she calmly. Language had
long since lost its power to impress her. "Why irritate
yourself and annoy me simply because I won't let you
tyrannize over me? You know you can't treat me as

if I were your property. I'm not your wife, and I don't have to be your mistress."

"Getting ready to break with me—eh?"

"If I wished to go, I'd tell you—and go."

"You'd give me the shake, would you?—without the slightest regard for all I've done for you!"

She refused to argue that again. "I hope I've outgrown doing weak gentle things through cowardice and pretending it's through goodness of heart."

"You've gotten hard—like stone."

"Like you—somewhat." And after a moment she added, "Anything that's strong is hard—isn't it? Can a man or a woman get anywhere without being able to be what you call 'hard' and what I call 'strong'?"

"Where do *you* want to get?" demanded he.

She disregarded his question, to finish saying what was in her mind—what she was saying rather to give herself a clear look at her own thoughts and purposes than to enlighten him about them. "I'm not a sheltered woman," pursued she. "I've got no one to save me from the consequences of doing nice, sweet, womanly things."

"You've got me," said he angrily.

"But why lean if I'm strong enough to stand alone? Why weaken myself just to gratify your mania for owning and bossing? But let me finish what I was saying. I never got any quarter because I was a woman. No woman does, as a matter of fact; and in the end, the more she uses her sex to help her shirk, the worse her punishment is. But in my case——

"I was brought up to play the weak female, to use my sex as my shield. And that was taken from me and—I needn't tell *you* how I was taught to give and take like a man—no, not like a man—for no man ever has to endure what a woman goes through if she is thrown on the world. Still, I'm not whining. Now that it's all over I'm the better for what I've been through. I've learned to use all a man's weapons and in addition I've got a woman's."

"As long as your looks last," sneered he.

"That will be longer than yours," said she pleasantly, "if you keep on with the automobiles and the champagne. And when my looks are gone, my woman's weapons. . .

"Why, I'll still have the man's weapons left—shan't I?—knowledge, and the ability to use it."

His expression of impotent fury mingled with compelled admiration and respect made his face about as unpleasant to look at as she had ever seen it. But she liked to look. His confession of her strength made her feel stronger. The sense of strength was a new sensation with her—new and delicious. Nor could the feeling that she was being somewhat cruel restrain her from enjoying it.

"I have never asked quarter," she went on. "I never shall. If fate gets me down, as it has many a time, why I'll be able to take my medicine without weeping or whining. I've never asked pity. I've never asked charity. That's why I'm here, Freddie—in this apartment, instead of in a filthy tenement attic—and in these clothes instead of in rags—and with you respecting me, instead of kicking me toward the gutter. Isn't that so?"

He was silent.

"Isn't it so?" she insisted.

"Yes," he admitted. And his handsome eyes looked the love so near to hate that fills a strong man for a strong woman when they clash and he cannot conquer. "No wonder I'm a fool about you," he muttered.

"I don't purpose that any man or woman shall use me," she went on, "in exchange for merely a few flatteries. I insist that if they use me, they must let me use them. I shan't be mean about it, but I shan't be altogether a fool, either. And what is a woman but a fool when she lets men use her for nothing but being called sweet and loving and womanly? Unless that's the best she can do, poor thing!"

"You needn't sneer at respectable women."

"I don't," replied she. "I've no sneers for anybody. I've discovered a great truth, Freddie—the deep-down equality of all human beings—all of them birds in the same wind and battling with it each as best he can. As for myself—with money, with a career that interests me, with position that'll give me any acquaintances and friends that are congenial, I don't care what is said of me."

As her plan unfolded itself fully to his understanding, which needed only a hint to enable it to grasp all, he forgot his rage for a moment in his interest and admiration. Said he:

"You've used me. Now you're going to use Brent— eh? Well—what will you give *him* in exchange?"

"He wants someone to act certain parts in certain plays."

"Is that *all* he wants?"

"He hasn't asked anything else."

"And if he did?"

"Don't be absurd. You know Brent."

"He's not in love with you," assented Palmer. "He doesn't want you that way. There's some woman somewhere, I've heard—and he doesn't care about anybody but her."

He was speaking in a careless, casual way, watching her out of the corner of his eye. And she, taken off guard, betrayed in her features the secret that was a secret even from herself. He sprang up with a bound, sprang at her, caught her up out of her chair, the fingers of one hand clasping her throat.

"I thought so!" he hissed. "You love him—damn you! You love him! You'd better look out, both of you!"

There came a knock at the door between her bedroom and that of Madame Clélie. Palmer released her, stood panting, with furious eyes on the door from which the sound had come. Susan called, "It's all right, Clélie, for the present." Then she said to Palmer, "I told Clélie to knock if she ever heard voices in this room— or any sound she didn't understand." She reseated herself, began to massage her throat where his fingers had clutched it. "It's fortunate my skin doesn't mar easily," she went on. "What were you saying?"

"I know the truth now. You love Brent. That's the milk in the cocoanut."

She reflected on this, apparently with perfect tranquillity, apparently with no memory of his furious threat against her and against Brent. She said:

"Perhaps I was simply piqued because there's another woman."

"You are jealous."

"I guess I was—a little."

"You admit that you love him, you——"

He checked himself on the first hissing breath of the foul epithet. She said tranquilly:

"Jealousy doesn't mean love. We're jealous in all sorts of ways—and of all sorts of things."

"Well—*he* cares nothing about *you*."

"Nothing."

"And never will. He'd despise a woman who had been——"

"Don't hesitate. Say it. I'm used to hearing it, Freddie—and to being it. And not 'had been' but 'is.' I still am, you know."

"You're not!" he cried. "And never were—and never could be—for some unknown reason, God knows why."

She shrugged her shoulders, lit another cigarette. He went on:

"You can't get it out of your head that because he's interested in you he's more or less stuck on you. That's the way with women. The truth is, he wants you merely to act in his plays."

"And I want that, too."

"You think I'm going to stand quietly by and let this thing go on—do you?"

She showed not the faintest sign of nervousness at this repetition, more carefully veiled, of his threat against her—and against Brent. She chose the only hopeful course; she went at him boldly and directly. Said she with amused carelessness:

"Why not? He doesn't want me. Even if I love him, I'm not giving him anything you want."

"How do you know what I want?" cried he, confused by this unexpected way of meeting his attack. "You think I'm simply a brute—with no fine instincts or feelings——"

She interrupted him with a laugh. "Don't be absurd, Freddie," said she. "You know perfectly well you and I don't call out the finer feelings in each other. If either of us wanted that sort of thing, we'd have to look elsewhere."

447

"You mean Brent—eh?"

She laughed with convincing derision. "What nonsense!" She put her arms round his neck, and her lips close to his. The violet-gray eyes were half closed, the perfume of the smooth amber-white skin, of the thick, wavy, dark hair, was in his nostrils. And in a languorous murmur she soothed his subjection to a deep sleep with, "As long as you give me what I want from you, and I give you what you want from me—why should we wrangle?"

And with a smile he acquiesced. She felt that she had ended the frightful danger—to Brent rather than to herself—that suddenly threatened from those wicked eyes of Palmer's. But it might easily come again. She did not dare relax her efforts, for in the succeeding days she saw that he was like one annoyed by a constant pricking from a pin hidden in the clothing and searched for in vain. He was no longer jealous of Brent. But while he didn't know what was troubling him, he did know that he was uncomfortable.

XXIII

IN but one important respect was Brent's original plan modified. Instead of getting her stage experience in France, Susan joined a London company making one of those dreary, weary, cheap and trashy tours of the smaller cities of the provinces with half a dozen plays by Jones, Pinero, and Shaw.

Clélie stayed in London, toiling at the language, determined to be ready to take the small part of French maid in Brent's play in the fall. Brent and Palmer accompanied Susan; and every day for several hours Brent and the stage manager—his real name was Thomas Boil and his professional name was Herbert Streathern—coached the patient but most unhappy Susan line by line, word by word, gesture by gesture, in the little parts she was playing. Palmer traveled with them, making a pretense of interest that ill concealed his boredom and irritation. This for three weeks; then he began to make trips to London to amuse himself with the sports, amateur and professional, with whom he easily made friends—some of them men in a position to be useful to him socially later on. He had not spoken of those social ambitions of his since Susan refused to go that way with him—but she knew he had them in mind as strongly as ever. He was the sort of man who must have an objective, and what other objective could there be for him who cared for and believed in the conventional ambitions and triumphs only—the successes that made the respectable world gape and grovel and envy?

"You'll not stick at this long," he said to Susan.

"I'm frightfully depressed," she admitted. "It's tiresome—and hard—and so hideously uncomfortable! And I've lost all sense of art or profession. Acting seems to be nothing but a trade, and a poor, cheap one at that."

He was not surprised, but was much encouraged by this candid account of her state of mind. Said he:

"It's my private opinion that only your obstinacy keeps you from giving it up straight off. Surely you must see it's nonsense. Drop it and come along—and be comfortable and happy. Why be obstinate? There's nothing in it."

"Perhaps it *is* obstinacy," said she. "I like to think it's something else."

"Drop it. You want to. You know you do."

"I want to, but I can't," replied she.

He recognized the tone, the expression of the eyes, the sudden showing of strength through the soft, young contour. And he desisted.

Never again could there be comfort, much less happiness, until she had tried out her reawakened ambition. She had given up all that had been occupying her since she left America with Freddie; she had abandoned herself to a life of toil. Certainly nothing could have been more tedious, more tormenting to sensitive nerves, than the schooling through which Brent was putting her. Its childishness revolted her and angered her. Experience had long since lowered very considerably the point at which her naturally sweet disposition ceased to be sweet—a process through which every good-tempered person must pass unless he or she is to be crushed and cast aside as a failure. There were days, many of them, when it took all her good sense,

all her fundamental faith in Brent, to restrain her from
an outbreak. Streathern regarded Brent as a crank,
and had to call into service all his humility as a poor
Englishman toward a rich man to keep from showing
his contempt. And Brent seemed to be—indeed was—
testing her forbearance to the uttermost. He offered
not the slightest explanation of his method. He simply
ordered her blindly to pursue the course he marked
out. She was sorely tempted to ask, to demand, explanations. But there stood out a quality in Brent
that made her resolve ooze away, as soon as she faced
him. Of one thing she was confident. Any lingering
suspicions Freddie might have had of Brent's interest
in her as a woman, or even of her being interested in
him as a man, must have been killed beyond resurrection. Freddie showed that he would have hated Brent,
would have burst out against him, for the unhuman,
inhuman way he was treating her, had it not been
that Brent was so admirably serving his design to
have her finally and forever disgusted and done with
the stage.

Finally there came a performance in which the audience—the gallery part of it—"booed" her—not the
play, not the other players, but her and no other.
Brent came along, apparently by accident, as she made
her exit. He halted before her and scanned her countenance with those all-seeing eyes of his. Said he:

"You heard them?"

"Of course," replied she.

"That was for you," said he—and he said it with
an absence of sympathy that made it brutal.

"For only me," said she—frivolously.

"You seem not to mind."

"Certainly I mind. I'm not made of wood or stone."

"Don't you think you'd better give it up?"

She looked at him with a steely light from the violet eyes, a light that had never been there before.

"Give up?" said she. "Not even if you give me up. This thing has got to be put through."

He simply nodded. "All right," he said. "It will be."

"That booing—it almost struck me dead. When it didn't, I for the first time felt sure I was going to win."

He nodded again, gave her one of his quick expressive, fleeting glances that somehow made her forget and forgive everything and feel fresh and eager to start in again. He said:

"When the booing began and you didn't break down and run off the stage, I knew that what I hoped and believed about you was true."

Streathern joined them. His large, soft eyes were full of sympathetic tears. He was so moved that he braved Brent. He said to Susan:

"It wasn't your fault, Miss Lenox. You were doing exactly as Mr. Brent ordered, when the booing broke out."

"Exactly," said Brent.

Streathern regarded him with a certain nervousness and veiled pity. Streathern had been brought into contact with many great men. He had found them, each and every one, with this same streak of wild folly, this habit of doing things that were to him obviously useless and ridiculous. It was a profound mystery to him why such men succeeded while he himself who never did such things remained in obscurity. The only explanation was the abysmal stupidity, ignorance, and folly of the masses of mankind. What a harbor of refuge that reflection has ever been for mediocrity's shattered and sinking vanity! Yet the one indisputable fact about the great geniuses of long ago is that in their own country and age "the common people heard them gladly." Streathern could not now close his mouth upon one last appeal on behalf of the clever and lovely and so amiable victim of Brent's mania.

"I say, Mr. Brent," pleaded he, "don't you think— Really now, if you'll permit a chap not without experience to say so—Don't you think that by drilling her so much and so—so *beastly* minutely—you're making her wooden—machine-like?"

"I hope so," said Brent, in a tone that sent Streathern scurrying away to a place where he could express himself unseen and unheard.

In her fifth week she began to improve. She felt at home on the stage; she felt at home in her part, whatever it happened to be. She was giving what could really be called a performance. Streathern, when he was sure Brent could not hear, congratulated her. "It's wonderfully plucky of you, my dear," said he, "quite amazingly plucky—to get yourself together and go straight ahead, in spite of what your American friend has been doing to you."

"In spite of it." cried Susan. "Why, don't you see that it's because of what he's been doing? I felt it, all the time. I see it now."

"Oh, really—do you think so?" said Streathern.

His tone made it a polite and extremely discreet way of telling her he thought she had become as mad as Brent. She did not try to explain to him why she was improving. In that week she advanced by long strides, and Brent was radiant.

"Now we'll teach you scales," said he. "We'll teach

you the mechanics of expressing every variety of emotion. Then we'll be ready to study a strong part."

She had known in the broad from the outset what Brent was trying to accomplish—that he was giving her the trade side of the art, was giving it to her quickly and systematically. But she did not appreciate how profoundly right he was until she was "learning scales." Then she understood why most so called "professional" performances are amateurish, haphazard, without any precision. She was learning to posture, and to utter every emotion so accurately that any spectator would recognize it at once.

"And in time your voice and your body," said Brent, "will become as much your servants as are Paderewski's ten fingers. He doesn't rely upon any such rot as inspiration. Nor does any master of any art. A mind can be inspired but not a body. It must be taught. You must first have a perfect instrument. Then, if you are a genius, your genius, having a perfect instrument to work with, will produce perfect results. To ignore or to neglect the mechanics of an art is to hamper or to kill inspiration. Geniuses—a few—and they not the greatest—have been too lazy to train their instruments. But anyone who is merely talented dares not take the risk. And you—we'd better assume—are merely talented."

Streathern, who had a deserved reputation as a coach, was disgusted with Brent's degradation of an art. As openly as he dared, he warned Susan against the danger of becoming a mere machine—a puppet, responding stiffly to the pulling of strings. But Susan had got over her momentary irritation against Brent, her doubt of his judgment in her particular case. She ignored Streathern's advice that she should be natural, that she should let her own temperament dictate variations on his cut and dried formulae for expression. She continued to do as she was bid.

"If you are *not* a natural born actress," said Brent, "at least you will be a good one—so good that most critics will call you great. And if you *are* a natural born genius at acting, you will soon put color in the cheeks of these dolls I'm giving you—and ease into their bodies—and nerves and muscles and blood in place of the strings."

In the seventh week he abruptly took her out of the company and up to London to have each day an hour of singing, an hour of dancing, and an hour of fencing. "You'll ruin her health," protested Freddie. "You're making her work like a ditch digger."

Brent replied, "If she hasn't the health, she's got to abandon the career. If she has health, this training will give it steadiness and solidity. If there's a weakness anywhere, it'll show itself and can be remedied."

And he piled the work on her, dictated her hours of sleep, her hours for rest and for walking, her diet— and little he gave her to eat. When he had her thoroughly broken to his regimen, he announced that business compelled his going immediately to America. "I shall be back in a month," said he.

"I think I'll run over with you," said Palmer. "Do you mind, Susan?"

"Clélie and I shall get on very well," she replied. She would be glad to have both out of the way that she might give her whole mind to the only thing that now interested her. For the first time she was experiencing the highest joy that comes to mortals, the only joy that endures and grows and defies all the calamities of circumstances—the joy of work congenial and developing.

"Yes—come along," said Brent to Palmer. "Here you'll be tempting her to break the rules." He added, "Not that you would succeed. She understands what it all means, now—and nothing could stop her. That's why I feel free to leave her."

"Yes, I understand," said Susan. She was gazing away into space; at sight of her expression Freddie turned hastily away.

On a Saturday morning Susan and Clélie, after waiting on the platform at Euston Station until the long, crowded train for Liverpool and the *Lusitania* disappeared, went back to the lodgings in Half Moon Street with a sudden sense of the vastness of London, of its loneliness and dreariness, of its awkward inhospitality to the stranger under its pall of foggy smoke. Susan was thinking of Brent's last words:

She had said, "I'll try to deserve all the pains you've taken, Mr. Brent."

"Yes, I have done a lot for you," he had replied. "I've put you beyond the reach of any of the calamities of life—beyond the need of any of its consolations. Don't forget that if the steamer goes down with all on board."

And then she had looked at him—and as Freddie's back was half turned, she hoped he had not seen—in fact, she was sure he had not, or she would not have dared. And Brent—had returned her look with his usual quizzical smile; but she had learned how to see through that mask. Then—she had submitted to Freddie's energetic embrace—had given her hand to Brent—"Good-by," she had said; and "Good luck," he.

Beyond the reach of *any* of the calamities? Beyond

the need of *any* of the consolations? Yes—it was almost literally true. She felt the big interest—the career—growing up within her, and expanding, and already overstepping all other interests and emotions.

Brent had left her and Clélie more to do than could be done; thus they had no time to bother either about the absent or about themselves. Looking back in after years on the days that Freddie was away, Susan could recall that from time to time she would find her mind wandering, as if groping in the darkness of its own cellars or closets for a lost thought, a missing link in some chain of thought. This even awakened her several times in the night—made her leap from sleep into acute and painful consciousness as if she had recalled and instantly forgotten some startling and terrible thing.

And when Freddie unexpectedly came—having taken passage on the *Lusitania* for the return voyage, after only six nights and five days in New York—she was astonished by her delight at seeing him, and by the kind of delight it was. For it rather seemed a sort of relief, as from a heavy burden of anxiety.

"Why didn't you wait and come with Brent?" asked she.

"Couldn't stand it," replied he. "I've grown clear away from New York—at least from the only New York I know. I don't like the boys any more. They bore me. They—offend me. And I know if I stayed on a few days they'd begin to suspect. No, it isn't Europe. It's—you. You're responsible for the change in me."

He was speaking entirely of the internal change, which indeed was great. For while he was still fond of all kinds of sporting, it was not in his former crude way; he had even become something of a connoisseur of pictures and was cultivating a respect for the purity of the English language that made him wince at Susan's and Brent's slang. But when he spoke thus frankly and feelingly of the change in him, Susan looked at him—and, not having seen him in two weeks and three days, she really saw him for the first time in many a month. She could not think of the internal change he spoke of for noting the external change. He had grown at least fifty pounds heavier than he had been when they came abroad. In one way this was an improvement; it gave him a dignity, an air of consequence in place of the boyish good looks of the days before the automobile and before the effects of high living began to show. But it made of him a different man in Susan's eyes—a man who now seemed almost a stranger to her.

"Yes, you *have* changed," replied she absently. And she went and examined herself in a mirror.

"You, too," said Freddie. "You don't look older—as I do. But—there's a—a—I can't describe it."

Susan could not see it. "I'm just the same," she insisted.

Palmer laughed. "You can't judge about yourself. But all this excitement—and studying—and thinking—and God knows what——You're not at all the woman I came abroad with."

The subject seemed to be making both uncomfortable; they dropped it.

Women are bred to attach enormous importance to their physical selves—so much so that many women have no other sense of self-respect, and regard themselves as possessing the entirety of virtue if they have chastity or can pretend to have it. The life Susan

458

had led upsets all this and forces a woman either utterly
to despise herself, even as she is despised of men, or
to discard the sex measure of feminine self-respect as
ridiculously inadequate, and to seek some other measure. Susan had sought this other measure, and had
found it. She was, therefore, not a little surprised to
find—after Freddie had been back three or four days
—that he was arousing in her the same sensations
which a strange man intimately about would have
aroused in her in the long past girlhood of innocence.
It was not physical repulsion; it was not a sense of
immorality. It was a kind of shyness, a feeling of violated modesty. She felt herself blushing if he came into
the room when she was dressing. As soon as she
awakened in the morning she sprang from bed beside
him and hastened into her dressing-room and closed
the door, resisting an impulse to lock it. Apparently
the feeling of physical modesty which she had thought
dead, killed to the last root, was not dead, was once
more stirring toward life.

"What are you blushing about?" asked he, when
she, passing through the bedroom, came suddenly upon
him, very scantily dressed.

She laughed confusedly and beat a hurried retreat.
She began to revolve the idea of separate bedrooms; she
resolved that when they moved again she would arrange
it on some pretext—and she was looking about for
a new place on the plea that their quarters in Half
Moon Street were too cramped. All this close upon
his return, for it was before the end of the first week
that she, taking a shower bath one morning, saw the
door of the bathroom opening to admit him, and cried
out sharply:

"Close that door!"

"It's I," Freddie called, to make himself heard above the noise of the water. "Shut off that water and listen."

She shut off the water, but instead of listening, she said, nervous but determined:

"Please close the door. I'll be out directly."

"Listen, I tell you," he cried, and she now noticed that his voice was curiously, arrestingly, shrill.

"Brent—has been hurt—badly hurt." She was dripping wet. She thrust her arms into her bathrobe, flung wide the partly open door. He was standing there, a newspaper in his trembling hand. "This is a dispatch from New York—dated yesterday," he began. "Listen," and he read:

"During an attempt to rob the house of Mr. Robert Brent, the distinguished playwright, early this morning, Mr. Brent was set upon and stabbed in a dozen places, his butler, James Fourget, was wounded, perhaps mortally, and his secretary, Mr. J. C. Garvey, was knocked insensible. The thieves made their escape. The police have several clues. Mr. Brent is hovering between life and death, with the chances against him."

Susan, leaning with all her weight against the door jamb, saw Palmer's white face going away from her, heard his agitated voice less and less distinctly—fell to the floor with a crash and knew no more.

When she came to, she was lying in the bed; about it or near it were Palmer, her maid, his valet, Clélie, several strangers. Her glance turned to Freddie's face and she looked into his eyes amid a profound silence. She saw in those eyes only intense anxiety and intense affection. He said:

"What is it, dear? You are all right. Only a fainting spell."

"Was that true?" she asked.

"Yes, but he'll pull through. The surgeons save everybody nowadays. I've cabled his secretary, Garvey, and to my lawyers. We'll have an answer soon. I've sent out for all the papers."

"She must not be agitated," interposed a medical looking man with stupid brown eyes and a thin brown beard sparsely veiling his gaunt and pasty face.

"Nonsense!" said Palmer, curtly. "My wife is not an invalid. Our closest friend has been almost killed. To keep the news from her would be to make her sick."

Susan closed her eyes. "Thank you," she murmured. "Send them all away—except Clélie. . . . Leave me alone with Clélie."

Pushing the others before him, Freddie moved toward the door into the hall. At the threshold he paused to say:

"Shall I bring the papers when they come?"

She hesitated. "No," she answered without opening her eyes. "Send them in. I want to read them, myself."

She lay quiet, Clélie stroking her brow. From time to time a shudder passed over her. When, in answer to a knock, Clélie took in the bundle of newspapers, she sat up in bed and read the meager dispatches. The long accounts were made long by the addition of facts about Brent's life. The short accounts added nothing to what she already knew. When she had read all, she sank back among the pillows and closed her eyes. A long, long silence in the room. Then a soft knock at the door. Clélie left the bedside to answer it, returned to say:

"Mr. Freddie wishes to come in with a telegram."

Susan started up wildly. Her eyes were wide and staring—a look of horror. "No—no!" she cried. Then she compressed her lips, passed her hand slowly over her brow. "Yes—tell him to come in."

Her gaze was upon the door until it opened, leaped to his face, to his eyes, the instant he appeared. He was smiling—hopefully, but not gayly.

"Garvey says"—and he read from a slip of paper in his hand—" 'None of the wounds necessarily mortal. Doctors refuse to commit themselves, but I believe he has a good chance.' "

He extended the cablegram that she might read for herself, and said, "He'll win, my dear. He has luck, and lucky people always win in big things."

Her gaze did not leave his face. One would have said that she had not heard, that she was still seeking what she had admitted him to learn. He sat down where Clélie had been, and said:

"There's only one thing for us to do, and that is to go over at once."

She closed her eyes. A baffled, puzzled expression was upon her deathly pale face.

"We can sail on the *Mauretania* Saturday," continued he. "I've telephoned and there are good rooms."

She turned her face away.

"Don't you feel equal to going?"

"As you say, we must."

"The trip can't do you any harm." His forced composure abruptly vanished and he cried out hysterically: "Good God! It's incredible." Then he got himself in hand again, and went on: "No wonder it bowled you out. I had my anxiety about you to break the shock. But you—— How do you feel now?"

"I'm going to dress."

"I'll send you in some brandy." He bent and kissed her. A shudder convulsed her—a shudder visible even through the covers. But he seemed not to note it, and went on: "I didn't realize how fond I was of Brent until I saw that thing in the paper. I almost fainted, myself. I gave Clélie a horrible scare."

"I thought you were having an attack," said Clélie. "My husband looked exactly as you did when he died that way."

Susan's strange eyes were gazing intently at him— the searching, baffled, persistently seeking look. She closed them as he turned from the bed. When she and Clélie were alone and she was dressing, she said:

"Freddie gave you a scare?"

"I was at breakfast," replied Clélie, "was pouring my coffee. He came into the room in his bathrobe—took up the papers from the table—opened to the foreign news as he always does. I happened to be looking at him"—Clélie flushed—"he is very handsome in that robe—and all at once he dropped the paper—grew white—staggered and fell into a chair. Exactly like my husband."

Susan, seated at her dressing-table, was staring absently out of the window. She shook her head impatiently, drew a long breath, went on with her toilet.

XXIV

A FEW minutes before the dinner hour she came into the drawing room. Palmer and Madame Délière were already there, near the fire which the unseasonable but by no means unusual coolness of the London summer evening made extremely comfortable—and, for Americans, necessary. Palmer stood with his back to the blaze, moodily smoking a cigarette. That evening his now almost huge form looked more degenerated than usual by the fat of high living and much automobiling. His fleshy face, handsome still and of a refined type, bore the traces of anxious sorrow. Clélie, sitting at the corner of the fireplace and absently turning the leaves of an illustrated French magazine, had in her own way an air as funereal as Freddie's. As Susan entered, they glanced at her.

Palmer uttered and half suppressed an ejaculation of amazement. Susan was dressed as for opera or ball —one of her best evening dresses, the greatest care in arranging her hair and the details of her toilette. Never had she been more beautiful. Her mode of life since she came abroad with Palmer, the thoughts that had been filling her brain and giving direction to her life since she accepted Brent as her guide and Brent's plans as her career, had combined to give her air of distinction the touch of the extraordinary—the touch that characterizes the comparatively few human beings who live the life above and apart from that of the common run—the life illuminated by imagination. At a glance one sees that they are not of the eaters, drinkers, sleepers, and seekers after the shallow easy pleasures money provides ready-made. They shine by their own light; the rest of mankind shines either by light reflected from them or not at all.

Looking at her that evening as she came into the comfortable, old-fashioned English room, with its somewhat heavy but undeniably dignified furniture and draperies, the least observant could not have said that she was in gala attire because she was in gala mood. Beneath the calm of her surface expression lay something widely different. Her face, slim and therefore almost beyond the reach of the attacks of time and worry, was of the type to which a haggard expression is becoming. Her eyes, large and dreamy, seemed to be seeing visions of unutterable sadness, and the scarlet streak of her mouth seemed to emphasize their pathos. She looked young, very young; yet there was also upon her features the stamp of experience, the experience of suffering. She did not notice the two by the fire, but went to the piano at the far end of the room and stood gazing out into the lovely twilight of the garden.

Freddie, who saw only the costume, said in an undertone to Clélie, "What sort of freak is this?"

Said Madame Délière: "An uncle of mine lost his wife. They were young and he loved her to distraction. Betweeen her death and the funeral he scandalized everybody by talking incessantly of the most trivial details—the cards, the mourning, the flowers, his own clothes. But the night of the funeral he killed himself."

Palmer winced as if Clélie had struck him. Then an expression of terror, of fear, came into his eyes. "You don't think she'd do that?" he muttered hoarsely.

"Certainly not," replied the young Frenchwoman. "I was simply trying to explain her. She dressed because she was unconscious of what she was doing. Real sorrow doesn't think about appearances." Then with quick tact she added: "Why should she kill herself? Monsieur Brent is getting well. Also, while she's a devoted friend of his, she doesn't love him, but you."

"I'm all upset," said Palmer, in confused apology.

He gazed fixedly at Susan—a straight, slim figure with the carriage and the poise of head that indicate self-confidence and pride. As he gazed Madame Clélie watched him with fascinated eyes. It was both thrilling and terrifying to see such love as he was revealing —a love more dangerous than hate. Palmer noted that he was observed, abruptly turned to face the fire.

A servant opened the doors into the dining-room, Madame Délière rose. "Come, Susan," said she.

Susan looked at her with unseeing eyes.

"Dinner is served."

"I do not care for dinner," said Susan, seating herself at the piano.

"Oh, but you——"

"Let her alone," said Freddie, curtly. "You and I will go in."

Susan, alone, dropped listless hands into her lap. How long she sat there motionless and with mind a blank she did not know. She was aroused by a sound in the hall—in the direction of the outer door of their apartment. She started up, instantly all alive and alert, and glided swiftly in the direction of the sound. A servant met her at the threshold. He had a cablegram on a tray.

"For Mr. Palmer," said he.

But she, not hearing, took the envelope and tore it

open. At a sweep her eyes took in the unevenly type-written words:

Brent died at half past two this afternoon.

GARVEY.

She gazed wonderingly at the servant, reread the cablegram. The servant said: "Shall I take it to Mr. Palmer, ma'am?"

"No. That is all, thanks," replied she.

And she walked slowly across the room to the fire. She shivered, adjusted one of the shoulder straps of her low-cut pale green dress. She read the cablegram a third time, laid it gently, thoughtfully, upon the mantel. "Brent died at half past two this afternoon." Died. Yes, there was no mistaking the meaning of those words. She knew that the message was true. But she did not feel it. She was seeing Brent as he had been when they said good-by. And it would take something more than a mere message to make her feel that the Brent so vividly alive, so redolent of life, of activity, of energy, of plans and projects, the Brent of health and strength, had ceased to be. "Brent died at half past two this afternoon." Except in the great crises we all act with a certain theatricalism, do the thing books and plays and the example of others have taught us to do. But in the great crises we do as we feel. Susan knew that Brent was dead. If he had meant less to her, she would have shrieked or fainted or burst into wild sobs. But not when he was her whole future. She *knew* he was dead, but she did not *believe* it. So she stood staring at the flames, and wondering why, when she knew such a frightful thing, she should remain calm. When she had heard that he was injured, she had felt, now she did not feel at all. Her body, her brain, went serenely on in their routine. The part of her that was her very self—had it died, and not Brent?

She turned her back to the fire, gazed toward the opposite wall. In a mirror there she saw the reflection of Palmer, at table in the adjoining room. A servant was holding a dish at his left and he was helping himself. She observed his every motion, observed his fattened body, his round and large face, the forming roll of fat at the back of his neck. All at once she grew cold—cold as she had not been since the night she and Etta Brashear walked the streets of Cincinnati. The ache of this cold, like the cold of death, was an agony. She shook from head to foot. She turned toward the mantel again, looked at the cablegram. But she did not take it in her hands. She could see—in the air, before her eyes—in clear, sharp lettering—"Brent died at half past two this afternoon. Garvey."

The sensation of cold faded into a sensation of approaching numbness. She went into the hall—to her own rooms. In the dressing-room her maid, Clémence, was putting away the afternoon things she had taken off. She stood at the dressing table, unclasping the string of pearls. She said to Clémence tranquilly:

"Please pack in the small trunk with the broad stripes three of my plainest street dresses—some underclothes—the things for a journey—only necessaries. Some very warm things, please, Clémence, I've suffered from cold, and I can't bear the idea of it. And please telephone to the—to the Cecil for a room and bath. When you have finished I shall pay you what I owe and a month's wages extra. I cannot afford to keep you any longer."

"But, madame"—Clémence fluttered in agitation—"Madame promised to take me to America."

"Telephone for the rooms for Miss Susan Lenox," said Susan. She was rapidly taking off her dress. "If I took you to America I should have to let you go as soon as we landed."

"But, madame—" Clémence advanced to assist her.

"Please pack the trunk," said Susan. "I am leaving here at once."

"I prefer to go to America, even if madame——"

"Very well. I'll take you. But you understand?"

"Perfectly, madame——"

A sound of hurrying footsteps and Palmer was at the threshold. His eyes were wild, his face distorted. His hair, usually carefully arranged over the rapidly growing bald spot above his brow, was disarranged in a manner that would have been ludicrous but for the terrible expression of his face. "Go!" he said harshly to the maid; and he stood fretting the knob until she hastened out and gave him the chance to close the door. Susan, calm and apparently unconscious of his presence, went on with her rapid change of costume. He lit a cigarette with fingers trembling, dropped heavily into a chair near the door. She, seated on the floor, was putting on boots.

When she had finished one and was beginning on the other he said stolidly:

"You think I did it"—not a question but an assertion.

"I know it," replied she. She was so seated that he was seeing her in profile.

"Yes—I did," he went on. He settled himself more deeply in the chair, crossed his legs. "And I am glad that I did."

She kept on at lacing the boot. There was nothing in her expression to indicate emotion, or even that she heard.

"I did it," continued he, "because I had the right. He invited it. He knew me—knew what to expect. I suppose he decided that you were worth taking the risk. It's strange what fools men—all men—we men— are about women. . . . Yes, he knew it. He didn't blame me."

She stopped lacing the boot, turned so that she could look at him.

"Do you remember his talking about me one day?" he went on, meeting her gaze naturally. "He said I was a survival of the Middle Ages—had a medieval Italian mind—said I would do anything to gain my end—and would have a clear conscience about it. Do you remember?"

"Yes."

"But you don't see why I had the right to kill him?"

A shiver passed over her. She turned away again, began again to lace the boot—but now her fingers were uncertain.

"I'll explain," pursued he. "You and I were getting along fine. He had had his chance with you and had lost it. Well, he comes over here—looks us up—puts himself between you and me—proceeds to take you away from me. Not in a square manly way but under the pretense of giving you a career. He made you restless—dissatisfied. He got you away from me. Isn't that so?"

She was sitting motionless now.

Palmer went on in the same harsh, jerky way:

"Now, nobody in the world—not even you—knew me better than Brent did. He knew what to expect—

if I caught on to what was doing. And I guess he knew I would be pretty sure to catch on."

"He never said a word to me that you couldn't have heard," said Susan.

"Of course not," retorted Palmer. "That isn't the question. It don't matter whether he wanted you for himself or for his plays. The point is that he took you away from me—he, my friend—and did it by stealth. You can't deny that."

"He offered me a chance for a career—that was all," said she. "He never asked for my love—or showed any interest in it. I gave him that."

He laughed—his old-time, gentle, sweet, wicked laugh. He said:

"Well—it'd have been better for him if you hadn't. All it did for him was to cost him his life."

Up she sprang. "Don't say that!" she cried passionately—so passionately that her whole body shook. "Do you suppose I don't know it? I know that I killed him. But I don't feel that he's dead. If I did, I'd not be able to live. But I can't! I can't! For me he is as much alive as ever."

"Try to think that—if it pleases you," sneered Palmer. "The fact remains that it was *you* who killed him."

Again she shivered. "Yes," she said, "I killed him."

"And that's why I hate you," Palmer went on, calm and deliberate—except his eyes; they were terrible. "A few minutes ago—when I was exulting that he would probably die—just then I found that opened cable on the mantel. Do you know what it did to me? It made me hate you. When I read it——" Freddie puffed at his cigarette in silence. She dropped weakly to the chair at the dressing table.

"Curse it!" he burst out. "I loved him. Yes, I was crazy about him—and am still. I'm glad I killed him. I'd do it again. I had to do it. He owed me his life. But that doesn't make me forgive *you*."

A long silence. Her fingers wandered among the articles spread upon the dressing table. He said:

"You're getting ready to leave?"

"I'm going to a hotel at once."

"Well, you needn't. I'm leaving. You're done with me. But I'm done with you." He rose, bent upon her his wicked glance, sneering and cruel. "You never want to see me again. No more do I ever want to see you again. I wish to God I never had seen you. You cost me the only friend I ever had that I cared about. And what's a woman beside a friend—a *man* friend? You've made a fool of me, as a woman always does of a man—always, by God! If she loves him, she destroys him. If she doesn't love him, he destroys himself."

Susan covered her face with her bare arms and sank down at the dressing table. "For pity's sake," she cried brokenly, "spare me—spare me!"

He seized her roughly by the shoulder. "Just flesh!" he said. "Beautiful flesh—but just female. And look what a fool you've made of me—and the best man in the world dead—over yonder! Spare you? Oh, you'll pull through all right. You'll pull through everything and anything—and come out stronger and better looking and better off. Spare you! Hell! I'd have killed you instead of him if I'd known I was going to hate you after I'd done the other thing. I'd do it yet—you dirty skirt!"

He jerked her unresisting form to its feet, gazed at her like an insane fiend. With a sob he seized her in his arms, crushed her against his breast, sunk his fingers deep into her hair, kissed it, grinding his teeth as he kissed. "I hate you, damn you—and I love you!" He flung her back into the chair—out of his life. "You'll never see me again!" And he fled from the room—from the house.

XXV

THE big ship issued from the Mersey into ugly
waters—into the weather that at all seasons
haunts and curses the coasts of Northern Europe. From Saturday until Wednesday Susan and
Madame Délière had true Atlantic seas and skies; and
the ship leaped and shivered and crashed along like
a brave cavalryman in the rear of a rout—fighting and
flying, flying and fighting. Four days of hours whose
every waking second lagged to record itself in a distinct pang of physical wretchedness; four days in
which all emotions not physical were suspended, in
which even the will to live, most tenacious of primal
instincts in a sane human being, yielded somewhat to
the general lassitude and disgust. Yet for Susan Lenox
four most fortunate days; for in them she underwent
a mental change that enabled her to emerge delivered
of the strain that threatened at every moment to cause
a snap.

On the fifth day her mind, crutched by her resum-
ing body, took up again its normal routine. She began to dress herself, to eat, to exercise—the mechanical
things first, as always—then to think. The grief
that had numbed her seemed to have been left behind
in England where it had suddenly struck her down—
England far away and vague across those immense and
infuriated waters, like the gulf of death between two
incarnations. No doubt that grief was awaiting her
at the other shores; no doubt there she would feel that
Brent was gone. But she would be better able to bear

474

the discovery. The body can be accustomed to the deadliest poisons, so that they become harmless—even useful—even a necessary aid to life. In the same way the mind can grow accustomed to the cruelest calamities, tolerate them, use them to attain a strength and power the hothoused soul never gets.

When a human being is abruptly plunged into an unnatural unconsciousness by mental or physical catastrophes, the greatest care is taken that the awakening to normal life again be slow, gradual, without shock. Otherwise the return would mean death or insanity or lifelong affliction with radical weakness. It may be that this sea voyage with its four days of agitations that lowered Susan's physical life to a harmony of wretchedness with her mental plight, and the succeeding days of gradual calming and restoration, acted upon her to save her from disaster. There will be those readers of her story who, judging her, perhaps, by themselves—as revealed in their judgments, rather than in their professions—will think it was quite unnecessary to awaken her gradually; they will declare her a hard-hearted person, caring deeply about no one but herself, or one of those curiosities of human nature that are interested only in things, not at all in persons, even in themselves. There may also be those who will see in her a soft and gentle heart for which her intelligence finally taught her to construct a shield —more or less effective—against buffetings which would have destroyed or, worse still, maimed her. These will feel that the sea voyage, the sea change, suspending the normal human life, the life on land, tided her over a crisis that otherwise must have been disastrous.

However this may be—and who dares claim the

definite knowledge of the mazes of human character and motive to be positive about the matter?—however it may be, on Thursday afternoon they steamed along a tranquil and glistening sea into the splendor and majesty of New York Harbor. And Susan was again her calm, sweet self, as the violet-gray eyes gazing pensively from the small, strongly-featured face plainly showed. Herself again, with the wound—deepest if not cruelest of her many wounds—covered and with its poison under control. She was ready again to begin to live—ready to fulfill our only certain mission on this earth, for we are not here to succumb and to die, but to adapt ourselves and live. And those who laud the succumbers and the diers—yea, even the blessed martyrs of sundry and divers fleeting issues usually delusions—may be paying ill-deserved tribute to vanity, obstinacy, lack of useful common sense, passion for futile and untimely agitation—or sheer cowardice. Truth—and what is truth but right living?—truth needs no martyrs; and the world needs not martyrs, not corpses rotting in unmarked or monumented graves, but intelligent men and women, healthy in body and mind, capable of leading the human race as fast as it is able to go in the direction of the best truth to which it is able at that time to aspire.

As the ship cleared Quarantine Susan stood on the main deck well forward, with Madame Clélie beside her. And up within her, defying all rebuke, surged the hope that cannot die in strong souls living in healthy bodies.

She had a momentary sense of shame, born of the feeling that it is basest, most heartless selfishness to live, to respond to the caress of keen air upon healthy skin, of glorious light upon healthy eyes, when there are others shut out and shut away from these joys forever. Then she said to herself, "But no one need apologize for being alive and for hoping. I must try to justify him for all he did for me."

A few miles of beautiful water highway between circling shores of green, and afar off through the mist Madame Clélie's fascinated eyes beheld a city of enchantment. It appeared and disappeared, reappeared only to disappear again, as its veil of azure mist was blown into thick or thin folds by the light breeze. One moment the Frenchwoman would think there was nothing ahead but more and ever more of the bay glittering in the summer sunlight. The next moment she would see again that city—or was it a mirage of a city?—towers, mighty walls, domes rising mass above mass, summit above summit, into the very heavens from the water's edge where there was a fringe of green. Surely the vision must be real; yet how could tiny man out of earth and upon earth rear in such enchantment of line and color those enormous masses, those peak-like piercings of the sky?

"Is that—*it?*" she asked in an awed undertone.

Susan nodded. She, too, was gazing spellbound. Her beloved City of the Sun.

"But it is beautiful—beautiful beyond belief. And I have always heard that New York was ugly."

"It is beautiful—and ugly—both beyond belief!" replied Susan.

"No wonder you love it!"

"Yes—I love it. I have loved it from the first moment I saw it. I've never stopped loving it—not even——" She did not finish her sentence but gazed dreamily at the city appearing and disappearing in its veils of thin, luminous mist. Her thoughts traveled again the journey of her life in New York. When she spoke again, it was to say:

"Yes—when I first saw it—that spring evening—I called it my City of the Stars, then, for I didn't know that it belonged to the sun—Yes, that spring evening I was happier than I ever had been—or ever shall be again."

"But you will be happy again, dear," said Clélie, tenderly pressing her arm.

A faint sad smile—sad but still a smile—made Susan's beautiful face lovely. "Yes, I shall be happy—not in those ways—but happy, for I shall be busy. . . . No, I don't take the tragic view of life—not at all. And as I've known misery, I don't try to hold to it."

"Leave that," said Clélie, "to those who have known only the comfortable make-believe miseries that rustle in crêpe and shed tears—whenever there's anyone by to see."

"Like the beggars who begin to whine and exhibit their aggravated sores as soon as a possible giver comes into view," said Susan. "I've learned to accept what comes, and to try to make the best of it, whatever it is. . . . I say I've learned. But have I? Does one ever change? I guess I was born that sort of philosopher."

She recalled how she put the Warhams out of her life as soon as she discovered what they really meant to her and she to them—how she had put Jeb Ferguson out of her life—how she had conquered the grief and desolation of the loss of Burlingham—how she had survived Etta's going away without her—the inner meaning of her episodes with Rod—with Freddie Palmer——

And now this last supreme test—with her soul rising up and gathering itself together and lifting its head in strength——

"Yes, I was born to make the best of things," she repeated.

"Then you were born lucky," sighed Clélie, who was of those who must lean if they would not fall and lie where they fell.

Susan gave a curious little laugh—with no mirth, with a great deal of mockery. "Do you know, I never thought so before, but I believe you're right," said she. Again she laughed in that queer way. "If you knew my life you'd think I was joking. But I'm not. The fact that I've survived and am what I am proves I was born lucky." Her tone changed, her expression became unreadable. "If it's lucky to be born able to live. And if that isn't luck, what is?"

She thought how Brent said she was born lucky because she had the talent that enables one to rise above the sordidness of that capitalism he so often denounced —the sordidness of the lot of its slaves, the sordidness of the lot of its masters. Brent! If it were he leaning beside her—if he and she were coming up the bay toward the City of the Sun!

A billow of heartsick desolation surged over her. Alone—always alone. And still alone. And always to be alone.

Garvey came aboard when the gangway was run out. He was in black wherever black could be displayed. But the grief shadowing his large, simple countenance had the stamp of the genuine. And it was genuine, of the most approved enervating kind. He had done nothing but grieve since his master's death—had left unattended all the matters the man he loved and grieved for would have wished put in order. Is it out of charity for the weakness of human nature and that we may think as well as possible of it—is that why we admire and praise most enthusiastically the kind of love and the kind of friendship and the kind of grief that manifest themselves in obstreperous feeling and wordiness, with no strength left for any attempt to *do?* As Garvey greeted them the tears filled Clélie's eyes and she turned away. But Susan gazed at him steadily; in her eyes there were no tears, but a look that made Garvey choke back sobs and bend his head to hide his expression. What he saw—or felt—behind her calmness filled him with awe, with a kind of terror. But he did not recognize what he saw as grief; it did not resemble any grief he had felt or had heard about.

"He made a will just before he died," he said to Susan. "He left everything to you."

Then she had not been mistaken. He had loved her, even as she loved him. She turned and walked quickly from them. She hastened into her cabin, closed the door and flung herself across the bed. And for the first time she gave way. In that storm her soul was like a little land bird in the clutch of a sea hurricane. She did not understand herself. She still had no sense that he was dead; yet had his dead body been lying there in her arms she could not have been more shaken by paroxysms of grief, without tears or sobs—grief that vents itself in shrieks and peals of horrible laughter-like screams—she smothered them in the pillows in which she buried her face. Clélie came, opened the door, glanced in, closed it. An hour passed—an hour and a half. Then Susan appeared on deck—amber-white pallor, calm, beautiful, the fashionable woman in traveling dress.

"I never before saw you with your lips not rouged!" exclaimed Clélie.

"You will never see them rouged again," said Susan.

"But it makes you look older."

"Not so old as I am," replied she.

And she busied herself about the details of the landing and the customs, waving aside Garvey and his eager urgings that she sit quietly and leave everything to him. In the carriage, on the way to the hotel, she roused herself from her apparently tranquil reverie and broke the strained silence by saying:

"How much shall I have?"

The question was merely the protruding end of a train of thought years long and pursued all that time with scarcely an interruption. It seemed abrupt; to Garvey it sounded brutal. Off his guard, he showed in flooding color and staring eye how profoundly it shocked him. Susan saw, but she did not explain; she was not keeping accounts in emotion with the world. She waited patiently. After a long pause he said in a tone that contained as much of rebuke as so mild a dependent dared express:

"He left about thirty thousand a year, Miss Lenox."

The exultant light that leaped to Susan's eye horrified him. It even disturbed Clélie, though she better understood Susan's nature and was not nearly so reverent as Garvey of the hypocrisies of conventionality. But Susan had long since lost the last trace of awe of the opinion of others. She was not seeking to convey an impression of grief. Grief was too real to her. She would as soon have burst out with voluble confession of the secret of her love for Brent. She saw what Garvey was thinking; but she was not concerned. She continued to be herself—natural and simple. And there was no reason why she should conceal as a thing to be ashamed of the fact that Brent had accomplished the purpose he intended, had filled her with honest exulta- tion—not with delight merely, not with triumph, but with that stronger and deeper joy which the unhoped- for pardon brings to the condemned man.

She must live on. The thought of suicide, of any form of giving up—the thought that instantly pos- sesses the weak and the diseased—could not find lodg- ment in that young, healthy body and mind of hers. She must live on; and suddenly she discovered that she could live *free!* Not after years of doubtful struggles, of reverses, of success so hardly won that she was left exhausted. But now—at once—*free!* The heavy shackles had been stricken off at a blow. She was free—forever free! Free, forever free, from the wolves of poverty and shame, of want and rags and filth, the wolves that had been pursuing her with swift, hideous padded stride, the wolves that more than once had dragged her down and torn and trampled her, and lapped her blood. Free to enter of her own right the world worth living in, the world from which all but a few are shut out, the world which only a few of those privileged to enter know how to enjoy. Free to live the life worth while—the life of leisure to work, instead of slaving to make leisure and luxury and comfort for others. Free to achieve something beside food, cloth- ing, and shelter. Free to live as *she* pleased, instead of for the pleasure of a master or masters. Free— free—free! The ecstasy of it surged up in her, for the moment possessing her and submerging even thought of how she had been freed.

She who had never acquired the habit of hypocrisy frankly exulted in countenance exultant beyond laughter. She could conceal her feelings, could refrain from expressing. But if she expressed at all, it must be her true self—what she honestly felt. Garvey hung his head in shame. He would not have believed Susan could be so unfeeling. He would not let his eyes see the painful sight. He would try to forget, would deny to himself that he had seen. For to his shallow, conventional nature Susan's expression could only mean delight in wealth, in the opportunity that now offered to idle and to luxuriate in the dead man's money, to realize the crude dreamings of those lesser minds whose initial impulses toward growth have been stifled by the routine our social system imposes upon all but the few with the strength to persist individual.

Free! She tried to summon the haunting vision of the old women with the tin cups of whisky reeling and staggering in time to the hunchback's playing. She could remember every detail, but these memories would not assemble even into a vivid picture—and the picture would have been far enough from the horror of actuality in the vision she formerly could not banish. As a menace, as a prophecy, the old women and the hunchback and the strumming piano had gone forever. Free —secure, independent—free!

After a long silence Garvey ventured stammeringly:

"He said to me—he asked me to request—he didn't make it a condition—just a wish—a hope, Miss Lenox—that if you could, and felt it strongly enough——"

"Wished what?" said Susan, with a sharp impatience that showed how her nerves were unstrung.

"That you'd go on—go on with the plays—with the acting."

The violet eyes expressed wonder. "Go on?" she

inquired, "Go on?" Then in a tone that made Clélie sob and Garvey's eyes fill she said:

"What else is there to live for, now?"

"I'm—I'm glad for his sake," stammered Garvey.

He was disconcerted by her smile. She made no other answer—aloud. For *his* sake! For her own sake, rather. What other life had she but the life *he* had given her? "And he knew I would," she said to herself. "He said that merely to let me know he left me entirely free. How like him, to do that!"

At the hotel she shut herself in; she saw no one, not even Clélie, for nearly a week. Then—she went to work —and worked like a reincarnation of Brent.

She inquired for Sperry, found that he and Rod had separated as they no longer needed each other; she went into a sort of partnership with Sperry for the production of Brent's plays—he, an excellent coach as well as stage director, helping her to finish her formal education for the stage. She played with success half a dozen of the already produced Brent plays. At the beginning of her second season she appeared in what has become her most famous part—*Roxy* in Brent's last play, "The Scandal." With the opening night her career of triumph began. Even the critics— therefore, not unnaturally, suspicious of an actress who was so beautiful, so beautifully dressed, so well supported, and so well outfitted with actor-proof plays —even the critics conceded her ability. She was worthy of the great character Brent had created—the way-ward, many-sided, ever gay *Roxy Grandon.*

When, at the first night of "The Scandal," the audience lingered, cheering Brent's picture thrown upon a drop, cheering Susan, calling her out again and again, refusing to leave the theater until it was announced that she could answer no more calls, as she had gone home—when she was thus finally and firmly established in her own right—she said to Sperry:

"Will you see to it that every sketch of me that appears tomorrow says that I am the natural daughter of Lorella Lenox?"

Sperry's Punch-like face reddened.

"I've been ashamed of that fact," she went on. "It has made me ashamed to be alive—in the bottom of my heart."

"Absurd," said Sperry.

"Exactly," replied Susan. "Absurd. Even stronger than my shame about it has been my shame that I could be so small as to feel ashamed of it. Now— tonight——" she was still in her dressing-room. As she paused they heard the faint faraway thunders of the applause of the lingering audience—"Listen!" she cried. "I am ashamed no longer. Sperry, *Ich bin ein Ich!*"

"I should say," laughed he. "All you have to say is 'Susan Lenox' and you answer all questions."

"At last I'm proud of it," she went on. "I've justified myself. I've justified my mother. I am proud of her, and she would be proud of me. So—see that it's done, Sperry."

"Sure," said he. "You're right."

He took her hand and kissed it. She laughed, patted him on the shoulder, kissed him on both cheeks in friendly, sisterly fashion.

He had just gone when a card was brought to her— "Dr. Robert Stevens"—with "Sutherland, Indiana," penciled underneath. Instantly she remembered, and had him brought to her—the man who had rescued her from death at her birth. He proved to be a quiet, elderly gentleman, subdued and aged beyond his fifty-five years by the monotonous life of the drowsy old town. He approached with a manner of embarrassed respect and deference, stammering old-fashioned compliments. But Susan was the simple, unaffected girl again, so natural that he soon felt as much at ease as with one of his patients in Sutherland.

She took him away in her car to her apartment for supper with her and Clélie, who was in the company, and Sperry. She kept him hour after hour, questioning him about everyone and everything in the old town, drawing him out, insisting upon more and more details. The morning papers were brought and they read the accounts of play and author and players. For once there was not a dissent; all the critics agreed that it was a great performance of a great play. And Susan made Sperry read aloud the finest and the longest of the accounts of Brent himself—his life, his death, his work, his lasting fame now peculiarly assured because in Susan Lenox there had been found a competent interpreter of his genius.

After the reading there fell silence. Susan, her pallid face and her luminous, inquiring violet eyes inscrutable, sat gazing into vacancy. At last Doctor Stevens moved uneasily and rose to go. Susan roused herself, accompanied him to the adjoining room. Said the old doctor:

"I've told you about everybody. But you've told me nothing about the most interesting Sutherlander of all—yourself."

Susan looked at him. And he saw the wound hidden from all the world—the wound she hid from herself as much of the time as she could. He, the doctor, the professional confessor, had seen such wounds often; in all the world there is hardly a heart without one. He said:

"Since sorrow is the common lot, I wonder that men can be so selfish or so unthinking as not to help each other in every way to its consolations. Poor creatures that we are—wandering in the dark, fighting desperately, not knowing friend from foe!"

"But I am glad that you saved me," said she.

"You have the consolations—success—fame—honor."

"There is no consolation," replied she in her grave sweet way. "I had the best. I—lost him. I shall spend my life in flying from myself."

After a pause she went on: "I shall never speak to anyone as I have spoken to you. You will understand all. I had the best—the man who could have given me all a woman seeks from a man—love, companionship, sympathy, the shelter of strong arms. I had that. I have lost it. So——"

A long pause. Then she added:

"Usually life is almost tasteless to me. Again—for an hour or two it is a little less so—until I remember what I have lost. Then—the taste is very bitter—very bitter."

And she turned away.

She is a famous actress, reputed great. Some day she will be indeed great—when she has the stage experience and the years. Except for Clélie, she is alone. Not that there have been no friendships in her life. There have even been passions. With men and women of her vigor and vitality, passion is inevitable. But those she admits find that she has little to give, and they go away, she making no effort to detain them;

or she finds that she has nothing to give, and sends them away as gently as may be. She has the reputation of caring for nothing but her art—and for the great establishment for orphans up the Hudson, into which about all her earnings go. The establishment is named for Brent and is dedicated to her mother. Is she happy? I do not know. I do not think she knows. Probably she is—as long as she can avoid pausing to think whether she is or not. What better happiness can intelligent mortal have, or hope for? Certainly she is triumphant, is lifted high above the storms that tortured her girlhood and early youth, the sordid woes that make life an unrelieved tragedy of calamity threatened and calamity realized for the masses of mankind. The last time I saw her——

It was a few evenings ago, and she was crossing the sidewalk before her house toward the big limousine that was to take her to the theater. She is still young; she looked even younger than she is. Her dress had the same exquisite quality that made her the talk of Paris in the days of her sojourn there. But it is not her dress that most interests me, nor the luxury and perfection of all her surroundings. It is not even her beauty—that is, the whole of her beauty.

Everything and every being that is individual in appearance has some one quality, trait, characteristic, which stands out above all the rest to make a climax of interest and charm. With the rose it is its perfume; with the bird, perhaps the scarlet or snowy feathers upon its breast. Among human beings who have the rare divine dower of clear individuality the crown and cap of distinction differs. In her—for me, at least— the consummate fascination is not in her eyes, though I am moved by the soft glory of their light, nor in the lovely oval contour of her sweet, healthily pallid face. No, it is in her mouth—sensitive, strong yet gentle, suggestive of all the passion and suffering and striving that have built up her life. Her mouth—the curve of it—I think it is, that sends from time to time the mysterious thrill through her audiences. And I imagine those who know her best look always first at those strangely pale lips, curved in a way that suggests bitterness melting into sympathy, sadness changing into mirth—a way that seems to say: "I have suffered—but, see! I have stood fast!"

Can a life teach any deeper lesson, give any higher inspiration?

As I was saying, the last time I saw her she was about to enter her automobile. I halted and watched the graceful movements with which she took her seat and gathered the robes about her. And then I noted her profile, by the light of the big lamps guarding her door. You know that profile? You have seen its same expression in every profile of successful man or woman who ever lived. Yes, she may be happy—doubtless is more happy than unhappy. But—I do not envy her—or any other of the sons and daughters of men who is blessed—and cursed—with imagination.

And Freddie—and Rod—and Etta—and the people of Sutherland—and all the rest who passed through her life and out? What does it matter? Some went up, some down—not without reason, but, alas! not for reason of desert. For the judgments of fate are, for the most part, not unlike blows from a lunatic striking out in the dark; if they land where they should, it is rarely and by sheer chance. Ruth's parents are dead; she is married to Sam Wright. He lost his father's money in wheat speculation in Chicago—in one of the most successful of the plutocracy's constantly recurring raids upon the hoardings of the middle class. They live in a little house in one of the back streets of Sutherland and he is head clerk in Arthur Sinclair's store—a position he owes to the fact that Sinclair is his rich brother-in-law. Ruth has children and she is happier in them than she realizes or than her discontented face and voice suggest. Etta is fat and contented, the mother of many, and fond of her fat, fussy August, the rich brewer. John Redmond—a congressman, a possession of the Beef Trust, I believe—but not so highly prized a possession as was his abler father.

Freddie? I saw him a year ago at the races at Auteuil. He is huge and loose and coarse, is in the way soon to die of Bright's disease, I suspect. There was a woman with him—very pretty, very *chic*. I saw no other woman similarly placed whose eyes held so assiduously, and without ever a wandering flutter, to the face of the man who was paying. But Freddie never noticed her. He chewed savagely at his cigar, looking about the while for things to grumble at or to curse. Rod? He is still writing indifferent plays with varying success. He long since wearied of Constance Francklyn, but she clings to him and, as she is a steady money-maker, he tolerates her.

Brent? He is statelily ensconced up at Woodlawn. Susan has never been to his grave—there. His grave in her heart—she avoids that too, when she can. But there are times—there always will be times——

If you doubt it, look at her profile.

Yes, she has learned to live. But—she has paid the price.

(14)